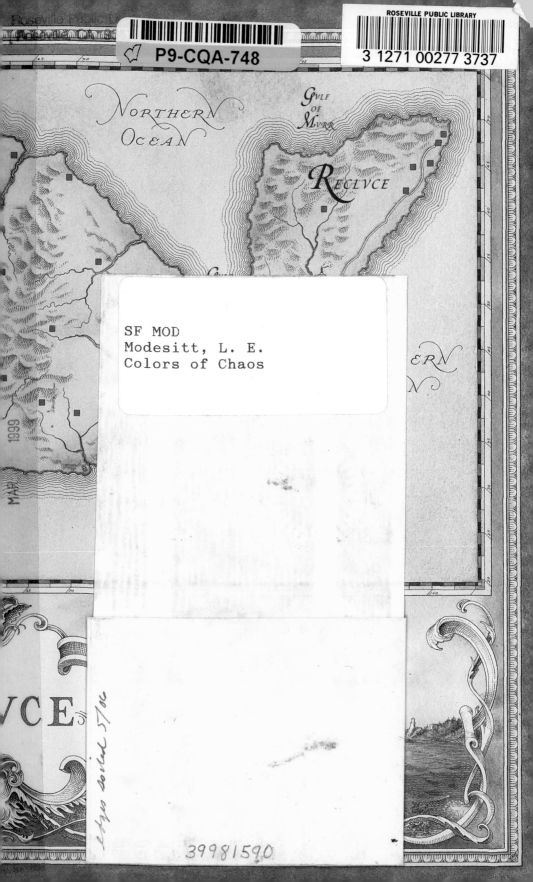

NORTHERN
OCEAN

GVLF
OF
MVRR

RECLVCE

NORTHERN OCEAN

MAR 1999

# COLORS
# OF
# CHAOS

# TOR BOOKS BY L. E. MODESITT, JR.

## THE SPELLSONG CYCLE
*The Soprano Sorceress*
*The Spellsong War*

## THE SAGA OF RECLUCE
*The Magic of Recluce*
*The Towers of the Sunset*
*The Magic Engineer*
*The Order War*
*The Death of Chaos*
*Fall of Angels*
*The Chaos Balance*
*The White Order*
*Colors of Chaos*

## THE ECOLITAN MATTER
*The Ecologic Envoy*
*The Ecolitan Operation*
*The Ecologic Secession*
*The Ecolitan Enigma*

## THE FOREVER HERO
*Dawn for a Distant Earth*
*The Silent Warrior*
*In Endless Twilight*

*Of Tangible Ghosts*
*The Ghost of the Revelator*

*The Timegod*
*Timediver's Dawn*

*The Green Progression*

*The Parafaith War*
*The Hammer of Darkness*
*Adiamante*
*Gravity Dreams**

*forthcoming

# L. E. Modesitt, Jr.

# COLORS
# OF
# CHAOS

**TOR** ®

A Tom Doherty Associates Book / New York

COLORS OF CHAOS

Edited by David G. Hartwell

A Tor Book
Published by Tom Doherty Associates, Inc.
175 Fifth Avenue
New York, NY 10010

Tor Books on the World Wide Web:
http://www.tor.com

Tor® is a registered trademark of Tom Doherty Associates, Inc.

Library of Congress Cataloging-in-Publication Data

Modesitt, L. E.
    Colors of Chaos / L. E. Modesitt, Jr.—1st ed.
        p.   cm.
    "A Tom Doherty Associates Book."
    ISBN 0-312-86767-0 (acid-free paper)
    I. Title.
PS3563.O264C65   1999
813'.54—dc21                                        98-43971
                                                        CIP

First Edition: January 1999

Printed in the United States of America

0   9   8   7   6   5   4   3   2   1

*In thanks and appreciation to Nesby Cornett Janes,*
*for all she made possible for others,*
*and especially in thanks for her daughter*

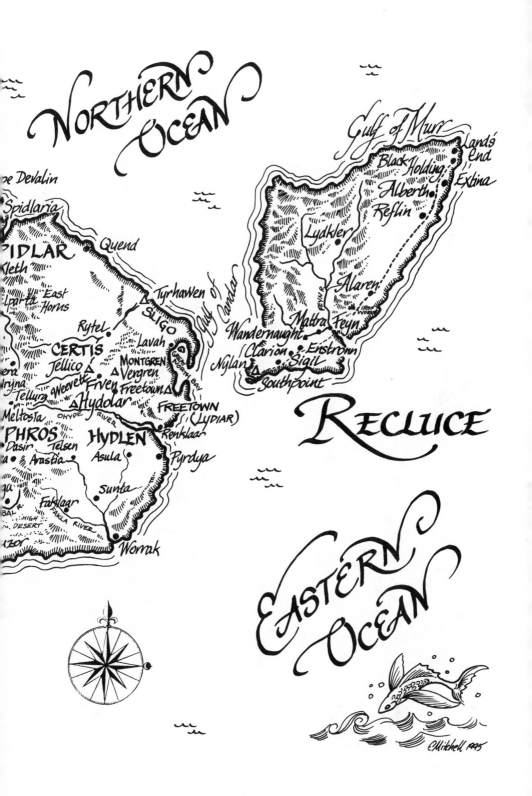

NORTHERN OCEAN

Gulf of Murr

e Devalin

Spidlaria

SPIDLAR

Kleth

Land's End

Black Holding

Alberth

Reflin

Extina

Quend

East
Horns

Lydkler

Sparta

Elparta

Tyrhaven

SLIGO

Alaren

Rytel

Lavah

CERTIS

Jellico

MONTGREN

Vergren

Fiven

Freetown

Hydolar

OHYDE RIVER

Weevett

Telura

Urjna

Meltosia

PHROS

Dasir

Telsen

Avastia

HYDLEN

Asula

Renklaar

Pyrdya

FREETOWN
(LYDIAR)

Wandernaught

Clarion

Nylan

Mattra

Feyn

IRON
WORKS

Erstronn

Sigil

Southpoint

Gulf of Candar

NORTH BAY

RECLUCE

Sunta

BAL

Faklaar

FAKLA RIVER

HIGH
DESERT

ZOR

Worrak

EASTERN
OCEAN

CMitchell 1995

# Characters

| | |
|---|---|
| *Nall* | Cerryl's aunt |
| *Syodor* | Cerryl's uncle |
| *Dylert* | Sawmill master, with whom Cerryl first apprenticed |
| *Brental* | Dylert's son |
| *Tellis* | Scrivener in Fairhaven |
| *Benthann* | Tellis's mistress |
| *Pattera* | Weaver girl |

## MAGES

| | |
|---|---|
| *Cerryl* | Mage of Fairhaven |
| *Sterol* | High Wizard of Fairhaven |
| *Kinowin* | Overmage of Fairhaven |
| *Jeslek* | Overmage of Fairhaven |
| *Anya* | Chief aide to Jeslek, niece of the factor Muneat |
| *Broka* | Master of anatomie |
| *Derka* | |
| *Disarj* | |
| *Esaak* | Master of mathematicks |
| *Eliasar* | Armsmaster of Fairhaven |
| *Fydel* | |
| *Gorsuch* | Mage adviser in Hydolar (Hydlen) |
| *Huroan* | Assistant chief Patrol mage, Fairhaven |
| *Isork* | Chief Patrol mage, Fairhaven |
| *Myral* | Master of sewers |
| *Redark* | |
| *Sedelos* | Mage adviser in Lydiar |
| *Shyren* | Mage adviser in Jellico (Certis) |

| | |
|---|---|
| *Sverlik* | Mage adviser in Fenard (Gallos), killed by Prefect Lyam |
| *Leyladin* | Black healer, daughter of Layel |
| *Bealtur* | Apprentice mage |
| *Faltar* | Former apprentice mage with Cerryl |
| *Heralt* | Former apprentice mage with Cerryl |
| *Lyasa* | Former apprentice mage with Cerryl |

## RULERS

| | |
|---|---|
| *Berofar* | Duke of Hydlen |
| *Estalin* | Duke of Lydiar |
| *Lyam* | Former prefect of Gallos, killed by Cerryl |
| *Syrma* | Prefect of Gallos |
| *Rystryr* | Viscount of Certis |

## FACTORS

| | |
|---|---|
| *Layel* | Leyladin's father, factor and trader in scarcities |
| *Muneat* | Richest factor in Fairhaven, Anya's uncle |
| *Jiolt* | One of the five wealthiest factors in Fairhaven, son Uleas is consort of Anya's sister, Nerya |
| *Scerzet* | One of the five wealthiest factors in Fairhaven |
| *Chorast* | One of the five wealthiest factors in Fairhaven |
| *Felemsol* | One of the five wealthiest factors in Fairhaven |
| *Loboll* | Wealthy Fairhaven trader |

# Colors
## of
# White

# I

Cerryl shifted his weight. He stood in the west corner of the small second-level rampart of the guardhouse before the north gates to the White City of Fairhaven. That was the only corner where the sun touched. His white leather jacket was fastened all the way up to his neck, and even with the heavy shirt and white wool tunic of a full mage underneath, he was cold.

He glanced out at the white granite highway that stretched north and, just beyond where he could see, curved eastward toward Lydiar. As the day had passed, it had warmed enough that his breath no longer formed a white cloud, but the north wind still cut through his white woolen trousers. His eyes went down to the armsmen in red-trimmed white tunics who stamped their boots and walked back and forth in front of the gates, waiting for travelers.

The rumbling of another set of wheels—iron ones—on the stone alerted Cerryl, and he looked up and out along the highway to study the approaching vehicle, a high-sided wagon painted cyan and cream, escorted by a full score of lancers in cyan livery, ten preceding and ten following the wagon. Cyan was the color of the Duke of Lydiar.

Cerryl couldn't help but wonder what was being conveyed to Fairhaven with so many lancers: Chests of golds owed for road taxes? Trade goods from the port at Lydiar as some sort of repayment? The ponderous approach of the wagon and the four horses indicated the load was heavy.

Slowly, slowly, the teamster in cyan eased the wagon up to the gates and the White armsmen. The Lydian lancers reined up on each side of the wagon and behind.

"Tariffs and goods for Fairhaven. Bound for the Wizards' Square," announced the captain of the Lydians, a squarish black-haired and bearded figure. He extended a scroll to the man in charge of the inspection and guard detail.

Cerryl took a deep breath and let his order/chaos senses study the wagon. Metal—coins in chests, as he had suspected, although there were but three chests. Under the dark gray canvas were also a dozen small barrels, more like quarter-barrels. Salt perhaps. Most salt came from Lydiar, the closest port, for all that it was two long days or three short ones.

The head gate guard glanced up at Cerryl, his eyes questioning the mage. Two of the lancers behind the Lydian officer followed his eyes. One swallowed as his eyes took in Cerryl's whites.

"That's what the scroll says, ser!" the detail leader called up to Cerryl.

"It's as they say, Diborl," Cerryl answered.

"You may pass," the head guard announced.

The wagon rolled past the guardhouse, and Cerryl listened. Listening was the most interesting part of the duty, at least usually.

". . . always have a mage here?"

"Always . . . Sometimes you see someone get turned to ashes . . ."

". . . you're jesting . . ."

"No . . . not something to jest at."

Cerryl hadn't had to use chaos fire on any person yet in his gate-guard duties, but he'd turned two wagons carrying contraband—one had iron blades hidden under the wagon bed—into ashes and sent the teamster and his assistant to the road crew, where they'd spend the rest of their lives helping push the Great White Highway through the West-horns.

The young mage shrugged. He doubted that either man had been the one who had planned the smuggling—or would have benefited much—but he'd seen Fenard and Jellico and grown up in Hrisbarg in the shadow of the played-out mines. He'd been a mill boy, a scrivener's apprentice, and a student mage under the overmage Jeslek. All those experiences had made one thing clear. Strict as the rules of the Guild were, harsh as the punishments could be, and sometimes as unfair as they had been, from what he'd seen the alternatives were worse.

After stamping his white boots again, Cerryl walked across the short porch, four steps, and turned back, hoping that keeping moving would keep him warmer. Sometimes, it did. Most times, it didn't.

He wanted to yawn. He'd thought sewer duty had been tiring, but it hadn't been half so tiring as being a gate guard. At least, in cleaning sewers he'd been able to perfect his control of chaos fire. As a gate mage, mostly he just watched from the tiny rampart on top of the guardhouse just out from the north gate. Also, the sewers were warmer in winter and cooler in summer. The sewers did stink, he reminded himself, sometimes a great deal.

"Ser?"

Cerryl glanced down.

Diborl looked up at the young mage. "We've got two here need medallions—a cart and a hauler's wagon."

"I'm coming down." Cerryl walked to the back of the porch area, where he descended the tiny and narrow circular stone staircase. He came out at the back of the guardroom. From there he entered the medallion room, where a wiry farmer with thinning brown hair stood. Behind him was a hauler in faded gray trousers and shirt.

The farmer had just handed his five coppers across the battered wooden counter to the medallion guard. Behind him, the hauler held a leather pouch, a pouch that could have held anywhere from several silvers to several golds, depending on the trade and the size of the wagon. That didn't include actual tariffs, either.

"Ser," said the guard to the farmer, "Vykay, there"—he pointed to another guard who held a drill, a hammer, and a pouch that Cerryl knew contained soft copper rivets—"he and the mage will attach the medallion."

"Just so as I can get going."

"It won't take but a moment," Cerryl assured the man, who looked to be close to the age of Tellis, the scrivener with whom Cerryl had apprenticed before the Guild had found him and made him a student mage.

The cart stood at the back of the guardhouse, a brown mule between the traces. The mule looked at Cerryl, and Cerryl looked back, then at the baskets of potatoes in the rear.

"Medallion should go on the sideboard around here." Vykay positioned the brass plate a handspan below the bottom of the driver's seat. "That be all right?"

"Might catch on stuff in the stable. A mite bit higher'd be better." The farmer nodded. "New wagon. Old one not much better than a stone boat no more."

The guard raised the medallion and glanced at Cerryl.

"That's fine."

With quick motions, the guard used a grease stick to mark the wood, then took out the hand drill and began to drill the holes for the rivets.

"Can remember when it was only three coppers," the farmer said to Cerryl. "Before your time, young mage." He offered a wintry smile. "Not be complaining, though. Do no good, and 'sides, I'd rather be using the White highways than those muddy cow paths they call roads."

Cerryl nodded, his eyes straying to the medallion Vykay had laid on the wagon seat—simple enough, just a rectangular plate with the outline of the White Tower stamped on it and the numeral 1, for winter, and the year.

"Just about ready, ser," Vykay announced, straightening, placing the medallion on the sideboard, and slipping the rivets/pins through the holes in the medallion and in the cart sideboard. Then came the offset clamps and two quick blows with the hammer. The guard glanced at Cerryl.

The White mage nodded and concentrated, raising a touch of chaos and infusing the medallion and rivets. He could feel the heat in his forehead, not enough to raise a sweat, but noticeable to him. "There." Cerryl turned to the farmer. "Your cart is allowed on all White highways for another year, ser. I must warn you that if anyone tampers with the medallion, you will need another. And . . . they could get hurt."

"I'd be knowing that, but I thank you." The farmer offered a brusque nod and took the leads to the mule, flicking them and leading the cart away, walking beside the mule, rather than riding.

Cerryl glanced at the second vehicle—a long and high gray wagon with bronze trim. The painted emblem on the side read: "Kyrest and Fyult, Grain Factors."

The hauler stood by the wagon. "If you could just replace . . ."

Vykay nodded and looked at Cerryl.

Cerryl extended his senses and bled away the remaining chaos, although there was so little left that no one would have been hurt, even if Vykay had removed the old medallion.

Vykay produced a chisel and, with two quick snaps, removed the old medallion and then replaced it with the new.

Cerryl added the chaos lock, then looked at the guard. "Is that all for now?"

"Yes, ser."

With a smile, Cerryl slipped away and back up to his perch on the second level of the guardhouse. He glanced back northward over the highway, momentarily empty near the gates, though he thought he saw another wagon in the distance making its way through the gray-leaved hills toward Fairhaven. Because of the alignment of the city, he found it strange that the north gate actually controlled the travelers from Hrisbarg and Lydiar and the far east of Candar. It was also strange, as he reflected upon it, how much straighter the Great White Highway was in Gallos and western Certis than near Fairhaven itself—yet Fairhaven was the home of the Guild and the mages who had labored centuries to build the great highways of eastern Candar.

Stamping his feet again, he walked back and forth on the walkway behind the rampart several more times, but his feet remained cold, almost numb.

The bell rang, its clear sound echoing on the rampart, but Cerryl had already stepped forward with the sound of wheels on stone once more.

A farm wagon stood before the guards. Three men in rough browns stood by the wagon. Three and a driver?

"What have you in the wagon?"

"Just our packs. We're headed to Junuy's to pick up some grain for the mill in Lavah."

Cerryl frowned. Lavah was on the north side of the Great North

Bay, a long ways to go for grain. His senses went down and out to the wagon, and he nodded to himself, marshaling chaos for what would come, knowing it would happen, and wishing vainly that it would not. "There's something in the space beneath the seat. Oils, I'd guess."

The driver grabbed an iron blade from beneath the wagon seat, and the gate guards brought up their shortswords automatically but stepped back.

Cerryl focused chaos on the driver, holding back for a moment, hoping the driver would drop the blade, but the man started to swing it forward.

*Whhhsttt!* The firebolt spewed over the figure so quickly he did not even scream. The blade *clunked* dully on the white granite paving stones beside the wagon. White ashes drifted across the charred wagon seat. The other three men did not move as the guards shackled them and led them into the barred holding room to wait for the Patrol wagon. The patrol would hold them until they were sent out on road duty.

Cerryl was glad they hadn't raised weapons. Killing the driver had been bad enough, and he wished the man had not raised the blade, but raising weapons against gate guards or mages was strictly forbidden, and rules were rules—even for mages.

Two other guards began to inspect the wagon, then pulled open a door.

"Good screeing, ser. Almost a score of scented oils—Hamorian, I'd say!" Diborl called up to the young mage.

Cerryl managed a nod. His head ached, throbbed. Myral had warned him about the backlash of using chaos against cold iron, but he'd not had that much choice if he wanted to ensure none of the guards were hurt. Absently, he had to wonder about his ability to sense the oils. No smuggler expected to get caught, and the hidden wagon compartment had been prepared well in advance, perhaps even used before. Did that mean other gate guards were less able, or lazy? Or looked the other way?

He pursed his lips, disliking all of the possibilities and understanding that he knew too little to determine which, if any, might be the most likely answer.

Below, the guards carried the jars of oil, probably glazed with a lead pigment, into the storage room. The confiscated goods were auctioned every eight-day, with the high bidder required to pay the taxes and tariffs—on top of the final bid. The golds raised went into road building and maintenance, or so Kinowin had told Cerryl.

Even if some smuggling succeeded, Cerryl still didn't understand why people tried to smuggle things past the gates—at least things made of metal. Cerryl knew his senses couldn't always distinguish spices from a wagon's wood or cloth. Leyladin, the blonde gray/Black mage who was the Hall's healer, might have been able to do that, but most White mages couldn't. But even the least talented White mage could sense metal through a cubit of solid wood.

He shook his head, fearing he knew the answer. The Guild kept its secrets, kept them well. Cerryl still recalled the fugitive who'd been turned to ashes by a Guild mage when Cerryl had been a mill boy for Dylert, watching through a slit in a closed lumber barn door.

As Diborl supervised, another guard brought out the two prisoners on cleanup detail to sweep away the ashes that remained of the wagon. Every morning one of the duty patrols brought out prisoners for cleanup detail, usually men who'd broken the peace somehow, but not enough to warrant road duty.

Cerryl rubbed his forehead, then turned and glanced at the western horizon. The sun was well above the low hills, well above, and the gates didn't close until full dark. Luckily, it was winter, and sunset came earlier. He couldn't imagine how long the duty day must be in the summer, and he wasn't looking forward to it.

The overmage Kinowin had told him that he would do gate duty, on and off, for a season or two every year for the first several years he was a full mage, perhaps longer—unless the Guild had another need for him. But what other need might the Guild have? Or what other skills could he develop? He definitely had no skills with arms or with the depths of the earth, as did Kinowin and Eliasar and Jeslek. And he wasn't a chaos healer, like Broka. The Guild didn't need mage scriveners, his only real skill.

So he could look forward to two or three years of watching wagons, to see who was trying to avoid paying road duties? Or trying to smuggle iron weapons or fine cloth or spices into the city?

He turned and paced back across the walkway, then returned, hoping the sun would set sooner than was likely. His eyes flickered toward the empty and cold highway, a highway that would have seemed warmer, much warmer, had Leyladin been anywhere nearer.

Yet even thinking of Leyladin didn't always help. She was a healer, and he was a White mage, and Black and White didn't always work out. Some Whites couldn't even touch Blacks without physical pain for both. He'd held her hands, but that was all. Would that be all?

He paced back across the porch again, almost angrily.

# II

. . . In time, as the winds shifted, and as the rains fell less upon Candar, and as the fair grasslands of Kyphros turned into high desert, and as the Stone Hills came to resemble the furnaces wherein metal is forged, others in the rest of the world came also to understand the dangers posed by the Black Isle.

Even the Emperor of far Hamor dispatched his fleets unto the Gulf of Candar, seeking the talismans of dark order borne by Creslin the Black so that they might be destroyed, lest the world suffer once more the same cataclysms as befell ancient Cyador.

Though warned by the those of the Guild of the great storms raised by the evil Creslin, the Emperor of Hamor thought that he alone would seize the talismans of order and thus raise Hamor to become first among all lands.

In his greed and arrogance, the emperor sent more than a score of vessels, all filled with armsmen and weapons of every type and size, and those ships sailed into the port known as Land's End and attacked the small keep therein, for Creslin was seeking the high and great winds far away.

Yet, even in Creslin's absence, Megaera the black-hearted raised mighty fires and turned many of the emperor's ships into funeral pyres for sailors and armsmen alike.

Creslin returned, with both his killing blade and the great winds, and all but a single ship perished, and all but a score of all those thousands of men who had sought the talismans of order perished as well.

The single ship that remained Creslin rebuilt and refitted, as the beginning to the Black fleets. . . .

*Colors of White*
(Manual of the Guild at Fairhaven)
Preface

# III

Cerryl nodded to the tower guards on duty, although he didn't know either by name, as he passed on his way to report to the overmage Kinowin.

"Good day, ser," the older guard returned.

Cerryl smiled politely, glad that this day was drawing to a close, although it hadn't been that eventful, unlike the time with the oil smugglers several eight-days before. Most days were quiet—and long.

Kinowin's quarters were on the lowest level of the tower—and the door was around the corner to the left from the guard station—Derka's door was the other way, not that Cerryl had been there, but Faltar had told him.

Outside of the time when Jeslek had tried to insist that Cerryl had not succeeded in accomplishing his magely task—or rather when Jeslek had insisted that he had not set such a task—and the High Wizard Sterol had brought in Kinowin, Myral, and Derka to judge the situation, Cerryl had never really had much conversation or contact with the stooped, silver-haired Derka. Then . . . Cerryl had seen how much power the kindly voice and stooped posture concealed.

Jeslek, thank the light, had been forced to admit he had set a magely task for Cerryl, whether he had so intended or not, and Sterol and the others had agreed that Cerryl was fit to be a full mage.

Cerryl snorted as he thought about it. If sneaking into a strange city and killing the ruler with chaos fire and escaping unseen didn't make for a magely task, he wasn't certain what did. Then, because he was an orphan from a suspect background, he'd been held to a more difficult standard in many ways—except for one thing. Sterol had known that Cerryl had used chaos fire before the Guild had found Cerryl, and the High Wizard had let that pass. Cerryl's father hadn't been so fortunate—which was why Cerryl had ended up an orphan almost right after he was born.

"Cerryl, ser," he announced as he rapped on the white oak door. He didn't mind reporting to Kinowin, the other Guild overmage that he knew of besides Jeslek, but that was because the big overmage had also surmounted poverty—and far more disciplinary actions than Cerryl—in becoming a mage.

"Come in," Kinowin's voice rumbled.

Cerryl eased into the room—so different from that of Myral or Jeslek. Myral's quarters were filled with books and Jeslek's almost bare of all but essentials. Kinowin's walls were filled with colored hangings of different types and styles, but all of them featuring shades of purple, accented with other colors. His books were limited to a single four-shelf case on the wall beside the sole window. Even the table that held his screeing glass was covered with a purple cloth—trimmed with green.

"I take it that nothing untoward happened today." Kinowin's lips curled into a friendly but sardonic smile, lifting slightly the purple blotch on his left cheek.

"No, ser. Not a thing. There weren't many wagons, and only the coach from Lydiar. Just two passengers, a grain merchant from Worrak and one from Ruzor."

"Wasn't there an olive merchant from Kyphros the other day?"

"Ah . . . two days ago, I think."

"Not much trade coming to Fairhaven at all, is there?" Kinowin nodded to the chair across from him. "We need to talk."

Cerryl's stomach tightened.

"No . . . you haven't done anything wrong, and the great Jeslek has been quiet so far as you are concerned. He's still out in Gallos raising more mountains. To protect the Great White Highway, he says . . ."

Cerryl wondered. Jeslek claimed that such a use of chaos was to show the force of the Guild to the prefect of Gallos, but Cerryl doubted such was the sole reason.

". . . also," continued Kinowin, "Jeslek's been reporting cattle theft in the northern part of Kyphros. His scrolls indicate that the locals are complaining that the thieves are being allowed to steal Analerian cattle and take them to Fenard for slaughter. He's sent a scroll to the new prefect—your 'friend' Syrma—suggesting that Gallos could use more evenhanded justice."

"Syrma won't like that, not from the little I saw."

"No, he won't, but Jeslek is convinced that Fairhaven must apply a stronger hand. Both Sterol and I agree . . . about the need for a greater presence." Kinowin offered a short laugh. "That brings up what we need to talk about. . . . Sterol and I were talking the other day, and we decided that some of the junior mages need to know more about what is happening. But . . . we're telling you each individually. I'd like you to keep this to yourself. You may discuss it with me, with Myral, with Sterol—and with Jeslek, of course. You may also talk with other junior mages, but only about things which have in fact already happened." Kinowin cocked his big head slightly to one side. "Do you understand?"

"Yes, ser." Cerryl frowned. "I think so. People are talking, but it's not always right what they're saying, and you need to make sure we understand what's really happening. But you don't want it spread all over the place, and there are some people who won't be told everything because they—" Cerryl stopped as he saw the glimmer in Kinowin's eyes. "I'm sorry, ser. Maybe I don't understand."

Kinowin laughed and shook his head. "You understand. You even understand the intrigue. No wonder Jeslek worries about you. Just don't share something like you just said with anyone but me or Myral."

Cerryl nodded slowly. He noted that the overmage had not mentioned the High Wizard Sterol or the overmage Jeslek.

Kinowin squared himself in his chair, put both elbows on the table, and leaned forward. "You know that Syrma is now the prefect of Gallos. Lyam's family—they are largely wool factors and timber merchants— is not pleased with the situation. Nor are the overcaptains of the Gallosian forces, especially a fellow by the name of Taynet. He's the most senior of the overcaptains. What this means for the Guild is that we really can't press Syrma for payment of all the golds that Lyam owed Fairhaven from when he was prefect."

Cerryl wasn't sure how the intrigue of Gallos had anything at all to do with him or the Guild, but Kinowin wasn't one for idle gossip.

"The traders in Gallos have been bringing in goods from Recluce through Spidlar—wool, spices, even copper. The Black traders have also been bringing in Austran cotton and linen—and it's cheaper than what comes from Hydlen. They're shipping that copper from Southport to Spidlaria cheaper than our traders can cart it across the Westhorns." Kinowin paused, cocking his head again, as if uncertain as to what else to say. "And they're using the profit to buy our grains and tubers. They can raise grain on Recluce, but not enough."

The junior mage waited.

"The Duke of Lydiar is beginning to expand the copper mines south of Hrisbarg . . . and might be persuaded to reopen the old iron mines. He's not happy about the cheaper copper . . . or the iron." Kinowin stopped. "Does this tell you anything?"

It told Cerryl a great deal—and nothing at all. Traders were always unhappy when someone else could sell cheaper, unless they were the ones who had the cheaper goods. Certainly Syrma would be in a hard position in Gallos. He'd become prefect because the Guild had effectively announced—through Cerryl's assassination of Lyam—that it was most unhappy with the Gallosians' use of the White highways without paying the tariffs. Jeslek's use of chaos to destroy one small Gallosian army had also pointed out that Gallos would have trouble using armsmen to defy Fairhaven. At the same time, the traders and merchants of Gallos were doubtless displeased with the thought of paying tariffs—and Lyam's family certainly wouldn't be in the best of humors.

"The situation isn't good and may not get better," Cerryl finally temporized. "What about the Viscount of Certis?"

"The viscount cares little about any mining or metals, or the wool. His concerns are oils, and right now his merchants can sell more oil than they can harvest and press. It costs the Certans about the same whether they get wool from Montgren or from Recluce through either Tyrhavven or Spidlaria."

Cerryl thought, half-wondering at the idea that he—an orphan raised by a disabled miner—would be worrying about merchants and traders and rulers as a member of the White Order of Fairhaven. Finally, he glanced at Kinowin. "I am only guessing, ser. Much of what supports the Guild and ties Candar together are the White highways. What you say tells me that if the prefect of Gallos supports us, he may be replaced. The Viscount of Certis does not care, and does not wish to offend, but may find it difficult to encourage his overcaptains to support us against Gallos." He paused. "What of the Duke of Hydlen?"

"Duke Berofar is old, and tired."

Cerryl swallowed. "War, then? Sooner or later?"

A grim smile crossed the overmage's face. "Although Jeslek and Sterol and I agree on little . . . we all fear such. And you are not to tell *anyone* that." Kinowin sat back in his chair, as if to let Cerryl digest what he had just said. After a moment, he continued. "You were with Jeslek when he used chaos to destroy the Gallosian lancers, were you not? How did Jeslek look after the battle?"

"It took all six of us, ser," Cerryl said carefully. "Jeslek did much more than anyone else."

"But you might not have won without all of you?"

"It would have been in much greater doubt," Cerryl admitted.

Kinowin laughed. "Well said, and with great care." The big mage stood and wandered to the window, looking into the shadows that fell across the Avenue to the east of the White Tower. "How many Gallosians were there?"

"Around twenty score."

"The prefect of Gallos can raise nearly twenty times that in lancers, if need be." Kinowin turned and faced the seated Cerryl. "The Viscount of Certis cannot match that, though he might come within fifty score. I doubt the Duke of Lydiar, for all his boasts, can raise more than one hundred score—trained lancers, that is. We have somewhere over two-hundred-fifty-score lancers and another hundred score of other armsmen and archers. Do you have any idea how many coins that takes each year?"

"No, ser."

"Were the pay chests for the year put together, just the pay chests, I would guess the total would easily exceed five-hundred-score golds."

Cerryl swallowed. The thought of that many golds, just for armsmen, left him speechless.

An ironic smile crossed Kinowin's face. "How many lancers did you kill in Gallos? You?"

"I didn't count, ser. I'd say a half-score, perhaps a few more."

"In one battle you killed more than some lancers do in years. You also clean sewers and water aqueducts. The other day you killed a man, kept some guards from being injured, and saved the Guild from being cheated on taxes and tariffs. Your stipend is more than ten times that of a senior lancer—because the Guild expects more than ten times as much from you." Kinowin paused. "There is a problem with that. Do you know what it is?"

Cerryl frowned. "The Guild isn't that big?"

The overmage nodded. "Yes, and Gallos as it is now is too large and too powerful, and all the tariffs and all the taxes will barely pay for our mages and our lancers. Yet we must ensure that Gallos pays its road taxes or soon none will do so. That is why Jeslek set you to kill Lyam and why he is raising mountains. And why Sterol must allow it."

Cerryl licked his lips. He had known that Jeslek had needed to raise the Little Easthorns for more than a vain show of power.

"I would not be overly surprised if we must send Eliasar and the White Lancers to Gallos before long. There must be someone to replace Sverlik, and that wizard must have enough force behind him to convince Syrma to treat with him."

"There must be a reason, ser, but can you tell me why we cannot raise the taxes and tariffs?"

"Cerryl . . . think . . . What did I tell you when you sat down?" Kinowin's face was expressionless.

The thin-faced and slender junior mage tried to recollect what the overmage had said. "Oh . . . because higher tariffs make the prices higher and people won't use the roads and pay any taxes?"

Kinowin nodded. "Roads are more costly than shipping, especially when the Blacks can call the winds to their beck."

Cerryl thought some more. "There are a lot of things you can't get from Recluce or by ship. Carpets from Sarronnyn and olives from Kyphros and brimstone from Hydlen."

"People forget the gains from the roads; they only think of the costs." Kinowin cleared his throat. "You need to think about those things. You can talk all you want to your friends about trade and tariffs." The overmage smiled. "Even to a certain blonde healer, but not a word about the pay chests or any thought of war. And not a word outside the Halls of the Mages."

"Yes, ser." Cerryl couldn't quite keep from flushing at the reference to Leyladin.

"Go get something to eat. Your guts are growling."

Cerryl rose and slipped out the door, noting that Kinowin had turned back to the window, hands clasped behind his back.

# IV

Cerryl glanced up as he started up the steps from the front foyer of the Halls of the Mages, his eyes going to the full-body stone images on the ledge just below the top of the wall—the images of the great mages, he guessed. He knew the stocky figure that was the second from the far left was Hartor, the High Wizard who had restructured the Guild to oppose Recluce. *As if it had done much good.*

He paused on the stone landing just outside the White Tower's first level. Did he hear a set of boots on the stone steps? He stepped into the lower level, where one of the guards he did know, Gostar, was talking to the boy in the red tunic of a messenger who sat on the stool behind the guards, waiting for a summons from one of the higher mages in the tower.

"Doesn't always take so long, lad." Gostar's eyes went to Cerryl. "The mage Cerryl here. He was a student mage for but two years."

The black-haired boy from the crèche looked away from Cerryl.

"It's true," Cerryl said. "Sometimes it's easier if it takes longer, though." His friend Faltar had taken nearly four years, but Faltar hadn't had to fight brigands in Fenard and sneak across a hostile land . . . or deal with Jeslek day in and day out. Cerryl frowned. Faltar also hadn't gotten a half-score of lancers killed, either.

"You see there, lad. All in the way you look at it," said Gostar heartily.

The messenger kept his eyes on the white granite floor tiles.

At the sound of boots coming down the tower steps, Cerryl glanced through the archway, and a broad smile filled his face as Leyladin descended the last few steps from the upper levels, wearing her green shirt, tunic, and trousers—even dark green boots. Her blonde hair, with the faintest of red highlights, had been cut shorter and was almost level with her chin.

"How is Myral?" asked Cerryl, not knowing quite what to say.

"Better today." After a moment of silence, Leyladin offered a smile, somehow both shy and friendly. "Can you come to dinner? Tonight?"

"I'd like that." Cerryl paused. "If you can wait a bit. I have to meet with Kinowin first. For the first season I do gate duty I have to talk to him after I finish. It shouldn't take that long."

A mischievous smile crossed her lips. "Father can wait that long."

"Your father?" Cerryl's throat felt thick.

"I've talked about you so much that he says he must meet you."

*Lucky me . . .* He could sense a chuckle from Gostar.

"I'll wait here with Gostar."

Cerryl nodded. "I hope it won't be long." He went to the left, past the guards and the still-mute young messenger.

"Lady mage . . . true he killed the prefect of Gallos all by himself?"

"It's said to be true." Leyladin's voice drifted after Cerryl.

"He looks . . . too nice . . ."

". . . a quiet mage . . ."

Appearances—was one of his problems that he looked like a polite young scrivener and not a mage who would upset the world. They said that the Black mage Creslin had been small. Was that why he'd killed—or had to kill—so many? Cerryl squared his shoulders as he stepped up to the overmage's door.

At the first *thrap* on the door, Kinowin replied, "Wait a moment, if you would, Cerryl."

"Yes, ser." Cerryl settled onto the bench outside the white oak door. Even if he hadn't done that much, it had been a long day, a very long day. The gates opened to wagons at sunrise. His eyes closed . . .

"Cerryl?"

He jerked awake and bolted upright. "Oh . . . I'm sorry."

Kinowin laughed once, gently. "That's all right. Being a gate mage is more tiring than most realize. That's why we give it to you younger mages. I wouldn't want to do it."

As Cerryl followed, still groggy, and closed the heavy door behind him, Kinowin walked to the window and looked out at the dark clouds looming to the east. Even the purple wall hanging seemed gloomy rather than striking.

Cerryl stood by the table, not wanting to sit down.

"Go ahead. Sit down." Kinowin did not turn from the window. "It's storming to the east." After a moment, he turned. "How did your day go?"

"It was quiet. I've seen farm wagons and even a stone wagon, but not many other kinds. There are more passengers on the coaches, and they look like factors."

"That should not surprise you."

Cerryl couldn't say he was surprised, but he also could not have said why he was not surprised.

"Do you know how the exchanges work?"

"Not very well. The factors make agreements to buy or sell goods in future seasons, sometimes for things that haven't even been grown or mined."

Kinowin stepped toward the table, then leaned forward and put his hands on the back of the chair. "The exchanges help smooth trade. I'd judge that is as good an explanation as any. The factors use the exchange in hopes of making coins or, when times are lean, to avoid losing too many coins. So . . . when things are unsettled, long before others realize there may be trouble, the factors are buying and selling those future goods. Will there be a famine in Certis or Southwind? The price of wheat corn two seasons from now goes up. The price of cattle goes down."

"Ah . . . the price of cattle goes down?"

Kinowin shrugged. "If the fields are brown and bare and grain is dear, the farmers and the holders must sell."

Cerryl wanted to shake his head. He'd never even considered such matters.

Kinowin flashed a sardonic smile. "To the blade's edge, Cerryl. To the blade's edge. The exchanges have been most busy lately. The price of future timber is going up. Do you know why?"

Cerryl looked at the overmage helplessly.

"Ships—it takes timber to build them, and they require the older, heavier oak and the long pole firs."

Cerryl understood.

"You see? Then tell me what that means."

"Well . . . if someone is building ships, but not so many traders are coming to Fairhaven, then they aren't building trading ships, but warships . . ."

"Both Recluce and Spidlar are building more ships. I'd say for trade. Others . . . are building ships because they are losing trade."

"Are we building ships? In Sligo?"

"Let me just say that I would be most surprised if the High Wizard had not contracted with the Sligan shipwrights for a few more vessels. That is something I would not mention to anyone."

"Yes, ser."

"Myral said you worked very hard to master a wide range of skills." Kinowin looked hard at Cerryl. "In the times we are living in, I would suggest you continue to work hard. Being a gate guard offers some time and opportunities for practice. You might see if you could master the illusion of not appearing where you stand. Although I have some suspicions you know something about that." Kinowin's eyes twinkled. "You might see if you could refine your chaos senses even more—see if you can determine by sense alone every item in an incoming wagon. I won't offer too many suggestions, but any skill you improve will improve others." The big mage straightened and let go of the chair.

"Yes, ser."

"I will see you tomorrow." Kinowin turned back to the window and the still-darkening clouds. A rumble of distant thunder muttered over Fairhaven.

Cerryl closed the door behind him.

". . . heard the door. Like as he won't be long, lady mage. Your words are kind . . ."

"Just remember . . ." Leyladin straightened from her conversation with the young messenger.

Gostar was no longer one of the duty guards and had been replaced by a White Guard Cerryl didn't know, a man with an angular face and a short-trimmed beard.

"Shall we go?" the blonde healer asked. "I'm hungry."

"So am I."

Leyladin turned and bestowed a parting smile on the messenger, getting a shy and faint one in return.

"You've made another friend." Cerryl glanced across the entry foyer of the front Hall as they descended the steps side by side.

"Most of them are lonely."

Cerryl wondered. The children of the mages in the crèche had each other. He'd never even really talked to another child near his own age until he'd been apprenticed to Dylert. Erhana had been snobbish, but she'd helped him learn his letters, and without that, he never would have become Tellis's apprentice—or been accepted into the Guild. Faltar had befriended Cerryl and become his first real friend, when Cerryl had first come to the Halls. That had been before Faltar had been seduced by Anya, but Faltar remained his friend. Friends were too hard to come by.

"You're quiet." Leyladin glanced at him. "Your childhood was lonelier, I know, but they're still lonely."

Cerryl almost stopped as he stepped off the last riser of the staircase and onto the polished stone floor tiles of the foyer floor but managed not to miss the step.

"That bothered you. Why?"

After a moment, he answered, "I just hadn't thought of it quite that way."

"I suppose I've had the luxury of being able to look at things without struggling for coins and food." The blonde shivered as they went down the steps to the walk beside the Avenue. "It's gotten colder."

"It has. Faltar said spring was coming."

In the early evening, darker than usual with the overhanging clouds, the Avenue was near-empty, with a sole rider plodding northward and away from the Wizards' Square. Cerryl fastened his white leather jacket halfway up as snowflakes drifted past them. He glanced over at Leyladin, wrapped in a dark green woolen cloak. Snowflakes—Cerryl didn't expect such in spring. Then, it was early spring, and the new leaves had barely budded, while the old leaves had barely begun to turn from gray to green. He could feel the slight headache that came with storms, not so severe as with a driving rainstorm, more like the twinge of a light rain.

"Storms affect you, don't they?"

"How did you know?"

"You told me, remember?"

Had he? He wasn't certain he had, but his life had changed so much, and so quickly, he sometimes felt he was just struggling to take in everything—like Kinowin's continuing lectures on trade and now more insistence on improving his skills.

The two walked quietly through the scattered flakes until they were less than a block from the south side of the Market Square.

"This way." Leyladin inclined her head to the left.

Another block found them turning north again.

"Here we are." She gestured.

Leyladin's house was not on the front row of homes on the Avenue below the Market Square, but in the slightly smaller dwellings one block behind those of Muneat and the more affluent factors. Instead of a dozen real glass windows across the front of the dwelling, there were merely four large arched windows on each side of the ornately carved red oak double doors, but each of the windows held several dozen small diamond-shaped glass panes set in lead. Each window sparkled from the lamps within the house.

The front of the house extended a good fifty cubits from side to side, and deeper than that, Cerryl suspected as Leyladin led him up the granite walk, a walk flanked just by winter-browned grass.

"The gardens are in the back," Leyladin answered his unspoken question. "Father said they were for us, not to display to passersby." The blonde mage opened the front door. "Soaris! Father! We're here."

She stepped into a bare foyer barely four cubits wide and twice that in length, with smooth stone walls on either side. Cerryl followed and closed the door. On the left wall was mounted a polished wooden beam, with pegs for jackets and cloaks. Against the right wall was a backless golden oak bench. Beside it was a boot scraper. A boot brush leaned against the wall stones.

Cerryl offered the brush to Leyladin, then took it after she finished and brushed his own boots. Then he took off his white jacket and hung it on one of the pegs.

A huge, heavy man wearing a blue overtunic appeared at the back of the narrow foyer. "Lady Leyladin, your father awaits you and your companion in the study."

"We will be right there, Soaris."

"Very good, lady." Soaris bowed again and departed.

Cerryl turned to her. "Lady Leyladin?"

The blonde mage blushed. "Some hold Father . . . in high regard. Since Mother died when I was young and my sisters are gone, I help Father by acting as lady of the household, since he has no consort."

Cerryl shook his head slowly. "I knew that you were well off . . ."

"Oh?" Leyladin arched her eyebrows. "From your peeking through the glass? I'll wager you didn't tell Sterol about that."

"I did," Cerryl confessed. "Except I didn't tell him who I looked at. You felt me. You told me that, remember? You were so strong that I stopped looking. I never dared try again."

"You were saying . . ." she said gently.

"Oh . . ." He shrugged. "I saw the silks and hangings. I thought you were the daughter of a wealthy merchant—but not so high as a lady." He grinned. "A lady and a mage and a healer. Far above this lowly junior mage."

"Stop it." The healer grimaced. "You're already more powerful than I am or will ever be. Let's see Father."

Cerryl followed her through the foyer arch into the main entry hall. The floors were blue-green marble squares, polished so smooth that the four bronze wall lamps and their sconces shed light from both the wall and the floor. The air smelled of trilia and roses—together with another scent, a lighter one. The walls, even the inside walls, were smoothed granite block to waist-level and white plaster above.

Green silks hung from the archway through which Leyladin led Cerryl into a long sitting room, one with two settees upholstered in green velvet and two matching and upholstered wooden armchairs. All were arranged around a long and low table of polished and inlaid woods. The table inlays had been designed to portray the image of a ship under full sail.

Cerryl paused as he studied the table and then the pair of matched cabinets against the wall, cabinets that almost framed the single picture in a silvered frame on the middle of the inside wall. The image was that of a smiling, narrow-faced woman with generous lips and long wavy blonde tresses. She wore a green vest embroidered in gold thread over a loose white silk shirt. The blue eyes seemed to follow Cerryl. He looked at Leyladin. "Your mother?"

She nodded. "That was her favorite outfit, and it's how I remember her."

The end of the sitting room held a hearth, with a brass screen before it. In the wall to the left of the hearth was an archway. Leyladin led Cerryl through the arch and then through a door to the right, ignoring the archway on the left. The study was but ten cubits on a side, perhaps five long paces, and three of the walls were paneled in dark-stained red oak. The forth and inside wall contained only shelves, though, but a third held scattered displays of books, the remainder holding decorative items—malachite vases, a curved silver pitcher, a narrow and ancient blade.

A heavy man rose from the desk in the corner, angled so that the heat from coals in the hearth bathed him where he had been sitting. The top of his head was bald and shining, and on each side of his head blond hair half-covered his ears. A wide smile burst from his clean-shaven face, and green eyes, lighter than those of his daughter, smiled with his mouth.

"Father, this is Cerryl. Cerryl, this is my father, Layel."

"So . . . you're one of the young mages?" Layel stepped around the polished dark wood of the desk and offered a polite head bow.

"A very junior mage among many." Cerryl bowed in return.

"He's got a sense of place, Daughter! Maybe too modest for the Halls, from all I've seen."

"He *is* modest."

"We should be eating. Meridis will be letting me know for days that I let the food suffer." Layel gestured and then let Leyladin lead the way out of the study and through the archway she and Cerryl had not taken on the way to the study.

"What are we having?" asked the blonde as they entered a small dining hall.

The dining hall was small only comparatively, thought Cerryl. While three places were set at one end, the long white golden table could have easily seated twenty. Each chair around the table was of the white golden oak, and each was upholstered in the dark green velvet. The pale white china sat upon place mats of light green linen, and matching linen napkins were set in holders beside the silver utensils flanking the china. Fluted crystal goblets were set by each plate.

"Your favorite," answered Layel, "the orange beef with the pear-apple noodles."

Orange beef? Pearapple noodles? Pearapples had been scarce enough in Cerryl's childhood, and to be savored on those few occasions when Uncle Syodor or Aunt Nall had produced one. Now Cerryl was about to have noodles made from them—as if they were as common as flour!

"I broke out some of the white wine from Linspros." Layel glanced at his daughter. "I needed some excuse for something that good. Couldn't very well drink it by myself."

The trader sat at the head, with Cerryl and Leyladin at each side, facing each other across the end of the table. No sooner had the three seated themselves than a gray-haired woman in the same type of blue overtunic that Soaris was wearing appeared with two large platters of the same fine white china, then scurried out and returned with two more.

Cerryl glanced across the offerings—thin cuts of beef interspersed with thinly sliced oranges and green leaves and covered with an orange glaze; fine white noodles; long green beans with nuts and butter; and dark bread.

Layel served himself the beef and noodles. After he had finished, Leyladin nodded at Cerryl. "Please."

"Can't say that, outside of the white, I'd be taking you for a mage." Layel took the big glass bottle and poured the clear wine into the three crystal goblets one after another.

Wine from glass bottles—another luxury Cerryl had heard about but never seen. "I know. I look more like a scrivener. I was once, an apprentice scrivener."

"Now that's something I don't know much about." Layel laughed. "Books, you can't buy 'em cheap. So I don't. Means I don't sell them, either. Don't have time to read them." He lifted his goblet. "To friends, daughters, and companions."

Cerryl followed their example but took only the smallest sip of the wine. Even with that sip, with the hint of bubbliness and the lemon-nut freshness, he could feel that it was far stronger than anything he'd ever tasted and far, far better.

"Ah . . . better than I remembered," said Layel.

"It *is* good." Leyladin lifted the porcelain platter that held the still-steaming dark bread and offered it to her father. Layel broke off a chunk, and the blonde offered the platter to Cerryl.

Cerryl took a chunk of the warm bread and glanced toward the older factor.

Layel smiled, as if waiting for Cerryl to speak.

"All of this . . . it's different from the Halls," Cerryl said slowly. "We don't see that much outside . . . I haven't anyway, even before I came to Fairhaven." He paused. "There's so much I've read about, but . . . Leyladin has told me you're a trader, and I don't know much about trading. What do you trade in?"

"Anything that sells, young mage. Anything that sells. You trade in grain, and if the harvest is bad, you lose everything. You trade in copper, and when someone opens or closes a mine, you lose. I trade in what I can buy cheap and sell dear." Layel refilled the crystal goblet before him and then Leyladin's. He glanced at Cerryl's goblet, still three-quarters full. "You haven't drunk much."

"With me, a little wine goes a long way, but it's very good. Very good."

"Father is not telling you everything. He hoards goods," Leyladin interjected with a smile, passing the pitcher with the orange glaze in it. "He buys them cheaply this season and sells them dearly the next. He has two large warehouses here and one in Lydiar."

"You'll be giving away all my secrets, Daughter."

"Just the two of you here?" Cerryl asked.

"Now. My brother Wertel has a house in Lydiar. He runs the business for Father there, and my sisters live with their consorts here in Fairhaven. I'm the youngest." Leyladin grinned. "And the most trouble."

"How could you say that, Daughter?" Layel shook his head in mock discouragement. "Trouble? You never brought in every stray dog in Fairhaven to heal it? You never had your head nearly split open because you would heal the fractious carriage horse? You never—"

"Father . . ."

"No . . . you couldn't find a nice fellow and give me grandchildren." The factor turned to Cerryl. "She had to become a healer. She was trying to heal everything—the dogs, the warehouse cat that got kicked by the mule, the watchman's daughter . . ."

Leyladin's face clouded ever so slightly at the last, but the expression passed so quickly Cerryl wasn't sure he'd seen it.

"Healers are far more scarce than White mages," Cerryl said brightly, taking a small mouthful of the beans and nuts with the fork that felt unfamiliar, copying Leyladin's usage. They were so tender he barely had to chew them, and they hadn't been cooked into mush in a stew pot.

"Would that it were like trade, where what is scarce is dear," mumbled Layel.

"Father . . . finish eating . . ." Leyladin grinned.

"Always on me, you and your mother. Best to enjoy good food."

"Talking with his mouth full is about his only bad habit," Leyladin said.

"And you've never let me forget it." Layel turned to Cerryl. "She'll find any of your ill ways and try to heal you of them. Fair warning I'm providing."

"Father . . ." Leyladin blushed.

"Turning the glass is fair for both."

Cerryl took another sip of the wine, amazed at how good it tasted, uncertain of what he should say.

Layel glanced at Cerryl. "I've embarrassed my daughter enough. She may know how you became a mage, but I do not. Perhaps you could shed a word or two about how you came to Fairhaven."

"I'm afraid that my life is quite common, compared to yours," Cerryl protested.

"Best we should judge that. A man's no judge of himself."

"Well . . . as Leyladin might have told you, I'm an orphan. Both my parents died when I was so young I remember neither. I was raised by my aunt and uncle . . ." Cerryl went on to detail his years at the mines, his apprenticeship at Dylert's mill, and then his work as an apprentice scrivener for Tellis. ". . . and then, one day, one of the overmages arrived at the shop and summoned me to meet with the High Wizard. He examined me and decided I was suitable to be a student mage. That took two years, and last harvest the Council made me a full mage . . . a very junior mage. Now I'm one of those who guard the gates to Fairhaven."

"Good thing, too." Layel shook his head. "I don't mind as paying the tariffs and taxes for the roads, but I'd mind more than a hogshead full of manure if the smugglers got off with using the roads and then coming into the city and selling for less than I could."

"Father . . . no one sells for less."

"They could. Aye, they could. Take stuff in Spidlaria and sneak through Axalt or take the old back roads from Tyrhavven, and afore you know it they'd be in the Market Square."

"Doesn't everyone pay the taxes?" Cerryl asked.

"No. Even all the mages in the Halls couldn't find every ferret who turns a good. That's not the task of the city patrol, either. They keep the peace, not the trade laws. Thank the light, don't need armsmen to make trade and tariffs work, not in the city, anyway. See . . . there's coins in Fairhaven, and the best roads are the White highways, the ones that can take the big wagons." Layel shrugged. "So traders and exchanges are here. Smaller traders can take carts over the back roads, but most times they can't carry that much, and the Traders' Guild makes sure the road gauges are kept."

"The road gauges?" asked Leyladin.

Cerryl had the feeling she had asked the question for him, but he was grateful. He'd never heard of the road gauges.

"You should remember, Daughter. If a road is more than four cubits wide, it's a highway, and the ruler must collect tariffs, and only those with the medallions may use it. See, that way, the pony traders have to go on the slow and muddy tracks that wind out of the way. And most times, a trader with fast teams and wagons is a prosperous trader, and the great highways are fast."

Cerryl nodded. Another fact he'd not known.

"Meridis! What have we for sweets?"

The serving woman reappeared. "Be you ready for sweets, ser?"

"Why'd you think I called?" Layel's stern expression dissolved into a chuckle.

"Father . . . you don't have to put on the stern front for company."

"Can't even be master in my own dwelling, not even over sweets." The trader glanced at Cerryl. "You'll see . . . leastwise, much as a mage can that way."

"Father . . ."

"Fellow ought to know." Layel turned to Meridis. "Sweets?"

"I baked a fresh nut and custard pie."

"Wonderful! It takes company for me to get my favorite."

"It does not," suggested Leyladin. "You always tell poor Meridis not to bother because you'd look like a shoat if she fixed it just for you."

"You see?" asked Layel. "An answer for everything."

Cerryl nodded, feeling somewhat overwhelmed by the banter and byplay.

"Then let's have it."

The empty dishes vanished into the next room, a kitchen, Cerryl thought, but he was far from certain about anything, and Meridis returned with three smaller china plates, each filled with a golden-crusted pie.

"Try it," urged the trader.

"It is good," added Leyladin. "Rich, but good."

Everything felt rich to Cerryl, but he took a small bite and then a larger one. Before he fully realized it, his plate was empty.

"See? Your mage friend agrees with me."

"It was . . . I've never tasted a sweet that good," Cerryl confessed. "In fact, I've never had a dinner so good."

Layel and Leyladin exchanged glances, and Leyladin added, "I'm so glad you enjoyed it. The Meal Hall isn't known for good food. Most of the full mages don't eat there unless they have to for some reason or another."

"I have noticed that," Cerryl said dryly. "I'm beginning to see why." He found himself yawning, perhaps because of the fullness in his stomach, or the warmth of the dining room, or the length of the day. "I'm sorry. It has been a long day."

"You have to be at the gates when they open for trade?" asked Layel.

"Yes. Otherwise they have to hold wagons until a mage arrives. I'd not want to face Kinowin if I caused that."

"Neither would I," said Leyladin with a laugh. "Perhaps . . . it may be getting late for you."

"Don't shoo him out."

"He has to rise early, Father."

Cerryl held up a hand. "Your daughter is doubtless correct. I've enjoyed the meal and the company . . . but I do have to be up before the sun."

Leyladin rose, and Cerryl followed her example, following her back through the house, lamps still burning in unused rooms, throwing shadows on polished and glistening floors.

In the foyer, he eased on his jacket, thinking about the short, but certainly chill, walk back to his cold room, a room that had seemed so luxurious—until he had seen Leyladin's house.

"What do you think?" asked Leyladin as she stood by the door.

"About what? Your father? He cares a great deal for you."

"Cerryl. You are as dense as that mule my father mentioned." A smile followed the words, but one that held concern, and her green eyes, dark in the dim light of the polished bronze lamps, fixed his.

He took a deep breath. "I don't know what to think. I could say pleasant things, and I would, to anyone but you. Right now . . . I'm . . . overwhelmed. I grew up an orphan in a two-room house. It was clean, but my pallet was on the stone floor, and my uncle felt lucky if he could grub a good piece of malachite and sell it for a silver once every few eight-days. I went to work in a mill not much past my tenth year, and I was lucky to have a pearapple to eat once or twice a year. Those noodles tonight—they were wonderful, but they probably used more pearapples than I've eaten in my whole life. I've never had good wine from bottles."

"Cerryl . . . I know that. I've known that from the beginning, but I couldn't keep pretending that I wasn't different." She reached out and touched his cheek. "With you . . . I don't want to pretend."

"That means more than you know." He offered a smile.

"I think I know that." She bent forward and brushed his cheek with her lips. "Good night. I'll see you soon."

As he walked through the night, through the light gusts of cold wind, through the intermittent snowflakes with the slight headache he'd almost forgotten, his thoughts swirled like the snow. What happened next? Could anything happen? Jeslek, Sterol, and Anya had all cautioned him again consorting with a Black. Yet Leyladin was a healer who was mostly Black, and he was a White mage—perhaps at best a White mage fringing toward gray. He repressed a slight shiver at that. No one liked gray mages, neither the White mages of Fairhaven nor the Black Order mages of Recluce.

He and Leyladin could hold hands . . . but how much more? Was she worried about that? Was that why she kept a certain distance?

He frowned as he kept walking. Her kiss had been warm, but not order-chaos conflict warm.

# V

Cerryl stretched, standing in the sun of the small guardhouse porch, glad that spring had returned. Even the hills in the distance were showing signs of full greening.

He sat down on the backed stool provided for him, just high enough to be able to see over the granite rampart. He kept his eyes open but concentrated on focusing the chaos energy of the sun into an ever-tighter line of pure chaos—something like a light lance, but no thicker than his index finger.

*Whst!* The barely audible hiss followed as the narrow line of golden fire cut into the granite at the bottom of the rampart, drilling into the hard stone. White dust oozed out onto the walkway.

Cerryl released the light dagger—or whatever it might be—and sat there quietly, sweating, although the day was not that warm, trying to cool off from his silent effort. The area under the rampart ledge wasn't that visible, and if anyone did look, he'd only assume that the stone-cutters had made an error and perhaps filled in with powdered stone that had leached away over time.

Kinowin had suggested he use his time to improve his skills . . . but how? And where? He couldn't very well have said that he'd mostly mastered the light cloak that left him invisible, certainly not in the Tower, where the walls had both eyes and ears. Nor did he wish to make known his light lances, and if he used those on guard duty, everyone in the Halls of the Mages—including Jeslek—would know in days.

Cerryl had wondered what other skills might be useful . . . that he could work on quietly. Somehow, focusing chaos into a tighter focus might help. At some time he wanted to try the light dagger against cold iron, but he dared not experiment with that where anyone could see or scree him. Chaos against iron would alert any mage nearby.

The sound of wagon wheels on the stones of the highway broke into his reverie, and he sat up straight, looking at the afternoon coach from Lydiar. The four passengers all filed out and stood by the guardhouse while Cerryl studied with his senses the boxes and bags roped to the top. Outside of one black case that held a set of iron knives, the bags were all filled with what seemed to be fabric or leather—things with a "soft" feel.

"Ser?" called the duty officer.

"The black bag has knives, but there's no rule against personal weapons."

The swarthy black-bearded trader in purple looked up at the thin mage, standing at the guardhouse upper rampart, back to the duty guard, then shook his head.

". . . see why you'd best not be smuggling?" asked the rotund Sligan in his embroidered jacket.

". . . demon-damned mages know what you eat for breakfast . . ."

"It makes your efforts more profitable," suggested the third man, a blond man in a gray tunic and trousers with high black boots, an outfit Cerryl didn't recognize.

"Smugglers don't take the White highways."

"If they don't, they'll not be carrying much."

"Let's go!" called the coach's driver.

As the coach pulled through the gates, the duty guard gave a broad smile to Cerryl. "That be keeping them thinking, ser."

"Let us hope so." Cerryl still wondered about the blond man in gray and black. The fellow could have been almost any age and showed neither order nor chaos. But something about him bothered Cerryl. Or was it that he just couldn't determine from where the fellow might hail?

Cerryl sat back down on the stool, fingering his smooth chin.

So many things were unsettled. Leyladin was off in Hydlen, and while he was pleased with his progress in using the light dagger, he felt he needed to come up with something more.

He'd have to think about it, not only about what other chaos skills he could hone or develop, but where so that others, Anya and Jeslek, especially, did not discover, not quickly, in any case.

# VI

Cerryl took a deep breath as he left Kinowin's quarters, not really knowing why, except that he was relieved that Kinowin hadn't pressed him again on improving his chaos-handling skills.

"It can't be that bad." Standing outside the overmage's door, Faltar grinned at Cerryl. "Wait for me. I won't be long."

"All right." Cerryl sat down on the small wooden bench as the blond mage stepped into Kinowin's quarters and shut the door behind him. Faltar was always so cheerful. Was that why he appealed to so many people? He certainly didn't have as much ability to handle chaos stuff as did either Lyasa or Cerryl, but all had been made full mages at the same time. Then, reflected Cerryl, it had taken Faltar four years. The slender mage leaned back against the wall and closed his eyes.

*Thud!*

Cerryl opened his eyes in time to see a red-haired apprentice mage, thin-faced and female, hurrying away from Kinowin's door. He sat up for a moment, but Faltar didn't appear, and he leaned back. Darkness, he was tired.

"Cerryl?"

Cerryl struggled awake. Gate-guard duty didn't help his sleep, and he hated to think what it might be like in summer when the days were longer. "I'm here. I think." He sat up on the bench and rubbed his eyes.

"Kinowin's already left. You were sleeping. I've been to the Meal Hall and back. They're having creamed lamb. Again." Faltar's lips curled. "I thought you might like to go out for dinner with me."

"I know how you like the lamb." Cerryl grinned, but his grin faded. "Do you ever eat in the Halls?"

"Not often."

"I don't see how you can eat in the city every night," Cerryl pointed out. "I can't."

"But you can," Faltar countered. "We get a gold every eight-day. That's ten silvers—or a hundred coppers. Most meals—except at Furenk's—cost five coppers or less. So you still have more than six silvers left over every eight-day, even if you ate away from the Halls every night." The blond mage smiled. "I'm not saying every night. Just tonight. Besides, what's coin for?"

Books, clothing, silk smallclothes to keep him warm on guard duty—Cerryl could think of quite a few things. Even a warm woolen blanket for the cold nights. Or a present for Leyladin. Still, he'd been careful, and he had nearly ten golds in his private strongbox. Faltar was right. Paying for a dinner out of the Halls now and again couldn't hurt. Leyladin was off on a trip to Hydolar—Duke Berofar was ailing and had requested a healer from Fairhaven. "Tonight—that sounds good."

"Let's try The Golden Ram. It's not far, and I'm starving."

"So am I." Cerryl stood and stretched, then followed Faltar out of the tower and past the guards and the messenger in red. Outside, the wind was gusting, almost warm, as they turned right leaving the front Hall and walked south along the Avenue past the White Tower.

"Spring is here," Faltar said pleasantly.

"Let us hope it remains this time."

The Golden Ram was less than a half-kay from the Wizards' Square. How many times had Cerryl walked past the inn on his way to and from his sewer cleaning duties? He probably couldn't have counted them. They stepped past the green signboard with the image of the golden ram and in through the left side of the double doors.

"Two of you?" asked the man in the faded blue vest standing by a small counter.

"Two, Veron," Faltar confirmed.

"The corner table." Veron gestured.

"I take it you come here often." Cerryl glanced around the long room as Faltar wended his way through the crowded room. In the other corner Cerryl caught sight of Eliasar and Kinowin, but neither acknowledged the younger mages, as they were apparently caught up in their own conversation. The public room contained all sorts of people, from young traders to lancer officers and even several couples.

"Ah . . . feels good to sit down." Faltar stretched circumspectly.

The serving girl, also wearing a blue vest, appeared at Faltar's elbow. "What'll you gents be having?"

"What's good?" asked the blond mage, looking at her, then at Cerryl.

"It all is, ser. I'd try the cutlets. They run three. A touch chewy, but tasty. Either the good ale or a red wine. Fresh barrel."

"I'll have the cutlets, with the good ale," Faltar said.

"The cutlets, but I'll try the red wine." Cerryl felt too hungry and tired to ask about other possibilities, but he'd drunk so much ale lately, or so it seemed, that he thought he'd try the wine.

"Two cutlets—they come with the roasted potatoes and bread—and an ale and a red. That be it?"

Both mages nodded, and the server bustled off.

"I didn't know you drank wine. Or is that the healer's influence?"

Cerryl found himself flushing.

"Oh . . . she'll change you yet."

"She probably already has," conceded Cerryl. "I don't see her much, what with her healing stuff and my gate duty."

*Thump! Thump!* Two mugs appeared on the table. "That'll be four, gents."

Cerryl fished out two coppers, as did Faltar. Both vanished, and so did the server.

"Gate duty is boring," said Faltar. "Sometimes you see odd things, though. This afternoon, I saw some Blacks—three of them. I think they were the ones that get exiled from Recluce."

"You let them in and didn't tell anyone?"

"Even I'm not that stupid." Faltar took a healthy swallow of the ale. "They were leaving, but I still told Kinowin when I got off duty. They didn't do anything wrong."

"What did he say?"

"He thanked me and sent an apprentice to tell Jeslek. What's her name, the new redhead?"

"Kiella? Oh . . . that's what she was doing."

"And I thought you slept through it all."

"I wasn't that sleepy."

"I could have roasted you with chaos, and you wouldn't have known it." Faltar grinned. "Anyway, two of them were blades, and one was a healer, it looked like."

"I imagine you looked very closely."

"It's not what you're thinking. One of the blades was a woman. Redheaded and good-looking from what I could tell, but she was big, taller than you, and had that look, like Eliasar does when he's slapping you around in weapons training. One was like Kinowin, big and blond, except he was even bigger. The healer was smaller, a young fellow, redheaded, almost shy."

"Here's the cutlets. That's another six." The serving woman in the blue vest set two heavy brown platters on the table, then glanced from Faltar to Cerryl.

Cerryl dug out another four coppers. Faltar did the same.

"And I'd be thanking you both." She slipped the coppers into her wallet and gave a broad smile, pausing for a moment before nodding and slipping away.

Cerryl frowned, then took a bite of the cutlet, chewing hard because it was tough, if tasty. He had his own ideas about the travelers from Recluce, but Kinowin had told him not to guess outside the Halls.

"What do you think?" asked Faltar.

"I just don't know. They make some of their Blacks, the ones that don't fit in, travel through Candar. That's what Myral told me once."

"That's the Blacks for you. You don't fit in, and they throw you out. I guess you can do that if you live on an island."

"Every place has rules," Cerryl pointed out, using his own dagger to cut the meat and then spear a chunk of the roasted potato. "That's why we have the city patrol."

"One of the mages who had been helping Eliasar when I became a student went with the Patrol. Klyat. He'd been an arms mage with the lancers."

"What does he do?"

Faltar shrugged. "I don't know. I haven't talked to him in a while, and he wouldn't say when I was a student. Keep the peace, I guess."

Cerryl nodded but wondered. He'd seldom seen the patrols, for all the talk about them when he'd been an apprentice.

"Recluce has always been trouble, from the time of Creslin on." Faltar chewed for a moment. "Now they're even shipping stuff from Austra and Nordla, and some of it's cheaper than what we can grow and make in Candar. Derka and Myral were always insisting we're going to have trouble with Recluce. Then these Blacks show up. Of course, it could be coincidence. These things happen." Faltar swallowed the last of his ale and lifted the mug.

"More?" asked the serving woman, drawn to the raised mug as a moth to light. "That'll be two."

Faltar fumbled out two coppers.

"Maybe . . . or it could be an order-chaos conflict."

"You just found about those, and now everything's an order-chaos conflict." Faltar laughed. "It could be trade."

"What does trade have to do with three wandering Blacks from Recluce?" Cerryl sipped the red wine, not nearly so clear or so good as that he'd had at Leyladin's house, trying to make it last.

"They could be spies. They'd been at the Traders' Square, looking for work as blades, supposedly."

"How did you find that out?"

Faltar raised his eyebrows. "I have my ways."

"I don't see that of young wanderers—they were young, weren't they?"

"The healer didn't look as old as you."

"That young?" Cerryl grinned. "Not ancient like you?"

*Thump!* The second ale slopped on the table. "Here you be." The server was leaving before she finished her words.

"Good ale." Faltar took another swallow. "I'm glad you recognize the wisdom of your elders."

"Maybe there's something there . . . but I don't think young travelers are the problem."

"Perhaps they're having troubles and throwing out more people. Did you think of that?"

"Then why would they be a problem for us?"

"I don't know. But there's something. There are shipwrights headed for Sligo . . ."

Cerryl looked hard at Faltar.

"Everyone in Fairhaven knows that," protested Faltar. "I heard it in the square."

"That may be . . . but if Kinowin—and he's still in the corner there— heard you . . ."

"You're probably right." Faltar sighed and took another swallow. "Still doesn't make much sense."

Many things didn't make sense to Cerryl. Fairhaven didn't have a port that was really its own but maintained warships and relied on trade, but Hydolar had three ports and didn't trade as much as the White City . . . and so it went.

He yawned. He felt like he happened to be yawning all the time. Was it just that the days were so long? Or was his practice with light daggers that tiring? "I suppose I'd better get back and get to bed."

"Summer will be easier. They split the day into two duties . . . but if you get first duty you have to be there before dawn, and if you get the afternoon one you guard well into evening. I'm going to stay here a bit."

"That's fine." Cerryl stood. "I'll talk to you later."

He walked slowly out, noting that Eliasar and Kinowin had been joined by another mage, one Cerryl didn't know, but that the three were eating and apparently joking.

Although it was full dark outside on the Avenue, the evening was warmer than it had been earlier in the day. Maybe Faltar was right, that spring had come to stay.

Back in the rear hall, as he reached for the latch to his door, his eyes went to the white-bronze plate mounted on the wall, where the Old Tongue script spelled out: "Cerryl."

Inside, he looked around—so much larger than any quarters he had ever had . . . and so bare compared to Leyladin's house. Two real shuttered windows, a wide desk, a wooden armchair with cushions, a full-size bed with cotton sheets and a red woolen blanket—even a rug by the bed, a washstand, a white oak wardrobe for his garments, and a bookcase against the wall beside the desk.

He closed the door, but Kinowin's advice continued to rattle around in his head—more skills. But what skills? He walked over to the bookcase and picked up his well-thumbed *Colors of White*, turning to the second half. He read slowly, skipping over the passages he'd read so well he knew them by heart, trying to find those he'd really not studied and those that had bored him. Finally, he settled into the chair, his jacket still on.

> . . . in all of the substance of the world are chaos and order found, and oft are they twisted together, so tightly that none, not even the greatest of mages, can separate them. Yet were they separated, such chaos would be without end. For the world is of chaos, and all the substance of this world is nothing more and nothing less than chaos bound into fixed form by order . . .

Cerryl frowned. If he understood what the words said, the writer meant that anything, even the book itself in which the words were scrived, was nothing more than chaos bound into its form by order.

He scratched his head. Yet light was nearly pure chaos—or as pure as could be stood by living things. An involuntary yawn broke his concentration. Tomorrow would come early, far too early. He set aside the book and disrobed, carefully hanging out his clothes.

For a time, he lay there in the luxury of the wide bed, the words of *Colors of White* twisting in his thoughts . . . "were they separated, such chaos would be without end . . . were they separated . . ."

While tomorrow would come early, he could look forward to the day after. That was his, as was every fourth day, and then he wouldn't have to struggle to rise before the sun with the predawn bells.

# VII

Cerryl stood at the edge of the Meal Hall, almost empty and nearly too late to get anything to eat. Finally, he went to the serving table and took a large chunk of bread, some cherry conserve so thick it was like molasses, and a pearapple, slightly soft.

As he turned, Esaak beckoned from a side table. Cerryl's heart fell. Was the older mage about to reproach him again for his mathematical deficiencies? He carried his platter and a mug of water toward the heavy and mostly bald mage.

"Young Cerryl . . ." Esaak shook his head. "You may be the worst mage in mathematicks in the history of the Guild."

"I'm still reading the book, ser."

"And doing the problems?"

"Only a few," Cerryl confessed.

Esaak laughed. "Not all mages can be engineers or mathematicians.

Just so long as you design no aqueducts or sewer tunnels." The deep-set eyes peered at the younger man. "Have you thought about what you would pursue? You do not strike me as the type to be a gate guard or an arms mage. Especially not for years on end."

*The study of light* . . . "I don't know. I really don't know what choices there might be. I know that Myral does much with water and sewers, and I think Kinowin follows trade, and you teach mathematicks . . ."

"Who taught Kinowin about trade, young Cerryl? I was watching ships unload in Lydiar and Renklaar before Kinowin was born."

"I'm sorry."

"No need to apologize. If you do not wish to spend your life sup-porting armsmen and lancers, you need to find a skill valuable to the Guild. Jeslek . . . he has studied the depths of the earth. How do you think he knows how to raise mountains?"

"I have seen him, but I don't possess that kind of power . . ."

"Remember"—Esaak raised his hand—"it must be practical as well as interesting. Best you think about it. You have time, but do not waste it." Esaak lumbered to his feet. "And I must instruct yet another un-tutored apprentice who thinks that numbers are but for counting coins. Good day, young Cerryl."

"Good day, ser." Cerryl waited until the older mage was on his way out of the hall before he sat down at the round table in the center, aware that Esaak had left and that, outside of the serving boys in red, he was alone.

He ate quickly, his thoughts flitting. *Light . . . how can that be practical, except for killing?* No, letting the Guild know about his skill with the light lances and daggers wasn't terribly appealing . . . or safe. His past experiences with Anya and Jeslek had taught him all too well that, according to the written and unspoken rules for jockeying for power—or survival—what had saved Cerryl was his mastery of skills the others had not known about and still did not know that he possessed.

The problem with hidden skills, though, was that he could end up being a gate guard forever, which was what Esaak had suggested would happen if he didn't show another useful talent. So how much talent and skill should he reveal, and how? What would be a safe yet useful skill?

After he swallowed the last of the bread and conserves, he left the Meal Hall and wandered along the corridor, glancing into the student common, where he used to study—empty except for the goateed Beal-tur, who glanced up at Cerryl, offered a polite smile, and returned to the tome before him.

Bealtur had been so certain he would be made a full mage before Cerryl, and he hadn't been. So had Kesrik, before Kesrik had been ma-neuvered into trying to trap Cerryl in a terrible mistake. Instead, Kesrik had been found out and destroyed in a blaze of fire by the High Wizard. Except . . . Cerryl knew full well that while Kesrik had probably tried to poison Cerryl, the brigands that had attacked Cerryl when he was on sewer duty had been sent by Anya, disguised as Kesrik. Cerryl still had no idea why the redheaded mage had tried that, but he watched her as closely as he could and avoided her as circumspectly as possible.

What else could he do? Most mages were restrained by the fact that the High Wizard, the two overmages, and a few others had the power to "truth-read" and discover plots. But Anya was under Jeslek's protection, and he was not only overmage but also possibly the most powerful chaos wielder in centuries. Cerryl's most reliable protection, until he mastered more chaos skills, was concealment, but developing skills and keeping them hidden could only get harder.

He crossed the courtyard to the last Hall, the one with the smallest rooms, and went up the steps to his own quarters, nearly all the way to the back. Once inside his room, he took a deep breath and extracted *Colors of White* from the bookcase. He had most of the day. Perhaps he could find some ideas there.

Perhaps . . .

# VIII

Cerryl walked past the fountain in the courtyard between the main Hall and the rear Hall. His feet ached, and his head throbbed—the former because he'd walked across the guardhouse ramparts too much during the day and the latter because he'd practiced using the light/ invisibility cloak too much. Kinowin had been perfunctory in his questions, as though the overmage's mind had been elsewhere, and Cerryl hadn't mentioned his aches, knowing that Kinowin wouldn't have been terribly sympathetic.

Despite the deep dusk, the courtyard was hot, and the fountain spray across Cerryl's face felt welcome.

"Hello there."

He looked up to see blonde hair and a green short-sleeved shirt and armless tunic of darker green—and another mage. Lyasa and Leyladin stood in a corner, also enjoying the cool of the fountain court. Cerryl turned and joined them, the immediacy of his various aches subsiding. "When did you get back?"

"I've been here all along." Lyasa grinned.

"This afternoon, a little past midday." Leyladin offered a warm smile. "I came in the southwest gate."

"Leyladin, Cerryl," Lyasa interjected, "I need to go. Anya has requested my presence for supper."

Cerryl winced.

"Her preferences don't run that way," said Lyasa lightly, "but it will be interesting to see what she wants."

"Be careful." Cerryl worried about anything involving Anya.

"I always have to be careful. That's the everyday rule for women . . . and Blacks." Lyasa nodded to Leyladin. "I hope we can talk before—"

"Tomorrow morning?"

"I can do that. It's my last free morning before I take over duty on the west gate." Lyasa grimaced.

"You're going on gate duty?" asked Cerryl.

"Don't all new mages? Kinowin was just waiting for Elsinot to finish a reasonable tour."

"Elsinot?" Another mage Cerryl didn't know, at least by name.

"Blocky, brown-haired—he seems nice enough. He'll take the relief duties now. You're lucky. You'll probably get morning duty in the summer."

Cerryl wasn't sure if that would be luck, to get up even earlier than he was now.

"I do have to go. I'd rather not give the esteemed Anya an excuse to be upset." Lyasa gave a half-wave as she stepped away from the pair.

"Have you eaten yet?" Cerryl studied the dancing green eyes, sparkling even in the gloom of the courtyard, and the wide mouth he thought of as kind. "We could go over to The Golden Ram."

"How about Furenk's?"

"Ah . . . all right."

"I have some silvers. That way you won't have to go back to your quarters. I'm hungry. Lyasa and I got to talking . . . and then it was dark."

"Your father's not expecting you?"

"No. He's in Vergren, and I told Meridis not to fix anything tonight." Leyladin smiled. "I was afraid she'd fix so much that I wouldn't be able to walk. She does that when I've been away." She turned toward the archway that led to the front Hall that fronted on the Wizards' Square.

Cerryl stepped up beside her. "I've missed you."

"I've missed you, too. It was interesting, but"—the blonde shrugged—"it's good to be back." A faint frown crossed her face and vanished.

The Avenue was dark as they crossed the square and headed east.

"You don't sound happy about it."

"I'm happy to be back. I wish Father had been here, but he had to go . . . something about problems with the lambing in Montgren."

"I thought he was a trader."

"He is, but the lambs born this year will affect wool in the years ahead. Also the price of grain and cattle . . . many things . . ."

Cerryl held back a sigh. Did the entire world revolve around coins and trade? The more he learned, the more it seemed as though it did. "How long will he be gone?"

"Soaris told me he left yesterday. That means an eight-day before he's back."

No signboard proclaimed Furenk's. Letters carved in a marble plaque beside the door to the two-story pink granite edifice stated: "The Inn at Fairhaven."

The two climbed the two wide pink marble steps and stepped inside. Cerryl glanced around, but before he could determine even where to go, a tall functionary in a pale blue cotton shirt and a dark blue vest appeared. "This way, Lady Leyladin, and you, ser." The man in blue turned and led the way to a table for two in the back dining room. He seated Leyladin.

Cerryl sat down across from her. The back dining room was empty, except for them.

"It's early," Leyladin said quietly.

"They obviously know you." Cerryl glanced around the room, which held only ten tables. Unlike the front room, where the polished tables were bare, all the tables in the rear dining area bore pale blue linen and full sets of cutlery. The rear dining area emphasized that Furenk's was the most expensive inn in Fairhaven, where all the wealthy factors stayed, and where Cerryl had dined once—with Faltar, for a dinner that had cost him three silvers, with a single goblet of wine and no real extras. That had been a dinner in the front room—not that Cerryl had even known about the rear dining area. A lighted small polished bronze lamp rested in the middle of each table, the ten the only illumination, giving the room a low and discreet illumination.

"This is the only inn in Fairhaven that Father will frequent. So . . . we're known here."

"Lady Leyladin." Cerryl wondered why the title bothered him.

"You make that sound so cold."

"I'm sorry."

"Lady . . . ser?" A thin older woman—also in the dark blue trousers and vest with the pale blue shirt—stood beside the table. "This evening, we have the special chicken breast or the tender beef over Furenk's pasta."

"The chicken," said Leyladin.

"I'll have that, too."

"And the good red wine," added the healer.

"The same." Cerryl didn't know what else to say.

The serving woman inclined her head and stepped away.

"What did Lyasa mean when she said she hoped you could talk before?" he asked after a moment of silence. "Before what?"

"Oh, Cerryl."

"Before what?"

"Before I leave for Lydiar."

"You just got back from Hydolar," Cerryl said, almost peevishly.

"I probably shouldn't have left there as soon as I did, but Gorsuch said it was clear that the Duke was much better."

"Gorsuch? Is he the mage there?"

"He's the mage and the Council's representative. He promised to summon me if things changed. Now I know why he and the High Wizard wanted me back in Fairhaven." Leyladin spread her hands, almost helplessly. "Sterol has requested that I attend Duke Estalin's only son. The boy is weak and ill from the bloody flux and does not seem to be improving."

"Why you?"

"I'm young and strong, devoted to Myral, and attracted to you. My father relies on the roads."

"What does all that about you—"

"Those are all reasons why I can be trusted to go to the seaport nearest to Recluce. Good healers are scarce enough in Candar."

"People leave . . . I suppose." Cerryl still wasn't sure why people would leave Fairhaven. The city was orderly, clean. Life was good so long as you obeyed the rules, but any land had rules. "I wish you weren't going."

"So do I."

Two fluted crystal goblets appeared on the table. "Here you be. Two of the good red. That'll be six."

"There." Leyladin slipped a silver onto the table before Cerryl could even reach his wallet. "I'll take care of it."

Four coppers reappeared on the table, but the blonde healer left them there.

"You'll let me get the dinner?" Cerryl didn't like relying on generosity, even Leyladin's.

"How about half of it?"

Cerryl wasn't sure even about that, but he nodded, then looked back into Leyladin's green eyes.

Leyladin took a sip from the goblet. "Not bad."

Cerryl followed her example. To him, the wine tasted excellent, better than any he'd had except for the dinner at Leyladin's. "It tastes good, but I've had a long day." He yawned.

"It's better like this, right now. You're so tired, anyway."

"I'm not that tired."

"You're yawning, and I just got back." Her eyes danced in the lamplight. "You're tired of me already?"

"That's not—" He shook his head. "You are impossible."

"I've tried to let you know that. So did my father. He agreed that I was the most trouble, if you recall."

"I seem to recall something like that."

The server slipped a heavy gilt-rimmed pale blue china plate in front of Leyladin and then one in front of Cerryl. One each was a boned chicken breast covered in a cream sauce. Beside the chicken was a dark rice that Cerryl had never seen, also topped with the cream sauce. A second small plate contained freshly cut slices of early peaches, covered with baby mint leaves and a clear glaze. Cerryl hoped he had enough silvers in his wallet. He nodded to the server. "Thank you."

"We hope you enjoy your dinner, ser and lady. Would you like anything else?"

Cerryl glanced at Leyladin and got the faintest of headshakes. "No, thank you."

The server nodded and left them alone in the quiet room, so quiet that only murmurs from the main dining area drifted to them.

Leyladin cut a small bit of chicken and tasted it, then smiled. "It's good."

Cerryl followed her example. The spice and cream chicken, flavored with orange, trilia, and peppers, was excellent. He saw why Faltar preferred eating out of the Halls, but then he had to wonder how his blond peer could afford such food. "I fear I could get too accustomed to this kind of food."

"Furenk serves better than at the duke's table in Hydolar. Much better." The healer grimaced. "Much of the food in the mages' Meal Hall is better than the duke's fare."

"That's another reason why you shouldn't go to Lydiar."

"Duke Estalin serves a better table. That's what Anya told me."

"How did she know you were going?"

"She was with Sterol when he requested that I go."

"Hmmmm . . ." Cerryl took another sip of the wine. "Do you get some sort of escort?"

"I had a full score of lancers to and from Hydolar."

"I got ten of Eliasar's worst when I went to Fenard." The White mage mock-snorted. "You are definitely of greater value to the Brotherhood."

"That was before the Council made you a full mage."

"Now, you think, I might get a full score of the worst?"

Leyladin half-laughed, half-chuckled at Cerryl's dry tone. "Perhaps a score and a half."

"You are so encouraging."

"I said I was trouble."

For a long moment Cerryl just looked across the low lamp into the deep green eyes, letting the silence draw out.

"Cerryl? Why were you looking at me like that?"

"Because you have beautiful eyes." *Because I could fall into them and never emerge.*

"Do you tell all the girls that?"

Cerryl flushed. "I've never told anyone that."

"I'm sorry. I must have sounded cruel. I didn't mean it that way." She looked down at the goblet in her long fingers.

"There haven't been—"

She held up a hand. "You don't have to explain. Sometimes I forget. That's all. How do you like the chicken? You didn't say."

*What did she forget? That I'm not the son of a trader or a merchant? That I haven't had mistresses and the like?* "Ah . . . the chicken . . . I liked it very much. The rice, too." He glanced down at the empty pale blue china. "And the peaches." That plate was equally empty, and he hoped he hadn't gulped them all down. He didn't even really remember eating them.

"The glaze was good."

He stifled a yawn, swallowing it and hoping Leyladin didn't notice.

"You're tired. I can tell that."

"I'm fine."

"You are tired, and you are going to walk me home. Then you are going to walk to your apartment and get a good night's sleep before you go on duty tomorrow." Leyladin rose, deftly leaving four silvers on the table.

"I was—"

"It's the least I can do if you think I'm going off to abandon you."

"I didn't say that."

"But you feel that way, and I don't want you to." She offered a warm smile. "Come on. I'm tired, too."

Cerryl found himself nodding, realizing that she had been traveling for at least two days—yet she looked wonderful. He wouldn't have appeared nearly so good. That he knew. He offered his arm as they stepped through the main dining area, now nearly filled.

"She's the lady healer . . . a White mage . . . could be a relative . . ."

". . . look good together, though . . ."

"Lady Leyladin . . . don't know him . . ."

In the foyer, the tall man in blue bowed. "Good evening, Lady Leyladin . . . ser."

Leyladin smiled and turned to the functionary. "Dassaor, this is the mage Cerryl. My father thinks most highly of him."

"No one would ever question your father's judgment, lady. We hope to see you both more often." Dassaor bowed.

Cerryl inclined his head ever so slightly. "Thank you, Dassaor."

Once they were outside and headed toward the Wizards' Square,

Cerryl glanced at the blonde healer. "You never told me your father thought highly of me."

"He does. He's amazed at you, particularly at how well you speak."

"I've worked hard at it. I didn't want to sound as though I'd just come from the mines."

"You've done more than that. Kinowin speaks well, but there's a roughness around his words. Yours are polished. You should feel pleased. Not because my father is amazed, but because of what you've made of yourself."

*What have I made of myself? A junior mage who must still watch his back and every hint of intrigue? A man who cannot even pay for the dinner of the woman he loves?* "I don't know that I've made that much of myself."

She laughed, gently. "You are hard in judging yourself."

The square was empty as they turned north on the Avenue.

"I guess I have to be. Whose judgment dare I trust?"

"You're wise there. I would not trust any other than Myral, and he is old and fading."

"You worry about him, don't you?"

"He's like an uncle of sorts . . . the only one I could talk to about the things a healer feels."

"You understand trade and your father, and you love him, but he doesn't really understand you?"

"He tries, but . . . no."

They turned west a long block below the Market Square, and Cerryl could see the lamps blazing in the windows of Layel's house.

"Will you let me know when you return? Do you know how long?"

"I will. I don't think it should be more than two eight-days. That's if it's the flux."

They both understood. If she could not help the boy heal, another two weeks of flux might well kill the child.

Leyladin turned at the door, taking Cerryl's hands, leaning forward, and brushing her cheek with her lips. "I enjoyed tonight."

"So did I."

He waited until the heavy door closed before he turned and began to walk back to the Halls of the Mages.

# IX

Cerryl stood beside one of the pillars at the rear and to the left side of the Council Chamber. He looked across the expanse of white tunics and robes, though the robes were generally preferred by older mages, such as Esaak and Myral. Each of the circular pillars that flanked the sides of the Council Chamber was of white granite, fluted, and flawless, except for flecks of gold. From the top of each pillar were draped red hangings, swagged from one pillar to the next. The base of each pillar was a cube of a shimmering gold stone. Polished white marble tiles, filled with golden swirls, comprised the chamber floor. Gold oak desks and their accompanying gold oak chairs flanked the center aisle. Despite the summer heat that baked Fairhaven outside the Halls of the Mages, the chamber remained comfortable.

The High Wizard Sterol stood on the golden-shot marble dais at the eastern end of the chamber, and flanking him were the two over-mages—Jeslek and Kinowin—the High Council, except that the three were always called the Council from what Cerryl could determine.

Sterol was speaking. ". . . Since last we assembled, many of our concerns have proved to be justified . . . particularly about the predatory nature of those plying trade from the Black Isle . . .

"Therefore, we are recommending to the Dukes of Lydiar and Hydlen, to the Council of Sligo, the Viscount of Certis, and the prefect of Gallos that they impose an additional surtax of 20 percent on goods arriving in ships bearing the flag of Hamor or the dark isle."

"Your pardon, High Wizard," puffed Esaak, rising from a desk in the second row. "How will that improve the revenues for the Guild?"

Sterol gestured toward his left. "Overmage Kinowin can better explain that."

"This surtax is not the best answer," admitted Kinowin, standing at the end of the first row. "At the moment, it is the only means we have to address the problem. As all of you know, highways are costlier to build and repair than the oceans and a few ports. What has been happening more and more is that importers in Candar, especially the Sligan and Spidlarian Councils, have been taking advantage of our roads and traders. The Black Isle and occasionally Hamorian merchants have been shipping goods to ports in Candar close to our roads. They sell these goods more cheaply because they do not bear the delivery costs in full. The Guild has almost eliminated brigands in eastern Candar, at least those who prey on the highways. At times, it costs less to ship wool from Land's End on Recluce to Lydiar than to carry it by wagon from Montgren. So . . . any good that must be grown, produced, or collected away from the highways . . ."

"Wait . . . you were just saying that our highways were being used against us, and now—"

"Patience, Broka . . . patience," said Kinowin tiredly. "Trade is complex. Let me explain. Those who buy goods are those who have coins. Those who have coins live in the cities. The cities are either ports or connected to ports by the White highways. Recluce is a much smaller place than Candar, and the Blacks use their arts to increase production of many goods, especially wool, oilseeds, and some fruits they dry. They also produce luxury goods that would otherwise come from across the Eastern Ocean. Their weather mages see the storms upon the seas, and they lose fewer ships. For all these reasons, many of their goods are much cheaper."

Cerryl wanted to rub his forehead. Never had he thought he would hear discussions on costs of trade in a meeting of the White mages. He turned toward the middle section of desks and caught a glimpse of Anya's red hair. Seated to her left was Faltar, his white-blond hair standing out even more than the red of Anya's. On Anya's right was the dark-bearded Fydel.

Mutterings began to rise around the chamber.

". . . can't he make it simple . . ."

". . . just send a fleet . . . if it's that much trouble . . ."

". . . send the lancers to Spidlaria and clean out their demon-damned Council . . ."

"Why do we even have to do anything about Recluce? All the Blacks do is sit on their island and cultivate order. Anyone who causes trouble gets thrown out—usually to our benefit." That came from a thin gray-haired woman in the middle of the chamber, one of the many that Cerryl did not recognize.

"We're not talking about an arms action now," Jeslek said mildly from where he stood beside Kinowin. "Aren't you tired of our gold going to Recluce so that the Blacks can use it to buy Bristan and Hamorian goods?"

"Their spices and wines are better and cheaper," a heavy voice rumbled from the back.

"So is some of their cabinetry," added another voice.

"And their wool—"

"If you can wear it, Myral!"

Abruptly the white-haired and sun-eyed Jeslek strode to the front of the dais beside Sterol. "Silence!" His eyes roved the room, chaos rising around him.

A faint smile played across Sterol's face as he slipped off the side of the dais and down the far side of the chamber behind the pillars.

"What Kinowin is saying is," Jeslek announced loudly, "that if we let people buy cheaper goods from Recluce traders, too many peasants and artisans in Candar will go hungry, and they won't pay their taxes, and we'll have trouble supporting the Guild and maintaining the highways."

"So ... what are you proposing, Jeslek?"

"Nothing major. Exactly what the High Wizard proposed. Just a 30 percent surtax on goods from Recluce."

"Thirty percent? He said 20. I'd rather drink that red swill from Kyphros," rumbled the bass voice.

"Precisely my point."

"That will increase the number of smugglers."

"We'll use some of the money to build up the fleet to stop that."

"And the rest? Does it go into your pocket, Jeslek?"

"Hardly. That's up to the Council, but I'd suggest that it be split between an increased stipend for Guild members, rebuilding the square, and funding the road construction. Would anyone else like a word?"

"Won't that just funnel more golds into Spidlar?"

"What about Sarronnyn ..."

"Southwind will love that ..."

Cerryl's eyes caught the flash of red as Anya slipped from her desk and through the pillars to follow Sterol. He frowned as the two mages vanished through the archway and out toward the foyer of the main Hall. Anya and the High Wizard—he definitely didn't like that. Leyladin had said something about Anya being there when Sterol had told her she was being sent to Lydiar. Was Anya everywhere?

"A moment," said Kinowin. "A moment. I know that the honorable Jeslek means well, but I would suggest that an increased stipend for any mages would be unwise right now. Most of the merchants would see the surtax as going entirely to our pockets, and that would cause more unrest."

The heavyset Myral stood and glanced around the chamber, waiting for the murmuring to subside.

Lyasa slipped up beside Cerryl. "You don't want to sit down?"

"I can sense what's going on better here."

"What *is* going on? Besides more taxes on things from Recluce?" The dark-haired and olive-eyed mage raised her jet-black eyebrows.

"Much more," he said in a low voice. "I just don't know what."

"That's always true," Lyasa agreed.

Both waited for Myral to speak.

Finally, the older mage coughed once, twice, and cleared his throat. "I am a few years older than most of you." Myral waited for the subdued chuckles to subside. "And, being older, have had more time to peruse the archives and the old records.

"Every generation or so, this arises. Why?" Myral shrugged. "I could not say, save perhaps that every generation of rulers of the lands of Candar must learn anew the price for unity in trade and peace. As the overmage Kinowin has said, and as the honorable Jeslek pointed out, a surtax is not the best answer. In fact, it should not be necessary, but necessary it is, because other lands, especially that of Spidlar, feel they should not contribute to the roads and order that hold Candar together. The most permanent answer would be for us to take Spidlar, as we were forced to take Montgren so many centuries before." Another shrug followed. "Alas, there are two other lands between our domains and those of Spidlar."

At Myral's woebegone look, another round of laughter filled the chamber.

"So . . . for the moment, I would say that it behooves us to request the surtax be levied. Then . . . we shall see those who are prudent and look to the future good of Candar and those who look to lining their wallets with golds, no matter how great the price their children may pay." Myral took a sweeping bow and seated himself.

A movement caught Cerryl's eyes, and he watched as Sterol eased his way back along the pillars on the south side of the Hall, reappearing at the side of the front of the dais, studying Jeslek.

Anya reappeared at her desk, and even from where Cerryl stood he could see the apologetic smile she flashed to Fydel and then to Faltar.

"She is good, in a sneaky way," murmured Lyasa. "You do have a vantage point here."

Cerryl nodded, pondering Myral's words—words that had sounded fine. Somehow what the older mage had said disturbed Cerryl, as if something did not scree true.

Darkness, he wished he knew more.

# X

Despite the darkness, Cerryl could feel the heat as he found himself struggling through a forest, but a forest like no other he had seen, one with trees taller than the Wizards' Tower, trees that he could sense but not see. He took a breath, then another, as he found his lungs laboring, as a cloying and sickly sweet scent permeated the air around him.

A long vine swung by his shoulder, then brushed the bare skin of his upper arm again. It turned woody like a liana, sending forth rootlets to cling to him as though he were one of the massive trees of the unfamiliar forest. The strange and cloying perfume grew stronger . . . so strong he could barely breathe, and his heart pounded in his chest.

Cerryl bolted upright in his bed, sweat streaming down his face, as if he were standing at his guard post in full summer sun. Or in a cook fire . . .

Chaos flickered from his locked door—a door he always kept locked when he slept—now that he could lock it, unlike when he'd been a student. He slipped toward the door, extending his senses. Without opening it, he could sense the white glow of chaos shielded, could feel the footsteps behind a light shield, could catch the faintest scent of sandalwood perfume.

Anya . . . headed along the corridor toward Faltar's room.

Cerryl forced himself to take a long and slow breath as he eased back to his bed, where he sat down slowly—suddenly shivering. After a moment, he wrapped the red woolen blanket around himself, then massaged his throbbing forehead with the fingers of his right hand.

". . . only a dream . . ." Except it wasn't, not exactly. The forest and the clinging vines had been a dream, but Anya had definitely been outside his door on her way to visit Faltar. He'd sensed her chaos aura before—on all the times when she'd visited Faltar when he and Cerryl had been only student mages. Now that Faltar was a full mage, albeit junior like Cerryl, there was no reason they couldn't sleep together, but Anya was still sneaking to see Faltar. That meant she didn't want it known she was seeing Faltar. Was she fearful of Sterol's jealousy? Cerryl shook his head slowly.

Lyasa had mentioned Anya and Jeslek—so how many mages was Anya bedding? Cerryl frowned, recalling the words of Benthann—the mistress of the scrivener Tellis, for whom he'd apprenticed before the Guild had found him. What had Benthann said? Something like . . .

"Sex is the only power a woman has in Fairhaven. Remember that. Even if she has a strong room full of coins or, light forbid, she's a mage, sex is the only real power a woman has . . . The only thing a man offers a woman, really, is power. Coins are power. Don't forget that. Sex for power, power for sex, that's the way the world works."

So . . . Anya, powerful a mage as she was, was trading sex for power? Or a future obligation or . . . something? Cerryl took a deep breath.

Darkness, he hoped it didn't turn out that way between him and Leyladin. It seemed different . . . but how would he know?

*You know . . . you have to trust yourself . . .* His lips tightened. That was easy enough to think, but he'd already seen how easy it was for people, even for himself, to deceive themselves.

*Will you be able to avoid deceiving yourself?* Still shivering under the blanket, he massaged his aching forehead, knowing that the morning would come all too early. Far, far, far too early.

# XI

Cerryl wiped his forehead. Even in the shaded part of the rampart area of the guardhouse he was hot, and summer had yet to come. The afternoons were getting warmer and warmer, and it would be at least another eight-day, from what he'd heard, before Kinowin split gate-guard duty into two rotations. With his luck, he'd probably get the hot late-afternoon duty.

*Creeaaakkkk . . .* He glanced out along the White highway to the north. A single cart rolled toward the gates. The gray donkey pulling it was led by a white-haired woman who plodded down the road almost as methodically as the beast.

Cerryl couldn't sense any medallion on the cart, and he leaned over the rampart. "Gyral?"

"Yes, ser?" The lanky detail leader glanced up.

"Do us both a favor and yell to that woman. Tell her that if she doesn't have a medallion and she gets close to the gates, I'll have to destroy her cart and take her donkey. Just tell her to turn around and take one of the farm roads—or something. Or that she'll need to get a medallion right now."

The White Guard frowned, then grinned. "You know her?"

"No. I just don't like taking things from old women. Maybe she doesn't know the laws."

"I don't know, ser. Some of them are pretty stubborn. I'll try." Gyral marched away from the two other guards toward the approaching peasant.

*Creaaakkk . . .* The cart carried several stacks of woven grass baskets and some of reeds. The woman made her way toward the gates, aided by a long wooden staff half again her height.

Gyral squared his shoulders. "Woman! You can't use the White roads without a medallion. If you come to the gates and you don't have the coppers for a medallion, then we'll have to take your cart and donkey."

"The roads be for all. That be what you White ninnies are always saying. I be one of the all, and I need to sell my baskets so that my family can live till harvest. And no spare coppers are you a-getting."

"You can't bring the cart in on the highway," Gyral answered. "Not without a medallion."

"There be no other way. Like as you know that."

"We'll have to take your cart and baskets." Gyral stepped backward.

"You and who else, young fellow?" The crone raised the walking stick and brandished it, waving it at the detail leader.

The lancer backed away and glanced toward Cerryl.

Cerryl gave an overlarge shrug and called down, "If that's the way she wants it!"

Donkey, cart, and woman creaked toward the gate with no sign of slowing.

"You have to stop," announced Gyral.

"I belong not to your White City, and, by the light, I'll sell where I please. The land gives me those rights, not some man who wears white and rides in a gold carriage." The crone swung the staff at Gyral and the guard beside him. Both backed away, although they had their shortswords out.

"Stand back!" snapped Cerryl.

Even the crone looked up.

Cerryl concentrated, trying to form a fireball that was part firelance, one that would strike the staff and not the woman.

*Whhssst!* The end of the staff vanished in flame, and then white ashes drifted across the stones.

The crone held a piece of wood no longer than a short truncheon, one that flamed. She dropped it on the granite paving stones before the guardhouse.

"Darkness and the Black angels take you!" The woman clawed at her belt, and a dark iron knife appeared as she launched herself at Gyral.

*Whhhsstt!* The firebolt enveloped the old woman, and when it subsided where the crone had stood was a faint greasy spot and a pile of white ashes that drifted in the light breeze.

"Stupid woman . . . mage tried to give her a chance."

"Don't buck 'em . . . not if you want to live . . ."

Cerryl leaned against the rampart stones, faintly nauseated. He straightened. "Unhitch the donkey and put it in the stable. Unload the baskets. They might be useful somewhere."

When the cart stood alone below the guardhouse, Cerryl loosed a last fireball, and, once more, only ashes remained, ashes and a few iron fittings that prisoner details carried away. The highway was empty again in the hot afternoon, and Cerryl sank onto the stool in the shade.

He wanted to shake his head. Even when you tried to explain the rules or help people, some of them just didn't believe. The taxes weren't new. They'd been there since the time of Creslin, something like three centuries or more, and there were still people who disputed them, who refused to accept the laws unless you used overwhelming force on them. Or, like the old woman, people who turned the words to what they wanted them to mean and then attacked when their interpretation was denied.

He hadn't had any choice at the end. Even for him, the rules were absolute. Anyone who attacked a gate guard died. Had he made it worse by trying to warn her? Or telling her she needed to pay for a medallion? Would it have been the same either way?

He wiped his forehead again, then glanced obliquely toward the sun, blazing in the green-blue sky. A long time until sunset—too long.

# XII

Kinowin had a new wall hanging—one with blue and purple diamonds pierced by black arrows, more like crossbow quarrels. The gently flickering light from the pair of wall lamps and the table lamp cast shadows from Kinowin and Cerryl across the hanging.

*Are we as insubstantial as those shadows?* Cerryl wondered.

The overmage followed Cerryl's eyes. "Do you like it?"

"The colors are . . . brilliant, I guess."

"It's Analerian. Jeslek sent it to me with his last dispatch to the Council. He knows I like hangings—and that I dislike being indebted to him." The big blond mage took a long pull from the overlarge mug on the edge of the screeing table. "Ah . . . getting hot too soon this year."

"Is he going to be High Wizard someday?" Cerryl had no doubts but wanted Kinowin's reaction and felt he could only seek it while he was still considered inexperienced.

Kinowin snorted. "The entire Guild decides that."

Cerryl had the feeling that the Guild agreed to support the strongest candidate.

"You don't think so, young Cerryl?"

"I do not know enough to agree or disagree, ser."

"Carefully said." The overmage pulled at his clean-shaven chin. "The Guild often recognizes the strongest mage as the most suitable."

Cerryl had understood early that the Guild wasn't about to deny any mage who was strong enough. Since Jeslek was strong enough to create small mountains, sooner or later he would be High Wizard.

Kinowin lifted the mug again, then looked at the younger mage. "Cerryl, you've been on gate duty for nearly two seasons. You're going to have morning duty at the north gate before long. It's a little earlier than I would like, but Bealtur, Heralt, and Myredin will be made full mages at the next Council meeting—that's but an eight-day from now."

Cerryl knew Heralt and Bealtur but not Myredin—except by sight and a few casual conversations in the eight-days.

"Heralt will take afternoon duty. He's the most dependable." The overmage studied Cerryl. "You know them. What do you think?"

"I don't know Myredin. I know that Heralt is solid and trustworthy."

"Carefully said ... once more." Kinowin laughed. "I'd like it if you didn't tell anyone. Most know, but I'd still like your silence."

"Yes, ser." Silence was usually a good idea, at least when an overmage requested it. *When Kinowin requested it,* Cerryl corrected himself mentally.

"Are you still upset about the old farm woman?"

"Yes." Cerryl thought and added, "I know that we have to hold to the laws. I wanted to warn her that she needed a medallion." He paused and cleared his throat. "What upset me was that she wouldn't listen. It's not as though the laws are new. But she wouldn't listen to anyone, and she drew a blade on a guard, and I had to turn her into ash."

"Everywhere there are laws," Kinowin said slowly. "We have laws. Hamor has laws. Even Recluce has laws. No land can long last without laws, and without the people obeying them. Not without thievery and killing and wastes in the streets. Yet, in every land, there are those who feel that they do not have to obey the laws. Some have so many coins that they attempt to buy their way around the laws. Some have armsmen, and some are like the old woman." The big overmage stood abruptly and walked to the window without speaking, as if he were debating what to say next.

Outside, the air was clear, and Cerryl could see the deep purple of the early-night sky past Kinowin's profile.

"The Guild has laws, too. We are the White Order, and yet ... some here also find it difficult to abide by those laws." Kinowin turned. "Sterol told you how difficult it was for an outsider to become a White mage, and yet, in some ways, you—and I—for the same reasons, understand better than those raised in the crèche the need for order. Yet order, because of the Blacks of Recluce, has a bad name in Fairhaven."

Cerryl tried not to hold his breath, knowing Kinowin might have more to say and afraid that if he spoke the older mage would stop. He still couldn't help but think about the old woman, though he knew he could have done nothing else, not as a junior mage and gate guard.

"The ways to corrupt order are many. The allure of sex, or power, or the desperate desire to be respected—they can all corrupt. Who of us does not wish to be loved and wanted and respected and powerful?" The overmage laughed. "If anyone tells you any of those are not appealing to him—or her—watch that mage most carefully."

"Ah ... yes, ser."

Kinowin turned. "Elsinot will stand your duty on the day the Council meets to confirm the new mages. I will summon you to the dais to tell the story of the old woman. Do not linger over it. Tell it briefly, but tell it with truth. Do you understand?"

"I will be there, ser. I cannot say I understand why."

A sardonic smile crossed Kinowin's face. "Let us just say that I see the need to let some of the brethren know that we are not universally loved and that our laws—fair as they are—do not seem fair to all." He gestured to the door. "I have kept you long enough."

Cerryl rose from the chair.

# XIII

The dark ships fitted by Creslin began to ply the Gulf of Candar, seizing all that they could and repaying none, yet all of the plunder laid up upon the stone piers of Land's End was not enough to feed and clothe and shelter all those who flocked to the once-desert isle.

The former dark guards of Westwind craved iron for their blades and blood to be shed upon those blades, and the wretched refuse from Renklaar and far Swartheld and Brysta and even those from Valmurl demanded that the Black mages feed and clothe them as befitted the wealthy.

To draw yet more coins from storm-battered and valiant Candar, Creslin sought greater enchantments and turned foul juice into a green brandy that so bewitched the mind and senses of all that betook of it that they would pay any number of coins to achieve yet another taste.

With those coins and those minted from the jewelry taken from captives, Creslin sent forth his vessels once more and had them pay whatever the grain factors of the ports of Candar asked, save that those who refused to trade found their warehouses torched by mysterious fires and flames that appeared from nowhere.

Yet even those coins were not enough, and the black-hearted Megaera mixed both the White and Black and swirled the oceans and had them cast forth all the coins and metals and previous goods that had sunk with the Hamorian fleet . . . disregarding the lost souls that wailed with the use of each silver, each copper . . .

> *Colors of White*
> (Manual of the Guild at Fairhaven)
> Preface

# XIV

As instructed by Kinowin, Cerryl sat behind a desk in the second row on the north side of the Council Hall, watching and listening as the meeting continued. Both Kinowin and Sterol stood on the dais, but Jeslek had remained in Gallos, and his place beside the High Wizard was vacant as mages stood and spoke and then reseated themselves.

"...we see no change in trading..."

"...a season has gone by, and still the Gallosian traders are accepting goods from Recluce."

"Not directly, Disarj. They ship the ironwork and spices to Spidlaria, and then the Spidlarians barge it upriver to Elparta."

"So? They still evade the surtax."

Sterol stepped forward, his hand raised. "Peace! The surtax was imposed here, not a season ago, but by the time scrolls were drafted and messengers sent it has been less than a handful of eight-days since all traders have been notified. Some traders may not yet know. They cannot summon ships back or change cargoes in a matter of eight-days."

"They will not change," snapped the frizzy-haired and balding Disarj. "A serpent will slither all its days."

"That may be," conceded the gray-haired Sterol, his hand touching his trimmed iron gray beard, his red-flecked brown eyes mild. "We have agreed that Eliasar should be dispatched to Fenard shortly with a suitable complement of lancers to offer encouragement to the new prefect."

"...make sure there are enough lancers for that encouragement..."

"...too bad young Cerryl didn't flame a few more..."

Cerryl winced at his name but kept his eyes on the High Wizard.

Sterol waited for a lull in the soft comments. "For us to act before the traders know of the tax will raise unrest even within our own lands."

"Our traders are already uneasy," pointed out the pudgy Isork. "They claim they lose coins every eight-day."

Kinowin stepped forward and nodded to Sterol, who nodded back.

The overmage cleared his throat. "We hear from the traders. That is truth. The traders are not all of those we govern. Those who have the coins or the power to reach us are not a tenth part of the people who depend on us—or from whom we draw our armsmen and lancers. Nor is everything always as peaceable as it seems, even within and around Fairhaven itself."

Low murmurs whispered across the chamber.

Kinowin squared himself on the dais. "One of our younger mages has been guarding the north gate. He told me of a meeting there. I also asked the guards, and all swore that it occurred exactly as told me. That is as it should be and speaks highly of the training he was given by the honorable Jeslek. Before we discuss matters further, I would like you to hear this story." He gestured to Cerryl, who stepped forward. "Up here, Cerryl, where all can hear you. Now . . . tell all of the Guild what you told me."

As Sterol eased off the south side of the dais, Cerryl stepped onto the gold-shot marble of the dais. He had to clear his throat before starting. He tried not to look at Anya, with Fydel seated beside her. Faltar was on duty at the south gate. Nor did Cerryl look at Myral, who was in the first row. "It was about two eight-days ago, and I was on duty. I looked out along the highway, and there was this old woman with a staff leading an old farm cart with some baskets in it. I could tell that she didn't have a medallion. She looked poor and maybe ill. So I called down to Gyral—he was the lead lancer on duty—and I asked him to warn her that she needed to either pay for a medallion or get off the highway." Cerryl cleared his throat gently, trying to overcome his nervousness before the assembled mages.

"She wouldn't stop or get off the highway. She yelled at all of us something like, 'The roads be for everyone!' She said she was a common person and she needed the road to sell her baskets so that her family could live until harvest and that she had no spare coppers for the White ninnies. I told her she'd have to give up the cart and the baskets, since she wouldn't pay for a medallion, and she screamed that the roads were for everyone. She took her staff and threatened the guards." Cerryl swallowed. "I used a firebolt and turned the staff into ashes. Then she screamed that darkness and the Black angels should take us. She grabbed a knife and attacked the guards. I had to flame her." Cerryl glanced toward Kinowin.

The overmage murmured, "Stay here for a moment." Then he turned to the Hall. "I think that young Cerryl was attempting to be both fair and understanding while upholding the laws and ways of Recluce."

". . . more than fair," came a murmur from somewhere.

". . . demon-damned peasants."

". . . ignorant beasts."

"Yet," continued Kinowin, his voice strengthening to silence the murmurs, "this peasant woman had no interest in his fairness or the laws. All she wanted was the easiest way to market and the most coins. Was she that different from the late Prefect Lyam? Or from all the smugglers who try to avoid taxes and tariffs? We meet, and too often, I think, we forget that the rules of law, and the need for such rules to ensure prosperity, they are merely nodded at even by those in Fairhaven. Too often our merchants take for granted the smoothness and the directness of our roads. Too often we do not see the anger at us, because we have forged a glorious city and prosperity for all Candar. Too often we would rather be loved than respected." Kinowin paused. "Before I let Cerryl resume his seat, are there any questions?"

A tall mage halfway back in the chamber rose. "You said that this woman called us 'White ninnies.' Did she use those words?"

"Yes, she did. She also said that she had rights under the land that no man dressed in white and riding in a gold carriage could take away."

Another mage—Isork—stood. "Did she actually say that the Black angels should take you?"

"Yes."

Isork sat down.

"Perhaps we should send Eliasar to Gallos sooner rather than later," suggested Fydel from the middle of the chamber, Anya practically whispering in his ear as the square-bearded mage spoke.

Sterol stepped back onto the dais from the columns at the south side of the chamber, waiting for another round of murmurs to die down. "The Council has decided that Eliasar should not depart until closer to harvest." He turned and gestured to Cerryl. "Remember what happened at the gates. Cerryl attempted to handle the old woman gently. The guards know that, and they will tell others. Unhappily, there will always be those who respect little but force. There will always be those who do not pay willingly for the prosperity and peace that the Guild has provided Candar. There will always be those who believe the lies and deceptions of the Black Isle. We cannot make all our people happy, but we can make them respect the Order. And that we will do.

"Many of you know that the overmage Jeslek is working in Gallos to ensure that the new prefect will indeed respect the Guild. We are also building more warships to patrol the gulf and the Eastern Ocean. All Gallos—and the Black traders—will respect Fairhaven before we are done. That will be the occasion to send Eliasar and the lancers." Sterol laughed. "Shortly, I will begin assigning mages to those warships that will be completed sometime this winter, and the Black traders will pay tariffs or they will not trade with Candar."

Kinowin nodded to Cerryl, who stepped down and back to his seat.

Sterol gave a nod to Kinowin, who returned it with one barely perceptible.

"Now that our business is complete," Sterol said in a warmer tone, "let us bring in the new mages."

Sterol waited on the dais, Kinowin to his right, as Esaak escorted the three figures in the tunics of student mages forward and down the center aisle of the chamber.

"High Wizard, I present the candidates for induction as full mages and members of the Guild." Esaak inclined his head, then stepped back and to the side.

Sterol let the silence draw out for a moment before speaking. "Bealtur, Heralt, and Myredin . . . you are here because you have studied, because you have learned the basic skills of magery, and because you have proved you understand the importance of the Guild to the future of all Candar . . ."

Cerryl smiled at the words that deviated not at all from those Sterol had employed when Cerryl himself had stood before the dais.

". . . we hold a special trust for all mages, to bring a better life to those who follow the White way, to further peace and prosperity, and to ensure that all our talents are used for the greater good, of both those in Fairhaven and those throughout Candar." Sterol paused, surveying the three. "Do you, of your own free will, promise to use your talents for the good of the Guild and for the good of Fairhaven, and of all Candar?"

There were three quiet assents.

"And do you faithfully promise to hold to the rules of the Guild, even when those rules may conflict with your personal and private desires?"

"Yes," answered the three simultaneously.

"Do you promise that you will do your personal best to ensure that chaos is never raised against the helpless and always to benefit the greater good?"

"Yes."

"And finally, do you promise that you will always stand by those in the Guild to ensure that mastery of the forces of chaos—and order—is limited to those who will use such abilities for good and not for personal gain and benefit?"

"Yes."

"In the powers of chaos and in the sight of the Guild, you are each a full mage of the White Order of Fairhaven . . ."

A shimmering touch of chaos brushed the sleeves of the three, and the red apprentice stripes were gone.

"Welcome, Bealtur, Heralt, and Myredin . . ." Sterol offered a broad smile and looked across the assembled group. "Now that we have welcomed the new mages, our business is over, and all may greet them."

Scattered murmurs broke out across the chamber.

Sterol glanced down at the three. "I'm very pleased that all of you have succeeded. You have different talents, and in the difficult days before the Guild we will need each of those talents, I suspect."

Cerryl waited for the older mages to congratulate the three before he stepped forward, beginning with the dark-eyed and curly-haired Heralt. "Congratulations, Heralt."

"Thank you. You and Kinowin made it easier."

Cerryl offered a smile. "Don't forget the High Wizard. He seeks talent." With a nod, Cerryl stepped up to Bealtur. "Congratulations."

"Thank you." The goateed young mage's words were polite, even, and without warmth.

"And congratulations to you." Cerryl nodded politely at Myredin. Myredin nodded back, his intense and slightly bulging gray eyes fixed somewhere beyond Cerryl.

Cerryl stepped back and to the side, back along the pillars on the north side of the chamber.

"I have a good feel about Heralt, too."

Cerryl turned. Kinowin and Myral stood behind the pillar. Myral inclined his head, and Cerryl joined the two.

"I'm sure you guessed that Kinowin wanted you to be seen," said Myral. "He could have told the story without you."

"I'm your protégé, ser?" asked Cerryl.

Kinowin smiled, almost ironically. "We need you to be seen and heard. I suggest you have something to say at the next meeting. Something that sounds most reasonable, with which few will disagree. Something about trade."

"Me?"

"You." Myral coughed, covering his mouth with the gray cloth he carried everywhere. After a moment, he added, "You have the shields to stand against Jeslek's anger, and he knows that. You have no ties to the traders of Fairhaven or elsewhere, and it is important that you be seen to have a mind."

*Whether I do or not . . . whether I'm just an ignorant orphan determined and lucky enough to have become a mage.*

Kinowin lowered his voice more. "Jeslek will be High Wizard by fall, if not before."

"Why not you?" blurted Cerryl.

"Your judgment of character is sound," said Myral with a chuckle, "but not of age. Kinowin is closer to my age than to Jeslek's. For him to use power as Jeslek does would kill him within a handful of years."

"We'll talk more later," said Kinowin, "but this is one of the few places where the three of us could talk for a moment without much notice." He raised his voice. "Thank you, young Cerryl."

"I did what I thought best," Cerryl replied with a bow, his voice also pitched to carry beyond the pillars.

Myral coughed and covered a smile as the young mage bowed again and turned, walking back along the pillars.

"Cerryl? Have you a moment?" The words arrived with the impact of the trilia and sandalwood fragrance used by Anya.

Cerryl offered a head bow to the red-haired mage. "For you, Anya, I always have time."

"Obvious but gracious, Cerryl, and I thank you for the effort."

"When one is young and unskilled as I, what else can I do?" He offered a shrug. "How might I help?"

"I was curious, just curious, mind you, about your encounter with the old woman. Were you given any instructions for situations such as that?"

"No. No one ever mentioned that I'd ever deal with old farm people. I was told about traders and haulers, and how to set up the medallions, and the general rates for wagon and cart sizes." Cerryl looked guilelessly at Anya, which was not difficult, since he spoke the truth.

"Why did you wish to warn off the old woman?"

"I didn't see any sense in destroying her cart and taking her baskets. They would add little to the treasury and would create bad feelings."

Anya nodded. "Yet you would judge when to break the rules?"

"I was not aware of breaking the rules." Cerryl could feel that Anya's questions were far from idle curiosity. "Anyone may bring a cart to the guardhouse to get a medallion, and gate guards are not allowed to destroy carts without medallions that do not come to the gates."

Anya laughed. "You could be more dangerous than Jeslek."

Cerryl bowed again. "I fear that I lack the mass of chaos that Jeslek can bring to bear upon all who would oppose him. Thus, I must think as best I can before I act."

Anya touched his shoulder. "Just keep thinking, Cerryl, and there will always be a place in the Guild for you." She flashed her brilliantly insincere smile, touched his shoulder again, warmly, and ducked away.

Cerryl wanted to wipe his forehead but didn't. The implication of Anya's remarks was certainly clear enough. He had thought that his life would get easier once he was a full mage, but he was beginning to have doubts about that, especially with all the undercurrents within the Guild.

And then to find out that Kinowin was far older than Jeslek—perhaps nearly so old as Myral? That was hard to believe, but Myral's words had held the feel and ring of truth, and that worried Cerryl.

# XV

As Cerryl crossed the courtyard in the early afternoon, his eyes went to the blonde-haired figure in green in the shadows behind the fountain.

"Leyladin!" He hurried over to her. "When did you get back?"

"Late last night." Her smile warmed him. "I slept for a while. I knew you were on duty early. Myral said you'd be here sometime after midday."

"I have to report to Kinowin for the first few days on summer duty. That's where I was. Tomorrow will be the last day of that."

"Have you seen him? Today?"

Cerryl grinned. "Just left his quarters."

"Could I entice you into something to eat at the house?" The green eyes danced.

"You could." *You could entice me into more than that . . .* "I haven't eaten much today."

"I'm ravenous. Let's go." Her eyebrows arched. "Don't expect me to be enticing in that way." A playful smile followed.

Even as Cerryl flushed, he wondered if his thoughts had been that obvious.

They walked past the fountain and its cooling spray and through the entry foyer of the front Hall and out onto the Avenue, turning north. As they passed the square, Cerryl glanced westward where white clouds were beginning to pile into the sky. "We might have some rain this afternoon."

"It rained almost every afternoon in Lydiar. There was mold everywhere." Leyladin shuddered. "It's a dirty place."

"Compared to Fairhaven, everywhere I've been is dirty."

A city patrol appeared ahead on the eastern side of the square, three guards in lancerlike uniforms, followed by a mage Cerryl didn't know, escorting a man in chains along a side street away from the Avenue.

"You don't see that very often," Leyladin said.

"The patrols? No. That's only the second or third time I've seen them since I've been in Fairhaven."

"Sometimes you forget there are patrols."

"Well . . . they do supply the prisoners who clean up the stable at the gate and the ashes if we have to destroy a wagon or cart."

"They do? I didn't know that."

Cerryl glanced sideways at her, but Leyladin seemed perfectly sincere. "You've lived here all your life."

"People here know the rules."

The White mage reflected. For the most part, people did know the rules and abided by them. They put their refuse in the rubbish wagons, their chamber pots in the sewage catches, and there were no brawls or fights in the streets. There were seldom any brigands, and no beggars or homeless urchins—not that he'd seen. He frowned. "What happens to the really poor people?"

"Most of them live on the southwest side of Fairhaven."

"I meant the ones without homes." In his almost five years in the city, Cerryl had been so busy he'd never really thought about the homeless. In the mine and farm country where he'd grown up people and children worked or died, and he'd never had the time to really explore Fairhaven.

"The Patrol sends them out of the city. If they come back, they go on the road crew, except for infants or small children. They go to the other crèche. When they get older, they get apprenticed somewhere." Leyladin made a vague gesture.

*The road crew? For life, like all the others?* He moistened his lips but concentrated on her words and offered a response. "Probably to the tanners and the renderers and trades like that."

"It's better than dying. It's a trade and a living."

Cerryl contained a wince. He could have been one of those children, but Leyladin was right. Even the road crew was better than dying, and not that much worse than grubbing in the fields for life—or working for a renderer.

"It's a pretty day, much nicer than in Lydiar."

"I'm sure," he answered.

South of the Market Square, Leyladin turned left, and they walked the block to her house. There the blonde healer took out a large brass key and inserted it in the lock. "Soaris is off today, and Father is back in Vergren again. Then he's going to Tyrhavven."

"He was in Vergren the last time I talked to you."

"He's worried about something, but he hasn't said much about it. I think it's timber this time. That's why he has to go to Sligo." Leyladin opened the door and held it open.

Inside was cooler than in the afternoon sun, much cooler, and Cerryl blotted away the dampness on his forehead, hoping he would cool inside the granite dwelling.

"Meridis!" The blonde walked through the foyer into the silk-hung entry hall and then through another door.

Cerryl followed her into the kitchen.

The gray-haired Meridis, wearing a pale blue shirt and no overtunic, looked up from the worktable where she was rolling out something. "Lady, I did not expect you so soon."

"We need something to eat. Nothing fancy. Fruit, cheese, some bread ..."

"Aye, those I can do." Meridis wiped her hands on the weathered gray apron cinched around her. "Go and sit down. Be but a bit. Even have some cool redberry. Now ... you sit down."

Feeling almost shooed from the kitchen, Cerryl followed Leyladin into a small room where a golden oak table with four chairs sat halfway into a hexagonal room, the outer three walls comprised of floor-to-ceiling windows facing north. Leyladin plopped down in a chair on one side of the table, her back to the windows.

Cerryl sat across from her. "Redberry?"

"I drink it when I can. Too much wine or ale, and I have trouble with healing. They say that the full Blacks on Recluce don't drink wine or ale or spirits."

Meridis appeared with a warm loaf of dark bread, a bowl filled with early peaches and green apples, and three wedges of cheese—one yellow, one yellow-white, and one pale white. Setting those down, she departed, only to return immediately with two platters and cutlery. A third trip brought two of the crystal goblets and two pitchers. "Redberry and golden ale. Now . . . eat afore you both melt." A brusque nod preceded her departure.

"Ah . . . she . . ."

"Meridis is family. She's not hesitated to let me know when she disapproved. She likes you. That's why the ale."

"How would she know?" Cerryl couldn't help frowning. "She's only seen me once—that I know of."

"She makes up her mind quickly. She doesn't change it easily." A smile crossed Leyladin's lips. "She's usually right. Not always, but enough that I'd never wager against her. Neither would Father." She poured ale for Cerryl and redberry for herself.

Cerryl waited for her to take a sip of her redberry before tasting the ale. "It's good. Then, everything here is good."

"Everything?" She arched her eyebrows.

"Everything."

"I'm glad you approve. Have some cheese . . . or something. You're pale."

Cerryl cut several slices of cheese off each wedge and nodded to her.

"Thank you." The healer took a wedge of the white and one of the yellow, then broke off a chunk of the dark bread.

Cerryl tried the pale white with bread. Before he knew it, he'd eaten three wedges of cheese with bread.

"You were hungry."

"It's been a long day," he admitted.

"Yesterday was for me. I just about fell into my bed last night."

"How is Duke Estalin's son?"

"He will recover. He wasn't that sick." Leyladin shook her head. "Sometimes . . ." She looked at Cerryl. "You heard about Duke Berofar, didn't you?"

He frowned. "Heard what? I don't hear that much, not on gate duty, and not when I really don't know that many of the full mages—the younger ones, I mean."

"It couldn't hurt to eat with a few others," she pointed out. "The more who know you as a real person . . ."

He nodded. That made sense. "What about Duke Berofar?"

"He died. Gorsuch . . . I just don't know."

"Don't know what?" Cerryl continued to feel that the more he learned about anything, the less he really knew. He took one of the green apples and cut it into wedges, then offered them to Leyladin.

"Thank you." She took one and ate it. "Berofar—he's from the old line out of Asula, and his first consort and his son and daughter died of the raging fever. That wasn't ten years ago, and that left him without an heir. I don't think he cares much for women. Still, he needed an heir, and that's why he consorted again. Young Uulrac was born at the turn of spring four years ago."

Cerryl ate two of the apple quarters and offered the last to the blonde healer. He cut another wedge of cheese for himself and listened.

"I think the Council will suggest that Gorsuch be one of the regents."

"He's the Council representative to Hydlen?"

She nodded. "Doesn't it seem strange to you?"

"What?"

"Jeslek has you kill Lyam—and Lyam wouldn't go along with the road taxes and tariffs, and the new prefect of Gallos knows that he could be removed if he doesn't. The old Viscount of Certis opposed our tariffs, and he and his entire family died of the bloody flux. Duke Berofar was trying not to provide levies and troops for us . . . and as soon as I'm tending one duke's son—where my absence would be a problem—Berofar dies . . ."

"Strange" wasn't the word Cerryl would have used. He could see the patterns once he had the facts. He just didn't know enough and wondered if he ever would. Fairhaven seemed so open and simple on the surface, like a calm ocean or lake, but most of what went on was below the surface. Was it that way everywhere?

"It's possible," he agreed.

Her eyebrows raised, as if in a question.

"That Sterol decided Berofar was a problem. I don't think any of the more powerful mages—Sterol, Jeslek, maybe Anya, or Kinowin—would stop for a moment to remove a ruler who might thwart Fairhaven."

"Doesn't that bother you?"

Cerryl shrugged, then took another swallow of the ale and refilled his goblet before answering. "It does, and it doesn't."

"That's a safe answer." Her tone was bitter.

"That's not what I meant. I haven't seen any place like Fairhaven. The streets are clean. There aren't many thieves. You can drink the water. You can buy most anything if you have the coins. People seem happy, most of them, and happier than the other places in Candar where I've been."

"That's because we push out those who are too poor or put them on road crews—or kill some of them if they make trouble."

"True. But what's the difference? In Fenard, the urchins live in the streets, and I'd wager most die young. Everyone has to worry about thieves and brigands, and there's flux and misery everywhere. There the prefect lets people die and others do the killing. Either way, the poor either find a way to make a living or die. Here, though, everyone else is better off as well, and I'm probably proof that an orphan has a chance."

"Don't you see, Cerryl, that's why you're a mage? So that Sterol and Jeslek can say that even a poor boy can rise to being a White mage?"

"What about Heralt? Or Kinowin? And I don't think Kiella exactly comes from coins."

Leyladin looked down at the polished white oak table. "It's the same thing."

"Maybe." He shook his head. "Maybe I am lucky. Am I supposed to turn away from it?"

"No. You have to make it better."

"Me? A junior mage who's a gate guard?"

"Myral said that you would be High Wizard."

"Me?"

"He has these visions."

Cerryl frowned again. *High Wizard? A boy whose father was a renegade? That's hardly likely.* "Once . . . he did mention that he'd seen the future, after the Guild had fallen, and that Candar was filled with mad chaos wielders . . . I wondered."

"Trust him. He sees more than he says."

"So does Kinowin," Cerryl said wryly, not wanting to think too much about Myral's visions for him, not at all. "In a different way."

"He does. Did you know that Kinowin's a lot older than he looks?"

"Myral told me that." Cerryl shook his head. "I wouldn't have believed it."

"Believe it. He's like Myral. Very careful about how and when he raises chaos. You should follow their example about that."

Cerryl nodded. He didn't want to mention that he'd already patterned his use of order and chaos after Myral's precepts—and what he managed to figure out from *Colors of White.* He cleared his throat, not wanting to dwell on the matters the healer had raised, not until he'd had a chance to think more. "I remember when I ate here before and I said how good everything was. You and your father looked at each other. That was because what you fixed was a simple meal for you, wasn't it?"

Leyladin looked down, then at him. "Yes. I was afraid if you saw a real full-course dinner, you'd be so upset that you'd never see me again."

"I'd see you again," he protested. "I'm here."

"I don't know, Cerryl. You . . . when we were at Furenk's . . . you were pretty stunned."

"I didn't know about the rear dining area. I'd eaten in the front before."

"And you'd wondered at that." Leyladin offered a small smile. "Didn't you?"

"Ah . . . yes," he admitted. "But I'm getting used to good food."

"Then you will stay for dinner?"

Cerryl flushed. "I'd be hard-pressed to leave, lady."

"I'm Leyladin, not lady." She grinned.

"I'm Cerryl, and I would be delighted to stay." He returned the grin. "Leyladin."

Her deep green eyes danced, and with her smile, warmth flowed up from within him.


# XVI

The sun had barely cleared the low hills to the east of Fairhaven when the heavy wagon rumbled through the north gates and onto the highway. Cerryl watched. The entire wagon bed was filled with brass fittings, ship parts of various sorts, headed for Lydiar.

Fittings for the warships Sterol had mentioned? No . . . those were being built somewhere in Sligo. But could there be others being built on the Great North Bay?

He shook his head. Again, he didn't even know enough to conjecture. How could he find out? Without asking anyone directly?

Leyladin had offered one suggestion—become friendly with more of the other younger mages. Some of them had to know things he didn't, and most people would talk, he'd discovered, with a slight bit of encouragement. That hadn't been his style, but . . . the more he saw, the more he understood the danger of being alone and aloof.

He glanced down at the white stones of the highway, arcing out to the north and then east, seeing the fine white dust that was everywhere in Fairhaven slowly settle back onto the stone. Then he walked across into the sunlight to warm up, knowing that before midmorning he'd be seeking the shade to cool off.

Below, Diborl watched as the prisoners from the city patrol swept the stones clean. Then another guard escorted them back to the holding room where they were kept between cleanup duties.

Not for the first time, Cerryl wondered exactly what the pair had done. Smuggling, disturbing the peace?

The creaking of another set of wheels alerted him.

Coming down the road from the direction of Hrisbarg were two farm carts and, farther behind them, yet another—the beginning of the line of produce vendors that would fill the markets before many folk were fully up and about.

He stood on the rampart and waited.

# XVII

Lyasa, Faltar, and Cerryl stood in the front foyer of the main Hall. Cerryl glanced toward the steps up to the White Tower, his eyes drifting momentarily to the upper ledge and the life-size statues of past great mages—most of whom he still did not recognize.

"Here he comes." Cerryl nodded to Faltar. "Let's ask him."

Heralt walked slowly down the steps from the White Tower into the front foyer of the Hall.

"Heralt?" called Cerryl. "We're going over to The Golden Ram. Why don't you join us?"

The dark-haired young mage lifted his head. "I'm tired. I thought I'd just eat in the Halls."

"All you get in the Meal Hall this late is stale bread and old cheese," Cerryl pointed out. "You don't have to stay with us long, and it won't be that late. I have morning duty, remember?"

Heralt offered a shy smile. "The Ram does sound better than bread and cheese or dried lamb."

"Dried lamb." Beside Cerryl, Faltar shook his head. "Any form of lamb . . ."

"Your feelings about mutton are well-known," said Lyasa. "Let's go. I'm hungry."

"Well . . ." Heralt shrugged and turned toward the other three.

The Golden Ram was half-empty by the time the four young mages settled around a circular table in one corner. Broka and another mage—both on their way out together—nodded.

"Good evening." Cerryl returned the nod and smiled.

Almost as soon as the three were seated, the serving woman was at Faltar's elbow, looking toward Cerryl and asking, "Drinks?"

"Ale," said Cerryl.

"Ale," agreed Faltar.

"Make that three."

"Four," added Lyasa.

"Fare's on the board. Ribs, fowl breast, or stew. Ribs and stew are two. Fowl's three."

Cerryl settled on the fowl, as did Faltar. Heralt had ribs and Lyasa stew, and the server with the swirled braid on the back of her head slipped back to the kitchen.

"You once said that your father was a merchant in Kyphros." Cerryl glanced at Heralt. "Do you see him much?"

Heralt laughed. "Kyphrien is rather far to travel . . . and he's not one for sending scrolls. My sister and I exchange messages, but not often."

"Here you be . . . four ales. That be eight."

Cerryl added three coppers to the pile. The server smiled and swept up a silver's worth of coppers. Lyasa had added the other extra copper.

"I wonder how people in Kyphros feel about the new mountains Jeslek is raising," mused Cerryl. He took the barest sip of the ale.

"The wool factors are worried." Heralt took a healthy swallow from his mug. "They say the Analerians have lost some of their flocks and that will make wool scarce." He shrugged. "Axista says it won't help prices, though, not so long as the Black Isle sends wool to Spidlar. That worries Father."

"Isn't their wool more expensive?"

"Not after all the tariffs on his. Or not much."

"Then, the road taxes and tariffs bother him?" Cerryl's tone was interested but not sharp.

"They bother everyone. They make prices higher, and people can buy less." Heralt took another sip of ale. "You didn't used to be interested in trade, Cerryl."

"I figure I'd better learn. That's what gate duty is all about, isn't it? Watching trade and trying to see who's smuggling?" Cerryl glanced to the white-blond Faltar. "You have any smugglers lately?"

"Not for an eight-day or so," Faltar mumbled as he finished a mouthful of ale. "This is better than Hall swill any day."

"More costly, as well," countered the curly-haired mage.

"You didn't mention smugglers," Cerryl prompted. "What were they trying to sneak past you?"

"Hides. Uncured hides to sell to the tanners," said Faltar.

"There can't be that much profit in hides," suggested Heralt. "Why smuggle them?"

"Because," added Lyasa, brushing a strand of jet-black hair off her forehead, "some gate guards have trouble discovering things that aren't made of metal or hard materials."

"And some don't look at that hard," added Faltar dryly. "From what I've heard."

*From Anya?* Cerryl wondered. Then he pondered how Faltar, usually so sensible, had fallen for the red-haired mage who apparently bedded half the Hall and cared little for any beyond the moment or what she could gain from using her body. *Is that why you still keep Faltar as a friend—because he's a friend despite Anya? Or because he's kept supporting you?* Still . . . Faltar's relationship with Anya meant that Cerryl had to be careful in some of what he said to the blond mage.

"How did you sense the hides?" asked Heralt.

"I didn't really sense them," admitted Faltar. "But there were some blades hidden under the wagon seat. Not enough to be contraband, but enough to make me worry. So I asked the guards to check the wagon. They knew where to look."

"They still couldn't have made more than a gold or so," protested Heralt.

"A single gold is more than some folk see in a year," Cerryl said.

"Spoken like a man who knows," said Lyasa.

"I made about three silvers in the whole time I was a scrivener's apprentice," Cerryl admitted. "The same when I worked at the mill." He laughed. "But I was at the mill a whole lot longer."

"I think I'd rather be a mage." Heralt took the last chunk of bread from the basket.

"Two fowls, ribs, and a stew." The four platters and two baskets of bread practically tumbled onto the polished but battered tabletop. "That be ten."

Cerryl fumbled out four coppers, wondering how often he could afford such luxury—despite Faltar's mathematicks.

"Thank you all." The serving woman scooped up the coins.

Faltar took a bite of the fowl and chewed noisily.

Across the table from Cerryl, Lyasa raised her eyebrows. "He only appears neat."

"Food's better than talk," mumbled Faltar. "Specially after a long duty day."

Cerryl used his dagger to slice off a strip of the chicken to pop into his mouth. Somehow it was both juicy and dry at the same time, but he was hungry enough that it didn't matter that much. Still, compared to the meals he'd had at Furenk's and Leyladin's, The Golden Ram's fare was definitely inferior. A mere two seasons before, he never would have thought that.

"This is better than Hall lamb any day," Faltar added.

"Better than stale bread, too." Cerryl grinned at Heralt.

"More costly, as well," countered the curly-haired mage.

"Mages aren't meant to die with coins," said Lyasa. "We can't leave them to anyone. You might as well enjoy what you eat."

"And drink," added Faltar.

"The other day, there was a big wagon that headed out toward Lydiar," Cerryl said. "Filled with worked brass. Ship fittings . . ."

"Has to be for the warships," replied Faltar after wiping his mouth and emptying his mug. He held the mug up for the server to see.

"I thought the Guild's ships were built in Sligo."

"Off that island in the Great North Bay. It's faster to use the highway to Lydiar and send heavy stuff by boat."

"That'll be two more," said the server as she took Faltar's mug.

"You'll have it," the blond mage promised, reaching for his belt purse.

"Ten ships seem like a lot," mused Cerryl.

"I know of at least seven solid ports in eastern Candar," Lyasa pointed out. "With time for supplies and transit, that's only one more ship to watch each port."

Put that way, reflected Cerryl, ten ships seemed almost too few.

"The only two ports that matter right now are Diev and Spidlaria ... maybe Quend," suggested Faltar.

"That's still only three ships for each port. The Northern Ocean is pretty big." Lyasa sipped her ale.

*Thump!* Another mug of ale appeared at Faltar's elbow. "Here you be."

The blond mage extended three coppers.

"How would you use the ships, Heralt?" Cerryl asked. "You know more about trade than most of us, I suspect."

The curly-haired and dark-eyed mage shrugged. "Lyasa's right. No one's going to smuggle through Lydiar or Renklaar. Ruzor or Worrak, maybe. That's only four or five places, but we'd have to mount a blockade, and the Blacks would try to use the weather. I don't know. I wonder if we could afford as many ships as we need. They say we've only got a score or so now. Ten more—that might do it." Heralt yawned. "Unless the Blacks build more ships, or better ones, or something like that."

"How could you build a better ship?" demanded Faltar. "A ship's a ship. If you make it faster, then it carries less cargo—or less armsmen—and there's not that much difference in speed under sail anyway. They all need the wind."

"Hamor uses slave galleys in the calmer parts of the Western Ocean," Lyasa said.

"Water's too rough here," insisted Faltar.

"Probably." Heralt yawned again. "I need some sleep."

"I'll walk back with you," said Cerryl. "Morning duty." He rose, then looked at Lyasa. "Are you coming?"

"I'll keep Faltar out of trouble."

"Me? Trouble?"

"Yes, you," she answered amiably.

Cerryl and Heralt slipped out into the fresher air, air still warm, with the faint fragrance of something.

"You think there's trouble coming?" Heralt asked as they headed toward the rear Hall, stifling yet another yawn.

"There's always trouble coming." Cerryl offered a laugh. "It's just taken me a while to understand that."

His eyes went to the northern sky and the pinpoints of light, distant lights supposedly, if *Colors of White* were correct, with suns similar to the one that brought chaos and light upon them.

Did they have their troubles? Did it matter?

He tried not to yawn as he started up the steps beside Heralt.

# XVIII

Cerryl blotted his forehead with the back of his forearm. Even in midmorning, the shadiest space behind the rampart of the guardhouse was almost unbearably hot. He felt sorry for Heralt, who would have to endure it all afternoon, with even less shade, although the dark-haired young mage was from Kyphros—to the south and far warmer than Fairhaven. Perhaps Heralt was better able to withstand the heat than Cerryl. Cerryl hoped so.

The green-blue sky was clear, with a haze toward the horizon that bespoke the promise of greater heat as the day went on. The air was still, hot, thick, weighing on Cerryl like a heavy blanket.

He glanced back toward Fairhaven, but the Avenue down toward the Wizards' Square was empty of all but a few riders and some folk on foot, none headed toward the gates themselves. He turned. The highway to Hrisbarg and Lydiar was equally deserted, a long, gently curving arc of deserted white stone in the midmorning glare.

Was that because it was summer? Or the result of the higher taxes and tariffs? Or had the High Wizard already started using warships somehow to enforce the taxes? He frowned. The taxes were levied in ports, such as Lydiar and Tyrhavven. How could the Guild levy a tariff or a tax on a ship's cargo if the goods were shipped elsewhere—to Spidlar or Sarronnyn?

*Creeakkk . . .*

Cerryl turned.

A thin figure led a donkey and cart off the side road a half-kay to the northwest and onto the highway toward the guardhouse. The young mage watched as the farmer led the cart around to the side of the guardhouse. The cart contained several baskets of greenery—beans?

"Ser? Another farmer for a medallion."

Cerryl nodded, turned, and started down the steps. *Another farmer?* As he reached the back medallion room, he asked, "Vykay? Have we had a lot of farmers lately?"

The thin guard looked at the other man, who had the ledger before him. "Sandur?"

"A moment." Sandur glanced at the waiting farmer. "That's five coppers for a cart, a silver for a full four-wheeled wagon."

"A cart be all I can pay for." The thin farmer pushed five coppers across the wooden surface of the counter behind which stood Sandur, the lancer acting as medallion guard. The medallion guard handed the bronze rectangle to Vykay but looked at the farmer. "Vykay and the mage will attach it to your cart, ser."

The farmer grunted.

Sandur turned the pages of the ledger, then glanced at Cerryl. "Says here . . . been six in the last eight-day. More than I recall."

Cerryl nodded to himself. The highway was emptier, and there were more farmers getting medallions. He turned to the farmer. "Your cart outside, ser?"

"By the door, young ser."

Cerryl led the way back out into the heat, followed by the farmer and Vykay with his drill, pouch, tools, and the medallion.

Cerryl waited beside the cart as Vykay drilled the holes for the medallion—another new medallion, no less.

More farmers than Sandur recalled? Again, Cerryl didn't know enough to determine whether that was just coincidence . . . or more. *As if you could really do anything about it.*

# XIX

Here you be. Ten for the lot." The serving woman set down the two mugs of wine and then the two of ale.

Cerryl glanced past her toward the archway that held the door into The Golden Ram, thinking he had seen Anya's red hair. He decided he'd seen but a glint of something off the bronze reflector of a wall lamp. He extended seven coppers before Leyladin could reach her wallet, eased the two mugs of ale across the table, then slid one of the mugs of wine before Leyladin.

Bealtur and Myredin each extended two coppers, and the serving woman swept them all up and headed back to the kitchen. Past her, in the far corner, past the cold hearth, sat Broka and Elsinot with a third, ginger-haired mage—Redark, Cerryl thought.

Cerryl reached under the table and squeezed Leyladin's hand, even as he looked at the two other mages. "How is guard duty going for you?"

The goateed Bealtur shrugged. "Mostly, it's boring."

Myredin's fine black hair drifted across his forehead. "I had a farmer walk up and ask why he had to pay for a medallion when his potatoes and maize fed the city. I told him everyone pays to trade. He wasn't happy, but he came back and bought a medallion."

"Does everyone pay? I sometimes wonder." Bealtur fingered his goatee, then took a sip of ale.

The serving woman set down four bowls. "Three each, twelve in all."

Cerryl frowned. "Stew used to be two, didn't it?"

"Was till last eight-day. Hioll says he can't get the fixings for what he used to." The server shrugged. "Whatever . . . he says what it is, and I tell you."

"And we pay," said Myredin.

"Better you than me, ser mage."

Cerryl grinned and extended his coins, as did the others.

After the server took the coppers and slipped away, Leyladin glanced at Cerryl. "Three for stew? There's not as much as there was last eight-day."

"Food must be getting dearer."

"It does anyway in the summer before harvest," added Myredin.

"What does this have to do with . . . anything?" mumbled Bealtur. "Guard duty is guard duty. It's boring."

"The farmers," Cerryl said. "More are selling goods in the city."

"They don't pay if they carry goods on their backs," said Leyladin.

"But they can't sell in the squares," pointed out Myredin. "Not without a cart, and you can't bring a cart into the city without a medallion."

"Some folk sell to people they know." Cerryl recalled a woman who had brought spices to Beryal when he had been working as an apprentice to Tellis. "They can do that."

"They have to know people. They can't peddle on the streets." Myredin's bulging eyes protruded a shade more as he took a deep swallow of ale. "More medallions mean more farmers selling in the squares."

"Have any of the older mages mentioned anything about more farmers getting medallions?"

His mouth full, Bealtur shook his head. So did Myredin.

"They wouldn't know, would they?" Leyladin dipped a chunk of bread into her stew. "Esaak—he reviews the Guild accounts, but it's only a few coppers for a farm medallion, isn't it?"

"Five," announced Myredin. "For a cart. A silver for a wagon, but most use carts."

"So," continued Leyladin, "if twoscore more farmers sought medallions, that would only be twenty silvers—two golds."

"I see what you mean." Bealtur nodded vigorously, his thin goatee almost swinging. "That's but two golds, and a factor's wagon alone is sometimes that."

"The accounts wouldn't show anything," Cerryl mused.

"Maybe you should say something at the next Guild meeting." Myredin glanced at Cerryl.

A glint flitted across Bealtur's eyes.

"Maybe . . ." *More likely I'll bring it up to Kinowin first.* Cerryl took a mouthful of stew, prompted by a growl from his stomach. "That's a few eight-days away. Let's see if we get more farmers wanting medallions."

"Oh, they all want them," said Myredin with a laugh. "Most won't pay for them. They know not how lucky they are. Those who make their trade in Fairhaven pay tariffs on their shops. The farm folk sell and run."

"And complain," added Bealtur.

Cerryl ate more of the stew with a chunk of the crusty white bread, then followed it with a sip of wine, glancing at Leyladin. "Do the traders and factors complain as much?"

She favored him with a wry smile. "No one complains more than traders. Traders are not happy unless they have something to complain about. They prefer to complain about those taxes or circumstances that allow them to ask for more coins for their goods, and of those they talk at great length."

"That I'd believe." Myredin took a gulp of ale.

"Of course," added Leyladin, eyes twinkling, "mages complain all the time about how much good they do for the people and how low the taxes they impose are for all the good they do. And they are not happy unless they can boast of how no one understands what they do."

Bealtur almost choked on his ale, swallowing hard and gasping for air.

"And healers?" asked Myredin.

"Oh . . . healers don't complain much." Leyladin grinned. "They suffer silently and think how ungrateful are all those that they have cured. Since they say nothing, few of their patients consider their fortune, and fewer still are willing to pay for their services."

"You, lady healer, are dangerous," pronounced Myredin.

"Me? A quiet and uncomplaining healer?"

"Very dangerous," added Bealtur with a smile, turning to Cerryl. "Best you watch out, Cerryl, or she'll heal you right out of being a mage."

"I wouldn't do that." Leyladin frowned, then looked straight at Bealtur. "Maybe I could try with you."

"Ha!" Myredin laughed. "Said she was dangerous."

Despite his best resolve, Cerryl found himself yawning.

"You . . . you have to get up tomorrow, don't you?" asked Leyladin.

"Sometime," he admitted.

"Sometime well before dawn."

"Yes."

"Then we'd better be going."

"I think we'll stay," said Bealtur.

Cerryl and Leyladin rose and made their way out, Cerryl noting that Broka and the others had already left. Cerryl pushed open the door and stepped into the slightly cooler night air, air that had been far warmer before dinner.

"They're trying to figure out why you asked them to join us." The blonde healer looked at Cerryl.

"It doesn't matter if they figure it out."

Cerryl and Leyladin walked slowly up the Avenue, arm in arm, enjoying the comparative cool of evening. He glanced around, but there was no one nearby. "Leyladin . . . would you do me a favor?"

"What sort of favor?"

"A magely favor. Just watch me for a moment." He let go of Leyladin's arm, stepped away from her, and stood there concentrating. He tried to let the light flow around him, not to direct it or create a full light shield that would render him invisible to the eyes but all too visible to any mage who could sense perturbations in the order-chaos fabric of the world.

"You're not quite there. My eyes . . . somehow they have trouble seeing you."

"What about your order senses? Do you feel any use of order or chaos?" Cerryl could feel the dampness on his forehead—another skill where he needed more practice.

"No. Not more than a tiny bit, and I couldn't feel that, I don't think, if I weren't right next to you. You're not there to order senses, either, though."

Cerryl let the light slip back to its normal flows.

The blonde healer blinked, shaking her head. "That was strange. I knew you were there, sort of, because you . . . are. I could see you, with my eyes, in a way, but I couldn't."

"Thank you." Cerryl extended his arm again.

"Why did you ask me?"

"I trust you." *And somehow I've always cared for you, from the first time I saw you through a glass when I was so young and didn't even know exactly what screeing was . . .*

"Why did you want me there tonight?" asked the healer.

"I like being with you." Cerryl grinned.

"I *know* that. But that's not the only reason."

"You know why," he answered.

"You don't want them to know." She shook her head. "And it was my suggestion."

"I listen," he pointed out, taking her hand as they walked around the south end of the Market Square. "I especially listen to you."

"I'm not sure whether I like it better when you do or you don't."

He could feel the humor in her words. "Well . . . if you don't want me to listen . . . I could try that."

"I could take another trip—say to Naclos," she countered.

"Naclos? That's where the druids are. People don't come back from there."

Leyladin shrugged playfully. "Then you wouldn't have to listen to me."

"Oh . . . now I *have* to listen to you?"

"No . . ."

He waited.

"Only if you want me to stay around." She squeezed his arm, then smiled.

Cerryl shook his head slowly.


# XX

Kinowin looked up from the table. "You had something odd happen? You only have to report to me once an eight-day, otherwise."

"It's not urgent," Cerryl ventured.

Kinowin smiled wryly. "Since you're already here, you might as well get on with it. Sit down."

Cerryl eased into the chair across the table from the big blond over-mage. "The other day, I had another farmer buy a medallion for his cart. The cart was older, but it had never had a medallion." Cerryl studied the older mage.

Kinowin nodded. "Farmers have been known to buy medallions."

"I checked the ledger. There have been almost a score since mid-summer. Last year there were five; the year before, seven." Cerryl shrugged. "I don't know where the older ledgers are."

"In the archives. Esaak could tell you where. Or Broka, I suspect." Kinowin stood and moved over toward his latest hanging, the one with the blue and purple diamonds pierced with the black quarrels, and his fingers touched the wool for an instant. Then he shook his head and continued to the window, where he stood silhouetted against the green-blue afternoon sky and the scattered white and gray clouds. "Did you tell the lancers what you were looking for?"

"No. An eight-day or so ago, I did ask if we'd had more farmers than usual. This time, I just asked if I could look through the ledgers."

"Good. Try to follow that example when you can. There are enough rumors in Fairhaven as it is."

"About the ships?" Cerryl asked. "Or about Prefect Syrma?"

"Those are the most common," Kinowin acknowledged. "What have you heard?"

"Only that the Guild is having trouble getting all the brasswork for the first ships."

"The first ships aren't the problem. They never are. Suppliers want the coins for the later vessels. They're happy to deliver at first. Then it gets harder." Kinowin turned from the window. "Why did you ask about the farmers?"

"It seemed like more wanted to sell in the city, and then The Golden Ram increased what it charged for meals."

"That's not surprising. There haven't been any rains in Hydlen south of Arastia since spring. Nor in southern Kyphros. Food prices are increasing."

"So farmers can get more by selling themselves, rather than to the factors?"

"They think so. Some do; some don't." Kinowin offered a wintry smile. "It's not a problem yet."

"I'm sorry I bothered you."

"That's not a problem." Kinowin fingered his chin. "Why don't you bring it up at the next Guild meeting? Except say that it could lead to worries in the city because the farmers are asking for more. That means that artisans will want more . . ."

"Oh . . ."

"We've already heard rumblings about that. But if you bring it up, it won't be as if I have a blade to whet."

Cerryl nodded.

"How is your healer friend?"

Cerryl shrugged. "I don't know. Sterol sent her to Jellico. Viscount Rystryr's son is ailing. No one knows why. She probably won't be back before harvest."

"I have no doubts the boy will recover, at least while she is there. Maladies seem far more common for heirs. They always have been." Kinowin's eyes flicked back to the roofs beyond the Halls.

Cerryl rose. "That was all. I'm sorry I bothered you."

"Don't be. You have a good feel for matters. You're just feeling things that haven't happened. They will. We haven't had as much rain as normal, either. It happens every few years, but people forget—except the factors." After a pause, Kinowin added, "I'll see you an eight-day from now, unless something important happens."

"Yes, ser."

As he walked down the steps to the foyer, Cerryl wanted to shake his head. Kinowin had as much as told him that food was going to become even dearer. Was that why Leyladin's father, Layel, was traveling all over eastern Candar? Arranging to buy grains and the like for more coins than in the past, but less than what the grains would actually fetch come harvest?

# XXI

Cerryl sat in his chair in his room in the warm afternoon, muggy from the brief rain that had bathed the city only long enough to steam it, looking through *Colors of White*.

Cerryl found himself continually returning to the Guild manual, despite the fact that the book offered but tantalizing glimpses of aspects of the world that made sense ... and suggested more. Yet for every time those glimpses led to something—such as his perfection of the light lances that Myral had said no other mage had developed in generations—there were a dozen times or more that he felt he had overlooked something. He took a deep breath and returned his eyes to the page open before him.

> ... and all the substance of this world is nothing more and nothing less than chaos bound into fixed form by order ...

Cerryl blinked, then continued onto the next page, forcing his eyes to read each word and his mind to fix each within his memory.

> ... Fire is a creation of chaos that in itself replicates chaos, releasing chaos as it destroys what it consumes. Yet the skeptic would say that fire and chaos are limited, in that not all substances can be consumed in fire ... That skeptic would be wrong, for in the presence of enough chaos, any substance will replicate the chaos beneath the surface of the world and the points of chaos we call stars ...
>
> As in all effort, that which is easy offers little benefit. So, too, with the power of chaos, for those substances with which chaos replication is difficult paradoxically contain the greatest concentrations of chaos ... could it but be released ...

*Thrap!*
Cerryl looked up from the book, almost with relief. "Yes?"
"Might I come in?" The voice was definitely feminine.
Cerryl marked his place with the strip of leather he used for such

and replaced the volume in the bookcase. He walked to the door and opened it.

Anya, wrapped in the strong scent of trilia and sandalwood, stepped into his room, her red hair flaming in the indirect light from the window. "You could close the door, Cerryl."

"Of course." Cerryl closed the door but did not slip the bolt shut.

She stepped over to the bed and surveyed it. "So neat. You are always neat and clean, as if you should have been born to the White."

"I had to learn what comes naturally to others, and I fear I lack the grace you exhibit so easily."

"You show much more grace than many born to the White." She turned toward the window, letting the light silhouette her well-proportioned form.

"You are kind." Cerryl inclined his head. "I would have to differ. Faltar shows far more grace than I, and you certainly know that."

"One could underestimate you, Cerryl." Anya smiled easily. "Almost. It is a pity you do not exhibit quite the . . . strength you did as a student."

"Strength is not terribly useful if it cannot be focused, Anya. You have shown me that there are other talents besides pure strength of chaos, though you have that in ample measure."

"Ah, Cerryl, one might almost wish you had more . . . innocence."

"Anya, I have more than enough innocence to get me in trouble. More I scarcely need." Cerryl's tone was wry as he stood by the bookcase.

She laughed. "Will you be at the Guild meeting?"

"Since it is in the afternoon, I hope to be."

"Jeslek will not be back, and I thought you might sit with me." She flashed the warm and false smile he had come to recognize. "And Fydel, of course, since Faltar will be on gate duty."

"I would certainly appreciate your tutelage, Anya. You are always so kind."

"I do not think you said yes." She smiled again, and the warm scent of trilia wafted around him.

"My heart would certainly say so." Cerryl offered a smile he hoped wasn't too false.

"Yet you have other commitments?"

"I know that I can be at the meeting." Cerryl shrugged. "Then, I will have to see."

Anya nodded. "I believe I understand. You know, Cerryl, that someday you will have to stand free of Myral and Kinowin. They are older, far older, than they might appear."

"I will look to you for guidance, then." *But not in the way you think . . . not at all.*

"I am flattered." Anya smiled her broadest smile once more, then slipped toward the door.

"You should be. I meant to flatter you. You deserve it." Cerryl opened the door for her.

"I do hope you will be able to join us."

"I appreciate your thoughtfulness."

With the door shut, Cerryl walked to his chair and sank into it with a deep sigh, sitting for several moments and trying to relax. Finally, he reclaimed *Colors of White* and opened it.

... for those substances with which chaos replication is difficult paradoxically contain the greatest concentrations of chaos ... could it but be released ... Yet the unbound chaos in the world must be concentrated most greatly were this to be done ...

*Thrap.*

Cerryl set the book down with another sigh, hoping Anya had not returned. "Yes?"

"Cerryl?"

"You can come in, Lyasa. Please." He set the book back in its place in the bookcase and walked to the door, opening it.

The black-haired Lyasa wrinkled her nose as she entered. "I thought so." Her eyes went to the bed. "Good."

"What did you want?"

"Just to make sure you survived your last visitor. Leyladin is my friend, too." Her olive-brown eyes rested on Cerryl. "I trust you more than most men, but Anya I trust not at all."

Cerryl had to smile.

"I'm not sure I find it amusing."

"I haven't trusted her since she found me in the street by the scrivener's," Cerryl admitted. "I see no point in angering her."

"She'll be angry if you don't bed her—sooner or later," predicted the black-haired mage.

"Not if I flatter her enough." Cerryl added, "I hope."

Lyasa dropped onto the bed. "You don't mind, do you? My feet hurt."

"Darkness, no. I haven't seen you lately. What have you been doing?" Cerryl turned the chair and sat down, leaning forward.

"After an eight-day or so, they decided my talents were better used elsewhere than on the gates—for a while. I'm working with Myral's masons on repairs to the offal treatment fountains and basins."

Cerryl winced. "That sounds worse than gate-guard duty."

"It stinks more, but I don't have to turn old ladies into ashes."

"I didn't want to . . ." *And try not to think about it too much . . . or for too long . . .*

"I know. Leyladin told me."

The silence drew out for a moment, and a brief breath of hot air gusted through the open window into the room for a moment before subsiding.

"I wonder . . . do the Blacks on Recluce have problems like we do?"

"They have problems," Cerryl asserted. "Everyone does. I doubt they're the same. They just throw out people who don't agree. Then we, or some other land, has to deal with them."

"We don't kill their exiles."

"They don't kill people who leave Fairhaven." He laughed. "Unless they agree with the Black doctrine, they just don't let them stay."

"We have to kill people who make trouble."

"I wouldn't be surprised if they don't do some killing, one way or another."

"I don't know." Lyasa ran her hand through her short and thick black hair. "I think it's harder for the Guild to govern Candar than for the Blacks to run their isle."

"Even eastern Candar is bigger," Cerryl pointed out. "I think Gallos alone is bigger than the whole isle."

"That's not it. You know what I think?"

"What?"

"That it's all because Creslin was a ruthless bastard. He killed off anyone who didn't agree right in the beginning, and they throw out dissenters, and they're on an isle. Nobody's left to disagree."

"Could be." Cerryl shrugged. "That would be Anya's style. Jeslek's, too, I think."

"Why are you telling me that?"

"Because I trust you."

"Have you told Faltar that?"

"No."

"He's your friend."

"You know why," Cerryl said with a laugh.

"Alas . . . men." Lyasa made a woeful face. "You are different. A little different."

Cerryl made a bowing gesture with his right hand. "My deepest gratitude, lady mage. If you would but convey that to the absent lady who is your friend . . ."

Lyasa shook her head, then yawned and stood. "I need a nap or something."

Cerryl rose and slipped toward the door.

"Whatever it is you do to keep her away, keep doing it."

*As if I'd ever dare to do anything else.* "Your request is my command." He put his hand on the door lever.

"Would that you had told me that before you met Leyladin."

"That couldn't happen. I've known her longer." Cerryl smiled at Lyasa's puzzlement as he opened the door. "Ask her."

"I just might."

As he closed the door, Cerryl glanced toward the bookcase, wondering if he would be able to read more than a page before being interrupted again. Finally, he sat and took out *Colors of White,* looking at the half-familiar words where the book opened:

> . . . iron, being that which draws free chaos unto it, never should it be employed around those who employ chaos for good, for it will drain chaos as it can . . .

He smiled ruefully. There were times when he'd felt that—when he'd had to climb the iron gate in Fenard while he had been holding a light shield, but usually iron did not burn him the way he knew it would Jeslek or Anya. He flipped back to his place marker and resumed his search.

# XXII

Cerryl stood in the shadows by the columns at the back of the north side of the Council Chamber, not erecting a light shield exactly, but letting the light sift, or blur, around him, as though he were not quite there. People's eyes shifted from him, and he could see them, if not clearly, unlike when he hid behind the total light shield, which rendered him invisible to all—except mages who looked for concentrations of order and chaos. That was one reason not to use the full light shield in the Halls, that and that it left him blind, except for his chaos-order senses. He couldn't explain the reasons for the difference, but Leyladin had assured him that no concentrations of order or chaos accompanied the effort, and she could sense such better than most Whites. With the blur shield he was now using he could see colors and forms, enough with his order senses, to recognize those he knew.

Esaak waddled in, accompanied by Myral, whose wheezing reached even Cerryl. After them came a mage wearing a crimson and gold sash. Gorsuch? Were the sashes to signify in what lands they represented the Guild?

Shyren appeared, his shock of graying sandy hair standing out and wearing a green sash—green for Certis. Eliasar, the battle mage, walked with him but did not wear a sash.

Then came the slender red-haired figure of Anya, accompanied by Fydel. She paused at the back of the chamber and peered around.

Cerryl almost held his breath, wanting to clutch the white marble column that partly shielded him.

"He's not here yet," Fydel said in a whisper, barely audible to Cerryl.

"I thought I had made it clear to him."

"That could be, but he still reports to Kinowin."

"Kinowin and Myral won't live forever," Anya hissed. "He will deal with us."

Cerryl shivered and waited. Once Anya, a puzzled expression on her face, finally walked down the aisle and seated herself beside Fydel, Cerryl let the light filter go and allowed himself to be cloaked only by shadows as the rest of the Guild entered the chamber.

"So you're here?" Lyasa slipped up beside Cerryl. "I didn't see you before."

"I've been here. I just didn't want to be seen at first."

"Why are you back here?" she asked in a low voice, her eyes going around the chamber, which was almost full. "You can't see everything from the back."

"I have a feeling."

"A feeling?"

"Just wait."

"If you say so."

For a time the two young mages stood in the shadows, watching. Then Cerryl smiled faintly as the sun-eyed and white-haired Jeslek strode into the chamber, marching up the center aisle, exuding the raw odor of chaos. "I thought so."

"Thought what?"

"Anya told me that Jeslek wouldn't be here and asked me to sit with her. She was looking for me earlier."

"What did you do to her? Besides refuse her advances? And her charms?"

"Isn't that enough?" he whispered dryly.

At the front of the chamber, Sterol stepped onto the dais, along with Kinowin and Jeslek.

"Let's go farther up." Cerryl slipped along the outer edge of the columns until he was within a dozen or so cubits of the gold-shot marble of the speaking dais.

". . . we face most difficult times, even more difficult than I had predicted at the last meeting." Sterol's face could have been carved out of granite when he paused, so hard did it appear. "Guild revenues have dwindled. At the same time, we have been forced into sending more lancers into Certis." He turned to Jeslek.

"The Great White Highway is now more protected than before, and by early fall we should have that protection completed." Jeslek's smile was dazzling. "Then we will bring in lancers to ensure that the prefect meets his obligations to Fairhaven."

"Bringing the lancers to Gallos will likely cost another 2,000 golds," Sterol snapped. "Two thousand golds to enforce what we should not have to enforce."

Kinowin and Jeslek nodded.

"Even raising mountains across the middle of Gallos has not fully convinced the prefect," Sterol continued. "His scrolls are polite, but his golds are not forthcoming."

"Because they are not forthcoming, the merchants and holders of Certis question why they should pay to maintain trade and highways," Kinowin added.

"As does, in a most polite way, Duke Estalin of Lydiar," inserted Jeslek smoothly, "though he is a longtime friend of the High Wizard. As did the late Duke Berofar, also a longtime friend of the High Wizard."

Cerryl shifted his weight.

"Don't say anything," suggested the black-haired White mage.

Standing by the third column back from the speaking circle on the right side of the room, Cerryl nodded and murmured, "That is good advice, Lyasa."

"With Sterol in the mood to incinerate anyone who disagrees, I'd wager it is."

*And with Anya watching closely for Jeslek's interests . . . and her own, whatever they may be.* "Unless one were to agree with the mighty High Wizard . . . and support him."

"You're too junior. They wouldn't even recognize you."

"It is better to be recognized." Cerryl shrugged and added in a low voice, "Then one's disappearance raises questions." He eased out to the side of the pillars on the north side of the chamber toward the dais.

"That's still dangerous."

"Life is dangerous. Death more so."

Kinowin raised a hand, then spoke. "Not all of us see the signs closer to Fairhaven itself, the very disturbing signs that are already appearing in our midst. You all know that I do not get around quite as I used to, but I do listen to those who do." He gestured to Cerryl. "You may recall Cerryl. He has been serving as a gate guard, and serving observantly. He mentioned something the other day, and I'd like him to tell it in his own words." Kinowin nodded. "Briefly, though, Cerryl."

Cerryl swallowed. "Several eight-days ago, we started getting more farmers buying medallions. One farmer sought a medallion for his cart. The cart was older, but it had never had a medallion. That seemed odd.

I checked the ledger. There have been more than a score of farmers just at the northeast guardhouse since midsummer. Last year there were five; the year before, seven." He turned to Kinowin.

"Thank you, Cerryl."

As Cerryl stepped down, Kinowin began to speak. "Cerryl got me thinking, and I went back over the records and ledgers. The most medallions given out from all guardhouses in a full year has been slightly over two score. This year, as of an eight-day ago, we have issued three score."

"Farmers are getting smarter . . ."

"What's the point?"

"The point, Isork, is simple. Farmers can pay five to ten coppers and make coins selling in the city. They couldn't before. Why? Because food prices are higher—much higher. Crops will be poor this year, especially in Hydlen and Kyphros. Tariff and tax collections on trade are less, because of what the Black Isle and Spidlar are doing. With crop prices going up, people have fewer coins to buy things, and that means Guild revenues are going down—as they already have . . ."

Cerryl reclaimed his spot beside the column.

Lyasa leaned over and whispered in his ear, "Don't say any more. Junior mages should be heard only on request."

Cerryl nodded, but his nod was of acknowledgment, not of agreement.

"You're going to get in trouble," she predicted.

"I've been in trouble my whole life," he whispered back, watching as Sterol resumed speaking.

"Recluce may have even tampered with the winds . . . to weaken us, and now with crops becoming scarce, they are shipping more and more goods into Spidlaria to evade the surtax. Lydiar is almost deserted at times, and so is Tyrhavven."

"While Spidlaria and Fenard prosper," Jeslek declaimed theatrically.

"Let them . . ." came a murmur from the back of the hall.

". . . don't need another war . . . not with the Blacks . . ."

Kinowin nodded.

The heavyset Myral heaved himself onto the dais, glancing around. "Those are fine words . . . but prosperity is not paid for with cowardice and ease. Most of you know me as the sewer mage, but we have less flux and raging fever than any city in Candar. Our people are healthy. Yet we cannot maintain sewers without masons and mages, and none of you would forgo your stipends. All that takes coins." Myral's eyes raked the chamber, and he coughed once, twice, clearing his throat before continuing.

"No sooner do we take action against Recluce than traitors here in Candar steal the livelihoods and the coppers from our people." The words of the heavyset and black-haired wizard garbed in white rumbled across the chamber.

"Proud words, Myral . . ."

". . . not the one to go with the lancers . . ."

"Silence!" snapped Sterol. "If you wish to speak, then stand forth and speak. Do not hide your words in murmurs and mumbles."

Cerryl smiled wryly, then stepped back onto the dais.

Kinowin opened his mouth, then shut it.

The trace of a smile crossed Jeslek's thin lips.

"I am most junior," Cerryl said. "And have been counseled to keep silent. So I will be brief. I stand with Myral." Cerryl kept his words level, almost soft, but loud enough to carry. "The renowned Jeslek and the noble Sterol have done their best to improve the lot of our people. Unlike many, I came from outside Fairhaven, and I know what great good Fairhaven represents. I have lived elsewhere. Can we do any less than support the work of the High Wizard and the overmages?"

"What's in it for you, Cerryl?" called Fydel.

Cerryl smiled softly, letting the clamor and snickers die down before speaking. "With such imposing figures as Jeslek and our High Wizard Sterol already expressing their concern . . . how about survival?" He grinned.

A patter of nervous laughter circled the chamber as he stepped off the low speaking stage and edged back toward his position by the third column.

"While I would not be so direct as gentle Cerryl . . ." began the next speaker, a man with white hair but an unlined and almost cherubic face.

Cerryl slowed as he neared the side of the chamber. Lyasa had slipped away, and a redheaded figure waited in the comparative dimness behind the post.

"Most effective, Cerryl." The voice was affectedly throaty.

"Thank you, Anya. I presume the effect was as you and the noble Sterol wanted." He smiled softly. "Or as you wanted, should I say."

"You flatter me." She returned the smile momentarily.

"Hardly. We do what we can. With your ability . . ." He shrugged. "Perhaps you will someday be High Wizard."

"Being High Wizard in these times might require rather . . . unique skills."

"That is certainly true, a point which Jeslek is certainly not adverse to making—repeatedly. I would prefer your approach, I suspect. That is why you would make a better High Wizard than the mighty Jeslek."

"A woman as High Wizard?" Anya's tone was almost mocking. "You do me high honor, indeed."

"I recognize your talent, dear lady." His smile was bland. "Your considerable talent."

"You are . . . sweet . . . Cerryl." She tilted her head. "Would you like to join me for a late supper—tomorrow evening?"

"Your wish is my desire."

"You are so obliging, Cerryl."

"When one is limited in sheer power of chaos, one must be of great service, Anya."

"I am so glad you understand that." She turned and stepped toward the broader Fydel, who waited, his hand touching his squared-off beard.

Cerryl smiled faintly, nodding to the square-bearded Fydel. As Fydel and Anya turned away, he shrugged and continued along the side aisle toward the back of the chamber, wondering how he could handle the dinner invitation he did not wish and feared greatly.

# XXIII

The upper room." Anya smiled brightly at Wescort, the owner of The Golden Ram.

"As you wish." Westcort bowed and lifted the braided golden silk rope that barred the staircase on the left side of the entry foyer to The Golden Ram.

Cerryl followed Westcort and Anya up the narrow stairs.

"Your request is our command." Westcort bowed again. "Would you like the wine now?"

"Please." Anya smiled.

The upper room was small, paneled in polished white oak and with its two windows hung in blue velvet. A deep blue cloth covered the single table, graced by a pair of crystal goblets and a full set of cutlery for each place. Two wall lamps lent a soft light to the room, and through the open window came a light breeze and the soft points of light shining through the evening along the southern part of the Avenue. The breeze carried the usual bitter-clean odor of chaos and stone, mixed with various other city scents—cooking, lamp oil, and greenery.

Anya seated herself, and Cerryl took the seat across from the red-haired mage.

"You were kind to join me." Anya smiled.

"You were most kind to invite me. I am a very inexperienced mage."

"What you did in the Council meeting was not inexperienced."

Cerryl smiled guilelessly. "What I did was because I *am*, dear lady. An experienced mage would not have needed to call attention to his powerlessness."

"Having less power than Jeslek does not mean you are without power," she pointed out, pausing as Westcort returned with a bottle of wine.

"This is the best of Telsen." He bowed.

"You may pour it, Westcort," Anya purred.

Westcort inclined his head and filled each of the goblets half-full of the dark red wine, leaving the bottle on the table. "You had requested the special cutlets with pearapple glaze . . . They will be here shortly."

"Thank you."

Westcort bowed again before retreating down the stairs.

Cerryl wasn't sure he wanted to know what favors or leverage Anya had used to make the proprietor so subservient, but his own experiences with her maneuvering, maneuvering that had resulted in Kesrik's death at Sterol's hands, left no doubt that Westcort knew her power.

"As I was saying, Cerryl, you are not without power. You merely cannot stand up to Jeslek."

Cerryl nodded, careful not to give away that he already had once, and survived.

"So you need friends and notice. You made yourself visible at a time when most young mages wait in the shadows. Why?" The bright smile followed. "You know that Jeslek is not fond of you and Kinowin is not fond of Jeslek. You support Kinowin and old Myral. They cannot stand up to Jeslek, either, but both are respected, and Jeslek would not dare remove them. So, while they live, he dare not remove you, now that both have quietly but clearly supported you." The redhead raised her goblet and sipped. "It was most cleverly done."

"I cannot say that I thought out anything that clearly." Cerryl shrugged, taking a sip of the wine, but not until after he had studied it with his chaos senses.

"Oh . . . you probably didn't, but you sensed it, and that is even more admirable, in many ways." Anya took another sip of wine. "This is very good. Enjoy it while you can."

Cerryl raised his eyebrows.

Anya laughed, not quite harshly. "That was not what I meant. The true chaos masters, like Sterol and Jeslek, are fortunate if they can enjoy more than a few swallows of good wine before the chaos in and around them begins to turn it to vinegar. Often very good vinegar, but vinegar nonetheless."

"I didn't know that."

"It is not something any would mention widely. But it's true."

"You must have a bit of that problem," Cerryl hazarded. "You are far more powerful than you reveal."

"Yes . . . and no." Anya shrugged, the goblet held momentarily in both hands. "Chaos power is not seen quite the same when held by women."

"Yet the Guild uses women—you, Lyasa, Shenan . . ."

A frown crossed Anya's face at the mention of Shenan, the Guild representative in Ruzor and supposedly Myral's younger sister. "Some of us . . ."

A discreet cough announced someone coming up the steps.

Westcort appeared with two plates, still so warm that Cerryl could sense the heat rising from them. The proprietor levered the white china onto the table, plates costlier than the heavy brown platters used in the main room below but far from the elegance of those Cerryl had seen in the back dining room at Furenk's. "The special cutlets . . . with the rice and mushrooms."

The woman server who followed added a basket of bread, a jar of conserve, and a second, opened, bottle of the same wine as in the first bottle.

Westcort placed a brass handbell on the table, equidistant from either, but on Anya's right. "If you need anything more . . ."

"Thank you, Westcort." The red-haired mage lifted her knife and the fork.

Cerryl followed her example, glad he'd had some experience with good cutlery, thanks to Leyladin, although, once again, the dinnerware was not so good as either that of Layel or that at Furenk's. Neither were the cutlets outstanding, if far better than the fare served below.

After taking several bites, Anya glanced at the younger mage. "You are surprising, Cerryl."

"I am who I am," he answered, not quite sure what he could say.

"Yes, you are." She flashed the warm, winning, and insincere smile. "That is what is surprising. You are an orphan raised by a miner and his consort—I did find that out, you know? Yet your speech bares no roughness. You worked in a mill and then for a scrivener. Yet you handle cutlery well, and your manners would grace any table. It is not what you are that is so surprising. It is what you are not." Another smile followed, less open, ironic, and more honest.

"What am I not?" Cerryl offered a gentle laugh.

"You are not rough, ill-spoken, and untutored. You do not—unlike others of a similar background—seek the more . . . violent avenues of advancement within the Guild."

"I was not aware I sought any." Cerryl took another small sip of the wine. "My ignorance has made me cautious."

"Ah . . . yes . . . caution. You are wise to be cautious now. Even Myral has hinted that the times are changing." She lifted the goblet and finished the wine in it.

Cerryl poured her another half-goblet, to the level that Westcort had initially.

"Myral is old, but more than a few times his visions have been true," mused Anya. "Some may be true but do not matter."

Cerryl frowned, then cut another section of cutlet, making sure the meat was well coated with the pearapple glaze before he put it to his mouth.

"They do not matter," Anya continued after a swallow of wine, "because they will happen long after you are dust. Does it matter that Fairhaven will be melted by a second sun—or that mad White chaos wielders will roam all of Candar? Or that Recluce will be sundered in twain by one of its own?"

"Perhaps it does. Perhaps, knowing such, we can change what might otherwise be."

"Perhaps." The tip of her tongue curled just over her perfect lips, and in the glow of the lamps her eyes seemed to flicker from pale gray to pale blue. "And perhaps not. Perhaps our actions in trying to avoid his visions are what will make them happen."

Cerryl almost shivered at that thought. How could one ever know which was the right course, then?

"That bothers you, doesn't it?" Anya smiled. "Better you enjoy the life you have than struggle to make right a future that your actions might equally make wrong."

Cerryl forced himself to take a slow sip of wine. "The wine is good."

"It is. There are better wines, but a good wine and a good life, lived now, are far more desirous than seeking a distant good that one's efforts may destroy as easily as create."

Cerryl tried to keep his head from spinning at the implications of Anya's words. *She's trying to upset you . . . and she's doing it . . . demon-damned darkness!* Finally, he said, "Do you think Myral is right about the times changing?"

She laughed, gently and generously. "Cerryl, all times change. How can Myral be wrong?"

"I know, but sometimes the changes are little, and sometimes . . ."

"Sometimes, the entire world changes?" She ate several bites of the rice before continuing. "Jeslek has raised mountains. You know. You were there when he began. No mage has ever done that. So times have changed." She lifted her shoulders, then dropped them theatrically. "Some things never change. Men will always want coins, and power, and beautiful women. Women will want what they want." Her eyes fixed Cerryl's. "What do you want from being a mage?"

Cerryl remained stock-still for a long moment before answering. "I don't know that I know."

"Best you find out before someone else chooses for you."

"It can be hard to choose when you know little of the choices," he pointed out.

"Well," she began, her voice light, "you could ask Myral and Ki-nowin to help you become a trade monitor. You'd probably end up in Quend, freezing half the year and using your glass to scree through cargo of fish and more fish. Or you could ask Eliasar for arms training—"

"And end up cutting off my own foot," he interjected with a laugh.

"Or you could work with Jeslek raising mountains and chaos, getting old before your time. Or you could spend the next half-score of years flaming old ladies from the gate ramparts . . ."

"You make few of the choices attractive," he pointed out.

"Exactly. All paths have drudgery. That is the problem with seeking fulfillment through one's skills in meeting the Guild's needs." Anya drained her wine.

Cerryl replenished her goblet, emptying the first bottle in adding but a touch to his own goblet, more to distract from the fact that he had drunk little than from any desire for more wine. "What would you suggest?"

"Ah . . . I won't. Not now, dearest Cerryl. I'm a cruel woman. You need to think about what I've said. You and Faltar and Lyasa and Myredin and Heralt and Bealtur, you all have to make your own choices. But no one tells you enough." Anya smiled the broad insincere smile.

Cerryl stiffened within.

"What I will tell you is that nothing is as it seems. Not the Guild, not Kinowin, not Myral, not Sterol, not even me. I'll tell you that. They won't." She took another swallow of the dark red wine. "No matter what anyone says, best you question it within yourself." Another swallow of wine followed. "Wine doesn't lie, Cerryl. We lie to ourselves; we lie to others. Wine lies to none." The bright smile was slightly off-center as Anya stared at Cerryl before lifting her glass once more and draining it.

Cerryl refilled it, almost absently. There was less than half of the second bottle remaining.

"You could be dangerous, Cerryl, but you're too kind. Even with those you trust not, you are kind. Best you be careful of that as well." Anya's pale eyes had turned darker, almost owlish, as she cradled the goblet in both hands.

*Too kind?* Cerryl swallowed a yawn.

"You are tired, and confused. Or partly confused. Or less confused than many, but still confused."

Confused? *Yes, but not in the way you think . . . dear Anya.*

"Run along, Cerryl. Run along back to your mine-cave-room." Anya gestured broadly. "Go back and be a cautious miner, and think." She laughed, this time almost raucously. "It won't help. It won't help at all."

Cerryl stood, then bowed slightly. "I am tired. Could I walk you back to the Hall?"

"Yes. You could. I would like that." Anya rose, gracefully despite all the wine she had drunk.

Cerryl followed Anya down the stairs, half-ready to reach for her if she fell, but the redhead swayed only slightly more than normal and with a grace that was almost seductive.

*Almost.*

"Good night, Westcort." Anya offered a head bow as she passed the proprietor.

"Good-night, Lady Anya . . . ser."

"Good night," Cerryl added. Since Westcort had not asked for coin, either Anya was known to be good for the debt . . . or she had already paid.

"You are wondering, are you not?" asked the redhead as Cerryl helped her up the steps to the front Hall. "You are wondering. Well . . . I will let you wonder."

The two walked slowly through the deserted front Hall, the sound of their boots echoing in the gloom barely relieved by the handful of scattered wall lamps, burning low and providing but a dim glow. The slight bite of the water-cooled air in the fountain courtyard was welcome and fleeting as they entered the second Hall.

"This way." Anya turned down a side Hall past the commons, one Cerryl had walked occasionally but seldom, since it led nowhere except to the next courtyard and since other routes were more direct. "We do have quarters in our own wing. Our own wing. It makes the bathing and the jakes more convenient."

Suddenly Anya stopped in front of a door. The bronze door plaque read: "Anya."

"Good night, Cerryl."

Anya slipped inside, and the bolt clicked shut.

Cerryl stood there for a moment. Had he heard a soft cry—or a laugh? He wasn't sure. He turned.

What had Anya wanted? To upset him? To find out more about him so that she or Sterol or Jeslek could manipulate him? She hadn't wanted him in bed. That was the only thing he was sure about—the only thing.

He walked slowly through the rear courtyard and into the farthest Hall, then up the stairs and along the corridor. He closed the door to his room slowly, wishing Leyladin were still in Fairhaven. He would have liked to talk to the blonde healer. Some things Anya had said about him had bothered him, accurate as they were, because they had been accurate and he wasn't sure why they had upset him.

Lyasa might help, but he'd have to be careful how much he said to the black-haired mage.

He yawned as he slowly began to disrobe. The predawn bell would ring soon—too soon.

# XXIV

. . . Some time passed, while Candar burned under the unrelenting sun and cloudless skies, and while the great rains harnessed by Creslin slowly transformed the desert lands of Recluce into a green that the isle had never known.

Even the banner of Recluce adopted by the Blacks was of darkness, that of a black blade and a black rose, crossed, as were the hearts and minds of Creslin and Megaera.

For, despite all the rain, all the coins and the ships that plied the Eastern Ocean to gather goods under the banner of Recluce, the isle was blighted, and its people hungered.

Once again, the Black leader of Recluce struck, a dark hammer of storms and ships that flowed through the Great North Bay under a fog that turned the day to night; and while the people of Lydiar struggled in the darkness, Creslin called down storms.

Mighty storms they were, so massive that they shivered the very stones of the Easthorns and created swamps and bogs west of Lydiar where none had been before, so powerful that their lightning shivered the keep of Lydiar into pieces of gravel.

The destruction rained upon Lydiar, and while it fell across every part of the city Creslin and his forces seized every ship and cargo in the port, and all the golds in the city, and all the food in the granaries, and all the dried fruits and meats in the warehouses.

Laughing, the Black sorcerer returned to Recluce, where he and the evil Megaera rejoiced in their plunder and divided it among all, save for the ships, which he armed and armored with the protections of order and sent out to demand tribute to Recluce from all upon the seas of the world . . .

*Colors of White*
(Manual of the Guild at Fairhaven)
Preface

# XXV

Have you granted any more medallions to farmers?" From where he stood with his back to the window Kinowin half-grinned at the younger mage.

"Yes, ser. Another six . . . so far. Only one of them had ever had one before. At least on the carts they presented."

"Any more incidents like that farm woman?" The blond mage touched his chin, then rubbed his jaw, his fingers remaining below the purplish blotch on his left cheek.

Cerryl shook his head, still wishing he hadn't had to flame the old woman, yet he doubted he could have done otherwise.

Kinowin stepped toward the table at which Cerryl sat, then turned and looked at the blue and purple hanging. After a moment, he added, "How was your late supper with Anya?"

"Disturbing, in a way."

"Why did you go with her?"

"I didn't think it wise to upset her too much."

A wry smile crossed Kinowin's face. "Anything you do that crosses her will upset her. You know that, don't you?"

"That's why I went. I'm sure to upset her sooner or later. I'd prefer later."

"Since you didn't fall into bed with her, did she talk to you about her paradox? It's not hers, really; it actually belongs to the first Black angel—Ryba. I find that rather symbolic . . ."

Cerryl swallowed. Was Kinowin saying that Anya was using the words of the first Black angel—the founder of Westwind and all its depredations? "About when Myral sees the future . . . is that . . . ?"

Kinowin nodded, then quoted, almost in falsetto, " 'Perhaps our actions in trying to avoid his visions are what will make them happen.' "

Cerryl winced.

"It's very effective," Kinowin mused. "I even fell for it . . . for a bit."

Cerryl couldn't imagine Kinowin falling for anything.

"It's very seductive. How can you know whether a vision is true? If it is not, and you oppose it, then do you bring it into being? Or . . . if it is true, and you oppose it, do you do the same? Because . . . if you can change things, how could the vision exist?"

The younger mage shivered. "Did Ryba . . . ?"

"Oh, yes. At least, if you can believe the *Book of Ayrlyn*. Some call it Ryba's curse."

"I thought that was a forbidden book."

"It is . . . until you're a Guild member. In a season or so I'll have you read it. You're not quite ready."

"Is it filled with lies, and I don't have enough knowledge to understand which are lies?"

"No. It's filled with truths, and you'll have a great deal of trouble understanding how truths can be lies." Kinowin snorted gently. "That's always been the problem we've had in the Guild." He eased away from the hanging and toward the single bookcase, stepping through the shaft of golden light wherein swirled white-golden specks of chaos dust. "A fact is. A stone exists." The overmage walked over to the bookcase and lifted a volume, then replaced it. "You see this book. It is." He laughed. "Sterol and Jeslek would die of mirth at rough-born and plainspoken Kinowin discussing truth. I have to laugh, too. What is truth? Oh, the philosophers will give you answers and words. But what no one—especially Myral—wants to admit is that there is no such thing as truth. That's where Anya is right. We take a belief that what we do is the good thing to do, and we call it the true way. The Blacks do the same."

Cerryl's eyes widened.

"I'm not saying that I believe the Blacks. They've created more bloodshed indirectly than Fairhaven has with all its lancers. They talk of peace and order, but Recluce was founded on the blade of the greatest swordsman and weather wizard of all time, and to this day no other ruler has slaughtered so many in the name of peace and order."

Cerryl waited.

"Men and women are not perfect. You have seen that. I'm certain Anya has told you about how all that most people want from life are coins or power or bodies in bed." Kinowin shook his head. "She's right. Those are what most people want. Where I differ from Anya is that I don't think the members of the Guild are or should be 'most people.' That is what the Guild was founded on." The overmage cleared his throat. "Did you know that in ancient Cyador, the first White land, west of the Westhorns, they had highways grander than ours, firewagons that sped tirelessly across them, and fireships that ruled the seas? Even the poorest of farmers had houses with stoves and water pumped from the ground. And the Blacks unleashed chaos and destroyed Cyador. They claim to be the supporters of order, yet they used chaos to destroy the greatest land Candar has ever known."

"*Colors of White* tells some of that." Cerryl's voice was neutral.

Kinowin walked to the window again, glancing out into the midafternoon light. "The idea of 'truth' is one of the most dangerous tools any ruler can use. The only problem is that declaring that there is no such thing as truth is even worse. Then people have no anchor and nothing to believe in." Kinowin turned to Cerryl. "You hear my words, but you don't understand. Not really."

Cerryl didn't know what to say.

"Has your healer friend talked to you about what she does besides healing?"

"No. She's still in Certis."

"I know that. Earlier, I meant." Kinowin shifted his weight so that he could look out the window and still watch Cerryl.

"Some things . . . like inspecting the water tunnels and using sleep spells on prisoners." Cerryl frowned. "I can't think of anything else."

Kinowin turned from the window to Cerryl. "Can you truth-read?"

"Truth-read?"

" 'Truth-read' isn't the right term, but everyone uses it. Tell when someone speaks what they believe to be the truth—or when their words do not match the chaos and order within them?"

Should he tell Kinowin? Cerryl shrugged. If Kinowin could sense what Cerryl could feel, the overmage already knew. "Most times."

"That will do. Your skills are being wasted on gate duty, and you need to learn more of how Fairhaven truly works. Myral and I have discussed this."

Cerryl could feel his stomach tightening.

"What do you know of the Patrol?"

"Not much. They keep the peace. They supply the prisoners for the cleanup details at the gates."

"You need to work with the Patrol. You have the skills, and Isork could use another mage. He and Huroan have but nine other mages, and that is far from sufficient."

"What . . . do I do?"

"Tomorrow will be your last day at the gates. The morning after, report to Isork. The main Patrol building is the two-story square building on the other side of The Golden Ram. He will be expecting you."

"Yes, ser."

Kinowin shook his head as he gestured. "You can go. I wouldn't tell anyone about our conversation. Sterol knows how I feel—and agrees partly. Jeslek and Anya will use it against you . . . later. There's nothing they can do to me."

Cerryl understood what Kinowin had not said—that none of the junior mages would understand. He wasn't sure *he* understood.

As he walked slowly down the steps to the front foyer, he took a deep breath. What he didn't understand at all was Kinowin. Anya—he could understand her wanting power, especially as a woman in the Guild and in Fairhaven. But why was Kinowin so concerned about *him?* There were anywhere from five to a half-score new mages that entered the Guild each year. *Is he concerned because you remind him of when he was younger? Or because he had too many unanswered questions when he was young? Unanswered questions? Why had he never answered the question of what you do when you see a vision of what will be? Because there is no answer?*

Cerryl pursed his lips and kept walking.

# XXVI

In the slanting light of early morning, Cerryl stepped through the plain white oak door into the Patrol building. Two Patrol guards stood at each side of the entry hall, each wearing a uniform identical to those of lancers, except for a wide red belt and a short truncheon in addition to the shortsword.

"Ser?" asked the Patrol guard on the right, with a close-cut black beard shot with streaks of white.

"I'm here to see Isork, the Patrol chief."

"Could I explain who you are to him, ser?"

"I'm Cerryl. Overmage Kinowin sent me."

"One moment." The patroller nodded. "I'll let Patrol Chief Isork know." He turned down the short and narrow hall he had guarded, rapped on a closed door, and entered.

Cerryl studied the entry hall—a rectangular and spare room only ten cubits on a side with two halls angling from the corners farthest from the entry door. Two backless oak benches were set against the side walls. A set of closed double oak doors on the back wall faced the entry. The floor was of featureless and time-polished granite that had faded to a dull gray. The only light came from the windows that flanked the door behind Cerryl.

The patroller emerged from the door at the end of the short hall. "This way, ser."

"Thank you." Cerryl inclined his head, then walked down the hall and entered the small room, no more than six cubits by ten. The pudgy-faced but broad-shouldered and muscular Isork sat behind a flat table-desk. A single vacant stool stood before the table, and against the wall to the left was a single four-shelf bookcase. A stack of parchmentlike papers, an inkwell and a quill holder, and a single volume were all that rested on the battered and oiled surface of the desk.

"Cerryl, to see you, ser."

Isork looked at Cerryl, studying him for a long and uncomfortable time with flat brown eyes that revealed nothing, then motioned to the single stool. "Sit down. You're young for Patrol duty—and slight." The pudgy but broad-shouldered mage shook his head. His short brown hair did not move. "Kinowin says you're an orphan. That right?"

"Yes, ser."

"You didn't call me 'ser' at the Council meeting."

"I wasn't to be working for you there, ser."

The trace of a smile crossed the pudgy mage's face. "So, off-duty, you believe you're equal to any mage?"

"No, ser. Not at all. I'm possibly better than some and not so good as others."

"What about me?"

"I don't know, ser. I'd say you'd have to be better than I am, but I don't know." Cerryl felt that he had to be honest, no matter how uncomfortable it was.

Isork shook his head again. "Who raised you?"

"My aunt and uncle. He was a master miner before they shut the mines."

"Where do they live?"

"They're both dead, ser. I was a mill boy for the lumber mill in Hrisbarg."

For the first time, Isork looked vaguely interested. "How did you get to Fairhaven, then?"

"I persuaded the mill master's daughter to teach me my letters, and after several years the mill master sent me here to Fairhaven to be an apprentice to Tellis the scrivener."

"And one of the mages who bought books from Tellis discovered you had the talent?"

"Yes, ser."

"Hmmm . . . Kinowin says that you're not the most powerful of the younger mages, but you're strong enough and you have the most control of your firebolts. That true?"

"I don't know what control others have. I can make mine go where I want them." Cerryl paused. "Unless it's more than a hundred cubits away. Then they don't always hit exactly where I want."

"When were you throwing chaos that far?"

"That was when I was a student and Jeslek took me to Gallos. We were attacked by some twenty-score Gallosian lancers."

Isork nodded again. "You killed some?"

"About a half-score that I know of."

"Kinowin said you've flamed some people on gate duty. Ever taken on a man with a blade or a spear?"

"Three, ser, when I was on sewer duty. Two had iron shields and blades. The other had a white-bronze spear."

"All at once?" Isork's bushy eyebrows rose.

"No, ser. The two with the iron blades at once, the one with the spear a little later."

Isork smiled ruefully. "Any other mages know of this?"

"Myral, Sterol, and Kinowin came right afterward. Some others might know. I don't know who they told."

"You didn't tell anyone?"

Cerryl frowned. "I think I told Lyasa and Faltar, but I didn't tell them much."

"Well . . . Kinowin's got a feel for this, and he's usually right. You just don't look like a Patrol mage. Even to me, you don't look like one, but you *feel* like one. Tight control over chaos, almost as if you don't have any, but I can feel the shields there. You keep it away from your body, don't you?"

"Yes, ser. Myral suggested it was better that way."

"It is. Most won't work hard enough to learn how. Why did you?"

"I'm not from Fairhaven."

"And you're not from coins or the crèche." Isork gave a knowing look at the slender mage. "Just like Kinowin. You have to do it better."

Cerryl waited.

"You'll do, and, light knows, good Patrol mages are hard to find. Half those I see want to fire everyone in sight, and the other half wait until they have to." Isork leaned back slightly. "What's the Patrol? No one knows, and everyone thinks they know what it should be. Our job is simple and hard. We're the bastards who keep the peace in Fairhaven, and we do whatever it takes. The basic rules are really simple. No bared blades anywhere in public in the city, and that's any blade except a dagger at table for eating or a blade used in trade, like at the tanner's. Some bravo has a blade out, he gets a quick warning. If he doesn't sheathe it, he's ash.

"No one attacks a Patrol with anything—except words—or he's ash. We see a fight, and we try to stop it. The mage—that's you—determines who's at fault. You can truth-read, can't you?" Isork looked at Cerryl.

"I can usually feel whether someone's words are true."

"Good. If there's any question, especially at first, you can summon me or Huroan. Most times, there's no question. Biggest problem is when some fellow starts beating his consort in public. If you fire him or stop him and send him on the road, the family can suffer. If you don't, like as not, sooner or later, he'll kill her or one of the kids. Or maim 'em so bad he might as well have killed 'em."

Cerryl raised his eyebrows.

"We bend the rules a little there. That's where we get the prisoners for the refuse wagons and the gate cleanup details. We try to get the idea across that rules are rules."

"Does it work?"

"From what I've seen . . . more than half the times, and that's better than anything else. If a fellow doesn't learn, well . . . sometimes the family can hold on without him, and at least they're alive."

"The other thing the Patrol does is judge things—the little things. That's what that chamber is for." Isork gestured to the white oak door to his left. "Folks sometimes disagree. So they come and ask me or Huroan to listen. We truth-read and try to sort it out. Most times, people just believe different things—no lies. When they find that out, and I'm sitting there, they can usually figure out an answer." A crooked smile crossed the Patrol chief's face. "We don't get many liars—usually those are from outside of Fairhaven."

"What do you do with the liars?"

"If they admit it . . . and make good . . . nothing. If they insist . . . well . . . they go on the road crew."

"Even wealthy merchants?"

A look of disgust crossed Isork's face. "They can offer a hundred golds in bond; then the High Wizard has to review it. Most times, that means they get out of Fairhaven." A smile reappeared. "But . . . see, if they don't come back and get judged by the High Wizard within a season, they lose the coins, and then, if they show up again and we find them, it's the road crew, and not even the High Wizard steps in then."

Cerryl nodded. *And the road crew is usually life at hard labor building the White highways.* He knew that much.

"We can't control what people do in their dwellings, but shops, squares, streets, places of business, inns, stables—those are public places as far as the Patrol goes.

"For the first couple of eight-days you'll be walking the streets with the best lead patroller we've got. That's Duarrl. Only one rule—if he asks you to flame someone . . . do it. He won't ask unless there's a good reason." Isork smiled. "It doesn't happen often, but I want you to understand. Also, the Patrol never argues in public. Do you understand that? So try not to order anything stupid. Your patrollers won't argue. They might suggest. Listen."

"Yes, ser."

"We don't take young lancers as patrollers. There's not a single patroller who's not at least a score and five. That means you're the youngest man in the Patrol. That bother you?"

"No, ser. I hope it doesn't bother too many patrollers."

"There's one other thing. There are rules for peacekeeping and for patrollers and Patrol mages. They're in here." Isork held up a slim volume, then set it down. "If Huroan or I decide that a Patrol mage has broken any of them, then the Council decides on discipline. Do you understand that?"

Cerryl nodded. He certainly didn't want to break any rules, not with Sterol and Jeslek able to discipline him.

"Good." Isork nodded, then lifted the slim volume from the desk once again and extended it to Cerryl. "Read as much of this as you can today. Be here tomorrow at dawn. First two eight-days, you'll go with

Duarrl on the morning patrol. That's mostly quiet, and that way you can learn where everything is in your section of the city—you'll get the southeast. That's where most things happen."

As he took the thin book, Cerryl wondered about why he would be given a section where the most things happened but said nothing.

"You wonder why the southeast?" Another crooked smile crossed Isork's lips. "That's where the low trades are, the poorer folk. More fights, but they respect the Patrol. They haven't got coins. Up in the northwest . . . well . . . best not to have a Patrol mage in a section where he has to deal with slick traders until he's got some experience under his belt."

"Do Patrol mages walk the streets all the time?" Cerryl couldn't recall ever seeing a mage with the patrols.

"No. Once you know your section, you'll be staying in your little room, just like I stay here. That way, your patrols can find you. You'll have ten patrols of four men reporting to you—except you're really there to back them up and protect them. Don't forget it. You'll have a set of guards, like here—and a messenger to find me in real trouble. Or to find you on the nights when you have the call."

"The call?"

"Oh . . . guess I forgot that. When you get the afternoon duty—that's really from midafternoon until midevening—you also have call. That means the messenger has to know where you're sleeping . . . or eating . . . wherever you are. Most nights nothing happens after midevening, but you'd best be where you say you are." Isork laughed. "In the Patrol, no one cares where that is or who you're with—just so long as the messenger can find you quick. Means you don't leave the city, and it's better if you're close to your section. Most mages just show the messenger their quarters, and that's where they are."

Cerryl nodded, feeling as though he were doing that far too often.

"One other thing . . . and I'll wager Kinowin didn't mention it. You get another gold an eight-day—and you'll earn every copper." Isork rose. "Tomorrow here at dawn."

"Yes, ser."

"You call me, Huroan, the overmages, and the High Wizard 'ser.' No one else in the Guild. And you call every person you meet on duty 'ser.' Strange world, isn't it?" The crooked smile faded. "Tomorrow."

Cerryl kept his face emotionless as he left the Patrol building and walked slowly toward the Wizards' Square. Once he was well away from the building, he opened the book and read the front page—"On Peacekeeping."

Another book like Myral's on sewage? Or philosophy like *Colors of White*? Or did it really have firm rules? Did the Guild have a manual for *everything*?

He closed the book and took a deep breath.

# XXVII

Duarrl was a head taller than Cerryl and half again as broad, clean-shaven with brown and gray hair and thin eyebrows that joined over his nose. Despite a bulk that threatened to burst out of the white tunic and crimson belt of a patroller, his face was long and narrow. He and Cerryl stood beside each other in Isork's office, while Isork stood behind the desk that contained little beside the quill and inkstand and another pile of paper and scrolls.

"Duarrl, this is Mage Cerryl," Isork began. "He's a bit young. Kinowin says he's talented. He killed those smugglers in the sewer last fall, the ones that had iron blades and shields."

Duarrl offered a minimal head bow. "Good. Mage who can't handle iron's not much use to the Patrol."

"He's also been in a full battle in Gallos—killed close to a score of purple lancers."

"Never liked those folk much," Duarrl grunted.

"I told you—he'll be taking the mornings from Fylker. Move him to the afternoon so Huroan and I aren't down there all the time."

"Be good." Duarrl smiled. "That way all of us can find you."

Isork spread a parchment map on the desk. "Like a sewer map. I'm sure you're familiar with those."

Cerryl nodded, then bent over, noting that red lines split the city in quarters. The north–south line was effectively the Avenue, and the east and west line ran outward from the Wizards' Square in each direction.

"You will have to find another inn to eat at." Isork grinned. "Least while you're on duty. The Golden Ram is just across the Avenue, but it's out of your section. Here's the section Patrol building." He pointed.

From what Cerryl could see, it was perhaps two blocks south and five blocks east of where Arkos the tanner had his shop.

"Your section has most of the tanners, some tinsmiths and copper-smiths, and some of about everything else except for big houses of wealthy factors. You should get to know it like the back of your forearm. Wouldn't hurt to spend some time screeing it as well. Use your glass before you have to." Isork turned to Duarrl. "Anything you'd like to add?"

"Well . . . like as a lot of hotheads in the southeast section . . . we try to yell first, give 'em a moment to understand we're Patrol. Makes it easier on all of us."

"They respect the Patrol, but it takes a moment for them to realize that they could be in trouble?" asked Cerryl.

"Right as light, ser. And, the boys, well . . . no sense in slicing up someone or forcing you to ash 'em, not if it not be needed."

*In short, look and think before you start throwing firebolts.* Cerryl nodded.

"Cerryl . . . a word while Duarrl talks to the Patrol." Isork cleared his throat and glanced at Duarrl. "Might tell 'em about him . . . what you think necessary."

"Yes, ser." Duarrl straightened.

Isork rolled up the map. As Duarrl closed the door, the Patrol chief offered a smile. "Not much to say. The reason you're here is so he can tell the patrollers what I told him to tell them. About you. They need to know that you've faced an iron blade and been in battle. Makes them feel better. Wouldn't be quite so necessary if . . ."

"If I looked more like you or Kinowin?"

Isork nodded. "True you faced down Jeslek?" The Patrol chief offered a wry smile. "It's not known to many . . . but I have talked to Kinowin."

After a momentary hesitation, Cerryl nodded. "I'd rather it not be known . . . unless you think it important."

"No one here but me needs to know that." Isork stood. "There was one other thing I didn't mention. Shouldn't be a problem, though, seeing you were a scrivener. The Patrol mage is the one who writes down the daily report. You have to finish that before you leave your shift and send it here by messenger. You don't start writing until you take over the morning duty, though. Next two eight-days, I want you learning everything you can about the southeast section—every inn, every spirit shop, every stable, and every warehouse. Any sewer tunnel you don't know."

"Yes, ser."

After a moment, Isork cocked his head to the side. "Let's go meet this morning's Patrol group. I don't expect you to remember all the names at once, but make an effort. Patrol mage is supposed to know every patroller by name and face."

"Ah . . . eight score?"

"About nine score, with the wagon drivers and everyone. We should have ten score, but . . ." Isork shrugged. "It's hard to get patrollers, too."

Cerryl opened the door, then waited for Isork to step around the desk. Duarrl and four men stood in a loose row in the entry hall. The four patrollers straightened slightly as Isork and Cerryl approached. Isork's eyes rested on each of the white-uniformed men in turn before he spoke.

"This is Mage Cerryl. Duarrl's told you some about him, I'm sure.

I'll tell you one more thing. He was raised in the mines and worked his way out of a sawmill." Isork nodded to Duarrl.

"Here they be, ser." Duarrl pointed to a tall and thin man with dark red hair and the faint trace of a scar above his left eyebrow. "Reyll."

"Noyr." The next patroller was squat, even shorter than Cerryl, but twice as broad, and his hair was jet-black, his eyes equally black.

"Churk." Churk offered a broad smile with his mouth, but the blue eyes remained distant under the short flax-gold hair.

"Praytt." After meeting Cerryl's eyes, the last patroller's green eyes flicked from side to side, as if he had to study everything around him all the time.

"All right, once we cross the Avenue, we'll do it like a sweep, except this is so Mage Cerryl knows what a sweep's like, and also so you don't forget." Duarrl grinned at the four patrollers. "First four blocks, Noyr and Praytt . . . you be in front of us. Reyll—the left alleyway, Churk, the right." He nodded sharply, and the four started for the doorway.

Isork looked at Cerryl and then at Duarrl. Cerryl understood—listen to Duarrl and try not to do anything stupid. Cerryl followed Duarrl out to the Avenue, out into a day that was already gusty, with a hint of chill, forecasting the cooler days of late fall after harvest. The six waited for a lumber wagon to rumble past before crossing the divided pavement of the Avenue. On the other side, Reyll and Churk eased away from the other four.

Cerryl had walked through some of the area east and south of the square on the last part of his sewer duty, but he'd walked through it, not studied it. So he tried to take in all the details poured forth by Duarrl.

"Vuyult—sells baskets and chairs, things woven from withies. Also sells withies themselves to the traders from Kyphros . . .

"There . . . the long warehouse with the gray timbers . . . used to belong to Hefkek . . . till he got bigger than his trouser . . . sold it to some brothers from Biehl . . . They grind all sorts of stuff . . . make pigments . . . Traders take 'em everywhere . . .

". . . Bavann . . . says they're all his daughters and cousins." Duarrl snorted. "Always different daughters and cousins, and they've stayed young, and his beard's gone from black to gray. Doesn't make trouble, though, and we're here to keep the peace, not to judge what folk do behind doors and walls . . ."

Cerryl had to nod at that, though he wondered at times if some of the mages didn't cross that line. After all, he hadn't exactly made any trouble, yet the Guild had sought him out and would have sent him to the road crew or killed him if he hadn't been acceptable to the Guild.

Duarrl stopped at the edge of a small square with a fountain. The water spurted out of a time-worn marble vase taller than a man. "They say this be the old square, the center of Fairhaven before the first Whites fled from the Westhorns." An apologetic smile crossed the patroller's thin face. "Not that I'd be knowing that, you understand, ser, but that be what the folk say."

"It could be true," Cerryl said. "I wouldn't know. That's the sort of thing no one would have a reason to lie about." He glanced around the near-empty square. An old man sat on the sunny side of the fountain basin, covered with a patched gray blanket, his eyes closed. Beside him rested a yellow dog with pointed ears, whose nose twitched as it surveyed the pavement.

A woman struggled down the narrow street to the east of the fountain, bent under a load of willow rods, while a cart pulled by a small donkey creaked past her and toward the square. On the far side, two boys, not even to Cerryl's chest, tossed a ball back and forth

"Good folk here," observed Duarrl. "Mostly from the countryside. Stay in the houses along the square for a time. Then they go back to the country or make enough coins to move north."

A black stone structure, almost cubical, stood at the far side of the square. Because it had been initially obscured by the fountain, Cerryl hadn't really seen it. The stones were dark gray, and the side of the wall that Cerryl saw was polished smooth—except in a handful of places where something had struck the stone and left a grayish gouge and radiating cracks.

"What's that?"

"Oh . . . that be a lodging house for laborers come from the country. Messil—he's Praytt's cousin or some such—runs it."

"That black stone?"

"Aye . . . said it was a Black Temple years and years back, long before Fairhaven looked as it did. Folks say at first no one could move the stones. A shame to waste it, Messil claims, saving only outsiders'd sleep there. Still, he runs a quiet lodging house."

A Black Temple in Fairhaven—they were scarce enough anywhere, and to find what had been one in the White City? Cerryl let his senses range over the building, finding only faint traces of the order that had once reinforced all the stones, but no more order than reinforced the stones and masonry of the Great White Highway.

"It probably was," Cerryl reflected.

"You know any of this part of the city, ser?" Duarrl asked deferentially.

"Not much south of Arkos's tannery—I've been in the potter's place. Lwelter's, I think."

"Old Lwelter died last season," Duarrl said.

"I met his son, but I don't remember his name."

"Flait be the one who has the shop now."

Cerryl nodded. "He wasn't exactly pleased when I appeared at his door."

"Begging your pardon, ser, but more than a few would rather not see the pure White at their door, much as they prefer the city itself."

"I was one of them," Cerryl confessed with a laugh. "I preferred not to encounter mages."

"You did not expect to be a mage?"

"No. I thought it impossible for a poor boy."

Duarrl nodded, then pointed ahead to a signboard hung out over the street, bearing the black outline of an oversized pot above a fire. "There be The Black Pot. Fansner's the keep. I'd not eat there. Good folk, but the fare . . ." He shook his head.

"Where would be a good place to eat?"

"The Broken Blade. Turgot has a good stew," mused Duarrl. "Then the bakery down the way there, Jeloran's. No signboard, but you can smell it. Nothing like The Ram or Furenk's. Sometimes, The Blue Heron be not too bad."

Cerryl watched as Reyll slipped out of yet another alleyway and shook his head.

"Alleys are clean today. Not always like that. Betimes, you be ashing rubbish and things may not be rubbish."

The mage nodded. Tossing rubbish in the streets or alleys was considered breaking the peace, because it could catch fire or harbor flux.

Duarrl pointed down the narrow street to the south. "Where the tin smugglers live. Second and third houses."

Cerryl's eyes followed the lead patroller's gesture, picking out the pale blue and pink plaster-fronted brick houses. "You let them live there?"

"Ser, we all *know* they smuggle tin in, but they don't use wagons, and the laws don't say anything about goods folk carry on themselves. 'Sides, how would the coppersmiths make their bronze—the little shops? They'd not be able to buy tin from the factors. A factor like Muneat, he won't sell tin in less than five stone lots. Chorast likewise."

"What else gets smuggled in like that?"

"Most anything, I'd guess, but so long as it's in small lots, and they don't use the sewers or break the peace . . ." Duarrl shrugged.

Cerryl kept listening, all too aware of how right Kinowin had been, of how little he truly knew about Fairhaven.

# XXVIII

After nearly an eight-day of walking the southeast quarter of Fairhaven, Cerryl was gaining an appreciation of just how much he hadn't known about the city—as well as very sore feet. So he was pleased to be able to ride the big chestnut out beyond the southernmost part of Fairhaven to where the sewers ended—at the southeastern side of Fairhaven, beyond and to the east of the southern gates.

A single white granite building stood on the edge of the plateau that marked the end of Fairhaven and overlooked the ponds and fountains. Cerryl tied his mount to one of the stone hitching blocks on the shaded east side of the stone building that was mostly warehouse.

Duarrl and Cerryl walked another fifty cubits south, to where they could survey what lay below. The four patrollers had dismounted but remained in the shade beside their tethered mounts.

"The other problem we get is the sewer outfalls. Have to check those regular-like. Isork thought you ought to be along. Otherwise he'd have to come, seeing as there's always the possibility of smugglers or some such."

"I found that out. I ran into smugglers—or brigands—when I was on sewer duty." Cerryl nodded. "Isork mentioned that, I think."

Duarrl laughed. "For a little mage, you been a lot of dirty places—mines, sawmills, sewers battles."

"I did spend a little time with a scrivener," Cerryl admitted. "That's where the Guild found me."

"Doesn't that beat all . . ." Duarrl shook his head.

For a moment Cerryl looked down across the tiered ponds and the fountains that sprayed foul water into the air to be cleansed by the chaos of the sun. A hint of ancient chaos seeped from beneath the granite that walled the slope—a hint that suggested the hillside was far from completely natural.

The sewage flowed directly from the two main tunnels into four settling ponds. The pond on the west end was empty of water, and a dozen prisoners shoveled the settled mix of offal, sludge, and other solids into handcarts, which were pulled by ropes to the side where the contents were loaded into a larger wagon. The solids were carted off to a dry gorge to the northeast of the city on eastern side of the hills where runoff would only seep into the higher grasslands southwest of Lydiar.

Cerryl studied the group but didn't see any sign of Lyasa. Perhaps she was not on duty yet or somewhere else in the vast sewer collection system. His eyes drifted downhill.

From the settling ponds the water flowed into channels that spread the sewer water into thin sheets that flowed down the flattened sloping granite inclines, exposed to the chaos of the sun, to be collected into another set of ponds that fed the lower fountains. Those fountains, in turn, flung the water into the air in fine sprays where the pure chaos of the sun would destroy much of the remaining unnatural chaos in the water.

The lowest tier of ponds remained covered mostly with water lilies, and the cleansed water flowed over the granite lips on the south side of the ponds and into another granite channel that led to the Haven River. Although Cerryl would not have wished to drink the cleansed water, Myral had often assured him that it was far cleaner than the water used for drinking in any other city in Candar. That reminded Cerryl to chaos-clean water from anywhere else in Candar or drink ale or wine.

"Glad we don't have to supervise that." Duarrl gestured toward the sewage workers. "Just provide the prisoners and a few guards."

"Disciplinary duty?" asked Cerryl.

The lead patroller nodded. "Little things—not showing up for duty, the first time, or being late a couple of times." He grinned at Cerryl. "The mages who supervise—they tell me that's disciplinary duty, too."

"So I've heard. I've not had to do refuse duty."

"Well ... let's go." Duarrl turned and motioned to the four patrollers.

Cerryl and Duarrl walked down the granite steps to the landing that held the grated bronze door covering the entrance to the sewer walkway. A second bronze grate covered the sewer tunnel itself, a grate that angled from the tunnel top out over the stone lip where the sewage dropped into the twin channels that split and carried the sewage to the two settling ponds. Two hundred cubits to the west was another tunnel and door.

Cerryl frowned as he studied the grated bronze door, then glanced at the stones of the extended walkway. He extended his senses to the gate, then turned to Duarrl. "Do you have a key? I turned mine in when I left sewer duty."

Duarrl fumbled through the ring on his belt. "Here ... I think that's it." He looked at the gate and then at Cerryl. "You think ... ?"

Cerryl smiled apologetically. "Someone's opened the gate, and not too long ago. There's blood on the stones and no chaos in the lock."

"Fellows," Duarrl turned, "we might have a problem here."

Cerryl turned the key and levered back the oversized grate door. He stood for a moment looking into the gloom. Behind him, four blades slid from their sheaths. After relocking the gate open, Cerryl squinted momentarily, then extended his order senses. Someone had been in the sewer tunnel recently—very recently.

At the end of the tunnel by the grate door, the walkway was wider than in the tunnels under the White City itself—nearly three cubits, almost wide enough for a cart, if a small one. At that thought, Cerryl looked down. Was there a trace of wheels in the slime?

"Ser? Ah . . . we can't see in the dark." Duarrl sounded apologetic. "If you'd wait a moment until I get a striker out . . ."

"I didn't know the patrollers carried lamps."

"Have to be two lamps with every patrol."

"Just hold out the lamps, then." Cerryl turned and waited for Reyll and Churk to extend their lamps. Hyjul and Saft stood back, as did Duarrl.

*Whst!* The tiny firebolt lit the first lamp wick. A second firebolt flared Churk's lamp into light.

"That do?" asked Cerryl

"Ah . . . yes, ser."

Cerryl could sense something, rubbish, a bundle, something, on the walkway perhaps thirty cubits ahead. As he walked, he began to gather chaos around him—not to him, as Jeslek might have done, but around him.

A scraping sound echoed down the wide tunnel, but not loud enough for a man. Cerryl could sense something on the walkway, and the sickening rotting odor was far worse than just sewage. The scraping had probably been rats.

"Let's have a lamp. There's nothing alive here."

Churk's small lamp was enough to reveal what Cerryl had feared.

Cerryl wanted to gag but swallowed silently. The corpse had been a man—he thought, although the stench was worse than that of the sewage that gurgled in the tunnel beside the walkway. The figure wore rags, but anything else—boots, belt, purse—had been stripped. His face and chest had been burned, so much that the features were a unrecognizable blackened mass.

"They forced him to open the lock," opined Duarrl.

"There are traces of chaos," Cerryl said. "Not a lot of blood. He probably died when the chaos exploded out of the lock."

Duarrl bent down but did not touch the body. "There's nothing on him. Not a thing." He straightened, then looked at Cerryl. "Might as well get rid of it. Can't see who it was. No sense in burying it."

Cerryl swallowed, then let the chaos swell, before releasing it.

*WHssst!*

When the flare of light subsided, all that remained was drifting ash, and a single copper lying on fire-scoured stone.

"They missed a copper." Duarrl snorted. "Churk . . . your turn, if you want it."

The flaxen-haired Churk bent down gingerly.

"Careful . . ." Cerryl cautioned. "It will be hot."

"Thank you, ser." Churk set his blade aside and took out a leather glove and picked up the coin, then straightened. "Hot enough that there be no flux clinging to it."

"No," said Duarrl. "Let's see if we find anything else ahead. Doubt that we will, but you never know."

Churk walked ahead, lamp in one hand, shortsword in the other.

After nearly four hundred cubits, past one set of stairs to a locked overhead grate, Duarrl stopped. "Not going to find anything now. Let's head back."

As they turned and started back in single file, Cerryl glanced through the gloom at Duarrl. "What do you think they were smuggling? They used a cart—a small one—but it was heavy enough."

"You could tell it was a cart?"

"There were traces . . . The wheels crushed some of the slime. That makes another form of chaos."

Someone swallowed in the darkness.

"See why you don't underestimate mages, fellows?" Duarrl laughed before looking toward Cerryl. "If they had a cart, had to be something heavy. Couldn't be finished goods, like woven wool or the like. Take too long to get the smell of sewer out. Arms of some sort, I'd guess. Maybe oils or perfumes. Had to be something worth killing over. Though folks like that'd kill for a few silvers."

Their steps echoed hollowly down the tunnel over the gurgle of the sewage as it pulsed toward the treatment ponds.

Once everyone was out, Cerryl took Duarrl's key. "I'll need one of these."

"You'll have it tomorrow, ser."

"Good." Cerryl locked the grated door closed, returned the key, then forced himself to gather an enormous bolt of chaos, forcing it into the heavy lock.

"This time . . . there won't be just one body." He kept his voice low enough so that only Duarrl could hear his words.

The lead patroller nodded.

To the west, the prisoners continued to fill the wagon with the sludge from the empty settling pond.

"We'll need to watch this more often," Duarrl said to Cerryl as they walked back to the sewer building—and the waiting horses.

Cerryl nodded. He had his own ideas. He doubted that the old entrance to the sewers off the Avenue—the one where he'd been attacked by brigands—had ever been sealed and he had to wonder why.

# XXIX

Cerryl picked up the note that lay on his bed, looking at the hand-writing on the folded parchment—parchment, not the cheap brown paper used by some merchants. "Cerryl," he murmured as he read the single name on the outside. Then he smiled as he saw the green wax seal. He broke it and read quickly, smiling more broadly at the green ink.

> ...returned to Fairhaven last night, and Father and I would like to have you for dinner tonight. According to Myral, you have not been assigned evening duty with the Patrol yet, and so we are hoping to see you tonight...

The note was signed with a flowing green "L." Cerryl folded it carefully, walked to his desk, and slipped it into the covered box that held his papers, including some few notes he had penned out on various subjects.

After washing up, he left his quarters and headed for the White Tower. The corridors were mostly empty, although he did pass the thin-faced apprentice Kiella in the fountain courtyard. "Good day, Kiella."

"Good day, ser." Her eyes did not meet Cerryl's, and she stepped aside quickly to let him pass, even with the space afforded by the oth-erwise-empty courtyard.

Cerryl nodded to the ginger-bearded Redark as the two passed in the foyer of the main Hall. Redark inclined his head in return, although his pale green eyes bore a faintly puzzled expression, as if he wondered who Cerryl might be.

Gostar—strangely, the only guard at the lower tower door, since there were usually two and a messenger—nodded as Cerryl reached the top of the steps from the foyer and approached him. "Good day, ser. You liking Patrol duty?"

"I've walked over most of the southeast part of Fairhaven," Cerryl admitted.

"You met my brother?"

"I don't know. I didn't know you had a brother in the Patrol."

"Name's Lostar."

"I don't think so, but I haven't met every patroller yet, and I don't know all the names of those I have met," Cerryl admitted. "I'm sup-posed to, but I haven't gotten that far."

"Looks like me."

"I'll keep that in mind." Cerryl glanced toward the steps. "You know if Myral's in?"

"Most times I wouldn't, but he just walked up a bit ago. Alone." Gostar grinned. "The High Wizard went somewhere in his coach. Didn't look so happy, but he hasn't lately. They say he's been getting scrolls from Overmage Jeslek."

"He's raising more mountains in Gallos, I think."

Gostar looked down. "Not one to say . . . don't seem as natural-like, though, ser."

"Neither chaos nor order taken to extremes is natural, Gostar. Sometimes necessary, but not natural." Cerryl grinned. "That's what Kinowin always says." *Not that Kinowin or Myral phrased it quite that way.*

Gostar looked up as boots sounded on the stones. A second guard appeared, one Cerryl did not know.

"Gostar . . . Oh, sorry, ser."

Cerryl smiled. "That's all right."

As the new Patrol mage headed up the stairs, he could pick up the first fragments of the conversation.

". . . wish the messenger'd get back. Hate running up and down for all of them . . ."

". . . go next time . . ."

". . . which mage was that?"

". . . named Cerryl . . . one of the real ones . . . say he was an orphan, sawmill brat . . . taught himself letters . . . made him a Patrol mage couple of eight-days ago . . ."

". . . tough little bastard then?"

". . . can hold his own, I'd say."

*Tough little bastard?* Cerryl wasn't at all sure about that, except maybe the "little" part.

*Thrap!* He rapped on Myral's door, conscious that he wasn't even winded from the steps. Maybe all the Patrol walking did have some benefits. "It's Cerryl."

"Oh . . . you can come on in."

Myral sat before the windows, half-shuttered, though the room was warm, sipping from a mug. Cider, Cerryl suspected, since that was almost all the older mage drank and the early apples had already been picked. Cerryl sat across the table from the half-bald, black-haired older mage.

"What can I do for you, now that you're in the Patrol?" Myral took a sip from his mug.

"I was just thinking. Do you know if that smuggler's entrance to the sewers was ever bricked up?"

A faint smile crossed Myral's mouth. "You still worry about sewers?"

"We found a dead body at the end of the sewers, in the tunnel just up from the treatment ponds. He was killed from chaos burns, then dragged inside."

"That's what the chaos locks are for," Myral said evenly, a hint of a smile behind his words. Abruptly the older mage coughed, several times, each cough more racking than the last.

Cerryl was on his feet before the attack subsided. "Are you all right?"

"No. But there's little enough you or I can do." Myral offered a wan smile. "The malady is age . . . age and chaos, as I have often told you." He blotted his mouth and lips with the heavy gray cloth. "You were asking about the tunnel. It has not been bricked up, and it will not be. Oh, you may find a line of bricks before the door in the basement of the factor's building adjoining it, but there will be another tunnel to it."

Cerryl nodded. He had thought as much.

"You do not look surprised, Cerryl. In ten years, you are the first merely to nod." Myral chuckled. "You may yet vindicate Kinowin's judgment."

"Who uses the tunnel, and what would happen if I caught them?" He didn't think it was wise to ask what Kinowin's judgment had been.

"A number of people doubtless use that door and tunnel, if infrequently, and I have no idea who they might be, though I tried for several years to determine just that. The only way to discover that would be to spend several dozen eight-days down there, and neither I nor the Guild had such time. As for catching them . . . those you caught would either be killed trying to escape or end up as road prisoners. There have been more than a score of such in the last few years."

Cerryl let himself lean back in the chair, waiting.

As the silence drew out, Myral coughed once, then began to speak. "The sewers keep Fairhaven clean and mostly free of the flux. They also offer roads for those who do not wish to be seen—if they will pay the price. Of course, they don't. They force some enemy or fool to open the grates. Now, what would happen if we bricked up that entrance?"

"They'd create another?"

"Precisely. And where might that be?"

Cerryl shrugged. He didn't know.

"Neither would I nor Sterol nor Kinowin nor Isork. Before long, we'd have masons in the sewers all the time. Actually, there are two such entrances to the sewer tunnels. The other one is in the northwest, on a secondary collector off the west main tunnel. We resist, even trap with chaos, any other attempts to breach the tunnels. Those we leave alone. It works better that way. There will always be smuggling and smugglers—so long as there are tariffs or taxes, or rules on goods. This way, only those with golds are successful—"

"Or those who carry goods on their bodies or in packs."

Myral nodded.

"How much smuggling is necessary?"

"Smuggling is unnecessary and to be frowned upon," Myral de-claimed, spoiling the ponderous tone with a smile that followed his words.

"You mean we can't stop it entirely? So we have to keep it limited to small quantities or those who have enough coins to exercise some degree of restraint?"

"I am not certain I could have said it quite so elegantly, young Cerryl. But, yes, that is the problem that has always faced the Guild." Myral coughed once again, more than a gentle sound, but less than the spasms that had racked him before.

"So I should be cautious?" Cerryl glanced past Myral to the clouds that seemed to be building north of the city.

"Any time you deal with people who would kill others for mere coins, or for power that will vanish even before they do, I would pro-ceed with great caution."

The mention of power that vanished was enough for Cerryl.

Myral coughed once more, then again.

Noting the paleness of the older mage, Cerryl asked, "Can I get anything? Should I send a messenger for the healer?"

"No. She was here earlier. There is little more she could do this day."

"Then you should lie down." The younger mage rose. "I will not tire you more."

"You tire me not. It is good to feel my advice and words are still worth heeding." Myral took a deep wheezing breath. "Still . . . some rest might aid."

Cerryl eased over to the heavyset older man and extended an arm.

Myral took it and levered himself from the chair. "Thank you." He took several steps and lowered himself onto the edge of the single bed in the corner. "Time was . . . didn't need an arm."

"Thank you for your advice." Cerryl wished he could do more, but he could sense that Myral just wished to be left alone. Cerryl closed the door, gently but firmly, and started down the stairs, passing one of the red-clad messengers at the first landing. The lad was headed up and gave Cerryl a tentative smile. Cerryl returned the smile.

On the way out of the tower, Cerryl nodded as he passed Gostar. The older guard nodded back but said nothing. Cerryl caught a few words between the two guards before he reached the bottom of the steps into the entry Hall.

". . . leastwise . . . recognizes that some of us . . . more than bodies with blades."

". . . ought to have more that didn't come from coins . . ."

Cerryl wondered about that as he crossed the entry Hall. Faltar had come from coins in a way, and so did Leyladin, and they were people who recognized that nonmages had worth and were people.

Once he was back in his room, Cerryl glanced out the window at the gathering clouds. While the land needed the rain, he hoped there weren't too many thunderstorms. Those hurt more than the gentle rains, though either would give him a headache.

He took a deep breath as he took the slim volume from his bookcase and opened it. He could read some before he left for Leyladin's house. He was fortunate enough that it would still be another season before he had afternoon duty. In the meantime, he really needed to reread *On Peacekeeping.* He'd hurried through it the first time, knowing he'd missed things. He tried to focus on the words.

> . . . peacekeeping is based upon keeping harmony among people . . . yet people though they look similar may not react in the same fashion when confronted by a patroller . . . or especially a Patrol mage . . .

That was true enough. He'd felt that himself. He continued to read, nodding as he went over passages that he recognized in some fashion.

> . . . no man may encroach upon the person or the property of another save with the express permission of the Council unless some person has been observed breaking the peace and flees . . . nor may any patroller enter the dwelling of any family, save as invited, or in pursuit of an observed peacebreaker or with the permission of the Council . . .

Cerryl frowned. Was that another reason why smugglers used the sewer tunnels? He wanted to shake his head. Being a Patrol mage wasn't turning out quite the way he had envisioned, and he'd barely begun. In fact, he hadn't. He would still be walking around the southeast section for another two days. He forced his eyes back to the pages before him.

> . . . a patroller or a Patrol mage who breaks the peace will be judged by the Council . . .

The book didn't give any penalties for peacebreaking, and that meant, from what Isork had said, that once someone had been found guilty of breaking the peace, judgment was in Isork's hands—or those of the Council. Cerryl shivered, despite the warmth of his room. He didn't know that he had a better answer, but he also knew he'd rather not have his fate in the hands of Sterol, Jeslek, and Kinowin.

Cerryl finally closed the book and rubbed his eyes, then stretched, and glanced out the window. The first evening bells would be ringing soon, and that meant he could leave for Leyladin's house—or mansion, more properly.

He washed up again, chaos-brushed his whites to remove any soil, concentrating on keeping the actual chaos from himself, and then stepped into the corridor outside his apartment—almost running into the black-haired Lyasa.

"Oh . . . I'm sorry."

"I know where you're going." Lyasa grinned at him. "That silly smile says it all." Her face sobered. "Be careful, Cerryl. You're both treading the edge, and I like you both."

"I know . . . We've been careful." *As if I had any choice . . .*

She glanced along the corridor, then lowered her voice. "Speaking of being careful, Jeslek is on his way back. Eliasar told me. He sounded worried."

"I thought he and Jeslek were close."

"Neither cares much for the High Wizard. That's no secret, but whoever's High Wizard no one cares much for." Lyasa shrugged. "Anya's been scuttling up to the High Wizard's apartment like a rat ferreting out a granary. She thinks her shields hide her, but who else wears that much scent?"

Cerryl almost choked but coughed instead.

"Are you all right?"

"I'm fine. I'm fine."

"It's true," hissed Lyasa. "Before long she'll be using red henna to hide the gray hair that her scheming brings."

"She can do that with chaos manipulation, I think," Cerryl replied in a low voice. "She may be already."

"Since she manipulates everything else," Lyasa raised both eyebrows, "that would be easy enough."

"You be careful," Cerryl suggested.

"I only speak such when I know she's on her back."

This time, Cerryl did choke, then had to cough his throat clear.

"About some things, Cerryl, you are still innocent."

"Not about *them*," he countered. "*Speaking* about them."

"I'll have to tell Leyladin that."

"I'm sure you will."

"You had better be moving. I wouldn't want you to be late." With a smile and a wink, she turned.

When Cerryl hurried into the fountain courtyard on his way to the front Hall and the Avenue, Bealtur was talking with Elsinot by the fountain.

Cerryl nodded as he passed and, after a moment, received nods in return. He could feel both sets of eyes on his back as he entered the front building of the Halls of the Mages.

The Market Square was nearly empty when he turned west off the Avenue toward the healer's dwelling. Most of the colorful carts were already packed, or close to it, and many had already left. Cerryl didn't recall the merchants and farmers packing up so early in previous summers, but then he hadn't been out of the Halls so much, either.

Again, as happened every time he approached Leyladin's house, he found his eyes taking in the four large arched windows across the front of the imposing dwelling, each window comprised of dozens of diamond-shaped glass panes set in lead, each pane sparkling. He didn't have to knock. Before he could lift the bronze knocker, the door opened.

"I'm glad you're here." The blonde healer smiled.

Cerryl smiled back. "So am I." He followed her through the silk-hung entry hall, through the orange-scented air of the long sitting room past the portrait of Leyladin's mother, and back into the red oak paneled study where Cerryl had first met Leyladin's father.

Layel stood up behind his desk as Cerryl entered. "Good evening, Cerryl. And a good evening it is this day."

"Yes, it is." Cerryl's eyes slipped toward Leyladin.

"Well . . . best we eat." Layel gestured, and the three headed into the adjoining dining hall.

Again the long white golden oak table that could have easily contained a score was set but for the three at the end nearest the door to the kitchen. The lamps were already lit, although the orange light of sunset still filled the room.

"Meridis . . ."

"I be here, and so is the soup." The gray-haired cook and server carried a white porcelain tureen out and set it on the corner of the table. "Now be seating yourself afore this gets cold."

Layel gestured and waited for Leyladin to sit. He and Cerryl sat nearly simultaneously.

Then, as Meridis ladled soup into the white china bowls, Layel poured a clear white wine from the big bottle into the three fluted crystal goblets.

The soup was almost a mustard brown, but tangy and certainly with no taste of the hot spice. Cerryl used the big spoon gingerly, then took another spoonful and one after that. "A good soup . . . what is it?"

"A pumpkin gourd soup." Leyladin extended the porcelain bread platter.

Cerryl took a chunk of the golden-crusted white bread.

"One of Meridis's many specialties," Leyladin added.

"She has so many that they cannot be termed specialties." Layel smiled at Meridis, who lifted the tureen and headed back to the kitchen.

Some time later, Cerryl looked up and found he had finished the soup and his bread without speaking.

"Patrol duty must be famishing."

"That and studying for Patrol duty. There is more to it than I had realized." Cerryl laughed. "I have found that to be true of everything I have done."

Layel added a laugh. "True it will be of anything of worth that you or I ever do."

"What about me?" Leyladin asked in a tone of mock demureness.

"Daughter, since you were born, there has always been more to you and what you do than meets the eye. Why would that change now?" Layel offered a sorrowful look.

Cerryl grinned.

Leyladin turned to him with the same demure expression. "You find that amusing, ser White mage?"

"No, Lady Leyladin . . . merely true. You set me back the first time I saw you, and nothing has changed."

A hearty belly laugh issued from Layel. "He knows you, Daughter. Indeed he does."

Leyladin offered a mock grimace, then smoothed her face back into demureness. "Alas, I am surrounded. Does not anyone understand my plight?"

Cerryl shook his head.

The gray-haired server returned to remove the soup bowls, then delivered three large platters—one with four fowl halves, each covered in an orange glaze; one with sliced potatoes covered with a white sauce; and the third with long slivers of what appeared to be roots covered in the white sauce.

"You didn't fix quilla?" Leyladin glanced from Meridis to her father.

"I do happen to like it, Daughter."

"It tastes like sawdust." The blonde grimaced.

"Then I like sawdust," replied the trader.

After the momentary silence, Layel served himself one of the fowl halves, then some of the potatoes and a heaping helping of quilla. He passed the last platter to Cerryl. "I was at the seasonal auction today. The one at the Patrol building."

Cerryl nodded and served himself fowl and potatoes and just a few slices of the smothered quilla.

"Did you bid on anything?" Leyladin took the fowl platter from Cerryl.

"I bid—and purchased—some rare oils and essences. Five golds and I got nearly a score of bottles of oil. Some fool had tried to smuggle them past the gates in a wagon with a false bottom." Layel smiled. "The gate guards are getting better, I think. That trick used to work."

"This was the auction of goods taken by the guards?" Cerryl took a sip of the fruit-tinged wine.

"Yes. They have one just before each season turn." Layel refilled his goblet. "I always go, if only to see what goods are so dear that they must be smuggled. I was taken by the clarity and perfection of these oils, though, and since none seemed to recognize their value . . ." The merchant shrugged. "Even with a gold's tax on my bid, I stand to triple my investment."

"What else was so dear," Cerryl asked, "that it was smuggled? I mean, that usually isn't?"

"That you can never tell. At the auction, there were the usual oddments—woven willow baskets, two barrels of soft wheat flour, three second-class hand-and-a-half blades, twoscore wool and linen carpets from Hamor . . . I bid on those, but Muneat's fellow took them. At what he bid, he can have them. Chorast didn't show. Usually he doesn't. Loboll sat there, didn't bid but once." Layel shoveled a mouthful of quilla down.

Leyladin winced almost imperceptibly.

Cerryl cut a small slice of the quilla and chewed, swallowing quickly after deciding that Leyladin was right—the quilla tasted even less appetizing than sawmill sawdust, more like sawdust mixed with axle grease. He'd inadvertently tasted enough of sawdust as a youth. He reached for the wine, ignoring the faint knowing smile that crossed her lips.

"Good stuff, quilla," Layel proclaimed. "You don't know what you're missing, dear." He speared the second half-fowl and transferred it to his plate.

"I'm quite happy not knowing." The healer cut a slice of the fowl.

"How do you find Patrol duty?" The factor took a healthy slice of fowl, then dipped it in glaze before eating.

"I'm not really on duty yet, not for a few more days. I'm still learning about the southeastern section of Fairhaven."

"That's where all the little smugglers are—tin, pigments, copper. Why, if you mages could tax them, you'd get half the coins you'd need for the roads."

Cerryl doubted that, but he nodded politely. "Everything seems quiet. Even the Market Square has fewer carts, and they leave early."

"That is true in late summer, every year, almost until harvest. Then there will be peddlers everywhere," predicted Leyladin, "but it will be quiet until then."

"Some of the factors have not been so quiet in recent days past," Layel volunteered. "Scerzet said that he would run any Spidlarian trader off the road, were any to cross his path."

"Oh?" Cerryl frowned.

" 'Tis simple. The Spidlarians—they do not lower their prices for wares. They match ours and then go a copper or two lower."

"They're actually pocketing extra coins in the amount that the tariffs raise your prices. Or just a few coppers less than that."

"So simple that a new-minted junior mage can see it." Layel beamed. "No matter how much we lower prices, they always can match our prices and make more coins."

"Do you think the Gallosians are encouraging them?" asked Leyladin.

"No, Daughter. The Gallosians, like all people, think of themselves. They will buy where they can buy the best quality for the fewest coins. Unless the White mages"—he inclined his head toward Cerryl—"unless they either force the Gallosians to pay more for goods traded through Spidlar or forbid their sale at all in Gallos, the Gallosians, as will all in Candar, will buy where they can most cheaply."

Cerryl could see more than a few problems.

As if anticipating Cerryl's thoughts, Layel continued, "Once goods are unloaded from a ship, to ensure all tariffs are paid is like catching smoke after it has left the chimney."

"The traders would not support a war against Gallos and Spidlar, would they?"

Layel shrugged. "Some, like the grain factors, see no difficulties. Recluce does not ship grain, and Austran grain is more dear than any grown in Candar. Nor is maize a problem. The wool factors would pay for war tomorrow—if not with many coins. So would the oilseed growers—those outside of the lowlands of Certis. The metals factors and, so I am told, the Duke of Lydiar are most wroth at the copper shipped from Southport."

*In short, it's like everything else . . . with no really clear answers.* Cerryl nodded.

"Few choices are there—to take either the city of Elparta or all of Spidlar . . . or see trade suffer and revenues for Fairhaven fall."

"Elparta?" Cerryl asked involuntarily.

"Aye . . . most of the trade to Gallos comes up the river to Elparta. Some goes to Certis through Axalt, but the pass beyond Axalt is narrow and can be patrolled, if need be. So, if the lancers took Elparta . . . then the surtaxes could be levied there."

"That would be somewhat difficult without the agreement of the prefect or the viscount and those of Axalt." Leyladin's tone was dry. "We would have to send lancers through the greater breadth of Gallos, or through Certis and Axalt."

Layel shrugged. "It will come to such. Not this year, but it will."

"Why do you think that?" asked Cerryl.

"The prefect will not oppose the Guild, not openly. But he will not send hordes of his own armsmen to collect our taxes, even though his own people gain vast sums of coin from the White highways. The Spidlarian traders will not impose or pay the tax, and they will sell where they can. The regular tax for them is half what it is for us. The only truly high taxes are the surtaxes, and yet they complain and complain."

"So we will have a war over taxes?"

"No. We will have a war over trade. That has always been the basis of war with Recluce. They can travel the seas more cheaply than we can build and travel the roads. And their magics allow them to create some goods more cheaply."

"Enough of this talk of war," Leyladin said abruptly. "If it comes, then we can talk of it. I'd rather talk even of wool carding and dyeing." She glanced at her father. "Or Aunt Kasia's tatwork and embroidery."

Cerryl smiled sheepishly. So did Layel.

"Who is your Aunt Kasia?" Cerryl finally asked, after enjoying several mouthfuls of the cheese-and-sauce-covered potatoes.

"Mother's youngest sister. She consorted with a landholder near Weevett. I spent a summer there, and she insisted that I learn the ladylike skills of tatting and embroidering. 'After all, dear, your children should be well turned out, and you should know how to teach them needle-and yarn work. All those coins your father has amassed may not last.' "

Cerryl found himself grinning at the blonde's mimicry of her aunt.

"It was a *very* long summer," Leyladin said dryly.

"What about your aunt?" asked Layel, looking at Cerryl. "She raised you, I understand."

"Aunt Nall?" Cerryl paused, then said slowly, "She wanted the best for me, but she didn't want me to be a mage. There wasn't a glass or a mirror in the house. She was always telling me that glasses were only for the high-and-mighty types of Fairhaven." His lips quirked as he lifted his goblet. "I feel far less than high-and-mighty."

"Would that more of 'em in the Halls felt that way. Much they've done for Candar and the city, but just folk with mighty skills—that's all they are." Layel lifted the leg—the sole remnant of fowl on his plate—and chewed on it.

*Folk with mighty skills?* Cerryl half-smiled at the thought, knowing that the very words would upset both Anya and Jeslek . . . and amuse Kinowin.

After the three finished, Meridis cleared away the china and returned with three dishes of a lumpy puddinglike dish.

"Bread pudding . . . good . . ." Layel smiled.

Leyladin took a small morsel of the pudding, then laid her spoon aside.

Cerryl took one modest mouthful—enjoying the combination of spices with the richness of the creamed and sweetened bread. Then he had another.

"See; even the White mages like bread pudding," Layel announced after his last mouthful.

"Not all mages," countered Leyladin. "It's too sweet for this one."

"I do have a fondness for sweets," Cerryl confessed, then blushed as he saw Leyladin flush.

"I have noticed," added Layel.

Leyladin shook her head. "You . . . you two."

Cerryl took the last bite of the pudding, trying not to look at her. "It is good."

"Next time, Daughter, you may pick the dessert, but occasionally your sire should have a choice."

"Yes, Father."

Contentedly full and relaxed, Cerryl found himself yawning, and he closed his mouth quickly.

"I saw that," Leyladin said. "When do you get up?"

"Before dawn," he admitted.

She glanced toward the window and the pitch-darkness beyond the lead-bordered glass diamonds. "You need to go."

"I suppose so."

"I am sure you will be back many times, Cerryl," said Layel, rising with Leyladin. "My daughter much prefers your company to mine."

"She has spoken quite well of your company," Cerryl managed as he rose from the velvet-upholstered white oak chair. "Often."

"Would that she did around me." Layel still smiled fondly at his daughter.

"Oh, Father . . ."

"See your mage off, dear."

Leyladin escorted Cerryl back through the silk-hung sitting room and front hall to the foyer. She opened the door.

"Thank you. The dinner was wonderful," Cerryl said. "And I did learn some new things from your father. I think I have each time."

"You always listen." Leyladin smiled.

"Are you going to be in Fairhaven for a while?"

"I hope so."

"So do I." *So do I!*

"I will be." She leaned forward and hugged him, then kissed him, this time gently on the lips.

His lips tingled—was it how he felt or the interplay of order and chaos?

"Both," she said, drawing back slightly.

"Both?" He shook his head.

"When we're that close, I can almost sense what you feel. That's why it will be a long time." She offered another warm smile. "Good night, Cerryl."

As he walked back to the Halls of the Mages, through the rain that had begun to fall, with the headache that had also begun to grow, he understood what she hadn't said. If they were ever to become closer, he could not handle chaos the way Jeslek or Anya or most of the Whites did. In fact, he'd probably have to get better at keeping chaos away from and out of his body.

Could he manage that? As a Patrol mage? As any kind of White mage? Without verging on the gray that the Guild—and Recluce—abhorred?

# XXX

Cerryl looked around the room, a space less than six cubits by nine—the duty room, it was called, with bare stone walls composed of faded pink granite blocks a cubit long and a half-cubit high. Both the walls and the cubit-square stone floor tiles were polished to a dull finish. A single high barred window no more than one cubit by two offered the only ventilation.

The single flat table that served as a desk contained two open-topped wooden boxes for scrolls and documents, an inkstand with a quill holder, a stack of blank coarse paper for reports, and a polished but ancient brass table lamp. The only other pieces of furniture were the straight-backed wooden armchair behind the desk and two backless oak chairs across the desk from it.

Cerryl set down *On Peacekeeping* and massaged his forehead.

"Ser?"

Cerryl glanced up to see a squad leader of one of the four-man patrols standing in the open doorway, a man of medium height with thick short brown hair and a sweeping mustache. Cerryl struggled for a moment with the name. "Yes, Fystl?"

Fystl stepped into the office and shifted from one foot to the other. "A problem, ser."

Cerryl stood. "Where?"

"Well, ser . . . it wasn't as though . . . ah . . . well . . . She said he didn't know what he was doing, but she stabbed him, and he bashed her with a staff . . . and right at the edge of the lower Market Square. What were we to do? We dragged 'em here for you to deal with."

"Are your patrollers all right?"

"Ah . . . Hurka, he got a slash—it's not deep, ser—and Veriot got some bruises from the staff."

Cerryl took a deep breath. His third day as a full Patrol mage, and there were two people he was supposed to turn into ash—according to the manual and the guidelines set forth by Isork. Yet Fystl wasn't acting as though the two were doomed, but apologetic.

"Maybe you should talk to them." Fystl looked down at the floor.

"You brought them here?"

"They're in the big room, yes, ser. Big fellow's name is Gerlaco; the woman's name is Jeyna."

"Gerlaco and Jeyna. Let's go." Cerryl followed Fystl out of the duty room and down the short corridor to the big room, the room where the patrols mustered in the morning and where offenders were brought to Cerryl for disposition, except the ones there were his first. As in the duty room, the walls of the assembly room were of stone, and the two head-high windows were barred. Unlike the duty room, there was no furniture. On the back wall was a stone platform elevated somewhat less than two cubits above the floor tiles. The space was approximately square, each wall twenty cubits long.

On the street side of the room—between the windows—three patrollers held a man in a ripped gray shirt, a figure towering well over four cubits. Even with his hands shackled, the three patrollers were having difficulty holding him still—that despite an undressed wound in the shoulder that had to have been painful.

On the other side of the room was a dark-haired woman who was tiny, reaching barely to Cerryl's shoulder.

Cerryl nodded to both as he walked across the room and climbed up on the platform. He felt silly doing it, but Isork had been firm about his speaking only from the stone platform. The Patrol mage cleared his throat, loudly. "Gerlaco . . . Jeyna."

The patrollers looked at him warily. So did the woman.

The big man spat on the floor. "I don't care if he's a White demon . . . no smooth-skinned youth is going to judge me . . ."

Cerryl decided to cut him off. He concentrated chaos and let fire flare from his fingertips.

"Tricks! All tricks. You're worse than the Black angels!"

The dark-haired woman flung herself on the floor almost at the base of the low platform. "Gerlaco's from Delapra. He doesn't understand! Don't kill him . . . please . . . He drank too much . . . Please . . ."

Cerryl could sense, even without trying, that she spoke the truth as she knew it.

"Kill someone . . . that boy? Ha!" The big man lunged toward Cerryl, getting close enough to one of the patrollers to twist his shackled arms and lash out with an elbow.

The patroller dropped like a stone, then sat on the stone floor cradling an arm that was wrenched or broken.

Cerryl kept his face stolid. His own appearance didn't help matters, but he really had no choice, not after everything.

"Stand back." Cerryl's voice was level.

"NOOO!!!!"

The patrollers backed away abruptly, almost thrusting the giant into the center of the assembly room.

Cerryl concentrated on focusing the chaos as tightly as possible, more like a light lance, but not quite. He didn't want to give that secret away.

*WHHSSTT!* A pillar of fire flared where the big man had stood.

"NOOO!!!" The woman sobbed from where she lay on the floor tiles.

"I'm sorry," Cerryl said quietly but firmly. "No one attacks a patroller. No one. It doesn't matter whether they're from Delapra or Recluce or Hamor." Somehow he kept his voice firm, even as he felt almost like shuddering. He shouldn't have had to do that, not on his first eightday as a Patrol mage. Not just because he was small and slender.

"Fystl . . . we'll talk in the office." Cerryl turned and walked out of the room that served as meeting place and judging space, leaving both the patrols and the woman.

". . . just like that . . . Wait till I tell Reyll."

". . . let the boys on tannery row know about this."

". . . like to see him on the streets, though . . ."

Ignoring the comments, he walked back down the few cubits of the corridor and into the duty room, sinking onto the padded leather cushion on the chair, the only bit of softness in the entire building, and the cushion wasn't all that yielding. He waited until Fystl closed the door, then gestured to one of the chairs.

Fystl sat, his eyes flicking every which way but not meeting Cerryl's.

"How many more like this can I expect until the word gets out that I'm just like every other Patrol mage?" Cerryl asked wearily.

"Ah . . . I don't know, ser. You handle 'em quick . . . maybe not many." Fystl shook his head. "Ser . . . was that a firebolt?"

"Yes," Cerryl lied. "Just a very controlled one. I didn't want anyone else hurt," he added more truthfully.

"Most clear the room." Fystl finally met Cerryl's eyes. "You that good all the time, ser?"

"Anywhere under fifty cubits."

A faint smile crossed the squad leader's face, then faded. "What about the woman?"

"He started it. She's been punished enough. Let her go."

Fystl nodded. "That be all, ser?"

"That's all."

"By your leave, ser?"

Cerryl rose. "Let me know if any problems come out of this."

"Won't be none, ser. Not a one." Fystl offered a half-bow, then turned and departed.

Cerryl hoped there wouldn't be, but hope often didn't match reality. He'd seen that often enough, especially with Uncle Syodor and Aunt Nall.

Cerryl looked at the short stack of papers he had put aside for a few moments to read *On Peacekeeping,* then leafed through them. He hadn't understood that another aspect of the drudgery of being a section Patrol mage was writing reports. Isork had mentioned reports, but understanding and doing were often two separate things. Cerryl had to write down any incident where the Patrol took someone into custody or where he used chaos to turn someone into ash or anything else he thought that Isork or the Council should know about.

Cerryl understood, belatedly, the stack of scrolls Isork had been reading when he had first met the Patrol chief. Slowly, he picked up the quill and dipped it into the ink. For a while, he'd decided he'd keep what amounted to a journal—jotting down notes as things happened throughout the day, then writing down at the end of his duty those matters that still seemed worth reporting.

His eyes flicked across the day's jottings . . . before the incident with Gerlaco.

> . . . brought in Kealf, accused of stealing apples. Kealf said under truth-read that Vilo wouldn't take his copper because he was from Sturba. Vilo agreed to take copper and pay a copper in damages to the Patrol.
>
> . . . one Azorf stole three loaves of bread. Caught by Nuryl's patrol. Sent to south prison for preparation and assignment to road duty.
>
> . . . vagrant who would not give name stole purse from Searlica, consort of the cooper Huntyl. Huntyl struck with barrel stave and hailed patrol (Sheffl—leader). Truth-read vagrant, committed theft. Sent to south prison for preparation and assignment to road duty . . .

Cerryl took his eyes off the notes and began to write, hoping he wouldn't have to detail turning too many peacebreakers into ash.

# XXXI

Cerryl took a large helping of creamed lamb from the Meal Hall's serving table and a full mug of the amber ale. At most of the tables around the room were apprentices, faces he did not know—except for the two redheads, Kiella and Kochar. The exception was the big circular table near the Meal Hall entrance, where Faltar, Lyasa, and Heralt sat, almost through with their meal. Lyasa waved to Cerryl, and he headed in their direction. He sat down and grinned as he noted the crumbs around Faltar's plate. "A touch of lamb with your bread?"

"I was too tired to go out, even with creamed mutton." Faltar grinned back. "I'm not a highly paid Patrol mage. I have to watch my coins."

"Someone told me that even junior mages could go out every night," Cerryl replied.

"He was wrong."

Heralt and Lyasa laughed at Faltar's woebegone expression.

"How does being a Patrol mage compare to gate duty?" Heralt—the curly-haired young mage originally from Kyphrien—took a sip of ale.

"Harder. Much harder," mumbled Cerryl between bites of lamb.

"You get off in midafternoon. You been over at the trader's place?" asked Faltar. "With your favorite healer?"

"No . . . walking the southeast section. Only way to get to know it well enough."

"By yourself?" asked Lyasa.

"As a Patrol mage, it wouldn't look all that good to have an escort off-duty." Cerryl's tone was dry. "I stay out of shadowed alleys and the taverns."

"He's still acting like an apprentice who has to learn everything," Faltar told Lyasa.

"He's also bringing in more coins, Faltar," she replied. "There might be some relation between the two."

"Never," said Faltar. "I couldn't imagine walking all over the city. My feet ache enough after guard duty."

"So does my head," admitted Heralt.

"Speaking of headaches." Lyasa turned to Cerryl. "Did you hear about Jeslek?"

"Besides his making mountains all over the middle of Gallos?"

"No. He's going to be High Wizard. We just heard."

Cerryl nearly choked and ended up covering his mouth to contain his coughs.

"You got a reaction there." Faltar grinned. "One of the few times I've seen Cerryl surprised."

Cerryl finished coughing and cleared his throat with a small swallow of ale. "I'm not surprised that he's High Wizard. I always thought he would be; but not nearly this soon."

"He marched up to Sterol's quarters and came down with the amulet," Faltar said.

"Kinowin has to approve it—and all the Guild," pointed out Heralt.

The other three looked at the curly-haired mage.

"I know. No one will oppose him," Heralt admitted.

"He's already wearing the amulet," pointed out Lyasa.

*You mean Anya is.* Cerryl shook his head at the vagrant thought. Why had he thought that? Jeslek was far more powerful than Anya, as strong as she was in chaos handling.

"I don't understand it," Faltar said quietly. "Derka says he's going back to Hydlen. Hydolar, actually."

"Derka's leaving Fairhaven?" asked Cerryl.

"Sterol's moving into Derka's chambers, too," Lyasa said. "That's what Kiella told me."

"I don't understand," added Heralt. "When Sterol was High Wizard, Jeslek kept his quarters as far from the Tower as possible. Now Sterol's going to be right under Jeslek."

Cerryl lifted a mug of the hall ale, definitely flat in comparison to that of The Golden Ram, and took a sip, then another.

"Three floors of solid stone," said Lyasa.

"Nothing compared to mountains," countered Faltar.

"Jeslek won't be there that much anyway," suggested Heralt. "He'll have to do something about Gallos and Spidlar."

"That's probably why Sterol let him have the amulet," suggested the black-haired Lyasa.

"But who will be the other overmage, to take Jeslek's place?" asked Faltar. "Does anyone know?"

"Anya would love that," offered Lyasa.

"I haven't heard," said Heralt. "Would Sterol take it?"

"No. He'd have to support Jeslek," Faltar said quickly.

Cerryl's eyes went to Faltar. That hadn't been Faltar's idea, he suspected, but said nothing.

"Cerryl? You aren't saying anything."

"What is there to say? Jeslek returns from Gallos, where he has created an entire range of chaos mountains. Suddenly, the honored Sterol relinquishes the amulet and recommends that the Guild approve Jeslek as High Wizard. No one knows who will be the new overmage, except that it's unlikely to be Sterol. What can a lowly mage such as I add to that?"

"I think you just did," said Lyasa.

Cerryl shook his head. "I said earlier that I always thought he'd be High Wizard. He just got there sooner than I thought."

"Like you," suggested Lyasa. "They say you're the youngest Patrol mage in generations."

*Probably all waiting for me to fail . . . could that be it? Could Jeslek have agreed to it to see if I'd fail?* Cerryl wanted to shiver. It certainly fit the way Jeslek operated. The new High Wizard set impossible tasks for mages he didn't like and then punished them when they failed, if they didn't die at the task. All the while, he quietly supported those less able who backed him. Seldom was there overt fighting among the White

Order, just positioning to cause others to fail or to be killed in ways not traceable to any mage. "That's only talk," Cerryl protested. "Besides, I have to stay a Patrol mage." *That's going to be the hard part.*

"You'll do fine on the Patrol," said Lyasa.

Cerryl hoped so. He stood.

"Where are you going?" asked Lyasa, grinning. "To a certain trader's home?"

"No. I have some reports to write and some things to read."

"Work, work, work . . ." Faltar's tone was light.

"Sometimes," Cerryl admitted. "Sometimes." He didn't look forward to reading more of *On Peacekeeping,* but he needed to finish it and learn it before real trouble arrived. With Jeslek back in Fairhaven, that could happen any time. Any time.

# XXXII

With ships from Recluce in every ocean and every gulf, each accompanied by a Black weather mage, the lands of Candar and their traders had no choices but to agree to trading with the Black Isle on terms most favorable to Creslin.

First to accede were the western lands, those where the Legend of the dark angels was held in higher regard; from Rulyarth the Tyrant of Sarronnyn sent a half-score of ships, laden with all manner of goods, and these the Tyrant bestowed upon Megaera as a consort gift, and prevailed with those gifts that Recluce grant more favor unto Sarronnyn.

From Southwind also came tribute, and copper, and scented oils like those that graced the consorts of the Emperor of Hamor, and hardy steeds bred in the pitiless sun of the Stone Hills.

Even the silver-haired druids of Naclos, they sent silksheen and the dark lorken wood prized by the Black crafters, prized though it could not be used by those of the way of prosperity and light, and the precious stones found nowhere but in the hidden depths of the Accursed Forest.

So began the alliance of the dark isle with the lands beyond the Westhorns, for even unto this day those whom the Black Isle has exiled in disfavor are not sent beyond the Westhorns, but unto those lands in less favor of the Blacks who fear to reject them lest the mages of Recluce turn the very seas and skies once more against Candar.

Over the generations has Recluce sent its questers and pilgrims to Candar, and some, even most, have found Candar pleasant and peaceful and to their liking, and they have remained and adopted the path to light and prosperity.

Thus, those who leave Recluce prove by their very value to Candar how admirable qualities are disparaged by the Black Isle and how little those who follow the twisted path of the dark order know of light and the true guide to understanding the world, and even what lies beyond our heavens . . .

> *Colors of White*
> (Manual of the Guild at Fairhaven)
> Preface

# XXXIII

A large fly buzzed slowly around the open doorway of the duty room, then settled through the grayness of dawn onto the dull-polished stone of the wall in the corner of the room by the single high and barred window. The faint breeze from the open window bore a chill that hinted at the approaching winter.

Cerryl stood and looked down at the flat desk-table, then at the unlit lamp, before calling, "Zubal!"

The thin messenger boy in red appeared in the doorway and bowed. "Yes, ser?"

"If anything comes up, I'll be spending the early part of the morning with Kesal's patrol. You know the area they'll be patrolling the next two eight-days?" According to Patrol rules, no patrol could spend more than three eight-days in a patrol area or return to that area until it had been rotated through the other nine areas in the section. Each year half the patrols in each section were rotated into another of the four geographical sectors of the city.

"Yes, ser. That's the potters and the tanneries and the masons."

"Good. You'll know where to find me if any of the other patrols need me."

Zubal's dark brown eyes dropped to the floor as he bowed. "Yes, ser." He eased out into the corridor to wait by the messenger's stool.

Cerryl stepped from behind the table, his eyes taking in the wooden document boxes, the stacks of paper, and the quill holder. Then he headed for the assembly room, passing the silent Zubal, who stood by his stool in the corridor.

One patrol—the one headed by the wide-mustached Fystl—was already filing out of the assembly room.

"Good day, ser," Fystl said with a nod.

"Good day, Fystl." Cerryl stepped into the assembly room, where the conversations—or briefings—dropped off, and glanced toward the patrol standing by the speaking stones. "Kesal? Might I have a word with you?"

"Yes, ser." The wiry patrol leader crossed the room and joined Cerryl in the corridor, his brown eyes meeting Cerryl's, questioning.

Cerryl took in the clean and smooth white uniform, the crimson patroller's belt, the brown hair sprinkled with gray, the carefully trimmed beard, and the rectangular and honest-looking face. "I'll be accompanying you for a time this morning. Zubal's the messenger, and he knows that."

"Accompanying us, ser?"

Behind Kesal, the other patrol leaders and their patrols filed out into the dawn.

Cerryl shrugged. "I can't learn the section sitting in the building, and the people can't learn about me, either."

"Ah . . . yes, ser."

"Kesal, I'm not here to do your job. I'm not here to look over your shoulder and tell you what to do. I am here to support you, and to let people know that I do." He nodded toward the assembly room. "Introduce me to your patrol."

Kesal nodded, clearly uncertain about a young Patrol mage who wanted to accompany a working patrol, then turned and walked through the open double doors of the assembly room toward the four men who remained in the room.

"Mage Cerryl will be accompanying us this morning," Kesal said blandly. "This is Chulk." The brown-haired and young-faced patroller nodded. Cerryl noted the wide red scar across the back of his large left hand.

"Bleren." Bleren was squat and white-skinned, with wispy strawberry blond hair and a gap-toothed smile.

"Olbel." The swarthy, olive-skinned patroller nodded, the curly black mustache waxed firmly in place, black eyes sparkling under coarse black hair.

"Pikek." The last man in the patrol—short-cut mahogany hair and square sideburns—favored Cerryl with an unvarying smile that did not include his pale gray-green eyes.

Cerryl didn't know quite what to say. He'd met all the patrollers in his duty section once, but briefly, and he'd learned the names from the duty rosters, but only a handful of faces fit with names, and none were in Kesal's patrol. After a moment, he said, "On and off, I'll be going with every patrol for a time." Then he nodded to Kesal, deciding against any more explanation.

"Let's go." Kesal stood aside.

So did Cerryl.

The four patrollers filed out of the room and the building, followed by Kesal. Then Cerryl walked beside Kesal as the patrol turned eastward, along the south side of the cross street from the avenue—the Way of the Tanners, a street Cerryl had traveled more than a few times as an apprentice to Tellis the scrivener. Although Arkos had been the only tanner Tellis had used, Arkos had competitors—Murkad, Viot, and Sieck—as well as others farther out the street to the east where Cerryl had not gone back then.

Chulk walked down the north side of the street while Olbel trailed Kesal and Cerryl. Pikek and Bleren were out of sight, checking the alley to the south of the street, mainly to ensure it was clean and clear of rubbish.

"How did you get to be patroller?" Cerryl asked.

"I was a lancer, but I got tired of riding all over Candar. That's a young man's game. I heard that the Patrol needed men, and I walked in on my home leave and asked. Mage Huroan said I could try, and I've been with the Patrol ever since. I know I'll get fed. Get to sleep in my own bed and sure live longer."

"Do all the patrollers come from the lancers?" Cerryl crossed the next side street, glancing southward along the row of still-closed doors as the orange glow of dawn sifted out of the east and over the city. The next block of the Way of the Tanners held various leatherworking shops—that much he recalled, although his memory was prompted by the faint scents of leather and tanning reagents.

Kesal rubbed his nose before answering. "No. They have to have had some duty, though. Infantry, gate guard, that sort of thing. We've even got a couple of mercs. The hard thing is learning the city. That's always hard, ser, at first, for the younger patrollers." Kesal smiled. "After ten years, now, doesn't matter where I patrol, I know people. Not all of them, but enough know me. That's good because when they rotate patrol leaders people with problems can still come to me."

Cerryl wasn't sure that Kesal's familiarity was necessarily that good. Then, how could any patrol system be perfect? If the patrollers became too attached to a patrol area, then they'd probably excuse too much because they liked people and wanted to be liked. If they weren't familiar enough with an area, then while little would happen in view of the patrollers, they'd also never find out the worst of the peacebreaking that happened in alleys and behind blank stone walls. "You can't be too friendly, and you can't be too distant?"

Kesal nodded. "When they get to know you, folks'll tell you things that they don't want happening around their dwellings. That's if you don't try to be their friend. Don't want the Patrol knowing too much, you, know."

Cerryl could understand that. Yes, he could. He'd certainly avoided the patrols, even as an apprentice. Then, as a chaos wielder who was the son of a renegade killed by the Guild, he'd had good reason. He suppressed a smile, one of rue and pain. *It almost makes no sense, that you are a White mage, when they killed your father . . . except those who did had no choice . . . except that you never knew him . . . except that he wanted to be a White mage . . . except that the only way to survive was to become a mage. And now you understand why what you feared must be.* After a moment, he added to himself, *Mostly.*

"Morning, Beykr." Kesal nodded to the stooped white-haired man who had propped open the door to a small shop graced with a wooden boot above the doorway. The walls beside the door were windowless.

"A good morning it is, Patroller Kesal." Beykr paused, then added, "And to you, too, ser mage."

"Thank you," Cerryl answered. "I hope it brings coins to you as well."

Beykr nodded politely before reentering the apparently dark shop.

"Makes good boots, I hear tell, but too rich for me." Kesal gestured eastward. "Miern—he's in the next block—makes mine. Sturdy, with heavy heels and thick soles. Fits me, too. One thing you don't go too cheap on is boots. Tell all the new men to set aside a few coppers every payday, more if they can, for boots."

After another block of closed doors, including Miern's, they paused as Pikek and Bleren approached from the south side street.

"Yes?" Kesal's voice was neutral.

"Ah . . . ser, there's a cart, and a dead horse." Bleren's voice was raspy. "Don't know why it was left there, not the cart anyway."

Kesal grinned. "Lucky we are that the section mage be with us, then."

Cerryl nodded wryly. He'd probably have to destroy the dead animal. There was no telling what sort of chaos it harbored.

"Chulk, Olbel . . . wait here."

Chulk crossed the empty street to wait at the corner with the dark-skinned Olbel while Cerryl and Kesal followed the other two patrollers.

Halfway up the alleyway, a horse lay tangled in the leather harness and across the left cart lead, just as the gap-toothed and squat Bleren had said. Cerryl frowned, letting his senses range over the horse. No real sense of chaos beyond that of a dead animal, but there was a residual sense of chaos on the cart seat. He stepped closer to the cart, its sides painted bright purple, with yellow trim. Dark reddish stains covered the wooden seat. Cerryl glanced at Kesal.

"Doesn't belong to anyone here. Brigands left it. Happens sometimes." Kesal glanced into the cart bed. "It's clean. Peddler."

Cerryl walked to the other side of the cart, where he found a blackened patch just below the seat and a gouge in the wood. The two brass rivets had been ripped out of the wood.

"They use a long iron bar, ser," Kesal said. "Rip off the medallion. That way we can't tell who it belonged to, not unless someone comes to us, and if it's a trader who travels around . . . could be a season or more."

"There's no flux or chaos in the horse. Looks like they just flogged it until it foundered and died."

"A waste . . . had to be city brigands," suggested Kesal.

Cerryl looked at the dead horse. Was that salt and sweat on its coat? Why would anyone push a horse that hard? Especially given what horses were worth? And how . . . within the confines of Fairhaven? After a moment, as the early-morning sunlight spilled into the alleyway, he let his senses range over the cart, trying to see if he could feel anything.

Something? The faintest sliver of order? Under the rear of the cart seat was a small fragment of cloth, not even so large as his thumbnail, that he eased from where it had lodged in a small split in the wood. Or had it been placed there? He studied the fragment, not just cloth— silksheen from Naclos. He'd only seen scarves of silksheen once, but they cost as much as a blade or a mount, some did.

"Silksheen," he murmured, letting Kesal see the fragment before slipping it into his belt wallet.

Kesal nodded sadly. "If that was what the cart carried, a duke's ransom or more, we'll be finding the body in the last sewer pond drained. They know which one will be last."

"They?"

"Whoever killed him."

Cerryl wanted to frown. That sort of peacebreaking wasn't supposed to happen in peaceful Fairhaven. Not at all, and Kesal acted as if it were common—or, at least, not uncommon. He tried to think. "Who would buy silksheen? Who could afford it?"

"No one in the southeast section." Kesal laughed ironically.

"How many bodies will there be in the settling ponds?"

"Hard to say, ser. Might not be any. Usually they find one or two, though."

Myral hadn't mentioned bodies in the ponds when Cerryl had learned all about the sewers from the older mage . . . just that Cerryl should look into any that he found in the sewers. Was that because entering the sewers meant breaking through chaos locks?

"No owner's marks on the horse, ser," Bleren announced.

"Unhitch the cart." Kesal turned to Pikek. "Once it's clear, you go to the main Patrol building and tell them to collect the cart. Then come back and find us." The lead patroller looked at Cerryl. "Someone will buy it at the auction."

Cerryl waited until the two patrollers had wrestled the cart and harness away from the dead horse. Pikek glanced at Kesal, getting a nod, and then turned and walked quickly westward and toward the Avenue.

"What be going on?" A man in brown peered out a door looking into the alley.

"Is this your cart?" asked Kesal.

"No, ser. Never saw it before." The man's eyes darted from Kesal to Cerryl and then to the cart before going back to Cerryl.

"Good. It was stolen."

"Ser, I never saw a purple cart like that—except ones in the Market Square." The man in brown closed the door with a *thud.*

"Ser, if you wouldn't mind . . ." Kesal glanced toward the dead horse.

"There's nothing else we can find out from the horse?"

"A ten-year-old chestnut, I'd guess. No markings, no ear notches—could be scores around Fairhaven. Unless someone reports the theft, we'll never find out."

Cerryl nodded, then studied the dead animal. After a moment, he gathered chaos around him, then released it.

*Whhsttt!* The dead horse vanished with the burst of chaos fire, and white ashes sifted across the worn paving stones of the alley.

"Bleren, you wait for the collectors," ordered Kesal.

"Yes, ser." The patroller brushed back his wispy strawberry blond hair and offered another gap-toothed smile.

"We'll be going east on the Tanners' Way then coming back on the Way of the Masons."

Bleren nodded.

As Cerryl and Kesal walked out of the alley and back to the street, Cerryl asked, "How often does this happen?"

"With the body missing? A couple of times a year. Usually, we find the body with the cart." Kesal laughed harshly. "Most times we still don't know who it is."

"Might not have even been silksheen in the cart," Cerryl hazarded.

"It probably was, or something just as costly. The cart bed was clean."

The two paused before crossing to the next block as a narrow wagon creaked by. The white-haired driver barely looked at the four patrollers. After the wagon turned westward on the Way of the Tanners, toward the Avenue, Chulk crossed back to the north side of the street.

Kesal took a deep breath, then shook his head, squinting into the low eastern sun. "Tannery row . . . could do without the smell."

Cerryl nodded, his eyes going to the familiar sign in the block ahead: ARKOS—TANNER. The iron grate was swung back from the ancient oak door, and the door stood ajar. Flanking the door were two iron-grated windows. The Patrol mage sniffed at the acrid odors drifting into the street from the vats concealed behind the recently white washed plaster walls, an acrid scent that mixed with the smell of greasy meat being fried somewhere nearby. How many times had he run from

Tellis's shop down to Arkos's to fetch parchment or vellum for some book or another? It almost seemed like another life. Then . . . it had been.

"You know the place?" asked Kesal.

"Yes. I used to fetch vellum for Master Tellis. Scriveners' apprentices get to know tanners."

"Maybe we should say 'good day' to him," suggested Kesal.

"He probably won't recognize me." Cerryl glanced at Kesal. "You think he's doing something to break the peace?"

"I don't know. He is from Spidlar, and too many strangers visit here. That's what Fystl told me, and I've seen a few myself over the past eight-day."

Was the patroller reflecting the Guild's growing dislike of Spidlar? Or was it just the bad reputation of Spidlarians? Or was Arkos indeed involved in some hidden form of peacebreaking? "Could he be smuggling?"

"He gets a lot of hides in wagons," reflected Kesal. "I don't worry about the hides, but you can put oils and things in leather containers, and most gate mages can't sense them. Unless the stuff is metal," he added.

"He's one of the better tanners," said Cerryl. "Why would he risk smuggling?"

"Why does anyone risk breaking the peace?" asked the wiry and bearded patrol leader, his voice dry.

"So you think it wouldn't hurt for Arkos to know that the Patrol is interested?"

"It never hurts to show interest. Specially before someone draws bare steel or bronze."

"And especially when you have a Patrol mage with you?"

Kesal grinned, then shrugged. "Well . . . ser." He turned to the swarthy Olbel. "We're going into the tanner's."

"I'll be out here." Olbel grinned, teeth white against his dusky skin.

The hatchet-faced Arkos seemed to shiver behind the worktable as Kesal and Cerryl entered the small front room. His eyes widened as they flicked from the patroller to the mage, and he bowed quickly. He did not look at Cerryl, but at Kesal.

The odor of frying meat was heavy, almost rancid, within the tanner's room, and Cerryl swallowed quietly.

"Ser Arkos," said the lead patroller jovially, "I just thought you'd like to meet one of the section Patrol mages. Mage Cerryl here is new to the southeast section."

"I am pleased to meet you, ser mage," Arkos said carefully, his luminous brown eyes meeting Cerryl's pale gray ones for but a moment.

"There have been a number of visitors here over the past eight-days," Kesal observed.

"My family—my cousins and their consorts—they have come from Kleth."

"From Kleth?" asked Kesal. "All that way to visit? Tanning must have become far more prosperous."

"Spidlar is not so good a place to be." Arkos shrugged. "And it will get less good. So they come to work for me. I do not need so many helpers, but . . ." He looked helplessly at Cerryl and then at Kesal. "Family is family."

"Have you seen any silksheen lately, Arkos?" Cerryl asked idly.

"Me, honored ser? How could I find the coins for such?"

Cerryl could sense the honesty behind that response, as he had with the tanner's response to Kesal's questions.

"Is Tellis still asking for your best vellum?"

Arkos's eyes narrowed momentarily. "Ah . . . yes, ser. Does he not always?"

"Always," Cerryl agreed. "Good day, ser Arkos."

"Good day, ser mage."

Back outside on the stone walk flanking the street, Kesal chuckled. "You worried him with the comment about vellum."

"He was telling the truth about his family. And about the silksheen."

"Good. One less problem to worry about."

*One less problem for the Patrol, but not necessarily for the Guild, not if people are already fleeing Spidlar.*

"We turn here—that's the next patrol area to the east."

The four walked down the north–south side street past three narrow plaster-fronted two-story houses that, while clean, bore the stamp of years. At the corner, Kesal glanced eastward along the Way of the Masons, where a heavy woman carried a basket on her head and dragged a blond child with one free hand. To the west, the street was empty, but two boys sat on a stone stoop three doorways to the west.

At the sight of the white and crimson, both youths eased inside, leaving a blank door.

Cerryl nodded. He could feel the residual chaos, although it was faint, very faint, and he made a mental note to send a scroll to Kinowin. The overmage was the only one he trusted to handle that fairly.

Two blocks later, they passed a shop with a signboard in black with a white pestle—an apothecary whose name Cerryl didn't recognize: LIKKET.

"What sort of apothecary is Likket?" asked the mage.

"Who knows? You see servants, women, and apprentices running in and out."

Cerryl fingered his chin. "Some apothecaries furnish different things. Nivor—his shop is on the other side of the Avenue—that was where Tellis got brimstone and oak galls to make ink. I heard that Rudint dealt mostly in oils for creams and unguents."

Kesal shrugged. "Can't say as I know. Seldom have trouble with apothecaries, and patrollers tend to learn things where they find trouble."

That made sense, but it bothered Cerryl, and, again, he couldn't exactly say why.

# XXXIV

In the afternoon quiet of the duty room, Cerryl looked at the blank sheet of paper before him and then at his informal journal beside it.

Dulkor brought in Aarhl, accused of stealing three barrels of molasses from the loading dock of the factor Hsian. Truth-read. Aarhl sent to south prison for preparation and assignment to road duty . . . Beggar without a name stole three coppers from youth on the Way of the Masons. Caught by Jiark's patrol and attacked Jiark with dagger. Turned to ash . . .

Cerryl began to write slowly, glad that the beggar remained only the third peacebreaker on whom he had been forced to use chaos fire during his first three eight-days as a Patrol mage for the southeast section. Using chaos fire troubled him, especially on beggars and old women. *Is it because you don't understand them?* Why would anyone attack a mage when the attack meant death? And why did people steal when most were caught and ended up spending their lives on the road crew? The beggar would have gotten better fare on the road than begging—and yet he wanted to die? Or he couldn't stand the thought of abiding by another's rules? *Yet everyone, even the High Wizard, lives by rules, and life would be sorry indeed without them.*

Cerryl shook his head. Yet he'd killed several score as an apprentice and a mage. The reasons did not make it easier, not much, but the alternative was worse. Still . . .

*One every eight-day? More than two score in a year?* He shook his head, hoping that his patrolling and firmness would reduce those numbers. From what he'd seen, he had few options. He kept writing. The first midafternoon bell had rung, and it wouldn't be long before Gyskas arrived.

Cerryl could sense that chaos that accompanied Gyskas long before the balding and graying older mage marched into the duty room with the second midafternoon bell, just as Cerryl was folding and sealing his daily report.

The oncoming duty mage nodded, and his deep-set green eyes swept the room. "Not too long a report?" He pushed fine brown and gray hair back off his high and receding forehead.

"No. One beggar took a knife to Jiark." Cerryl shrugged. "How many do you have to flame every eight-day?"

"On this shift?" Gyskas frowned as Cerryl stood. "Two or three. Mostly outsiders. Our people know what happens if they attack a patroller." He took a deep breath. "It gets to you sometimes, but you can't have a set of rules that's harder on locals than on outsiders."

Cerryl stepped around the flat desk and called, "Wielt!" Waiting for the sandy-blond youth, he added, "If you figure we've got four sections with two shifts . . ."

"Fortunately, it doesn't work that way. There's more peacebreaking here than in the other three combined. Lucky us."

*Or is it more peacebreaking of the kind that comes to the Patrol's attention?* Cerryl wondered.

The messenger appeared in the duty room doorway.

"If you would, take this to Mage Isork or Huroan at the main Patrol building." Cerryl handed the folded and sealed daily report to the stocky messenger in red.

"Yes, ser." Wielt turned to Gyskas. "Voar is in the assembly room, ser."

"Thank you," Gyskas turned his eyes back to Cerryl, coughing once. "Tomorrow's your off-day?"

"The day after tomorrow. I think Dujak . . ."

"That's right. He's covering most of the morning off-days this season, here and in the southwest section." Gyskas glanced toward the chair.

"Oh . . . sorry." Cerryl stepped around the desk. "Have a good afternoon and evening."

"It's never that good, Cerryl. You'll see." Gyskas gave the younger mage a twisted smile. "Say . . . in a year or so. Enjoy morning duty while you still can."

Cerryl nodded before turning and leaving the duty room, nodding to the black-haired Voar, who stood by the messenger stool. Then Cerryl walked past the assembly room and through the doors.

Several off-duty patrollers followed Cerryl outside, where the wind had picked up under a dark gray sky, and the air held a damp chill. After a smile and a nod, Cerryl headed west toward the Avenue, picking up the low murmurs they exchanged as they left.

". . . didn't wait for Isork to ash that beggar . . ."

". . . not like Klyat last spring . . ."

"... bet he's going walking through the section again."

"... least you don't have to explain where something happened."

Cerryl kept from nodding as the low voices died out behind him. When he reached the Avenue, he stopped for a moment and watched.

A long canvas-covered wagon creaked northward, pulled by a four-horse team. Beside the driver sat a guard with a spear. A pair of mounted guards rode behind. All four wore a green livery Cerryl hadn't seen before.

He extended his perceptions, and from what he could tell the wagon held bales of cleaned and carded wool. Wool—so late in the year? Or had it come from Kyphros on its way to Lydiar? He shook his head. The wool had to have come from Montgren. Was it being shipped later in the year just because prices were likely to be higher? But why all the guards?

After the wagon passed he turned south, down toward the Way of the Tanners, walking through the drizzle that had begun, ignoring the faint headache the light rain created. Cerryl walked slowly along the Way of the Tanners, just looking.

The incident with the purple cart still bothered him. No one had claimed it from the Patrol storage, and no one had reported either a cart or a person or silksheen missing, not according to Huroan. Medallions weren't that cheap either.

Three youths leaning against the brick wall on the other side of the street, the north side, watched him as he neared. Cerryl studied the three, none that much younger than he was. The tallest wore a faded gray vest over a worn brown shirt and patched brown trousers. His curly hair looked oily and dirty. The smallest wore drab gray, blotched white as if from spills from some kind of caustic or acetic. The third wore a sheepherder's jacket.

Abruptly the tallest spat on the sidewalk.

Cerryl wanted to sigh. Instead, he concentrated, then flashed a fire-bolt to the pavement where the spittle had landed.

With the flash, all three youths straightened.

Cerryl smiled broadly.

The three remained immobile as he passed on the far side of the street.

"... hate 'em ..."

"... uppity Whites ..."

"... careful ... can be touchy ..."

Cerryl let his perceptions linger with the three until he was a good fifty paces east of them.

Eventually, he turned into Likket's shop.

The apothecary looked up from a table containing several piles of what appeared to be bark as the mage entered. "Ser?"

"I'm Cerryl, Likket. I know what some of the apothecaries do, but what sorts of things do you provide?"

Likket looked at Cerryl for a long moment. Cerryl looked back steadily until the older man's eyes dropped.

"I provide potions, some to loosen the bowels, some to tighten them, others to loosen the muscles, others to ease pain, ser. Here . . . here is the willow bark."

*Willow bark? Wasn't there something about that in one of the books you copied for Tellis?*

"The elixir from willow bark is most useful in lowering fevers from the flux and pains in limbs. Sometimes, it aids in pains in the head."

"You don't provide dyes for cottons or wools, then?"

Likket shook his head in a way that suggested the question was ridiculous.

"Nivor provides the basics for scriveners' inks."

"Most dyers would not trust an apothecary with any such knowledge, ser mage."

"What about silksheen?"

"That cannot be dyed. Surely you would know that?" Likket squinted at Cerryl.

"I'm one of the newer Patrol mages." Cerryl offered an embarrassed smile. "I know about scriving and timber and a few other things, but not about fabrics and dyes and potions for pain. Is there anything stronger than willow bark?"

"Stronger, aye. Poppy juice or powder in wine—it be far stronger." Likket cackled. "Strong enough to let some folk sleep on a stone boat. That's only for those already a-dying of mortification."

Cerryl nodded. "You mentioned other potions?"

"Ah . . ." Likket held up a hand blown glass bottle, stoppered with a cork. "This manchieniel syrup . . . if made from the green leaves, it tightens the bowel. But if made from the brown-gray leaves, it loosens them mightily . . ."

Cerryl smiled and waited for Likket to say more.

The rain had begun to fall more heavily when Cerryl left the apothecary's, and his skull had begun to throb. He turned westward and began to walk back toward the Avenue and the Halls of the Mages.

Once inside the front foyer and out of the damp, he nodded to Kochar as Jeslek's redheaded apprentice rushed by in the direction of the courtyard and, presumably, the Meal Hall.

"Good day, Kochar."

"Good day, ser," Kochar said quickly, with only a brief pause, and he hurried past Cerryl and toward the Meal Hall.

Cerryl crossed the fountain courtyard and took the side Hall to the rear courtyard and entered his own building. He was opening his door when Faltar appeared in the corridor.

"It's creamed lamb again. Let's go over to The Ram."

Cerryl thought, his hand touching his clean-shaven chin.

"I asked Leyladin for you. She'll meet us there in a bit." Faltar grinned, looking vaguely raffish with a lock of blond hair almost across his left eyebrow. "She was coming down from treating Myral."

"Where is she now?"

"She went to her house. I would, too, if I had a palace like that. You go there often?"

"Not often. Sterol had been sending her all over Candar, and I've not been going many places right now."

"They say only Muneat's dwelling and maybe those of Chorast, Scerzet, and Jiolt are grander. Loboll . . . who would know?"

"I wouldn't." Once, when he had been Tellis's apprentice, Cerryl had delivered a book to the factor Muneat, and the factor's front hall had certainly appeared grand to him back then, but he'd not seen any of the rest of the mansion. Nor did he know the dwellings of the others Faltar had mentioned.

"Are you coming?" Faltar raised his eyebrows.

"I think the lamb in the Meal Hall can serve others," Cerryl said. "Let me wash up first."

"I'll meet you at The Ram," Faltar said. "Oh . . . Heralt's coming. Is that all right?"

Wondering why Faltar would even ask, Cerryl answered, "Of course. I like Heralt."

"Good. We'll see you there." With a broad and self-satisfied smile, Faltar turned.

Cerryl slipped into the gloom of his room, closing the door and sinking into the chair before his desk for a moment. His feet ached. He still couldn't imagine spending all his duty on his feet for year after year, the way most patrollers did. Then, he couldn't imagine doing *any-thing* year after year.

He took a deep breath and massaged his still-aching forehead.

*Thrap.*

Slowly, he rose and trudged toward the scent of sandalwood and trilia that seeped into his room even before he opened the door.

"Might I come in?" Anya smiled her brilliant and patently false smile.

"Of course." Cerryl gestured for her to enter.

The redhead swept past him and sat on the edge of his bed.

Cerryl turned the chair to face her and sat down. "I haven't seen you in a while."

"How do you like being a Patrol mage?" asked Anya.

"So far, it's been interesting." He offered a smile, hoping it was more genuine than hers. "What have you been doing?"

"Helping Sterol and Jeslek. Drafting scrolls . . . that sort of thing."

"You must have a fine hand."

"Not so fine as a former scrivener, but it suffices. I did learn a few things before the Guild found me."

"You're from Fairhaven, then?"

"Most mages are." Anya leaned forward, yet somehow the white tunic clung even more suggestively to her form. "You know, once Jeslek officially becomes High Wizard, the Guild will need another overmage?"

"Would you like my support?"

Anya laughed, twice, two musical notes, perfect in pitch, yet ringing off-key. "No. I doubt the Guild would feel secure with a woman as overmage."

"Who might be considered?" Cerryl shifted his weight on the chair.

"Eliasar, Redark, Esaak, perhaps Myral or Broka." Anya shrugged. "A few others."

"You're more powerful than any of them." Cerryl paused. "Or is that the reason why you would rather not be considered?"

"You are perceptive—if still somewhat naive." She paused. "Do you wish to be a Patrol mage all your life?"

"I hadn't thought about it."

The redhead stood. "You might."

Cerryl stood as well. "You never said who might be a good candidate for overmage. Perhaps I should suggest Fydel, then."

"I'd prefer you didn't." Anya smiled again as she reached for the door latch. "But you can certainly suggest anyone you wish."

"I doubt I will be suggesting anyone," Cerryl said, holding the door that she had opened. "But I did want your opinion."

"Expressing opinions too early is seldom wise." She flashed Cerryl a smile. "Good evening, Cerryl."

"Good evening, Anya."

He closed the door slowly. *She doesn't want you suggesting her or Fydel . . . or anyone. But why should your opinion matter at all?* As he sat down again, he nodded. The message had been clear enough: *Don't support anyone of great chaos power for overmage.*

Cerryl stood. At least Leyladin would be at The Golden Ram.

After he shaved, washed, and changed his shirt and tunic, he gathered himself together, stepping out into the empty corridor, half-afraid Anya would swoop down again. He half-smiled, then closed his door.

A few moments later, he walked into the fountain courtyard, enjoying the faint breeze, enough to cool but not to chill.

"Cerryl?"

The young mage turned. Fydel stood by the fountain in the fading light of early evening, the spray cascading into the circular granite basin behind him.

"How do you like the Patrol?" asked the square-bearded mage.

"So far, it's interesting. Better than gate-guard duty." Cerryl laughed. "I'm not exactly the arms type, like you or Eliasar. Are you going back to Gallos with Jeslek?"

"Jeslek hasn't said anything about going back. Where did you hear that?"

"I didn't hear anything," Cerryl admitted. "I'm just guessing, but from what I saw when I was there with you I don't think that even Jeslek's creation of those mountains will be enough to convince the new prefect to collect road taxes and tariffs."

"That may be," answered Fydel, shaking his head, "but the High Wizard hasn't said anything. *I* certainly wouldn't wish to guess his actions publicly." Fydel's eyes seemed lost under the bushy eyebrows that arched as he spoke.

"I was but asking."

"Jeslek thinks quite highly of your *skills*."

Cerryl caught the ever-so-slight emphasis on the word "skills" before he answered. "Mine are poor indeed compared to his."

"He knows that, also. That is another reason why he respects you among the younger mages."

Cerryl didn't bother to comment on Fydel's lying, a twisting of chaos so obvious almost any mage could have caught it. "He respects you most highly."

"I do what I can for him." Fydel bobbed his head. "Well, I must be going. I trust you continue to find Patrol duty interesting, although it's sometimes better if something like that doesn't intrigue you overly. Patrol duty is really meant to be what it is, just simple peacekeeping." With another nod, Fydel smiled, his white teeth bright in the fading luminescence of twilight.

Cerryl passed through the courtyard and then through the entry foyer to reach the Avenue, turning south toward the inn.

Why had Fydel stopped him? The older mage had been waiting for Cerryl. To tell him what?

*That he should stick to the simpler aspects of peacekeeping?* That was clear. *Why* wasn't at all clear.

Faltar, Lyasa, and Leyladin sat at the round table in the corner by the front window of The Golden Ram.

"It took you long enough!" Faltar exclaimed. "I ordered an ale for you." He pointed to the mug before the empty seat.

"Thank you." Cerryl sat down, between Leyladin and Faltar, glad to take his weight off his boots.

"Now your friend is here," announced a stocky serving woman, who had seemed to materialize at Cerryl's shoulder, "what would ye mages be having?"

Faltar inclined his head to Lyasa.

"The stew," answered the black-haired woman, exchanging a brief glance across the table with Leyladin.

"The fowl, whatever it is," said Leyladin.

"The fowl," repeated Faltar, followed by Heralt.

"The stew," Cerryl said, trusting Lyasa's judgment, since he knew Leyladin cared little for any kind of inn stew.

"Two stews, three fowls." The server swept away.

"What kept you?" Faltar persisted.

"How about cleanliness and exhaustion?" Cerryl offered a tired grin.

"Unlike some who think but of their guts," quipped Lyasa, with a pointed look at Faltar.

"Ah, I am slandered most unfairly."

"Most fairly, I'd say," suggested Heralt.

"All rumor and gossip," declared the blond White mage. "All of it."

"Speaking of gossip . . . did you know that Jeslek's announced a special meeting of the Guild next eight-day?" asked Lyasa. "No one knows what it's about. It's a night meeting. That's so most of the Guild can be there."

Cerryl took a long, slow swallow of his ale.

"Maybe it's so we can approve him as High Wizard. That might be nice." Faltar snorted over his mug of ale.

"You wouldn't be quite so bold if he were here," said Lyasa.

"He's not."

"No—but Bealtur just walked in." Lyasa smiled.

Faltar choked, then looked over his shoulder. "That wasn't fair."

"He could have," suggested Leyladin. "Or Fydel, or Anya, or Myredin . . ."

"All right." Faltar looked at the mug he held. "Will you let me drink now?"

"I might." Lyasa grinned.

"Here you be!" announced the server. "Three fowl, two stew. Three each for the stew, four for the fowl. And two baskets of the light bread. Dark's a copper more."

"Light will be fine," Heralt said.

Cerryl frowned as he pulled out coins, handing three to Faltar and three to the server. The last time he'd had the stew, the price had been but two coppers and the fowl had been three.

"That's right," Leyladin whispered into his ear. "Prices are higher."

"Thanks be to ye." With a smile, the server departed.

"Was the ale three?" Cerryl asked Faltar.

Faltar nodded, his mouth already full of fowl.

Cerryl bent forward. He was hungry, not having eaten since morning. When he straightened again, his bowl was nearly empty, and he'd also finished two large chunks of rye bread.

"You were hungry." Leyladin offered a smile over a platter of fowl of which she had seemingly only eaten but a third.

"Very hungry," Cerryl admitted before taking a swallow of the ale.

"We were talking of gossip," suggested Lyasa.

"At the moment, Jeslek is both High Wizard and overmage," mused Heralt.

"Who will they select?" asked Faltar.

"It's who *we* select," corrected Lyasa. "We have to select both, even if no one will choose other than Jeslek for High Wizard."

"But the overmage?" asked Leyladin, almost indifferently.

"Who knows?" Lyasa lifted jet-black eyebrows. "Kinowin is still the other overmage. So maybe Jeslek will suggest someone."

"He won't," offered Heralt. "He's taken being High Wizard. He'll let the Guild select someone."

"But who?" asked Faltar. "Myral's too old. Derka won't come back from Hydolar. Jeslek's going to need to send Eliasar to Gallos. Esaak doesn't care about anything but mathematicks."

"Anya?" suggested Heralt.

"She'd like that." Lyasa laughed. "But she won't be chosen."

"Then who?"

Cerryl leaned back in the chair, trying to ignore the headache from the rain and the concerns raised by Anya's visit. He also tried to stifle a yawn but did not quite succeed.

Leyladin leaned closed to him and whispered, "You need to leave, don't you?"

He nodded slightly.

"Are we boring you, Cerryl?" Faltar asked.

"I was up before dawn, and I walked some of the section after duty. I'm tired." He forced a smile. "Not bored."

Leyladin stood. "I had to spend more time with Myral, and I'm about to fall over."

Cerryl rose slowly. "I'm sorry. I am tired."

Lyasa smiled. "Bedtime, then."

Cerryl found himself flushing.

"Go on, you two. We understand." Faltar grinned broadly.

Cerryl could sense Leyladin's embarrassment as well. "Faltar . . . not everyone has quite the same approach as you do."

"Ha!" said Heralt. "He's got you, Faltar."

"Everyone gets me," grumbled the blond mage good-naturedly as Cerryl followed Leyladin out of The Golden Ram.

Out in the lamp-punctuated misty darkness, the blonde healer turned to Cerryl. "You don't have to walk me home. You're tired."

"It's but a few blocks, really, and the exercise will do me good."

"You're lying. Your feet hurt, and your head aches, and the fog and rain don't help." Her voice was soft, and a smile followed.

"Never lie to a Black mage," he said. "I still would feel better if I walked you home."

"I can accept that." Leyladin smiled. "Perhaps you could come to dinner, the night after tomorrow? Father should be back by then."

"Back? Is he off again?"

"He's in Lydiar, something about brass fittings and about getting armsmen for a ship bound for Summerdock."

"He's been traveling more lately."

"He says he has to."

After a short silence, Cerryl glanced to his left at the bulk of the White Tower, almost glowing with the power of chaos through the drizzle and mist.

"You're worried. Why?" Leyladin glanced up the Avenue.

"Anya came to see me." Cerryl's pale gray eyes followed her green ones. "Fydel stopped me in the courtyard on the way to The Ram. Neither one of them has spoken to me in eight-days. Or longer."

"What did they say?" Leyladin glanced toward the Market Square, dark and wreathed in a foglike mist.

"Nothing. Well . . . not quite. Anya delivered a veiled hint that it would be better if the next overmage happened to be one that wouldn't challenge Jeslek in power. Fydel? He as much as told me that I shouldn't get too involved in anything beyond simple peacekeeping."

"Hmmmm . . . and what are you up to, dear Cerryl?"

"I'm not up to anything. I am worried about that missing cart. That's the one I told you about."

"I asked Father. He didn't know about anyone missing, at least not anyone he trades with."

Cerryl shrugged. "I don't see why Fydel would even care."

"Fydel doesn't. Anya might. Muneat's her uncle."

Cerryl swallowed. "I asked her where she came from. She never answered."

"Her father died several years ago. Of the flux. So did all her brothers. She has a younger sister who is the consort of Jiolt's oldest, Uleas or something."

"Who is Jiolt? All I know is that he's a rich factor." Cerryl took Leyladin's arm to guide her across a puddle as they turned westward from the befogged and darkened Market Square. Feeling her warmth so close to him, he wished, not for the first time, that he could hold her more than the few brief embraces she permitted.

Leyladin cleared her throat. "Jiolt . . . Father doesn't talk about him much. He's one of the governors of the Grain Exchange, but he factors other things, like Father, whatever interests him—wool, linen, tin, but not copper . . . oils, but only the rare ones . . . that sort of thing. Like

Muneat, but Jiolt has three sons, where Muneat's only living heir is Devo, and he's not all that bright."

"Why do all you female mages come from trading families?"

"Lyasa doesn't."

"I wasn't sure. She never told me."

"Nor me, but I know all the trading families. So if she does, it's not from Fairhaven or Lydiar or Vergren."

Cerryl nodded.

"She does not come from poverty. She is mannered and not ill-used." Leyladin laughed softly, almost bitterly. "Only those talented daughters who come from coins survive." Her eyes went to the lamps by the doorway of her house, less than fifty cubits ahead.

"Few enough chaos-talented boys without coins survive," Cerryl said quietly, thinking of his father.

"I'm sorry, Cerryl. I did not mean it that way."

"I know."

At her doorway, her arms went around him. "Go home, and please get some rest."

"I will." He returned the embrace, enjoying momentarily the warmth and even the order that infused her.

Her lips touched his, warmly but briefly, before she leaned away from him. "Good night."

"Good night."

Somehow, the evening seemed damper and colder on the walk back to his empty apartment.

# XXXV

Cerryl walked quickly across the foyer toward the tower steps. The day hadn't been that bad, but he was glad that it had been quiet. Only a few celebrating mercenaries at The Battered Cask, and they'd quieted down even before he'd gotten there after the summons from Coreg, the lead area patroller. Both the innkeeper and Coreg recommended that Cerryl but warn them, and Cerryl had heeded the recommendation, if warily. Everyone had seemed relieved at that. Cerryl wondered if he'd have trouble later—or if Gyskas would.

Cerryl shook his head as he started up the steps to the lowest level of the White Tower. *You still don't have enough experience.*

Neither guard was more than passingly familiar, and Cerryl nodded politely as he passed and began the climb to Myral's quarters, hoping the older mage happened to be there.

He paused outside Myral's door, then knocked once. *Thrap.*

After a moment came the familiar voice: "You can come, in, Cerryl."

Cerryl opened the door, then closed it behind him. Myral sat by his table, a mug of hot cider before him.

"To what do I owe this visit?" Myral smiled, then half-choked and lapsed into a series of deep and retching coughs.

Cerryl bolted toward Myral. The older mage held up a hand even as the heavy retching coughs subsided. Cerryl stood, waiting for Myral to stop coughing, glancing toward the windows shuttered against the chill breeze and then at the older man. After a time, Myral cleared his throat and took the smallest of sips from the mug.

"Are you all right?" Cerryl asked.

"I swallowed wrong. It happens with age. Now ... what do you wish?"

"I thought you could help me."

"All I can provide these days is information, and you know that." Myral smiled. "So what knowledge can this aging mage provide?" He gestured toward the chair across the table from him, then lifted the mug of cider.

Cerryl seated himself. "I need to know more about tariffs and trade."

"For the Patrol?" Myral raised his eyebrows. "For peacekeeping?"

"For peacekeeping. Over an eight-day ago, we found an abandoned cart—a painted and well-kept cart. There was blood on the seat, and a scrap of silksheen under the seat, and traces of chaos." Cerryl went on to explain how nothing else had turned up, but not about Fydel's veiled suggestion that such interest was beyond peacekeeping. "It keeps bothering me, but I don't know exactly why. So I thought about you."

Myral lowered the mug of hot cider and chuckled. "I am flattered. So many mages forget us relics once they become full members of the Guild."

"I know I have much to learn."

"You are one of the few who understands that." After a pause, Myral asked, "Why do you think taxes and tariffs have anything to do with this strange cart?"

"The silksheen ... I guess."

Myral frowned. "Do you have that scrap of silksheen?"

Cerryl glanced around, then nodded. "No one else seemed to care."

"Look at it, closely."

The younger mage extracted the fragment from his white leather belt wallet and studied it for a time. "It was cut ..."

"Exactly. Silksheen looks fragile, but you cannot rip it. It takes a sharp blade to cut it, a very sharp blade." Myral took another sip of the cider, letting the vapor wreathe his face.

That meant the fragment had been placed under the seat deliberately. *But why?* After another look at the fabric, Cerryl replaced it in his wallet.

"We think of silksheen as a fabric because it is soft and beautiful and lasts," Myral said slowly. "Yet I understand the druids use it for ropes and harnesses for its strength."

"When a small scarf can cost over a gold?"

"What is a rope that will not break worth? Or a scarf that will outlast its wearer?"

"Is it so valuable that anyone would stoop to murder?"

"That is your judgment. I would not, not for a length of fabric, no matter how beautiful, no matter how strong."

"Some might."

"Every man has a price, especially those who value everything in terms of coins." Myral sipped his cider. "You know what I can say about silksheen."

Cerryl waited, then finally spoke. "About taxes ... I know what the golds go for—armsmen, stipends for mages—but I really have no idea how many golds are needed by the Guild."

Myral shook his head. "Guess."

"Fifteen thousand? Every year?"

The older mage's eyes widened. "You are low by a third or more, perhaps by a half these days, but most would not guess a fifth part of that."

Cerryl permitted himself a slight smile, amazed that his overestimation had fallen so far short. "The medallions ... they bring in only but a thousand golds a year, two at most. I cannot imagine twenty thousand golds or more. Where would one keep it?"

"We do not. Nearly so fast as it arrives, it must depart. You get your golds every eight-day, do you not?"

"Yes."

"So does every other mage. The White Lancers get their coppers and silvers, and the masons, and the cooks, and the haulers ... and everyone spends all or part of them, and more taxes are levied on that spending, and the golds return."

Cerryl nodded. That made sense.

"So where do we get more than five hundred golds an eight-day?"

"Taxes on the factors and merchants and artisans?"

"Who else? There are far more peasants and street peddlers, but how would we collect such taxes?"

That also made sense.

Myral took a long swallow of the hot cider, then held the mug just below his chin, letting the vapor on the damp day wreathe his cheeks before speaking. "Fairhaven is more than a city, and less than a land. That is its strength and its weakness. We do not collect tithes from the landowners the way that the Duke of Lydiar or the Viscount of Certis do. Instead, we must tax those who sell goods in the city, and those who carry goods into it, as well as those who carry goods out of it. Yet we cannot drive the merchants away. Of this Sterol and those before him were most aware." Myral shrugged. "Traders are supposed to pay a tenth of their profits in taxes, a tenth of what they clear after paying for their goods and those who work for them. They also pay for trade medallions—"

"The most anyone pays is four golds a wagon a year," Cerryl pointed out. "That is not a large sum for a well-off trader."

"They would have you believe differently. They grudge every gold even while they insist the Guild close the roads to all traders but those of Fairhaven."

"Perhaps the Guild should charge more for the goods of those from elsewhere."

Myral shook his head. "It is not possible, or necessary. There are those who sell large amounts of goods to factors in Fairhaven, and those factors pay taxes on the goods. Those who wish to use the roads but who never come to Fairhaven, they pay a tax, but it is but half of a tenth, and only for those who trade more than two hundred golds a year. Those with small amounts of goods who sell in the squares, the golds they pay for medallions are those we would not see otherwise."

Cerryl thought for a moment. "Except for goods such as silksheen."

"That is true, but there are few such." Myral adjusted the white wool lap blanket across his legs.

"Gold . . . jewels?"

"A few others, but most would not dare to carry them in carts." Myral smiled. "Few would dare to carry silksheen, save that the Tyrant of Sarronnyn has made it dear."

Cerryl raised his eyebrows.

"Silksheen is traded in two places—in the trading fields east of the Stone Hills and at the port of Diehl. So half goes to Sarronnyn, and all those who have coins and ships haggle over the other half at Diehl. The druids will not sell to any who represent Fairhaven." Myral shrugged. "They know who tells the truth and who does not, and will not trade again with those who deceive them."

"So silksheen is very, very dear here?"

"When it is found at all. That should tell you all you need to know about silksheen, more than enough."

*More than enough? What has he told me?* Cerryl cleared his throat, feeling warm in the close confines of Myral's room, a room that always seemed hot to him and too cold to the aging mage. "Fairhaven is clean, and you can drink the water. The streets are safe. It is a good place to live."

Myral smiled. "Ah . . . for whom?"

Cerryl frowned. "For everyone."

"Think, Cerryl. Those with coins . . . can they not purchase whatever they need wherever they live? What do those thousands of golds purchase them that they could not purchase less dearly elsewhere?"

"Then why do they not depart?"

"Who would buy their goods?"

The conversation was turning in the direction Cerryl had disliked when he had been an apprentice, where Myral and the others had asked question after question, never answering any.

"Who is better off—the poor artisan in Fairhaven or the poor artisan in Fenard?"

"The one here, of course."

"Who lives in more luxury—the High Wizard or the prefect of Gallos?"

"The prefect."

"So who benefits most from the Guild?" Myral smiled crookedly.

"Oh . . ."

"And who pays most of the golds?"

Cerryl nodded.

"Remember, Cerryl, most of those golds the factors and merchants pay . . . where do they come from?"

"From those who buy their goods." Cerryl wanted to shake his head. Myral was running his mind in circles. There were few very wealthy factors, and that meant that most goods were bought by those who had less.

"Taxes are not what they always seem," Myral lectured. "The merchant who pays them charges them to those who buy his wares. Yet he feels that they come from his pocket, even though his buyers supply the coin." The balding mage sipped his cider. "You need to think about that. Confusion wars with confusion upon your face."

Cerryl offered a twisted smile, then asked, "Why do the gate guards report to the overmage, rather than the Patrol chief?"

"Did Isork raise that with you?" asked Myral dryly.

"No. Not even indirectly. I hadn't even thought about it. It just popped into my thoughts."

"Be most careful where you express any such unguarded thoughts. In any event, the Patrol chief does report to Overmage Kinowin, as do the gate guards." Myral coughed once. "Now . . . this old mage needs a respite. Off with you."

Cerryl rose. "Thank you for once again enlightening and confusing me." He grinned.

"It's not enlightenment if it is not confusing," Myral answered.

After closing the door, Cerryl stood on the stone landing for a moment, trying to gather together his scattered thoughts. The factors, merchants, and artisans paid 10 percent of their earnings to the Guild. He pursed his lips. How much had Tellis made? Fifty . . . a hundred golds a year? Five to ten golds to the Guild, and Cerryl had known another ten scriveners... That would only be a hundred golds. But if each group of artisans paid a hundred golds... there were weavers, potters, coopers, basket makers, woodworkers, fullers, apothecaries, jewelers, coppersmiths, and tinsmiths and all sorts of other smiths...

"Still..." Most of the taxes had to fall on the larger traders and factors. But what did that have to do with the purple cart, silksheen, and the fact that Fydel had warned him away from more than simple peacekeeping?

He walked slowly down the tower steps.

"Few would dare to carry silksheen..." For some reason, those words remained in his thoughts.

Why? *Who had the coins to buy silksheen?* Cerryl shook his head. It was obvious, so obvious he should have seen it earlier, far earlier, but mages who had been scriveners and sawmill boys did not think in such terms, not naturally. He knew in general terms where the silksheen had gone and possibly even to whom in particular, but why was an unanswered question. He had trouble believing that even the wealthiest of factors would accept silksheen gotten from peacebreakers merely for coins.

He frowned. Why not? There was nothing in the manual or the codes against purchasing stolen goods—or goods of dubious origin. Was that because it was impossible to prove that goods were stolen? Or for some other reason?

Every question raised another.

As he walked toward his room he massaged his forehead slowly. At least, he'd get to have dinner with Leyladin the next evening. Perhaps that would help... one way or another, if he could get his thoughts together.

# XXXVI

It is always a treat to dine here." Cerryl looked across the blond wooden table to his left, at Layel.

"You are kind, Cerryl." Leyladin passed the white china bread platter to Cerryl, then served herself one of the half fowl breasts wrapped in wafer-thin ham and covered with melted white cheese, topped with an off-white mustard dill sauce. After that, she served some buttered nut beans to Cerryl and then to herself.

"I meant it." Cerryl took a chunk of bread and set the bread platter to the right of the balding and clean-shaven factor, who had begun to sample his own fowl breast.

"Thank you," answered Leyladin.

"Good dish Meridis turned out," mumbled Layel.

Cerryl served himself one of the fowl breasts and cut a slice, following the example of the other two at the table. He took a bite, agreeing silently with Layel's assessment.

"It *is* good." Leyladin smiled. "That's because she knew Cerryl was coming."

"More likely that she knew you wanted it to be good," suggested Cerryl.

"Doesn't matter," responded Layel, "why it's good."

Cerryl took another slice of the fowl dish and ate it, nodding, then followed that with the beans and some bread.

"Except that I should tell Meridis," pointed out Leyladin.

"You will anyway," said her father. "You always let her know when you especially like things."

"She makes her likes known?" asked Cerryl, giving the blonde healer a quick grin.

"She hasn't shown you that yet, young mage?" Layel laughed. "If she hasn't, she will."

"Silks and jewelry . . . or herbs and potions?"

"Silks?" Leyladin raised her eyebrows.

"She hasn't had much use for the silks lately," said Layel.

Leyladin frowned, and Layel laughed softly. "Daughter, what was . . . well . . . it was."

After a moment, Cerryl spoke. "One time, when I was an apprentice mage, I saw some silksheen scarves in the Market Square." He shook his head. "I made the mistake of asking how much they were. It was a mistake for an apprentice, anyway."

"It would be a mistake for most," said Layel. "Though it would seem odd for there to be silksheen in a common market."

"I've seen it there a handful of times, but not often, and not in the past few seasons," Cerryl answered carefully. "Does anyone know much about how they make silksheen?" He took a slow sip of the white wine and waited.

"The druids of Naclos make it, or so I have been told," answered Layel. "They will only trade with those of Recluce and some few traders out of Sarronnyn. So we can procure it here only through them."

"You have silk hangings here . . ."

"Silk, not silksheen," answered Leyladin with a laugh. "All the silk in the house would not pay for a pair of silksheen gowns."

"All the silk hung in the house," corrected Layel. "Not all the silk gowns." He smiled fondly at his daughter, but his eyes twinkled.

Leyladin flushed. "I don't wear them often anymore."

Layel raised his eyebrows. "Now. That is true. Perhaps I should have them made into tunics and trousers."

"Perhaps," agreed Leyladin.

"Or give them to your niece when she is grown."

"Father, I do believe you are you trying to irritate me." Leyladin smiled and handed the fowl platter to her father. "Do have some more fowl."

"If silksheen is that costly," Cerryl pursued, "I'm surprised that I ever saw it in the Market Square." He paused. "Where would one find it, then?"

Layel shrugged. "It is too dear for my purposes. I would not deal in something that only a handful of men could or would buy. Muneat has bought silksheen in the past. He has a nephew—well, he's not exactly a nephew; the fellow's consort is Muneat's niece, but he's Jiolt's youngest son, and he factors all manner of rare and scarce items."

Cerryl hid his nod and observed, "Silksheen sounds too dear for most. What do you find the best things for trade?"

"Me? What the good might be matters little, save that I can purchase it for many fewer coins than I can sell it and that there are many who would buy. Copper when new ships are being built; grain before others know that the crops will fail; tin or zinc whenever it is cheap; silver in the winter, for it is always cheaper then." Layel spread his hands. "You see, I will reveal all."

Cerryl smiled. "Not quite, for you have not revealed how you know when a good is cheaper and will become more dear."

"Father has not ever told *me* that; he just seems to know." Leyladin glanced across the table. "Are you both finished with your dinner?"

"If there be something special for sweets, Daughter."

Cerryl reluctantly decided against another fowl breast, knowing he would sleep uneasily with its weight in his gut. "Yes, thank you."

"Meridis?"

"Could you hearty men not eat more?" asked the cook as she appeared in her blue livery.

"A full breast I had," answered Layel, "and richer than anything I've had in days it was. Quite enough, thank you."

"Excellent," added Cerryl.

Meridis took the platters with a smile. "A yam molasses pie we have, though as getting enough of the sweet molasses was a chore, and dearer than you would have liked, Master Layel. Each eight-day a few more coppers it takes, or silvers." The door closed behind her.

"They've raised prices at The Golden Ram again," Cerryl said. "That's twice this year."

"Aye, and it may happen yet again." The factor shook his head.

"But enough of such. Leyladin tells me that you are a bright flame in the Patrol. How came that?"

Cerryl spread his hands. "Scarcely a bright flame, just a very junior Patrol mage who has much to learn." He paused as Meridis set what seemed to be a quarter of a golden brown pie before him and then before Layel. A smaller section went before Leyladin.

"There you be, and I be not expecting more than crumbs returning to the kitchen." The door closed behind Meridis.

Leyladin laughed. "She means that."

Cerryl looked at the huge chunk of pastry and filling. So much for trying to spare his gut. He looked helplessly at Leyladin, then said, "You have to eat all of yours, too."

The healer glanced down and swallowed. "Me?"

"She looked at you, too," Cerryl pressed, with a grin.

"If I must . . ." Leyladin offered a groan.

"Such sounds from the woman who as a child ate an entire half-pie," Layel offered.

"That was then," the healer said. "Much has changed."

*Indeed it has,* reflected Cerryl as he began to eat the sweet. *Indeed it has.* He was not looking forward to returning to the Halls, not by himself.

# XXXVII

Cerryl glanced from his notes to his half-written daily report to Isork, then at the doorway as Isork himself stepped into the small duty room.

"Ser." Cerryl stood immediately. "I didn't know you were coming." He gestured at the desk. "I was just finishing my report. Gyskas should be here before long."

"I didn't come to see Gyskas." Isork slipped into the chair across the desk. "Sit down."

Cerryl sat.

"I understand you occasionally still walk with one of the patrols?"

"Yes, ser. Not too often . . . but every so often. I don't tell them before that day when, or why . . . I just do it."

"Why?"

"Ser . . . I couldn't say exactly," Cerryl fudged, "but . . . it feels better when I do. People know I'm young, and I felt that they had to know I intended to learn the city and keep the peace."

"You also walk the section by yourself when you aren't on duty."

"Yes, ser. I don't know that I'm helping much . . . Nothing seems to happen when I go with any patroller . . ."

"You're keeping the peace if nothing happens." Isork laughed. "When you're on duty, even when you don't patrol, almost nothing happens."

"Ser . . . you said that people respected the Patrol here. I just wanted to make sure that they still did."

"Oh, they respect you. So do the patrollers. They see you walking the streets by yourself, checking out things—"

"I'm still trying to learn where everything is," Cerryl explained. "I don't want to have my lead patrollers trying to explain where something happened."

"We need more mages who've been through whatever you've been through." Isork shook his head. "Your patrollers call you their tough little sawmill bastard. First new Patrol mage in three years that I can keep. First one who's either patrolling or where he's supposed to be, too." The pudgy-looking but muscular Patrol chief glanced around the room, then frowned. "Don't let that go to your head. You've still got a lot to learn, but you're on the right road."

"Thank you, ser." Cerryl waited, suspecting from the Patrol chief's body position that Isork had more to say.

After a moment, Isork looked at Cerryl. "I heard you were asking about silksheen."

Cerryl didn't bother to ask how the senior Patrol mage knew. "Someone killed a trader and stole some silksheen. It's costly, and there couldn't be many places where it could be sold. No one reported anyone missing or any cart being stolen. So I thought people who handled silksheen might know."

Isork nodded slowly. "Asking general questions discreetly is fine. I'd appreciate it if you would tell me if you find out anything. Silksheen, as I am most assured you have discovered, is only traded by two or three merchants in all of Fairhaven. They are quite close to many of the senior mages."

Cerryl returned the nod. "I did discover that, and I have no reason to make further inquiries." *Not now, and certainly not in any direct way, not after what I found out so far.*

"You've got a good head on your shoulders." Isork rose. "I enjoy reading your reports." After another smile, he nodded a last time, turned, and left the duty room.

Cerryl swallowed. *Not a very good head, not at all.*

# XXXVIII

Cerryl strode through the open double doors of the section building's assembly room and crossed the floor to the speaking stones, ignoring the murmurs from the four patrollers to the right of the entryway. He stepped up on the stones and looked out at the small group. His eyes fixed on lead patroller Sheffl. "What happens to be the problem?"

The muscular patroller cleared his throat. "Ser mage, these two men cannot agree. They stopped us on patrol." He raised his eyebrows and half-smiled, gesturing to the two shorter figures who stood on either side of him.

A squat, fair-skinned, and red-haired man dressed in brown glared at the other man. The second had short gray hair, was tanned as if he worked in the open often, and wore faded blue trousers and a sleeveless blue vest. The tanned man in the vest ignored the glares from the squat man, and his eyes rested on Cerryl.

"They were arguing?" Cerryl asked the patroller. "Close to breaking the peace?"

"You might say that, ser." Sheffl's limp black hair flopped across his forehead with the nod he gave. "Karfl—he's the mason there, in the blue vest—he was waving a stone hammer a lot. Queas was reaching for a staff. He was really yelling, could hear him from the back alley. Thought maybe . . ." The lead patroller shrugged.

Beside the double doors, just inside the room, the other four patrollers waited, watching, their faces indicating various degrees of boredom and interest.

Cerryl looked at the tanned mason. "Why were you arguing?"

"Demon-damned artisans . . . be all the same. Queas . . . he said he be a-tradin' a set of china pieces, ten platters and ten mugs and two pitchers, if I would repair and rebuild the stone wall at the back of his courtyard." Karfl shrugged. "Should have known better. Got the wall done, and a bit of work it was, too. Some fool had backed a wagon through it, mud-brick and not fired brick or stone. Then Queas offers me ten platters and two pitchers and says I should be lucky. Only did it because I wanted the set as a consort gift for my daughter Viaya. Can't have a consort gift without mugs." Another shrug followed.

"I see." Cerryl could sense the man's belief that the situation was as he had told the Patrol mage. After a moment, Cerryl glanced at Queas. "What do you have to say?"

"I offered him ten platters, yes, and two pitchers, but not the mugs,"

Queas replied. "I am a poor potter, and I had the platters already. So the pitchers I had to throw and fire and glaze. Pitchers, they are not easy, not if you want their handles to be strong. But the pitchers, they are good, good enough to sell anywhere. So are the platters."

Cerryl held up a hand. "Did you offer him the platters and the pitchers when you first talked about how you would repay him for repairing the wall?"

"That is what I said, ser mage."

Cerryl frowned, catching something about the words. "Did you tell him that you were offering ten platters and two pitchers, or did you say you were offering him a set of ten and two pitchers?"

"A set of ten, it is ten platters."

Cerryl turned to Karfl. "What did you think he said to you?"

"A set of ten, and that means platters and mugs. Some places, it be even ten small plates as well, but I weren't expecting that."

Cerryl pursed his lips. Demons! People arguing over the meaning of what a set was. He directed his next words to Queas: "If a merchant, like Likket or Nivor, or Tellis the scrivener, asked you for a full set of ten pieces of china . . . what would he expect to get?" Cerryl's eyes focused on the potter, as did his senses.

Queas shifted his weight from one foot to the other. "Ah . . . but . . . ser mage . . . Karfl is not . . . ah . . . he is a mason."

"You have a different meaning for masons?"

Queas bowed his head. "I will make ten mugs. It will take an eight-day, though. I cannot fire and glaze properly, not with the work I have accepted coins for . . . not sooner."

Cerryl looked toward Karfl.

"An eight-day don't matter, ser mage. Just so as I can get a proper consort gift for Viaya." The mason squared his shoulders.

Cerryl addressed the two. "I trust this will not come before the Patrol again."

"No, ser mage," murmured Queas.

"Not 'less he don't deliver the mugs," stated Karfl.

Cerryl nodded to Sheffl. The lead patroller gestured to the door, and Karfl marched out, followed by a subdued Queas.

". . . mages got some uses."

Cerryl smiled faintly as he heard Karfl's muttered comment. He wasn't sure he wanted to hear what Queas might be saying or thinking.

Back in the duty room, Cerryl sank into the high-backed chair. Sometimes, even when people heard the same words, they still didn't agree. Sometimes people, like Queas, were too quick to interpret words in the way that they wished. He took a deep breath. At least, he hadn't had to put them on road duty or refuse duty or flame them.

At the scritching sound, he looked up.

Weilt paused in the doorway. "Ser?"

"Yes, Weilt . . . come on in." Cerryl gestured to the chair. "Sit down. Your feet have to be sore."

The blond messenger glanced around the duty room, then leaned forward and murmured, "Ser . . . you have to be careful."

Cerryl frowned. "Careful? I always try to be careful." His words were low, probably because the messenger's had been also.

Weilt whispered, "It's not in the southwest, ser." He straightened and said loudly, "Will that be all, ser mage?"

Cerryl swallowed, then answered. "Ah . . ." He raised his voice: "That's all for now, Weilt."

"Thank you, ser." Weilt left quickly.

"Be careful," Cerryl murmured. *And not in the southwest section . . .* Why? His inquiries about silksheen? Why would that upset people? Yet Isork had suggested care. Where had Weilt heard what he'd heard? Cerryl smiled. Messengers often overheard things, he imagined.

He frowned.

As with so many other things in Fairhaven, much more was hidden than revealed. He needed to talk to Leyladin, if he could, since she was the only one beside Myral and Kinowin he trusted. But Myral was failing, and Kinowin was Isork's superior. That left Leyladin, yet . . . he worried about bringing her too much into the intrigues.


# XXXIX

Cerryl stepped out of the foyer and down the stone steps onto the paved sidewalk beside the Avenue, turning north into the cold rain that seemed to get heavier with each step. Not wanting to discuss all the warnings he'd received in the Halls of the Mages, where all too many might overhear, he'd asked Leyladin the evening before if he could stop by her house after his duty. With a smile, she had agreed.

"You just didn't realize it would be raining," he muttered to himself. Ahead, the colored carts in the Market Square were shrouded in rain and mist rising from the pavement warmed by the vanished sunlight. His eyes flicked through the fall rain, and he forced himself to concentrate despite the headache the storm had brought. He turned westward on the street south of the square. Someone was watching him—not quite as in a screeing glass, but definitely watching. Cerryl could half-feel, half-sense the observation, and he studied the line of walls fronting the house to his right.

A blurred figure, half-concealed by a tree limb, stood at the corner of the wall less than thirty cubits away. A figure holding something . . . a bow?

Abruptly, and as quickly as he could, Cerryl raised a wall of chaos all the way around him—or tried to—and lurched forward and toward the nearer section of the wall, where he hoped the archer could not get a clear shot. He half-tripped, half-dropped to his knees.

Pain flared through his left shoulder.

On his knees, still a half-dozen cubits from the wall, he overlooked the burning of the heavy shaft in his arm. His eyes narrowed toward the figure in blue nocking yet another shaft.

Anger flared through Cerryl, and chaos flowed after the anger.

*Whhhstt!* The bowman flared into a pillar of fire, white ashes dropping across the wall with the rain.

Cerryl forced himself to concentrate, somehow focusing chaos wrapped in order around the iron, using that raw force to expel/destroy the arrow. White stars flashed across his eyes, and he closed them, but for a moment.

Opening his eyes, ignoring the stabbing in his arm, he staggered upright, then looked down at the redness welling from the wound across the white of his shirt and tunic. He clasped his right hand over the wound, hoping it would help staunch the blood.

He put one foot in front of the other, then repeated the action until he found himself tottering up the stone walk to Leyladin's door.

He had barely let the knocker fall when she appeared.

"I felt it! What happened?" Her eyes and senses encompassed him.

"Darkness! Take my arm."

She helped him inside through the foyer and the front hall, leaving drippings of mud and blood, and laid him out on the settee in the front room to the left of the foyer—the pale blue silk-hung room he'd never entered.

"I'll get blood on—" he protested.

"Hush." She concentrated, and he could feel the order and the warmth from her infusing his upper arm and shoulder, even as she gently cut away the white fabric from around the wound. "It's not as bad as it could have been."

"I blocked some of it—just not quick enough."

"I need to clean this and then stitch it up. The muscle is ripped up, but it's not so deep as I'd thought. You must have done something to hold it off."

"Told . . . you . . ."

"Hush . . ." She pressed a cloth against the wound. "Hold this. I'll be right back."

Cerryl held the cloth, listening to Leyladin as she entered the kitchen.

"...a bottle of the brandy, Meridis! I don't care what Father says ...It works."

Even before the words died out, the healer was back with a small case, a bottle, and a clean white cloth. "First, we need to clean off the blood and everything else."

The cork came from the bottle, and Cerryl wanted to scream as the liquid sloshed across the wound.

"Sorry ... dear one ... but it helps. No one's quite sure why, but with both brandy and order most wounds heal cleanly."

Cerryl didn't like the word "most."

"Don't squirm. There's still cloth in the wound, and I need to get it out ... chaos behind it ... not much, but it will grow if I don't ..."

Cerryl kept his teeth clamped together, hoping he wasn't biting his tongue, feeling the sweat bead on his forehead and the salt run into the corners of his eyes.

"There—that's the worst of it. Now ... more brandy and some order ..."

Cerryl winced again, in spite of himself. "That hurt more than the arrow."

"You will recover." Leyladin forced a laugh. "Now ... just rest for a moment. You need it and so do I." She sat down on the floor beside the settee. "Should I send a messenger to Isork?"

"Not yet ..." Cerryl didn't know when would be a good time, if ever. "Kinowin ... later."

"Lady Leyladin. You be white." Meridis scurried into the sitting room, carrying a tray of bread and cheese and a bottle of wine and two goblets. "Ser Cerryl ... you look like some nourishment might not hurt."

The tray went on the floor beside Leyladin, who took a small knife and began to cut wedges off the block of white cheese.

Cerryl smiled as Leyladin handed him a small wedge of cheese, then chewed it slowly, realizing just how tired and hungry he felt. He glanced at the healer—as pale as Meridis had said.

"Healing is hard work, I see."

"Harder than most reckon," she said after swallowing. "Much harder, sometimes." She passed a chunk of bread.

"Thank you," he said quietly. "I was lucky you were here."

"Fortunate, not lucky, that you'd asked me to be here." After passing him a glass of wine and taking it back after he had swallowed some, she asked, "Do you know who did it?"

"I was so angry that I lashed out. A bowman in blue, I think, but he's ashes. He was nocking another shaft. Didn't wait to find out."

"Blue ... that's the color of a half-score of houses."

"Not the blue Meridis wears, or Soaris. A brighter, deeper blue."

Leyladin's eyes narrowed briefly, but she did not speak.

"I think I'd better get back to the Halls," Cerryl said.

"You can stay here . . ." Leyladin insisted. "You should stay here."

Cerryl shook his head. "No . . . I'll be fine in my own quarters."

"You weren't fine walking here."

"It happened on the street, not in the Halls. I don't think it would be good for me to stay here."

"Then I'll tell Myral and have him look after you somehow. He can tell Kinowin." The healer cocked her head to the side, then nodded. "You shouldn't be going back, but you surely should not be walking. I'll send Meridis to summon the carriage."

Cerryl didn't argue that point, taking another swallow of wine as Leyladin scurried out to the kitchen. He was no longer dizzy, but the aching in his arm and his head had grown even stronger, more throbbing.

"The carriage will be ready shortly." Leyladin looked at the tray on the floor. "Can you eat more?"

"Yes."

"Then you should." She handed him another slice of the white cheese.

When Meridis announced the coach was ready, Cerryl had finished most of the bread and cheese, as well as a full goblet of wine. As he walked slowly through the front hallway, Meridis looked at him. "I can't believe anyone would try to attack a mage. I can't believe it. What is the world coming to?"

"What it has always been," said Leyladin crossly.

Cerryl continued walking out to the coach, through the rain that had subsided to a drizzle, feeling slightly light-headed. Because of his use of chaos? The wound? The treatment? All three? He wasn't sure, and it didn't matter.

Soaris sat in the driver's seat, studying both Cerryl and Leyladin as they walked toward him. A footman armed with a shortsword watched impassively as Cerryl climbed into the coach. Leyladin slipped inside, closed the door, and sat beside him.

The carriage eased forward, gently, for which Cerryl was most grateful, and the rain began to splat more loudly on the roof.

After the coach pulled up at the front entrance to the Halls of the Mages and they stepped out, Soaris announced, "We will wait here for you, Lady Leyladin."

"Thank you, Soaris." She nodded before stepping up beside Cerryl's injured left arm and shoulder, almost as if to shield the wound from casual view.

Cerryl walked deliberately up the stairs and through the entryway to the front Hall, then through the foyer, Leyladin at his elbow. The two reached the fountain courtyard before encountering anyone.

Lyasa, standing by the fountain, as if waiting for someone, turned. Her eyes widened, and she hurried toward Cerryl. "What happened to you?" she whispered, her eyes going to the dressing and the blood splattered across Cerryl's tunic.

"Later," said Leyladin.

Lyasa swung around and walked on Cerryl's right. He was glad of both women's help on the stairs up to the floor that held his quarters, and he sank gratefully onto his bed, where Leyladin arranged the pillow to prop him up slightly.

"You stay with him," Leyladin said to Lyasa. "I'm going to tell Myral."

As the door closed, the black-haired Lyasa pulled the chair over to the bed and sat down. "What happened?"

"An archer shot me," Cerryl said dryly from the bed. "He's ash, but it took a little effort for me to get to Leyladin."

"An arrow—with an iron head—and you're walking?"

"Leyladin's a good healer."

"Not that good." She frowned. "An archer attacking a mage—in Fairhaven? That's not good."

"It isn't the first time," Cerryl recalled the armed men who had attacked him when he had been an apprentice mage cleaning out sewer tunnels.

"Cerryl, for someone so quiet, you upset too many people."

"I wasn't trying." Cerryl closed his eyes, but his head seemed to spin, and he quickly opened them.

The door latch clicked, and both Lyasa and Cerryl turned their heads.

Kinowin stepped into the room and glanced at Lyasa. The dark-haired mage rose from the chair, nodded, and stepped outside, closing the door.

"How do you feel?" asked Kinowin.

"I've felt better," Cerryl admitted. "I was lucky Leyladin wasn't that far away."

"It was more than luck." Kinowin settled into the chair that Lyasa had vacated. "I've put a guard outside your door with instructions to admit only the healer, Myral, me, and of course," he added sardonically, "the High Wizard. A guard wouldn't stop any talented mage, but then Jeslek and I could quiz every member of the Guild, and that thought will stop anyone with any such thoughts."

Cerryl hoped so. He needed some rest, some sleep without worry.

"Do you have any idea why this happened?" asked the overmage. "I talked to Isork, and he didn't think it was related to your Patrol duties in the southeast section."

"Did he say it that way?" asked Cerryl.

"Yes. I noted that. Do you want to explain?"

Cerryl let his breath out with a slow sigh, ignoring both the throbbing headache and the dull soreness in his arm.

"I think you'd best explain," Kinowin suggested with a chuckle.

"It all started with the purple cart," Cerryl began, launching into a retelling of the chaos traces, the blood, and the fragment of silksheen. "When the messenger warned me, then I began to watch everyone. I just didn't watch closely enough."

"Not many mages survive shafts with large iron heads," said Kinowin. "Wasn't that what struck you?"

"I know it was iron. It hurt, and it burned. But he was nocking another shaft. So I ashed him first."

"This was during the rain, wasn't it?"

"That does seem odd." Cerryl recalled the archers when he'd gone to Gallos with Jeslek. They'd never strung their bows in the rain. Then, they hadn't been attacked in the rain.

"Someone was out for you, and they knew about mages. We don't handle chaos as well in the rain, and iron shafts often can kill some mages outright." Kinowin raised his eyebrows. "I would let your inquiries about silksheen die away. For now, at least."

"I already told Isork that," Cerryl said, fearing he sounded like he was whining. He hated whining.

"Isork wasn't ever the problem." Kinowin rose. "Rest. I'd like you at the meeting the day after tomorrow."

"Yes, ser."

"It won't be that bad."

*No. It will be worse.*

Kinowin rose, giving Cerryl a knowing nod, and left. The door latch clicked shut.

After a time, Cerryl closed his eyes.

# XL

At the knock on the door and the click of the latch, Cerryl sat up straighter from where he was stretched out on the bed and set down *On Peacekeeping*. "Yes?"

Leyladin stepped into the room, and a cool breeze flowed from the open high window until she closed the door. "You look like you're feeling better."

"I am. You're a good healer."

"You helped." She smiled.

For a moment Cerryl just looked at her, amazed that she was the same woman he'd seen by chance in a screeing glass when he'd been but a child.

"Let me see the arm." Leyladin bent over Cerryl and examined his right shoulder, both with her eyes and with her senses.

He could feel the dark shafts of order, slightly uncomfortable, but not painful.

"There's some leftover chaos there. Just hold still."

"I *am* holding still."

"There. I don't think it will recur, but I'll check tomorrow before you leave for the Guild meeting." Leyladin took a slow, deep breath.

"How—"

"Because Myral told me to." The blonde healer smiled.

"Sit down for a moment. I know healing is work."

"Just for a moment. I still have to see Myral." The blonde healer eased into the straight-backed chair.

"How is he?"

Leyladin shook her head. "Not as well as I would like. Each day, the cough gets stronger, and he gets weaker, but there's no illness. The chaos has taken its toll on him." She shrugged. "He's been more careful than most, at least in the recent years, but White mages don't live that long." Her eyes studied Cerryl.

"I'm trying. I've followed his advice."

"You and Kinowin are about the only ones."

"Jeslek almost flaunts his power. He doesn't have to; everyone knows he's the strongest."

"Everyone does," Leyladin said blandly, raising one eyebrow as she looked at Cerryl.

"You—" Cerryl paused, wondering how she knew he was avoiding displaying his own abilities.

"It's hard to keep things from a healer."

"I'm discovering that." *Along with many other things.*

"You know," she said quietly, "you're not really a White mage."

Cerryl frowned.

"You look White to most, but you're not. There's no core of chaos within you. That's why that heavy iron arrowhead didn't kill you." Leyladin smiled. "You can handle chaos, but you can also handle order. You're a gray mage."

Cerryl winced. "Don't tell anyone. You know what Jeslek and Sterol would do to me if that came out. I've enough difficulties anyway."

"Myral and Kinowin already know. They won't say anything. They're like you. Why do you think they look out for you?"

"Because I'm not always trying to prove I'm the master of chaos," Cerryl suggested.

"That doesn't hurt." Leyladin stretched, then stood. "I feel better, and I need to see Myral." She walked to the bed, bent down, and brushed his cheek with her lips. "Just be careful."

"I will."

Once the door closed, Cerryl leaned back against the pillows. An iron arrowhead, a large one, and an attack against a mage. He nodded slowly to himself. If the attack succeeded, no one would trace the killer, because no one would be able to find the archer. If it failed, as it had, there wasn't enough of the archer left to determine who had hired him. That meant some mage who knew Cerryl all too well, and Cerryl was fairly sure which one it was. But he still didn't understand why.

After a deep breath, he picked up *On Peacekeeping*. So far, he hadn't found even veiled references to smuggling and stolen goods. Since it was his third time through the book, he doubted he would, but learning more about peacekeeping couldn't hurt. Besides, he felt guilty about someone else having to take his duty, but Leyladin and Kinowin had insisted that a few days' recuperation would be better for everyone.

# XLI

The first order of this meeting is to affirm Jeslek as High Wizard," announced Kinowin, standing alone on the polished gold-shot marble dais of the Council Chamber. "Is there any member of the Guild who wishes to propose another member as High Wizard?"

In the silence that followed, Kinowin studied the Council Chamber, his eyes covering the gold oak desks and red-cushioned gold oak seats at the front, then scanning the polished white granite columns at the sides for any mages who might be standing there under the swagged crimson hangings. Finally, he announced, "Seeing as no other candidate has been proposed, as overmage and representative of the Council, I declare that the new High Wizard is the honorable Jeslek." The tall blond mage gestured toward the front row, motioning Jeslek up to the dais.

Jeslek bowed, then straightened. "Thank you all for your support." He paused and studied the chamber. "I have two matters to discuss. The first is a tribute. I would like to announce that my predecessor, Sterol, will be honored for his service to Fairhaven and the Guild by having his image added to those facing the Tower. We can do no less for a great mage."

From his seat at the north end of the third row Cerryl watched, with Heralt to his right.

"Second, this is a time when the Guild faces great dangers," Jeslek announced. "These dangers do not seem real to some. Yet even one of our own Guild members has been attacked—in Fairhaven, less than two blocks from the Halls of the Mages."

Cerryl wondered if Jeslek would call him to the dais or give the impression that anyone could have been attacked by leaving the mage "victim" nameless.

"Some of you know who was attacked; some do not; but a name matters little when a full mage is attacked with iron-headed arrows in Fairhaven itself. It could have been any mage . . ."

Cerryl wanted to snort at that, but he kept his mouth shut and his face expressionless, his eyes on the center part of the second row where Anya and Fydel sat. Faltar probably would have been there, had he not been one of the very few not able to attend, because he had the evening gate duty.

Myral sat in the front row, forward and to the right of Anya. He seemed healthy, despite Leyladin's concerns. At the other end of the front row, almost in front of Cerryl, sat Sterol, quietly watching Jeslek, a cold and ironic smile on his face.

"Why doesn't he name you?" whispered Heralt to Cerryl.

"More effective if he doesn't," Cerryl answered.

"Why is this occurring?" demanded the new High Wizard. "It has happened because those in Recluce have never respected Fairhaven and because the traders of Spidlar would listen to the Black angels in hopes of filling their wallets with golds they deserve not."

"How do we know this had anything to do with Spidlar?" asked Disarj.

Cerryl's eyes went farther back in the chamber, settling on Isork, who nodded very slightly at the question raised by the frizzy-haired mage.

"Nothing is certain," Anya said, rising slowly from where she had been sitting in the second row of the Council Chamber. "But a fragment of a blue cloak was found, as was a bow of the type used by Spidlarian mercenaries. One of those mercenaries entered the city not long before Cerryl was attacked." She shrugged.

". . . was Cerryl . . . was it?"

". . . why him?"

A fleeting expression of annoyance crossed Jeslek's face but vanished even more quickly. Cerryl wondered why Anya had named him, then nodded. By giving his name she had subtly linked him to an attack by Spidlar and strengthened the impression that Spidlar had been the absolute cause of the attack—even though Cerryl knew that was not the case, even if he had no way of proving otherwise.

"This is something that should not be countenanced," suggested Fydel, standing up from beside where Anya had reseated herself.

"We need more proof!" came a call from the back, a voice Cerryl did not recognize.

"What kind of proof do you want?" demanded Anya, turning to face the rear of the chamber. "Every eight-day, more Black ships and more Black goods pour into Spidlar. Every eight-day, the prefect of Gallos becomes more and more reluctant to pay the road tariffs. Every eight-day, our own traders complain more about how they cannot sell their goods and pay their taxes. Do you wish to wait until the lancers of Gallos seize the Great White Highway? Or until the Guild cannot pay your stipend?" The redhead's voice dripped scorn.

"Then how are we to deal with Spidlar?" asked Disarj.

"How are we to deal with Recluce?" came from another voice somewhere near the front of the chamber.

"Repeal the surtax," suggested yet another anonymous voice from the midbenches of the Council Chamber.

Cerryl brushed his mouth with his hand, as if to cover a cough, rather than the smile he felt.

Jeslek swiveled toward the voice. "Who suggested that?"

There was no answer.

"If you don't want the Spidlarians or the Blacks making golds, then you'll be making the Hamorians and the Nordlans rich," suggested Myral from the first row. "Or the Suthyans and the Sarronnese. Trade is like water. It has to go somewhere."

"Why can't it flow here?" demanded Jeslek.

"That is easier said than done."

"Why not increase the tax on Recluce goods?" asked another White wizard.

"Think again," said Esaak, his voice rumbling. "That surtax is a hundred percent already."

"So? Those are spices, wines, luxury goods. Besides, who can wear their wool anyway? People will pay still more, and the Treasury will benefit, but not the Hamorians and Nordlans."

"Couldn't we use the tax to build a larger fleet?"

"We could build even more ships, but why do we need any more?" Cerryl found himself asking, amazed that he had spoken.

"To cut off outside trade to Recluce, of course," snorted Jeslek, young-looking despite the white hair and golden eyes. His eyes pinned Cerryl momentarily.

Anya glanced sideways at Cerryl, as if to suggest silence might be better for the young mage.

Her look irritated him enough that Cerryl continued. "That would have worked three centuries ago, but after Creslin we had neither ships nor money. It won't work now. All Recluce is doing now is buying our grain from the Nordlans. The Nordlans pick it up in Hydolar and ship it to Recluce. Then the Blacks sell their stuff to the Nordlans in return. It costs them more, but we lose all that trade."

"That's Jeslek's point," offered Anya in the silence that followed. "Unless we cut off trade to Recluce, we lose."

Heralt jabbed Cerryl in the ribs as Cerryl reseated himself. "You're probably right, but Anya looks like she'd consider hiring the next mercenary archer to shoot you."

Cerryl refrained from answering that, just nodded at Heralt, then added, "I won't say any more."

"Good idea."

"All that is fine in theory," snorted Myral, wiping his bald pate with another of his gray cloths. "But I have yet to see something which will work. Nor did any of our predecessors. Do you honestly think, Jeslek, that previous councils have approved of the growing power of Recluce? Did they lose scores of ships and thousands of troops on purpose?"

"Of course not." Jeslek frowned, then smiled. "But, remember, the Blacks cannot use the winds now—even if they had a Creslin. What if we put more wizards on our ships?"

"How many would that take?"

"Not that many. That way, we could blockade Recluce. The Nordlans won't make enough off the island to want to lose ships." Jeslek's face bore a smug look, the look of a man who has discovered a solution.

In the third row the ponderous Esaak stood and offered a wide shrug. "That may be, Jeslek. Bring the Council a plan. For such an expenditure of coin, we should see a plan."

Cerryl shivered. Even for Esaak to ask Jeslek to justify himself to the Guild was risky indeed.

Jeslek still smiled as he nodded. "I will indeed. In the interim, however, to protect our interests in Gallos, I will be dispatching the mage Eliasar with an honor guard of a thousand White Lancers to Gallos, in order to encourage the prefect Syrma to remit those revenues owed the Guild. I will be accompanying Eliasar." The High Wizard smiled. "Now, we need to consider the selection of an overmage to fill the vacant position on the Council."

Anya smiled as well, her eyes on Esaak, but her smile was one for which Cerryl cared little.

"Are there any suggestions for a new overmage?" asked Kinowin, stepping forward on the dais, ignoring the round of murmurs following Jeslek's announcement.

Cerryl wanted to shake his head. Jeslek was effectively announcing that, one way or another, he was going to ensure coins from Gallos, even if he had to use his chaos power to turn the city of Fernard into rubble. The so-called honor guard was large enough to protect Jeslek long enough for him to destroy Fenard, if need be. Cerryl was certain that the prefect Syrma would see it the same way.

Kinowin waited for the whispers to die away before repeating his question. "Are there any suggestions for a new overmage?"

Did Jeslek feel he had no choice? Were matters that bad? From what Cerryl could tell, part of the Guild's problem lay in the basic structure of order and chaos—and the geography of the world. Recluce didn't need as many armsmen as Fairhaven and the countries of Candar because it was an island and because the Black Order contained weather mages who could destroy the ships of any land that tried to invade the isle. So Recluce didn't have to spend as many coins on armsmen. Likewise, Recluce simply exiled anyone who didn't conform. On the other hand, the Brotherhood had to maintain highways and ships . . . and lancers and gate guards, and wizard envoys to the other lands of Candar.

Still . . . he was missing something. There had to be a way to make it possible for the goods of Candar not to be costlier than those of other lands. There had to be a way.

He laughed to himself. Why was he so worried? He was a Patrol mage, a very junior one, and no one was really going to listen to him, even if he did come up with a solution. Not right now, anyway.

"What's so amusing?" whispered Lyasa, sliding up to his seat, standing by the pillar to his left.

"I was having great thoughts and then realized that it will be quite a few years before anyone will listen to such."

"Fewer than you think, the way things are headed."

"What do you mean?" he whispered.

Lyasa shook her head. "Not now."

"The Council is asking for suggestions," Kinowin stated even more loudly.

"How about Disarj? He's had a lot to say," suggested Fydel.

Disarj rose to his feet. "I lack the experience of, say, the honorable Fydel and so must decline. Perhaps Fydel should be considered."

"No one will want it," murmured Lyasa. "They'll have to choose between Kinowin and Jeslek on everything."

"I wouldn't want to," murmured Heralt.

"You might be right," Cerryl whispered back.

"How about Esaak?"

Cerryl didn't see who asked the question, but Esaak stood more abruptly than Cerryl would have believed. "High Wizard Jeslek deserves someone with greater youth and vigor than these old bones can muster." After a pause, he smiled. "Someone like the honorable Redark, who is young enough to provide strength, old enough to have caution, and deliberative enough to provide balance." Esaak gestured toward the green-eyed and ginger-bearded Redark.

Redark smiled, warmly.

"That's perfect," hissed Lyasa. "He can't decide what he wants to eat most days. He'll do whatever Jeslek wants because he's not smart enough to understand Kinowin and won't admit it."

Cerryl looked at Lyasa quizzically.

"Believe me. I know."

The bleak tone in the black-haired mage's voice convinced Cerryl, as did the quiet and muted sighs that swept the chamber.

"Are there any other suggestions?" asked Kinowin, turning to Jeslek.

Jeslek offered the smallest of shrugs.

"Since there are no other suggestions, and since the honorable Redark is a full and qualified member of the Guild, the Council accepts him as overmage." Kinowin inclined his head to Jeslek.

*Is that blotch on Kinowin's cheek more flushed?* Cerryl wondered, admiring Kinowin for his poise in what had to be a strained situation, a very strained situation.

Redark rose and stepped down the aisle toward the dais.

"They threw him out of the Patrol, years ago," Lyasa added.

"How did you know that?" hissed Heralt.

"Derka told me before he left for Hydolar." She shook her head. "Some say he's Jeslek's cousin, but no one really knows."

Cerryl moistened his lips, his eyes on Anya, seeing the cold smile in profile—a very cold smile.

# XLII

The thin dressing on his arm felt like it bulged even under the loose shirt. Cerryl glanced at his shoulder and the white tunic and shirt that revealed nothing, then studied the flat desk. Even though he'd been out an eight-day, the desk looked the same as ever—the two empty wooden boxes, the inkwell and quill stand, the lamp, and a stack of rough paper.

Zubal peered into the duty room. "You all right now, ser?"

"I'm fine," he told the messenger. "I'll spend a little time patrolling, with Nuryl, this morning, I think."

"Yes, ser." Zubal bobbed his head and withdrew.

After another look at the empty desk, Cerryl shifted his weight, put his white Patrol jacket back on, and then walked through the predawn gloom to the assembly room.

"He's back . . ."

". . . told you wouldn't be long."

Cerryl beckoned to Nuryl.

The area Patrol leader slipped away from his men and over to Cerryl. "You're going with us, ser?" Nuryl's eyes went to Cerryl's shoulder.

"It's not as though I have to swing a blade," Cerryl pointed out. "Besides, you're all out there every day." He grinned.

After a moment, Nuryl smiled back, then nodded, and returned to his men. "Let's go."

Cerryl listened to the comments from Fystl's and Sheffl's men, the only groups that remained, as he walked out of the assembly room beside Nuryl.

". . . wouldn't go out after taking a war arrow . . . not that soon."

". . . why they get the coins . . ."

". . . told you he was a tough little bastard."

Somehow Cerryl didn't think of himself as tough in the way someone like Eliasar was, or even as Kinowin must have been in his younger days, both men physically imposing and appearing able to break smaller figures in pieces. Even Jeslek was fairly imposing, at least compared to Cerryl.

Outside, the streets were still damp with water from the storm of the previous night, glistening almost silver in the gray light just before dawn.

# XLIII

Fat white flakes of snow drifted down, some sliding off Cerryl's oil-polished white leather jacket, others melting when they struck the stones of the Avenue or the walkway. Cerryl glanced ahead and to the side, alert for anything unusual, his eyes and senses changing focus continually as he walked northward toward Leyladin's.

The Market Square was nearly deserted under the fall of fluffy snow, with but a handful of painted carts clustered in the center. As Cerryl turned westward just south of the square, he surveyed the wall from which he had been shot. The trees, with their shrunken and wizened gray winter leaves, now offered little cover. A thin layer of white covered grass and shrubs, but not stone roads, walkways, or tile roofs.

He continued westward.

A thin line of white smoke rose from the center chimney of Leyladin's house, but the shutters remained open, the glass windows shut. Cerryl remained half-amazed at all the glass windows in Fairhaven—amazed and grateful that even the Halls of the Mages had them.

Soaris opened the door. "How be the arm, ser mage?"

"Much better, Soaris. Much better. I appreciated your handling of the carriage. I didn't thank you at the time, but I trust you understand I wasn't feeling as well as I might have."

"I understand, ser." Not a trace of a smile crossed the houseman's face, though his eyes betrayed a slight twinkle as he stepped back and opened the door fully. "Lady Leyladin asked that you wait in the right-hand sitting room. Her healing duties at the Tower took somewhat longer than she had thought."

Following Soaris, Cerryl sat down in one of the velvet upholstered armchairs, the one facing the silver-framed picture on the inside wall. This time he had a chance to study the portrait of Leyladin's mother. The smile was warmer than Cerryl remembered and the blonde hair longer and more golden than Leyladin's reddish-tinted hair. The gold threads on the green vest had been carefully reproduced by the artist, so faithfully that even a loose thread near the side pocket showed. The woman's blue eyes held the same common sense and wisdom as her daughter's, but not the laughter.

Had life somehow been hard for Leyladin's mother? Harder than for the daughter? Cerryl wondered, his own eyes meeting those of the painting. After a moment, he looked away, reviewing the elegant furnishings—the settee, the other armchair, the matching cabinets of polished dark wood, and the low inlaid table before him. All were spotless, as if the room were never used—and almost as though it never had been.

The scent in the room was that of Leyladin, light and flowery, with a hint of depth.

After a time, at the sound of leather slippers on the marble of the hall, he turned and stood. "You look beautiful."

"I look tired." A fleeting and crooked smile crossed her lips, erasing for an instant the darkness beneath her eyes.

"You still look beautiful."

"You're kind." In silklike green shirt and trousers, with a heavier but sleeveless vest of purple wool, the healer sat on the green velvet settee and touched the place beside her. "Sit by me . . . please."

"Don't look so serious," he pleaded as he settled beside her.

"I *am* serious. I can't laugh all the time."

Cerryl waited.

"I know you care for me, Cerryl, and I care for you. We keep seeing each other, but we don't say too much. We look like lovers to others, but we don't talk like lovers."

"I thought you didn't want me to," Cerryl said slowly. "I thought, because I'm White and you're Black, we had to be very careful, and I don't want to hurt you."

Leyladin's eyes shimmered, as if she were close to tears. She tightened her lips, then turned so her eyes met his.

Cerryl looked into her eyes, feeling again as if he were falling into their green depths.

"Cerryl."

Although her voice was gentle, he almost jumped. "Yes?" He tried not to look at her so intently. "I'm sorry. Sometimes, I feel like I could get lost in your eyes."

"That sounds like you're trying to be a poet. Or a lancer officer with a maid he's just met." The words were tempered with another smile, a gentle one with a hint of laughter.

Cerryl winced. "That's not what I meant. That's how I feel, but I wasn't trying . . . You're getting . . . when you do that . . . but you don't . . ." He sighed and stopped, finally shrugging. "I can't say what I mean."

"Try it again," she suggested gently. "Just say the words. Don't try to impress me or convince me. Say what you mean."

He swallowed. "I did. I do feel like I could get lost in your eyes. I didn't say it to make you feel anything. It's the way I feel. I don't know how to be a poet. Sometimes, I still feel like I have to watch every word so that I don't sound like a miner or a mill boy."

"That is what makes it so difficult." She looked down. "If only, if only you were not a mage and I a healer."

"We are what we are. Does it matter?" Cerryl reached out and took Leyladin's hand. "I can hold your hand. Do you feel any chaos there? Any burning?"

"That's now," she said quietly. "What about next season? Or next year?"

"I'm doing everything Myral taught me, and you can touch him to heal him."

"Myral isn't my consort."

"White mages can't have consorts," he responded. "You know that."

"But Black healers can," she pointed out.

Cerryl swallowed. "Are you saying, because I'm a White mage . . ." Cerryl swallowed once, then again, feeling his stomach turn in a sickening sense of despair.

"I'm not throwing that at you. I'm not considering becoming anyone else's consort, but whether it's recognized or not, I want that sort of relationship."

Cerryl nodded, wondering how he could ever fill that role. How could she ever consider a mere Patrol mage as anything more than a friend? How could he have hoped for more?

"Cerryl . . . dear one . . . you *are* dear to me."

"More like a friend, I fear," he said hoarsely.

"I would not hug a friend so, nor bestow the lightest of kisses."

"Then . . . ?" He shrugged helplessly.

"I want you, but I want you as though you were my consort. I want you to be able to hold me, no matter what you have done as a mage. I do not want a man who holds chaos and her power as his mistress while he says he is my consort."

Cerryl nodded slowly. With her words he could scarcely argue, yet . . . was what she wanted even possible?

"Don't look so downcast. You've barely over a score of years. We do have time to see if that is what you also wish." She smiled warmly, her green eyes twinkling. "Besides, Meridis has fixed a pork roast, stuffed with apples and spiced bread dressing, just for us. And no quilla."

"Your father? Isn't he here?" For the moment Cerryl was stunned, stunned at Leyladin's directness and stunned at where all that she had said might lead them. He grasped at her father's absence, at anything to give himself some space to let himself take in her earlier words.

"Father remains in Lydiar, making arrangements for his ships." She leaned forward and brushed his cheek with her lips, then rose from the settee. "I'm hungry. Myral was worse, and it took a long time."

"I think the Guild meeting tired him. I talked to him the other night, and he almost fell asleep. It was barely dark."

"He has to sleep so much, these days." She shook her head as she led the way to the dining hall.

The room had two place settings, across from each other at the end toward the kitchen. The rest of the long white golden table shimmered in the lights from the wall lamps as the light from the windows faded with the coming of evening. Cerryl gestured to the white golden oak chair and waited until Leyladin seated herself on the dark green velvet upholstered seat.

Then he sat, careful not to brush the pale white china that rested upon a place mat of light green linen. Following Leyladin's example, he took the green linen napkin and laid it in his lap. Since the amber wine bottle was already uncorked, he filled her fluted crystal goblet, then his own.

Lifting his glass, he said, "To you." *What else can I say?*

"To you, dear one." She lifted her glass in turn.

They both sipped.

The kitchen door opened.

"About time it is . . . Much longer and it'd be dry as dust and as hard as bone." Meridis set two platters on the table, then returned with another. "And there be honey cake for later. Enjoy."

"Thank you," offered Cerryl.

"No thanks to me, but thanks to the lady. Be her wish, only my doing." The gruff words were belied by the broad smile before the cook vanished into the kitchen.

Leyladin took two of the already-sliced sections of roast and stuffing, each covered with a clear apple glaze, then tendered the serving platter to Cerryl. His arm twinged as he took the platter, but he set the serving dish down carefully and served himself.

Leyladin leaned forward and served the cabbage rolls to Cerryl. "I saw that."

"The arm's better. That only happens every so often."

"Likely tale." She flashed a warm grin.

"Most likely."

After another silence that seemed to stretch out, he took a sip of the wine, then offered, "I didn't know your father had ships."

"He has three. He uses them mainly for what he calls long-voyage trading. Prices change too quickly across Candar. He sends the three out for goods that can't come from Candar or Recluce."

Cerryl frowned, trying to think what goods might not come from either, considering that the Black mages could reputedly grow just about anything. "Such as?" he finally asked.

"There are some dyes . . . There's a crimson one that comes from crushed insects that only live in the southern jungles of Hamor and a deep purple one that the Austrans get from some sort of mussel." The blonde took a sip of wine. "And silver, now that the silver mines in Kyphros are worn out. There's a dark wood, like lorken, very rare— that comes from Hamor."

"I think I understand," Cerryl said. "It's like the way he trades, things that others would like that he can get more cheaply with his own ships."

"How do you like the roast?"

"It's good. Would you like some more, before I eat it all?"

"Just one more slice," she said.

Cerryl served her one slice and then took the last two for himself.

"What are we going to do?" he finally asked, after glancing down at a clean platter, surprised not that he had eaten so much, but that he did not feel stuffed. "The two of us?"

"Listen to Myral," she said. "He told me that we shouldn't hurry, not right now, not until you understand how to handle your power better. He told me not to worry." She shook her head. "He's dying, and he told me not to worry."

Cerryl lifted the goblet but did not drink, his eyes on the still-falling white beyond the window. "There's not much other choice, is there?"

"No. I trust Myral. Sometimes . . . he sees things."

Cerryl trusted Myral's sight, but even so, that left the question of what to do about it, and Anya's arguments and Kinowin's counterarguments ran through his mind.

"What are you thinking?"

"Kinowin called it something like Ryba's curse. If you see a vision, and if it's true, how do you make it come true? By doing what you planned to do or doing something different?"

"What did Kinowin say?" asked Leyladin.

"He never answered the question."

"What do you think?" she pursued, fingers loosely circled around the crystal stem of the wine goblet.

"I don't know what to think." He pursed his lips, then let his breath out slowly. "I suppose . . . I suppose you—we—do what we think is best and hope."

"Do you think waiting to become lovers is wrong?"

"No . . . I don't like it, but you and Myral are probably right." *About that, anyway . . .* "I cannot say I am pleased, though."

"Nor I." Leyladin leaned forward so that her hand could reach across the table and grasp his. "But we can be together."

Cerryl nodded slowly, then smiled.

# Colors
# of the
# Guild

# XLIV

Cerryl scripted out the last of his daily report, his eyes running over the hand-written letters whose narrowness Tellis had insisted upon so long ago—at least it seemed so long ago.

A gust of hot wind from the high window that was barely open brushed his hair, and he glanced up. It had been more than a year, more like a year and a season, since he had become a Patrol mage, and he was still on morning duty. Another fall and another harvest was coming in another handful of eight-days, and little had changed. He still walked the streets with the area patrols occasionally, and while peacebreaking had dropped for a time, the number of offenders had seemed unchanged for the past two seasons.

There was still the occasional cart or wagon with goods and driver missing, but no other traces—and while Cerryl had kept personal records, he had not ventured beyond what Fydel would have called "simple peacekeeping." Cerryl had his ideas, but without proof and/or more understanding, his ideas were but ideas. He'd learned early that to those without power patience was a necessity, however little he liked waiting. The incident with the iron arrow had reemphasized that lesson.

That also applied to Leyladin. He and Leyladin saw each other more frequently, but a sense of reserve had built between them, an unspoken wall. Behind everything Cerryl felt forces were building, forces he could not see but certainly could feel.

His eyes went to the Patrol report before him:

> ... Guarl, who is a laborer for the tanner Huyter, stole five loaves of bread from the baker Sidor. Guarl was caught by Duarrl's patrol. Guarl claimed he needed the bread for his consort and children ... given refuse duty for four eight-days ...

Cerryl shook his head—he'd bent the rules on that one, but his truth-read had shown Guarl to be honest and desperate. Afterward, Cerryl had gone to the tanner's and asked Huyter about Guarl. The tanner had said that he had only been able to pay his laborers half their normal pay because he had no coins left. The boot makers were getting their leather from a factor named Kosior, supposedly made from hides from Hydlen, where the maize crop had failed and the late rains had devastated the grasslands earlier parched by the late-summer drought. After a second year of grassland and crop failure, rather than have the cattle starve, Hydlenese farmers had sold many for slaughter, with the meat salted and the hides sold for what they would bring.

"So . . ." Cerryl murmured to himself, "cheap leather comes to Fair-haven, and tanners cannot pay their laborers. The Blacks use their ships to bring cheaper goods to Spidlar and then use the coins to buy scarce grain." He shook his head. "And I keep the simple peace in the south-east sector." He folded the report.

After a moment, he blotted his forehead, then called, "Orial?"

The messenger in red appeared.

"Here's the daily report for the Patrol chief."

"I'm leaving, ser." With a smile, the redhead bowed and scurried out and down the corridor.

Cerryl stood. Gyskas had not arrived yet, since the older mage no longer hurried to relieve Cerryl, an indirect compliment or acceptance, Cerryl supposed.

He walked back and forth in front of the table-desk. Myral had cautioned patience, and so had Leyladin. Having few choices, and none better, Cerryl had been patient.

Jeslek remained High Wizard and had accompanied Eliasar to Fen-ard—and then returned, with a chest of golds from Prefect Syrma. Most of the "honor guard" of White Lancers had also returned, but according to Jeslek's reports at the seasonal Guild meetings, the golds had contin-ued to come from Fenard and Certis. Nothing came from Spidlar but cheaper goods smuggled on back roads, followed by protests that the prefect could not spare the armsmen to patrol every road in the des-mesne of Gallos. Less loud demurrals came from the Viscount of Certis.

Cerryl paused in his pacing as he sensed the rush of chaos that accompanied Gyskas.

"Anything new?" asked the balding older mage, blotting dampness off his high forehead.

"I put a tanner's laborer on the refuse crew."

"Beating a woman?"

"Stole some bread for his family because he wasn't paid."

Gyskas frowned. "That should be road crew."

"I know, but I truth-read him. Child and mother are sick; they don't have enough coins. The tanner can't pay because of the cheap leather from Hydlen." Cerryl shrugged. "I couldn't let him go, but . . ."

"Cerryl, be careful that you don't get in the habit of bending the rules. Especially now. We're going to see more of that." Gyskas took a deep breath. "I still say that whatever Jeslek did in raising those moun-tains changed the weather, and it's hurt the crops and grass. Bread's a copper for two of the big loaves. Ale at four coppers at The Ram?"

"I don't see as many carts in the Market Square, either," Cerryl pointed out.

"They don't want to travel the roads when they can get as much or more in Hydlen or Spidlar."

"Would you?" asked the younger mage.

"Probably not, but this can't go on."

"The High Wizard's waiting until both the wealthy factors and the poor traders see that."

"He's waited long enough." Gyskas walked around the table-desk and pulled out the chair. "I'll see you tomorrow."

"Till tomorrow." Cerryl nodded and left, passing the assembly room before the second shift patrols filed out.

The wind on the street was hot and dry, as always in the height of late summer. Cerryl turned south, toward the Way of the Tanners, eyes and senses studying everything as he moved quickly along one block, then another.

"Afternoon, ser Cerryl!" called the washerwoman who had set her basket on the narrow porch of Esad's—a store of odd items, neither a chandlery nor a miller's market nor a weaver's shop, but a place that held items partaking selectedly of all.

"I hope it has been a good one for you," he answered, not recalling her name but knowing he had seen her in the assembly room a season back for something.

"Some days are good, some bad, but Ikor does not beat me now. The foul words—those he may keep and use." She smiled and lifted the basket.

Cerryl nodded and resumed walking.

When he reached the Way of the Tanners, he turned eastward and continued on for another two blocks until he reached a narrow building with a single window and a wooden boot hung over the doorway. He stepped under the wooden boot over the open entry and into the shop.

The black-haired boot maker at the bench looked up. "Ser Cerryl, your boots were ready the day before yesterday."

"I know. I had to take part of a duty in the northeast section." Cerryl shrugged. Isork had only let Cerryl cover the time until dinner, saying that it wasn't Cerryl's lack of experience, but that he didn't want to overwork anyone. So Cerryl had taken the first part and Klyat the second, while Wascot recovered from a flux from bad food.

"They say there be more peacebreaking there in the past eight-days," offered the boot maker, turning toward the shelf on the wall where rested a pair of white and thick-soled Patrol boots. He lifted the boots off the shoulder-high shelf and turned back to Cerryl. "You keep the peace good here. Fairer 'n most, too."

"I try, Miern."

"That'll be a gold, you know?"

Cerryl extracted a gold and a half-silver from his wallet. "There."

"You need not—"

"Good boots are worth it." Cerryl reached for the boots.

"For that . . . at least . . ." Miern fumbled under the workbench and came out with a worn cloth sack. ". . . don't need this anyway." The boot maker put the boots in the gray sack, splotched with faded patches nearly white, and extended the sack.

"Thank you."

"Got to take care of those who pay in these days." Miern smiled.

"Is it that bad for you? Someone told me that leather is getting cheaper," Cerryl ventured.

"Cow leather," Miern affirmed. "I make my boots, the sturdy ones, from bull leather. Don't care for that cheap leather from Hydlen. One thing that Beykr and I agree on."

The Patrol mage had to grin. "I didn't know as you agreed on anything."

"Precious little, ser mage. Precious little."

"Thank you, Miern," Cerryl said again.

"Thanks be to you, ser mage."

Cerryl stepped out onto the walk that flanked the Way of the Tanners and turned westward, toward the White Tower and the Halls of the Mages.

Ahead of him, he could see clouds building and darkening. He hoped the storms weren't too bad. With harvest hardly begun, a heavy storm could ruin much of the wheat corn, and that would only lead to higher prices, prices that had continued to rise since the previous winter, driving up the price of bread and, unhappily for him, the amount of small theft, even if other forms of peacebreaking seemed to be declining in his section.

Leyladin was waiting in the fountain court at the Halls of the Mages, as she did when she could.

Cerryl couldn't help smiling, and smiling more broadly when she smiled back. "You still make me smile."

"Good. You weren't here yesterday or the day before. I was afraid I'd done something."

"No. Wascot was sick, and I had to take the first part of his afternoon duty. Isork took the second part one night, and Huroan did last night, but it was late when I got back." He paused. "You have something to tell me? What's wrong?"

"It's not that bad. The High Wizard has requested I go back to Hydlen. The young duke is ailing, and Gorsuch suspects all is not well."

Cerryl frowned. "That sounds like a different turn on an old tale."

"I think as much, also."

Neither needed to spell it out. The old Duke, Berofar, had died just after Leyladin had been there to care for his son Uulrac, and both Cerryl and Leyladin had suspected Gorsuch, as the Guild representative to Hydlen, had not been uninvolved. Yet now Gorsuch was practically demanding Leyladin return.

Cerryl nodded. Of course, an underage ruler needed a regent. If the boy died, then one of his older cousins would become duke and Gorsuch would return to being an adviser, if that, and Jeslek would have to contend with a more independent duke who probably had no love of Fairhaven. "Uulrac's six?"

"Something like that."

"When do you leave?"

"Tomorrow morning."

That didn't surprise Cerryl much, either. "Perhaps you should move to Hydolar and I should petition to become Gorsuch's assistant."

"You have to stay here."

"Why? Myral's visions?" *Why does she keep bringing them up? . . . I'm no Jeslek, or even a Kinowin.*

"And other things," she replied obliquely. "Can you join me and Father for an early dinner?"

"I'd be happy to, and even happier were you able to invite me for tomorrow."

"Perhaps you could come as soon as you wash up. Then we could talk."

"I will hurry." Cerryl bowed.

"So will I." She squeezed his hand.

Cerryl strode quickly to his room, where he stripped to little more than smallclothes, and marched to the bathing room. The cold water felt good, even for shaving.

Back in his quarters, still stripped to the waist as he dried and changed, Cerryl's eyes went to the scar across his shoulder—barely a thin white line, yet it had been a wide red welt. Had it healed so well because of Leyladin's continual presence?

And now she was headed off, just as matters seemed to be getting worse throughout Candar. Hydolar . . . again?

He shook his head and donned a clean white shirt, then a crimson-trimmed sleeveless white tunic and the red patroller's belt. Some of the Patrol mages didn't wear the red belts, but the belt felt right to Cerryl.

He hurried down the corridor and out of the Halls, nodding to a few that he passed—Myredin and Bealtur and Disarj. He saw Redark from behind, but since the overmage didn't turn, Cerryl didn't feel as though he had to acknowledge the High Council member.

After stopping for a moment on the shaded walk outside Leyladin's to catch his breath and to cool off, Cerryl knocked firmly.

Soaris opened the carved and polished door for Cerryl and bowed. "Good afternoon, ser Cerryl."

"Good afternoon, Soaris." Cerryl found the coolness of the house was refreshing as he stepped through the foyer and into the marble-tiled entry hall.

"I'm in here, Cerryl." Leyladin waited, on the settee before the portrait of her mother.

Cerryl's eyes went from daughter to mother and back again before he sat down beside the blonde healer. "How are you feeling? You look very serious."

"I talked to Myral this morning."

Cerryl waited.

"He doesn't think he'll see the end of the troubles ahead."

"We're likely to have troubles for many years," Cerryl pointed out. "That's what I see, and that could be a long time. He could be around for years."

"Cerryl. He's getting weaker."

"You're worried that if you go . . . but if you stayed . . . ?"

She nodded. "He might survive, and I don't know that's what Jeslek wants."

"Jeslek has a problem. If Uulrac dies, things can't help but get worse in Hydlen. If Myral dies, some will say that Jeslek invented Uulrac's illness." He paused. "Do you think . . . ?"

"No. Jeslek *is* worried about the boy. But he also doesn't care much for Myral. If Myral dies, who will speak out?"

"I will."

"You do already, but the older mages don't listen, except for Kinowin and a few of the Patrol types."

Cerryl patted Leyladin on the knee, mostly because he had no idea what he could do or say.

She sighed. "Usually there have been more than one or two Black healers in Fairhaven, but the numbers are fewer and fewer."

"They go to Recluce?" Cerryl frowned. "There was a Black healer that came through here last year."

"One of their exiles or pilgrims? Even if we could find him, he couldn't take Fairhaven. Sometimes I even get headaches so bad that I can't see, and I was born here."

"You haven't told me that . . . I've never sensed . . ."

"I've not let anyone see that." She turned directly to him. "How could I let any word of that get to Jeslek?"

"Maybe it's better for you to go to Hydolar."

"It's not better for Myral or you."

"I'll be fine. I can look in on Myral."

"You will, won't you?"

"I promise. I'm not a healer, but I'll let you know by messenger if you're needed."

"If he gets really sick, and Uulrac's not too bad . . ."

Cerryl nodded, not knowing for what he hoped.

"So how are the two not-quite lovers?" boomed Layel from the entry hall.

"Just talking, Father." Leyladin's voice was cheerful, with a forced spirit Cerryl could sense was painful.

"Are you two ready to eat? Been a long day at the Exchange, and I'm starved."

"If you would tell Meridis, Father, we'll be right there."

"That I can do, Daughter. That I can." With a loud chuckle, Layel left the entry hall.

"You have to be careful, Cerryl. More cautious than ever before."

"I know."

Leyladin stood. "Father will be calling again if we don't get to the dining hall." She grinned. "Food is almost as important as trade to him."

"Almost?" Cerryl raised his eyebrows as he took Leyladin's arm.

"Sometimes, it's more important."

They walked from the sitting room to the dining hall, where Layel stood behind the head chair.

"Good! We can eat." The factor seated himself, as did the others, Cerryl waiting slightly for Leyladin.

No sooner than the three were seated did Meridis appear with a large steep-sided china bowl that she set before Layel.

"Meridis? What might this be?"

"Fowl casserole, ser."

"Fowl casserole? That be a dinner?" Layel glanced at Meridis.

"Begging your pardon, Master Layel, but all the beef is tough and stringy, and so are the fowl in the market. Stewed and with wine and spices and cheese, and even the broad mushrooms . . ."

Layel lifted his hands. "You did the best you could, and for that I am grateful."

Meridis returned to the kitchen and came back with another platter, which she set before Layel. "Quilla, as you wished."

"That is better." A broad smile crossed the factor's face.

Standing behind Layel, Meridis rolled her eyes, then set the bread platter before Leyladin, before again retreating to the kitchen.

"You said it was a long day at the Exchange?" Cerryl said as he poured the white wine from the clear bottle into the factor's goblet.

"Yes . . . ah, thank you."

"Why might it have been so long?" Leyladin asked, her eyes twinkling.

"Grain prices . . . they go up, and then down a little, and then up . . . Recluce is buying more grain in Sarronnyn. That means—" Layel eased half the quilla on the platter onto his own plate, then glanced at Leyladin. "You won't be eating this, I know."

"Recluce is buying more grain," Cerryl prompted.

"There isn't enough left to ship to Hydlen at the old price, and that means that grain prices, and the prices of flour and bread, will rise all through the fall and winter, even until next harvest, perchance. Ah . . . would that I had seen it earlier. Saw it early enough for a modest gain, but, oh, had I seen it far earlier." The factor shook his head and spooned out a moderate helping of the casserole, his nose wrinkling slightly.

After Leyladin served herself, Cerryl took a modest helping, as well as bread and but a small serving of quilla, a serving he hoped he could eat without merely choking it down. He started with the casserole and found himself taking another bite. "This is good."

"Meridis makes a good casserole . . . when Father lets her."

"A man's food is meat untainted with all such delicacies, or where such delicacies add to the flavor and do not bury it," Layel mumbled through a mouthful of quilla.

"I often prefer the delicacies," Leyladin said.

"I like both," Cerryl confessed—truthfully, since he'd had little enough of either growing up.

"Spoken like a mage." Layel laughed.

"He *is* a mage, a very good mage." Leyladin took a sip of wine.

"I work at it."

"Everything takes work. Trading does."

"How did you get started being a factor?" Cerryl asked.

"Long time ago . . . my father, he was a cloth merchant, one step above a weaver, and I asked myself, 'If Da is a merchant, why can't I be a factor?' I went to the Market Square and watched what people bought and what they paid . . . and when they bought, and I saved every copper until I could go to the weavers in the late spring, for that is when times were the worst, and buy all that I could, and I saved it until after harvest . . ."

Cerryl and Leyladin listened as Layel spun out his tale of rising from the son of a cloth merchant to a powerful factor. Layel barely paused when Meridis cleared the empty dishes and returned with three cups of egg custard.

"Egg custard?"

"You told me to take care with the honey and the molasses, that they would be hard to come by in the seasons ahead," answered the cook.

"So I did. So I did. Egg custard. There's worse. There's no custard, and no eggs," mused Layel. "And, you know, there were times like that. Bought my first coaster . . . and lost her on the second voyage . . . Folk said I was failed. They were wrong . . ."

Leyladin smiled at Cerryl.

He smiled back.

". . . wrong 'cause I had coins saved, not enough for another ship, not then, but I took a share in an Austran spice trader that ran the Black

Isle leg—can't do that now . . . no, you can't. Can't do this, and can't do that . . . world's not the same now, not by a long bolt . . ."

Later, when the lamps cast all the light in the house and in the front foyer, Leyladin and Cerryl stood by the door.

"I'm sorry it's so late," Leyladin apologized. "Father, he was so pleased to be able to tell someone how he got to be a factor. You have to get up early."

"So do you. I don't have to ride to Hydolar." Cerryl wrapped his arms around Leyladin, ignoring her wish for an almost chaste hug for just a moment before releasing her. "Be careful, very careful." *Myral doesn't have any visions about you, Leyladin.* He concealed a wince at the thought that he might be accepting what Myral had said.

"I'll be fine."

"Make sure that you are," he insisted.

"You take care of yourself, and watch out for Jeslek and Anya." For the first time, her lips met his, warm—and loving. "And keep doing what Myral told you . . . I want to be able to kiss you again."

*So do I.* Cerryl held her for a long time, without speaking.


# XLV

Cerryl paused at the top landing of the White Tower, wondering again why, after more than a year of ignoring Cerryl, Jeslek had summoned him.

Hertyl was the guard outside the High Wizard's chamber, and he nodded at Cerryl, then opened the door. Cerryl nodded back and stepped into the chambers of the High Wizard. Behind him, the door closed with an ominous *thud.*

Jeslek's white hair shimmered, and his sun-gold eyes yet glittered out of the youthful face. He gestured to the chair by the table that held the screeing glass, a glass that had been recently used, Cerryl knew, from the residual chaos that swirled unseen around it.

"Please have a seat, Cerryl."

"Thank you, ser." Cerryl noted the rain running down the thick glass of the tower windows, a warm rain, but still unwelcome for the steam that would cloak the city later—and his headache.

"Mock politeness does not become you or any mage, Cerryl, except upon ceremonial occasions." Jeslek took the chair across the table. His eyes bored into the younger mage. "There is little point in wasting time with evasions and maneuvers. I do not care for, shall we say, your careful approach to handling chaos. You do not care for my use of chaos

on a massive scale. We both, however, wish that Fairhaven prosper."
The High Wizard paused.

"That is true."

"You cannot, or will not, raise chaos in huge measure. You have
shields strong enough to withstand that amount of chaos. Thus, I cannot
destroy you with chaos, nor you me. You cannot lead Fairhaven, but,
young as you are, you could keep it from being led."

Cerryl detected a certain amount of untruth in Jeslek's words but
merely nodded that he had heard what the High Wizard said. Cerryl
glanced in the direction of the toy on the shelf, a detailed miniature of
a windmill with a small black iron crank. His eyes opened—black iron,
bursting with order. Yet the toy, or model, or whatever it was, had been
finely detailed, so finely that it looked as though it could pump water.

"Oh, that? A small part of the problem in Spidlar, one you as a
Patrol mage need not concern yourself with. Not at present." Jeslek
flashed a smile.

"Black mages in Spidlar?"

"As of now, there are three Blacks in Spidlar, Cerryl, a smith and
two armsmen. There may be a Black healer as well. It is strange. We
have all this difficulty with Spidlar, and there are all these Blacks there.
It's not your concern, but it will be discussed at the next Guild meeting."
Jeslek smiled. "The smith's name is Dorrin, not that it should concern
you, but . . . I will satisfy your curiosity. This time."

"Yes, ser." Cerryl took his eyes from the model, but the amount of
order concentrated in it bothered him, disturbing him almost as much
as had there been an equal amount of chaos focused there. A smith
named Dorrin? A Black smith? Why had Jeslek mentioned the name?
To see if Cerryl knew?

"You do not know this smith's name?"

"No, ser." Cerryl repressed a frown.

"That, at least, is to your benefit." Jeslek paused. "Now . . . do you
wish to stand in my way?"

"No. I still have much to learn."

"Ah . . . you remain the honest mage." Jeslek laughed. "And you
have avoided Anya's bed."

"That seemed best, given my youth."

"How do you find the Patrol?"

"I continue to learn, especially about Fairhaven, and I find that
good, for I was not raised here."

"That is good for any mage, even those raised here." Jeslek's eyes
glittered momentarily. "You follow Myral too closely, Cerryl."

"Myral? I respect his understanding."

"His understanding—with that I have no quibble." The High Wizard smiled lazily. "Few mages have understood so much as Myral. Yet
few have been so frozen into inaction by such understanding. Myral is

too cautious. There is a time to strike and a time to wait. Myral would always wait."

"He is cautious," Cerryl temporized. "You feel it is time to strike."

Jeslek nodded abruptly. "If we do not show that Fairhaven is to be feared, and not just respected, the rulers of eastern Candar will ignore every White mage in their courts."

"Is that really why you raised the Little Easthorns?"

"Is that what they're calling them? Diminishing me by calling them little?"

"To divide Gallos," Cerryl continued, as if he had not heard Jeslek's comment. "It's too big to hold together with a mountain range down the middle."

"Have you seen the Market Square, Cerryl? Each eight-day there are fewer traders there. Do you know why? Because goods are short, and they can obtain more in Hydlen or Kyphros, and they do not have to pay the road taxes. After years of benefiting from our roads and efforts, they turn away, and the rulers in some other lands encourage them. Some would change the rulers in other lands."

"As in Hydlen?"

"Or Gallos. Even after my visit with Eliasar and the creation of the chaos mountains, the Gallosian merchants bridle. They would forget the years they benefited from the White highways and reject their just debts."

"That will happen, ser," Cerryl suggested, "unless they are compelled otherwise."

"What do you suggest, then, O wise young mage?"

"You have far greater experience. I cannot suggest. I only know that most men respond to swords or silvers or chaos, not to words. We cannot raise enough golds, not now."

Jeslek's sun-gold eyes meet the pale gray ones of the younger mage, surveying him deliberately. "Did you know that matters in Spidlar are getting worse? I understand that brigands ride every back road."

"I had not heard that. I cannot say I am surprised. It would be to our interest that brigands be found there."

"Do you know that, since Spidlar refuses to act, the Viscount of Certis sent forces to control them?"

"I take it that his efforts have been less than totally successful."

Jeslek's eyes glittered more intently, and Cerryl wondered if he had presumed too much.

*Probably . . . but you can't back down.*

"You could be dangerous, Cerryl, if you weren't a disciple of Myral's."

"You know I don't have the kind of chaos power you do."

"I know that you have never raised such power. I know that you do not wish to do so." Jeslek raised his eyebrows. "You avoid using chaos more than you have to. That is wise, assuming you retain the ability to wield it when you have no choice. Ah, yes, young Cerryl, there will be a time when you have no alternative but to raise chaos in force." A twisted smile crossed the High Wizard's face, and his fingers touched the amulet that hung around his neck. "That is where Myral and even Kinowin are mistaken. But you need not listen to me. Just watch."

"I will," Cerryl said quietly.

"I know you will." With another smile, Jeslek rose. "I trust you will continue your hard work with the Patrol."

"I plan to, ser."

"No mock politeness, Cerryl."

"You are the High Wizard." *And the office deserves respect.*

"You are wise to remember that." Jeslek gestured toward the door. "I will see you again when the time is ready. It may not be that long. You do have certain . . . skills . . . the Guild may need."

"I stand ready to assist the Guild."

"Good."

Cerryl inclined his head, then turned and left, his senses and shields ready. Outside, when Hertyl closed the door, Cerryl took a silent but slow, deep breath. *What did he want? To tell me he knew I could withstand his chaos? To warn me? To test me? And why did he ask about the smith?*

Cerryl wanted to shake his head as he went down the steps. Jeslek was very different from Sterol, very different, but then he'd known that since he had been an apprentice mage. Cerryl only wished he understood more of what he knew existed but could not see.

Outside, the rain splattered on the Tower, and on the steps Cerryl rubbed his aching head. His eyes flicked southward, in the general direction of Hydolar, and he took a deep breath and continued down the stone steps toward the entry Hall.

# XLVI

Cerryl was trudging the last few cubits toward his room when a blond figure appeared in the corridor.

"I'm going to eat in. Do you want to join me?" asked Faltar.

"Eating in?" Cerryl raised his eyebrows. "Have I heard your words?"

"The Golden Ram—everywhere—the prices are higher, and my stipend is but a gold an eight-day. I had to get new boots, and I couldn't believe how much more they cost this time . . ." Faltar shook his head.

Cerryl glanced down. "They look good. Where did you get them?"

"From Beykr, down on the Way of the Tanners."

The smaller mage laughed. "I get mine from Miern. He's a block farther east. The boot soles and heels are thicker and a good two silvers cheaper, maybe more. I've been told they fit better, too."

"Now you tell me."

"You didn't ask." Cerryl grinned. "I'll go with you. Leyladin's still in Hydolar, and my stipend doesn't go so far, either. I wear out boots faster on Patrol duty."

"You still walking the streets?"

"I don't know the city well enough, not by far. I wasn't born here, remember. Wait a moment, and let me wash up."

Faltar leaned against the stone wall of the corridor. "Try to hurry. I'm hungry and I might lose the courage to face the Meal Hall."

"Courage doesn't matter if you have no coins to eat elsewhere. I'll hurry." Since his own gut was growling, Cerryl washed quickly.

Faltar was still leaning against the wall when Cerryl emerged from his room. "Good."

The two walked down the steps to the main level and across the rear courtyard.

"How's gate duty going?"

"Boring," admitted Faltar. "Always the same. Most of the owners of the wagons and carts are honest, but there's always someone who thinks we can't find oils or spices or silver. I don't understand. The cost of a full-trade medallion isn't that high."

"The problem's not here, I think," mused Cerryl. "Fairhaven isn't the only land—or city—that levies taxes, and you can't remove a medallion and then replace it. Not without the gate mages sensing it."

"Oh . . . that means two wagons and a place to keep them?"

"More than that. The big factors do that all the time. Why do you think the wagons we see here are always so clean? The carpet merchants, on the other hand, they apply for a new medallion every time they come."

Faltar nodded. "I knew that, but I hadn't thought about why."

"They only come once or twice a year, and an extra two golds is cheaper than two wagons." Cerryl frowned. *Do they wait when they remove the medallions, or does someone get hurt?*

Faltar sniffed as they entered the Meal Hall. "It's not lamb. I can smell that."

"Stew—with dried beef." Cerryl stepped toward the serving table.

"Sorry, ser." An apprentice scuttled out of the way.

"Go ahead." Cerryl laughed, gesturing to the table. "We've time."

"Thank you, ser." The apprentice scurried to ladle stew across the bread on his platter, then grabbed another chunk, before pouring a mug of ale from the battered gray pitcher.

"Not much better than sauced mutton."

"I'd prefer the mutton," Cerryl said, ladling the lumpy brownish mixture across a chunk of bread.

"Never," said Faltar.

Cerryl half-smiled and poured a mug of the ale, then made his way to one of the smaller side tables. In the corner he saw Kochar and Kiella, both redheads eating slowly and talking. Before long, Kochar would be a full mage, Cerryl thought, if he didn't do something at the last moment to upset Jeslek. He couldn't say that he knew the handful of other student mages—there seemed to be fewer than when he and Faltar had been students.

". . . say he's a Patrol mage . . ."

". . . don't know the other one . . ."

The words drifted from one of the circular center tables. Cerryl smiled to himself. As a student, he'd never known by name the younger full mages. He wouldn't be responsible for an apprentice for years, if ever, and he ate at the Meal Hall infrequently and quickly. It might be more often if the costs of food in Fairhaven kept increasing, though.

Faltar slid into the chair across from Cerryl and took a mouthful of stew. He frowned. "You might be right. I never thought lamb could be better than *anything.*"

"You see fewer traders through the gates now?" Cerryl took a mouthful of the tough rye bread, then finally tried the stew. His mouth puckered with the saltiness, and he reached for the ale.

"I don't see as many as last year, even in the winter. There aren't as many people on the roads, except for lancers. More are headed west."

"Gallos?"

Faltar shook his head, his mouth full. After swallowing, he answered, "Certis."

That made sense, in a way, because Jeslek had more control over Viscount Rystryr. "Jeslek saw me yesterday."

"What did he want? You're not his favorite."

"To make sure I wouldn't cross him."

"Why do you worry him?" asked Faltar, making a face at the mouthful of stew he swallowed. "Bitter . . . too salty."

"He's worried about Spidlar," answered Cerryl, ignoring the thrust of Faltar's question. "That's what he told me. He as much as said that the viscount is raiding Spidlar and losing armsmen. He thinks Spidlar is getting support from Recluce."

"That won't set well with the Guild. It sounds like the viscount wants Spidlar for himself. What is our High Wizard going to do?"

"He didn't say, except it didn't matter for a Patrol mage. Not yet."

"Good of him," mumbled Faltar. "This isn't stew. It's swill."

"It's better than that. I know."

"Don't remind me. I'm glad I didn't have to find the Guild the way you did." Faltar spooned in another mouthful. "I'd be careful. That 'not yet' sounds like he's thinking up something special for you. He's never liked you since you forced Sterol to override him and let you become a full mage."

"You're in a hurry," Cerryl observed. "You have plans for this evening?"

"Maybe." Faltar flushed.

"A certain redheaded mage?"

"No more than you're interested in a certain blonde healer."

Cerryl laughed. "There may be more compatibility between two Whites."

"Is that still a problem?"

"I understand it's always been a problem, unless approached carefully. Leyladin is very careful, and I cannot say I fault her."

"Cerryl the methodical."

Cerryl shrugged.

Faltar swallowed the last of his stew, then chewed a final mouthful of bread, washing it down with a swig of ale. "You don't mind if I go . . . ?"

"Go. I've no one to get ready for, and I'd rather not gulp this down." With a nod, Faltar rose and slipped away.

Cerryl looked across the now mostly empty Meal Hall. He liked Faltar, but he was so besotted with Anya that what Cerryl could mention to him was limited. Cerryl took another small mouthful of bread, wondering how Leyladin was doing, hoping she had been successful in healing young Uulrac and that she would be back before too long. Somehow, he doubted it would be either simple or quick. Nothing seemed to be, not involving the Guild.

Finally, he stood and walked toward the corridor toward the front Hall of the Mages. He could walk up the Avenue in the twilight.

Cerryl paused at the edge of the fountain courtyard, where two figures stood in the shadows beyond the fountain in the far corner, shielded by darkness and spray. Their postures bothered him, and he cast forth his perceptions, as gently and dispersed as possible. At the same time, he used his skills to blur over his chaos-order image, so that unless another mage looked right at him with concentration, he wouldn't even seem to be there.

"You sleep with whoever grants you power for the moment," said the taller figure.

"You fawn over whoever grants you favor, Fydel. Tell me there's a difference. You prefer to sleep with me, but you certainly don't sleep alone much," Anya replied.

"That's different. You make Jeslek think he's the only chaos focus since Cyador, and now every little thing in Spidlar has him feeling personally slighted. He almost killed me over that black toy."

"You kept it from him for a season, and the letters from the smith to the lady trader. That was not wise, Fydel. Don't blame me or Jeslek for your stupidity."

"Do you *want* Jeslek spewing chaos all over Candar?"

"He already has, and he intends to bring all the lands of eastern Candar under Fairhaven. After the way they're treating the Guild, do you blame him? Do you want your stipend cut?" Anya moved closer to Fydel. "I know this is a hard time." She touched his face. "I won't be owned, Fydel, but I will make it up to you. Not tonight. Later."

Cerryl eased away before the two realized he had been using his chaos-order senses to spy.

Slowly, his thoughts swirling, he walked back to his empty room, all idea of walking up the Avenue discarded. What had he been missing in his efforts to become the best possible Patrol mage? What was really going on in the Guild and with Spidlar? Black iron so strong it warped the feeling in the High Wizard's room? Made by a Black smith who wrote letters that Fydel had kept from Jeslek. No wonder Jeslek had let the smith's name drop—Dorrin, was it? To see if Cerryl were plotting with Fydel?

Cerryl swallowed.

That didn't even take into account that the Black smith was tied up with a lady trader—and there were lady traders? Were traders involved in everything? Blacks settling in Spidlar? Certan forces raiding Spidlar? And he'd seen none of it?

He shook his head. What could he do? What should he do? What could a junior Patrol mage do?

He wished Leyladin were back. He needed someone to talk to, someone who understood more than he did and someone whom he could trust.

# XLVII

Cerryl glanced across the Avenue at the main entrance to the Halls of the Mages, silhouetted against the late-afternoon sun, and then at the White Tower, his eyes studying the outside of the topmost floor, the apartment of the High Wizard. Was more chaos swirling around the tower, or was he just becoming increasingly sensitive to chaos?

He crossed the eastern section of the Avenue, ahead of a slow-moving and empty green-trimmed wagon drawn by a pair of matched grays, then continued across the south side of the square and across the empty western half of the Avenue.

Another day of being a Patrol mage, another day of dealing with petty theft of bread, a barrel of flour—and in neither case had the Patrol found the thief, or thieves. No one had seen anything, and by the time Fystl had gotten Cerryl to the shop, somehow all those who might have seen anything had vanished. That bothered Cerryl. So did the slight but slow increase in such peacebreaking.

He blotted his damp forehead as he entered the cool stone walls of the front foyer, glancing ahead to his left, toward the empty steps to the White Tower. Once through the foyer, he crossed the fountain courtyard, grateful for the cooling mist of the fountain, and made his way through the middle Hall, past two apprentice mages he did not know, and into the rear courtyard.

"Cerryl?" Anya stood in the shade by the arched entryway to the rear Hall.

"Anya . . . greetings."

"How was your day, Cerryl? Do you remain as fond of being a Patrol mage as you were a year ago?"

"I do." Cerryl paused, then added quickly, "You know, I've never asked exactly what you do. I mean, Faltar guards gates; I'm a Patrol mage; Esaak teaches mathematicks." He shrugged. "You seem most talented and yet . . . mysterious."

"I'm only mysterious because I'm a woman and no one asks a woman what she does. Right now, I'm an assistant to the High Wizard. I used to teach knife fighting to the lancer officers, and before that I was the assistant mage for the water aqueducts." A bright smile crossed Anya's creamy-complected face.

"Much more impressive than being a Patrol mage, I must admit." Cerryl's eyes went to the battered sheath at Anya's waist. Somehow, the knife belonged there, unfortunately. "How might I be of service?"

"You really shouldn't use that phrase, Cerryl." Anya smiled crookedly. "Actually, I just wished to talk to you for a moment."

Cerryl managed not to flush. "You always bear interesting views."

"I am glad you think so."

"I do."

"Good." The smile returned, the one Cerryl distrusted thoroughly. "I am sure you know how difficult matters in Spidlar and Gallos are getting."

"I had heard that, but matters here in Fairhaven are not so good as they might be, either. Nor in Hydlen."

"You are having difficulty in your Patrol section?" asked Anya.

"Less trouble than most." *But I spend more time working at it.*

"That surprises me not, Cerryl, nor the High Wizard." She paused. "You also know that Myral is ailing, and that Kinowin is not so young as he might appear."

"I have heard such."

"Fairhaven has not mustered all its lancers in generations, and those who have seen battle are either few or old."

Cerryl nodded, not enjoying the implications. "Eliasar has experience, much experience."

"Eliasar will offer all he has. It might not reflect well on those others who have even limited experience, should they avoid using that experience when it is needed."

"I can see that."

"Good. I hope you learn much more about peacekeeping in the few eight-days ahead. I trust I haven't kept you."

"Ah . . . no. Not at all."

"Good afternoon, Cerryl." Anya flashed a last deceitfully honest-looking smile, then inclined her head and slipped past Cerryl and toward the middle Hall, leaving behind the heavy scents of sandalwood and trilia.

Cerryl pursed his lips, then entered the rear Hall and made for the steps to the upper level. He had barely entered his room and seated himself on the edge of the bed when there was a *thrap* on the door.

"Yes?"

"It's Lyasa. May I come in?"

"Come on in." Cerryl rose to his feet to greet the black-haired mage. "I see that Anya had something to say."

"I see that you're looking out for my interests." Cerryl grinned and gestured to the chair.

"I don't know about yours. Leyladin is my friend. What did Anya want this time?"

"To warn me without being obvious about it."

"About what?"

"That Jeslek is going to ask me to go with him to take over Spidlar, perhaps reduce some of it to rubble, and that it would be bad for my future, and probably my health, to refuse."

"I cannot imagine that going on a war campaign to Spidlar and Gallos would be very healthful."

"They may ask you as well," mused Cerryl. "Anya mentioned that few mages had any experience in battle, and you were with us in Gallos. You're strong with chaos."

"Not so strong as you or Anya." A frown crossed Lyasa's face, and darkness settled in the deep brown eyes. Then she smiled. "But I could definitely keep a watch on you that way."

"You certainly could."

"Nothing's going to happen soon. If they aren't bringing in wagons and extra mounts now, they can't be ready before late fall or early winter. Jeslek would be a fool to mount a campaign before spring, and he's no fool."

"He's not a fool, but he doesn't always do what others expect."

"Have you heard from Leyladin?"

Cerryl shook his head.

"You could scree her, you know?"

"I don't know. That feels a bit like . . . peeping."

A grin flashed across Lyasa's face. "Good for you. But she wouldn't mind a quick look in the day or afternoon, I suspect. It would show you care." The black-haired woman rose from the chair. "I'm supposed to meet with Kinowin, something about aqueducts."

"Better than sewers."

"I'll see."

After Lyasa left; Cerryl stood and looked at the glass on his desk. Where should be begin? What was he looking for? And why? *Because nothing's quite right and you need the practice because you've been neglecting screeing.*

Finally, he sat down and studied the glass.

Could he see Leyladin, as Lyasa had suggested?

He concentrated on finding order, the solid black order he equated with her. He felt two pulls, amid smaller pulses of order. He settled for the stronger sense of order and let his mind focus on order, solid black order.

The silver mists filling the glass before him parted, more easily than he recalled, showing a red-haired man with a hammer in his hands, working an anvil. Order seemed to well from the glass.

Was this the smith Jeslek had mentioned? Was he the same one Anya had talked to Fydel about? The one tied up with a woman trader? Cerryl doubted there could be any other embodying such order, yet the red-haired smith didn't seem either much younger or older than Cerryl himself.

If possible, the smith embodied order as much as Jeslek did chaos.

Cerryl watched the even rhythm of the hammer for a time, then released the image, realizing belatedly that sweat poured down his face.

After a time, he tried the glass again and was rewarded with an image of a blonde healer sitting across a table from a brown-haired boy with a face too thin for his age and eyes sunken too deep below fine eyebrows.

Leyladin looked healthy, but Cerryl worried about her charge and what that could mean for Fairhaven—and Leyladin and him.

Slowly, he let the image slip away. He sat at the desk for a time, a long time.

# XLVIII

Cerryl studied the screeing glass, knowing he should practice more. He didn't want to try to look at Leyladin too often. He knew that would upset her because she could probably sense his efforts. After all, she had sensed his first attempt when he was a youth, and Cerryl himself could tell when someone was using a glass to capture his image.

He frowned. Did the young Black smith know he was being observed? How could he not? That brought up another question. Jeslek had insisted there were three Blacks in Spidlar, but Cerryl had only been able to use the glass to find the smith. That meant the other two didn't marshal nearly the order that either the smith or Leyladin did. So why was Jeslek so concerned? Were they better arms commanders than those of Certis or Fairhaven? Cerryl had no way of determining that and enough more immediate worries—such as Leyladin and Patrol duty. His duty hadn't been quite so bad for the past two days, perhaps because he'd been spending more time on the streets again. How long could he do that? It made it more difficult for all the area patrols he didn't accompany to find him, and it wasn't fair to them for him to be out of the building too long. Yet his being on the street definitely reduced even the minor peacebreaking.

He took a deep breath and looked toward the window, where the afternoon light and a warm breeze poured into the room. Then he looked down at the glass again.

*Thrap.*

For practice, Cerryl concentrated on the glass, attempting to see who stood on the other side of the white oak door. As the mists parted, the image of a messenger in red appeared, a round-faced girl who was new, at least to Cerryl.

He let the image lapse and stood, quickly walking to the door and opening it. "Yes?"

"Mage Cerryl, ser?"

"That's me."

"The overmage Kinowin bids you come immediately. He wants you to hurry. He will meet you at the mage Myral's quarters as soon as you can get there."

Cerryl swallowed, then stepped out of the room and closed the door. "Thank you!" he called over his shoulder as he began to hurry toward the stairs, not quite at a run.

He dodged around Kiella entering the fountain court and almost ran down another apprentice in the front foyer. Cerryl slowed his pace as he neared the steps to the tower. It wouldn't do any good for him to race up to Myral's and arrive so out of breath that all he could do would be to stand and pant.

He was still slightly breathless when Kinowin opened Myral's door.

"I'm glad you hurried," the overmage whispered. "Cerryl's here," he added in a louder voice as he closed the door.

Myral lay on his bed, wearing a white robe, one so heavy that Cerryl would have sweated to death, yet the older mage had a blanket over him and shivered as Cerryl neared the bed.

"Glad . . . you came." The words were barely audible.

Cerryl knelt on the floor by the bed, letting his fingers touch Myral's all too pale forehead. Cerryl kept his face composed and concerned, with a superficial calmness he hung onto as necessary for the moment. Cerryl struggled to try to raise order, as he did chaos, outside himself, and to impose that flickering black fragment on the flux that was ravaging Myral.

"Helps . . . a little . . . for a few moments . . . know . . . there's too much chaos in my body. Before long . . ." Myral gasped. "For a White mage, it has been a good life."

"Just relax," Cerryl said quietly.

"I hoped for you . . . did not tell . . . the truth . . ." Another series of gasps followed. "None . . . none . . . since Cyador . . . hold chaos light like you could have . . . did not want . . . tell you . . ."

"I know . . . I found out."

"So . . . sorry . . . sad to see you lose . . . that . . ."

Cerryl touched Myral's shoulder. "Everything has worked out. Please don't worry."

". . . still worry."

Cerryl glanced toward the door, then bent toward Myral's ear, whispering low. "Chaos light can be shielded. Don't worry, old friend and mentor."

"Yes." A smile crossed the older mage's face as Cerryl eased his lips from Myral's ear, a smile that faded under another attack of coughing.

Cerryl could sense that Myral's entire body pulsed with the unseen deep and angry red of a chaos flux, and but a few dark threads of order bound that chaos, threads that he had strengthened momentarily, yet they had frayed almost immediately.

Myral coughed another time, then seemed to convulse, then slumped back onto the bed.

Even as Cerryl watched, wide-eyed, sparkles of chaos flared, and the body of the older mage collapsed into dust, and even the dust seemed to sift into nothingness.

"From chaos and unto chaos," murmured Kinowin, "that is from whence we come and where we go, for unto none is given the everlasting light of the eternal sun of chaos." His voice broke on the last words, and he turned toward the closed and shuttered window.

Cerryl stood slowly.

In time, Kinowin turned.

"Even for him, there was too much chaos at the end," Cerryl said. "I couldn't do any more. I don't know how."

"You know more than you admit," said Kinowin quietly. "The healer?"

"I've watched her. I have to do it outside myself. It's harder that way, and I couldn't do enough. If she'd been here . . . if she had just been here . . ."

The overmage shook his head. "Perhaps a few days more, if she had been here. No more than that. Even the best of the Blacks can but retard death. Perhaps someday . . . perhaps . . . but not now."

"I tried," Cerryl added. "I did."

"I know. What did you tell him at the end? That you were more than you seemed?" asked Kinowin.

His eyes burning, Cerryl nodded. "He deserved to know that . . . he did."

"No one else will know," Kinowin said. "I'm glad you told him." The older mage covered the vanishing white dust that had been Myral with the heavy white blanket. "You can't do more here; best you go for now. Do not seem to grieve for Myral though you do. Leave the Halls until you are calm. Jeslek and Anya would use that against you, and Myral would not wish that."

"What of you?"

"I am older, and all know I grieve. Let them sense my grief."

Cerryl could see the wetness on the older mage's cheeks. Finally, he turned. "Only because he would wish it."

"I know."

Cerryl blotted his face and somehow managed to keep his expression blank through the entry Hall and until he was on the Avenue, marching northward through the early twilight.

*You should have spent more time with him. He knew so much, and no one else cared—except Kinowin and Leyladin, and she couldn't even be there. You should have looked in on him more. You promised Leyladin . . . but it happened so suddenly . . .*

He kept walking up the Avenue, eyes not quite seeing, but his senses instinctively extended, looking for chaos or danger—the habit a result of the attempt on his life the year before and the skills he'd had to develop as a Patrol mage.

Myral was gone . . . not even a body, nothing but sparkling dust that had sifted into nothingness before his eyes. Nothingness. Was that what happened to all White mages?

He stepped aside for a woman and a child, not really seeing either, and kept walking.

All living things are composed of order and chaos; this has been since the beginning and will be until the end.

Likewise, every single thing under the sun which has form must partake in some degree of order, for without order there is no form.

In similar measure, every object which lives, or which has lived, or which gives heat or sustenance, must embody some element of chaos, for without chaos there is not heat, nor light, nor life.

Chaos itself, were one able to apply the lost and Great Mathematicks of vanished Cyador, could be described in symbols as precisely as those used in calculating the forces a building or a bridge must endure; yet even with such precise calculations, chaos would never appear the same in any situation, no matter how minutely all the objects it entered were shaped, weighed, and measured.

That is the nature of chaos, that it can be described, precisely, yet never predicted.

Order, contrariwise, can never be precisely described, for order creates a form dependent upon the objects wherein it is found and the amount of chaos present; yet the result of more and more order being introduced into an object remains always the same, for if of unliving material, the object will cease to change while that order remains, and if living, the excess of order will lead to death.

Thus, order can be predicted but not described.

In living creatures, excessive order will result in death, yet because a creature cannot live without embodying chaos, once it dies, for lack of adequate chaos, the body will collapse into small segments of ordered objects.

If the creature embodied great chaos, suddenly lost, this collapse will occur so speedily that the body will seem to vanish into dust. If great order exists, the same will occur, as a gathering of great order into a small compass cannot be maintained without the influence of chaos . . .

*Colors of White*
(Manual of the Guild at Fairhaven)
Part Two

# L

Cerryl stood, wearily, as Gyskas stepped into the duty room.

"You look tired," said the older mage.

"It's been a long day. I'm spending more time on the streets. It's the only way to keep the small theft down." Cerryl eased from behind the table-desk.

"So am I, in the early part of the shift. People almost look the other way when it's a loaf of bread or a few pieces of fruit."

"Except for the baker," said Cerryl, "and people don't lift things when the merchant's looking."

"Coins are getting scarcer, and they're hungry. Between the problems in Hydlen and the Spidlar and Recluce business, it could be a long winter."

Cerryl nodded.

"I heard old Myral died. You know, the sewer mage?"

"I know. I learned much from him." Cerryl managed to keep his voice even. "I hadn't seen him much lately." *And you should have, and now it's too late.* "He was sicker than anyone thought."

"I guess so. He was around forever. It seemed that way." Gyskas offered a brief smile. "Good fellow—even taught me a trick or two."

*Good fellow . . . taught me a trick or two, and before long no one will remember except in a vague way.* "He was good." Cerryl forced a shrug. "It's all yours. I'll wander through the section on my way back to the Halls."

"Suit yourself." Gyskas smiled. "Make my duty easier. Thank you."

Out in the street, the air was hot—and still—more like late summer than early fall. Cerryl turned southward.

". . . the mage . . . the little one."

". . . the tough one."

Cerryl smiled at the two youths on the porch but kept walking. Was he thought tough because he was often out on the streets? He didn't feel tough, not at all.

The street was hot, and the sweat began to ooze even more down his neck and back.

*Why did Myral's death upset you so much?* He shook his head as he turned westward along the Way of the Masons—anything to avoid going back to the Halls too early. *Because his is the first death of anyone who believed in you when you've been there?* He wondered. He'd loved his uncle and aunt, but they had died in a fire, kays and kays away, and he hadn't even found out for half a season. He'd never seen their bodies, and there wasn't even a place he could call theirs. Dylert, the sawmill master, he'd died sometime two years back, but while Cerryl had respected Dylert, he hadn't loved him. He'd seen enough death. He'd dealt death. *Death always happened to others . . . but it doesn't, does it?*

A figure in brown dashed from the side street, followed by a man in blue, who grasped the youth practically in front of Cerryl.

"No!" The youth saw Cerryl's white and the red belt, and the color drained from his face.

"Ser mage, this one—he stole a half-basket of potatoes right from the kitchen door." The gray-haired man glared at the boy, then turned to Cerryl, not loosening his grip on the dirty brown-haired figure— scarcely ten years old, Cerryl guessed.

The Patrol mage repressed a sigh and looked at the trembling but defiant boy.

"I don't care. You mages don't be doing anything for us. My sis, she's wasting, and Ma, she scrubs all day and can't get coppers for bread, not enough."

"That's what they all say," snapped the man.

Cerryl could sense the truth of what the boy said and his fear. What could he do? If he took him in, it was surely the road crew . . . a warning?

Almost without thinking, Cerryl concentrated, forming chaos, focusing it into a tight circle, then extended it toward the wide-eyed youth, who tried to move.

"Hold still, or I'll blind you!" snapped Cerryl.

The youth swallowed but stopped squirming.

There was a faint sizzle as the chaos touched the boy's forehead.

"NO!" The youth slipped into a dead faint.

The man's face blanked as he looked at the circular brand on the boy's forehead.

"Did you get your potatoes back?" Cerryl asked tiredly.

"Ah, yes, ser."

"I'll take care of the peacebreaker." Cerryl bent and lifted the thin figure.

"Ah, yes, ser."

Behind the blankness of the other's face Cerryl could sense the fear, close to terror, as the man backed away.

*What have you done? You can't let him go, not without all of them risking a mere brand for food. Idiot! What were you thinking?*

He started walking, carrying his burden, until he reached the corner. *Now what?* With a sigh, Cerryl turned northward, in the direction of the section Patrol building. Already the thin figure was weighing him down.

The boy stirred, moaned.

Even after four blocks, Cerryl could feel his eyes burning and his stomach churning as he carried the half-conscious figure into the section building.

Gyskas stepped out of the duty room. "What have you there?"

"A peacebreaker. Child tried to steal potatoes because his family was starving."

"You truth-read that."

"Yes. Unhappily."

"That burn is chaos fire."

"Yes," Cerryl admitted. "A bad idea of mine. I thought about letting him go with the burn to mark him. Now . . . I don't know."

"We'll have to send him to south prison."

"I don't like it."

"We don't have much choice," pointed out the older mage.

"I suppose not." Cerryl took a deep breath.

"I can handle it from here," Gyskas said.

"Maybe you'd better. I'm not thinking very well." *Is that the truth!*

"It's not . . ." Gyskas broke off his words.

"I know. We can't afford not to think. Thank you. I'll see you tomorrow." *I hope.*

Cerryl walked slowly out of the building and turned westward, toward the Avenue, toward the Halls of the Mages, his stomach still churning, his heart feeling pressed by lead on all sides, each step an effort.

*How could you have been so stupid?*

*Because you were upset.*

*That's not good enough.*

He kept walking, walking until he reached his room and sank into the chair before his desk. After a time, he looked up, then down at the screeing glass on his desk, reflecting only the ceiling. How had he made such a mess of the day? *Just because you were upset . . . because Myral died?* There had to be more.

*Thrap.*

Out of a blind need to practice, to do something, he focused on the glass. Lyasa waited outside.

"Come in, Lyasa." He stood by the table, waiting.

She opened the door. "You know, Cerryl, I hate that."

"People screeing to see who's there? I'm sorry. I've just been trying to practice using the glass. I don't do that much in Patrol work. Not that I'll be doing that much longer, I suspect."

"What?"

He shrugged tiredly. "I made a mistake. I was too hard on a child caught stealing. I mean, I was trying not to be, but it didn't work out that way, and he's going to end up on the road crew, and it's my fault, and there didn't seem to be anything else I could do."

"They won't get rid of you for that."

"I don't know. I touched him with chaos, meant to warn him, but I burned him, and I shouldn't have tried it."

Lyasa winced. "You didn't mean to."

"No. Not exactly. But rules are rules, and I didn't do what I was supposed to, and I'll have to pay for that."

"Outside of the . . . burn, was anyone hurt? Did you do . . . ?"

"Anything else stupid? No. I should have thought about things, should have taken him to the section building, but I was thinking about Myral, and I was upset, and then I thought about this . . . child . . . on the road crew." He lifted his hands helplessly. "I just didn't think, and I've tried to be so careful."

"Cerryl . . . you can't be so careful that you never feel."

"Feeling—that's what caused the problem. If I hadn't been feeling . . ."

"About Myral?"

He nodded.

"Does Leyladin know? That was what I came to ask you about."

"I sent her a message scroll about Myral. There wasn't much else I could do. I wish Leyladin could use a glass."

"Blacks can't—not easily—and healers especially have a hard time."

"I know. It sounds simple in *Colors of White*. 'Screeing is the gathering of chaotic light patterned by the order of the world . . .' " He shook his head.

"You're still upset about Myral."

"Yes," he admitted. "I don't know why. I mean, I know why I'm upset, but not why I am *so* upset. So upset that I couldn't even remember the rules of peacekeeping." He laughed bitterly.

"Because you respected him and you haven't found many mages to respect," suggested Lyasa.

"That's probably part of it. Except why did I go out and do something he wouldn't have respected?"

"Were you trying to break the rules?"

"No. Yes. How can I say? I didn't want the boy to go on the road crew. But I didn't want to—I couldn't—let him go. If you let one get away with stealing, with all the hunger, they'll all be stealing." Cerryl shook his head. "I don't . . . Maybe I'm not meant to be a Patrol mage. That . . . demons! I probably won't be much longer."

"You're making too much out of this. You still brought him in, didn't you? And he'll go on the road crew?"

"I'm sure he will." Cerryl couldn't tell Lyasa of the horrified look in Gyskas's eyes or the sickening sense of despair he himself had felt. He just shook his head.

"Then what is the problem?"

"You don't break the rules, not if you're a Patrol mage. How can anyone trust the mages if we don't keep the rules we make? Things are bad enough already, and it's harvesttime. What will they be like by midwinter?"

"Worse," admitted Lyasa. "But you didn't make them that way. You made a mistake. We all make mistakes."

Cerryl just shook his head. "Sometimes . . . sometimes, you can't afford mistakes." *Not me . . . not if everyone's watching to see if you do . . . hoping you will.*

She reached out and touched his shoulder. "I'm sorry. Is there anything I can do?"

"No. Not now." He straightened. "I did what I did. We'll have to see what happens. I just hope it's not too bad." *How can it not be bad when discipline is going to come from Jeslek and Redark?*

"If you need anyone to talk to, I'm around."

"Thank you." He swallowed. "I mean it."

Lyasa offered a soft smile before she left.

Cerryl sat down heavily, half-staring at the blank screeing glass.


# LI

Cerryl looked up from the table-desk as Isork appeared in the doorway. As the chief Patrol mage shut the door to the duty room behind him, Cerryl stood. "Ser."

"Cerryl . . ." The chief Patrol mage's voice was soft, almost regretful. "Gyskas reported what happened yesterday afternoon."

"I thought he would, ser." Cerryl lifted a sealed message from the desk, stepped forward, and extended it. "Here is my report. I doubt they differ in any great degree."

Isork continued to stand as he unfolded the sheet and read it. Seemingly he read it a second time; then he handed it back to Cerryl. "I prefer Gyskas's report, and I think you would as well. He was somewhat more charitable to you than you have been to yourself. That speaks well of you, but there is no sense in making matters worse."

"Yes, ser." Cerryl folded the report into his belt.

"Cerryl, I am sorry. But we cannot change the rules of peacekeeping."

"I understand that, ser. Especially now. But nothing seemed to fit. He didn't resist taking, and he didn't attack me. He was telling the truth. Am I supposed to put him on the road gang because he had to choose between letting his sister starve or stealing?"

"We cannot let peacebreaking occur." Isork offered a half-smile.

"No matter what the reason. People often have good reasons to break the peace. Sometimes, as now, the Guild may even be partly at fault. It's easy to keep the peace when times are good. It's harder when times are bad. Yet it is even more important that Fairhaven remain calm in the troubled times."

*How can it remain calm when more and more people cannot find enough to eat?*

"I know you were upset by Myral's death. Kinowin told me when I saw him early this morning. But you have to do your duty, according to the rules, no matter what you feel. I can't have mages branding people. What were you thinking?"

"I wasn't thinking, ser. For a moment, I thought of just using the brand to remind him, but I realized that wouldn't work. So I carried him back here. I should have put him on the refuse crew, I suppose, but I wasn't thinking. It happened so quickly."

"No . . . what you should have done was send him to the south prison for transfer to the road crew. Without branding him." Isork smiled. "Then, we could have arranged for him to escape on the way to the highway work. We will anyway, but we'll have to make sure he doesn't escape until he is well, well away from here, probably into Kyphros."

Cerryl's mouth opened.

"That's the second lesson. We're not totally unfeeling—but what we do has to *look* like it is totally unfeeling, totally impartial. The adjustments have to be made in a way that doesn't appear to compromise the system."

"Now what do I do?" Cerryl sighed. "I'm sure the word will be out that there is a crazy Patrol mage."

"We could get around that, in time, after a disciplinary assignment and relocation to another section. What this points out is that you're too young and too creative," Isork said, "to stay as a Patrol section mage. You think too much. Sooner or later, the thinking will push you into doing something else. You've already made a few decisions that were a bit creative, like putting people on the refuse crew that other mages would have sent to the road crew." Isork shook his head. "The Patrol doesn't air its refuse or its laundry in public. You won't see open disciplinary hearings for Patrol mages—or patrollers. That sort of thing only undermines public trust. It's simple. Patrol mages and patrollers are fully accountable, and all know they are."

Thinking about facing the three Council members, Cerryl held in a shiver. "I'm sorry. I didn't mean to cause you trouble." He lifted his hands.

"We'll make another adjustment. I've talked to Kinowin, or I wouldn't be here. The word is that you have been disciplined, and it will be passed. We will use you to point out to people that that even mages do not break the rules. You will report to the High Wizard and the overmages at noon for your disciplinary assignment."

Cerryl swallowed. *Just for not knowing ... for showing what you thought was care.*

"It's not because you cared, Cerryl. Most of the Patrol mages care, believe it or not. It's because you didn't think of the consequences for others." Isork added, almost dryly, "If you have to break the rules, don't do it in public, and make sure it doesn't have obvious bad public consequences that come back to you or the Guild."

"It was stupid."

"Yes, it was. But we all have done stupid things, and most of us survive them and learn from them. I trust you will, too." Isork offered a consoling smile. "Now ... you'd better get moving. The High Wizard is expecting you. I'm taking the rest of your duty."

"I'm sorry. I didn't mean for you ..."

"That's part of being Patrol chief." After a moment, the muscular older mage added, "That's part of being in charge of anything. If things go wrong, you're the one who has to set it right and do what's necessary. I chose you, and I'd choose you again—except I wouldn't have let you go back on duty right after Myral's death, and you would have had time to learn in your heart as well as in your head why the rules have to be maintained." Isork shrugged. "So ... I have to do extra duty because you seemed so good that I didn't realize that you looked toward Myral as an uncle or other close relative. We don't let anyone on duty after a consort or brother or a sister dies, or a parent, if patrollers or mages know their parents. It's because things like this can happen."

Cerryl looked at the floor.

"It's always better to avoid problems than to solve them. Remember that, too." Isork's tone turned brisk. "Now ... on your way. And don't worry too much. Both Kinowin and I think you'll be an asset to the Guild. You just need more seasoning. We were too eager because the Patrol is shorthanded. Now ... go."

"Yes, ser."

"You can leave the door open."

Cerryl gave what he hoped was a formal nod and left.

*He's almost as upset with himself as with me ... because ... he didn't see enough?* Despite his own fears, Cerryl wanted to shake his head.

# LII

Cerryl stood on the topmost landing of the White Tower, imperceptibly shifting his weight from one foot to the other and trying not to look at the closed white oak door or at Cerryl.

"You may send in the mage Cerryl."

Straightening his shoulders, Cerryl walked into the High Wizard's chambers.

There was one empty chair at the table around which sat the High Wizard and the two overmages. Jeslek gestured to the empty place. Cerryl sat down gingerly. Absently, he realized that the black iron toy windmill had vanished. *Because its order warped things too much even for Jeslek?*

"We had thought of you to take Myral's place in monitoring the sewers, for a time," Jeslek began, "before you attempted to remake the rules for peacekeeping by yourself."

Cerryl nodded impassively. There was no point in confessing he just hadn't thought; that was probably considered worse than being too free with the rules. The less he tried to defend his stupidity the better, and he was only beginning to understand the enormity of that stupidity.

"The Patrol is already short of mages," Kinowin said, "and you do have various talents. The problem facing the Council is how to use those talents without giving the impression of rewarding you for stupidity. Extreme stupidity."

Cerryl wanted to wince.

"I had thought of assigning you to one of the blockade ships, but ships are even more disciplined than the Patrol, and you would be too free to be . . . creative there," added Jeslek.

Blockade ships? Cerryl tried to keep his mouth in place.

Redark merely nodded, as if that were expected of him.

"So you will be assigned to the west gate, for double duty, both duties, for the next two eight-days. That should reduce the time you have to offer creative solutions to problems we do not have. After that, the Council will consider how you might best serve the Guild." Jeslek's smile was not particularly cruel but almost dispassionate. "And you will keep a report of every single vehicle that enters and leaves the gates, with its general cargo, and you will *not* delay any wagon or cart. You will also abide strictly by the rules of gatekeeping. Do you understand?"

"Yes, ser." Cerryl almost wanted to sigh in relief.

"Also, you will receive no stipend for those two eight-days, and your stipend thereafter will be reduced to the minimum for a full mage."

"Your golds for this past eight-day, and the minimum you would have received for the next two eight-days, will go to the family of the boy you branded," Kinowin added. "If they cannot be found, then the coins will be used to purchase bread for the poor and distributed by the patrollers of the southeast section."

Cerryl almost nodded in agreement.

"Do you find that equitable?" asked Redark.

"Yes, ser."

"We thought you would," said Jeslek. "Also, for the next two eight-days you are to remain within the Halls when you are not on duty or going to and from duty."

"Yes, ser."

"Finally, you are to write a fully reasoned statement on why exceeding the rules is dangerous to both the Guild and the individual mage, and you will present it to Overmage Kinowin for his review and for his later examination of you," added Redark. "You have an eight-day to compose the argument. You will present yourself for the examination at his leisure after he has read your argument."

Cerryl nodded.

"What your future may be in the Guild and whether you have a future depend entirely upon your conduct over the next eight-days," added Jeslek.

*That,* that Cerryl had understood from Jeslek's opening words. Cerryl also understood he had been fortunate to have *any* real chance at redeeming himself. Isork had made the rules clear enough at the beginning, and Cerryl had lived in Fairhaven and in the Halls long enough to know that overtly breaking rules was scarcely wise and often not survived—as in Kesrik's unfortunate case.


# LIII

Cerryl shifted his weight on the stool and squinted into the setting sun, shading his eyes as he studied the White highway that headed west for perhaps five kays before it split, one branch going west-northwest to Weevett and on to Vergren while the main road proceeded westward through southern Certis toward the Easthorns.

After only three days, his feet hurt, and his head ached from duty that lasted from before dawn until the midevening bell. His eyes went to the sheets of paper roughly bound in twine that served as his record of wagons and carts. He'd never realized how many went through the west gate even in slow times, not until he'd had to write down each one.

He glanced at the latest entries.

> . . . Muneat and Sons, factors, blue wagon, bearing hard wheat flour from Certis to Fairhaven, medallion in place . . .
> Sekis, spice merchant, cart, from Hydlen, bearing spices and herbs, applied for medallion . . .

His face was salty from the sweat that had dried on his face, salt that mixed with continuing sweat in the late-afternoon heat. While the farmers might be glad of the dry and warm weather for their harvest, it made the second level of the guardhouse hot—far hotter than the second level at the north guardhouse, he'd decided. The area around Fairhaven had been spared the devastating rains that had ruined so much of Hydlen's crops, but the local crops couldn't make up for the losses elsewhere in Candar. The year before had brought drought, but too much rain had followed the year and a half of dryness, with equally disastrous results.

His eyes turned west again. The road arrowed toward the guard-house, a line of blinding pinkish white in the last of the full afternoon light.

Somewhere out on the road he could see a shape through the glare, another wagon, or cart, headed in toward the White City. He strained eyes and perceptions, but all he could sense was something moving. After a time, he could hear the faint rumble of iron wheels, and that meant a heavy wagon.

Reluctantly Cerryl stood so that he had a better view, leaning forward and resting one hand on the stone wall of the rampart, waiting as the wagon rumbled northward toward the gate.

Two guards rode before the wagon, drawn by four horses. The wagon itself was of oiled wood, not painted, and filled with barrels roped in place behind the driver and a third guard who sat beside the teamster.

Cerryl extended his senses, but the barrels seemed to be filled with flour, or meal, and the chaos lock around the medallion remained tight, strong enough that it was less than a season old.

The driver flicked the leads, and the team slowed, rumbling to a halt before the guardhouse.

The lead guard stepped toward the driver.

"I be the trader Hytul, bound from Rytel, with flour for the factor Jiolt."

The lead guard—Besolar—glanced toward the guardhouse rampart and Cerryl.

"Nothing but flour in the barrels," Cerryl confirmed. "Nothing under the seat. The medallion is fine."

The two guards beside Besolar looked into the wagon bed and underneath the seat, as if to confirm what Cerryl had said. They nodded at Besolar.

As the wagon rolled past and through the gate, Cerryl sat down on the stool and picked up his list, adding yet another entry:

...Hytul, trader, oiled wagon, four-horse team, bearing soft cake flour from Rytel (Certis) to Fairhaven, for the factor Jiolt, medallion in place...

After he finished writing, he leaned back slightly, his eyes closing almost inadvertently. He jerked upright, stifling a yawn. Dark demons, he was tired, and he still had another bell to go before the gate closed to wagons and carts.

Afraid he'd fall asleep on the stool, he stood once more, wincing as he put weight on his feet, and walked to the edge of the rampart, looking out to where the sun had begun to drop below the low hills to the west of the White highway.

*Three days, and you have more than an eight-day and a half to go.* He turned and looked toward Fairhaven. Darkness! How quickly life could change, and unpredictably. *Except you could predict that stupidity does lead to problems.* He stifled another yawn and began to walk back and forth across the short stretch of the guardhouse rampart.

# LIV

Cerryl walked tiredly down the corridor and into his room, glancing around. One eight-day almost done—one more day—and one to go, but he still had to finish the written argument for Kinowin. His stomach growled.

There hadn't been any food left out at the Meal Hall, and he hadn't seen any street vendors or even an open chandlery on the way back from the south gate. That had been the way things had been going lately—ever since Myral's death.

*But you didn't cause his death. How could there be any connection?* Or was the connection that, with Myral's death, there was no one to offer subtle advice to counterbalance the scheming that pervaded the Halls? He turned back and closed the open door. Wondering wasn't going to get the last of his writing done. His stomach growled again.

He should have saved some of the cheese he'd bought at the chandlery two days earlier. He'd been lucky to catch the owner leaving a closed shop, but he couldn't count on that often. *Should have . . . should have . . . should haves don't matter.*

He took a deep breath and sank into the chair to take the weight off his aching feet. The blank screeing glass reflected nothing, not in the darkness of the room.

Almost as soon as Cerryl slumped into the chair, Faltar peered in the door, and dim light from the corridor gave the room a gloomy cast.

"Hungry?" asked the blond mage.

Beside Faltar, Lyasa held the door but did not speak.

"I can't leave the Halls," Cerryl said tiredly. "You know that."

"We know." Faltar stepped into the room, followed by Lyasa. He had a full loaf of bread in one hand, the other behind his back. Lyasa carried something wrapped in cloth.

"A half-wedge of white cheese," she announced, setting it on the desk beside the bread Faltar deposited. Then she lit the bronze lamp with a spark of chaos. "We need a little light to get rid of the gloom."

Faltar set the bread beside the cheese one-handed.

Cerryl looked at the bread and cheese, feeling his mouth water.

Faltar grinned and produced a mug from behind his back. "And ale! Warm and a little flat, but we do what we can."

"Thank you. You didn't have to do this," Cerryl protested, smiling even as he did. "You didn't."

"We did if we didn't want you to starve. Jeslek's been telling the serving boys not to leave anything out after dinner, and it's hard to find any street vendors in the middle of the evening." Faltar's mouth twisted. "I know. I've had enough evening duty."

"They were hard on you," said Faltar, perching on the side of one end of the bed. "After all, the boy was a peacebreaker, wasn't he? He'd have lost a hand or his life in Certis."

Lyasa sat on the other end while Cerryl used his belt knife to slice a sliver of the cheese—still cool—and eat it with a chunk of bread.

"No." Cerryl shook his head after swallowing. "Not so hard as they could have been. I wasn't thinking. Besides, Fairhaven isn't Certis." He took a sip of the ale. "Even this tastes good."

Faltar glanced at the stack of papers on the corner of the desk. "Surely you're still not writing Patrol reports?"

"No. Part of my punishment. I have to write an argument on why transgressions on the part of the individual mage are bad for the mage and the Guild."

Lyasa grimaced. "Jeslek's treating you like an apprentice."

"Probably. But I made a mistake even an apprentice shouldn't have made. How can I complain about the punishment?"

"I hate to be so blunt," Faltar said. "But if what you did was so bad, why are you still around?"

Cerryl swallowed more of the bread and cheese before laughing harshly. "I don't know, but I can guess. First, I only hurt and did not injure permanently a poor boy who was already a peacebreaker. Second, the Guild can blame me and give the family of a proven peacebreaker four golds as recompense—and that's more than they probably see in years. Third, the trading situation and the problems with Spidlar, Hydlen, and Gallos are getting worse, and Jeslek is going to need every mage he can find. If I get through this, I'll probably be going with the lancers somewhere. That will get me out of Fairhaven for long enough for everyone to forget—if I even survive." Cerryl shrugged, then took another sip of the warm ale. "Thank you both again. I wasn't sure how I was going to get through tonight." *It's hard enough to write something when you feel good; it's near impossible when you're tired and hungry.*

"You have to finish that tonight?" asked Lyasa, pointing toward the stack of papers.

"I've been working on it for the last five days. I have to give it to Kinowin in the morning—or leave it for him."

"As soon as you eat, we're leaving, then."

Faltar looked at Cerryl, then at the papers. "I still say it's not fair."

"I wasn't really fair to the boy," Cerryl said. "And he'll hate the Guild forever."

"It won't matter on the road crew," Faltar answered.

"You never know," Cerryl temporized, not wanting to reveal Isork's planned "adjustment." He added after a moment, "Besides, I'll know."

After Cerryl had eaten what he needed—about half the cheese and the bread—and drunk most of the ale, Faltar and Lyasa stood and departed.

In the silence and the dim light of the lamp he barely needed, Cerryl glanced at his scrawled words on the rough paper, then at the blank parchment before him.

Finally, he began to write, sifting words from the draft and thoughts from his mind.

After a time, he looked at the parchment and read over the words:

Each mage holds some power to marshal chaos, and that chaos can change or even destroy the lives of others . . . For those with such power, to live and work together requires trust. Trust among those who can marshal chaos requires that the use of chaos power be restricted to what all have agreed is needful. Rules describe what is needful . . .

Cerryl paused. That wasn't an argument. What he had so far just said why rules were necessary. So why was exceeding the rules dangerous? *Because Jeslek and the Council will destroy you unless you're powerful enough to destroy them.*

His lips twisted crookedly. He certainly couldn't write that out. *Because if you get away with it, others will try?* He picked up the quill, sharpened it with his bronze penknife, then dipped it into the inkstand.

> If a mage transgresses the rules of the Guild, he must be punished, for if he be not so disciplined, others well might follow his example, each in greater measure than the previous transgressor. Thus, a transgression of the rules must subject either the transgressor to punishment or the Guild to an example leading to greater transgression. Likewise, by transgressing, a mage places himself outside the protection of the Guild and exposes himself to possible retribution for his transgression . . .

Cerryl replaced the quill in the holder. Was that really true? He rubbed his forehead, then looked at the parchment. The night would be long and the gate duty the next day longer.

# LV

Cerryl stepped into Kinowin's quarters, still dusty and hot from a long day on his guard duty. He was more worried about what Kinowin might decide than the three days left on his double duty assignment.

"Sit down. You look as though you could use the rest." Kinowin poured something from the gray pitcher into a second mug. "And something to drink."

"Thank you, ser." Cerryl sat gingerly and looked at the mug.

A single bronze lamp in a wall sconce supplied a faint illumination to the lower tower room, and a light breeze drifted through the open window and from the darkness beyond.

"Drink it. It's but fresh cider. Call it a tribute to Myral." Kinowin leaned forward and lifted his own mug. After drinking, he added, "One of the few crops not damaged or destroyed this harvest."

Cerryl took a swallow of the cider, welcoming the cool tang on his dry and dusty throat.

"You were asked to present an argument. The argument was why exceeding the rules was dangerous to a mage and to the Guild." Kinowin lifted the parchment. "This is better than I expected, Cerryl. It is also far better than Redark, Esaak, or Broka thought possible. They suggested to Jeslek that, with experience, some years from now, you might be considered to offer some instruction in explaining why the Guild is important to apprentices." Kinowin's face crinkled into a smile. "They emphasized the part about some years in the future." The overmage set the parchment back on the table, then stood and paced toward the window, pausing and glancing at the red and gold hanging, rather than the blue and purple one Cerryl knew he usually surveyed.

"You thought about what you wrote. That was clear. It was so clear that one could almost ask why you broke the rules of peacekeeping. It was clear enough to let any know you had learned from this error. I did not have to let the three see what you wrote. Beyond showing them that you had gained from your experience, why do you think I shared your words?"

Cerryl swallowed. He had ideas, but dare he express them?

"Go on."

"Because you wanted others to see my value and the value of your judgment about me?"

Kinowin turned back to Cerryl. "You could be the greatest mage in many years. No matter how great you might be, you are but a single person. Is Jeslek a greater mage than Isork?"

"Ah . . . I would judge so."

"How could Jeslek consider the problems in Spidlar and Gallos if he could not rely on Isork to keep the peace?"

Cerryl could see where Kinowin's words led.

"Is the High Wizard a greater mage than Esaak? Certainly, but does Jeslek have time to instruct in mathematicks?" The overmage coughed to clear his throat. "My questions are simple. So simple that even an untutored peasant boy in Fenard could answer them. Yet ruler after ruler, generation after generation, is undone because he cannot or will not find others he can trust to do all the duties that hold a land together."

Cerryl nodded. "That is also why there must be rules. So that all can work together."

"You have great skills, Cerryl," Kinowin continued, looking out the window, rather than at the younger mage. "As I know too well, possession of skills others do not have usually leads to equally great mistakes. Sometimes, such mistakes are not discovered because they are so large that no one realizes matters could have been otherwise. Other times, they seem very stupid because others do not understand the thoughts behind them."

"Mine was stupid," Cerryl admitted.

"You were worried about being more than a Patrol mage, were you not? About people going hungry? About the unfairness of sending a boy much as you might have been to the road crew? All for trying to feed a sick sister?"

"I did think about that."

"In being a mage, you must always balance what must be done now with where that will lead. If you do not survive what you do now, you will not reach the future. If you do not think now about where you go, you will have precious few choices when you reach next year or the years after. But . . . at your age, you have to survive." Kinowin laughed gently. "Survive long enough, and few will gainsay your dreams."

Cerryl knew that Kinowin was saying far more than his words and that the overmage did not expect a direct answer. "I thank you for sharing your wisdom."

"Wisdom? I doubt that."

"What happens now?" Cerryl asked carefully.

"For the moment, after you finish your double duty, you will remain as a gate guard, but only the morning duty. In the afternoons, once you have eaten, you will present yourself to the High Wizard. You will be serving as his assistant. You will *not* receive any additional stipend for that. Not now. The moment you finish your last double duty, the restriction on remaining in the Halls is lifted—but not until then."

"Yes, ser. Do you know what the High Wizard expects?"

"Outside of reminding you of your place? And me of my lack of judgment in recommending you for the Patrol?" Kinowin's tone was dry. "For all his faults, Jeslek takes his position most seriously. He sincerely believes that the trade difficulties with Spidlar and Recluce represent a basic problem that Fairhaven must address, and soon. He has continued Sterol's policy of opening the Guild to all with possible talent, but that is making things worse right now."

"Lack of coins?"

"The Treasury is being depleted, and the road tariff payments from other lands are arriving later and later." Kinowin turned back toward the window and the scattered points of light beyond. "For what the Guild does we have never had enough mages of great talent, and each one that we lose . . ." He shook his head. "Myral was a great, great loss, though most will not understand why. Too many think that a great chaos wielder is a great mage." Kinowin's eyes fixed on Cerryl. "Jeslek is more than a mage who can unleash great amounts of chaos. I do not always agree with him, but he thinks as much of Fairhaven as himself."

"I will do my best for him."

"Good." Kinowin pivoted on one foot to face Cerryl. "Do your best and watch all corners, from the moment you leave here." Kinowin's lips offered his crooked smile, or one that seemed so because of the blotch on his cheek. "All mages need to watch all shadows in the years to come. Now go get some sleep."

Cerryl rose from the chair. "Thank you."

"You'll thank me—and Myral—well enough by surviving, thank you." Kinowin walked toward the door. "You have a few years to learn. Use them."

Cerryl nodded again.

What Kinowin had said, and not said, echoed through Cerryl's mind as he headed down the main steps from the White Tower to the front entry foyer. In effect, the overmage had told him, in several different ways, to do Jeslek's bidding and to survive. And to learn. The last reference to Myral had not been accidental or sentimental, not at all.

Cerryl shivered. What had Myral seen and passed on to Kinowin? How could Cerryl believe that he would do great things, as Kinowin had vaguely suggested, or become High Wizard, as Myral had told Leyladin? How . . . when he could not see the simplest things necessary to survive?

He shook his head. *Do what you have to do and survive.* He looked toward the empty foyer, extending his perceptions, but the Hall was empty for the moment. *You'd better get back into the habit of studying everything again.*

He smiled. At least, he had a future to look out for—if he made no more stupid mistakes. *If . . .*

# LVI

After gulping down some leftover bread and cheese from the Meal Hall and washing up quickly, Cerryl hurried up the steps to the upper level of the White Tower, glad that his gate-guard duty was only a normal duty period, rather than two.

The guard outside the High Wizard's chambers was neither Gostar nor Hertyl, but a grizzle-bearded veteran unfamiliar to Cerryl, who studied Cerryl suspiciously, his hand on the short iron blade. "Ser?"

"Cerryl. I'm here as directed by Overmage Kinowin." Cerryl stood there, conscious that he no longer wore the wide red belt of a Patrol mage and was no more than a very junior mage—once again. He was also conscious that the guard wore an iron shortsword, not one of white bronze, and that, he thought, was new. *Why? Does Jeslek fear attack from other mages?* A single guard with an iron blade would not stop most mages. Cerryl repressed a frown.

The guard stepped to the door and rapped once. "A Mage Cerryl is here, ser. He says the overmage Kinowin sent him."

"He's expected, but have him wait out there."

"Yes, ser." The guard nodded and gestured to the bench. "If you would like a seat, ser?"

"Thank you." Cerryl dropped onto the seat. His feet were still sore. He wondered if they'd ever recover.

After a time, Redark left the chamber, glancing briefly at Cerryl but saying nothing. Then Anya departed, offering a dazzling smile but no words, leaving a faint scent of sandalwood lingering around the upper landing.

The guard didn't speak, and Cerryl didn't feel like trying to make conversation. *What does Jeslek want from you? Why would you be his personal assistant, especially after Sterol used you against him? So he can watch you closely?* That didn't seem to make sense, but Cerryl wasn't sure what did—except Kinowin's words about doing what was necessary to survive.

In time, perhaps midafternoon, Jeslek opened the door. "You may come in, Cerryl."

A red-haired student mage—Kochar—stood by the table as Cerryl entered.

"Kochar . . . you may go. I will see you in the morning." Jeslek gave a perfunctory nod to the apprentice mage.

"Yes, ser."

After the door closed, the High Wizard turned to Cerryl. "Kochar will be starting sewer duty in the next few days. He is getting more and more able," Jeslek announced as he glanced at the table and the blank glass. "For a brief time Esaak has agreed to take over those duties that Myral had held."

Cerryl waited.

"For the moment, Cerryl, I have little enough for you. You may have the rest of the afternoon to do as you please. I would like you here every afternoon after your morning duty. You will listen. You will observe. You will not speak of what you see or hear here. You will offer no statements, no advice, no words whatsoever, unless you are asked. You may ask an occasional question. Choose it carefully." Jeslek's smile was hard and bright. "Do you understand?"

"Yes, ser."

"Good. I will see you tomorrow."

Cerryl bowed slightly, then turned, his shields ready, though he knew Jeslek had raised no chaos, and slipped from the High Wizard's chambers and back toward his own quarters.

He needed to rest—and think.

# LVII

After his duty, Cerryl hurried, but did not run, back to the Halls of the Mages. There he ate alone. That was because any of those he knew well enough to sit with were on duty or elsewhere and he had no desire to exchange meaningless words. He gulped down rye bread and cheese and fresh pearapples before returning to the rear Hall, where he washed. Then he made his way to the top of the White Tower, where Gostar guarded the High Wizard's chamber.

"Be not here, Mage Cerryl. None of them," offered Gostar.

"I guess I'll wait." Cerryl sat down on the bench. Despite the smooth polished oak surface and probably generations of usage, there was a faint grittiness to the wood. Cerryl looked down. Was everything around the tower slightly gritty? The effect of too much chaos? He frowned.

Gostar glanced around, then lowered his voice. "Begging your pardon, ser. Some say that you were removed from the Patrol for hurting a boy; some say it was because the High Wizard cares little for you . . ."

Cerryl looked at Gostar. What could he say? Finally, he answered. "The boy stole some bread. I didn't want to send him to the road crew and I put a small brand on his forehead to warn him, but he ended up on the road crew anyway. I was wrong, and he ended up in the same place with a brand on his forehead."

Gostar looked at Cerryl and nodded, apparently neither pleased nor displeased.

Cerryl couldn't detect whether the guard was upset or relieved and sat on the bench, waiting for Jeslek and whatever the High Wizard wanted Cerryl to do. This time, he had to wait but a short time before Jeslek returned, trailed by Anya and Redark and Kinowin.

Behind the group followed one of the messengers in red from the crèche, who glanced at the bench before which Cerryl stood.

Without speaking, Jeslek motioned for Cerryl to follow the group into his chambers. Once all were inside, after Cerryl closed the door, Jeslek handed a scroll to Cerryl. "Read it while we talk."

While the four sat at the chairs around the table, Cerryl stationed himself by the wall closest to Jeslek's right hand and began to read through the scroll, focusing on the parts that followed the flowery greeting.

... knowing that we of Gallos have the highest regard for the White Brotherhood of Fairhaven and for those highways which the Brotherhood has developed and maintained to ensure peace and prosperity for Fairhaven and, to a lesser but still important degree, for other lands in Candar ...

... fair trade is considered vital to all lands, particularly those of us not so blessed as Fairhaven ...

... yet a tax upon the craftsmen and merchants of Gallos, for that is what the tariffs levied for the use of the White highways must in all fairness be termed, such a tax falls heavily upon a land already troubled by the whims of nature ... and in all fairness, we must suggest, cannot be long maintained by any ruler in Gallos even in deference for past services as great as constructing the highways that all could use to greater benefit were not tariffs levied upon the users ...

... all know of the past power and glory of Fairhaven, and few would wish to believe that any in present-day Fairhaven would stoop to preserve unpopular and unnecessary tariffs through banditry or raids upon neighbors or neighbors of neighbors ...

... moreover, no power in Gallos could stand against its people and their unwillingness to be taxed for that from which they see little benefit ...

The seal and signature were those of Syrma, prefect of Gallos.

*Great benefit from the highways, yet the people see no benefit?* Cerryl puzzled over the apparent contradictions even as he continued to listen to the four around the table.

"It's a veiled threat," Kinowin observed. "He's saying that he knows Fairhaven is behind the banditry and raids on Spidlarian traders." His fingers touched the purple blotch on his left cheek momentarily.

"What are we supposed to do?" asked the ginger-bearded Redark. "Just let them take over the highways and still maintain them out of our vast treasury and generosity?" Bitterness dripped from his words.

"What do you—and Sterol—think, Anya?" Jeslek asked the red-haired mage. "I am certain you know the thoughts of the former and esteemed High Wizard."

"You grant me too much insight, ser." Anya smiled.

"Then, what do you think?"

"My thoughts matter little. What matters not is truth. What matters is what those with whom we must deal think. They seem to think that we have less power than in years past and that they can avoid paying their obligations. Unless we can compel them in some fashion, they will not pay." Anya finished her statement with a brisk nod.

Kinowin nodded with her, but Redark frowned.

"Gallos is lagging," Jeslek said. "I've already sent messages to Gorsuch, as regent for young Duke Uulrac, Duke Estalin, Viscount Rystryr, suggesting that it may be necessary for them to raise levies to deal with the problem of Spidlar."

"They won't do it—except for Gorsuch," interjected Kinowin. "They all think it's our problem."

"That is very clear," said the High Wizard. "The problem is Syrma. Rystryr will do as we suggest if given a push. Gorsuch will also."

While Gorsuch would do exactly as Jeslek told him, Cerryl reflected, Gorsuch's direct power lasted only so long as Uulrac remained alive. Pushing Gorsuch to require levies might well shorten the sickly young duke's life span—and possibly Leyladin's. The young mage pursed his lips and continued to listen.

"Syrma's power as prefect is recent, and he must defer to others, especially to those of coins and the great factors who continue to profit from the trade with Recluce and Spidlar. So we will ask for levies, and he will demur. He will not refuse. He will say that it is early yet and that he respects Fairhaven." Jeslek snorted. "He may say anything, but he will not post the listings."

"And then what do we do?" asked Redark.

"We find a way to convince them all."

"You wouldn't turn Fenard into a mountain, I trust?" said Kinowin, his voice dry.

"Not Fenard. What would be the point? All those golds we need would be lost." Jeslek smiled. "No. We need another more . . . subtle reminder for our friend Syrma. I will have to think about that." His eyes flicked toward Cerryl, if but momentarily. "We will talk that over later, when I have a better thought of what might be required."

The cold expression behind the High Wizard's smiling mouth chilled Cerryl, but the younger mage kept on his face a look of mild interest.

"Now, we need to review what coins we must disburse in the next season." Jeslek glanced at Redark. "Do you have the numbers I asked for, Redark?"

"Yes, ser." From somewhere Redark produced a set of papers, placing one in front of each of the others at the table. "You see . . . there are the golds required to fit the last three ships and the extras for the White Lancers. Below are what must be spent on the Guild, or stipends, and support, and there are the requirements for supplies for the masons, and for the Patrol and for the sewers and aqueducts . . ."

Cerryl stifled a yawn. He had the feeling that the meeting would be getting duller.

# LVIII

Cerryl stood by the wall, trying to avoid Anya's glance, as Kinowin and Redark walked into the High Wizard's chambers. Fydel stood with his back to the bookcase on the other side of the table.

"Why did you want us here now? You gave us little warning," said Redark as he slumped into a seat at the table.

Kinowin took the chair between Anya and Redark but said nothing, his eyes on the white-haired, sun-eyes High Wizard.

"You may recall that I have been concerned that Recluce was playing a larger part in Spidlar than those in Gallos or Recluce would admit," Jeslek said easily.

"You have said that for several years, as I recall," replied Kinowin. "There has been little proof."

"I hope that I am about to remedy that." Jeslek nodded toward Anya and the screeing glass that still held residual chaos from the red-haired mage's earlier efforts. "Anya has been following certain activities in Spidlar, and she tells me that it appears likely that we will be witnessing just how certain matters have escaped the notice of our neighbor the Viscount Rystryr. I have also asked Fydel to be present, since he will be involved more in Gallos."

Kinowin's eyebrows flickered, Cerryl noted, but the overmage did not speak.

"Let us watch now." Jeslek gestured to the glass where the white-silver mists swirled away to reveal the brown fall grasses of the upland meadows somewhere north of Fenard and south of Elparta. In the center of the mirror, a trader's wagon plodded southward. A red-haired woman drove the wagon, and a man rode beside her, hunched and shrouded in a dark cloak.

Over the top of the hill waited another group, wearing the dark green tunics of Certis. As the wagon neared the hill crest, the riders fanned and charged toward the two traders.

Just as quickly, the redhead halted the wagon, and two men with bows stood in the wagon bed, throwing off brown cloths and aiming their arrows at the charging raiders. A pair of swords appeared in the hands of the redhead, and from behind the raiders Spidlarian guards appeared, led by a blond giant who strewed bodies before him.

Not a single Certan raider survived. As the shovels appeared for grave digging, Jeslek waved his hand, and the image vanished from the mirror. "Bah . . . no magic at all. Just good tactics and cleverness. No one survives; no bodies are found, and the rumor spreads that the Spid-larians are using magic."

"It doesn't exactly help to tell that to either the viscount or the prefect," observed Anya from the chair closest to the window.

"Or to admit it took more than a season and magic to figure it out," added Fydel. "That's hard when they claim to have lost nearly a hundred men over the last two seasons."

"Do we know who is responsible?" asked Cerryl deferentially, with a nod toward the High Wizard. "Beyond the obvious?" He gestured toward the blank mirror.

"Our . . . sources . . . in Spidlar would indicate that most of the damage has been caused by one squad formed for this purpose last spring. Supposedly, the squad leader and assistant are outcasts from Recluce. Those are the big blond warrior and the redhead who drove the wagon."

"Supposedly? That's rich! They exile two people, and those two people just happen to be in the right spot to block everything. Do you really believe that, honored Jeslek?" asked Fydel.

Jeslek did not correct Fydel's mathematicks. "I said supposedly. There is also the Black mage who is a smith in Spidlar. You may recall his name, Fydel. Dorrin, is it not?"

"I believe so," Fydel replied blandly.

Cerryl refrained from wincing.

"What do you plan to do?" asked Redark.

"Now . . . nothing." The High Wizard held up a hand, as if to forestall objections. "I'm not playing Jenred's waiting game. But do any of you really want a winter war? It nears the end of fall already."

Headshakes crossed the tower room. A frown accompanied Kinowin's headshake.

"Once the roads clear in spring, I will personally direct our forces in the invasion of Spidlar. Over the winter, we should step up efforts to close off as much trade as we can—and, as possible, minimize the impact of Recluce's meddling. The newest ships should help in this matter." Jeslek smiled at Fydel, then at Redark. "We need to make it a hard winter indeed in Spidlar. We also need to use the winter to ensure that the other lands of eastern Candar will provide the golds that they should."

"Spidlar isn't the real enemy; Recluce is," reminded Fydel.

"You and I know who the real enemies are." Jeslek smiled with his mouth. "And their time will come."

"So clever, and so cryptic," murmured Anya under her breath.

Jeslek's eyes fell on her, and her lips closed. His eyes glittered, and she shivered. Fydel swallowed, and Cerryl looked out the tower window, wishing that he had not spoken at all, though he did have leave to ask a question and that had been his first in more than three eight-days.

"Are there others from Recluce in Spidlar?" asked Kinowin.

"We do not know of others, but the number of Austran traders carrying goods from Recluce has increased. We need to close off the ports until the winter ice appears. Then we need to make sure that those traders do not begin to use Ruzor."

"You do not trust the prefect?" asked Redark.

"Would you?" Jeslek smiled broadly.

From the one time Cerryl had observed Prefect Syrma, he had to agree with the High Wizard.

"I would not impose further upon you." Jeslek gestured toward the overmage Redark. "You have seen what there was to see."

Redark lifted himself from the chair. "Would that the prefect had seen that. It would help more than us seeing it."

"The prefect will see what he needs to see, I am certain." Jeslek turned to Fydel. "You may go, Fydel, Anya."

"Yes, ser."

"And you also, Cerryl. A word with you, Kinowin."

Cerryl nodded and followed Redark, Fydel, and Anya out of the tower chambers.

Redark clumped down the steps alone.

Fydel glanced at Anya. "That Black blade was good."

The chamber guard remained impassive, but the blond messenger on the bench listened, wide-eyed.

"I worry more about his ideas than his blade," Anya said. "Too many Certans are dead for it to be luck."

Cerryl agreed with that as well. With a nod to the pair, he started down the stone steps. His feet hurt from an already-long day, and his stomach was growling.

Even though his feet hurt, he had to frown. Once again, the smith who was a Black had come up—and had been dismissed. But why was Jeslek not worried about the smith? Or did the High Wizard have something else in mind?

Cerryl shook his head.

# LIX

Grateful for the cool breeze that had finally brought more comfort to Fairhaven and the Halls of the Mages, after the unseasonably hot days following harvest, Cerryl walked slowly up the steps toward Jeslek's chambers.

For once, Cerryl was allowed inside immediately, and Jeslek sat at the table alone, sipping wine from a goblet, rather than a mug. A scroll lay on the table, one with ribbons, and fragments from a broken wax seal lay on the wood beside the scroll.

"Good day, Cerryl."

"Good day, High Wizard." Cerryl stationed himself in his normal position by the wall.

"You have been in Fairhaven now without traveling for well over a year now, well over a year. Is that not so?"

"Yes, ser."

"Yes . . . I think some travel would be good for you."

The younger mage waited.

"Cerryl. You removed Lyam rather effectively, as I recall." Jeslek's sun-gold orbs met Cerryl's pale gray eyes.

"Yes, ser. At your command, ser."

"Ah, yes . . . I recall something about that." Jeslek straightened, then sat back in the chair. "No matter." He lifted the scroll that lay before him. A fragment of green wax skittered off the table. "I have just received word that young Uulrac suffered a seizure and died in his bath—rather suddenly and tragically."

Cerryl swallowed.

"You foresaw that, did you not? I saw your face when we discussed the impudent scroll from Syrma."

"I had feared such would occur, ser. But I did not know, and I was cautioned only to observe."

"Wise of you, very wise. I like the fact that you do listen, Cerryl. There still may be a future in the Guild for you. Now . . . one Ferobar, a cousin of Uulrac's, has proclaimed himself Duke of Hydlen. Do you know of him?"

"No, ser."

"His origins lie in Renklaar, and his allegiances appear to lie with the traders of that port. In fact, those allegiances may well be the reason for poor Uulrac's untimely death." Jeslek raised his eyebrows. "I see you understand."

"I have listened."

"You are known to be fond of the Lady Leyladin, are you not? Well . . . she remains in Hydolar. Duke Ferobar has declared her under protective guard. I doubt he values her that highly, but to anger one of the leading factors of Candar would not be wise. Nor would killing a healer set well even with his own folk." Jeslek took a sip of the wine he had not offered to Cerryl, his lips curling ever so slightly, as if the wine were sour. "Gorsuch barely escaped with his life and has returned to Fairhaven, for the time. I will be sending Fydel and Anya—and you—to Hydolar to escort the valued healer Lady Leyladin back to Fairhaven." Jeslek smiled. "I will also be sending tenscore White Lancers."

Cerryl had the sinking feeling he knew what was coming next.

"You will be going as Fydel's assistant, as will Anya, and that should leave you somewhat free . . . to be creative." Another smile followed. "The Guild would certainly benefit by the disappearance of Duke Ferobar."

"Ser . . . High Wizard?"

"Yes, Mage Cerryl?"

"If you as High Wizard feel that Duke Ferobar is a danger to Fairhaven, and if you order me to remove Duke Ferobar, I will do all in my power to do so. I understand why you would not wish such an effort to be made public, but I would appreciate it greatly if the two other members of the High Council were so informed." Cerryl stiffened, ready to raise his shields if Jeslek decided to lift chaos.

A lazy smile crossed Jeslek's face. "You do learn, Cerryl. I must grant you that. And you do not challenge my authority as High Wizard. Very well, I so order you, and I will inform both Redark and Kinowin. You may discuss this with Kinowin; he may have ideas, and I know you will feel less unhappy if you can discuss it with him. All of you will leave tomorrow morning at first light. You have the remainder of the day to prepare." The High Wizard paused. "Anya will also have a special charge, and you are to assist her as she sees fit, except when it might hamper your duties to me. You may also request her aid, provided it does not hamper her charge. I have already told her such."

"Yes, ser."

"Send in the messenger as you depart."

"Yes, ser." Cerryl bowed, then turned.

Outside, he nodded to the brown-haired and stocky young messenger in red. "The High Wizard desires a messenger."

"Yes, ser."

Cerryl walked straight down the steps to Kinowin's chambers, hoping the overmage might be in. Luckily for Cerryl, he was.

"You look like twisted chaos, Cerryl," Kinowin greeted Cerryl as the younger mage stepped into his chamber.

"I have the High Wizard's leave to discuss something with you."

"Something that disturbs you, I can see." The right corner of the overmage's mouth lifted ironically.

"Duke Uulrac died. Jeslek suspects it was murder."

"How could it be anything else these days?" Kinowin's lips twisted more fully, then smoothed into a faint smile. He gestured to the chair on the other side of the table. "Sit down. What you have to say will doubtless take a bit."

"You recall what Jeslek required of me in Fenard? With the old Prefect Lyam? He has ordered me to undertake a similar task in Hydolar . . ." Cerryl continued to detail his assignment. ". . . and since Jeslek thought your advice might be beneficial—"

"You are here." Kinowin's lips tightened. "I cannot say that any of this surprises me. Nor can I fault Jeslek's desire to remove Ferobar without the use of armsmen. Such a removal will send a message to his successor—and to Syrma. For a time, at least, and Jeslek must have time to gather more golds."

"If I can remove Ferobar."

Kinowin laughed. "You can do that easily enough. What you must do is remove him after you have already left Hydolar."

"After I have left Hydolar?"

"You would not wish your fellow mages to be attacked, would you? Nor the Lady Leyladin?"

"No. Of course not."

"Also . . . few will suspect danger *after* three White mages have left Hydolar."

Cerryl nodded. "An illusion?"

"Yes. Anya is quite good at them, and she will relish doing you a favor in Jeslek's service. Also . . . you must make sure that no trace of Ferobar remains, except perhaps ashes."

"Confusion?"

"If none are sure if or when he died, your escape will be far easier. There are enough factions in Hydlen that none dare attempt to impersonate him. Finally," Kinowin added with a shrug, "disappearance upsets rulers and would-be rulers far more than death, which most expect to claim them sooner or later."

Cerryl nodded. The overmage's words made great sense.

"When do you leave? Tomorrow?"

"First light."

"You'd better prepare." Kinowin rose. "You might wish to take a warm jacket with winter hovering on the horizon."

Cerryl stood and replied. "Thank you."

"Thank me when you return."

# LX

Anya and Fydel, already mounted, looked at Cerryl in the orange light of dawn. Cerryl glanced at the big chestnut gelding and the red and white livery. Finally, he swallowed and pulled himself into the saddle. He shifted his weight, but the saddle was as hard and as unyielding as he had recalled.

Fydel nodded to the lancer officer on the bay beside him. "Let us depart, Captain Reaz. We have a long-enough ride ahead."

A cold breeze out of the north blew at Cerryl's back as he urged the gelding after the other two Whites. Kinowin had been right; winter was on its way. Behind him, he could hear the sound of lancers riding nearly in unison as the column left the stable courtyards and turned onto the Avenue south of the Halls of the Mages.

Cerryl found himself riding beside Anya.

They had almost reached the south gate to Fairhaven before either spoke.

"Whatever you may be doing for Jeslek," Anya said quietly, "I do suggest that you do it with great success and devotion."

"I intend to," Cerryl answered as quietly.

"And I would not let your feelings for the Lady Leyladin interfere. After all, Cerryl, there's no real future between a Black and a White."

"I've been told that," Cerryl answered. "Right now, she is a friend." *Because that's all she'll let it be.*

"Blacks who are friends can be useful, so long as you do not turn your back for too long. Also, Blacks who are linked to great factors can be even more useful, if you use your head and not your heart."

The sound of hoofs echoed down the Avenue as the column rode toward the south gate, the one Cerryl had spent guarding for too long. Even after making his maps of Candar as an apprentice—a time that felt more and more distant—it felt strange to be riding west to reach Hydolar, west for a time on the Great White Highway and then southwest on one of the lesser White highways until they reached the Ohyde River and Hydolar.

"Have you thought more about Myral's great visions?" asked Anya, in a normal tone. "You can see where they led him."

"I don't know anyone who has escaped dying," Cerryl pointed out. "Myral lived longer than most mages. His knowledge was useful for that."

"A few years. Someday . . . someday, a strong White mage will be able to live longer, far longer."

The cold certainty of Anya's words bothered Cerryl. "I suppose that's possible. I suppose it's also possible that a strong Black healer might manage the same."

A strange expression, one Cerryl couldn't define, flitted across the redhead's face, so quickly Cerryl almost missed it.

"That might be so, but you are a White, and you should follow your own path. Especially now." She smiled, overly sweetly. "Jeslek expects you to bring honor to the Guild."

*Honor? Power perhaps, but hardly honor.* Then, he reflected, Fairhaven needed more power. The Guild—

"What are you thinking?" Anya asked.

"About power," he answered truthfully. "About how the Guild needs power more than honor. If we were stronger, then we wouldn't have to worry about having Guild representatives killed or chased out of other lands. We could suggest trade policies that would benefit all Candar and not have to argue and send lancers and wizards back and forth across Candar."

Anya laughed. "You sound just like Jeslek. Perhaps he did pick better than he knew."

"It's true," Cerryl said stubbornly, wondering why he felt he had to defend his ideas against Anya.

"Oh . . . Cerryl, you and Jeslek will struggle and dream, and nothing will change. We can only change that close around us for comfort or personal triumph. The world will be what it will be."

Was there a trace of something else in her sardonic words? Envy? Pity? Cerryl couldn't tell.

Instead he shifted his weight in the saddle, trying not to think about just how sore he would be by the end of the day.

# LXI

Even by midmorning of the second day, Cerryl's legs ached and his thighs burned. He'd never ridden before becoming a student mage, and outside of his one trip to and from Fenard as an apprentice, he'd never spent much time on horseback.

Fairhaven had faded into the low fall-golden hills behind them early on the first day, and since then they had ridden through low hills and valleys, and more low hills and valleys, each browner than the one before, as though drought and the coming winter had taken their toll.

The heavy fall rains that had washed out so many crops, especially in Hydlen, had come—briefly—and gone, too late to help the land and too early for the next growing season, and the dryness had returned.

Cerryl could hear Captain Reaz talking to Fydel.

"... used to be greener here, far greener ...

"... demon-damned Blacks meddling with the weather again."

Cerryl had his doubts. More likely something about the mountains Jeslek had created in Gallos had as much to do with the unseasonable weather in Candar, and in Hydlen, as did anything the Blacks had done. Then, that wasn't exactly something he dared say.

"... meddle with everything ... just ought to stay on their accursed isle."

Cerryl glanced from the two ahead of him to Anya, riding in silence beside him, her jaw-length red hair disarrayed by the light and warm breeze that now blew from the south. After a moment, he cleared his throat. "Jeslek told you that I had a task to do for him in Hydolar."

"He did." Anya nodded briskly, from where she rode beside him, as though her thoughts were elsewhere. She turned to him, and her eyes focused on the younger mage. "He also said that I could call upon you."

"He did," Cerryl agreed. "So long as it did not hinder my ability to complete my charge to him."

"He did say that."

"I would like to request your assistance, Anya," Cerryl said, careful to keep his words formal, for reasons he could not say but felt nonetheless.

"With what?"

"A seeming of myself ... when the time is ready. That's all."

"A seeming of you? Even Fydel could do that." Anya laughed. "I will ask the same of you ... in time. A favor, that is. To help me shift the ground slightly. Far less than in Gallos."

Cerryl nodded.

"Have you thought more about the future?" An amused smile crossed Anya's lips.

"I have been advised to think most strongly about the present. By several," he added after a moment. "I might not see any future if I don't."

She laughed again, softly and ironically. "It is strange how a few seasons can change a man."

"We learn," Cerryl said, blocking his annoyance from Anya's possible truth-reading.

"That doesn't matter, either. Not most of the time."

"Why?" asked Cerryl, intrigued in spite of himself. *Besides, it is a long ride.*

"Learning affects only what you do. If you teach others, you change others. That was what Myral believed." Anya's face grew distant, her eyes elsewhere. "That doesn't work, I've found. People only learn what they want to learn, or what they will accept. So most of that learning is wasted. Most of life is wasted if you try to help others. They take and do not appreciate. They reject the knowledge that you have struggled to gain, and they will walk on you or kill you for a silver—or less." After her words came the bright smile. "Just watch closely, Cerryl. You'll see what I mean. If you dare to look." Her eyes swept to the road ahead, as if to signify that she had said what she would say.

Despite the sun that fell across him, Cerryl suddenly felt cold, even before the wind picked up, and very alone, even though tenscore lancers rode behind him.

# LXII

Fydel and Captain Reaz had reined up on the last low rise before the road dipped southward in a gradual slope toward the red walls of Hydolar, circled on three sides by those walls and on the fourth by the River Ohyde. Beside the road, stretching toward the walls, were browned fields, so brown Cerryl couldn't be certain whether they were grain fields or meadows burned brown by the unseasonably hot sun that had baked the land through the late summer and the past autumn. Only a handful of peasants' cots were scattered across the fields, marked as much by the taller gray-leaved and wilted trees around them as by the huts' earth-brick walls and thatched roofs.

Cerryl studied the city's high stone walls. To the southwest, beyond those walls, the River Ohyde glittered in the late-afternoon winter sun. On the far side of the river Cerryl thought he saw trees, even a patch of woods on a hill, but of that he was uncertain.

"They've closed the gates," observed the captain.

"That's not terribly welcoming. Do you think they plan to attack if we approach?" asked Fydel.

Reaz shrugged. "I could not say."

Fydel turned in the saddle and addressed Anya. "Can you and Cerryl cast chaos fire at the gates if they open them to attack?"

"Not from this far. That's more than a key from here," answered the redhead.

Fydel looked at Cerryl.

"Anya's right. We might be able to loft a few fireballs that far, but it would be hard to hit the gate."

"Fydel," Anya said quietly, "it's not likely that any duke would attack a force of White Lancers unless he had to. Why don't we ride closer and ask for the return of the healer? Cerryl and I will be ready to cast chaos fire if you need it." She smiled crookedly.

"We ride on!" called Reaz. "Be ready to lift lances."

"Ready to lift lances . . . Ready to lift lances . . ." The command echoed down the lancers behind Cerryl.

Reaz dropped his hand, and the column started forward again.

Anya edged her mount closer to Cerryl. "Be ready to offer me assistance."

Cerryl raised his eyebrows. "I thought we were going to request the healer's return."

"We are. We also need to show Duke Ferobar that Fairhaven will not be mocked."

"How?" asked Cerryl, honestly curious as to what the redhead had in mind for humbling the new Duke of Hydlen.

"How might Duke Ferobar feel if the east tower—there— collapsed?" Anya pointed.

Cerryl followed her finger. "He might send all his lancers after us."

"He might," Anya said, with a smile.

"We're to request the Lady Leyladin first, Anya," snapped Fydel, again turning in the saddle. "Once we have her, then you two can carry out whatever Jeslek laid upon you."

"Or . . . if they won't release her," speculated Anya.

"That, too," grudged Fydel.

Cerryl studied the red walls as they rode closer, noting how the air seemed to waver over the walls in the afternoon sunlight, even though it was cool, almost cold, on the plain outside the city, and how glints of light off helmets reflected from the parapets. Yet his senses told him that but a comparative handful of armsmen manned the ramparts.

Somewhere around two hundred cubits from the closed and iron-banded gates, Reaz and Fydel reined up. Cerryl, his eyes on the fifty-cubit-tall walls, managed to stop the gelding short of crashing into the older mage or swerving into Anya.

"Get the herald," Fydel ordered.

"Herald!"

A squat figure with close-cropped mud-colored hair and jowls, flowing out of his uniform, answered the summons, reining up beside the captain.

"The mage has a message for you to convey," said Reaz.

"Yes, ser."

Fydel rode forward from the others, ever so slightly, and began to talk to the herald, repeating his words time after time.

Shortly, the herald eased his mount away from the column and drew forth a long horn from his lanceholder. He bugled the call. Cerryl winced at the off-key tones but wondered if they would have hurt any less had they been on key.

There was no response from the high walls.

The herald bugled again.

After the third call, a series of notes echoed back.

"On behalf of the High Wizard of Fairhaven, we have come to provide an escort for the healer and Lady Leyladin to return to her home in Fairhaven." The herald's clear tones carried toward the walls and the gate.

"Wait," came back the answer.

Cerryl shifted his weight in the saddle, his eyes on the high red walls, then upon Anya. He was gratified to notice that Anya's eyes were also upon the walls and that chaos smoldered around her, as if she were uncertain as to what the Hydlenese might do.

"They could refuse to return Leyladin," he offered, not hoping that, but wanting Anya's reaction.

"Then, we could bring down all the walls."

"How?"

"Just help the ground and stone beneath the foundations shift . . . You can use chaos as if it were butter or a grease, you know. It flows; it's not stiff like order."

Cerryl frowned. That made sense, but he hadn't thought about it in that way—as he hadn't about so many things, he kept discovering.

Out of the corner of his eye he could see Captain Reaz shifting in his saddle. Was the good captain uneasy about what might happen as well?

The cool wind flowed around the mages and the lancers, and the walls remained silent. Not a sound came from the browned fields beside the road, except for the faint whistle of the wind. Cerryl hunched up inside his jacket for a moment.

A triplet of horn notes echoed from the walls, followed by a call: "How would the great Duke Ferobar know that you are what you claim?"

Fydel whispered to the herald, and the man echoed his words: "Who else would bring tenscore White Lancers?"

"Any brigand of means could dress men in white."

Anya smiled cruelly. "Tell him he shall have his answer in but a few moments."

"Just splash the gates in chaos fire," Fydel snapped. "We want the healer first."

"As you wish." Anya turned to Cerryl. "Make ready."

Cerryl nodded and began to raise chaos, careful to keep it around him but well away from his body, easing it from the earth, careful to match what Anya mustered.

"Now!" commanded the redhead.

Cerryl released his chaos fire with Anya's. The two fireballs arched toward the walls, then merged. A wave of flame splashed and crested nearly to the top of the walls above the closed gates.

As the chaos flame subsided, sections of the gates continued to burn, gray and black smoke rising from the wood into the cool afternoon air. Cerryl could smell the bitter scent of burning wood and chaos and even feel some of the heat, carried on the wind toward them. A patch of dried grass ten cubits or so from the side of the road by the causeway leading to the gate began to burn, then died as the flames consumed the last of the grass.

"Ask them again," Fydel told the herald.

Sweat dripped from the heavy man's face as he rode forward once more and bugled, then called, "On behalf of the High Wizard of Fair-haven, we have come to provide an escort for the healer and Lady Leyladin to return to her home in Fairhaven. You have requested proof, and we have provided it!"

No answer came from the walls, save that men began to dash buckets of water from the parapets toward the gates beneath. Slowly, the flames vanished, until only few parts of the gates steamed and smoldered.

After more buckets of water, even the steam and smoke vanished, but the wind carried the smell of wet ash to Cerryl. He shifted his weight once more in the hard saddle.

A trumpet call echoed from the wall. "The Lady Leyladin will join you shortly. Once she reaches you, the hospitality of the duke is withdrawn, and none of the White persuasion are welcome in Hydlen once you depart on your return."

"What hospitality?" muttered Fydel. He turned to the herald. "Tell them we await the lady healer and will depart only when she is safe with us."

The herald wiped his brow, then bugled and repeated the message.

"An attack for sure." Anya turned to Cerryl. "Shortly after Leyladin rides to us. Are you ready to cast fire at the gates when they emerge?"

Nodding, Cerryl blotted his forehead. Suddenly, despite the cool wind from behind him, the sun seemed to burn the back of his neck.

The gates creaked ajar, and a single figure on a black mount rode forth. Cerryl caught his breath, but the blonde hair and the unmistakable sense of order that surrounded her reassured him.

"We need to get her away from the walls," he said to Fydel.

"We all need to get away from the walls." The square-bearded mage glanced toward Anya. "You two had better prepare. We are not staying a moment, longer than we must. I would rather not rely on chaos fire against the lancers the duke could muster."

Recalling Fydel's feeble attempts in Gallos two years earlier, Cerryl could understand the older mage's concerns. Cerryl glanced at Anya.

"She's close enough now. Follow me." Anya's face seemed unreachable, her eyes glazed over.

Cerryl swallowed and tried to send his own perceptions after Anya's, following her line of chaos toward the large chunks of bedrock underlying the tower. *How did she know?*

Somewhere, he could hear Fydel talking to Captain Reaz and then to the herald. He could also sense the growing order as Leyladin's mount trotted swiftly toward the lancers.

"Lancers, turn about!"

". . . turn about! . . . Turn about!"

Cerryl could sense how Anya eased chaos in the lines between the rocks and how she concentrated chaos in one rock, shifting it from one to another, and he tried to replicate her actions.

The ground shivered as one soft rock deep beneath the tower collapsed in upon itself.

Seemingly in the distance, the herald bugled again as Leyladin reached Fydel.

"Lady Leyladin, are you all right?" asked the bearded mage.

"I'm tired and hungry, and worried, but I'm otherwise right."

After a second triplet, the herald called, his voice not quite shaking, "Remember the might of Fairhaven, and do not think to challenge it again, lest the full might of the High Wizard fall upon you. You have been warned!"

Fydel glanced in Cerryl's and Anya's direction.

Cerryl could feel the sweat pouring off his forehead as well as down the back of his neck, could feel the rocks shifting beneath the tower. Another section of the deeper rock collapsed, but the tower shivered.

Cerryl thought of water . . .

What about letting water meet chaos? Even as he channeled more chaos beneath the tower, he also sought a stream of water, easing it edging from the levels below the rock toward the chaos he built, forcing them together, more and more tightly.

*HSSSSttt!! Crumptt!* A section of ground exploded out from beneath the base of the tower walls, and steam sprayed upward, the heat welling even toward the lancers.

"Ride! Let us ride!" ordered Fydel. "Too close."

The ground shook more violently, then trembled several times more. With a rumble, more stones slid out from the bottom of the tower. Others seemed to crumble and fragment.

Hot droplets of rain cascaded down around the mages.

Screams that might have been were lost in the roar of falling and grinding stone.

The ground shook yet again.

"That's enough!" snapped Anya, reeling in her saddle as she wheeled her mount.

Cerryl shook his head.

"Are you all right?" Leyladin eased her mount next to Cerryl's.

"We must ride!" snapped Fydel.

Cerryl reached for Leyladin's hand. "Are *you* all right?"

"I'm fine. I'm glad to see you."

"I have to go. I'll catch up with you later." *If I can.*

"Fydel, catch his seeming!" ordered Anya.

Confusion crossed Leyladin's face as Cerryl thrust the gelding's reins at the healer and slipped from the saddle.

"Ride with them. You have to go."

"Healer!" snapped Fydel.

Cerryl staggered to the side of the road, his sight cut off as he lifted his light shields to keep the Hydlenese from seeing him, though a part of his mind pointed out that they wouldn't see much in all the dust.

Behind him, the thrumming of hoofs faded as Leyladin and the White Lancers rode eastward and back toward Fairhaven.

A few more patters of hot rain dropped around him, and he moistened his lips to try to keep from coughing. Why weren't there any riders coming after the lancers?

He cast his senses toward the massive gates, then smiled. Anya or he or something they had done had buckled the causeway enough that the gates could only open partway.

The dusty and saddle-sore mage walked slowly toward the gates, placing his feet carefully and using his chaos-order senses to guide him.

As the rumbling of displaced stone had stopped, he could hear screams and moans from the east—from his left. *Was toppling the tower necessary?*

He tightened his lips and kept walking toward the gates.

A half-dozen mounts trotted along the road, then reined up.

"Bastards . . . gone . . ."

"Not about to chase 'em with half squad."

"No others . . . ?"

Cerryl eased along the side of the causeway, trying to move silently, not to raise dust with his boots to undo the effect of the light shield, but the attention of the lancers was to the north.

". . . stables went . . . lot of 'em . . . White demons!"

Cerryl edged around the still-warm wood of the singed gates and along the stones of the archway behind the gates. A dozen armsmen stood at the far end, glancing through the archway toward the lancers on the causeway and then to the east toward the fallen walls and towers.

Step by unseen step, the young mage eased his way along the stones and toward the open inner gate.

Just short of the gates, he stopped and flattened himself against the wall stones as a clatter of hoofs echoed through the shadowed archway. Another squad of lancers rode past him, the last rider so close he could have touched the mount without stretching.

After another deep breath, he eased along the timbers of the open inner gate and then along the inside of the outer walls for another fifty cubits, where he slumped into a recess formed between two stone columns that provided some additional support to the gates or archway.

For a time he just sat there, unseen behind his light barriers and unseeing, wondering what he was doing in Hydolar. *Wasn't destroying a tower and killing people enough of a warning?*

He took a deep breath.

# LXIII

Finally, Cerryl stood, partly sheltered between the stone buttresses for the gate, wincing at his sore muscles, hoping he was ready to find Duke Ferobar.

Comments still swirled from the lancers and armsmen by the gates, now arrayed in groups, as if waiting for some sort of orders.

"White bastards . . . kill 'em all!"

". . . don't mess with them wizards."

". . . can't tell us what to do."

"They just did, Muyt, and I'd wager that nothing happens."

A grim smile crossed Cerryl's lips. That was certainly what Jeslek hoped for, but even Cerryl doubted the effect would last long. In Fairhaven, peacebreakers went to the road crew or were turned to ash. The next day or eight-day, there were more peacebreakers—not nearly so many as he'd seen elsewhere, but they were there, and he doubted that people in Hydlen were that different.

Taking a last deep breath, beneath his full light shields, he stepped gingerly across the open space before the gate area and into the shadows on the west side of the street facing the gate. There Cerryl dropped the full shield and eased around himself the blurring or bending effect that seemed to cause others' eyes to slide away from him, as if he were not there, and, incidentally, allowed him to see.

He walked down what seemed to be the main street, old and reeking of raw sewage and far narrower than even the streets of Jellico or Fenard. The second stories of many houses or shops protruded another cubit more into the street than the street-level walls of the buildings, giving the street an even gloomier appearance. Most of the walls appeared to be timber or planks or woven withies roughly plastered over and once painted and now faded and peeling.

"Spices . . . good spices for poor meat . . ."

"Oils . . . oils here . . ." A wizened woman swung an aged and stained wicker basket as she chanted.

Cerryl winced. He wouldn't have wanted anything the woman sold.

A small brown dog darted from one alleyway and past Cerryl before disappearing behind a hunchbacked peddler. Beyond the peddler two women stood on a narrow raised porch, though Cerryl couldn't determine what the shop was.

"Deris! The Whites brought down the east tower—that's what Gurold said—and then they rode off, just like that. Delivered some message to the new duke . . ."

"Should I care? This is what? The third duke since winter? Bread still be too dear, and getting dearer."

"Dearer yet, if the duke must raise coins from us to rebuild his fine tower."

Cerryl eased past the women and the porch, frowning at their words. The combination of the hubbub, the smells, and the confining nature of the street had already given him the beginning of a headache, and their words did not help. He was already tired after a long day of riding.

Perhaps a block later, where the street widened fractionally, a small boy looked up, his eyes wide, clearly seeing the mage, then ran down the alleyway toward a woman.

"Mama . . . mama . . . a demon . . . saw a demon . . ."

Cerryl slipped the full light shield in place, tiring as it was. Relying on his chaos-order senses, he barely managed to keep from stepping into the open sewer, staggering back into the street, and almost careening against yet another hawker, who glanced one way, and then the other, before repeating his call. Cerryl hoped he wouldn't have to continue too far without sight.

"Roasted maize, roasted maize . . ."

The woman took several steps toward the main street, holding tightly to her son's hand. "Demons aren't real, Kuriat. We don't have demons in Hydlen, sweet."

Cerryl kept walking, going another block before switching back to the less tiring blur screen. He wished he had been able to enter the city to fetch Leyladin. His task would have been far easier. Already his feet ached, although the walking seemed to help the cramping in his thighs that the more than three days of riding had created.

He'd thought about a disguise, but any stranger would have been marked in Hydolar. Besides, where would he have changed in the midst of the lancers, and how soon before rumors seeped out?

Cerryl had no idea where he was headed, except that his limited screeing before he had left Fairhaven had shown that the larger buildings were almost next to the river, on a low bluff on the western side. The duke's palace had to be one of them, but which one was something else he needed to know.

Again, he didn't know enough. He hadn't even known enough to know what he needed to learn. A low snort escaped him, and he glanced around, but none of the people on the street paid any attention, wrapped as they were in their own doings.

He frowned. Less than a half a kay from the collapsed tower, and no one seemed to care. Then he shrugged. He'd had to ash one peacebreaker on the open streets in Fairhaven, and some people hadn't even stopped doing business. People didn't change that much from city to city, at least not in Candar. *Do they anywhere?*

A block farther, he finally had to stop and slip down as alleyway to relieve himself—that would have been peacebreaking in Fairhaven. Many things would have been different in the White City.

Ahead he could see an open-fronted shop, with loaves of bread. His mouth watered as he stepped toward the shop, noting some smaller loaves of a darker bread on the side.

Again he eased the full light shield in place, ignoring the increased headache, and slipped his hand out for one of the loaves. It was warm to the touch, and he kept walking, as silently as possible.

"Mora! There's a loaf missing . . ."

"Thief!"

Cerryl continued onward, ignoring the bustle behind him but feeling slightly guilty for stealing the bread. Yet he was hungry, and he couldn't afford to appear to anyone in Hydolar. *You could have left a copper.*

He should have, but he decided against retracing his steps. *You should have.* He took a deep breath and kept walking. After another block, he broke off a piece. The small loaf was a heavy bread and almost too sweet, but he ate chunks slowly as he walked southward.

"Watch where ye tread," snapped a voice at knee-height.

Cerryl glanced back, taking a breath of relief as he saw the beggar hunched against the wall was blind. He kept walking.

After another kay or so, the street widened into an avenue with a square ahead. Beyond the square were three buildings, but the center building was the largest, fronted by a high brick wall, pierced with an iron gate, swung half-back. A guard in green stood on each side of the gate.

Cerryl stood beneath the wall, perhaps thirty cubits from the guards. Another man lounged against the wall less than a dozen cubits from Cerryl. For a time, the mage watched the street, finishing the warm loaf of bread as he did. He could feel the chill as the sun dropped below the walls and left the street in shadows.

Three riders approached the gate, all in gold and green, looking as if they would enter the courtyard beyond the wall. Cerryl shifted to the full light screen, noting that the bread had reduced his headache to a faint ache. After a moment, he stepped along the wall, trying to reach the gate in order to follow the riders through the archway.

He ended up almost running, but the sound of hoofs covered his scuffling enough, and the heavy breathing of the mounts was louder than his as he walked behind the three mounts and their uniformed riders—but not too closely—into the palace courtyard.

At the mounting block at the foot of the wide stone steps, a single rider dismounted, glancing back at the other two. "I know not how long I will be."

"The duke will not be pleased, ser," offered one of the men remaining mounted.

"No duke is ever totally pleased, Niarso." The officer who dismounted turned toward the steps.

Cerryl eased around the mounts, trying to follow the officer up the steps and through the entrance to the palace. He kept the shield up as he edged along the edges of the square columns that flanked the main entrance. Inside, the building was darker and cooler, enough that Cerryl almost shivered.

Cerryl could sense a figure in some sort of uniform, a gold and green surcoat over armed-striped leathers, marching stiffly, as if he were headed somewhere important. With a shrug, Cerryl followed the officer—if that were what he happened to be.

At the top of the steps and along another corridor, Cerryl found himself standing in a shadowed corner of the Great Hall. The officer stepped out toward a group of figures on a dais at one end of the room.

Cerryl edged, as he could, along the side of the hall, slipping from column to column.

"Ser?" The officer Cerryl had followed bowed before Ferobar—or the man Cerryl suspected to be Ferobar.

Ferobar was scarcely taller than Cerryl; that the young mage could sense, even from the side of the room. The duke was silent as the officer straightened and remained silent for a bit longer before he addressed the officer. "You did not send lancers after them?"

"Half the mounts of the nearest lancers were destroyed by the collapse of the tower. It would have taken a half-day to send for the Yeannotan horse. We had but four squads mounted, and I would not send four squads against tenscore White Lancers and three White wizards." The officer bowed again. "Not so late in the day, either."

Ferobar glared at the tall officer. "You are dismissed, Captain. I do not expect to see you in Hydolar by morning."

Even from where he stood, Cerryl could sense the chaos of near-uncontrolled anger from the lancer officer.

Ferobar looked beyond the captain and raised his voice. "There will be no evening meal in the hall, not tonight, not after the disgrace of the lancers." Ferobar turned and departed from the dais, leaving on the far side, but Cerryl could not have followed him, not without risking being discovered. So he let his senses follow the duke so long as he could, toward the staircase beyond the smaller east door of the Great Hall.

Slowly, the hall emptied until but a single guard stood in the archway from the main north corridor.

Cubit by cubit, Cerryl eased his way along the wall toward the open east door, then stepped into the small side hall. He could sense no one around. Standing in the dark shadows, he dropped the light screens and glanced up the stairs.

Breathing deeply, he rubbed his forehead, then raised his shields again and, by chaos senses and feel, made his way to the upper level and into a long and narrow corridor. Perhaps fifty cubits away, to his right, two guards were stationed outside a door.

Between them and him was a wide chest, almost a cabinet or sideboard of some sort, against the same side of the corridor as the door to what he believed was the duke's chamber. Cerryl eased across the polished stone floor of the corridor and toward the cabinet, finally stopping next to it, where he felt slightly less exposed. He knew that most people couldn't see through the full light shield, but it still bothered him to walk past people with only the sense in his own mind and feelings that he could not be seen. He could be heard and smelled—he knew that from his experiences in sniffing Anya's sandalwood scent, except he doubted he smelled anywhere that pleasant at the moment. Then, all of Hydolar seemed to reek, so who would notice?

The two guards remained silent and the corridor empty.

Cerryl frowned. He could kill the guards, but that didn't feel right. Even so, it was far too early in the evening. *First, you must survive.* Kinowin's words slipped into his mind. But even if he could kill them, could he do it silently enough? Besides, he suspected there was a cold iron bolt behind the door.

Well, the duke had to eat, sooner or later. Cerryl sat down on the floor against the side of the wide cabinet or sideboard. He was tired, and he needed to rest.

"What have you there?" asked one of the guards, his voice echoing down the corridor.

Cerryl shook himself fully awake, wondering if he'd let his shields drop. Then he smiled. Despite the tapers on wall sconces, the corridor was so dark someone would have had to have fallen over him to see him.

"The duke's evening cider, and hot it is. You be wanting to make it cold?"

Cerryl shivered. Either the woman hadn't even seen him or she had come up another staircase. He swallowed and checked his shields. Then he eased to his feet and slipped along the stone floor next to the wall on the far side of the corridor until he was almost behind the serving woman.

She turned and frowned, and he held his breath, standing less than two cubits behind her, in front of some sort of framed picture, holding his breath.

"Thought someone was there . . ." she murmured.

"Only the picture, Misty. Only the picture," laughed one of the guards.

The other rapped on the door. "Misty with some cider, sire. Do you wish—" He turned. "He wants the cider." He reached for the heavy iron latch.

Cerryl could hear a bolt being withdrawn on the inside.

The guard on the right offered a half-bow to the serving woman. Cerryl waited until he straightened, then boldly stepped after the serving woman with the tray—barely slipping into the room before the heavy wooden door *clunked* shut behind him.

At the end of the room to Cerryl's right was a huge hearth, in which burned a low fire. Cerryl felt warmer, glad for the heat after his wait in the chill outer corridor. Before the fire, on a faded green settee, sat Ferobar, a volume of some sort in his hand. On the table to the duke's right was a brass lamp, emitting less light than the fire. The table to the left held a bowl of fruit and little else Cerryl could sense. The wall opposite the door held four windows, each with a window seat beneath, each window seat covered with an upholstered cushion. All the windows were closed and shuttered.

"Your cider be here, sire." Her voice trembled, and the mug rattled against the pitcher on the tray.

"Bring it here, Misty." The man's voice had an edge like the big blade of Dylert's mill just before it was ready to crack.

Cerryl could sense a figure, more than four cubits tall, and broad, standing to the right of the door. The young mage edged to the left, away from the huge guard, flattening himself against the paneled wall that adjoined the door, hoping his shields would suffice in the dim light.

The server set the tray on the table beside the bowl of fruit, then straightened.

The duke poured from the pitcher and took a sip. "Could you not have gotten it hotter?"

"Near bubbling it was, ser, and I hurried, fast as I could."

"You may go, Misty." A weariness filled Ferobar's voice.

The tall guard withdrew the bolt, only long enough for the server to depart, then slid it back in place.

Cerryl used his order-chaos senses to study the room, trying to get a better impression. The ceiling was not that high, perhaps five cubits, and the chamber was no more than fifteen cubits long and ten wide. The wall opposite the hearth held bookshelves, but less than half the wooden shelves held volumes. A musty odor filled the room, enough to make his nose itch.

"They think I'm a tool of the merchants of Renklaar, you know?"

Cerryl almost jumped at the words, seemingly addressed to him, before he realized that Ferobar had turned on the settee and was talking to the hulking guard who remained on the inside of the door.

"I'm no man's tool. I am the rightful Duke of Hydlen. I should have been all these years. It's late, but I know what to do. Yes, I do. Merchants . . . all they think of is how to pile one coin upon another. Do they think of whether they will have coin if Fairhaven increases the levies?" There was a pause while the duke slurped some cider, then ate something from the table. A biscuit? Fruit?

Cerryl couldn't tell, not with the strain of holding the screens and his increasing headache. Yet he had the feeling that the sooner he acted, the better. *The sooner you act in a way that will let you escape and survive.*

"It's too bad you can't speak, Girtol, but it's not, because I couldn't talk to you otherwise." Ferobar laughed, with an edge that sent a chill down Cerryl's back. "You'd be far less use to me were you able to speak. Nor I to you, my old friend. Fortunate it was that I saved you those years back, fortunate for us both, and more fortunate now that I am duke." Another cackling laugh issued from the thin lips.

Cerryl could sense that Ferobar was not that old, in fact probably not more than a half-score of years older than he was. Ferobar poured another mug of the cider, his face turned back to the low fire in the hearth.

"Already my bones are chill, chill knowing that none are happy with their duke. The merchants will not be pleased, because we have not the vessels to break the blockade of the White demons. The demons are not pleased, even though I returned their healer, because Hydlen cannot pay what they demand in tariffs. The people are not pleased that I will not lower taxes. The armsmen are not pleased that I could not stop the destruction of the east tower . . ." Ferobar gulped a swallow of cider.

"Should I sleep? How can I sleep? Sleep . . . what is sleep? A small death that claims us each night." Ferobar slurped more cider, then turned to Girtol once more. "Seat yourself, dear Girtol. If my fate worries you, place that chair before the door."

Wordlessly the big guard pulled a massive oak chair in place before the door and sat down, his eyes not leaving the duke.

"You can sleep, Girtol, unlike your master."

Cerryl thought. How could he remove the duke without alerting the mute guard? Even a mute guard could alert those outside. And if Cerryl removed the guard, surely the duke would seek aid.

Cerryl stifled a yawn. He was tired, dead tired. His feet ached. His head throbbed, and he had to finish his task and get out of the duke's palace.

Ferobar poured yet another mug of cider, his eyes on the low fire that was slowly burning down.

The young mage waited, hidden behind his light shields, fighting exhaustion, impatience, and a headache.

Still, in time, Ferobar's head eased forward, lolling on his shoulders.

Cerryl straightened, turned toward the hulking guard, dropped his shields, and focused chaos into the tight light lance that he had developed in the sewers and used so sparingly in the years since. The light seared into the mute guard before he could even open his mouth, leaving nothing but ash atop the muscular torso that slumped into the wooden chair.

Cerryl turned and threw a second bolt at the yet-dozing Ferobar. There was a dull and muted thump as the body pitched forward onto the carpet before the settee.

The young mage held his breath, momentarily, but there was no sound from without the chamber. He padded toward the duke and, standing back but slightly, concentrated chaos on the body until nothing remained but drifting white ash and a belt knife. He left the belt knife where it lay and turned back to the unfortunate Girtol. Another burst of chaos, and another set of drifting ash resulted.

Then, Cerryl took a moment to drink the remainder of the lukewarm cider from the pitcher and slip two apples from the bowl into his tunic before easing toward the door beside the hearth. He opened it gingerly, assuming that the next room was a bedchamber, nodding as his senses revealed the same.

The bedchamber had no other doors, but there was a window. Cerryl eased to the window, then stood on the window seat. The window overlooked a roof, and the drop was less than three cubits. Cerryl eased the window open with a sigh and wiggled out into the darkness, dangling his feet, then letting go.

His boots skidded as he hit, and he clutched at the still-warm roof tiles, somehow slowing his descent on the sloping roof.

*Now what?*

He listened, but everything around him sounded the same—no yells or screams or lamps or lanterns.

He crawled slowly along the roof away from the duke's window. After another forty cubits, the roof ended. He peered over the edge, seeing a drop of far too many cubits, then looked back up the slope of the roof toward the broad chimney.

Even in the darkness, he could see the stepped design, and the intervals were not that great. He crept upward on the warm and dusty tiles until he reached the chimney, then lowered himself, dangling until his boot toes touched the bricks below. Then he unclamped his fingers and let his feet take his weight. After resting a moment, he repeated the process with the next part of the chimney.

The last drop, to a small unlit courtyard, was a good five cubits. He hit with a thud, and the shock ran from his boots to his thighs, which threatened to crumple. Wobbling for a moment, he staggered several steps, then looked around. He was on the back side of the palace and could sense the river beyond the wall ahead of him.

He turned toward the west end of the courtyard, walking in the darker shadows, those areas untouched by the infrequent wall lamps. The courtyard seemed to go on and on.

A yawn took him and he had to yawn again. As he leaned against the wall, breathing hard, from both fear and exhaustion, he could feel his eyes wanting to close. He took another breath and continued westward.

How long he wound through courtyards with closed doors he wasn't certain, but a different scent drifted through his nostrils, one of horses and hay. *Stable?*

Stables usually had haylofts . . .

He eased toward the stable and was gratified to see that the door was ajar.

Easing the light-blurring shield around him—he could not have held a full light shield—he stepped through the door, glancing around. Finally, he eased past the stable boy, dozing on a round bale of hay by the door, and past two rows of stalls until he came to a ladder. Hay around the ladder suggested a loft above. Slowly, he eased his way up to the top of the loft ladder and across the rough planks.

In a dusty corner that felt as though it had been neglected for days, he sat down, rubbing his nose, trying to keep from sneezing. Slowly he ate one apple and then the other. The growling in his stomach lessened.

He thought about taking off his boots but, too tired to make the effort to hold off sleep, lay back on the small bit of straw left in the loft.

# LXIV

Cerryl bolted awake, his head aching, his nose stuffed up, and almost unable to breathe. Outside, the light was barely gray, so he hadn't slept that long, or it felt like he hadn't. He shivered inside his jacket.

Below, he could hear voices, young voices.

". . . why leave so friggin' early?"

". . . don't say anything . . ."

The young mage rubbed his eyes, then eased toward the ladder. His stomach growled and he could feel a tightness, almost a cramping, in his guts below his stomach. His headache wasn't the one that came with overuse of chaos, or rainstorms, but a leaden aching.

*Not going to get better while you're in Hydolar . . . that's for sure.* He peered below into the gloom of the stable.

The stable boys were saddling several mounts and, after each was saddled, leading it out into the courtyard. Cerryl didn't hear voices in the courtyard.

With a deep sigh, he summoned the light shield and then felt his way down the ladder onto the main level. His feet slipped on the greasy-feeling clay of the stable floor, and he had to grab the ladder to steady himself.

The ladder squeaked as the wood slipped on the edge of the loft above.

"What was that?" One of the stable boys looked from the stall where he saddled another mount.

"Nothing. There's no one here. None of 'em get up this early, except for Pierdum."

". . . dumb bastard."

"Careful, he'd beat you as soon as spit."

Cerryl walked carefully along the edge of the stalls, toward the open door, feeling his way step-by-step. The stable wasn't clean, the way those in the Halls were, but almost rancid, and that didn't help the cramps and churning in his gut.

He couldn't help but wonder . . . why hadn't there been any outcry from the adjoining palace? Or did the duke habitually sleep late? Or did no one wish to break down the bolted door?

The thoughts gave an urgency to Cerryl's desire to escape the city.

"Don't forget the ration packs, and don't eat anything. One biscuit missing and it's a caning for sure." The youth led another mount past Cerryl.

*Whuffff...*

"Better stuff in those than the lower table in the kitchen."

"Course...They're officers."

"Something's upsetting them. The horses," said the boy leading the mount. "Like a wild dog or something."

"Haven't seen none."

"Keep a look." The shorter stable boy tied the mount to the long hitching rail outside the stable.

Once he passed on returning to the interior, Cerryl stepped outside quickly and hurried to the corner of the building, where he lowered the full light shield into the vision-blurring screen. He studied the courtyard.

After a moment, he nodded to himself. The gate in the courtyard wall looked unguarded, and beyond the gate was Hydolar. He watched as the other stable boy tied another mount at the end of the rail.

" 'Nother to go." The youth turned back toward the stable.

"Better start mucking after that," came from inside.

Cerryl eased toward the end mount, a chestnut. Once he was certain both stable boys were completely inside the stable, Cerryl untied the reins and scrambled into the chestnut's saddle.

*Wuuuffff...* The horse seemed to back off.

Cerryl patted his shoulder firmly. "Easy, fellow...easy..." Then he urged the mount toward the open gate from the stable yard. He couldn't hold a full light shield, not with the growing sharp pains in his gut and the leaden headache, and even keeping his blurring efforts was hard. He only hoped that, if people saw him, their vision would show nothing out of the ordinary, just a blurred image of a rider on a lancer mount.

*Can't afford to get sick...not in Hydolar...*

He rode quickly across the courtyard and toward the courtyard gate.

"Who was that!"

"Took the chestnut. Not Mierkal...always late..."

"Shit!...What'll we tell him?"

As he passed through the gate, Cerryl felt badly for the stable boys, but not badly enough to remain in Hydolar any longer than he had to, not at all.

The street leading back to the north gate of the city was far less crowded, and, thankfully, his blurring effort was working enough that not a soul of the handful of people he passed in the orange light of dawn even seemed to look in his direction. The faint mist that lay over the city, perhaps from the river, might have helped as well.

The cramping in his gut was worse, and so was the headache as he rode out through the city gates.

"...know that lancer?" came from the gatehouse.

"... can't see him well ... wants to ride out alone ... that's the duke's problem ..."

"... still."

"... what lancer, Jiut? Didn't see no lancer, did you?"

A tight smile crossed Cerryl's face as the chestnut carried him down the gentle slope of the causeway to the road that would carry him back to Fairhaven. He was out of Hydolar. *With two long, long days' ride to go ... or three ...*

He rubbed his forehead, but it helped the headache not at all. Nor the growling in his stomach and lower gut. Perhaps if he ate something from the ration pack? He turned in the saddle and fumbled out a hard biscuit, hoping some food would reduce his shivering as well.

# LXV

Cerryl yawned. Twilight had passed into full evening, and every span of his body ached, starting with the crown of his head all the way to toes that threatened to cramp within his boots. The night was still, cool, but not yet cold, and with the stillness he could hear a few scattered insects in the dry fields flanking the road. *Insects? In winter? More likely rodents.*

He'd hoped to make the Great White Highway before long, but the stretch of road he traveled had no kay markers and no towns, just dark humps in the fields that were the cots and houses of peasants and herders. He wished he'd been able to ask for a detachment of lancers to wait for him, but that would have alerted the Hydlenese, and the lancers wouldn't have kept quiet about it, either—and it was clear that Jeslek wanted mystery.

Cerryl patted the stolen horse on the shoulder. He needed to find another place somewhere to deal with his bodily necessities—again! He preferred a spot not exactly on the open road, although he had yet to see all that many travelers.

He hoped his vision-blurring skills had been good enough to ensure that those few who had seen a rider would not remember any details, except that the mount was that of a lancer of Hydlen. A disappearing duke wasn't much good to the Guild—or Jeslek—if people noticed a White mage traveling back from Hydlen. Once he was close to the Great White Highway, it wouldn't matter, but ... until then ... few should see him.

His guts twisted again—violently—and he shivered.

He glanced around. Was that a clump of bushes ahead, where he could tie the mount? Already the big beast had tried to leave him twice, and once he'd had to lunge for the reins. Clearly, the animal belonged to someone and Cerryl wasn't that someone.

Cerryl dismounted and led the beast toward the bushes. His guts contracted, sending a wave of pain through his torso, and his fingers fumbled with the leather reins. He reached for them, and his boot caught on a root, and he sprawled on the ground, dust welling up around him, his fingers losing the leathers.

He stumbled to his feet, but the horse was trotting down the road. "Here, fellow . . ." Cerryl rasped. "Here, fellow."

The horse did not turn but kept moving back southward.

Cerryl walked more quickly. So did the horse.

Cerryl tried to trot, but the chestnut picked up his feet even more quickly.

After a time, Cerryl stood, panting, in the darkness of an empty road, watching the dark blur that was a horse moving southward, in the direction of Hydolar.

Cerryl shook his head. He faced a long and hungry walk back to Fairhaven, with little more than a handful of silvers and coppers in his wallet.

Not only that, but he could hear the rumbling in his lower gut and sense the continuing pain. The bread he had stolen? Or the strain of the whole effort on little sleep and less food? Or the apples from the duke's fruit bowl? Had they been poisoned? He laughed harshly. Indeed, that would be an irony.

His guts twisted again, and he looked for a more promising and private place, stumbling off the road and toward another clump of bushes beyond the shoulder of the road by perhaps a dozen cubits or more.

When he had recovered, Cerryl stumbled back to the road, clenched his teeth, and kept walking, trying to hold himself together for a bit longer, looking for a place to rest before he resumed what was going to be a long walk, one far too long.

The night was looking far less than restful or promising, and it was getting colder. He shivered again, despite the heavy riding jacket.

# LXVI

In the welcome, if slight, warmth of the midmorning sun Cerryl walked along the side of the Great White Highway. He'd been walking since dawn, and his boots were cut and dusty, and his feet ached. His whole body ached, but not so badly as two days before, when he doubted he had walked more than five or six kays, or the day before, when he might have covered more than ten to finally reach the Great White Highway.

Along the way, he had found some water and a few fruits that he snitched from crofters' trees, but he was weaker than he would have liked, and his vision had a tendency to blur, still. The cramps in his lower gut had continued, as had his shivering, but had lessened in the last day. *Not enough by far.* He wasn't sure what had happened. Even when he'd eaten bad food as a child, the gut flux hadn't been as painful as the initial cramps had been this time. *Perhaps you've gotten too used to good food?*

He gave himself a weary headshake and kept walking, looking back to see if he could make out any trace of travelers.

On the highway he hoped he could pick up a ride with some carter or teamster. *You hope . . .*

He'd been walking, on and off, with rests that tended to get longer each time, since dawn, but he hadn't seen a single wagon or team, not one, not even a lancer group. He wasn't the most experienced traveler, but the lack of other travelers bothered him.

After what felt like another kay but was probably far less than that, he stopped and turned to survey the road. A faint dark spot had appeared on the shimmering pink-white stone of the highway, a spot seemingly too big to be a single rider.

Hoping it was a wagon whose driver he could persuade to carry him back to Fairhaven, Cerryl turned and walked another few hundred cubits, then looked back. The spot had turned into a wagon, accompanied by two riders.

Cerryl took a deep breath and walked some more.

Then, he turned and stood, waiting under a sun that was too cool for his chilled body, a body that was sweating beneath the white leather jacket, even as he fought off shivers.

As the wagon neared, it slowed and stopped . . . well back of Cerryl. The wagon bed was of a light wood, recently oiled, and a canvas was roped over the contents. Cerryl could sense, but not see, the Guild medallion on the far side of the wagon bed. Two guards reined up their mounts beside the driver, both with their blades out.

"Those White garments mean something?" asked the driver, raising his voice.

Cerryl mustered a bit of chaos, ignoring the increasing headache and the stars that seemed to flash in front of his face, then flared it into a fireball that he flung in the direction of Fairhaven. "Just that I'm a footsore mage, trying to get back to Fairhaven."

"What might you be doing here, ser mage, if a humble trader might ask?" The wagon driver peered at Cerryl.

"I was in rough country, and my mount went down," Cerryl lied. "So I hiked here to the highway and hoped I could find a ride back to Fairhaven." He offered a grin. "I could provide some additional protection."

"Wouldn't dare do less than offer you a seat. Not much, but better than by shank's mare." The teamster shook his head. "Almost worth it to see a mage walking."

The two mounted guards concealed smiles.

"Might as well hop up here. Name's Narst."

"Cerryl." Cerryl forced himself up onto the hard wagon seat. It felt wonderful.

The teamster flicked the leads, and the wagon rumbled from a creep into a solid pace. "Thought you folks always went in large groups, seeing as you be so well liked."

"Those who are more senior and better liked do indeed travel in large groups. Some of us are sent out by ourselves." Cerryl shrugged. "I've been a full mage but two-odd years, and we do the smaller tasks, deliver special messages, guard the city gates . . ."

"And you?" asked Narst.

"Coming back from delivering something. Thought I could go a different way. Didn't work out that way."

The teamster smiled. "You young fellows . . . even mages. No shortcuts in life, none that work well, no ways."

"I've been finding that out lately." Cerryl took a deep breath.

"There be water in the jug behind the seat. Look as you could use some."

"Thank you."

After Cerryl took several swallows, gratefully, he asked, "If I wouldn't be intruding, might I ask what you are trading in?"

"No surprises there, ser mage. Bolts of brocade from Sarronnyn, gold and silver threaded through the rich green and blue. What doesn't go to Muneat I can always sell in Lydiar."

"You started in Fenard?"

"Aye." Narst shook his head. "Always they want brocade for the coins one would spend on coarse wool. Save for Willum, but he's out of Spidlar and cold as the stone, done in by brigands. So needs I must travel farther to the east with more than I'd wish."

"They say there have been more brigands in Spidlar lately."

Narst frowned, then said flatly, "Some go so far as to say those brigands wear green under their gray."

Cerryl returned the frown. "I'd not heard that. Has the viscount some quarrel with Spidlar?"

"Who might know that, ser mage, save the viscount himself? Would you be knowing him?"

"No. I saw him once, years ago, when I was an apprentice. I was at the bottom of the table." Cerryl forced a laugh. "A long table. I could not see him clearly, nor hear his words."

Narst paused, then spoke slowly, deliberately. "I know not if this be true. Yet some say it be so. They tell me that upon each tariff collected by him upon those who use the White roads in Certis, upon each, he adds another part, claiming this be required by the White Brothers, save they never see it."

"That I had not heard, but I will see that it is heard by those who should know in Fairhaven." Cerryl didn't have to counterfeit that frown. The last thing the Guild needed was blame for taxes it wasn't getting and that were lining Viscount Rystryr's pockets or strong rooms.

"That disturbs you?" asked Narst.

"Greatly. It is hard enough to raise the coins to keep the roads open and in good repair. Many already feel that the tariffs are too high. To find that the tariffs are yet higher and that anyone would use the Guild as a way to take more coins from those who trade and those who buy their goods . . ." Cerryl broke off, afraid he was getting too windy, perhaps because he was too tired. "I'm sorry. Let's just say it is not good."

"That it be." Narst nodded and lapsed into silence.

So did Cerryl, hoping he could last the distance to Fairhaven under a winter sun that offered little besides light.

# LXVII

Cerryl roused himself out of a state of stupor and exhaustion as the wagon rumbled up the Avenue and neared the Halls of the Mages. The sky was fading into dark purple.

"If you could stop somewhere near the square there . . ." Cerryl forced himself erect on the hard wagon seat.

"That I can do, ser mage. That I can."

After the wagon halted, Cerryl eased off the seat and turned to

Narst. "I thank you." He extended his last silvers and clasped them into the trader's hand. "I wish it were more, but I cannot tell you how grateful I am."

"You need not pay me . . ."

"I would not feel right if I did not," Cerryl said. "Mages are not wealthy. If I were, it would be more. Success in your trading." He smiled, though he was seeing stars before his eyes. "More than success."

He could hear the guards as he turned to the steps of Halls.

". . . more amazing yet . . . a mage who pays."

". . . he be human . . . and I hope to the light he remains such."

The faint praise bothered Cerryl nearly as much as curses would have, but he had to watch every step, afraid he would trip and fall on his way through the front foyer and to the fountain court. The chill of the spray from the fountain sent him into another bout of shivering.

The two apprentice mages he passed steered away from him, and Myredin nodded but did not speak. Ceryl was too tired to worry about it and crossed the rear courtyard to his own Hall.

Lyasa came scurrying as Cerryl limped toward the steps to his quarters and to where he could get water and a good bath. He wanted those more than food.

"Demon-darkness . . . what . . . ? You're sick . . ."

"I'm getting better." That was true. He felt far better than the day before. Or the day before that. "Two days ago, I wasn't sure I'd live."

"What happened?" Lyasa followed Cerryl for a moment, then took his arm as he made his way to his door.

"Not much sleep, bad food, flux, lost mount, lots of walking . . . long trip back from Hydolar." He opened his door. His room appeared unchanged. "I need a bath."

"You need some food and wine." Lyasa studied him. "You're going to fall over."

"Am not." He sank into the chair in front of the desk. "Need to see Jeslek, too."

"Now?"

"I have to."

"You're stubborn." Lyasa sighed. "I'll find something for you while you bathe."

"Thank you."

Lyasa offered another sigh before turning.

Cerryl struggled through a bath, shaving, and changing into fresh whites, wondering if the soiled set he had dragged across Candar could ever be gotten clean, especially the jacket. He was pulling on boots that had seen better days when Lyasa returned with a tray.

"Eat slowly," she commanded, setting the tray on the desk before him. "I couldn't get any wine. If Leyladin could see you now . . ."

Cerryl started with small mouthfuls of bread, interspersed with slivers of cheese. Shortly the stars flashing before his eyes subsided, as did the worst of the light-headedness. Abruptly he stopped. "I'm full."

"You didn't eat that much. Just what *have* you eaten lately?"

"Very little." Cerryl took a healthy sip of the redberry, probably better for him than ale or wine in his present condition. "I have to see Jeslek."

"Can't it wait?"

"When the High Wizard told me to report as soon as I returned?"

Lyasa gave an exasperated sigh. "Mages . . ."

"You're a mage, too."

"Don't remind me."

"I'm sorry."

"It's not your fault. Just go and see Jeslek, and then come back here and get into bed—and eat some more if you can."

"Yes, Aunt Lyasa." Cerryl grinned.

Lyasa grimaced.

Cerryl pulled himself to his feet. Lyasa watched as he walked slowly out the door and down the corridor. Going down the steps to the main level wasn't that bad. Nor was crossing the courtyards and making his way back through the front Hall and foyer. The flights of steps to the top of the White Tower took all the strength he had, or so it seemed.

Hertyl glanced up as Cerryl dragged himself toward Jeslek's door and the ever-present guard.

"Tell the High Wizard I have returned." Cerryl slumped onto the bench next to the messenger, who eased to the end away from the mage.

Hertyl rapped on the door. "The mage Cerryl has returned, sire. He awaits your pleasure."

For the first time Cerryl could recall, Jeslek opened the door. His eyes swept over Cerryl. "Come in."

Cerryl forced himself to his feet and followed the High Wizard inside.

After he closed the door, Jeslek gestured to the chair across the table from the one he took. "Sit down. You look worn out."

Cerryl sat and looked at the High Wizard, behind whom, through the glass of the window, Cerryl could see scattered points of light across the city. "Thank you. It was a long trip, and harder than I thought. The duke barred the city to us . . ."

"Anya reported that." Jeslek's face clouded. "That I had not expected. *Never* has that occurred, not once since the founding of the Order."

After the silence, Cerryl continued. "As you ordered, I removed the duke. Then I climbed down the roof and left the chamber bolted and empty. I couldn't close the window behind me . . ." Cerryl went on to explain his return, not omitting, but not dwelling on in detail, his bout with the flux and his having to walk and ride the last two-thirds of the journey.

"You didn't tell the merchant anything?" probed Jeslek.

"Only that I was junior mage and that we ran errands, did small tasks, and that I'd lost my mount in rough ground."

"Best you could have done." The High Wizard pursed his lips. "Duke Ferobar is dead—and vanished? You are certain?" Jeslek's eyes centered on Cerryl.

"Yes, ser. So is his personal guard, but no others."

"Where did this happen?

"At night, in his personal chambers. I had to hide there and wait for a time until he dozed."

"Did you leave any traces of your presence?"

"Except for a sense of chaos, no, ser."

Jeslek nodded, and a smile crossed his lips. "Good. I had hoped the silence out of Hydolar had meant your success, but it is good to know that." He reached for the scroll on the table and extended it to Cerryl. "Read this. Is it accurate?"

Cerryl had to force himself to focus on the black script, and his eyes wanted to skip over words.

> ... Duke Ferobar mocked his own people by murdering the rightful Duke Uulrac. He mocked Fairhaven by attempting to murder a representative of the High Wizard, and by imprisoning an innocent healer, and then by closing the city gates on emissaries of the Guild ...
>
> ... Duke Ferobar has been removed to where none will ever see him again, and the east tower of Hydolar has been destroyed. These actions should remind the new Duke of Hydlen of his duties to the people of his land and to the Guild. We trust that the road duties will be paid immediately. We also trust that an additional sum of 1,000 golds will be paid to recompense the Guild for its efforts to set matters as they should have been ...

"Yes, ser. I mean, the part about what happened to the duke is. He's ash, and no one will ever see him again." Cerryl swallowed.

"I would prefer not to level the city, but I will, if I must." Jeslek smiled, almost sadly. "Fairhaven can no longer be perceived as weak or tolerant of lapses of obligations by other lands. Weakness leads to either defeat or the need to be more ruthless than strength would have been."

"Oh ..." Cerryl shook his head. "I heard something else. The trader who gave me a ride ... he said that people were saying that Rystryr had raised the road tariffs and was keeping the increase but telling everyone that it was going to Fairhaven." He shrugged. "He was telling what he thought was the truth."

"I had heard some such along those lines from others." The High Wizard nodded. "We will look into that. Now . . . you are weak and ill. Do not worry about gate-guard duty. We have a few new mages. Take the next eight-day to rest and recover. Come to me when you are well."

"Yes, ser." Cerryl managed to get to his feet and out of the High Wizard's chambers without staggering.

Going down the stairs was also no problem, unlike climbing the last steps back up to his room, which left him panting and his vision filled with stars.

Leyladin was waiting when Cerryl trudged into his room.

"Oh . . . Cerryl . . . just lie down."

Cerryl didn't argue, just stretched out on his bed.

Leyladin pulled off his boots, shaking her head. He could feel her order senses probing him, ever so gently.

"Feels good to lie down."

"It's almost as though someone poisoned you."

"Maybe they did," he said hoarsely, explaining about the apples from Duke Ferobar's fruit bowl.

"The poisoners weren't very good. You can do that to apples, but the fluxes conflict, especially for a mage. If they'd put that in pastry, you wouldn't be here." Her hand was cool on his forehead. "Don't talk now. You can tell me everything later."

He lay back on the bed, just glad to be there, glad she was there.

# LXVIII

Cerryl took a long and slow sip of the ale, enjoying it as if he'd hadn't expected to ever taste it again. *That's a bit of self-pity.* With a wry smile, his eyes flicked toward the entry of The Golden Ram, where he could see Myredin and Bealtur leaving. He did not wave to the pair. "This tastes good."

"You should not drink too much," Leyladin said from where she sat at the circular table beside Cerryl.

"Always the healer," added Heralt, his dark eyes smiling.

"Someone has to be."

Cerryl finished the last of his stew, mopping it up with a chunk of bread, glad that both headaches and the poison-induced flux had faded away. He was still weak, he'd discovered, but was getting stronger.

"The words around the tower are that the Duke of Hydlen vanished," Heralt offered. "Has anyone heard who might be the new duke?"

"No one stepped forward this time," Lyasa pointed out.

"What do you think?" Cerryl turned to Leyladin. "You've spent more time in Hydolar than anyone."

The blonde healer lifted her shoulders and smiled shyly. "No one talked to me that much."

"I'll bet you listened." Cerryl grinned.

"Out with it, Leyladin," demanded Lyasa, pushing a lock of jet-black hair off her forehead.

"No one wants to be duke," the blonde finally said. "The traders control both Hydolar and Renklaar, and they don't like our taxes. The High Wizard has demanded immediate payment of the tariffs and a thousand golds in damages. Whoever is duke will have to collect those taxes or face disappearing. He'll also have to rebuild the tower that Anya destroyed, and that will take more coins."

Heralt pursed his lips, then took a swallow of ale. "I'd not like to be in his boots."

"That's because they don't understand the order of chaos," Cerryl said absently.

Leyladin's face darkened momentarily, and she quickly added, "I don't think anyone in Hydlen understands much of anything, except the traders, and all they want is more coins."

"That's what most people want," pointed out Heralt.

Cerryl glanced across the table toward Heralt, reaching out under the table and squeezing Leyladin's hand.

The four looked up as a blond figure in white made his way past the other tables toward the corner.

Faltar pulled over another chair to join the group. "I'm sorry, but I had to pull extra duty. Fydel took Buar with him to Gallos."

"Fydel went to Gallos?" asked Cerryl.

"Right after he and Anya brought Leyladin back," Faltar confirmed. "Something's going on. Eliasar's back, and he's training new lancers. A bunch of them. Some are mercenaries, I think."

"Most are mercenaries," Heralt added.

Faltar raised his arm to catch the attention of the serving girl. "The stew and some ale."

She nodded and kept moving.

"Another ale," said Heralt.

"Another here," added Lyasa

"Three ales and a stew. Be a moment." The girl did turn toward the kitchen then.

"Don't think Buar's that good," Faltar observed, looking toward the kitchen. "Hope she hurries with the ale. Buar, he'll do whatever a senior mage wants, though."

"Don't we all, right now?" asked Cerryl.

Faltar laughed. "Right you are."

"You know, Cerryl," Heralt began slowly, "we don't really know how you ended up here in such sorry condition."

Cerryl took another swallow of ale before he began. "You know I went to Hydolar with Anya and Fydel to get Leyladin, and I was supposed to help Anya."

"You said that before. You and Anya brought down one of the towers."

"Nobody told me that," interjected Faltar.

"The east tower," Cerryl said. "The idea was to tell the duke that he was lucky—that the Guild could bring the whole city down. Jeslek also wanted me to do something in the city. But he didn't realize that we wouldn't even be allowed inside the walls. That's never happened before." Cerryl shrugged. "I did what I was supposed to do and stole a mount to get back. But somewhere I ate some bad food and got a terrible flux. Then, when I was trying to ... well ... anyway ..." He flushed slightly. "The horse got away, and I had to walk back to the Great White Highway, and I managed to get a trader to give me a ride the rest of the way back. Very embarrassing to admit I lost my mount."

*Thump! Thump! Thump!* "Three ales. That's four each."

"Four for an ale, hard to believe," muttered Faltar as he eased out the coppers.

"Stew be ready next." The server scooped up the coins and slipped off to deliver a mug to the adjoining table.

"Ah ... that's good," said Faltar. "Good after a dusty day."

Lyasa took a swallow from her second mug without commenting.

"So ... you did whatever Jeslek told you and then you lost your mount?" Heralt shook his head. "That doesn't seem like you."

"He was sick," Leyladin said. "Very sick. I don't see how he managed it."

"Wait a moment," Faltar said. "Cerryl goes to Hydolar, and then ..."

"Faltar, that's all I can say. All right?" Cerryl's eyes fixed the blond mage's.

"Oh ..." Faltar swallowed, then nodded.

For a moment there was silence around the table.

"I've been gone," Cerryl broke the silence. "What's happened with Spidlar?"

"Three more ships on the blockade," Lyasa said. "I overheard Redark saying that banditry was rising in Spidlar, and now that the ice has closed in, the winter will be even harder than usual."

Cerryl frowned. For some reason, the red-haired smith flicked into his thoughts. Did Black smiths have the same problems as White mages? Somehow, he suspected the man had problems, but not the same ones.

"You sit there in your own thoughts, Cerryl. You're so quiet," Lyasa observed, "but you're the only one in the Guild who's been the target of an assassin, been advanced and then demoted, and had to escape from two unfriendly cities."

Cerryl shrugged. "What can I say? I keep making mistakes."

Faltar laughed.

Even Heralt smiled.

"I'm not sure I accept that," Lyasa said. "We all make mistakes. Even Jeslek makes mistakes."

"I don't know," mused Cerryl, trying to change the subject. "The High Wizard has a real problem. The Guild has been trying to make life in Candar better. Look at Fairhaven. It's cleaner, the people are more prosperous; and there's less peacebreaking. It's almost as if other rulers don't want prosperity."

"They don't," said Leyladin. "They're not interested in prosperity for their people. Look at Jeslek's quarters. They're small. The Duke of Lydiar has a palace. So does the Duke of Hydolar. Even the great factors in Fairhaven do not have mansions the way they do in Lydiar or Renklaar."

If Leyladin considered her father's dwelling modest, and she had seen both factors' dwellings and palaces elsewhere, Cerryl could imagine that the mansions of factors elsewhere must be grand indeed.

"How can a ruler not be concerned about his people?" asked Faltar.

"Most are concerned only that the people pay their taxes." Heralt snorted. "The Guild has a problem. People in Fairhaven don't know how well off they are, and those outside of Fairhaven don't know how much better off they could be under the Guild. Because we can raise chaos, people fear us, and their rulers make sure that we're always the bad ones." He gulped the last of his ale. "Look at Cerryl. He made a mistake on the Patrol—a little one. If a guard bashed a beggar in Fenard or Kyphrien, do you think they'd punish the guard? I demon-darkness know that they don't. Same in Lydiar. Cerryl didn't even do that. Yet we're those fearsome mages who turn people into ash."

Cerryl nodded ever so slightly. What Heralt said made sense, but how many people saw what he'd seen? He rubbed his forehead. He was still more tired than he would have liked.

"Cerryl needs to go," Leyladin announced, standing and half-tugging Cerryl to his feet.

"Still the healer," said Heralt.

"Someone has to take care of him," the healer answered.

"And you're that someone," Lyasa replied.

"Who better?" Leyladin raised her eyebrows.

"Better you than us," said Faltar. "Good night."

"Good night." Cerryl gave a smile and a nod.

The air outside was cooler, cold enough to hint at snow—but far fresher than inside The Golden Ram. Cerryl fastened his jacket.

They walked up the Avenue past the Halls of the Mages, a light and cooler breeze slipping around them.

"I can walk home by myself," Leyladin protested.

"I know you can, but I'd feel better if I walked with you, and you don't want me to worry, do you?"

The blonde laughed. "You are impossible."

"I'm very possible.

"You have to be careful. Jeslek will want you to do something else even more dangerous next time." After a pause, she added, "You shouldn't have made that comment about the order of chaos. Jeslek and Anya would use that against you."

Cerryl sighed. "I know. I'm still tired, and I'm not on guard as I should be."

"What did you mean by that? About the order of chaos?"

"Oh . . . it's obvious if you think about it. Any city, any land, has to have order within it. You can't make a city work without it. There have to be rules, and rules are a form of order. Things like aqueducts and sewers are a form of order. So is peacekeeping. But no one in Fairhaven wants to admit that we need order as much as the Blacks on Recluce do. And," he added with a laugh, "they need chaos, at least some, as much as we do."

Leyladin shivered. "Don't say that around Jeslek. He really will find something horribly dangerous for you to do. And if you do that, the next task he gives you will be even worse."

"He might."

"He will."

"I can take my time getting better."

"I already told him and Kinowin that it would take more than an eight-day. I said that you'd been poisoned and that if they pushed you too soon you wouldn't be able to do as much. And I told Jeslek that I'd told Kinowin and some others that." Leyladin offered a satisfied chuckle. "He wasn't that happy about it, but right now I'm the only healer he has."

"That was wicked." Cerryl squeezed her hand. "I'm grateful that you did."

They turned onto the street leading to Leyladin's dwelling. *Modest dwelling?*

"You meant it about the big houses of the factors in Lydiar?"

"Oh, yes. Kiriol's house is easily three times the size of ours, and his is far from the largest."

Cerryl's lips quirked into a crooked smile lost in the darkness as they walked up the stones to the door.

After Leyladin hugged him and gave him a single warm kiss, Cerryl walked slowly back toward the Halls of the Mages, noting that the warmth of the past few days had faded and that the wind was getting chill again.

Jeslek—what if anything, could Cerryl do about the High Wizard? Jeslek faced a hard situation as High Wizard, and with that Cerryl sympathized. *But you don't want to get killed to solve his problems.*

He shook his head. All he could do was watch and be patient and try to survive. *And hope and be ready if you get the chance.*

# LXIX

Cerryl sat down at the table across from the High Wizard and waited for Jeslek to speak. His fingers brushed the wood of the seat, feeling the slightly gritty white dust that never left the tower, no matter how often it was swept and mopped. Outside the White Tower, as he watched, the light sleet that had been falling, pattering against the glass, stopped, and the indirect sunlight bathing the city brightened.

The white-haired and sun-eyed High Wizard studied Cerryl silently before speaking. "Cerryl, the healer Leyladin has told me that you should have a few more days' respite from heavy physical effort, but that you are capable of doing less taxing things."

"I feel better," Cerryl said firmly, not wanting to admit too much weakness but knowing that he wasn't yet up to another of Jeslek's special tasks.

"Good." Jeslek smiled. "I have a duty that will not tax your body much, but it will help the Guild. You should be interested in it, since you were one of those who brought the matter to my ear. I would like you to use the screeing glass as best you can to see what you can discover about the handling of road taxes and tariffs in Certis. The matters of which you spoke earlier."

Cerryl concealed a swallow. "Yes, ser."

"Even if you discover little, you should become more proficient with the glass. It is a most useful tool, as you will find." Jeslek rubbed his chin. "I would expect you would learn something. You have learned so much in other ways." Jeslek flashed a smile, then stood. "I will not tire you more."

Cerryl stood as well and glanced out the window, noting that the sun had come out again.

"When you find something, let me know."

"Yes, ser." Cerryl gave a small bow before he turned and departed.

Going down the steps was far easier than climbing them had been.

He found Leyladin and Lyasa standing in a sunlit corner in the rear courtyard, in a spot where the cold breeze did not penetrate, although the floor tiles were moist and the courtyard smelled damp, not quite musty.

Lyasa glanced from Cerryl to Leyladin and back to Cerryl. "I need to be going."

"You don't have to go," Cerryl said.

"I really do." Lyasa smiled at Leyladin. "I'll talk to you later, or tomorrow."

Cerryl had the feeling he was missing things, but he was still tired and not ready to puzzle them out. After the black-haired mage left, he sat down on the bench beside Leyladin.

"What's the trouble?" she asked.

"Jeslek wants me to do something. It's not hard, but I can't do it."

"You? The one who's figured out all sorts of new things?"

"I've never had much luck with this. He wants me to use the glass to scree out how Rystryr is taking road tariff coins for his own use. Or how his people are."

"You could do that," Leyladin affirmed.

"I don't even know how to use the glass to find matters that don't have chaos and order—"

"Cerryl," Leyladin corrected, "everything is order and chaos. It's only different combinations. You have to think of it like that."

Cerryl rubbed his forehead, then pushed back the fine brown hair that was getting too long. "I understand that, but how do I *do* it?"

"You practice until you figure out how." She smiled. "Like everything else. If others can do it, so can you. The opposite isn't true, for which you should be grateful."

He nodded slowly.

"You're tired, but you can do it. Do you want me to come with you?"

"No. I suspect Lyasa will be back, and I don't have much to say, right now."

"And you worried that you can't do this perfectly, the way you want to do everything."

Cerryl gave a wry nod.

"You can." Her smile was warm. "You will."

He walked slowly back to his quarters, holding onto her words of support. He was tired, but ... he had to learn something else. *Is life just always learning something else?* He paused as the answer came unbidden: *It is if you want to survive and prosper.* He took a deep breath and started up the steps, his thoughts scattered. How could he discover whom to follow in the glass? If he began with those who concentrated chaos ...

Shyren—the Guild mage in Jellico. Surely the man had enough chaos around him for Cerryl to use the glass to find him. Shyren had to meet with other people, and, with effort, perhaps Cerryl could call up their images once he had seen them with Shyren. *Perhaps . . .*

# LXX

The figure Cerryl watched in the screeing glass strode down a narrow stone-walled corridor, lit dimly by scattered lamps, then quickly crossed a courtyard through a rain that blurred the image in the glass, before entering yet another building and climbing a wide staircase into the ornate dining hall that Cerryl recognized. He took a deep breath and let go of the image, not looking as the image of the mage in white faded, as did the silver mists surrounding Shyren. Fascinating as the searching was getting, Cerryl's head ached, and he needed to eat.

Half-amazed at the growing darkness in his room, Cerryl rubbed his forehead. Was it already after sunset? That meant he was too late for the evening repast in the Meal Hall. He pushed back the chair from the table, whose polished wood felt gritty to his touch. Then he stood and walked to the window. His stomach growled, reminding him more emphatically that he needed to find something to eat.

He wished he'd been able to see Leyladin, but, again, she was off to Lydiar because Duke Estalin was worried about his son once more— another bout of something. Cerryl understood why Jeslek wanted her there, especially with the continuing mess in Hydolar and all Jeslek's concerns about Spidlar, but the younger mage wasn't totally pleased with her absence.

His stomach growled again, and he turned and pulled his white cold-weather jacket out of his wardrobe. He looked down and wiggled his toes in the new boots that had almost depleted his purse. He still had enough for a bite at The Ram, and tomorrow he could draw his stipend.

At the door, his eyes went back to the glass.

He could keep following Shyren, although he was certain the mage knew he was being tracked by the glass, but Cerryl had to wonder if there weren't a better way to see if he could discover what was happening with the golds of the Certan road duties. He shook his head. He wanted to find out who handled the golds, but he couldn't exactly call up images of coins. Coins weren't really composed of active order or chaos, the way people were. Of course, they often created chaos.

He frowned. They created chaos. Could he use the glass or his senses to find lines or concentrations of chaos, the kind that might be created by those who had coins?

Chaos . . . the glass was still easier to use when chaos was involved, unless the concentration of order was strong—as with the redheaded smith in Diev. Something about the smith bothered Cerryl, but he couldn't say what. His looks at the smith had shown that Dorrin had built his own smithy and a barn. Clearly, the smith planned to stay in Spidlar, yet the house and smithy weren't built like they were outposts for more Blacks to follow. Were they built for the lady trader? But he had yet to scree the woman. Where was she?

Cerryl massaged the back of his neck. Woolgathering about the smith wasn't going to get him fed. He closed the door and walked along the corridor toward the steps down to the main level and the rear courtyard. The ongoing chill of winter had seeped into the building, and he fastened his jacket as he walked.

# LXXI

The dwelling in the screeing glass before Cerryl was three stories tall, built of timber and stone, with diamond-shaped leaded glass panes in the long and narrow windows. At the mounting block before the dwelling was a carriage drawn by two matched grays. A man in a dark gray cloak trimmed in silver brocade stepped from the carriage and under the archway.

Cerryl glanced up at the rap on his door.

"Ser?" The high voice had to be that of a messenger.

With a sigh, one of those he was issuing all too often lately, Cerryl rose from his table-desk, letting the image lapse, and walked to the door, opening it.

"Ser, the High Wizard requests your presence as soon as you can be there." The lad in red bowed twice, his eyes avoiding Cerryl's.

"I'll be right there."

"Thank you, ser." The messenger scurried back down the corridor.

Cerryl straightened his shirt, tunic, and belt, then left his quarters and walked quickly through the Halls of the Mages. He could hear the mumble of apprentices in the commons and in the library, but he did not peer in as he passed. The corridors and courtyards were empty, except for one mage—Elsinot. The two nodded to each other as they passed in the front foyer. Then Cerryl started up to the White Tower.

The duty guard was one Cerryl did not know. "Ser?"

"The mage Cerryl. The High Wizard requested my presence."

"One moment, ser." The guard rapped on the door and announced, "The mage Cerryl, at your request, High Wizard."

"Bid him enter."

"You may enter." The guard held the door.

Cerryl closed the door firmly, careful not to slam it. Jeslek, seated at the table, did not rise but pointed to the chair across the polished wood from him.

"You summoned me?" said Cerryl as he seated himself.

"I did. What have you discovered? About the road coins? Have you found anything?"

How could Cerryl explain?

"Ah . . . yes . . . and no, ser." He pursed his lips, then frowned. Finally, he plunged in. "I have seen things in the glass that would suggest road taxes in Certis are not going where they should, but I could not say for certain that such is so. I could not tell you how many coins are not reaching either the viscount or the Guild."

"Go on." Jeslek sounded almost bored or as if he had expected something of the sort.

"The man who seems to be the finance minister, he lives in a house that could be a palace. Two of those who seem to work for him, they also live in houses larger than those of the grandest of factors here in Fairhaven . . ."

"Good." Jeslek nodded. "You are making progress. I would like you to see what more you can discover in the next eight-day." After a hesitation, the High Wizard asked, "How are you feeling?"

"Much better. I still get tired more easily than I used to, but in a few more days I hope . . ."

"You have at least an eight-day. If you can discern more before that, I would like to be informed."

"Yes, ser."

Jeslek stood. "Until later, Cerryl."

Caught by surprise, Cerryl sat for a moment, then stood. "Yes, ser."

His head seemed almost to spin as he walked out of Jeslek's chambers. While the High Wizard had not been caustic or cruel, as he had seemed at times in the past, he had definitely been preoccupied. Were matters in Spidlar getting worse? Or was it Hydlen?

Cerryl walked slowly down the stone steps of the White Tower, still trying to figure out what had bothered him about the quick meeting. Jeslek almost hadn't seemed to care, yet he had summoned Cerryl.

The first dinner bell rang, echoing through the front foyer. In a way, that amused the brown-haired mage, because few, if any, in the front Hall or the White Tower ever ate in the Meal Hall.

At the moment, the Meal Hall didn't sound too bad, because his coins were limited and Leyladin had yet to return from Lydiar. His infrequent and quick looks with the glass had shown a healthier-looking boy with her, presumably Duke Estalin's son. So Cerryl hoped it wouldn't be too long before she returned. In the meantime, he would eat in the Halls and save his coins.

Heralt was already at the serving table when Cerryl reached the Meal Hall. Seeing the creamed mutton, Cerryl smiled, imagining Faltar's choice words about the meat. After filling his plate and taking a healthy chunk of the rye-and-grain bread and a mug of the weak ale, Cerryl joined Heralt at one of the side tables.

Cerryl nodded as he sat, then took a mouthful of bread. He couldn't face starting with the mutton, hungry as he was. Next he sipped the ale, followed at last by some of the creamed mutton, which gave off an orangish smell. *Orange?* He didn't want to think about it. After several mouthfuls, he turned to Heralt. "How is guard duty going?"

Heralt looked blankly at Cerryl for a moment, then glanced around the as yet sparsely filled Meal Hall before speaking, his voice lowered. "Things are getting bad. They brought in a trader. Traders dress pretty much the same. Her hair was short, almost like a man's, and she wore ... you know. But she's a woman, and the lancers brought her in through my gate. They had her bound. It ... just didn't feel right."

"How did you know she was a trader?"

"I was guessing, but it bothered me." Heralt shrugged. "So I asked Fydel why they were bringing in a trader."

"And?" The fact that Fydel was bringing back a woman dressed as a trader bothered Cerryl ... something he should be remembering.

"He told me to ask Jeslek."

"That's odd," mused the gray-eyed mage. "If she owed road taxes, they didn't need to bring her here. If she attacked a mage, she'd be ash already." Female trader? He swallowed—was it the one tied up with the smith that Jeslek, Anya, and Fydel all worried about?

"You look like you know something—like you were hit in the face with a staff," Heralt observed.

"I'm not sure, but ... if ... well ... There's a female trader that Anya was worried about."

Heralt glanced around the Hall again, then at the line of five apprentices who had suddenly appeared at the serving table. "I wouldn't want to be a woman Anya didn't like, not one who wasn't a mage."

"Nor I. But I don't know why she doesn't like this one," Cerryl admitted, "except that this woman trader, if she's the same one, knows a Black smith."

"I don't like it." Heralt grimaced. "The prefect of Gallos not quite defying the Guild, the old prefect killing Sverlik, the Duke of Hydlen killing the old duke—he was just a child—and trying to kill Gorsuch and then disappearing. Things are getting bad."

*Worse*, Cerryl corrected mentally, *much worse, even if you can't prove it*. "It looks that way."

"Why?" asked Heralt. "There have been bad years for crops before. That's not new. There have been viscounts and prefects and dukes who have disputed the road tariffs before. That's not new. There have been traders here in Fairhaven that didn't like the Guild, and that's not new. Recluce has been there for something like twenty-five-score years, always an enemy. Yet we have more mages and more White highways than ever before, and most people in Candar are better off." The dark-eyed mage spread his hands.

"I don't know why." Cerryl paused. He had been about to say that it seemed no one respected the Guild as much, but was that it? How could the other lands in Candar—and Recluce—not respect Fairhaven after the example of the enormous power demonstrated by Jeslek in creating the Little Easthorns? "I don't know."

Heralt stood. "I have to go." He grinned. "I'll see you later."

"Who is she?"

Heralt just shook his head.

"You're not saying? Wise man."

Heralt grinned, then turned.

Cerryl finished the last of his dinner alone at the table, ignoring the chatter of the apprentices.

Instead of going back to his room after eating, Cerryl went back through the fountain courtyard, and the cold and windblown spray, and into the front Hall. He took the steps to the lowest level of the White Tower and eased around the corridor past the guards to Kinowin's quarters, where he knocked.

"You can come in, Cerryl."

Cerryl closed the door behind him.

Kinowin looked up. He was standing by the bookshelves and studying a volume half-open in his huge hand. "I hope this isn't about that Patrol business. You have to talk to Isork about that, if you want to rejoin the Patrol. And it would have to be a year or more from now."

"No, ser. It's not about the Patrol. Not that I know of."

Kinowin glanced at the pages before him, then closed the book. "Then sit down."

Cerryl sat, his nose twitching. Was it the dust from the old volume Kinowin held? He rubbed his nose, and the itch subsided but did not go away totally.

Kinowin walked toward the window, his back to the purple and blue hanging, his eyes focused out through the thick glass of the window closed against the early-evening chill. "What is it?"

"Fydel and the lancers brought in a trader, a woman trader."

"That bothers you?"

"Yes," Cerryl answered directly. "I cannot see any reason for it, not even with all the problems that the Guild faces. Fydel could discipline a trader without using a full lancer detachment."

"Strange, yes." The overmage nodded without looking at Cerryl. The younger mage waited.

"Overmage or not, Cerryl, I am not privy to all that is done for the High Wizard."

"Yes, ser."

"Why does a simple trader bother you?" asked Kinowin, finally turning from the window.

How much should he tell Kinowin? He cleared his throat. "Some time ago, I overheard a remark by Anya about a female trader who was linked to the smith in Spidlar—the Black one that Jeslek is following. The one called . . . Dorrin, I believe."

Kinowin raised his bushy blond eyebrows. "Yes?"

Cerryl shrugged. "It's not my task. Yet it disturbs me, and I don't know why."

"Those who get involved in what is not their task . . . What happened with the Patrol, Cerryl?"

Cerryl winced inwardly at the implied reprimand. "Ser, I have done nothing, nor will I. I know that when something bothers me, such as this, there is a problem. I can do nothing. But I thought you should know, if you did not already. All I can do is bring it to your attention."

Kinowin gave a soft laugh. "So you will make this problem mine?"

Encouraged by the open, humorous tone of the overmage's laugh, Cerryl gave a wry smile. "Yes, ser. I do not know where else to turn, and you are far more capable at such than I."

"Cerryl, that sounds like Anya. Why don't you say what you mean?"

Cerryl swallowed. "It bothers me. I think it will not help the Guild. I don't know why, but I feel strongly. Who else can I let know?"

"That's more honest . . . and more disturbing." Kinowin paced back to the other side of the room, pausing and fingering a green and silver hanging featuring interlocking triangles. "All I can say is that I will inquire, in my own fashion." He turned and looked at Cerryl. "Is that enough?"

Cerryl stood. "Yes, ser. That's all I can ask."

"It's more than you can ask, Cerryl, but I trust your feelings about the Guild. Now . . . let a poor overmage have a few moments to read."

Cerryl stood, a rueful smile on his face. With a bow he left, heading back to the uncertainty of his room and a screeing glass that showed more and more and revealed less and less.

# LXXII

Cerryl looked at the chaos swirling across the glass, disrupting his search for Leyladin. Maybe he needed a moment of rest. He stood and paced back and forth across his room. Then he took a sip of water from the mug on the desk.

Finally, he reseated himself before the glass, but he could sense strong patterns of chaos, far closer than Lydiar—or Certis. Something was wrong in Fairhaven, perhaps even in the Halls . . . subtly wrong, and wrong at the moment. *But what? Do you really want to know?*

He looked down at the silvered mirror on the desk, hoping to trace out the wrongness through the glass. The mists parted, and Cerryl's mouth opened as he saw the image in the glass.

*Cracckkkk!* The White Guard continued to lash the figure strapped facedown on the long table, and a line of red slashed across the legs.

A white-haired White wizard's hands moved, as if to fight back something. The mage's forehead shimmered with sweat, and he glanced at a mirror on a small table, tilted toward him.

Cerryl frowned, but he could not make out the image in the mirror. He could discern that the White wizard was Jeslek and that Anya stood beside him. The lash cut across the bare shoulders of the figure strapped on the table, and the prisoner shuddered.

The wizard frowned, glanced at Anya.

She shook her head and spoke briefly.

Instead of responding, Jeslek took a sip from a mug. His face tightened in concentration, and he nodded to the guard. The whip snapped across the woman's bare back.

Jeslek wiped his forehead and nodded once more to the guard.

Another lash cracked across the woman's back.

The smile on Anya's face turned Cerryl's guts, and he swallowed. By the time he looked again, the guard had unstrapped the unconscious woman and lifted her over his shoulders like a sack. The guard followed Fydel from the lower tower room.

Cerryl quickly let the image lapse, hoping that Jeslek and Anya had been too preoccupied to notice or, if they had, too much so to determine which mage had been observing. Despite the chill in his room, sweat beaded across his forehead, and his guts still threatened to rise into his throat.

*What can you do? You've told Kinowin, and if Jeslek finds out that you're spying on him . . .*

For a time Cerryl sat before the blank glass. Then he stood, squared his shoulders, and walked to the window, looking out as fluffy flakes of snow drifted down past the heavy glass.

After a time, he turned, wiped his forehead, and walked to his door, heading toward the fountain court. He stood by the archway for some time, knowing that Anya would come—should come—sooner or later.

At last, he sensed the wave of chaos that accompanied Anya as she crossed the front foyer of the Halls of the Mages and headed toward the fountain court.

Looking worried and as if he were not paying attention, he started across the courtyard at an angle, ignoring the snow that fluttered down and melted on the stones.

"Cerryl! Watch where you're going. You almost ran into me." Anya looked at Cerryl intently. "You meant to catch my attention."

"Of course." Cerryl grinned. "I couldn't keep that from you." The scent of sandalwood and trilia was almost overpowering, but he couldn't let that distract him.

"But why?" Anya seemed genuinely curious.

"Do you have a moment?" He pointed toward the bench beyond the fountain before he realized, belatedly, it was wet. He stopped short of sitting as he drew her toward it.

"You intrigue me, Cerryl. A moment only." Still, she followed him, and they both stood beside the bench.

The gray-eyed mage looked directly at Anya. "War or conflict takes force. If you kill the trader woman, you will force that Black smith, whatever his name may be—"

"Dorrin," Anya said with an amused smile. "Dorrin."

"To attack Fairhaven. Can't you sense just how much order he embodies? He carries as much order as Jeslek does chaos."

"Cerryl . . . you can see much, but there is a great deal which you do not see." Anya flashed the bright and false smile. "Of course, the smith embodies great order. But you always did have a soft spot for victims. That was what caused you trouble with the Patrol. Let me assure you that the trader lady will return to her smith, and she will survive."

"Then why did you have Jeslek torture her?"

"Cerryl . . . do you know what Jeslek would do to you if I mentioned this?"

The younger mage forced a smile, blocking his true feelings as he had learned to do so long before in order to survive. "Anya . . . I would tell him that you told me, and he would believe me."

Anya's smile faded. "You surprise me, Cerryl. What is the trader woman to you?"

"Nothing. I've never met her. I'm worried about Fairhaven."

For a time the redhead studied Cerryl. Finally, a half-smile crossed her lips. "You really do. You really are like Jeslek. I never would have expected it."

Cerryl distrusted the second smile, even more than the first.

"She will go back to her smith. Never fear. And nothing more need be said. Do you understand?"

Cerryl understood that he could not trust Anya, but that she told the truth so far as the lady trader's return went. There was more there, but he didn't know what else to ask or how to follow up on what he had learned. So he nodded.

"Good." Anya turned and left him standing there.

Once she had left the court, Cerryl took a deep breath. What else could he have done? He couldn't have approached Jeslek or Kinowin again, and certainly not Fydel. Only Anya was devious enough that she had enough to hide from Jeslek. *You hope . . .*

Slowly . . . he turned and started back to his room.

# LXXIII

Cerryl stepped up to the door, but it opened before he could lift the knocker, and Leyladin was in his arms. He held on for a long time.

Finally, she stepped back. "It's cold out. You could come in."

"I came as soon as I got your message."

"I can see that." She smiled, with a warmth that made him forget the chill and the slush in the streets through which he'd walked, then stepped back.

They walked into the sitting room to the right of the entry hall. A fire had been laid in the hearth, and the warmth was welcome to Cerryl. A faintly aromatic smell from the fire filled the air, not quite pine, but something resinous.

Leyladin settled onto the settee, and Cerryl sat beside her.

"It's gotten cold and stayed that way."

"It's winter," Cerryl suggested with a laugh.

"The weather is colder than usual."

"The whole year's been strange." Cerryl turned on the settee. "When will your father be home?"

"Not for a bit." Leyladin paused. "You almost don't seem glad to see me, not after the first few moments."

"It's not that." Cerryl looked past the healer, toward the painting of her mother, and the image's blue eyes seemed to bore into him.

"You're upset. More troubles with Jeslek?"

"Not exactly . . ." He pursed his lips.

"What don't you want to tell me?"

"It's not that." He paused. "You can't tell anyone, not even Lyasa."

"I won't." A smile danced across her lips. "Not even Lyasa."

"Fydel captured a woman trader and brought her back . . ." Cerryl detailed all that he knew. ". . . and when they whipped her, Jeslek was twisting chaos . . . I could sense it, so much that I almost couldn't scree at the time. I couldn't go to Kinowin again, and I couldn't exactly question the High Wizard. So I confronted Anya. She told me that the woman was being returned to the smith. She is on her way back. I checked." Cerryl shook his head. "I don't understand any of this. I've told Kinowin, but I can't press him on it, not after the mess I made of the Patrol."

"And you can't let Jeslek know you saw him torture this woman."

"I don't see how; do you?"

"Not in your position, Cerryl." Leyladin shook her head.

Cerryl glanced at the image of the healer's mother, but the eyes remained bleak blue and fixed upon him.

"Jeslek tortured the smith's woman," Leyladin said slowly. "It doesn't make Jeslek look very good."

"No, it doesn't."

"That doesn't further your order of chaos."

Cerryl took a deep breath. What could he say?

"You could say that he will pay for it," suggested the blonde.

"He may."

"You could say that you could do nothing."

"For now, I fear I have done what I can. I may have made matters worse, both for her and for me. I did not know until the torture was almost over. I couldn't even have run there fast enough to shorten what they did." Cerryl shrugged despondently. "Her torture will enrage this Dorrin. He appears to be a man who will find an answer, no matter what the cost. I hope I am not too near when he does."

"He is similar to you, then." Leyladin laughed, flirtatiously yet distantly.

Cerryl looked at the floor.

"How do you feel about this . . . torture?"

"It was wrong."

"No . . . what does it make you feel?"

"What difference does that make? I don't exactly have the power to do anything."

"Fear, rage, anger, despair—they're like chaos within you. You keep what you feel about everything to yourself. Sooner or later, Cerryl, you'll have to trust someone."

"I trust you."

"You trust me with what has happened, but I have to pull out of you what you feel."

"That's hard for me."

"I know." The blonde healer slipped an arm around him and hugged him for but a moment. "You've never had anyone to share with, have you?"

"No."

"You need to learn."

"We are already."

Leyladin frowned. "What do you mean?"

"A while back, I was thinking something, but I never said it. You answered what I was thinking."

"It must have been obvious." She gave a soft and humorous laugh.

"Perhaps it was." Cerryl wasn't sure but forbore saying more as the front door thudded against the foyer wall.

"Cold as a winter road out there, it is!" Layel called as he stamped his feet in the entry foyer. Then he stepped into the sitting room and strode past the two on the settee and stood before the hearth. "Nothing like a warm hearth after a cold ride."

"Where were you riding from?" asked Cerryl.

"Just from Muneat's warehouse. It's on the far northwest, but the wind has picked up, and I fear cold and more snow. He had some brocade, goodly stuff, but a goodly price as well."

"You didn't buy any," Leyladin said with a laugh.

"I buy as little as I can when the price is dear, no matter how someone tells me it will become dearer." The balding blond trader shook his head. "If it becomes dearer, all too often, none have the coins to purchase. So I buy what I can that others will have coins for." He turned so his backside was warmed by the hearth. "Little enough of that, these days. What a world! Still there is no duke in Hydolar, and brigands are everywhere on the roads out of and into Spidlar. One of the best traders I know, fine fellow, Willum was, always had goods of a differing streak—he's dead, killed by brigands. Never been to his warehouse, some small port in Spidlar—Diev, that's it. Met him in Elparta or Axum, handful of times, and he's gone."

Cerryl frowned. He'd heard the name somewhere, but he couldn't recall where.

"You know him?" asked Layel.

"No, ser. I've heard the name, but I can't remember where."

"Then there's Freidr . . . factor in Jellico, sent me a scroll wanting to know why your Guild was insisting all warehouses in Jellico be inspected." Layel raised his eyebrows.

"I didn't know anything about that," Cerryl confessed.

"No matter. I'm warmer. Is dinner ready?" the factor asked his daughter.

"Let me check with Meridis." Leyladin rose and headed for the kitchen.

"You looked most shocked, young Cerryl, when I spoke of inspections."

"I was, ser. I'd never heard of that before."

"Neither had I; neither had I. Sorry place the world be getting to. Would that those Black angels on Recluce leave us well enough alone."

Cerryl refrained from commenting that he wasn't certain all the problem lay with Recluce.

Leyladin reappeared, standing in the archway by the hearth. "Meridis is more than ready. She wanted to know what took you." The healer grinned at her father.

"Blasted woman. What took me? Gaining the coins to pay for the food and her stipend—that's what took me . . ." Layel broke off as he saw the twinkle in Leyladin's eyes. "Daughter, you will order me to death."

"Not me."

Layel glanced at Cerryl. "Daughters! Let us eat."

Leyladin and Cerryl exchanged glances, their mouths offering amused smiles beneath momentarily laughing eyes.

# LXXIV

Wondering why Kinowin had summoned him, Cerryl rapped on the overmage's door. *Has he discovered something about the woman trader? Or the smith?*

"Come in, Cerryl."

Cerryl entered and closed the door behind him. The room was warm, despite the chill outside the White Tower and he lack of a hearth within the overmage's chamber. With the warmth was the scent of something almost astringent, healerlike.

"You summoned me?"

Kinowin gestured to a chair, and Cerryl sat, still wondering.

"Cerryl," said the overmage. "Jeslek has suggested to me that you accompany the expedition to Spidlar."

"Me? A former Patrol mage who couldn't abide by the rules?" Cerryl kept his voice dubious, but not sarcastic, because sarcasm would annoy Kinowin. Why had Jeslek not told Cerryl himself? The High Wizard had not hesitated to do so in the past.

"Few in the lancers know that, but most would deem that a benefit. Jeslek claims he'll need someone to restore peace in the bigger towns, but someone who's seen battles and will be useful. He implied that someone who would not be missed in other ways would be more suitable."

Cerryl winced. "He wants me out of his way and to disappear when he's safely conquered Spidlar."

"That may be. But . . . if you do well, and survive, you most likely won't have to worry about arrows from side streets for the rest of your life. Or being sent out to remove fractious rulers single-handedly." Kinowin's tone was half-humorous, half-serious. He frowned. "You know, do you not, that a new duke has yet to emerge in Hydolar? Nor have the road tariffs been paid."

"I didn't know. I don't think I'm surprised. Are you suggesting that Jeslek might send me back there if I don't go with the expedition to Spidlar?"

"I could not presume to guess the High Wizard's intent." Kinowin's eyes twinkled, and an ironic smile appeared—briefly.

"What do you think Myral would have said?" Cerryl asked.

"He would have suggested you go. I'm certain of that." Kinowin offered a gentle smile.

Cerryl grinned and then shrugged. "I'll go." *Not that there was much choice.* "Is there anything special I should take that I don't know enough to think about?"

Kinowin cocked his head. "Patience. After that, a spare pair of boots and an extra good wool blanket. You'll be going before the High Wizard with Fydel to Jellico. You and Fydel will accompany the Certan levies and their commanders from Jellico to Spidlar, when the time comes."

"Just us?"

"You'll have a large detachment of White Lancers, but most will be with Jeslek, I understand. He has some plan in mind. He hasn't disclosed it, and I doubt he will."

"He must be . . . preoccupied."

"Not to tell you himself?" The overmage sipped something from his mug, though it did not seem like cider or yellow fir tea to Cerryl. "He will, in time, but he is only one mage, and matters have gotten far from simple in recent eight-days. Far from simple." Kinowin set the mug down on the table and glanced toward the purple and blue hanging.

"The woman trader went back to Spidlar," Cerryl ventured.

"I know. That was a time back. I doubt Jeslek's plan will work, but there's little either of us can do. Not now and not at this distance. I fear it may turn upon him, and I told him so, though he did not consult me, either, before undertaking it." Kinowin shook his head. "You can do nothing. Not now. Concentrate on what you can do."

*That's hard . . . and getting harder.* "I'll try."

"You'd better try harder . . . if you want to survive this next year." Kinowin lifted the mug once more. "That was all I wanted to tell you."

"Thank you." Cerryl rose, still filled with doubts and questions, so many that he couldn't have centered on one at that moment. As he left, he could still smell the astringent odor. Was Kinowin drinking something because he was ill? Or to prevent illness?

The thought of the Guild without Kinowin as overmage sent a chill down Cerryl's back as he headed for the steps out of the Tower.

# LXXV

We're going to Furenk's tonight," Leyladin had told Cerryl, in the firm tone that brooked no argument. "I'm paying, and you're going to enjoy the food and the wine."

The two walked down the Avenue, carefully avoiding the few patches of ice remaining on the paving stones. The air bore the trace of an acrid odor, one Cerryl would have described as that of damp chaos, though he had no idea how chaos could have been damp.

"It's been a cold winter," said Leyladin.

"It was a warm harvest and a hot summer, though."

"Hydolar was beastly. I'm glad you came and got me."

"How was Duke Ferobar?"

"I don't know. I never saw him. I think he was fearful of mages. I'd rather not talk about it anymore. I was glad to see you. I was even halfway glad to see Anya."

"That is something."

Leyladin's eyebrows rose. "Fydel is nice enough, but he'll only do what he's told. You and Anya will do what you think is necessary. Jeslek sent Anya to make sure Hydlen paid. He sent you to make sure the duke paid."

"You don't like him."

"No, I don't, but . . ." She left the sentence unfinished.

"You're not sure which is worse—Sterol's caution or Jeslek's actions?"

"Something like that." The blonde gestured toward the archway. The marble plaque at Furenk's was unchanged, still proclaiming: "The Inn at Fairhaven," although the pink marble steps were damp from the mist that had followed the cold rain.

Despite the season, the entry area held the faint scent of flowers. *Incense?* wondered Cerryl, although he saw no braziers.

As had occurred the last time, a tall functionary in a pale blue cotton shirt and a dark blue vest appeared. "Lady Leyladin, Mage Cerryl, how good to see you both."

As Cerryl wondered how the man in blue knew his name, the functionary took both their coats and then led the way to a corner table in the back dining room. He seated Leyladin.

Cerryl sat down across from the blonde healer. Again, the ten tables of the back dining room were empty, except for the one where they sat. The pale blue linen was spotless and ironed smooth. The polished bronze lamp in the middle of the table cast a warm but faint glow, and the hearth in the middle of the wall held a moderately high fire that removed all trace of chill from the back dining area.

"It's as elegant as I remember. Like you," offered Cerryl.

"You're elegant, too, you know." Leyladin smiled. "I didn't want to share you tonight. Father would have talked and talked and talked about trade and how bad things are getting."

"They are, but . . . I'm glad we're here."

"Lady . . . ser?" A heavyset woman in the dark blue trousers and vest with the pale blue shirt appeared beside the table. "This evening, we have the special sliced beef with mushrooms and pearapples or a rack of lamb, young lamb glazed in minted apple."

"The lamb," said Leyladin, "and a bottle of the Kyphran gold wine."

"The beef."

After the server left, Cerryl looked across the table at the blonde in green, at the deep green eyes he often felt he could fall into. He smiled.

"Why the smile?"

"You."

"Good. I'm glad. You know, you never tell me about what it was like growing up outside of Fairhaven."

"Hard. Not terrible . . . but hard in a way. I had to fetch water from the spring above the mines. The ones below ran green and yellow sometimes and smelled of brimstone. The house . . . it was nicer than many, even in Hrisbarg. Uncle Syodar took the best from the mine buildings after the old duke closed the mines . . ." Cerryl continued to offer his impressions of the mines and growing up there. ". . . something sad about a place where so many men had worked, and then where only my uncle was left." He paused as the server returned with the wine.

Leyladin sipped the first drops, then nodded and let the server fill each goblet half-full.

Cerryl lifted the goblet and took a sip, smiling as he tasted the Kyphran gold wine, a wine that smelled and tasted like it held faint traces of the best fruits of spring, summer, and fall swirled together. "This is good, maybe the best wine I've tasted."

"I've always liked it. Father said I should." Leyladin grinned. "It's four silvers a bottle."

Cerryl swallowed—almost half a gold for a single bottle? "No wonder it's good."

"Enjoy it." Leyladin lifted her goblet.

After a moment, Cerryl took another sip. Four silvers or not, it was good. "What do you think about Kinowin telling me Jeslek wants me to go to Jellico and then Spidlar?"

"He doesn't want you too close to him here in Fairhaven, perhaps anywhere. I think he's afraid of you, in a way."

"Me?"

"No false modesty, Cerryl. None of the younger mages have your strength or talent."

"Still . . ." he mused.

"Had I thought of it, I would have expected that Jeslek wanted you to go with the forces to Spidlar." Leyladin tightened her lips. "He may even let it be known that you are the mage who removed two rulers."

Cerryl frowned. He had thought of that. "But if he does, then, if he has to have anyone, not just me, but anyone, do that again, it makes it harder."

"There is that." Her eyebrows arched.

"You don't trust him?"

"I trust him to do what benefits him. You benefit him—now. You won't always, you know."

"I know." He took another sip of the golden wine, trying to separate out the flavors . . . and failing.

"So long as he has problems . . ."

"That could be a while. I still don't quite understand how things got so bad. Heralt was pointing out that nothing is new. I mean, we've had bad crops, problems with Recluce, ungrateful rulers, trade difficulties . . . sometimes all at once, but the Guild hasn't had to fight half of Candar in one form or another."

"No mage has created mountains before," she answered.

"I wondered about that." He looked up as the server returned with two plates. "Part of the reason is that it's easier to manipulate chaos within the ground than pull pure chaos from the ground and cast it like a firebolt. Part is, I think, that Jeslek wants to split Gallos in two with the mountains. I said that, and he didn't correct me."

The heavyset woman placed the lamb before Leyladin and the beef before Cerryl.

"Thank you," Leyladin said.

"Will there be anything else, lady, ser?"

Cerryl and Leyladin exchanged glances. Then Cerryl spoke. "No, thank you."

The gray-eyed mage cut a small sliver of the beef and chewed it slowly. "Also good."

"Try a bite of the lamb." Leyladin extended a morsel.

After clearing his mouth with a sip of the wine, he ate the lamb.

"Good. Better than the beef, I think, but not much." He recalled Faltar and his aversion to lamb, then pushed away the thought.

After a short silence, Leyladin said, "You think too highly of Jeslek, even as you worry about him."

Cerryl frowned. "Do you really think that? Why?"

"You seem to think Jeslek thinks beyond himself. I have doubts of that. Either way, he would have you with him to do those tasks he would rather not do. So would Anya, for different reasons."

Cerryl offered an enigmatic smile.

"You aren't listening. You always give me that order-cursed smile when you don't want to tell me I'm wrong. Anya is pure poison, especially for you. Everything she says is twisted, but you listen to everyone, and then you have to figure it out. You usually do, but while you're trying to understand it all, you can do stupid things . . ." Leyladin shook her head. "I don't know why I bother."

"I don't trust her, either. I have few choices. I would rather stay with you." Cerryl sighed slowly. "There. Is that better?"

"It's more honest," said Leyladin. "Why don't you try it?"

"What? Honesty?" Cerryl laughed gently. "I have. It doesn't work. Except with you, and you're a Black."

"You were honest with Myral. You're honest with Kinowin."

"I never lied. I've misled them both with partial truths." Cerryl's mouth twisted. "In that way, Jeslek is honest. He doesn't pretend to be listening. He can afford that. You can, you know, when you're the most powerful White wizard in recorded history."

"What about the ancient Whites?"

"I don't trust legends. In any case, that knowledge has mostly been lost." Cerryl finished the last of his beef and pearapples and then wiped up the sauce with a scrap of bread. "That was outstanding. Thank you."

"You're welcome. Now you understand why I like to come here."

"I do." He frowned.

"What's the matter?"

"Oh, nothing. You said I'd understand, and I do, but most people don't. People talk about understanding," the gray-eyed wizard mused. "What they mean is that they want you to understand what they want or believe enough so that you'll change. Understanding itself doesn't change anything."

"You are cynical."

"Truth isn't cynical, Leyladin."

"Enough of truth or cynicism. We don't have that much time left." She gestured toward the server, who had peered into the rear dining area, then waited for the woman to approach.

"Yes, lady?"

"What of sweets?"

"We have a honey cake and an egg custard glazed with the rare raw sugar of Hamor."

"The egg custard," Leyladin ordered.

"I'd like that also." Cerryl nodded in agreement.

With a smile, the server turned. Cerryl refilled both their goblets, emptying the bottle. "I've enjoyed the meal . . . and the company."

"I liked the company, too. But not another word about the Guild."

"Yes, lady." He smiled at her.

"What was your uncle like? You've never said, except that he was a master miner."

"He was a miner. His words were rough, and his heart was good. He believed in doing his best in working. Dylert—the mill master— once said that he admired him above all the other craft masters. I didn't know he was a master crafter until after I'd left the mines."

"Did he know you'd be a mage?"

"He and Aunt Nall both knew I had the talent. They tried to keep glasses away from me when I was young."

"Wise of them."

"I didn't think so at the time." Cerryl laughed, then paused as the server arrived with the egg custards, each in a circular dish covered with a hard and dark brown glaze.

Leyladin raised her eyebrows at the server and mouthed something.

"Seven and five, lady."

"Thank you." The healer turned to Cerryl and smiled. "Go ahead. Try it."

The glaze was powerfully sweet, sweeter even than honey, contrasting with the subdued richness of the custard.

"Rich . . . but good," he finally said, looking at the empty dish.

"I take it you like rich but good?"

Cerryl flushed.

"I like it when you do that." She giggled.

"I'm glad you do." He could feel that he was still red.

She reached across the table and touched his hand. She was still smiling. "Let me enjoy this . . . now."

He had to smile back. "I guess I do like rich . . . and good."

She giggled again.

Cerryl tried not to wince as Leyladin left eight silvers on the table for the server—almost his stipend for an entire eight-day. Instead, after they donned the jackets that the server had returned to them, he offered his arm as they left the rear dining area and walked through the half-filled front area.

"Lady Leyladin . . . He's a mage . . . don't know his name . . . Patrollers say he's one not to anger . . ."

". . . fair . . . though . . ."

"...her father...almost as many coins as Jiolt..."

Cerryl wondered if he'd ever get used to the whispers and the speculations that seemed to trail him. As they stepped out into the dark and chill, he bent toward Leyladin. "Thank you again. It was wonderful."

"I'm glad." For a moment she leaned her head against his, and he could smell the faint floral scent and the scent of the woman he loved—and wondered if he would ever have, except as a friend.

They walked slowly back up the Avenue and then westward toward Leyladin's house. The wind was colder, wet, raw, promising another winter storm before long.

Leyladin took Cerryl's hand. "Promise me that you'll follow Kinowin's advice for now. Not always—just for the next year or so."

"You have visions, too?" He smiled gently, squeezing her fingers gently.

"Not visions, feelings."

"I trust them, and I'll do my best."

"Don't humor me."

"I'm not. Sometimes...I can't always do what I want. I didn't want to deal with either the prefect or Duke Ferobar. I didn't get that much of a choice."

She squeezed his hand, and they walked up the stone walk toward the door of the house she considered modest—compared to those of factors in other cities.

# LXXVI

Cerryl settled into the chair uneasily, waiting for Jeslek to speak, his eyes half on the heavy flakes of wet late-winter snow that plummeted past the windows of the White Tower.

"Overmage Kinowin has already told you that I'll like you to accompany the expedition against Spidlar." Jeslek smiled tightly, seeming almost coiled like a serpent in his chair, for all that he appeared to be sitting normally across his table from Cerryl. "Anya has also told me that you have discovered on your own the order strength of the young smith Dorrin—and that you have concerns that he may act against the Guild."

Cerryl forced a shrug. *What can you say?* After a moment, he answered, his words deliberate. "The smith left Recluce, and he forges items embodying great order. I found that out in trying to find out where the road coins were going."

"So? They are still only toys and implements for crafters." Jeslek raised his eyebrows.

"He has built a home and a smithy and a barn. I doubt that he wishes to return to Recluce. Perhaps, with what he has forged, he cannot." Cerryl hoped he was as correct as his words sounded.

"That is most likely the case."

"Well, he carries a great deal of order, and if he has nowhere else to turn, and if the Guild attacks where he lives, he might feel compelled to act against us."

"That is also true—but he is an order smith. He cannot even make edged weapons. I doubt he will be more than a nuisance. I worry far more about the two who have become officers. They have already done much damage." Jeslek frowned briefly. "Have you made any more discoveries about the misdirected road tariffs?"

"I've found a few more people in the viscount's court that seem to have prospered more than there is any way to find through a glass. It's hard from here, and not knowing much about them," Cerryl admitted, shifting his weight on the hard chair.

"We will be gathering levies in Jellico, and you can continue your efforts there as well, since you will have little else to do until we actually begin the campaign against Spidlar." The High Wizard's sun-gold eyes glittered, and for a moment Cerryl thought he could smell chaos and brimstone in the tower.

"When do we leave, ser?"

"You and Fydel will leave in an eight-day. I need to attend to some matters in Hydolar—such as the missing road tariffs and the thousand golds for damages. Nonetheless, I intend to have everyone in Jellico before the turn of spring—except for the last group of White Lancers Eliasar is training."

"You are going?"

"Of course. The rulers of other lands do not seem to fear a High Wizard who remains in Fairhaven. This time, it will be different. Much different. As the traders of Hydolar will discover first—to their peril." The sun-gold eyes glittered.

"Yes, ser."

"You may go and begin to prepare, Cerryl."

The younger mage nodded.

"Cerryl . . . best you recall that all has saved you is your devotion to Fairhaven. That devotion should remain most firm."

"It will, High Wizard. It will."

"I thought as much. Good day, Cerryl."

# LXXVII

Cerryl and Leyladin stood in the entry foyer of her house. Outside, a cold drizzle fell through the darkness, the mist rising from the stone walks and roads thick enough to blot out the lamps from the adjoining houses.

"I enjoyed dinner, and being here . . . again." Cerryl dropped his hand from the door and took her hands. Her fingers were cool in his.

"Father talked too much . . ." A wry smile flashed across her lips and vanished.

"It was all right. He doesn't have too many people to talk to, I wouldn't imagine. Not besides you."

Leyladin frowned.

"What's the matter?"

"Sometimes . . ." She offered a small sigh, taking her hands back, but not moving away. "Sometimes, I'm not good at being patient, either. I wish I were."

"You could come. Jeslek wouldn't mind having a healer."

"No. If I come, then you can't do what you must. You won't look out for yourself, and then we'll have no chance at all." Her words were firm. "I don't like it. But I know."

Cerryl wanted to shake his head. "Know what?"

"You're leaving tomorrow. How do you feel about that?" Leyladin asked.

"Worried. You didn't answer my question."

"Worried about what?" Her deep green eyes glinted.

"Leaving you, of course."

"Ha! You said that because I expected it."

Cerryl forced an enigmatic smile.

"Don't do that." She frowned. "I can't tell if you're teasing or if you're still giving me that order-cursed smile because you don't want to disagree with me."

Cerryl grinned. "You're beautiful when your eyes flash like that."

"They will flash. I know Anya's going with Jeslek, after they deal with Hydolar, but you'll end up in Spidlar together—or close enough. She's still pure poison, especially for you. She may smile, but she hates you, partly because you don't manipulate easily and partly because of me. She can't stand the thought that a White mage could love—and touch—a Black."

"I can see that . . . Is that why you can't come?"

"Partly. Kinowin also asked that I not go."

Cerryl concealed a swallow. At times, it seemed as though he were still the mill boy or the apprentice and everyone else knew what was happening and and he could only catch glimpses. Even when he asked and searched, he got no answers or answers that weren't answers at all. "Did he say why?"

"He said it would be a war, a war that Candar had not seen the like of and would not again until Fairhaven fell, and that would be many more generations. Many more."

*From anyone but Kinowin . . .* "He said that?"

"He told me that my going wouldn't be good for me or for you. He was most firm." Her eyes glinted with anger, anger Cerryl could feel before it faded. "Most firm."

Leyladin smiled sadly and put her arms around Cerryl. "He also said you had much to do and to learn . . . if Myral's visions were to come to pass."

"What about us?"

"If they don't . . ." Her eyes misted in the dim light.

Cerryl hugged her to him, even more tightly, so tightly he almost felt that black and white, or black and gray, twisted around each other in the dimness. Their lips met, and there was no hesitation, not for either.

# Colors of Candar

# LXXVIII

Standing in the stable courtyard at the far rear of the Halls of the Mages, Cerryl looked at the mount and at the white and red livery. He'd never been that comfortable on a horse, probably because he'd never been in the saddle until he'd become a student mage. His last effort on horseback had resulted in a long, long walk.

Finally, he mounted and eased his mount over beside Fydel's, dreading the ride ahead. At least the gelding seemed more tractable than the beast he'd stolen in Hydolar.

Although the dawn wind blew out of the northeast, damp and cold, but not strong, his jacket kept him warm. *So far . . .* He looked around. A half-score of lancers sat mounted by the gate from the courtyard.

Fydel glanced at Cerryl, then toward the small group of lancers. "Best we be going now."

"Where are all the lancers?" Cerryl asked.

"Most of them are at the South Barracks. We'll meet them there."

"Fifty score?"

"Half that. The others will come with the High Wizard when he deems it necessary." Fydel urged his mount forward.

Cerryl flicked the gelding's reins to catch up to the older mage. He hadn't missed the tinge of bitterness in the square-bearded mage's voice. "After he takes them to Hydolar?"

"After he takes them to Hydolar and brings down another tower to prove his mightiness—and takes the coins necessary to wage this war. It has been too long since the powers of chaos were unleashed." Fydel shrugged as he turned his mount onto the Avenue. "In generations, only Gallos has felt them—when we were last there." He snorted. "For all that, for the destruction of near on twenty-score lancers, the prefect yet ignores Fairhaven when he thinks he can do so, and less than two years have passed. The viscount bows in perfect obeisance and does as he pleases. We have twice removed the Dukes of Hydolar, and yet the merchants believe not our power." Another snort followed.

*Are all rulers moved only by considering which forces are the greatest?* Cerryl felt as bleak as the gray morning.

The gelding's hoofs clopped dully on the white stone of the Avenue, a stone that seemed lifeless in the gray before dawn.

# LXXIX

Beyond the wide stone bridge that spanned the River Jellicor, trails of white and gray smoke rose over the walls of Jellico, walls set less than half a kay north of the bridge. The gray sky, the walls that seemed like smeared charcoal in the fading light, and the smoke all imparted an air of gloom to the walled city. The smooth stone ramparts rose more than forty cubits above the causeway that ran to the gates.

Cerryl glanced down at the river from the big gelding as the column crossed the bridge. Even the water was gray. On the far shore, the western shore, they turned almost northeast for a few hundred cubits before the road turned again and ran straight west toward the granite walls. The gates—red oak and ironbound—were open, but the well-oiled iron grooves testified to their ability to be closed quickly. A half-score of armsmen clad in gray and brown leathers and with armless green overtunics waited by the gates. One of them was a woman, looking as hardened as the men.

Cerryl's eyes widened as a White Guard appeared behind the squad, surveying the arrivals, then bowing slightly to Fydel as the senior mage reined up. Fydel inclined his head, and Cerryl followed his example, wondering why he'd not seen White Guards on his earlier trip. Or had he just not noticed?

"The mages Fydel and Cerryl, preceding the High Wizard Jeslek on his visit to the viscount," rumbled Fydel.

The guard apparently in charge looked from the pair of mages to the long column of lancers that reached back nearly to the bridge. Then he looked back to Fydel. "Ah . . . you are most welcome, noble mages. You know your way to the palace barracks?"

"We have been there before," replied Fydel with a smile.

As they started through the gates, Cerryl looked up. As on his last visit, archers in green with bows watched the column of riders from the ramparts on the walls above. One looked away quickly as Cerryl's eyes surveyed him.

Even narrower and meaner were the houses and shops of Jellico than Cerryl remembered, barely wide enough for three or four mounts abreast, if the riders and horses on each side scraped the fired brick walls. Under the late-afternoon gray sky, the three-story structures appeared to loom higher than they were, pressing in on Cerryl. A wagon stood before a shop on the right and Fydel and Cerryl had to pass it single file. A handful of men and women stood on the far side of the wagon, and their eyes went to the white jackets of the mages and then to the uniforms of the lancers who followed.

"... more of those Whites."

"... leave well enough alone."

"... tariffs and taxes ... all they want."

"... hush! They can hear you, and find you ..."

Cerryl wanted to laugh, if bitterly, at the last remarks, suspecting that all too many of the taxes the locals paid were collected in the name of the Guild but went to the prefect and his establishment. *Suspecting it and proving it are two very different mounts.*

Jellico had an odor, more muted than on his last visit, but still holding the smells from the open sewers running beside the buildings on the right of the street and burned grease, tanning acids, and mold, plus others Cerryl could not identify—and did not wish to try. He shifted his weight in the saddle, glad he did not have to remain on horseback that much longer.

The odors shifted to a mixture more pleasant when the column wound its way around the north side of the Market Square, where the scent of roast fowl mixed with scented oils and incense, almost drowning out the less aromatic odors of the streets. It was late enough, Cerryl saw, that many of the peddlers had already left, and most of those remaining in the square were packing bags and a few carts.

The small hill on the west end of Jellico held the sprawling buildings of the viscount's palace and the associated buildings, barracks and stables, all surrounded by another set of granite walls smoother and more polished than those of the city.

Fydel nodded to the guards standing by the archway holding the open lower gates, ignoring the squad of crossbowmen on the false rampart above. Once inside the long tunnel-like archway, Cerryl could feel as well as hear the echoes of hoofs.

Within the courtyard, the heavyset Shyren waited, clearly having used his glass to determine their arrival. The gray light made the pasty complexion of the Guild's representative to Certis even whiter, and his hair, sandy blond mixed with white, appeared nearly all white.

"Greetings, Shyren!" called Fydel.

"Greetings," answered the gray-and-sandy-haired wizard. "I'm glad you made it through the gates before nightfall."

"So are we." Fydel bent his head forward, as if stretching his neck.

"You and Cerryl—you'll be in the guest barracks. You know where those are?"

Fydel nodded.

So did Cerryl, but the fact that Shyren knew his name made him wonder what other information had been conveyed to Shyren—and by whom and why.

"I'll show you which rooms are yours in a moment." Shyren looked at Teras as the lancer captain reined up behind the two mages. "Take your mounts through the archway there and through the next one to the rear courtyard. There will be an undercaptain there to show you the quartering arrangements."

"Yes, ser." Captain Teras raised his arm. "Through the arch, by twos. After me!"

Shyren looked up at Fydel. "How was the trip?"

"Damp and cold."

"Not so cold as Spidlar these days—or Sligo, either." Shyren flashed a crooked smile that Cerryl distrusted almost as much as he did Anya's. "Winter ice has been hard on Spidlar—that and the brigands that attack traders headed suchways."

The two mages waited until the line of lancers had disappeared, then rode slowly across the still-damp stones of the courtyard and through the archway into a second courtyard, a square a good hundred cubits on a side, surrounded by window-studded stone walls rising a good five stories.

Fydel reined up before the guest stable, and he and Cerryl dismounted. Cerryl surveyed the courtyard, noting again how every building seemed to join every other one and how all looked about the same from outside—flat stone walls with small windows.

Shyren gave a perfunctory smile. "You've been here before. You both get captain's rooms. The ostlers will take care of your mounts once you unload them."

After he wearily unstrapped his bedroll and pack, Cerryl followed Fydel and Shyren across the courtyard and through a weathered bailey door. Then came the two flights of steps he remembered and another narrow stone corridor to a rounded corner of the building.

"You have the first two rooms. The first three are generally for mages. They're a shade larger and fresher." Shyren smiled again. "You're expected for dinner with the viscount. Fydel, you'll sit with me until Jeslek arrives, because you brought in the lancers."

"And then I return to my proper place with the captains?" The sarcasm in the square-bearded mage's voice was heavy and bitter.

"Of course. We all have but moments of glory." Shyren's response was light, but Cerryl could sense a deep bitterness behind the words. The Guild representative turned to Cerryl. "You are considered a senior captain, but the juniormost of those."

Cerryl nodded.

"They could not do less, knowing you have been, as they put it, blooded in battle." Shyren cleared his throat. "Dinner's at the second bell. I will see you then." With a nod, the heavy mage turned and waddled back around the corner.

Fydel looked at Cerryl; Cerryl offered an ironic smile.

Then Fydel laughed. "You see more than most, young Cerryl. You do indeed." He turned toward the first door.

Cerryl walked to the second, lifted the latch, and stepped inside. There he lowered his bedroll and pack onto the stone floor inside the door and surveyed the place—smaller than his quarters in Fairhaven, with a single window, shuttered. The furniture consisted of a narrow pallet bed, a battered wardrobe, a washstand and pitcher, and a lamp on a brass bracket. Two heavy blankets were folded at the foot of the bed, and an oval braided rug lay on the floor by the bed. A chamber pot stood in the corner, while a heavy wooden bar leaned against the wall behind the door.

Apparently even captains needed to bar their rooms in Certis.

Cerryl closed the door and began to unpack. He had the feeling he would be in Jellico for more than just a few days—and he would be busy with his screeing glass all too often, unfortunately.

# LXXX

At the second bell, Cerryl slipped out of his room to find Fydel waiting. Without a word, the two walked down the corridor and descended to the courtyard, crossing the lamp-illumined stones to the far side. There the pair of guards nodded.

At the top of the steps leading up from the courtyard, the two mages passed the first of the guards in green and gold. Above the pink marble wainscoting, the walls were finished in green silk fabric. Gilt-framed pictures spaced at five-cubit intervals held portraits of mounted viscounts in green uniforms.

At the end of the corridor was an archway into a dining hall, a good fifty cubits long and half that in width. As they entered the hall, Cerryl found his mouth watering at the scent of cooking meat.

Near the head of the table stood Shyren, speaking quietly with Viscount Rystryr, a big and broad-shouldered man who wore a gaudy green and gold tunic. His ruddy cheeks seemed flushed, perhaps from riding in the chill, and he sported a bushy beard under thick blond hair. A fire roared in the marble fireplace at the foot of the table. There were gathered a half-score of Certan officers, who barely graced Fydel and Cerryl with a glance, occupied as they were in conversation with the White Lancer captain, Teras.

Shyren caught sight of Fydel and nudged the viscount.

A smile replaced Rystryr's serious demeanor, and his hearty voice boomed out, "Welcome to Jellico, Mage Fydel! We welcome you and your lancers, and Captain Teras."

"We thank you," replied Fydel. "The hospitality of Certis is legend, and welcome."

"Since all are here, let us eat." Rystryr gestured toward the table.

Cerryl glanced along the table, looking for his name, and found it on a bronze-framed slate bearing a statuette of a captain—far nearer the head of the table than he had anticipated. His name was chalked in Old Tongue script, "Carrl," the same spelling as on his last visit years before.

Fydel and Shyren sat on the right and left of the viscount, while an officer in green and gold sat beside Fydel. Beside Shyren sat a man clad in black and red and beside him a white-haired man in gray and gold. Below the officer beside Fydel sat the hulking Teras.

As a full mage, even a junior one, Cerryl apparently ranked near the top of the various captains, as he found his place only five spaces down from Fydel on the same side. According to the place slates, the name of the sandy-haired captain on his left was Setken and the younger black-haired captain to Cerryl's right was Dierl.

With his mouth dry, Cerryl sat and waited for the wine to arrive, hoping it wouldn't be long before the nearest pitcher made its way to him.

"What kind of mage are you, if I might inquire?" asked the dark-haired Dierl.

"We're all White, except for a healer or two."

"No, I meant . . . chaos or arms or earth or . . . that sort of thing."

"Well . . . I've done all of those."

"You've been in battle or you wouldn't be this far up the table. Isn't that right?"

"Yes."

"Ever killed a man?"

Cerryl winced.

"You haven't?" pursued Dierl, an edge to his voice.

Cerryl tried not to sigh or explain that he wasn't exactly fond of killing. "Ah . . . I don't know. Somewhere between two and three score."

Dierl's mouth shut abruptly.

"You had to ask, Dierl." A smile crossed the face of the redhead across the table from Cerryl. "I'm Honsak."

"I'm Cerryl," the mage answered, realizing the other could not see his place slate.

"Is it fair to ask if you've faced off against an armsman in close combat or been wounded?"

"Both," Cerryl answered, deciding not to elaborate more than necessary.

"Blade?"

"Arrow in the shoulder."

"What about the men you faced? Did they use cold iron?"

"They did, and they're dead."

"Now that you've established his background," called a voice from down the table, "could you more senior captains pass the wine?"

Laughter followed the comment.

Honsak filled his goblet and then Cerryl's and handed the wine down. Two serving platters followed the wine, one with slabs of beef covered in a brown gravy, one with potatoes. A basket of bread came next. Cerryl filled his plate, then began to eat as the others did.

"You were here years back, were you not?" asked one of the more junior captains across and down the table from Cerryl.

"Yes, over two years ago."

"Wasn't there a redheaded woman mage?"

"Anya—yes, she was here," Cerryl admitted.

"Is she still a mage . . . or what . . . ?"

"Anya? She's a very powerful mage," Cerryl said dryly. "I understand she will be here before long. She'll come with the High Wizard."

"Slekyr said she had her own ideas about men."

Cerryl couldn't help but smile. "She's been known to like handsome captains, I'm told, but I'd be careful. She brought down one of the big towers of Hydolar."

"Ah . . . does she throw chaos fire?"

Cerryl grinned. "She has done much of that—but only against enemies, and Certis is certainly filled with friends."

"Best stay on her good side, Deltry," said another captain.

Another round of laughter filled the middle of the table, and Deltry flushed.

"I'm new to this sort of thing . . ." Cerryl began as the laughter died away, looking at Honsak.

"You mean, staff type work?" asked the redhead.

Cerryl nodded, hoping he wasn't stretching things too much. "And I haven't really worked with other lands' captains. I was curious. For example, how often do you pay people, and who holds the coins?"

"Everyone but us," came from somewhere.

A general guffaw, if muted, followed the remark.

"All the coins are held in the strong rooms in the palace, and the viscount's finance minister provides them every two eight-days to Overcaptain Levior—he's the arms purser—the fellow up there in uniform beside your mage."

"What if you're away from your barracks?"

"They love that. You get all the pay you've earned when you get back, but no one gets the pay of those who don't come back. Well . . . half goes to a consort, if there is one, but few consort with armsmen or lancers."

"Is the finance minister one of those up there with the viscount?"

"I don't know," answered Honsak. "Issel, is the finance minister the fellow in gray?"

Issel, who sat across and one place up the table from Cerryl, turned in the direction of the viscount and frowned, but for a moment. "That's him, old Dursus himself."

Cerryl fixed the name and face. "Does the finance minister have much to do with you?"

"As little as he can, and us with him. He doesn't collect enough coins, and they say we don't get paid. Hasn't happened yet."

"He must have a lot of assistants," ventured Cerryl, looking at Issel.

"Only one I know of is Pullid. He's the fellow in gray and scarlet farther down toward us."

*Pullid and Dursus* . . . "What sort of field rations do you usually get?" Cerryl continued, deciding to steer the conversation away from finances.

"If we're out more than an eight-day, whatever we can find," said Setken from Cerryl's left. "Less 'n that, it's hard biscuits, yellow cheese, and a few strips of dried beef. Plus anything you can stuff into your saddlebags, if you get enough warning and every other officer hasn't been out scrounging for his men. What about you Whites?"

"Pretty much the same, except the cheese is hard white, and we usually get some dried fruits. Hard as darkness to chew, but it helps."

"Dried fruits. Maybe we could—"

"Don't even think about it, Honsak," interrupted the sandy-haired Setken. "Dursus would have you sent to garrison duty in Quend before you could even find Overcaptain Gised. 'Dried fruit for armsmen? Ridiculous. Far too many coins.' "

At Setken's impersonation of Dursus even Cerryl found himself smiling.

"Coins, always the coins," muttered Honsak.

"That's true everywhere, I think," Cerryl agreed, after finishing the last of his wine and glancing around for the pitcher. "There are never enough coins."

"Even for you Whites?"

"Especially for us Whites," Cerryl said, noting the mix of surprised and frankly incredulous looks. "We only get road taxes and tariffs on the merchants in Fairhaven. We don't have any peasants to tax, and we have no ports and only one city."

"But the road taxes . . . ?"

"It costs a good many coins to build and maintain the roads," Cerryl pointed out, adding, "All of the Halls of the Mages would fit within one portion of the viscount's palace."

"Have you seen other great cities besides Jellico and Fairhaven?" asked Setken smoothly, clearly wishing to steer the conversation in another direction.

"I've seen Fenard and Hydolar," Cerryl admitted.

"And how did you find them?"

Resigning himself to a continued discussion of pleasantries, Cerryl replied, "I would say that the walls of Jellico are among the more impressive..."

As he spoke, Cerryl's eyes wandered to the head of the table, where the Viscount Rystryr leaned toward Fydel, apparently making some sort of point with his fist. Cerryl kept talking, suspecting that he would need many more innocuous subjects and humorous comments to see himself through his days in Jellico. *Many, many more.*

# LXXXI

Cerryl glanced down at the glass on the oval braided rug, watching the mists clear, showing a blonde healer in green sitting at a desk, her head cocked to one side, a sheet of paper before her. A broad smile crossed her face, and she lifted her fingers to her lips and then blew the kiss outward.

Cerryl smiled and let the image fade, knowing she had sensed his presence.

After a time, he looked down at the glass again, concentrating until the silver mists formed and then spread, showing a figure in scarlet and gray. The man sat in a carriage, but Cerryl could not tell where the carriage was bound.

A time later, he tried again, concentrating on a more distant view of Pullid, but the glass merely showed the carriage nearing the viscount's palace, the image blurred by the intermittent spring snow flurries fluttering down.

Cerryl pulled on his white jacket with a shrug and made his way through the corridors toward the front courtyard where he had seen the mounting block for carriages. There he waited with the two pair of armsmen who guarded what appeared to be the entrance to the viscount's part of the sprawling warren of buildings.

Cerryl stepped forward as Pullid eased out of the carriage. "Ser Pullid?"

The bulky man in gray and scarlet turned. "I do not believe I know you, ser mage. Young ser mage."

Cerryl ignored the condescending tone. "I was hoping you might bring your vast knowledge of finance to my aid." He offered what he hoped was a warm smile.

Pullid merely scowled. "What would a mage need to know of finance?"

"Well . . . we do raise some coins, through the assistance of rulers like the viscount, of course, in order to build and maintain the great White highways. All say you are the one who is most important in assisting Finance Minister Dursus and that you know the best ways to ensure the collection of tariffs and such. We have had some difficulty in Montgren," Cerryl lied, "and I thought I might ask for your advice."

Pullid continued to frown without responding.

Cerryl could read the man's thoughts from his face. He didn't want to offend a mage, particularly one brought on a war campaign, since that meant one able to turn him to ash. But Pullid clearly did not wish to talk to Cerryl.

"I wondered . . . obviously the viscount has roads of his own to maintain. Is that a separate tariff, or do you collect them both together?"

"We would not dare to collect taxes more than once." Pullid offered a slightly off-key laugh. "Even once is difficult enough."

Cerryl nodded as he gained a definite feel for the man.

"Now . . . if you will excuse me . . ."

"Of course." Cerryl bowed, if but slightly.

Back in his guest quarters, he took out the glass. Perhaps he had stirred Pullid into action. The next image was that of Pullid talking to the finance minister, but from what Cerryl could tell, Dursus seemed unmoved, talking easily, before finally motioning Pullid out of the paneled study or office. Pullid walked until he reached a smaller, a much smaller, paneled room, where he sat behind a table for a long time, long enough that Cerryl finally had to let the image lapse before his head threatened to burst.

His problem still remained. How could he prove the viscount was diverting coins? Everything Cerryl felt told him that it was happening, but he had not one single vision or item even remotely close to proof. Most likely, his efforts had only made everyone nervous and unhappy with one mage named Cerryl. Yet if he didn't push, how would he find anything in a city where he knew no one?

He sat on the bed and massaged his neck and forehead, trying to massage away the headache.

Perhaps later.

# LXXXII

Cerryl sat on the edge of the bed and looked down at the glass that rested on the braided oval rug—a rug that might once have been green but now appeared gray. The silver mists vanished, and he was left with a blank glass reflecting the timbered ceiling. He was getting nowhere through screeing.

His brief interchange with Pullid had led nowhere, nor had his repeated attempts to track the man with the screeing glass. Finance Minister Dursus never seemed to leave the palace, except to be driven to and from his luxurious home on the hill south of the one on which the prefect's palace perched. While Pullid traveled to meet a number of people, even armsmen and those who appeared to be tax collectors, Cerryl could never see any trace of coins, let alone anything other than conversations, usually brief. He wished he could hear what he watched, but the glass did not allow such.

In the three days since their arrival, the viscount had hosted no more meals. Cerryl and Fydel had eaten with the Certan officers on a less formal and far less sumptuous basis in a stone-walled hall in the lower level of the barracks building. Cerryl had already explored the barracks building in which he and Fydel were housed, finding it more than half-empty but with the feel of recently having been more fully utilized. Were the absent armsmen and officers those harassing Spidlar in one way or another?

Speculating and observing through the glass wasn't going to reveal any more than it had. Of that Cerryl was rapidly being convinced. Either he couldn't see what was going on or he couldn't recognize it. He somehow needed to find another approach.

Cerryl leaned back on the bed.

He'd been trying to find out things from those who collected the taxes and tariffs . . . and finding nothing. That could be because he didn't know what to look for and where or because the collectors knew he or someone was watching and could simply outwait him.

Who paid the tariffs?

Those who had coins, and the ones most likely to have coins were factors and traders. Cerryl, unhappily, hadn't met that many traders, either inside or outside Fairhaven. In fact, Narst, the trader he'd begged a ride from on his rather painful journey from Hydolar to Fairhaven, was probably the only real trader Cerryl had met, just as Layel was the only real factor he knew.

Narst had mentioned some names... The one from Spidlar wouldn't do, but what had been the name in Jellico? Fedor? No... Freidr, or something like that.

*You can't do any worse than you're doing so far.*

He struggled to his feet and pulled on the white jacket. While his room was cool, outside would be cold and wet from the spring snow flurries. After closing his door, he made his way down the corridor and steps to the courtyard and to the stable.

He stood for a moment outside the stable, then cleared his throat. Finally, he whistled.

A pale face appeared. "Ah, yes, ser?"

"I'm going riding," Cerryl told the ostler.

"Oh, you've the big gentle gelding?"

"That's right."

"Be a few moments, ser."

"I'll wait."

Cerryl studied the courtyard, sensing the age of the structures that surrounded the stable, seemingly far older than even the ancient buildings of Fairhaven.

"Here he be." The ostler led out the gelding.

Cerryl glanced at the red and white livery, wondering if he would be better off without such an announcement, then shrugged. "Thank you."

The ostler nodded.

The gelding *whuffed* as Cerryl swung himself into the saddle, then walked easily toward the archway from the courtyard. From the low gray sky occasional intermittent fat flakes of snow fell, all melting almost instantly upon hitting the stones of the street. A few patches of white clung to sections of roofs. Cerryl guided the gelding downhill and eastward to the Market Square.

He reined up beside the porch of a store, where an older man, dressed in dark blue was talking with a younger bearded man.

Both turned as they became aware of the rider watching them.

"Ser mage?"

"I'm looking for a trader. Freidr or some such," Cerryl offered.

"Freidr?" The younger man frowned.

The older one nodded. "Son of Fearkl."

"Could you tell me where his place is?"

"Like as I recall, not that many trade as much with him as his sire, the narrow street off the north corner of the square—back there." The older man pointed. "His place is about a hundred cubits off the square. It be a plain building without a sign."

"How will I tell if it doesn't have a sign?" Cerryl asked.

"Between the cooper's and Wrys the silversmith's. Should have said that."

"Thank you both." Cerryl inclined his head.

"Freidr . . . a trader? Fop and a fool . . . sister a better man than he be."

"Takes all kinds, Biuskr."

The trader's sister a better man? Cerryl frowned but kept his eyes on the north side of the street, ignoring for the most part the bustle of the square to his right. The corner street was narrow, barely wide enough for a wagon and a mount at the same time, and the building was ancient. How long had the family been in factoring?

Cerryl dismounted and tied the gelding to the iron ring set in the stone post almost at the door, then rapped loudly. There was no answer. He waited a time, then rapped again.

Finally, the door opened, but Cerryl could see the heavy chains on the inside of the antique oak. Behind the chains stood a thin woman with fine blond hair twisted into a single braid down her back. Wispy hairs escaped both the braid and the sides of her head. "Yes, ser?"

"I'm looking for the trader Freidr."

Her eyes widened, not meeting Cerryl's, and she swallowed. "A moment, ser, a moment, I assure you he will be here." The door was not closed quite all the way, as if to make a statement, but the iron chains remained in place, forming an arc between door and frame.

"Who be it now?" came a rough voice from the dimness beyond the door.

". . . one of *them* . . . another one . . . didn't say . . ."

A pale face appeared behind the chains. "I'm Freidr."

"I'd like to speak to you, then," Cerryl said politely.

After a moment, the man loosened the chains, held the door, and stepped back. Short and squat, he wore a new dark blue tunic and matching trousers. His boots glistened even in the gloom of the small foyer.

Cerryl took in the dark beard and the cold blue eyes, eyes that did not meet his gaze, though they almost seemed to. The man was hiding something, but why was he afraid of Cerryl? *Surely not just because I'm a mage?*

"Might as well go to the office." Freidr closed the door, replaced the chains in their slots, and turned to his right, heading down a narrow passageway, then turning into a small room. The trader closed the door after Cerryl entered.

An ancient oil lamp set in a green-tinged copper bracket on the wall spilled light across the space. On one wall was a cage of iron bars with heavy wooden racks behind it. The three strongboxes behind the iron seemed almost lost in the rack shelves that could have held nearly a score.

Freidr sat behind the table-desk, his arms on the table, waiting. Cerryl took one of the antique wooden straight-backed chairs, a chair that felt as old as the building that held it.

"How might I help you?" Freidr offered a professional smile, but his eyes still did not quite meet Cerryl's.

"The trader Narst mentioned you," Cerryl offered.

"I'm a factor who deals with many traders." Freidr presented an apologetic smile.

"I am sure you do. You also deal with the prefect's tax collectors."

"Every factor must do so, especially with the road taxes imposed by the Guild at Fairhaven." Despite the chill in the room, perspiration had already begun to seep from the dark-bearded factor's forehead.

"Do you keep records of the taxes you pay?" Cerryl raised his eyebrows.

"Surely you're not suggesting . . . You already had the warehouse searched."

"*I* didn't have anything searched," Cerryl pointed out, wondering just what had been going on in Jellico that Freidr was so fearful of a young White mage.

"No . . . you might as well have . . . The prefect's inspectors did."

"Was it Pullid?" Cerryl tried to keep his tone casual.

"He stood there, but you think he'd dirty his hands? I don't know their names, the ones who went over the accounts. They said they were looking for goods stolen from you White mages."

Cerryl looked at the sweating trader, then smiled. "Why don't you just show me the tax records?"

"You'll take them. Then what will I do when Pullid comes back next year?"

"I won't take them," Cerryl assured him. "I'm looking for something very different. It appears . . . Let me just say that there are irregularities in the tariff records. It would help . . . and I'm sure you'd want to be helpful." As he smiled more broadly, Cerryl felt as though he were acting just like Anya.

Freidr sighed.

Cerryl let his senses range ahead of the trader as the man turned and lifted out a ledger and an old wooden box, one that reeked of age.

"Here . . ." The factor offered another sigh as he pushed the ledger toward Cerryl. "You can see. I've paid them all—every last one."

Cerryl scanned the receipts, mentally totaled the numbers . . . then frowned. One was signed with another name—Liedral.

"Liedral—that's your . . . sister . . ." A cold feeling settled over Cerryl, and his eyes felt like ice as he looked at the factor.

Freidr cringed in the chair, as though he had been struck. "I did what you people wanted . . . what the other bearded . . ."

"Fydel, you mean?" Cerryl asked.

"That's what he said his name was . . ."

Cerryl forced himself to be calm, although he wasn't sure why he was getting agitated. He hadn't done anything. He hadn't even been able to see what had happened until it was over and done. *You still feel guilty . . . because the Guild did it and you feel it was wrong?* "The matter with your sister is something entirely different. This deals with golds. You have paid on the order of 15 percent of your receipts—at least is what you claim."

"It's 15 percent . . . and it's of everything. Pullid, he went through everything . . . everything. That's what you mages require."

Cerryl nodded. "And he told you that he would send one of us after you if you didn't show everything?"

"He didn't have to . . . We know that."

Cerryl forced a smile. "Would you mind telling me how you know that?"

"We just do . . ." Freidr's eyes flicked from side to side, never meeting Cerryl's.

"How long have you been paying 15 percent?"

"I don't know . . . five years . . . The records are there." Despair flooded the factor's face.

Cerryl wanted to shake his head. "It doesn't matter. There will be records." He stood. "Thank you."

Then he paused, before looking back at Freidr. "Can you think of any other traders who had their warehouses scrutinized in the way yours has been?

"Ah . . . no . . ."

"You're lying." Cerryl hated to do it, but he gathered enough chaos to create a small fireball above his raised left index finger.

Freidr paled.

"Do you recall?" Cerryl gave another Anya-like smile, still disliking himself for it.

"I don't . . . know . . . not for certain . . . but Pastid . . . and Triok . . . they were muttering something."

"Pastid and Triok . . . where might I find them?"

"Pastid—he's on the other side of the Market Square, where this street is, except it's the Silver Way there, about three hundred cubits. His place is next to a coppersmith's—Gued, I think. Triok—he's on the Way of the Weavers, or the north part, north of the palace."

Cerryl inclined his head. "I trust that is correct."

"It is . . . I tell you it is."

"Good."

"Is that all, ser?"

"That's all." Cerryl smiled. *For now.* He unlatched the door, letting his chaos senses scan the narrow passage before he opened the door and stepped out. The small hall was empty.

Freidr followed him, at a slight distance, letting Cerryl open the front door.

"Thank you again," Cerryl told the factor as he left.

The door shut quickly, and Cerryl could hear the chains rattled into place. It wasn't absolute proof—but 15 percent? According to what Myral had told him, the highest Guild tax on merchants outside of Fairhaven, and only the large ones, was a third of that. Even the Guild tax on factors in Fairhaven was but a tenth part.

Cerryl untied the gelding and mounted quickly. The intermittent snow had given way to a light rain of fat raindrops, splatting on the road stones. He turned his mount back westward.

What he had discovered also raised a few questions. Did Shyren know? If not, why not? Or if he did, why hadn't he told Jeslek? And if Shyren had told Jeslek, what sort of scheme was Jeslek attempting?

Though Cerryl rapped on Pastid's door, there was no answer. Cerryl rode around and down the back alley, but the rear loading doors were also locked and bolted from the inside. Finally, with the sun dropping over the western walls of the city, he headed back toward the viscount's palace.

The ostler took the gelding without comment. Cerryl crossed the courtyard again and walked up the steps.

Shyren stood at the top, a lazy smile on his face. "Out for a ride, I understand?" the older mage said mildly.

"There's little enough for me to do in the barracks and palace," Cerryl answered with a laugh. "So I rode around the city a bit, asked a few questions, and tried to get more familiar with it."

"You young mages . . . I suppose that's wise. You never know where you might be going. Still . . . a place like Jellico has its dangers for those who don't know its ways." Shyren's eyes glittered ever so slightly. "They are not what one might suppose."

"I'm sure that's true. Is there any place you would suggest I take care?" Cerryl asked politely.

"Everywhere and nowhere." Shyren laughed softly, a sound almost sibilant. "Where coins are involved, or folk think they are, any step could be dangerous. And other lands are not near so . . . well tended as Fairhaven. What you would call peace is never achieved here, nor will it ever be." The heavyset mage shrugged. "We Guild representatives do what we can, but we are limited—most limited."

"I can see that might be a problem."

"It is." Another smile, almost regretful, crossed Shyren's face. "I had come to tell you and Fydel that I just received a message from the High Wizard. He plans to reach Jellico in five days."

"Thank you."

"I thought you might like to know." Shyren started to turn, as if to head down the stone steps, then paused. "I would suggest great care on your rides, young Cerryl. Five days is scarce enough to learn Jellico, and White mages are not held in near so high esteem here as in Fairhaven. While all may be fair to your face, watch your back."

"I appreciate your words, and your concern." Cerryl inclined his head.

After the Guild representative had left, Cerryl rubbed his chin. *Definitely a message. Do you have to worry about arrows and traps? Or worse?*

He took a deep breath and headed toward his room, his chaos senses extended. His room was empty, but the residual sense of disorder gave him the definite impression that Shyren had spent some time there. He smiled to himself. The longer he was in the Guild, the more he understood that he and perhaps Kinowin were among the very few Whites who could sense residual chaos. *Why? Because you're among the few who keep yourselves separate from chaos?* Leyladin could, and probably most Blacks. *Another skill to keep hidden . . . and if you develop more, they might be enough. But enough for what?*

He shook his head.

As the first bell rang, he decided he needed to hurry if he wanted to wash up before the evening meal.

# LXXXIII

Cerryl blinked and let the image in the glass fade. Still nothing of substance had come from his efforts to follow Pullid and Dursus in the screeing glass. He picked up the glass, warm to the touch in the cold barracks room, and replaced it in the wardrobe. He glanced toward the barred and shuttered window. He might as well ride out—despite the wind and rain—to see if he could talk to either Triok or Pastid. Neither trader had been around for the past two days—Triok's consort had insisted she expected him any day, while Pastid's building remained locked.

After reclaiming his jacket, Cerryl left his stark barracks room and made his way down the stone steps and across the rain-splashed stones of the courtyard. The ostler nodded as he walked up, then disappeared into the stable. Cerryl glanced around the courtyard and at the miniature pools of water between the paving stones, pools occasionally rippled by the light rain that still fell. While he waited, he cast his senses toward the walls but could discern only a guard and no chaos. Then he shifted his weight and glanced around again, as he had been ever since Shyren's words about the dangers of Jellico. *The real dangers of Jellico are within these walls.*

"Here he be, ser mage." The ostler led out the gelding, still with the definitely bedraggled white and red livery.

The streets of Jellico seemed fractionally less crowded as Cerryl rode slowly out of the gates and turned the gelding north and toward Pastid's warehouse. Pastid remained absent, the building locked.

With a deep breath Cerryl eased his mount back west and toward the lower hill, the back side of which held Triok's establishment. The rain continued to spit out of the low clouds, intermittently, but the dark gray clouds promised a heavier fall before long. Cerryl continued to scan the areas through which he rode north and west of the viscount's palace, with both his eyes and his chaos senses, feeling, somehow, somewhere, a slight increase in chaos. Was Jeslek nearing? Or something else?

Triok's building resembled what Cerryl would have thought a trader's place to be, with a small and narrow two-story brick dwelling attached to a timbered warehouse with a tile roof. A muscular bearded man was standing at one end of the wagon before the loading doors, shifting bales of something from under the canvas covering the wagon bed to the open loading door of the warehouse.

Cerryl dismounted and led the gelding toward the man. "Trader Triok?"

"None other, ser mage," grunted Triok as he moved another bale.

"Your consort may have told you that I'd been trying to see you for the past few days—"

"That she did. That she did." Triok straightened after setting down the bale and frowned. "Don't be knowing what you Whites be wanting of me. Pay my tariffs and taxes. Don't go your way often, but better this way." He gestured toward the medallion on the wagon.

Cerryl nodded. "I just wanted to ask a few questions. You only pay one set of taxes, except for the medallion, but they're collected by the viscount's men—Pullid's men, actually."

"Been that way for years. Afore Pullid was Zastor. Don't remember the fellow afore him."

"Do you remember when the rate was a tenth?"

Triok frowned. "Not been that long ago. Three, four years, 'cause that was the year the brigands got Siljir in the pass heading down to Passera."

"Do you recall when the rate went from a twentieth to a tenth part?"

Triok laughed. "Not that old, young ser mage, not by a mighty bow shot."

Cerryl nodded. "How do you find the White highways?"

"Like 'em. Don't like the tariff, have to say." Triok looked toward the gray sky and then the warehouse door, as if to indicate he had better matters to attend to than educating a young White mage, preferably before it began to rain even harder. "Be good if we had a road into Spidlar . . . once the troubles there are over," he added quickly.

"I'll convey that." Cerryl smiled. "Thank you." He led the gelding back from the wagon slightly before remounting.

". . . what was that about?" Triok's consort stood inside the loading door.

"Don't know . . . care less . . . but didn't take many moments, least-wise . . ."

Cerryl frowned. Myral had said the tariff for large outland merchants was a twentieth, but it had been collected as a tenth for years, and none in the Guild had known or cared. Somewhere over three years ago, the rate had been raised in Certis to 15 percent. Why? And why then? *Wasn't that when Rystryr became viscount? Or had that been afterward?*

He kept riding, headed eastward until he reached a larger street to take him back to the viscount's palace, still wondering, his gray eyes scanning the streets, the scattered shops, and the mostly shuttered windows.

Cerryl halted the gelding just before the corner of the larger street that led southward to the viscount's palace. While he didn't exactly sense chaos, what he did feel was unease, something he could not describe. As he studied the empty street ahead, he mustered chaos around him.

*Empty? When has any street in Jellico been empty?*

He glanced toward the top of the wall to his left, a good three cubits above his head, even mounted, not a house wall, but a wall enclosing a courtyard of some sort.

A dark figure peered over the wall, bearing something . . .

Cerryl swallowed and flung chaos, then turned to the other side and flung a second wall of chaos fire. *Whhhstt!*

*Sprung! Sprung!*

Crossbow bolts and chaos fire met. Both figures on the walls vanished.

*Clunk! Clunk!*

The crossbow bolts clattered along the damp paving stones. Belatedly Cerryl could feel the rain began to mist down around him, so light as to barely cause a twinge in his skull.

Cerryl raised the light-blurring screen and simultaneously urged his mount ahead and around the corner, raising yet more chaos, but the street remained empty for almost a block. He was breathing heavily as he rode carefully southward for a block. The street ahead, across the way that he knew led eastward to the market, was also empty, and he turned eastward to find a less direct—and more crowded—way back to the palace.

After another few hundred cubits, with the main square in sight, he reined up, leaving the light-blurring screens up. He remained on the gelding, trying to catch his breath.

He sniffed, smelling something beyond the sewage and filth and roasting fowl, something burning. Two wagons, each pulled by a single

horse, careened down the street into the Market Square and then eastward. A building was burning to the northeast of the square, down the
street where the trader Freidr had his establishment. Cerryl swallowed,
then eased his mount in the direction of the wagons, reining up once
more well back of the building where flames flickered from a single
window.

A group of men in gray threw buckets of water on the roofs of the
surrounding buildings, then, as the fire did not seem to grow, began to
dump buckets on the warehouse itself. The rain began to fall even more
heavily, and cold water seeped down the back of Cerryl's neck. He
shivered in the saddle but did not urge the gelding any nearer to the
dying fire or the men who fought it. The thin blonde woman sobbed
under the overhang of the cooper's shop, holding an infant while Cerryl
watched.

To Cerryl's surprise, the fire guttered out, but he realized part of
that was because the fire had apparently started in the office and the
office walls were stone. The combination of the rain and the bucket
brigade had managed to quench the flames before they spread.

Cerryl nodded to himself—chaos fire.

Still keeping the blur screen up, he turned his mount and headed
back toward the viscount's palace. Once inside the second courtyard,
he reined up outside the stable and dismounted.

"Ser?" asked an ostler he did not know or recognize.

"I'm Cerryl, returning my mount for grooming and stabling." He
offered a polite smile.

"Oh . . . you be one of the mages. Yes, ser. I'll be taking him, then,
and Firklat will be back shortly."

Cerryl could sense the confused groom was telling the truth and
handed over the reins. "Thank you."

"Our duty, ser. Our duty." The groom bowed.

Cerryl inclined his head in response, then slipped through the doorway and up the steps toward his own room—still as stark and empty
as ever. Where was Shyren's room—and was the mage around? Again,
Cerryl could offer many reasons for his suspicions of Shyren, but not a
single featherweight of proof.

Cerryl wasn't about to ask anyone, because everyone remembered
a mage who asked questions. Rather, he decided to continue his explo-
rations of the viscount's palace.

The corridors of the wing that held the formal dining hall were
deserted, except for a single guard, who barely looked up as Cerryl
walked past briskly, his pace indicating he was in a hurry to reach a
definite destination. While the dining wing held other chambers, including what seemed to have been a council space of sorts, all were
empty.

Cerryl moved to the next wing, the old wing, where he passed two guards, directly inside the entry arch, both of whom studied him and dismissed him as he started up the stone staircase that was roughly four cubits wide, not wide enough for an official staircase yet seemingly too wide for mere servitors to use.

Shyren's apartments were on the second floor of the old wing of the palace. At least, Cerryl would have called it old from the sense of aged chaos exuding from the stones.

The young mage glanced up and down the narrow corridor, but there was no one around. The door was secured by a simple bronze lock, one Cerryl recognized. *A sewer lock, for darkness' sake!* Just like all the locks that guarded the sewers of Fairhaven and, like them, filled with a knot of chaos. But the lock was not closed, just turned so that it appeared closed.

Cerryl frowned, then shuddered as his chaos senses discovered the less obvious line of chaos—a line of force strong enough to destroy even a strong mage, were such a mage caught unaware.

Cerryl wrapped the light-blurring screen around himself, then eased up to the trapped lock and slid away the two concentrations of chaos. He studied the door again before opening it and leaving it ajar.

Finally, he slipped inside, smiling wryly as he quickly surveyed the room—or rooms. The anteroom contained an inlaid desk with a matching wooden armchair and a thick red velvet cushion. On each side of the desktop was a polished bronze lamp. There were two matching onyx inkstands and a quill holder as well. Three golden oak bookshelves stretching nearly five cubits high and each one almost as wide were set against the rear stone wall, and all three were packed with leather-bound volumes.

His ears and senses alert for anyone approaching, Cerryl slipped into the second room—the bedchamber. A heavy and dark red velvet curtain blocked most of the light from the wide window, but even without the light, Cerryl could see the high bedstead that did not fill a fifth part of the room. The hangings on the high four-postered bed were red and golden satins, and filmy golden silks screened the bed itself. A diaphanous gown lay across the red velvet cushion that turned the long chest at the foot of the bed into a settee of sorts.

To the right of the man-high hearth opposite the bed was a small table, set for a dinner for two.

Cerryl stopped studying the furnishings and began to use his senses to survey the room. Even more chaos lay within the chest by the bed—chaos and metal. The young mage swallowed. The chest was literally filled with gold. He could sense that without even touching the ancient and polished white oak. He could also feel an even larger mass of chaos coiled under the lid of the chest.

With a nod, he turned. What he had discovered would have to do. He dared not linger longer.

Shyren's quarters were far more opulent than the High Wizard's, and no wonder, with all the gold the old mage possessed.

As Cerryl replaced the lock and the two chaos traps, he wanted to smile. Shyren had one problem. As a White mage, he had to keep at least some, if not all, of his gains near him. Who else dared he trust with such an amount of gold?

Clutching the light-blurring screen, Cerryl turned back down the corridor, descending the stairs and passing the guards on his way back out into the front courtyard.

Behind him, he could hear the low voices of the guards.

"Who was that?"

"I don't know . . . looked like he belonged here. One of Dursus's people, I guess."

"Too many folk we don't know these days."

Cerryl nodded. He hoped so.

Back in his room, he took out the glass and laid it on the worn green braided rug and searched for Shyren, finding the mage in the viscount's chambers. Almost before the mists had fully parted and revealed the image of Shyren in one of the council chambers with Dursus and the viscount, Cerryl let the screeing glass turn blank.

Then he put the glass away and stepped out into the hall.

"You're as wet as a drowned cat." Fydel stood by the door to his own chamber. "Where have you been?"

"Riding in Jellico, trying to learn the city." Cerryl paused, but only momentarily, noting that Fydel appeared almost as wet as he did. "You've been out, too."

"Making arrangements to ensure nothing disturbs our efforts against Spidlar." Fydel shrugged. "I'm going to talk with Teras—in the rear courtyard by the building where the viscount meets with all his ministers. Do you want to come? You probably ought to. Someone ought to know about the provisions' plans besides me. Neither Jeslek nor Anya will pay any attention." Fydel's tone was bitter, as it often seemed to be, reflected Cerryl.

*Why not? That's about where you want to go.* "If I won't be in the way."

"No. You might as well hear what you'll have to do sooner or later, anyway." The square-bearded mage gave a faint smile and turned, as if expecting Cerryl to follow him.

Cerryl did. If Fydel's errand didn't lead him to where he could find Shyren, he'd find some other pretext. It couldn't be that hard.

He didn't have to invent another pretext, for as they crossed the second courtyard, on the side under the overhang that protected them from the rain, another figure in white appeared, heading in the opposite direction, but on the far side of the courtyard.

"Fydel . . . I need just a word with Shyren."

"I'll wait here—if you won't be long."

"Only a moment." Cerryl turned and angled toward the heavy older mage through the rain that had turned to drizzle.

Shyren slowed, then stopped.

"Mage Shyren." Cerryl inclined his head.

"Young Cerryl, you seemed to be headed toward me." Shyren smiled falsely. "And how has your stay in Jellico been thus far?"

"Rather unsettling, I must admit. Some fellows let loose with crossbow quarrels—aimed at me, I fear."

"You do not seem terribly injured. Are you certain that you were the target?"

Cerryl shrugged. "There was no one else upon the street, and the white jacket of a mage is difficult to mistake." Cerryl shrugged. "Unless they might have been seeking another. You wouldn't have any idea who else they might have sought?"

"It is to avoid such mishaps that I have made it a practice never to ride the streets. Carriages are much less prone to slings and arrows, as it were. Mages should stick to magery, not adventure, especially not adventure in unfamiliar cities."

With his senses concentrated on Shyren, Cerryl could feel the twisting, the deception, not quite like a lie, and he wanted to nod. Instead, he inclined his head, blocking all of his own feelings and responding as if he were accepting in a heartfelt way Shyren's words. "So you had told me, and while I had thought that I might make Jellico less unfamiliar, it appears that your advice was most correct. I intend to remain within both the walls of the palace and the exact dimensions of my assignment here as an assistant to Mage Fydel." He inclined his head in the direction of the archway where Fydel stood. "Perhaps that will ensure less attention."

"I can assure you that so long as you confine yourself to that charge any attention you receive will be far more to your benefit. Few appreciate mages extending their talents to where they are unnecessary and unwanted. Especially young mages." A sympathetic smile, false as those that preceded it, filled the heavyset mage's face.

"I do appreciate your advice, ser Shyren, and will follow it most scrupulously." Cerryl bowed. "These recent events have made clear its value."

"Ah . . . yes . . . I am glad you have found that. We all need to do that which we do best. I am most certain Jeslek will be pleased with this . . ." A last smile crossed the older mage's lips. "Now, if you will excuse me, as I am tending to a difficulty facing the prefect . . ."

"Of course." Cerryl bowed and scraped once more, obsequiously.

"What was that all about?" asked Fydel as Cerryl returned.

"I was conveying to Shyren the value of his advice."

Fydel raised his eyebrows but did not speak. Then he turned, and Cerryl followed him, conscious that Shyren's eyes followed him, for all that the older mage had spoken of needing to be excused.

# LXXXIV

Under another gray afternoon sky, Cerryl and Fydel stood in the second courtyard of the viscount's palace, waiting as Jeslek and Anya rode through the archway, followed by the first of the White Lancers, headed by a captain unfamiliar to Cerryl.

Shyren, who stood a good thirty cubits to the left of the two younger mages, raised his arm. "Hail to the High Wizard." His voice was friendly and loud, pitched to reach Jeslek.

Jeslek rode forward, seemingly toward Shyren, with Anya keeping her mount abreast of the white-haired and sun-eyed mage. Then Jeslek guided his mount aside, back toward Cerryl. As he reined up, Jeslek turned to Anya. "You know what to do." He vaulted out of the saddle and strode up to Cerryl, flinging the reins in the direction of a lancer who followed. "Come over here."

Anya rode across in front of Shyren and Fydel, raising chaos as she did. "A moment, Shyren. Jeslek has something to deal with."

Cerryl caught the glimpse of a smile on the heavy mage's face before Jeslek drew Cerryl aside, under the overhang of the courtyard across from the stable entrance and away from the other three mages. "Shyren has sent a scroll saying you are a danger to the Guild and that if you are not disgraced and removed, none of the traders will continue to pay tariffs to Fairhaven. What did you do?" asked Jeslek.

Cerryl smiled. "I discovered what happened to the tariff coins."

"And what have you discovered about the coins?" asked the High Wizard with the lazy smile that concealed anger.

"I take it that coins are getting to be a difficulty." Cerryl forced himself to keep his voice light while keeping his emotions shielded. He also stood ready to divert any chaos Jeslek might muster. "Even after collecting a thousand golds from Hydlen."

"Two thousand," Jeslek corrected, with a tight smile. "I raised the cost since I had to travel there. The new duke had to lose another tower and the northern gates before he saw the wisdom of paying damages and raising the call for levies."

"I see." Cerryl paused, noting the further tightening in Jeslek's jaw, then added, "Did you know that prefect has been collecting a tariff laid at the Guild's door?"

"We've never been able to stop that," the High Wizard admitted with a half-rueful smile that vanished as quickly as it had appeared. "Is that all?"

"Of 15 percent," Cerryl added. "Since Rystryr became viscount. Roughly, anyway."

Jeslek's smile faded. "And?"

"I haven't found where it all went, but there is a rather large chest filled with golds and secured with the largest chaos lock I've ever seen." Cerryl offered a smile. "It's in Shyren's bedchamber."

Cerryl had walked by Shyren's quarters, earlier in the day, behind his blur shield, but the chaos locks, and the chest, remained in place, from what he could tell. He only hoped that Shyren were not more devious than he appeared, or at least that Shyren believed Cerryl comparatively inexperienced, more like a younger version of Fydel.

"You think such is still there, now that he knows you know?" Jeslek's eyes flicked sideways in the direction of where Anya engaged Shyren, though the High Wizard's head did not move.

"It was this morning, and I believe he thinks I am a less adept version of Fydel. He did pay some crossbowmen to kill me. I can't prove that, though." Cerryl shrugged.

Jeslek's crooked smile returned. "I think you should escort me to Shyren's quarters. Now."

Cerryl glanced back.

"Anya will ensure Shyren is occupied for a time. She is quite good at that. Shall we go?"

Cerryl led the way.

The bronze lock on Shyren's door remained chaos-trapped, as it had been every time before when Cerryl had checked.

"The lock is never locked but always twined with chaos," Cerryl said as he eased the chaos out of the bronze, letting it dissipate before opening the door.

"Rather luxurious," said Jeslek, "more so in person than through a glass."

Cerryl stepped toward the bedchamber, his own shields still in place.

"Shields, yet. You do not trust your own High Wizard, Cerryl?" asked Jeslek.

"I have no reason to trust anyone," Cerryl pointed out. "Here is the chest." He gestured the white oak chest, then lifted the velvet cushion that covered the lid.

"Allow me," Jeslek said dryly, stepping forward and bleeding away the chaos inside the chest. "A chest more than two cubits long and half as deep, all filled. This may be even more golds than we brought from Hydlen."

Cerryl hoped so.

Abruptly the High Wizard stepped back behind the hangings of the four-poster bed as the door to the outer chamber *snicked* open. Cerryl found himself standing alone by the open chest as Shyren stood in the door to the bedchamber, breathing heavily, his face flushed.

Cerryl prepared himself.

"What are you doing here?" Shyren raised chaos as he spoke. "You're just his tool, Cerryl. You don't understand. No, you're a meddler in things you don't understand. You will not meddle longer, and I will not be swept aside by an arrogant upstart!"

*Whhstt!* Chaos flame sheeted around Cerryl's shields. Behind him, the satin hangings of the big bed began to char, then to smolder.

"Oh . . . you actually know shields." Shyren flung a larger firebolt that slammed toward Cerryl.

The younger mage smiled and let his shields catch the chaos energy before adding his own power, turning the force, and narrowing the fires into a bolt of concentrated chaos that drove through the older mage's shields as if they did not exist.

"Ohhh . . ." The brief murmur of surprise was cut off as Shyren's form flared in chaos flame, then fell in fine white dust. All that remained on the stone floor was a white-bronze dagger, glowing.

Anya stepped into the room. "He insisted. You did tell me not to destroy him."

Cerryl turned, not lowering his shields, to see Jeslek's reaction as the High Wizard stepped out from behind the bed.

"Cerryl managed well enough. Better than I would have thought, actually."

"He has that habit," returned the red-haired mage, almost as if Cerryl were not present. She moved easily toward the chest at the foot of the bedstead.

"I might ask what these are doing here," said Jeslek, gesturing toward golds lying in the chest he had opened, "save I fear we all know. There must be 3,000 golds there." The High Wizard straightened and favored Cerryl with a smile. "We will proceed to the viscount. You will agree with everything I say. It will be better that way." His eyes went to Anya. "You will remain here to ensure that no others succeed in lightening the Guild's purses."

"So long as I'm not blamed for this mess," Cerryl agreed warily.

"No . . . poor Shyren. He forgot that gold is not power." Jeslek glanced at the chest, ignoring Anya, then back at Cerryl. "Who else might have some more golds?"

"The finance minister, Dursus, and his assistant Pullid. Pullid actually collects the taxes. I found that out from a local trader. Shyren found I'd talked to the trader and killed him and burned part of his warehouse." Cerryl had his doubts about who had killed Freidr, but it was clearly better to place the blame on Shyren than on the other suspect.

"You have been diligent," observed Jeslek. "That is definitely one of your virtues." He gave a brisk nod. "We should visit the viscount. Come, Cerryl."

The two walked down the corridor from Shyren's chambers, down another set of steps, then across a high-ceilinged vaulted circular hall and through a set of pillars past two guards in green and gold.

Another fifty cubits down the lamp-lit hall, Jeslek paused before a set of double doors, where two more guards blocked the way.

One of the guards took in the two mages in white and the amulet around Jeslek's neck then offered, "His Mightiness requested he not be disturbed."

"Tell him the High Wizard of Fairhaven would like to see him. Now." Although Jeslek's tone was mild, the words almost steamed with the power of chaos.

The guard inched back. "He did say . . ."

Jeslek smiled, and a tongue of flame leapt from the floor before the guard. "Tell him."

The other guard, without speaking, turned and rapped on the heavy door. After a moment, he bellowed, "The High Wizard seeks the viscount immediately!"

After another pause, the guard opened the door.

As the two mages passed, Cerryl noticed the dampness on the foreheads of both guards. He would not have wanted to be in their boots.

The viscount rose from the gilt chair set behind a broad gilt table, setting down a scroll as he did. "My dear High Wizard, I had expected to see you at dinner. You and your red-haired assistant."

Jeslek stepped forward while Cerryl closed the study door behind them, then eased up almost even with the High Wizard.

"My dear viscount, perhaps you have seen one of my mages. This is Cerryl. He was sent here not only to help prepare for the invasion of Spidlar, but to resolve some . . . irregularities . . . in the handling of road tariff golds." Jeslek flashed his brilliant smile at the blond and burly viscount.

At each corner of the table stood a guard with an iron blade, and both watched Jeslek.

"Irregularities, you say?" Rystryr's voice was thoughtful, barely rumbling in the confines of the private study.

"Yes. Apparently, Shyren entered into an agreement with your finance minister, one Dursus, I believe, and perhaps his assistant." Jeslek turned to Cerryl. "What was his name?"

"Pullid." Cerryl kept his eyes on the guards and his order-chaos senses on the crossbowman hidden behind the lattice to the right.

"And what of Shyren? Should he not be here to address such . . . irregularities? I do not see him." Rystryr raised his bushy eyebrows.

"And you will not," said Jeslek. "Those of the Guild who line their chests at the cost of the Guild usually do not survive."

"Ah . . . yes. I could see how that would not set well with the Guild." Rystryr nodded blandly.

Cerryl could sense both dismay and concern behind the words, though the viscount's voice remained dispassionate.

"No, it does not. The Guild acts for the good of all of Candar, not for the good of a single man or a single land. Some find it difficult to understand such," added Jeslek in a tone that seemed almost musing. "Until they act against the Guild, thinking that we do not see or understand." The bright and false smile followed. "Unlike you, Rystryr. I am most certain you understand."

"Of course I understand. How could I do otherwise? You and the lovely Anya have made that most clear."

"We are most glad of that." Jeslek frowned. "You will, of course, seize the golds taken by this Dursus and his assistant and return them to Fairhaven. I would judge you should be able to find 5,000, at the very least, before releasing such brigands to the mercy of chaos." Another smile appeared on the white-haired wizard's face. "Five thousand, at least."

"That might be difficult."

"Oh . . . I am most certain that you will find a way to trace such coins and return them. Most certain. And I do look forward to seeing the posting of all of the spring levy notices in the next few days," Jeslek said mildly. "Under the circumstances, I think that would be wise, do you not agree?"

"We but awaited your arrival, High Wizard, and we will let all know that both Certis and Fairhaven are opposed to the troubles created by the Spidlarian Council of Traders." Rystryr smiled back.

*He's going to make sure everyone in Certis knows he was pushed,* Cerryl reflected. *Is that wise?* The younger mage wasn't sure but wondered if admitting you bowed to a stronger neighbor might not create even more discontent.

"That will suffice." Jeslek smiled even more broadly.

"We look forward to seeing you all this evening." Rystryr nodded politely.

"And we you, my dear viscount." Jeslek turned.

Cerryl followed his lead but his senses on the concealed crossbowman until they were out of the study and well down the corridor headed back toward Shyren's chamber.

"The viscount was part of it, wasn't he?" Cerryl asked.

"If I suggested directly that he had been part of this," Jeslek shrugged, "then we would need a new viscount—and now is not the time for that. He has been warned in a way that will keep him honest for a time. But only for a time. No ruler stays honest."

Cerryl was inwardly amused at that. *There's no difference between honesty over power and honesty over coins.*

"We will need to exercise more control over those such as the viscount, especially after we deal with Spidlar. Especially then."

Cerryl kept pace with the taller High Wizard.

"We leave tomorrow, and not a word of this, not that I should have to tell you such."

"Yes, ser."

Jeslek's long strides across the stone tiles of the courtyard were noiseless, and only Cerryl's boots clumped in the late-afternoon grayness.


# LXXXV

Cerryl found himself beside Fydel and behind Anya and Jeslek as the White force rode out from the north gates of Jellico with the sun barely rising over the eastern walls. The flat fields beyond the causeway and flanking the road were damp and brown, with furrows that showed seed to have been planted, seed that had perhaps an eight-day before it would show green against the rich dark brown of the tilled bottomland. The road itself was damp packed clay, not the smooth stone of a White highway, and rutted from wagons and carts.

The High Wizard turned in the saddle, again and again, until all the lancers and the wagons were more than five kays beyond the causeway and well onto the road that followed the western bank of the River Jellicor. Even then, Jeslek continued to glance back every so often.

At the head of the first block of lancers, directly behind the mages, rode Captain Senglat. Somewhere near the middle of the column, by the second white and crimson banner, rode Teras, the other captain.

At least the spring rains meant that there was little dust, reflected Cerryl. Then, the softer clay might well slow the wagons at the rear of the column. Farther north, too, the river might be flowing higher with the meltwaters from the Easthorns and the run off from the rains, perhaps high enough to flood the road and create additional delays. The scattered trees that bordered the river had begun to show new leaves and the gray winter leaves had begun to green, giving the trees a mottled appearance.

Cerryl rode silently, lost in his own speculations, while a low conversation continued between Anya and Jeslek.

"He'll send the levies . . . Cerryl made sure of that . . ."

". . . over four thousand in the chest . . ."

". . . help . . . for a while . . . so will the 5,000 Rystryr will send to Fairhaven . . ."

". . . think he will?"

Jeslek laughed, harshly, jolting Cerryl out of his reverie. "He will. I made sure that someone told him about Lyam, the former prefect of Gallos, and about the late Duke Berofar. Rystryr will do exactly as he is told—for the next year or so. Rulers have such short memories. So we shall have to keep providing reminders." Another laugh followed, softer than the first.

*Do rulers have shorter memories, or do we just notice their faults because they are obvious?* Cerryl didn't know but strongly suspected the latter.

The sun stood clear of the eastern horizon, shedding a golden light across the green-blue sky, when the road widened slightly and Jeslek motioned for Cerryl and Fydel to ride abreast of him and Anya.

"Fydel, you and Cerryl will travel with the main body of lancers, and Anya and I will lead the van. Once we are another ten kays north on this river road, well away from Jellico, we will part. You two and Teras will care for the heavy wagons and the extra provisions. We will await you at Axalt."

"Axalt?" asked Fydel. "We are headed through the Easthorns there?"

"That is the shortest way to Spidlar without traversing Gallos," answered the white-haired High Wizard. "We shall assure ourselves that the road to and through Axalt will be clear for the Certan levies that will follow in another four or five eight-days, after the spring planting is complete."

As Jeslek spoke, Cerryl glanced over his shoulder, back at the nearly vanished walls of Jellico.

"Axalt has never allowed lancers and armsmen . . ." Fydel's voice trailed off as Anya's pale eyes fixed on him from where she rode, half-turned in the saddle to follow the conversation.

"Axalt has not heeded our advice, nor paid any tariffs. Axalt has certain tariffs of its own to pay." The High Wizard smiled. "Axalt will pay."

Cerryl winced inwardly at Jeslek's expression. The gray-eyed younger mage had a good idea of exactly what sort of tariffs the High Wizard meant to levy upon the mountain city.

Jeslek drew ahead of the other mages once more, momentarily, until Anya joined him, and the two rode silently in front of Cerryl and Fydel.

More than another kay passed before Cerryl eased his own gelding forward. "Who will replace Shyren in Jellico? Or has that been decided?" Cerryl finally asked the High Wizard.

Jeslek did not turn, nor answer immediately, but Cerryl continued to ride on Jeslek's quarter until the High Wizard turned slightly in the saddle. "I have sent a summons to Gorsuch. He, at least, understands what happens when lands do not heed Fairhaven. Just as you now understand the need for rules in governing and in peacekeeping."

Jeslek nodded curtly, then eased his mount farther ahead of Fydel and Cerryl, back beside Anya, and behind Senglat. The captain had moved up in the column and now rode behind the half-score of fore-riders, not really a true vanguard, at least not yet.

*Why the mention of rules and peacekeeping on an invasion force?* Cerryl frowned, teasing the thoughts back and forth and finding no ready answers, finding his thoughts more on a blonde healer as he wondered how Leyladin was, half-wishing he were still in Fairhaven, and fully wishing he could talk to her and to see her laughing deep green eyes and hear her words. Instead, he took a long and slow breath and shifted his weight in the saddle.

# LXXXVI

Cerryl guided the gelding around the gray rock on the right side of the road, a pile of squarish irregular stones that was nearly to his mount's shoulder and left but enough passage for little more than a single rider at a time. As he followed Fydel, he glanced up at the rock face to the north of the road that tracked the winding canyon cut by the river. The darker rock and the line of gray stone indicated that the rockfall was recent, and the second he and Fydel had encountered in the last kay of riding. Each time they had been required to stop while the trailing lancers removed enough rock to allow the supply wagons to pass.

The younger mage cast his chaos senses ahead, but he could find nothing he would not have expected and no sign of other riders, except for Captain Teras and the twenty-odd-score lancers and the wagons. The canyon walls were high enough that shadows cast by the not-quite-midmorning sun still covered the road. Occasionally, in sections of the road where pockets of chill remained, Cerryl's breath steamed in the shadows.

Once past the rocks, Cerryl drew his mount alongside Fydel's. "Those rockfalls seem large."

"You always get rock coming loose in spring," Fydel answered. "The ice breaks it loose. It's worse in the Westhorns."

Cerryl looked back and up at the cliff. He still wasn't sure that so much rock could have been broken loose by meltwater or ice. His eyes dropped to the cold foaming water to the left of the road—high, but still within its banks and comfortably below the level of the road. Only the brush within three or four cubits of the water had been flattened by an earlier and higher stream flow. That could change with a hot rain or a series of hot days. There was still all too much snow in the higher reaches of the Easthorns that flanked the canyon area they traveled.

*Rawwwkk!* A black vulcrow flapped off the end of a dead pine trunk that had fallen against an older and healthier fir.

"Scavengers . . ." muttered Fydel.

Cerryl half-stood in the stirrups, then settled back down and tried to get more comfortable in the saddle.

Neither man spoke for another kay or so—until they reached a third and far larger rockfall in a fractionally wider section of the canyon. The rock slide had ripped trees off the canyon wall and bought down chunks of granite from the left side of the canyon, filling most of the streambed and creating a small lake that stretched upstream. The new lake's surface had risen almost to the level of the road itself.

"We need to get through here quickly." Fydel turned and looked at Teras.

"We're still waiting for the supply wagons," Teras pointed out. "The water isn't rising that fast. There's enough water, and it's near enough to water the horses. We've the space to gather." He pointed ahead to the right of the road and an open and cleared space that had obviously been used as a staging point or a campsite, with fire rings and clay packed by all too many hoofs. "It might be a good time to stand down."

A frown crossed Fydel's face, but he nodded. "So long as we can mount up quickly if needed."

"That we can do." Teras nodded to the herald beside him, who took out his horn and bugled a call that Cerryl had come to recognize as the stand-down signal.

After taking advantage of his position at the head of the column and watering his mount, Cerryl rode farther up the road. He was glad to be able to dismount and stretch his legs in a different way and to refill his water bottles. He was also careful to chaos-boil them, even if he had to wait before drinking the water—and it was hot even then.

Fydel joined him, dismounting easily.

"Don't know why you bother," said Fydel. "The water isn't that bad up here."

"It can't hurt." Cerryl shrugged, still holding the chestnut's reins. "Besides, I don't feel right about those rock slides. Who knows what else might have fallen into the water?"

"You'll never be an arms mage if you worry about that sort of thing." Fydel laughed once.

*You'll never live to be an old arms mage if you don't.* "That could be," Cerryl said.

After a time, the creaking and groaning of wagons filled the wider space in the canyon that was becoming a lake.

Finally, Fydel drew Teras aside. "As soon as the wagon beasts are watered, we need to move on," Fydel ordered Teras. "The water is almost up to the road."

"It will take a little time, but we'll hurry best we can, Mage Fydel," Teras answered deliberately.

The sun had risen well above the canyon walls before the wagons and their teams had been watered, fed, and rested, and the water from the new lake was lapping at the side of the road as Fydel and Cerryl rode westward through the stream canyon. The road still rose, if more gently than before, and the murmurings from the lancers were louder as the day progressed.

While they had seen signs of the passage of Jeslek's force—hoofprints and droppings—no messengers had reached them, and outside of the sound of the stream and the intermittent calls of vulcrows and the infrequent squawk of a traitor bird the only sounds came from the force of lancers that Fydel and Cerryl led deeper and deeper into the Easthorns.

Then, after a narrow defile, the road curved and widened into what appeared to be a small valley. There, under a single crimson and white banner, a squad of White Lancers waited.

Cerryl nodded to himself as he saw the tumbled walls beyond and the trails of smoke that curled into the clear green-blue of the sky above. The rock slides that had obstructed the road had not been caused just by thawing and meltwater, and Axalt had definitely paid Jeslek's tariffs.

"The High Wizard has made his point," Fydel observed. "Others will heed what has befallen Axalt."

"I wonder," murmured Cerryl. "I wonder." It had taken the disappearance and death of one duke and the destruction of two towers before the Dukes of Hydlen had understood the power of Fairhaven, and then only reluctantly. Would the devastation of one small mountain city really change the minds of the Traders' Council of Spidlar?

"Mages Fydel and Cerryl?" asked the lancer subofficer who rode forward toward the white and crimson banners that followed the two mages.

"The same," answered Fydel.

"The High Wizard has continued toward Elparta. He would have you meet his forces just beyond the Easthorns. He also requests that you make prudent haste."

"Prudent haste? That we can do." Fydel nodded and cleared his throat, turning in the saddle to Teras.

While the two talked, Cerryl's eyes took in the jumbled heaps of rocks that had once been walls, dwellings, warehouses . . . who knew what. The stench of death, while faint, was present and would grow, even in the cool under the clear skies. The scattering smoke trails whispered upward.

Cerryl thought he saw a crouched figure scuttle from one pile of rubble to another, but long as he looked again, he could see no other movement. Then, he wouldn't have moved either, not after what Jeslek had done to Axalt. He turned back toward Fydel.

"There's no reason to tarry here," observed the square-bearded mage.

Cerryl glanced over the devastation. "No. I would guess not."

Somewhat later, as the lancer column wound upward toward the end of the valley, picking its way through and around the rubble, Cerryl could hear the murmurings from the lancers who rode behind them.

". . . didn't leave much for us."

". . . didn't leave much for anyone."

*Will Jeslek leave much for anyone?* Cerryl eased himself into another position in the too-hard saddle and kept riding.

# LXXXVII

From where he rode beside Fydel, leading the White Lancers and halfway down the hillside, Cerryl could see a hamlet ahead, little more than a gathering of huts in a depression between the rolling hills. From around the huts rose the smoke of cook fires, and farther out Cerryl could discern scores of mounts confined, either in rough corrals or on tie-lines. The hamlet itself lay perhaps ten kays westward from the end of the canyon that had led them from fallen Axalt into Spidlar.

Cerryl glanced back over the line of lancers, in the direction of the supply wagons still out of sight behind the hill he and Fydel were descending on the winding clay track that barely resembled a road. Behind them, the snow and ice of the Easthorns' higher reaches almost merged with the puffy white clouds that had begun to drift in from the north.

Cerryl hoped the clouds didn't bring rain—or not too much. He turned and studied the road ahead and the hillside that seemed to alternate between rocks, scrub bushes, and patches of grass—a land suited mostly to grazing, if that. He squinted, trying to see farther westward where several of the more distant hills appeared to be wooded, but the hills faded as the gelding carried him downhill.

A half-kay or so outside the unnamed hamlet, the road flattened and widened somewhat. With the more level ground came the scents of horses and smoke and other less savory evidences of human habitation.

In the hamlet itself, Jeslek and Anya stood outside a rough-timbered dwelling slightly larger than the handful of others, perhaps twenty cubits in breadth and ten deep and boasting a clay-chinked stone chimney. Cerryl could sense the residual of the chaos used to clean the dwelling

"So . . . you have arrived." Jeslek's sun-eyes glittered. "At last. We have been here near on two days."

"We made prudent haste," answered Fydel. "It took longer because of the rock slides and the rising waters. And the supply wagons you left for us to escort."

"You passed through Axalt?" The High Wizard's eyes traveled from Fydel to Cerryl and then back to the dark-bearded mage.

*How else could we have gone?* Then Cerryl realized, belatedly, that Jeslek wanted an acknowledgment of some sort. "We saw the destruction you wrought, High Wizard. Nothing remains of Axalt."

Jeslek snorted. "I have sent a message to the Traders' Council of Spidlar, suggesting that they heed what befell Axalt."

"They will not," said Anya, standing beside Jeslek, her flame-red hair fluttering in the light and chill wind that blew out of the Easthorns and across the rolling hills of southeastern Spidlar. "They scarce will have learned that we have arrived here. Nor will they credit all the levies to follow until they have seen them in battle."

Jeslek gestured toward the cots and small barns behind him. "Battle? It will be eight-days before we see any battle. By then, we will have advanced half the distance to Elparta."

"What would you have us do?" asked Fydel.

"Best you quarter with us," offered the High Wizard, "though we will be here for but a few days, while we refresh mounts and make repairs." Jeslek glanced at Teras. "You had best consult with Senglat as to where you should camp your force and rest their mounts."

From where he had drawn his mount up next to Cerryl Teras nodded acknowledgment. "As you suggest, High Wizard."

"Shortly, we will discuss how we will proceed to bring Spidlar into the fold."

Cerryl dismounted wearily. Any respite would be more than welcome, but he doubted that Spidlar—or any land—would come into the fold all that willingly.

# LXXXVIII

Cerryl sat on the hard bench beside Anya, across the rough-cut trestle table from Jeslek and Fydel. A light rain fell outside the small house, and occasional gusts of damp and cool morning air filtered through the open door.

The High Wizard was half-turned on the other bench, his eyes fixed on Fydel. "There are only two roads from Axalt into Spidlar. The northern road goes to Kleth and the southern one to Elparta. They both split from the one leading out of this pigsty. The fork is about ten kays to the west of where we are now. There's a town there, if you can term it such."

The dark-bearded Fydel nodded.

"You and Cerryl will hold that town while Anya and I will lead the advance on Elparta, once the first levies arrive."

"Why don't we just take the northern route and be done with it?" asked Fydel.

"Because the northern road is even worse than this track, and because we'll need the river to move the levies down to Kleth and Spidlaria," Anya answered for Jeslek.

Cerryl wanted to hold his breath, so strong was the odor of trilia and sandalwood despite the breeze from the open door.

"Which levies? Aren't the Certans coming through what's left of Axalt? Can't they hold the town? That's what levies are best at, anyway." Fydel shrugged.

"Rystryr's levies are coming through Axalt, but we don't want that Black arms commander coming out of the north and hitting them before they even get to the river."

"Honored High Wizard . . ." Fydel paused, then added, "I fail to understand. If we took the northern route—"

"Then this Black would hold Elparta," interrupted Jeslek, "and he would control the river and be able to attack either our forces or the Gallosian levies. As I have told you, Fydel, he is an excellent field commander."

Anya smiled her blindingly false smile. "We also wouldn't have any Gallosian levies because they wouldn't march downriver into Spidlar. We wouldn't be there to lead them, and the agreement for levies requires the White Lancers to provide horse support. Or do you propose that we abandon half the ground armsmen that we have already called in?"

"As for the Certan levies, you and Cerryl have to provide the escort and horse support, and that means you will be quartered at the town at the road fork, whatever its name might be." Jeslek raised his snow-white eyebrows. "As Anya has pointed out, we also have to have a way for the Gallosian levies to enter Spidlar, and that has to be by the river or the river roads. That means we have to reach the river, and that's where Elparta is."

"So we do the dirty work—"

Jeslek's eyes flashed.

"Whatever you wish, High Wizard," Fydel said quickly.

"I am High Wizard, Fydel, and it would behoove you to recall that." Jeslek's voice moderated. "Have you a better way of ensuring that *all* the levies are joined?" After a moment of silence, Jeslek nodded, almost to himself. "I thought not. Now . . . we are to expect the first Certan levies in an eight-day. Until they arrive, Anya and I will advance as far as we can without engaging any large Spidlarian forces. You will scree the north road and run patrols to ensure that we are not flanked . . ."

Cerryl continued to listen, still wondering precisely why Jeslek had insisted on Cerryl's own presence. The breeze died, and, again, he found himself overwhelmed with the scents of sandalwood and trilia.

# LXXXIX

Cerryl walked slowly toward the cook fire behind the squarish house, looking toward the south. Although the fields and meadows were green, the color that faded with the sun as he studied the land had been the lighter green of early spring, and the evening was getting chill, like every evening since they had left Jellico.

Cerryl eased up closer to the cook fire, stopping to the right of Fydel and Anya. He sniffed the scent of a mutton stew of some sort.

"How did it go today?" asked Anya, tendering a mug of something to the square-bearded mage.

"The same as yesterday, and the day before." Fydel shook his head, his eyes going to the west, where the purple of the sky deepened. "I wish the darkness-damned Certans would get here. If they don't . . ."

"If they don't . . . what?" asked Jeslek as he strode up to the fire. "Do you want to go back and fetch them?"

"It might be better than trying to fend off the raids from that Black renegade," suggested Fydel dourly.

"We won't have to wait that long. The first detachment has reached the ruins of Axalt." Jeslek glanced at the lancer cook. "How long?"

"A bit longer for the stew, ser." The cook looked down at the boot-packed ground around the stones of the cook-fire ring. "I'm sorry."

*Everything took longer,* reflected Cerryl silently. *Everywhere.*

"Did you lose anyone today?" asked Anya, glancing back to the square-bearded mage.

"Not today. One lancer took an arrow in the thigh, but it wasn't deep. We never saw the archer."

Cerryl frowned but said nothing. How could Fydel not see an archer?

"You think it's easy?" snapped Fydel as he turned to the younger mage. "You try one of the road patrols. The blue bastards don't stay in one place. You go down one road, and some archers are firing at your squad from the woods to your rear. If you try to clear out the woods, you lose more men because they can't make any speed on horseback there. If you avoid the woods, you can't get anywhere. The fields are still muddy." Fydel looked at Cerryl. "Tomorrow . . . you should come with us. You'll see. Darkness, you'll see."

"Perhaps you should, Cerryl," Jeslek said. "It will give you an idea of just how you will handle peacekeeping once we take Elparta. There's not much else you can do until the levies get here."

"Yes, ser." The last thing Cerryl wanted to do was ride along roads that weren't even lanes trying to keep raiding parties away from the camp.

"And you can flame any archer you see," Jeslek said with a smile, "since you seem to find it so easy."

Fydel laughed. Even Anya smiled.

Cerryl took a long, slow breath, then looked toward the cauldron, hoping it wouldn't be that long before the mutton stew was ready. He had to wonder how he could get in trouble without even speaking. Were his expressions that obvious, or were Fydel and Jeslek once more out to put him in situations where he was more likely to fail? As he waited for the stew to finish, he forced a pleasant smile onto his face.

# XC

Just because he'd given Fydel a questioning look the night before, now Cerryl found himself back on the gelding, his muscles no longer aching but only moderately sore. Fydel's score of lancers rode northward on a road that was more trail than road, a track of dusty gray clay that rose in powdery clouds with each hoof that struck it, a track barely able to take two riders abreast. Despite the full morning sunlight, the day was pleasant, although Cerryl suspected that the afternoon would be hotter and far less pleasant.

On the east side of the road was a piled stone wall, no more than two cubits high. Behind the stone was a higher meadow, where fresh green shoots twined up between the frayed and brown stalks of the previous year. To the downhill and left side of the road was a field that had been plowed, but which showed no regular growth, just scattered splotches of green against the dry tan soil.

Cerryl wondered if the arrival of the White Lancers had driven off the peasants before they could plant.

"See? There's no one there. Or you think there isn't. Except they're there . . . waiting with some dark angel trap." From where he rode to the left of Cerryl Fydel snorted.

Glancing across the open terrain, Cerryl had to wonder where the Spidlarian forces would even hide. He couldn't detect any chaos or order that could have been used to conceal riders or armsmen on foot.

"They don't use magery," Fydel answered the unspoken question. "You'll see."

As they continued northwest on the narrow road, the cultivated fields gave way to more woodlots or woods and meadows—and peasant cots even more widely scattered.

A fly buzzed past Cerryl's face, and the gelding's tail swished to brush the offending insect away, sending it back to plague Cerryl. He swatted at it several times before it flew elsewhere; then he blotted his forehead.

After a time, the road dipped into a swale, with a small marsh below the road to the left. A brook ran from the east through a depression in the road. A good thirty cubits upstream from the road was a clump of bushes, the small new leaves barely unfurled and the second-year leaves still half-gray.

"They hide in places like that. Well . . . they won't hide any longer." Fydel's face screwed up in concentration.

Cerryl could feel the chaos buildup. "There's nothing there."

"There won't be," grunted the older wizard.

*Whhhstt!* The fireball arced out and fell onto the clump of bushes. Chaos flames spurted into the sky as the bushes flared red. A puff of flame fluttered from the bushes before arching into the ground and dissolving into white ashes that fell into an oval on the brown and green grass. Cerryl swallowed as he realized that the brief flame puff had been a bird of some sort.

The flame tongues where the bushes had been died away almost immediately, leaving reddish embers and thin trails of black and gray smoke that wound skyward. The acrid scent of burning brush and winter leaves filled the air, then died away as the light breeze scattered the ashes, even before Cerryl and the lancers reached the marshy area.

"Easier that way," grunted Fydel. "Doesn't leave them anywhere to hide."

Cerryl hadn't seen that much cover, not any sufficient to conceal any force large enough to threaten even a score of lancers. "How big a force do they have?"

"Around here? A score perhaps, but they don't ever send that many—just a few archers. They loose some shafts, and they're gone. They don't use magery, and you can't use a glass to find something that disturbs neither order nor chaos."

Cerryl nodded, his eyes flicking to the left at the ashes and wisps of smoke that had been marsh bushes, then to the road. Another hill, higher than the one the troop had just descended rose beyond the stream, and the road angled eastward and began to climb once more.

The murmurs from the lancers who rode behind Teras drifted up to Cerryl over the dust-muffled sound of hoofs.

"... up and down ... up and down ..."

"... got two mages today ... Mayhap that'll help."

"Don't count on mages ..."

"Ready lance or blade's best defense for a lancer."

Cerryl rubbed his nose, trying to stop the itching. *Kkkchew* ... He rubbed his nose.

From the next high point in the road Cerryl looked northward. Ahead, the road turned eastward as it curved down and around the hillside toward a broad valley filled with meadows where scattered purple wildflowers dotted the green. Beyond the meadows was a forest or woods that stretched up the hillsides. Nearer, below the road to the left, the grass was sparser. Occasional bushes—still showing furled winter-gray leaves and bare branches—bordered the uphill side of the road.

Cerryl glanced toward the valley, leaning forward in the saddle and squinting to make out the forms in the meadows.

"Cattle," observed Fydel. "We might be able to send out a wagon and bring in some for rations." He paused. "If they're still here ... if the blue bastards haven't set them up as a trap." He turned in the saddle and added in a louder voice to Teras, "Woods ahead—and cattle. Have them ready for anything."

"Arms ready!" ordered Teras.

"Arms ready."

Cerryl took a deep breath, then exhaled. From behind one of the bushes farther uphill—exactly where Cerryl couldn't see—an arrow arched down toward the small column.

*Whhhsttt!* Cerryl loosed chaos, almost without thinking.

The metal arrowhead, glowing red, tumbled into the road dirt, less than a dozen cubits before Cerryl's mount.

"Arms!" The order came from Teras.

About a half-score of lancers galloped past Cerryl and off the road in the direction from which the shaft had come.

"Quick there," said Fydel. "Lucky you were looking that way."

"You said they might do something." Cerryl tried to reach out with his order-chaos senses but could find no indication of anyone, especially not the ordered blackness of a Black mage.

He listened. After a moment, he could hear hoofs on harder ground, sounds that vanished almost immediately, as did the half-score lancers.

Fydel and Teras kept riding downhill toward the meadows and the cattle that grazed there. Since they did, as did the lancers who followed, so did Cerryl, but he kept his eyes and senses alert for order or chaos concentrations—or more arrows.

The road and the valley remained unchanged—until the lancer detachment rejoined Fydel and the others halfway down the road to the valley.

"They were gone, ser," reported the subofficer who had led the half-score lancers back to rejoin. He offered a nod to Captain Teras. "Would have foundered our mounts trying to catch them."

"Fall in, at the end," said Teras laconically.

"Yes, ser."

The lancers rejoined the column.

"Lucky this time," Fydel said dourly. "Won't always be looking in the right direction when someone looses a shaft."

"I'll take good luck when we can have it," replied Teras from beside the square-bearded mage, "especially against attackers who loose shafts and then flee."

"We need more levies. That way we could just move ahead and take over all these hamlets." Fydel grinned at Cerryl. "Then you could worry about peacekeeping and this sort of thing."

"Thank you," the younger mage answered. "I appreciate your faith."

"Think nothing of it." Fydel's grin broadened.

"We might get some fresh beef out of this patrol," suggested Teras. "The men will appreciate that."

"We all will," said Fydel.

*Except for the peasants who lose their animals.* Cerryl just nodded and blotted his forehead again.

# XCI

Jeslek looked around the small cot, his eyes flashing in the gloom, first at Anya, then Fydel, and finally resting momentarily on Cerryl. As Anya smiled behind the High Wizard, Cerryl could sense he wasn't likely to enjoy what was coming.

"Fydel was most impressed with your ability to sense the blues." Jeslek smiled a bright smile that was as false as Anya's well-practiced expression.

Cerryl waited.

"You have also had experience in directing patrollers and in battle," Jeslek continued. "I would be most remiss if I did not employ such talents." Another smile followed as the High Wizard pointed to the map flattened on the crude trestle table, barely illuminated by the single brass lamp on the wood beside it. "Here is southern Spidlar. The main body of our forces will be traveling westward to Elparta. To begin with, the levies will come through the Easthorns from Rytel. We must protect this section of road from the mountains to where our forces are, and eventually to Elparta." Jeslek offered a perfunctory nod. "It makes little sense for you to accompany us, Cerryl, not now. It also makes less sense for Fydel to patrol the entire road between our forces and the Easthorns."

"You wish me to patrol a section of the road?" asked Cerryl not quite guilelessly.

"Fydel will command the patrols immediately to the rear of the main body of forces and from the town to the west of the fork hamlet."

Fydel nodded.

"You will patrol the section you recently traveled, from the mountains through this town to the fork hamlet and halfway to the next town."

"That is about fifteen kays west of here," Anya interjected.

"You will have twoscore White Lancers and two subofficers." Jeslek smiled again. "You have been most creative in the past, and I am certain you will use that skill to Fairhaven's advantage once again."

"Two score . . ." mused Cerryl.

"Fydel will be closer to the Black arms commander's forces and will need a somewhat larger force." Jeslek lifted the stones holding down the corners of the map, one at a time, then rolled it up. "I do not propose to have large groups of lancers strung out across Spidlar. You and Fydel are to stop any attacks, when possible without losing many lancers, to avoid battle when you cannot, and to ensure that any levies traveling the road are warned well in advance of any possible attacks that you cannot turn." Jeslek paused before his final words.

"With your skills, Cerryl, I am certain you can handle such a mundane task."

Behind the High Wizard, Anya smiled through the dim lamplight.

"I appreciate your trust and confidence." *Wonderful! You're in charge of more road than Fydel and with fewer lancers. Yet another opportunity for failure and disgrace, especially against an experienced Black commander.*

# XCII

The breeze from outside the small cot was warm already, even though the sun was barely above the horizon. Cerryl could hear someone feeding the horses and the clanking of a cook pot. His eyes dropped to the screeing glass upon the time-worn wood before him, and he leaned forward on the bench, slowly sketching from it what he could on the rough map beside the glass. He paused and dipped the quill in the traveling inkstand once more, then added another dashed line that represented a narrow trail. His maps suffered in accuracy, but making them was another way beside riding every cubit of trail and road to learn more about Spidlar. He particularly tried to follow and note on his crude maps the narrow trails that were not exactly roads. Those were the ones that an experienced lancer leader might well use against someone—like Cerryl—who did not know the land, especially in dry weather.

He shook his head and went back to screeing. Finally, after his fingers began to tremble, he let the image of a patch of land to the northwest of his encampment fade, and he put his hands in his head, closing his eyes for a time.

A bit later, he smiled and reached for another place. Leyladin's image swirled through the mists, and a puzzled look crossed her face. Then came a smile, a broad smile, and her fingers touched her lips. Behind her, Cerryl could see the green silk hangings of her room.

After a moment, Cerryl let the image fade, a wistful smile upon his own lips. While he could sense when someone used a glass to scree him, he still wondered how Leyladin could sense he was the one looking at her, but, in a way, she'd known him first through the glass and had always recognized his screeing. *What else has she always known?*

He frowned and studied the blankness before him on the rough wooden trestle table. The glass showed him no riders in blue, no armsmen in each of the hamlets he screed—those within a day's ride of the road between Axalt and the staging town where he and his small detachment of lancers were based. His screeings did not mean that his lancers might not face ambushes, only that there were no large bodies of armsmen that near.

*They're all making Jeslek's advance difficult, that's why.* Cerryl wiped his forehead, damp with the effort of working with the glass, then took a swig from his water bottle.

He concentrated again, thinking about the smith in distant Diev, whose focused order radiated across the kays separating them.

The red-haired smith was beside his forge, drawing wire, and Cerryl could sense the order in that wire even through the glass. Like Leyladin, Dorrin glanced up as his image strengthened in the glass before Cerryl. Unlike the blonde healer, the smith scowled, but briefly, before returning to drawing wire.

"Ordered black iron wire," murmured the gray-eyed mage, shaking his head. What Dorrin was doing would cause great troubles for the White forces moving toward Elparta, even if Cerryl did not yet understand how. That he could feel. *Does Jeslek know? Or care?*

Cerryl stood and packed the mirror back into its carrying case.

# XCIII

While the morning cook fires were building, Cerryl took the screeing glass from its case and set it on the trestle table—the beginning of his daily pattern. The already-warm wind gusted through the open door, swirling Cerryl's white trousers around his legs and boots and carrying the odor of green wood into the cot.

He rubbed his nose, then pulled the bench out so that he could sit as he called up the images he needed—and as he added to the rough maps he continued to draw. He had sketched in most of the side roads and trails that fed into the main road between Axalt and Elparta, and there were far more of them than he ever would have guessed before he'd begun his informal project.

He frowned as he looked at the blank glass, deciding against seeking Leyladin until he was finished with a drafting session and with scanning the nearby hamlets. That way, at least, he could end with a pleasant visage.

He found one more trail, winding through the rolling hills and leading almost to the main road where Jeslek and his forces massed a good forty kays to the southeast of Elparta along the hills that separated Gallos and Spidlar. After Cerryl added that to the map, he began to look for the latest supply wagons from Certis. Those were encamped somewhere in the Easthorns short of ruined Axalt. Finally, he began to scree the nearby hamlets.

The first two attempts showed still-empty hamlets. Even before the silver mists cleared on his third effort, a good four-, perhaps fivescore mounted armsmen wearing blue tunics or vests appeared in the glass, saddling their mounts and preparing to ride.

Cerryl couldn't tell exactly where they were, but they looked to be on the road leading to the crossroads just beyond the hamlet where he'd made his headquarters—less than a half-day's ride on what passed for one of the better roads in the area.

The brown-haired mage forced himself to finish checking the other locales before he returned to the image of the mounted armsmen. After studying the image again, he slowly stood and wiped his suddenly damp forehead. From what he could tell, no inordinate order or chaos accompanied the armsmen, and the glass wasn't wrong. At least, it usually wasn't.

*You hope it's not.* He swallowed and walked out of the cot, glancing around the hamlet, the few buildings swathed in the orange of postdawn, lancers gathering beyond the cook fires for their rations.

"Ser?" asked the young lancer serving as a messenger.

"Oh . . . I need Hiser and Ferek. Right now."

"Yes, ser."

As the lancer scurried off, Cerryl massaged his clean-shaven chin. Even in the field, he hated the itchiness of a beard, although sometimes he skipped shaving a day or two with the white-bronze razor that Leyladin had given him years before.

*Has it been that long?*

Hiser was the first to arrive, his lank blond hair flopping across his forehead. The older Ferek followed, brushing back thinning red hair streaked liberally with white.

"We've finally got visitors," Cerryl said. "Probably fivescore Spidlarian lancers. They look like they're on the road to the fork, maybe a half-day's hard ride."

"That's more than we have." Ferek looked speculatively at Cerryl. Hiser nodded.

"I'm not really an armsman," Cerryl ventured, "but it seems to me that we want to meet them somewhere that favors us, where they can't easily ride around us and where they have to ride uphill to reach us." He paused. "And where I can throw firebolts at them."

"There's that bunch of hills about two kays beyond where the road forks," suggested Hiser.

Cerryl nodded. It might work. "Ferek . . . you get the men ready, and Hiser and I and a few lancers will ride out there now to see how we can best set up."

"Set up . . . what's to set up?" Ferek mumbled to Hiser as the two walked back in the direction of the corral and the lancers, some of whom were still eating.

Hiser murmured something, but Cerryl didn't catch his words. The mage turned back to the cot, where he again called up the image of the Spidlarian lancers, now clearly riding southward. He let the image go, slipped the glass into its case, then stepped out of the cot. He walked down to the pole and post corral, stopping by the cook fire to grab a biscuit and some hard yellow cheese, which he wolfed down and chased with water. When he reached the corral, the gelding was already saddled and tied, waiting.

Hiser was mounted, as were five lancers.

"We're ready, ser."

Cerryl strapped the glass into a saddlebag and then mounted. The sun had climbed clear of the low hills to the east and blazed out of the clear green-blue morning sky, indicating a day that would be long and hot.

"Do you know how hard they're riding?" Hiser asked.

"They're walking their mounts."

As they rode westward past the untended fields and meadows, Cerryl could hear Ferek's voice behind them as he addressed the majority of the lancers.

"No more raids. These be armsmen, and lots of 'em. A good wizard helps, but he'll not do everything."

*Not do everything? Let's hope I don't have to.* Cerryl still recalled the battles in Gallos, when he'd been an apprentice. It had taken three wizards and three apprentices to defeat the Gallosian lancers. *There were a few more Gallosian lancers there than here.* But that battle still pointed out the limits of using chaos fire. The bigger the battle, the less use it was, because drawing chaos from the land and air exhausted the White wizard before all the armsmen on the other side were turned to ash.

The early-morning wind had died, and the morning was still and damp, although there had been no rain in several days. Cerryl shifted his weight in the saddle, his eyes on where the road forked ahead.

Cerryl, Hiser, and the quarter-score lancers took the north fork, the one that wound its way toward Kleth—eventually. After they had ridden up and down three of the long and gentle rises that barely qualified as hills, the day had gotten warm enough that Cerryl was sweating, and what little breeze there had been had long since died away. The road was empty, and the only tracks were those of Cerryl's patrols.

In time, the seven reined up on the hillside that Hiser had thought might be suitable for what he had envisioned. The young mage glanced at the subofficer.

"See . . . this is the right place," Hiser said. "We could form up on the right in that meadow . . . make them ride up—or charge down."

Without speaking, Cerryl surveyed the ground to the northwest. Was Hiser right? Could they use the terrain to their advantage? How? Height wasn't enough by itself. The road went through a narrower space between the two rolling hills. On the north side was an open meadow and on the south a woods or woodlot, thick enough to slow and split riders. Any decent officer would see that and go another way, and Cerryl couldn't count on stupidity on the part of the Spidlarians.

"Let's ride along the road to the next rise," the mage suggested.

A brief frown crossed Hiser's face.

"You were right about the place," Cerryl said, "but if we wait here, it will be obvious to them. I'm wondering if the next rise looks like high ground but would show that we could be flanked."

Hiser nodded. "So we'd form up and then give a little attack and fall back."

"We might just fall back," Cerryl said. "I'd rather avoid losing men we don't have to lose. It would also give them the idea I don't know what I'm doing." *You don't, anyway.* He concealed the wince at his own self-doubt.

"Make them hasty . . . you think?"

"Something like that, just so they don't think too much."

Cerryl rode down through the long and gentle slope of the meadow for nearly half a kay, noting that despite the lush grass, the ground appeared flat and firm.

"They could ride up this easy," said Hiser. "Course . . . we could ride down easier."

"Let's hope they think so." Cerryl turned his mount back uphill.

After dismounting near the single oak near the road—he thought it was a oak—Cerryl took out the glass and laid it on its case in the shadow of the tree, then motioned for Hiser to join him.

As the image swam into the glass, Cerryl could hear the lancer subofficer swallow. The Spidlarian lancers were still on the road headed toward Cerryl. They were not straining their mounts but moving at a good walking pace.

"Watching their mounts, they are," observed Hiser.

"A cautious leader." *And that's trouble.* Cerryl released the image. "We might as well relax until Ferek and the others get here."

"Stand down," Hiser ordered the five lancers.

Cerryl sat down in the shade, leaning against a crooked oak root that had risen aboveground. He had the feeling he'd best rest while he could.

Well before midmorning, Ferek and the balance of Cerryl's lancers arrived.

"The hill the last back is a better place," Ferek offered brusquely as he reined up beside the oak, looking down at Cerryl, who had not remounted the gelding.

"You're right," Cerryl agreed amiably. "We won't fight here. I don't want them to see that, though. If they do, they might try something else." *That I wouldn't be able to puzzle out quickly enough.*

Ferek scratched his beard. "Tire the mounts some to ride back there if they're chasing us."

"They've ridden farther, much farther," Cerryl pointed out, "and it will be a time before they arrive—at least midday." He paused. "If you rest and water the mounts in the stream there, will they be ready?"

Ferek looked toward the stream that crossed the southeastern side of the long meadow. "Easy. Do it in squads, I would."

"Then why don't you start now?" Cerryl smiled.

Hiser covered his mouth and coughed to hide a smile.

Ferek swung his bay around and ordered, "Water time. Stand down in squads! Water. Be quick now."

Cerryl rode the gelding back to the sole oak tree near the road on the crest of the rise and dismounted. He took out the glass and called up the image of the Spidlarians—who appeared nearer. Overhead, the leaves rustled briefly, then stilled again.

It was almost noon before the Spidlarian force appeared on the more distant hill—and reined up as the riders saw the short line of Cerryl's lancers, all mounted and apparently ready to repulse any attack or to attack themselves.

"Mayhap they won't come forward," said Ferek, from Cerryl's right. "Or they'll let their mounts get their wind."

"It could be. We'll have to see." Cerryl blotted more of the dampness from his forehead and the back of his neck and stood slightly in the stirrups, trying to loosen trousers that clung too tightly, welded to his body by heat and sweat.

As Ferek's lancers had done, the Spidlarians cautiously watered their mounts in small groups, clearly not letting any horse drink much, before re-forming on the rise across the meadow from Cerryl's forces.

Slightly before midafternoon, the larger Spidlarian force slowly began to move, taking the slightly lower sections of the long meadow, then moving up. A group of archers rode halfway up the meadow and started to dismount and string their bows.

"Don't like that, ser," Ferek said.

Cerryl concentrated.

*Whhhssttt.* A firebolt arched and fell on one side of the archers.

One man flared into flame, and the others fell back a good hundred cubits.

Cerryl frowned. The archers were at the edge of his range, especially for accuracy, but he didn't want them getting too close.

Still more than a kay away, the blue lancers split into groups of perhaps four riders and spread from one another as they walked their mounts slowly uphill and across the gentle slope of the rise. The hot sun glinted from their bared blades.

"They be not together," mumbled Ferek.

"I thought that might happen." Cerryl nodded. The Spidlarians knew or suspected that the Fairhaven forces had a White wizard; so they would not charge in mass where a single firebolt could wreak damage on more than a handful. Still, they would have to mass at some point before they reached Cerryl's force . . . but that could be almost at the last moment on the gentle meadow. They wouldn't be able to keep that spread out once they reached the narrower section of the vale the road traveled between the hills to the southeast.

"There are a lot more of them . . ." ventured Ferek.

Cerryl smiled faintly. "When they get to those bushes, down by the dead tree, we'll turn and ride back along the road."

Ferek frowned. "Why'd we ride up this far?"

"So they wouldn't see how the road goes through that narrow place behind us." Cerryl repressed a sigh. He'd already told Ferek once. "All right, have the men follow me back to the second hill—all but the two squads with Hiser." He paused. "You ready, Hiser?"

"Yes, ser." The subofficer gave a quick nod, his eyes going to the lancers who flanked him.

*Whhssst!* Cerryl arched another fireball toward the Spidlarians. It fell well short, as he knew it would, but the lancers slowed as the green grass burned for a time, with a thick grayish smoke that quickly faded and then dissipated. "Let's fall back." Cerryl turned the gelding. "Hiser . . . have your group hold here as long as you can without losing anyone, then ride back to our position."

That would spend the horses more than Cerryl would have liked, but he didn't want a fallback to turn into a pell-mell retreat, and having two squads remaining to "hold" the lower rise might ensure a more orderly retreat. *If you're lucky.*

"We'll hold 'em long enough for you to re-form, ser," Hiser promised.

"Don't hold too long," Cerryl answered. "The idea is to avoid losing men."

Hiser nodded.

Cerryl wanted to wince. "I meant that."

"Yes, ser."

With a nod, Cerryl turned the chestnut and rode alongside Ferek, glancing over his shoulder. With the "retreat" of the White Lancers, the Spidlarian forces began to urge their mounts into a quick trot up the hillside.

Cerryl reined up, then cast a last firebolt. *Whhsttt!*

"Aeiii . . ."

More by luck than skill, the wobbly sphere of chaos fire enveloped a blue lancer more than twenty cubits in front of the others. Cerryl was gratified to note that the blues' advance slowed.

Almost with each of the gelding's hoofbeats on the road through the vale toward the higher hill to the southeast Cerryl looked back over his shoulder, nearly bouncing off the trotting mount. The dust burned his eyes, and his throat felt almost clogged with the reddish stuff.

After what seemed the entire afternoon, Ferek's lancers turned and re-formed on the higher hillcrest, barely getting into formation before Hiser's squad galloped back uphill, at least several men short.

"Lost a few, ser," Hiser said as he wheeled and drew up beside Cerryl. "The blues are a-coming fast."

"Let's hope they're coming fast enough." Cerryl began to muster chaos around him, so much that he could feel the air tingle.

Although the quick-moving Spidlarians were still more than half a kay away from Cerryl's position on a still relatively low crest, now more than twenty cubits higher than the road below, the first Spidlarian lancers found themselves riding closer and closer together, forced nearer and nearer to one another by the narrowing of the swale that wasn't really even a true valley.

*Whhsstt!* The firebolt arced into the middle of the horsemen, flaring into a mushroom-shaped flame.

The screams were faint and quick, but the riders swerved around the blazing figures and the grass on either side of the road, and the Spidlarian advance slowed just slightly.

"Darkness . . . he got near on a score . . ."

*More like half that.* Cerryl concentrated and loosed a second firebolt. *Whhssstt!*

Some of the riders saw the chaos fire, and those at the edge of the Spidlarian formation split off and galloped up the lower hill to the south of Cerryl's force, then turned back to the west.

Abruptly, at the trumpet triplet that rang out across the hill, the remainder of the riders turned away.

"Why they do that? Just because of a few blasts of flame?" Ferek scratched his white-streaked red beard.

"I figure they lost near on a score right there," suggested Hiser.

"They saw the trap and backed off. They'll look for another way to get at us."

Cerryl knew the younger subofficer was right. He just had to figure out how and where the Spidlarians would strike again. *If you can.*

# XCIV

Overhead, a handful of widely scattered and white puffy clouds barely moved through the green-blue sky. The air was hot and damp from the soaking rains of the day before, and the road clay remained dark, but not sloppy, except in the handful of places where muddy water had puddled.

The road ran from east to west along a low ridge that bisected a meadow and formed the southern boundary of the vale. A stream, surrounded by wet ground and intermittent marshy spots, wound back and forth across the center of the lower ground. Irregular clumps of low bushes dotted the marshy ground.

On the far west end of the open valley were a half-score cots, outbuildings, and cultivated fields that showed lines of green. A handful of figures appeared to be toiling in those fields, and a thin line of smoke rose from the chimney of one cot. The presence of peasants was a measure of just how far north he and his lancers had followed the Spidlarians, Cerryl reflected.

The White mage reined up and studied the vale, trying to ignore the damp midday heat and the sweat that bathed him.

Cerryl could see the Spidlarian forces on the western end of the ridge that formed the northern horizon. "Looks like they're all there."

"If we try to get to them, we'll have to ride down into the valley and back up the other side," Ferek pointed out. "We ride to them . . . and we'll lose men. They got archers."

"We don't try right now," suggested Cerryl. "Just let them see that we're here. They'd have to ride through the marshy ground below to reach us, and they won't do that." *Just like we won't. Besides, if they tried it, you wouldn't have any trouble dropping more firebolts on them, and they know that.*

"No way to fight."

"We're not interested in fighting unless we can win," Cerryl pointed out. "We're keeping them from getting to the supply wagons and from harassing any levies traveling to support the High Wizard." *If any more ever show up.*

Cerryl shifted his weight in the saddle and studied the blue-clad figures on the far ridge. After a time, he shifted his weight again. The Spidlarians did not move. A brief whisper of a breeze passed over the White mage. Then the air was still and sodden once more.

Finally, Cerryl dismounted.

"Ser?" asked Hiser.

"I want to see if they're all really there." Cerryl took out the leather case and set the mirror on the grass. He knelt beside it and concentrated.

Ferek and Hiser dismounted and stood on the road behind Cerryl. From there they could see the screeing glass.

As Cerryl had suspected, behind the two or three squads silhouetted on the near horizon the majority of the Spidlarians were slipping down the far side of the ridge and forming up on a narrow trail that seemed to lead back eastward. *Probably south as well, and they're trying to get behind us and toward the supply road.*

"They'd be a-sneaking off," opined Ferek.

"So they can flank us," suggested Hiser.

Cerryl nodded and tried another image, hoping to trace out the trail where the Spidlarians were assembling. He needed to see where it led— and if there were a way in which he could block them from the Axalt– Elparta road, a way that didn't cost him any of his too-few lancers.

The narrow road or trail where the Spidlarians were marshaling wound southeast, behind a line of rises too gentle to be hills. Perhaps the way was a farm road of some sort—or the longer and original road—since it rejoined the road Cerryl and his lancers had taken, per- haps four kays to the east.

Cerryl frowned as he let the road image fade. He rubbed his fore- head. Did he dare move his lancers while some of the blue forces were still observing them?

He squinted in the bright afternoon light, trying to call up the image of the Spidlarian lancers once more. His head ached by the time the silver mists cleared and he had a sightly misty image of the opposing force. Sweat dribbled down the back of his neck and oozed down his forehead.

The Spidlarians had started to move southeast, and at almost a quick trot, and the last blue squads had vanished from the ridge.

Cerryl lifted the glass and began to pack it. "Ferek, Hiser, have the men turn. We're headed back to that higher hill three kays or so back, the one with the low bluff just beyond the rodent pond."

The two subofficers mounted.

"Form up! We're headed back." Ferek's deep voice rumbled across the ridge.

"Form up!" echoed Hiser.

Cerryl slipped the glass into the saddlebag and remounted, easing the gelding up beside Hiser and riding beside the young subofficer to the head of the column headed back to the southeast.

"Ride to one place . . . wait . . . watch him throw a fireball. Then turn and ride some more . . ."

"Shut up, Burean . . . Ride all day if'n it be saving my ass."

*You hope you're saving them,* Cerryl thought. *If you're not . . . ?* But what choice did he have against a larger force that he needed to keep from the supply lines?

Cerryl found his eyes drifting to the north and east as he rode beside the two subofficers, back along the same stretch of road that they had ridden that same morning. He couldn't sense the Spidlarians, nor hear any sign of another force, but his eyes flicked in the direction of the trail road nonetheless. The sounds of the mounts drowned out any murmurs of insects or birdcalls—if there were any.

"You sure they be headed back this way, ser?" inquired Hiser, his voice deferential.

*No.* "As sure as anything is, Hiser."

The blond subofficer nodded.

"I'll check again in a while," Cerryl said, "once we get back to the higher ground on the road."

"Always take the high ground." Ferek bobbed his head.

Cerryl was sweating more heavily when he reined up on the grassy bluff, flanked by gentle grassy slopes that slanted downward to the narrow trail where he expected the Spidlarians to appear. He frowned. While he'd remembered the central bluff and the overlook well enough, he hadn't recalled how gentle the inclines were on each side.

He glanced over his shoulder back along the road and the higher ground where his force had mustered. Farther to the southeast, the small pond created by the water rodents glimmered silver between two rises, almost like a distant screeing glass. He turned in the saddle, looking sideways at Ferek. "This overlooks where the trail joins up . . . but our road is better, and we should have gotten here before them. I'm going to try the glass again."

With another look to the trail road below, he slipped out of the saddle and tried the glass. The headache that came with the image of Spidlarian lancers was worse than the last, and flashes of light sparkled in his eyes, light that bore the white of chaos, chaos not from the sun.

A quick study of the image in the glass reassured him that the Spidlarians continued on their track, with a handful of scouts out ahead, and he released the image as quickly as he could, trying not to stagger as he collected the glass and straightened.

His tunic was damp through, and the headache remained. Behind him he could hear the murmurs of the lancers and the breathing of their mounts, at least those nearby. The horses probably needed water, but he dared not let them seek the stream farther back along the road, not when the Spidlarians were approaching.

From where he stood on the road Cerryl glanced up at the two subofficers. "Ferek . . . have the men stay down on that side of the hill—just below the crest. I don't want the Spidlarians to see them."

Ferek's salt-and-pepper eyebrows lifted.

"I want to give them a little surprise. I can't if they see our lancers."

After a moment the older subofficer nodded, then turned his mount.

"The same for your company, Hiser."

"Yes, ser."

Cerryl rubbed his forehead, then stepped toward the gelding to re-pack the glass. He found his hands trembling. When had he last eaten? He tended to forget that mustering either order or chaos—or using the glass to spy out the enemy—required that he eat more often.

Tiredly he pulled a stale, hard biscuit from his saddlebag and chewed slowly, moistening his mouth with occasional swallows from his water bottle, his eyes on the trail road. Abruptly he shook his head and remounted, turning the gelding back down the road, just far enough that he could barely see the trail on which he hoped the Spid-larians continued to ride toward him.

He fumbled out another road biscuit and crunched on it, until all that remained were crumbs. Unhappily, the headache remained also, if slightly diminished.

A whispering sound intruded on Cerryl, the faintest of whispers, and he pulled himself more erect in the saddle. No longer was he sore each evening from riding, but even all his recent riding experience hadn't made him any less susceptible to fatigue.

Cerryl motioned to the subofficers for quiet, watching the trail road, waiting as the lead Spidlarian scouts appeared, followed by a vanguard of perhaps half a squad. Shortly, as the scouts disappeared from view under the short bluff, Cerryl began to gather chaos to himself as he eased the gelding uphill.

*Whhhstt!* A firebolt arched out toward the angled trail, splashing across the damp clay well back of the lead Spidlarian scouts, but short of the main body of riders. Cerryl eased the gelding back downhill a few dozen cubits and flattened himself against his mount's neck and mane, trusting that the opposing lancers would ride a few dozen cubits farther.

As the sounds of mounts grew louder, and as Hiser and Ferek glanced worriedly at him, Cerryl rode back uphill and out onto the downslope that led to the narrow bluff overlooking the trail—just in time to see several scouts point in his direction.

A half-score mounted archers spurred their mounts along the gentle slopes that flanked the bluff overlook, angling their mounts in toward him.

*You waited too long.* Cerryl mustered chaos once more and focused it on the two leading lancers—into a narrow beam of lance fire.

Both archers went down, vanishing into ashes, leaving a thin line of black smoke rising into the clear afternoon sky.

*Whhsttt!* Cerryl followed the light lancer with another firebolt, one that sprayed across the lancers behind and downslope of the archers.

Greasy black smoke seemed to puddle around the front lines of the blue-clad lancers, swirling back upon itself in the damp and still air.

An arrow hissed past the mage's shoulder, and Cerryl jerked around in the saddle to see another pair of archers renocking their bows from mounts less than a hundred cubits to his right—almost as high on the grassy inclines to the west of the bluff as he was on the center.

His mind felt as clumsy as frozen hands had on cold mornings at the mill as he struggled to raise more chaos and fling it against the two bowmen.

*Whhstt!* Small as the firebolt was, the White mage's aim was good enough to turn one archer into flames and ash and send the second spurring his mount down the grassy slope. The retreating archer tried to beat flames out with one hand and guide his careening mount with the other.

Squinting into the afternoon sun, Cerryl ignored the smell of burned flesh and focused on the blue-clad lancers nearly half a kay away on the trail road, lancers who seemed to be turning.

After a deep breath, Cerryl launched another large firebolt.

*Wwhhhssttt!* The globe of fire arched sedately over the grassy slope and dropped, splashing chaos fire across the second line of Spidlarians and their mounts.

Cerryl reeled in the saddle, points of light flashing before his eyes and his head throbbing. When he could see, he found that Hiser had ridden up beside him.

"They've turned, ser. You killed another half-score."

*Only another five score to go.* Cerryl nodded slowly. "Send a scout to watch the trail on the far side. We need to make sure that they're actually moving back."

"Yes, ser." Hiser rode back toward where his company had been mustered, waiting.

The gray-eyed mage struggled to get to his water bottle, his fingers trembling so much that he had to concentrate totally on unstoppering the bottle. He drank slowly, and the water seemed to reduce his shakiness and the frequency of the flashes before his eyes, but not the headache or the bone-weariness he felt.

The sun was clearly nearing late afternoon, hanging over the low hills to the west, when Hiser returned.

Cerryl glanced up, taking in the sun and the shadows cast by the scattered trees and bushes. Had that much of the day gone?

"They're going," announced Hiser. "One of the scouts says they're heading back along the road to Kleth."

"For now," Cerryl said. *For now.* He took a long and deep breath. One thing was becoming increasingly clear. Chaos fire was far more suited to either ambush or defense, not to direct-on attacks, not unless he could count on the enemy remaining massed in one place, and that seemed unlikely, to say the least.

The constant use of chaos, even on a small scale, seemed to be close to unworkable—at least for him—no matter how much order or chaos he could handle at longer intervals. He didn't even want to think about why he was out in the backlands, fighting off Spidlarian armsmen with far too few White Lancers for the task, needing to muster chaos all too often—or about the lengthening separation from Leyladin.

# XCV

In the orange-tinged light that followed dawn, Cerryl looked down at the glass on the rough-planked trestle table, rubbing his eyes. Over the past three eight-days, he hadn't slept that well, not with the constant tracking of the Spidlarian forces and his efforts to keep them away from the supply road, especially with another set of Certan wagons moving out of the Easthorns and toward Elparta.

Because he knew he would never get back to it with all the screeing facing him, he permitted himself the luxury of a quick look in the glass for Leyladin, seeking that distant focus of order somehow faintly gray, rather than the pure black of Dorrin the smith. Was that because she lived amidst chaos? Or for some other reason? *Why is there no mention of gray anywhere, not in any of the books or by any of the senior mages? Even as a warning?*

The mists cleared from the glass, and, almost as if she had been waiting, the red-golden-haired healer smiled from where she sat in a green dressing gown at the writing table in her silk-hung room. The room still amazed Cerryl, but he smiled as well, even knowing that she could not sense his expression, but because he was cheered by her smile. After a long look, he let the image go and looked at the blank glass on the table for a moment.

Finally, after taking a swig of water from his nearly empty bottle, he began to concentrate, scanning one by one the hamlets that bordered the supply road. All were vacant, as they had been since spring.

Cerryl rubbed his forehead once more, again wondering where the Spidlarians had gone. He stood and walked to the hearth, where he took a water bottle off the shelf and took a deep swallow. After that, he went back to the table and the screeing glass.

In time, he found the Spidlarian force, breaking camp in a higher meadow amid leaved trees, rather than evergreens. From what he could tell, they had doubled back north and west, midway between Fydel's patrols and those of Cerryl, but more than forty kays north of the Elparta–Axalt road.

Cerryl consulted his rough map, then nodded. There was a trail, not really a road, that angled toward the Elparta road. He suspected that Jeslek probably wouldn't have paid that much attention to the trail. *But he will if you allow the wagons to be taken or his flank to be attacked.* Cerryl pursed his lips. *Could there be another force joining them?*

With a sigh, he turned back to the glass, squinting as his eyes watered and the inevitable headache began to build.

There was another force, smaller than the first, but still twice the size of what Cerryl had, angling in from the west. Both blue forces would reach the Axalt–Elparta road at about the same point. *Unless you stop them.*

But how? His eyes watering, Cerryl massaged his forehead. Using pure chaos—particularly firebolts—definitely limited how many armsmen he could take on, especially at once. He took a last swallow from the bottle, then stood and walked to the open door.

In the stillness, the air outside the cot was already warmer than inside the rough wooden building as Cerryl walked toward the cook fires. The aroma of roasted mutton drifted toward him.

Standing by the rough pole corral fence, Ferek lowered the chunk of greasy meat he was eating. "You'd not be looking all that pleased this morning, Mage Cerryl," observed the subofficer. "Have the blues gone into the Easthorns now, trying to reach the road?"

"I think not." Cerryl motioned to Hiser.

The blond subofficer swallowed the last morsels of the hard bread he had been eating and walked toward the mage and the older subofficer.

Cerryl's headache and watering eyes reminded him that he also needed to eat, and the mage stepped aside toward the plank propped on two tree sections that served as a provision board. Cerryl took almost half a small loaf of bread and used his white-bronze belt-knife to laboriously cut a chunk of the dry white cheese that seemed nearly as hard as the wood on which it rested.

The bread, though warm, was dry, and Cerryl had to struggle to swallow a mouthful. He wished he'd brought his water bottle from the cot, but he managed to gnaw off a corner of the cheese before he turned back to the subofficers and swallowed before speaking. "There are two forces now, the one we've been chasing and another one, maybe half the size of the first. They're headed toward the Elparta road, maybe forty kays west of here."

"That'd be a solid two-day ride," said Hiser.

"It should be three for them." *You hope.*

"Together . . . what? Fourfold our numbers?" asked Ferek.

"Could be more than that," Cerryl admitted. "We have to keep them from getting to where they can attack Jeslek and the other lancers from behind."

"Take some mighty good working to do that." Ferek's tone was bland.

Hiser just looked at Cerryl, his mouth expressionless but concern in his eyes.

"We'll find a way." Cerryl offered a smile he did not feel. "After you finish eating, get the men ready. We'll need to start as soon as we can. I'd like them to have a chance to rest before we face the blues."

The blond Hiser nodded, then tugged at his short beard. "We leave anything here?"

Cerryl shook his head. If they beat back the Spidlarians, they'd need to stay closer to Jeslek's force, and if they didn't . . .

"One way or the other . . . no sense in that," agreed Ferek, mumbling his words over another mouthful of the greasy mutton.

Cerryl took another mouthful of bread and a chunk of the hard white cheese, chewing carefully.

"They won't ride away this time," predicted Hiser.

"No, I don't think so either." Cerryl could feel some of the worst of the headache subsiding. *You have to remember to eat . . .*

"I'll have them cook down the rest of the mutton." Ferek turned toward the cook fires.

"I'll pass the word," Hiser answered. "Be a bit, still."

"I know," Cerryl mumbled through the last of the hard cheese. He turned and walked slowly back to the cot to pack his own gear, thinking about Hiser's words. How could he deal with close to eightscore lancers who knew how to avoid firebolts?

Hr frowned as he paused inside the cot's doorway, his eyes going to the glass he'd left on the table. What about rearranging order and chaos? Wouldn't that be less tiring than extracting chaos and flinging it? *How would that help you in a battle or skirmish?*

Cerryl shrugged as he packed the glass and peered around the dusty room. *You'd better find some way.*

With a last glance at the empty trestle table, he turned and stepped back into the cool morning air, hoping that the day would remain pleasant, rather than turn sweltering.

# XCVI

The hazy clouds of morning had thickened and turned into heavy gray masses that filled most of the sky, with but occasional patches of blue-tinged green. Despite the clouds, the day was warm and sultry, without even a hint of a breeze. The light rain of the morning had given way first to mist and then to the damp heat that permeated everything.

Cerryl felt that if he so much as lifted an arm or shifted his grip on the gelding's reins, he would burst into sudden sweat.

"Damp," murmured Hiser. "Makes it seem hotter."

"Get hotter yet 'fore summer's over," answered Ferek.

"This is where they join." Cerryl reined up and surveyed the road and the draw that held the narrower way that the Spidlarians traveled from the north. He shook his head, thinking about how the narrow strip of clay actually curved eastward for several kays, around the hills, before swinging west and south to join the Elparta–Axalt road.

Behind him, the column slowed and stopped. The scouts had already vanished behind the woods a kay or so ahead, around which the main road curved.

"They won't be coming that way," suggested Ferek, spitting onto the patchy grass of the main road's shoulder. One hand gestured toward the wooded hills to the right of the road and toward the defile that held the narrower road from the northwest.

"How would you come?" asked Cerryl.

"Those fields back a ways . . . they be a trace steep, but they be open. They slope to the main road. I'd bring the mounts up that way. Specially after knowing what you done to 'em in narrow places."

From his mount to Cerryl's left Hiser nodded.

What Ferek said made sense, but would the Spidlarians see it that way? And if they did, what could Cerryl do with an open field? As Cerryl recalled the meadows, the slope from the narrow road was up-hill. Would any lancers advance uphill?

Cerryl dismounted and handed the gelding's reins to one of the lancers drawn up behind Hiser. Then he extracted the glass and set it on an even patch of ground on top of its leather case. With the heavy clouds overhead, there was no direct sunshine to worry about.

Cerryl concentrated on the glass, trying to bring up the Image of the Spidlarians, ignoring the perspiration that intensified when he attempted screeing or employing either order or chaos. Slowly, the silver mists cleared, and an image of lancers appeared. From what he could tell, they remained on the same road as before, heading in a generally southward direction, but at least a day north of where Cerryl and his forces were positioned.

*You hope.* Then, Cerryl had been screeing and hoping a great deal over the past several eight-days. Finally, he repacked the glass, pausing to massage his forehead for a moment.

"Ser?" asked Hiser.

"They're still riding this way." Cerryl remounted and looked eastward. "We should ride back to those fields," he decided. "Not everyone, just a half-score or so. The others can stand down here."

"Now?" asked Hiser.

"The blues won't be here for almost another day, not at the pace they're making."

"What if they go across the hills to cut off distance? They could do that," suggested Hiser.

"Don't think so," offered Ferek. "From what the mage has shown in the glass, that north way be open. Till the last few kays, leastwise. Cross the hills, and too many places there for a mage to hide and throw fire."

"Best we lay out the encampment," suggested Ferek.

"And send out scouts and pickets," added Hiser.

"Ferek," Cerryl ordered, "you take care of setting up the encampment. Hiser will lead the half-score lancers from his company who will ride back to that meadow field with me."

"Yes, ser." Ferek nodded. "Men could use an early stop and some rest. We'll have it all set up when you get back."

Cerryl turned his mount back eastward, letting Hiser ride ahead of him and issue the commands to select the half-score of lancers that would accompany the two of them. He would have preferred to stop and rest himself.

*How are you going to handle a force that could be five or six times yours? Especially when they know how to attack a White mage?* Cerryl shifted his weight in the saddle. He didn't have any answers, just hoped that there was something about the fields that would give him an idea.

Hiser eased his mount up beside Cerryl as the smaller group separated from the longer column of White Lancers. For a time the only sounds were the plodding of hoofs, the breathing of horses, and scattered murmurs of the lancers trailing the two.

"How are we going to face some tenscore lancers? Can you destroy them all with wizard fire, ser?" Hiser finally asked.

"Not if they spread out the way they usually do. That's why we're riding back there. I need to see what else I might do."

When they reached their destination, Cerryl could sense that it was well past midafternoon, despite the still-thick gray clouds.

Once he reined up, a long vulcrow cawed and flapped away from the higher grass downhill from the main road. Cerryl studied the slanting fields once more. He let his order-chaos senses slide under the long, sloping field, probing for concentrations of order or chaos, but the ground felt no different from any other patch of soil, except that some order seemed slightly more concentrated near the small stream to the west of the lower road that lay beyond the broad and slanting meadow.

Through a small gap in the clouds a thin line of sunlight arrowed across the afternoon, briefly lighting the edge of the hardwoods that defined the eastern edge of the meadow, a meadow nearly a kay wide. The light faded as swiftly as it had appeared, and the green leaves of the woods appeared gray-green once more.

The distance between the two roads was closer to two kays, and to Cerryl's eyes the main road appeared nearly two hundred cubits higher than the other, far narrower road, which wound back into the lower woods to the north and west. The lower road flanked the stream for perhaps four kays before actually meeting the main road to the west, and both stream and road wound through relatively thick woods.

"Two hundred cubits higher, even, maybe," Cerryl murmured to himself. The slope between the two roads was greater than Ferek had thought and than Cerryl had recalled.

"A bit steep to bring up a mount," suggested Hiser.

"Could be, but it's nearly two kays, and they can spread out. If they take the road, they get bunched together." Cerryl shrugged. "If they do, we go back to where the camp is. Between the hill gap and the woods, their lancers will get all bunched up."

"They'd not like that."

*Less than coming up the meadow.* Cerryl rode the gelding slowly out and down into the meadow. While the ground was uneven in places, the footing seemed firm and the slope not so steep as it had appeared from the higher road.

The grass was thick and green, nearly knee-high. Later in the year it would burn well, but not now. What if he loosed the order bounds right beneath the surface? What would that do? Cerryl frowned. He couldn't just leave order free. Could he shift it into other parts of the ground?

He swallowed and tried to reshift some of the order and chaos, strengthening the ground beneath the surface in thin lines and then breaking the order ties in other places.

*Grrrrr...* The ground shifted ever so slightly, and Cerryl swallowed.

"What was that?" asked Hiser.

Cerryl didn't answer, struggling as he was with his battle to change the order-chaos balance of the rocks and subsoil, shift the strengths and the bonds that had knit the ground together. Sweat rolled down his forehead, and he absently blotted it away from his eyes.

A flock of blue-winged birds fluttered from the hardwoods, shrieking as they did. A sudden *buzzing* filled the sodden air, and dozens of flying grasshoppers rose out of the grass and hummed their way eastward and north, away from the ground Cerryl strained to alter. A single deer bolted downhill, then turned as she saw the White riders and bounded back into the woods.

"... little closer and we'd a had a good meal ..."

"... real good meal ..."

"... better be still ... He's got that look."

"So's Hiser."

Cerryl squinted and blocked away the low-voiced comments from the lancer squad. Even as he continued his efforts, he began to sense a roiling, almost a boiling, and an ebb and flow or order and chaos, far, far deeper than the subsoil where he worked.

Coils and lines of black order wound around unseen but clearly felt fountains of chaos that rose and fell sporadically in the depths beneath the meadow. Should he send his senses below? Would it help?

*No ... not now. Too much to do here.* He forced his concentration back to the task at hand.

In the end, the meadow grass concealed a churned mass of clay beneath a thin layer of soil holding the long green grass, clay that, Cerryl suspected, more nearly resembled quicksand than clay. Cerryl had also left just enough support in thin pillars and layers of order to hold a few riders and mounts—in case the Spidlarians wanted to scout the meadow. Some of that order he would have to shift later.

The thoroughly sweat-soaked mage finally took a deep breath in the late-afternoon air, then another. He closed his eyes for several moments, perhaps longer, to shut out the sparkling flashes of light that disrupted his vision, before turning in the saddle to Hiser. "Make sure that no one rides across that meadow. It's likely to be the last ride they take." Cerryl's tone was dry as he turned back toward his horse.

"Ah, yes, ser."

Cerryl remounted the gelding, his thoughts still on the sense of entwined order and chaos that he had sensed deep below the meadow. *How far into the depths do they extend?* He shook his head. Those speculations would have to wait. Besides, his entire body was screaming that he'd done enough, more than enough. He turned to Hiser. "We'll head west, back beyond where the trees start. That way, if they send out scouts, they won't see us anywhere near the fields."

"There be nothing 'tween them and the next wagons and levies, then," pointed out the blond subofficer, tugging at his beard.

"We travel faster than they do. If they turn east, we can catch them unless they want to founder their mounts, and then..." Cerryl shrugged dramatically.

*And in the meantime, we wait...*


# XCVII

In the gray light of another cloudy morning just past dawn, Cerryl stood and packed the screeing glass back into its case, his eyes going to the two subofficers. "They're still on the road. Both groups have joined, and I make out a good ten score, perhaps twelve score."

"Another score in scouts and a score more in their van," suggested Ferek.

Cerryl offered a casual shrug he didn't entirely feel. "It won't matter if they come up the meadow." *What if they don't? How do you assure that they climb the meadow?* He took a deep breath, conscious that even the air smelled and felt dampish, moldy, despite the warmth already apparent.

Ferek and Hiser exchanged wary glances.

"Can you think of any way to ensure that they climb the meadow?" Cerryl glanced toward the trees to the south of the camp, then toward the thin clouds of the eastern sky and the light that seeped up behind them. The air remained hot and still, almost as though it had cooled little over night, and the odor of overcooked biscuits seeped around him.

"If'n their captain thought we were a-waiting..." mused Ferek. "Along the end of the narrow road, that be."

Cerryl massaged his forehead. All the order-chaos manipulations and screeing were extracting their price. His tunic and trousers were looser, and his eyes burned almost all the time, not to mention the headaches and the flashes of light that sparked before his eyes. *Using the glass before eating doesn't help.... you know?* "I need to eat."

"Not much but dried mutton, hard cheese, and harder biscuits," offered Hiser. "Cooked them too long, someway."

"That's fine." Cerryl set the glass case beside his bedroll, then straightened, turned, and walked a dozen paces toward the rough-hewn serving plank, where he took two biscuits. The brownish oval of the first was so hard that when he tried to gnaw off a corner, his upper teeth slid off the biscuit and he nearly bit his lip.

"I said they were hard, ser," offered Hiser, who had followed him.

Cerryl unsheathed his knife and hacked off a tan chunk that seemed closer to wood than food, then put it in his mouth and took a swallow of water to moisten the rock-hard biscuit. One taste of the dried mutton jerky was enough to persuade him to try another biscuit and more of the hard and musty cheese.

The light flashes before his eyes stopped after the second biscuit, and the headache diminished but did not disappear. His stomach did stop growling. After he finished the third hard biscuit, Cerryl turned to Ferek, who had waited for the mage to finish eating. "What if you took twoscore lancers and rode them down that narrow road and then back ... and left a couple of scouts on fast mounts where the road curves back to the west?"

Hiser grinned. "You mean where the blues could see them?"

Cerryl nodded. "That might give them the idea to climb the field, especially if we're not in sight on the road above the fields."

"Have to pull back pretty far so as their scout not be seeing us," offered Ferek.

"You can put most of the lancers a kay or so back, even farther," suggested Cerryl. "We'll need some trees or a small woods for a screen. Otherwise, their scouts will see us."

"What if they overrun you? You can't throw firebolts at all of them," Hiser pointed out.

"If they don't try the meadow ... there's no way we have enough lancers to stop them. I can use the glass to scout them." *And get more headaches.* "We might as well take another look right now."

Cerryl walked back to where he had left his bedroll and the leather-cased glass, picking both up. The bedroll needed a real washing—not just a brushing with chaos to remove the worst of odors and dirt—but Cerryl doubted he'd have a chance for that anytime soon. He'd already spent more than a season in Spidlar, and all of it had been spent patrolling one section of road in support of Jeslek's advance on Elparta. *Is Fydel having the same problems? Does it matter?*

One way or another, it was clear that Jeslek was having great difficulty, though Cerryl had no idea precisely why. Dorrin, the redheaded Black smith, had remained far to the north in Diev, and Cerryl had found no hint of any other order concentrations in Spidlar. Was the Black arms commander that good? Good enough to slow or stop the High Wizard and all the chaos at Jeslek's command?

The two subofficers followed the mage.

"Ferek, I'd like you to come with us, but have your men wait here at the camp. We don't need them riding back and forth and tiring their mounts." Cerryl strapped his bedroll in place behind the gelding's saddle, then put the glass and its case into the one saddlebag. The other carried one set of riding whites and some smallclothes, both more soiled than what he wore. Chaos-cleaning, after a while, just didn't remove everything.

"I'll get the company ready," said Hiser.

"Dierso can get mine ready while I ride with you," added Ferek.

As both subofficers left Cerryl to his own preparations, the White mage studied the encampment, with the mounts on tie-lines run from the trees behind the clearing and the half-dozen fire rings for cooking. The lancers doubling as cooks had already begun to bank the fires and douse them with water from the small stream.

Cerryl remembered to check the gelding's bridle and girths before he mounted and surveyed the area again, this time from the saddle, as he waited for Ferek and Hiser and his company of lancers to join him.

The day had brightened and warmed even more when Cerryl reined up on the main road, well back from the sloping meadow that lay between the two roads. He nodded to himself as he did, then turned to the two subofficers. "We'll pull back to the south—to the thicker trees there." He pointed to a dense grove several hundred cubits to his right. "Just your companies, Hiser. And we'll circle them in from the east, so that there are no tracks across the grass between the road and the trees." He turned to the older subcaptain. "You take your company from where we camped back to where the roads join and bring them along the lower road—but just to the edge of the woods there, where the lower road curves—then pull back and form up to defend the draw where the two roads join. That way, maybe the Spidlarians will get the impression that the rest of us are lurking farther back—or in the lower woods."

Ferek nodded. "Be me, I'd worry about that."

"I don't think they'll reach us until early this afternoon, but I'll send a messenger if it's going to be earlier." Cerryl paused. "If you find out anything you think I should know . . ."

"Don't worry, ser. I'll send you a messenger."

As Ferek turned his mount back to the west, accompanied by two lancers, Cerryl and Hiser continued eastward along the main road for almost a kay, until they reached another series of fields, each with cots by the road—almost, but not quite, a hamlet of sorts.

Cerryl saw no one, and the shutters of the nearest cot remained closed, as they had the day before when Cerryl's forces had first passed and the fields were empty.

"If we go along that track there," Cerryl pointed, "it won't be as noticed, and at the end of the fields we can turn back west."

"Singles now," Hiser ordered, letting Cerryl lead the way.

The White mage could sense no one in the cot, but he kept looking as he rode past along the clay trace beside the field. The only thing that moved was an orangish cat that jumped off a woodpile and into the green stalks of maize nearest the shuttered cot.

". . . ride and hide . . . ride and sneak."

"Shut up, Birnil . . . Most of us are still here . . . not like when Eliasar wanted to teach the Sligans a lesson."

"No lessons here."

Cerryl turned in the saddle and called, loudly enough for his voice to carry, "The tutoring's not over yet!"

Hiser grinned, and the muttering died away. The lancers followed Cerryl more quietly as he turned the gelding back westward. The riding was slower through the loosely wooded and overgrown regrowth area and toward the thicker section of woods opposite the chaos-trapped meadow that Cerryl hoped the Spidlarians would take to reach the main Axalt–Elparta road.

Once the company reached the denser and mainly oak woods, Cerryl turned in the saddle, inclining his head toward the blond subofficer. "They can stand down for a while."

"I'll tell them."

When the young subofficer returned from arranging his men, he watched as Cerryl took out the screeing glass and set it in a darker space between two oak roots.

Cerryl scanned the silver-framed image in the glass, but where the lower road bordered the steeply sloping meadow remained empty, with no sign of riders—or anything else.

Hiser glanced at Cerryl.

"Not yet."

Cerryl checked the glass periodically until, sometime slightly after midday, a single rider in blue trotted down the lower road, his head turning from side to side as he studied the meadow without halting. The scout passed on and disappeared around the curve where the lower road entered the woods to the west.

Before long a second scout followed.

Cerryl let the image lapse and straightened from studying the glass, half-leaning against the rough bark of the old tree

"It can't be long," suggested Hiser in a low voice.

"Midafternoon," said Cerryl.

After a time, the scouts returned, heading back toward the main Spidlarian force, Cerryl surmised. Before long, another scout appeared, this one studying the meadow and then riding up through the tall grass to the top.

Cerryl held his breath, but the chaos-altered ground supported mount and rider. The scout studied the road, and the hoofprints that led eastward, and rode to the east for close to half a kay before returning and descending the grassy slope to the lower road. He also vanished, headed back toward the main body of Spidlarian lancers.

As Cerryl had predicted, the full column of mounted Spidlarians eventually reached the sloping meadow slightly past midafternoon. The long column halted at the base of the meadow.

Finally, yet another pair of scouts rode up through the grass and up onto the main road. One turned west, the other east. They also returned and rode down the meadow to the main body.

As the glass showed the Spidlarians re-forming to climb the grassy slope, Cerryl could at last hear the sounds of voices, low voices, more like the intermittent and muted hum of insects. When the riders in the column turned, so that they presented a wide front in riding up the sloping meadow, Cerryl released the image in the screeing glass and extended his perceptions, removing the last order props that supported the top layer of grass and soil, beginning near the main road at the top of the slope.

"More than I thought . . ." murmured Hiser.

*More than you thought, either.* "That's why we needed something different," answered Cerryl, finding sweat dripping from his forehead in the sweltering afternoon, despite his position in the cooler and darker woods. He waited, his head throbbing, deciding not to undermine the lower part of the slope yet. That should wait.

Abruptly he shook his head. He wasn't thinking. Sitting in the woods wouldn't help much if some of the Spidlarian lancers did avoid his chaos-ooze trap. And how would he know when to remove the order supports on the lower section?

"We need to mount up . . . have the lancers ready for any that do manage to get up the slope."

Hiser nodded. "I thought so, ser. The company is ready."

Cerryl packed the glass in quick motions and untied the gelding from the sapling beside the oak, mounting hastily and heading toward the road. *Now it won't matter, but you should have thought of that earlier. Why didn't you? Because you've used so much order and chaos that you can't think?*

He snorted as he urged his mount northward.

He could hear the faint first screams of Spidlarian mounts as they plunged through the thin crust of soil and grass, screams that were cut off as horses and riders were swallowed by the chaotic ooze.

Cerryl spurred his mount toward the main road and the top of the rise overlooking the meadow and the lower road, where he reined up and tried to grasp the situation.

Perhaps two-thirds of the blue lancers had pulled up short of the upper ooze-filled part of the sloping meadow. The remainder had apparently vanished into the churning dark ooze in the midpart of the deep meadow grass.

Cerryl took a deep breath and forced himself to concentrate, ignoring his already-pounding head and sliding his order senses to the lower part of the meadow, well behind where the bulk of the remaining blue forces were struggling to quiet scattered and spooked mounts and turn to retreat.

A dozen riders at the eastern side of the Spidlarian line started back toward the road—right over the area where Cerryl had removed the bonds that held both soil and clay together.

All dropped into more of the quicksand bog–like chaotic ooze that replaced the tall grass. One rider climbed to the top of his mount's saddle and flung himself sideways. He fell flat onto the dark mass and lay there scrambling for an instant before vanishing under the dark brown ooze.

To the west, almost a score of riders rode sideways toward the woods, getting beyond the trapped chaos ground just before Cerryl completed the encirclement.

*Whhhssttt!* Cerryl arched a firebolt over and downhill from the blue lancers, forcing them to turn away from the chaos fire and smoldering grass and shrubs at the edge of the meadow. "You need to get them," the mage gasped at Hiser, even as he flung a second firebolt down across the meadow. "Stay close to the trees."

*Whhhsttt!* One blue lancer screamed as the flames engulfed him and his mount, but the rest of the score or so struggled uphill and through the woods.

Cerryl struggled to finish undermining the slope, now that the remaining Spidlarian lancers were surrounded by the ooze trap.

*Don't think about it . . . just do it.*

Hiser's men swept down through the thinner trees on the western side of the meadow.

*Whhssstt!* Cerryl launched another firebolt below the escaping Spidlarians—to ensure they kept coming uphill—and then another—at the Spidlarians themselves.

*Whhhsttt!* He shivered in the gelding's saddle, casting a last firebolt to aid Hiser's company before the two groups of lancers met among the thinner trees.

Despite the flashes of light across Cerryl's eyes and the blurring of his vision, the odor of burning flesh, the cries, and the screams of wounded mounts—those were enough to confirm his accuracy. He sat on the gelding, just holding himself in the saddle as he heard the clash of blades below him.

He began to see again—if intermittently—enough to make out when the last of the blue-clad lancers slumped in his saddle. Enough to see that Hiser's men led four empty-saddled mounts back up through the trees.

Cerryl forced himself to scan the killing ground.

Three horsemen galloped downhill along the eastern edge of the meadow, close to the trees. Cerryl wasn't sure where they had come from. Returning scouts perhaps, now trying to flee the carnage?

One scout turned his mount slightly westward, toward the ooze-covered ground, as if to avoid a fallen limb or something else. The horse jerked forward, issuing a scream, and then both mount and rider vanished into the dark brown ooze that extended even closer to the woods.

Neither of the remaining riders even looked back at the scream.

Cerryl forced himself to take a deep breath before casting forth the narrow focused fire lance that he'd hidden for years from Jeslek. The first beam lanced through the trailing rider and caught the leg of the leading horse, who went down in a heap.

The surviving blue lancer vaulted clear of the falling mount, somehow, but Cerryl's second fire lance caught him before he reached the trees.

Swaying in the saddle, Cerryl rode slowly along the main road, looking down at the dark mass of ooze that had swallowed over a hundred riders and mounts, both looking to see destruction and hoping he needed to raise no more chaos and devastation.

Hiser rode to met him at the midpoint of the road above what had been a meadow. "Ser? There were but three left."

"I . . . just did . . . what . . . they did . . . all last year." *So you want to be like them?* Cerryl leaned forward in the saddle, emptying his guts on the grass by the shoulder of the road. Then he straightened, ignoring the churning in his empty stomach. He steeled himself and concentrated, removing the barriers he had built, letting order flood back into the ground. The ooze shivered, once, twice, and slowly seemed to solidify.

On his mount beside Cerryl, Hiser gave a shudder. "Terrible . . . no one will guess what lies buried there."

"Terrible . . ." murmured another lancer.

Cerryl was less sure of that. Armsmen, lancers, even mages died in wars and skirmishes. Was any one death less terrible than another?

*Crack!* A line of lightning flashed to or from the hillside where he had incinerated the last of the Spidlarian lancers. The ground shivered, and a light and acrid mist drifted from the foglike clouds that had formed over the battle area.

Cerryl's eyes burned, and stars flashed across whatever he could see. He turned the gelding, hoping he could ride long enough so that they could rejoin Ferek and his company.

"You be looking like darkness, ser."

"Probably." Cerryl felt like darkness, if not worse, barely able to stay in his saddle. Yet he had neither lifted a blade nor repulsed one. He wanted to shake his head, wondering what Eliasar and the other arms mages might have thought. But he rejected the gesture, feeling that his head might roll off his shoulders if he moved it suddenly.

He could have used a healer—especially a certain healer.

As he followed the subofficer back toward Ferek's company, back toward the camp and the bedroll he knew he needed, he could not help but overhear some of the lancer comments.

"...blues were stupid."

"...see why the High Wizard left him."

"...patrollers said he was tough."

Cerryl didn't feel tough, just exhausted—and stupid and lucky. He'd made too many mistakes in trying to execute his plan and had to use far too much chaos as a result. He wondered when the next attackers would arrive—and from where. And if he would ever learn the best way to handle situations where he was overmatched in forces.

*Why don't they just pay their tariffs? We all lose this way.* He shivered as he rode, his vision so blurred he was almost blind. *Why? Why can't they see?*

Neither the late-afternoon heat, nor the clouds that had begun to break up, nor the stench of death in his nostrils provided any answer.

# XVCIII

Cerryl looked down at the glass on the trestle table, a table narrower than the table he had used in the last cot he had appropriated. Both table and cot were newer as well—but not much—and equally battered. The glass had turned up blank, as had every other attempt he had made for more than an eight-day.

He massaged his forehead, then closed his eyes, becoming more aware of the mixed odors of manure and cook-fire smoke drifting in through the open cot doorway on the warm early-morning breeze. With the smoke came the odor of cooked mutton—always cooked mutton. Cerryl even missed the hard cheese, now that the last of that had been eaten.

*No sign of any more Spidlarians . . . why?* After nearly a season of chasing the blue lancers, there were no more to be found. One battle—and that wiped out all that they could send to southeast Spidlar? Or were they mustering a far larger force? It couldn't be Cerryl's failure to scree, not when he could still call up Leyladin's image or that of the red-haired smith Dorrin in Diev.

Cerryl he opened his eyes, trying to ignore the faint headache that never seemed to fade completely anymore. Then he stood and stretched.

A message to Jeslek, that was what he needed to write and send off, stating the apparent situation and asking if the High Wizard needed Cerryl and his lancers. He walked slowly to the cot doorway and then across the hoof-packed clay toward the cook fires. The hard biscuits he had eaten at dawn weren't enough, and he needed more to eat. He would have to choke down the strong-tasting mutton, like it or not.

"Some mutton, ser?" asked the lancer cook.

"Yes, thank you." Cerryl took the fat-dripping chunk, leaning forward as he chewed off a tough mouthful to keep the grease from his whites.

"Any sign of more Spidlarians?" The broad-shouldered Hiser stepped toward the slender White mage.

Ferek turned from where he stood on the far side of the cook-fire ring, gnawing on a chunk of the dark meat, waiting for Cerryl's answer.

"There aren't any close. They're all around Elparta, or downriver at Kleth."

"Don't make sense," mumbled Ferek. "We're easier pickings than the High Wizard and all those Certan levies."

"There aren't that many around Elparta," Cerryl said.

"Beats me, then, why it be that the High Wizard hasn't taken the place."

"He's trying not to level it, I'd guess," Cerryl said.

"Didn't stop him none at Axalt," pointed out Ferek, with a hoarse laugh that cracked.

"Mayhap that be why," answered Hiser. "Having the river and the piers'd make our task the easier."

Cerryl took another bite of the mutton, wondering whether that were the entire reason. Or had the Black armsleader been more difficult to find and subdue than Jeslek had initially calculated?

"He don't take Elparta soon, and we'll be here like all winter and then a fair piece." Ferek's voice was dry. "We be not getting many of the lancers and levies from Hydlen, either."

"Those in Hydolar care only for their own lands and coins," Hiser said, adding after a laugh, "and everyone else's women."

"Sons of clipped-coined cutpurses, every one," Ferek declared, " 'cept those who like their sows better than their women."

Cerryl shook his head, if minutely. A long and hot summer going nowhere was leading to a long fall and winter, with short supplies and shorter tempers among the lancers.

# XCIX

Cerryl stood in the doorway to the one-room cot that served as meeting place, bedchamber, and rain shelter. In the dim light of the late-summer twilight he reread the scroll that had arrived earlier in the afternoon with the messenger from Jeslek.

While there may appear to be no Spidlarian forces near the road and lands you hold for Fairhaven . . . when the Black Isle is involved, appearances may be indeed deceiving . . . We should never be so deceived . . .

Your skills and presence are not required for the taking of Elparta, and it would be foolish for the Guild to hazard all of its brethren in Spidlar near Elparta unless such is required by events . . .

I remain convinced that events do not yet require the massive use of chaos against Elparta . . . Until summoned, you are to remain near the midpoint of that portion of the main road lying between the Easthorns and the present position of our forces . . . to secure it for safe usage by all those who answer to Fairhaven, and to ensure that all who use the road do answer to the White City . . .

*An inquiry, and you get assigned another twenty kays or more of road to patrol?* Cerryl glanced up from the scroll and massaged his forehead with his left hand. From what he gleaned from the lancers who had brought Jeslek's scroll, the White Lancers and the Certan levies had advanced to within thirty kays of Elparta and the river—or closer. But they had been there for nearly three eight-days, and nothing had happened. Jeslek had not pressed an attack, nor had the arms commander of the Spidlarians.

*Why not?* Jeslek had never hesitated to employ force against others when it served its purpose, or his. Did he lack the levies he had been promised by the prefect of Gallos and the Duke of Hydlen?

Cerryl's fingers went to his chin. Groups of Certan levies—and supply wagons—had passed every few eight-days, but not a single armsman from Hydlen. Gallosian levies would have come to Jeslek directly from the south—if any had.

Cerryl began to reroll the scroll as Hiser walked toward the cot. "Good evening, Hiser."

"Evening, ser. Not trying to be too nosy, ser, but you got a scroll a bit ago."

"From the High Wizard," Cerryl admitted. "He wants us to keep guarding the road, even farther west now."

"We haven't seen a blue in two eight-days, could be longer."

"That doesn't mean we couldn't. Or won't."

"So we're still staying here, ser?" asked Hiser.

"For now." Cerryl gestured vaguely with the loosely rolled scroll. "The High Wizard remains concerned that the Black Isle has some secret way to attack from his rear or to destroy all the White mages if they are in one place. So we will remain here."

The young blond subofficer shrugged. "It could be worse. We're taking fewer losses than those with the High Wizard."

"Is that what the messengers are saying?"

"The blues—or that Black warleader, they say his name is Brede or some such—are using knives you can't see to cut lancers out of their saddles. They pose as peasants or merchants and then shoot unsuspecting lancers in the back. The men are angry." A sad smile crossed Hiser's face. "Ours but grumble."

"Better grumbling than dead." Brede . . . he's causing enough trouble that even the men know his name?

"Most think that way." Hiser nodded, then looked to the north and the lingering red in the western part of the northern sky. "Might be getting some rain."

"The air feels damp," Cerryl agreed. What else can you say? Besides that you don't know what the High Wizard is doing—or why?

# C

Slightly past midafternoon, well after the morning patrol, Cerryl was grooming the gelding, something he did less well than he would have liked, when one of the lancer scouts rode up to the crude corral.

"Ser? That supply wagon? It's for us." The thin redhead's words burst forth.

Cerryl looked up.

"That's what the lead guard said. He asked if I was one of your'n. He did, and then he said he had stuff, but you had to claim it."

"I guess I'd better get there. How far out are they?" The mage set aside the brush and began to saddle the gelding.

"Three kays east or so."

"I'll be ready in a few moments." A supply wagon for them? Coming all the way from Fairhaven? When he had first seen the wagon in the screeing glass, he had assumed that it held some form of supplies and luxuries for the High Wizard.

Once he had the gelding saddled, Cerryl and the lancer scout rode not quite directly into a cool wind out of the northeast. The grasses beside the road bent in the steady wind, and the air held that indefinable scent that promised fall before summer had ended—a mixture of heavy grass, leaves ready to winter-turn gray, late-blooming flowers, and the touch of mold from the first grasses and fallen leaves already decaying.

The mounted guard before the wagon consisted of five White Lancers and five guards in green. All slowed, as did the wagon, when Cerryl rode up, accompanied by the red-haired scout and followed by Ferek and a half-score lancers.

"Ser mage? I be Ersad, senior trade guard for Ser Layel," said the white-bearded guard in green, riding at the front of the column beside a lancer subofficer. "You are Cerryl?"

"I'm Cerryl."

"He's Cerryl," blurted the scout.

Behind the scout, Ferek laughed, once, but gently. "He is Cerryl, White mage and commander of the two companies that hold the road for Fairhaven and its friends."

Both the subofficer and the older guard looked coldly at the scout, who flushed and clamped his lips together.

The older green-vested guard leader inclined his head, studied Cerryl for a moment, then extended a scroll. "We have supplies for you and your lancers from ser Layal and Lady Leyladin."

"We are most grateful." Cerryl inclined his head and took the scroll but did not break the green wax of the seal as he slipped the scroll into his tunic. "And we appreciate your effort in bringing them all this long way to us."

"Our task, ser mage."

Cerryl turned his mount and rode alongside the older guard.

Ferek brought his escort around behind the high-sided and canvas-covered wagon, past the circular emblem of Layel, painted in gold over the green of the wagon body.

"How was the journey?" Cerryl addressed the trader's lead guard, then nodded toward the lancer subofficer.

"Better than it will be after season turn," replied the guard in green, a far darker green than that Leyladin affected. "We trust we will be able to deliver the other supplies to the High Wizard and be back through the Easthorns by then."

"The High Wizard is but three, perhaps four days to the west—on this road."

"Hmmmm . . . close timing for the Easthorns, but may chaos favor us."

"Chaos and prosperity be with you," Cerryl answered. "You are most welcome to camp here tonight. What we have is simple, but the lancers would hear of what happens in Fairhaven."

"We shall do so." The lead merchant guard nodded, as did the lancer subofficer who rode beside him.

When they reached the encampment, Cerryl watched from his saddle as the barrels were rolled into the small structure that had once been a barn and now served as a storehouse—barrels of flour, of salted pork, of maize meal, even a small barrel of dried fruit and one of roasted and salted nuts.

"There are also two baskets for you, ser," the green-vested guard said as one of the armsmen in green approached with two circular wicker baskets tied in rope. Each cylindrical basket was not quite two cubits high and a cubit across.

"Ah . . . could you set them by the door of that cot there?" asked Cerryl, gesturing toward the cot that served as his conference room, bedchamber, and screeing place.

"Yes, ser."

Once the wagon had been unloaded and the merchant guards and the lancers were establishing their camp, Cerryl rode to the corral and dismounted.

"The men are pleased already." Ferek had already dismounted, and he turned to the mage. "How did . . . ah . . . Merchants are not known to favor the White Tower . . ."

"Ser Layel is one who does." Cerryl smiled.

"We need watch the dried fruit. Too much will turn their bowels to water." Ferek frowned.

"As you see fit, Ferek. Ration it out so that there is some in the eight-days ahead."

Hiser marched toward them. "Those . . . are they truly for us?"

Cerryl nodded.

"The trader Layel sent them to Mage Cerryl and his men." Ferek grinned. "Even more so, I am glad to be termed such."

"He sent supplies to the High Wizard as well," Cerryl pointed out.

"Only to keep the High Wizard from feeling slighted, I wager," said Hiser.

Cerryl wasn't about to take that wager. "Layel would like to be thought supportive of the White Tower."

"I'll make sure the men know he sent the food—and the fruit and nuts." Hiser grinned.

"That would be good." Cerryl unsaddled the gelding, then led the horse into the corral, where he took off the bridle. He patted his mount's shoulder, and the horse snorted, then tossed his head, before trotting away and toward the water trough.

Cerryl walked back to his cot. There he extracted the scroll and broke the seal. He unrolled the short length of parchment, looking at the flowing characters set so precisely in green ink—green ink for a green-eyed healer.

Dearest . . .

*Dearest?* Cerryl swallowed. *You didn't expect that.*

Sending you provisions is doubtless breaking some Guild or lancer rule, but few will complain if your men benefit. Most is for them, and you, as their commander, except for the two baskets for you . . .

I have also sensed your presence, gently, over the seasons, and that presence has come to mean much to me, in spite of the differences between us. Kinowin has told me of your duties patrolling the road, and we both feel that is for the best in these days, though you will be in Elparta before winter, we feel . . .

*In Elparta before winter?* Did that mean Jeslek was about to take the city at last? How would she and Kinowin know that for certain? Even glasses did not show what *might* be.

Ersad can be trusted to return any scroll to me . . .

Cerryl grinned. That was definitely a suggestion.

I miss you and look forward to your return, no matter the seasons that may pass or the distances that separate our bodies . . .

Cerryl swallowed, and his eyes burned.

After a time, he brought the two baskets into the cot. He untied the hemp rope on the first basket carefully, coiling it and setting it on the bench beside the trestle table for what uses it might serve in the season ahead.

The first basket contained personal items—several bars of oil soap, wrapped in waxed parchment, two sets of new smallclothes, a set of new whites, and a pair of sturdy white boots, made by his own boot maker.

In the second basket were waxed packets of things—several of hard white cheese, what looked to be travel bread, and packages of dried fruit wrapped in waxed linen.

None of it meant as much as the single word at the top of the scroll.

After he closed the baskets, he took out the portable inkwell and a quill and one of his remaining sheets of parchment, then sat at the trestle table.

*How will you reduce all you want to say into a single scroll?*

He shrugged, then grinned, looking at the off-white parchment lying on the wood before him. *Dearest* . . . The single word ran through him, and his grin broadened into a wide smile.

# CI

Cerryl stood and walked around the cot, his jacket fastened almost to his neck. His breath had been steaming in the cold morning air just after dawn, but the small fire he had built and the fall sun had warmed the unseasonably cool day enough that he no longer resembled a chimney with each breath as midmorning approached.

Although the cold rain had passed, Cerryl had called off road patrols for the next few days, relying instead on his screeing and upon the mud and pooled water on the roads and trails to delay or halt any possible Spidlarian force. *What force? The blues shouldn't have enough lancers to hold even Elparta.*

At the hearth, still warm with coals from the small morning fire, Cerryl paused. Despite the closed plank door, the wind still seeped through the cracking and badly chinked mud bricks of the wall, around the warped and the mis-hung door, and up under the roof sills, leaching away the slight heat of the hearth fire.

His first attempts had shown only muddy and empty roads around their hamlet and encampment, although the images of the western side seemed to display less water and mud. Still, nothing remotely resembling the opposing Spidlarians appeared anywhere. Nor was there any trace of the concentrated order that accompanied Black mages—not any closer than Dorrin, the smith in Diev, and he was about as far from Cerryl as one could get and still remain within the boundaries of Spidlar.

Cerryl let the glass go blank once more, then paced back to the fire and then to the door, which he opened. A light but cold wind enveloped him, despite the sunshine from a sun that did little to warm him. The green-blue sky seemed more like that of winter than early fall.

*Would the winter be as much colder than usual as the fall was showing?* Cerryl shivered. That kind of cold he could do without. He closed the door and walked back toward the table.

After massaging his forehead, Cerryl stood and looked down at the glass, silver against the time-smoothed wood. He concentrated, thinking about Elparta and Fydel, rather than Jeslek, since the square-bearded mage was hardly sensitive enough to notice he was being watched through a glass.

The silver mists formed and parted to reveal an image.

The scene in the glass was clear enough—too clear.

A large mass of villagers . . . peasants . . . locals—whatever Cerryl wanted to call them, they were people, and they were being herded along the road. From what Cerryl could tell, the lancers who flanked them were urging them westward along the road.

*Why?*

Cerryl brushed thin brown hair back off his forehead. Why would Jeslek herd people ahead of the White Lancers? To keep the Spidlarians from attacking? To use the people as a shield to reduce the casualties to the levies and the White Lancers?

*Is Jeslek that short of lancers and armsmen?*

For several moments more Cerryl watched, until he could sense the beginning of yet another headache. Then he let the image slide away until the glass reflected only the ceiling beams of the cot and the underside of the branch and thatch roof.

Villagers or people being herded along a road toward something? *Why?* Again, the question leapt into his thoughts. Because of the Black warleader or something the Black smith had created to use against Jeslek and the White Lancers?

Cerryl fingered his chin. Was that why Jeslek was so adamant that Cerryl remain to guard the road? Because the Blacks had developed something that couldn't be felt or seen with a glass?

He shook his head, knowing that he didn't know enough but sensing that what Jeslek was doing with the people would cost someone more, a great deal more, before the war in Spidlar was over.

*Are you just saying that because you disagree with what he's doing? Or because you honestly feel that way? What if Jeslek is right?*

Cerryl brushed his thin and too-long hair back off his forehead again. He probably should groom the gelding and then talk to Hiser and Ferek and wait for any instructions from Jeslek. *If they ever come.*


# CII

Standing between Ferek and Hiser, Cerryl studied the provisions remaining in the shed—one half-barrel of wheat flour, in which he'd had to use chaos to kill off the weevils twice already, and less than a quarter of a barrel of maize meal. The last of the dried fruit and nuts had gone nearly two eight-days previous.

The shed, whose gap-boarded walls had been rough-caulked with moss and mud, smelled of moss, mud, and mold, despite the efforts of various lancers to keep it swept and dry. A spiderweb glistened in the corner above the remaining barrels, trembling ever so slightly in the light breeze that swirled through the shed itself.

The roll of distant thunder rumbled across the valley, and for reasons he couldn't place Cerryl thought about chaos and the people Jeslek had been herding down the road. Three days had passed, and there had been no scrolls or orders from the High Wizard—and nothing in the glass, except images of White forces circled around the walls and closed gates of Elparta.

Cerryl blinked and tried to catch what the subofficers said.

"... not enough for even half an eight-day, not with proper-like rations," finished Ferek.

"We'll be needing more coin, ser Cerryl," offered Hiser, "or we'll be having to forage off the local folk again. Be having to do that sooner, excepting for the provisions your friends sent us."

Cerryl should have looked into the supplies more closely, but all the screeing and waiting and worrying had distracted him, tired as he was from all the effort required to use the glass so much and so often.

A wave of unseen white, a fading echo of some distant and massive use of chaos, swept across Cerryl as he stood in the small provisions shed. He fought off the shudder. *What has Jeslek done? Raised more mountains?*

Hiser looked at Cerryl. "You all right, ser? Matters ... stuff, it be not that bad yet."

The mage shook his head. "It wasn't ... isn't that. Someone is using chaos—too much."

Not quite rolling his eyes, Ferek glanced at the younger subofficer.

"My being able to sense those sorts of things has kept most of your company alive, Ferek." Cerryl's voice was mild, even though he wanted to yell at the man. Then, was that because he worried about what Jeslek—or someone—might have done?

Hiser glared at Ferek.

"Ah ... begging your pardon, ser ... didn't mean ..." Ferek stammered out the words.

"That's all right, Ferek," Cerryl said quietly. "Even most lancer officers don't understand." He paused. "I'll send a scroll to the High Wizard stating our situation and asking for coins so that we don't have to take from the locals. If he doesn't respond, then we do what we have to." *But you hope it doesn't come to that.*

"Some of the fellows said there's a boar rooting in the woods over and down by the creek feeding the bigger stream." Ferek offered. "Wild-like, I mean."

"Well ... if they can bring it in, that's better than taking from the nearby hamlets."

"They can, and it's enough to stretch things, the cooks say."

"Fine. I'll send off another message sent to the High Wizard." Cerryl half-turned. "I'll be in my cot. Need to see why all that chaos ..."

"Yes, ser."

The White mage who'd never wanted to be an arms mage walked through the fine, cool mist that promised to turn into a full cold rain before twilight, back toward the cot he had grown to know too well over more than two seasons.

After closing the door, he set several sticks and a log in the hearth and tweaked them into flame with the smallest touch of chaos. Then he uncased the screeing glass and set it on the table.

As the faint heat from the hearth tried to beat back the chill seeping in around the door and the closed shutters, Cerryl concentrated on the glass and upon the chaos he had felt so strongly earlier.

The silver mists swirled into place, then lifted to reveal another kind of chaos—a city on a river, with gray stone walls toppled as if swept down by a giant's hand and water puddling in the streets, a raging torrent running down the River Gallos, except the Spidlarians called it the River Spidlar, or most of them did, from what Cerryl recalled.

After a year, after saying he would not destroy any cities after Axalt, Jeslek had done just that. He had raised another wave of chaos and brought down another city—or part of it, since the glass showed some structures untouched.

*Why? Because the Black warleader was good enough to hold off an entire White force with a fraction of the men and equipment?*

Rubbing his forehead and standing with his back to the growing warmth of the hearth, Cerryl let the image slip from the glass.

What had really happened in the campaign for Elparta? Cerryl was convinced there were too many details he didn't know. *And things you really won't want to know?*

"That, too," he murmured to the empty glass. "That, too."

Then he took out ink and quill and parchment. Regardless of what had happened in Elparta, he still needed to inform Jeslek about the provisions needs of his lancers.

His eyes flicked westward as he reseated himself at the table.

# CIII

The aroma of roasting pork mixed with the dampness of the mist that had hugged the hamlet area for more than an eight-day. Cerryl half-smiled as he walked from the cot toward the cook fires, his eyes going to the low clouds that continued to roll westward out of the Easthorns. The morning patrol had been cold and damp, but every patrol lately had been that way.

He rubbed his forehead, trying to hasten the departure of the headache that followed every prolonged effort with the glass, efforts that continued to show no signs of either more supplies and levies or of Spidlarian forces near the Axalt–Elparta road.

Would the rest of the fall be filled with damp and rain? *Darkness hard on the harvest . . . if there even is one.* Or early snows? Cerryl shivered at that thought, and his fingers went to the buttons on his jacket, a jacket that looked more splotched tan than white after two seasons in the field.

"We found three of 'em, a sow, an old boar and a younger one," said Ferek with a wide grin as Cerryl approached.

"I can smell that."

"We left the young sow for now. Be a while yet, but the men can wait." The older subofficer gestured toward the clouds. "You want a road patrol this afternoon?"

"Just to those cots to the east. Some of the folk have returned."

"After the men eat?" asked Ferek. "Pork'll do 'em good." He grinned. "Kieral found near on a stone of potatoes in the side field there, at the back. Missed them earlier."

"That's only good for a few meals," mused Hiser, from beside Ferek.

"Take 'em where we can get 'em." Ferek nodded emphatically.

"The message should reach the High Wizard tomorrow." *You hope.* "Late this afternoon is fine for the patrol."

The three looked up at the sound of hoofs. Three lancers rode toward the corral and the cook fires. The lead rider wore the sash of a messenger.

"A message for Mage Cerryl from the High Wizard," gasped the lean young lancer, extending a scroll.

As he took the rolled and sealed scroll, Cerryl noted absently that one of the lancers who rode with the messenger was a woman, older and hard-faced. "I have it. Why don't you three dismount? We'll be having a hearty midday meal, and I imagine it will be welcome after a cold ride."

"Thank you," the messenger answered.

The other two lancers nodded . . . and dismounted.

Cerryl stepped away from the cook fire that held two cauldrons filled with potatoes. The two boars were being turned on makeshift spits at the other two fires. After breaking the seal, he began to read.

Greetings, Cerryl,

As you may surmise from this, your presence is needed in Elparta, your presence and your particular skills. Now that Fairhaven controls Elparta and the River Gallos, as I trust you have discovered through your glass, protection of the road from Axalt is less important and provided as much by our control of both Elparta and the upper reaches of the river . . .

We expect that you will decamp immediately and make your way with prudent haste to rejoin us here in Elparta . . .

Jeslek had signed the scroll, but the signature was almost a scrawl, unlike the more precise lettering of earlier messages. *The impact of using so much chaos, or because he's hurried?*

That also brought up the question of who had written the scroll itself. Anya? There hadn't been any scriveners coming along the main road, nor any apprentice mages, and Cerryl doubted that Jeslek would have trusted Fydel to write anything. Then, he trusted Anya less than either Fydel or the High Wizard.

Cerryl rerolled the scroll and thrust it inside his jacket, then stepped forward.

Both Ferek and Hiser were waiting, but neither said a word, though their eyes were filled with questions.

"The High Wizard has summoned us to Elparta. We will depart at dawn." Cerryl smiled. "There's time enough to enjoy the boar."

"Good," said Ferek.

Hiser nodded politely.

". . . about time," came from one of the lancers loitering by the adjoining cook fire.

". . . that blue commander . . . wonder if they got him . . ."

". . . never happen . . . say he's a giant . . ."

". . . won't have to freeze here anyway . . ."

After what his glass had shown of Elparta, Cerryl had the feeling that wintering over in Elparta—for that was surely what Jeslek had in mind—would scarcely be that warm. It would require at least some labor to repair enough of the city to house those lancers and levies stationed there through the cold seasons. And the following spring and summer would only bring more difficulty with the blues and their near-mythical commander.

# CIV

As he rode downhill and westward, Cerryl saw the flattened trees and shrubs before he glimpsed the River Gallos. Despite the weak midday sun and the cold wind from the east, a sickly smell rose from the mud that covered the floodplain.

Once below the eroded bluff that years before had slumped into a gentle incline, the road turned and ran along the ancient levee north toward Elparta, wide enough to allow four horses abreast—or two wagons wheel-to-wheel.

"Two abreast, Hiser," Cerryl ordered, not wanting any of the mounts walking through the stinking mud bordering the road, already repacked into a solid clay surface from heavy traffic. Here and there on the slope above the river were heaps of thatch and planks or water-smoothed mud bricks that had once been cots or outbuildings. Cerryl tried not to breathe deeply.

"Demon-darkness stench," Ferek commented. "Worse inside the walls, I'd wager."

"Surrender couldn't have been this bad," said Hiser.

Of that Cerryl wasn't certain. He glanced ahead toward the slumped outline of what had been city walls. A full company of lancers, dismounted, was gathered just outside the rubble.

One of the city gates lay broken against the rubble of one guard tower. Only the iron straps of the other remained, blackened and thrown across the shattered planks of the first gate. Cerryl nodded. Jeslek—or Fydel or Anya—had taken out some wrath on the gate.

On a makeshift platform beside the opening into the city stood a lancer officer. "The High Wizard is in the high house on the hill." Captain Teras inclined his head to Cerryl, then gestured over his shoulder. "He expects you. I will see your men are quartered . . . with what we have."

"Thank you."

"Dester and Huyl will guide you. The ways are not what they once were." Only the faintest tinge of irony colored the voice of the hulking lancer officer.

Cerryl turned in the saddle. "Don't let the men run loose, no matter what anyone says. If they're allowed the freedom of the place, make sure they go in threes."

"I would second that, Subofficers," Teras added.

"Yes, ser," Hiser and Ferek answered almost simultaneously.

"I be Dester, ser. This way, if you would." Dester was a rail-thin figure with a gray goatee who eased his mount alongside and then slightly in front of Cerryl's gelding.

The other lancer, a true white-bronze lance in his holder, merely nodded as he joined them.

Some sections of the stone walls of Elparta had toppled inward, and the dwellings and other structures within fifty cubits of the walls were largely rubble as well. As Ferek had predicted, the odor was higher once past the walls.

"Is anything left standing?" Cerryl asked.

"Most east of the river walls, especially beyond the merchants' hill. That's where we're taking you, ser. Doors don't fit lots of places. Some of the fellows like that." Dester sniffed, almost in disapproval.

Huyl remained silent.

The street had been broad for a city not designed by White mages, but the piles of fallen roof tiles and rubble from walls had narrowed it to little more than space for two mounts. Huyl fell back.

Cerryl found his hands going to his dagger, and he shook his head. Better chaos than a dagger, but he hoped he had to use neither.

A long scream echoed from somewhere to the left of where Cerryl rode, a long and despairing scream. He turned his head to look down the half-blocked lane off the main street, but the cobblestones were deserted, and he saw neither lancers nor a woman. The scream had told him enough, and there was little he could do. Still . . . his stomach clenched.

Slowly, the three made their way along the main street, for perhaps three-quarters of a kay, before turning eastward. After several hundred cubits, the side avenue began to slope gently uphill, ending another 300 cubits farther east at an open brick-and-stone gateway guarded by four lancers.

"Here be the High Wizard's headquarters and quarters," announced Dester. "And we'll be a-heading back."

"Thank you."

With a nod, Cerryl rode through the gates. Another set of lancers were stationed by the carved doors to the mansion. As he dismounted and tied the gelding to a hitching post carved in the likeness of a red deer, Cerryl glanced around. The walls around the large house, larger even than Layel's, had been roughly patched and the courtyard cleared of fallen brick and roof tiles.

One of the second-story windows was missing shutters, and a thin crack ran across the stone facade of the dwelling on the left side of the arched front doorway where the two lancers stood.

Before Cerryl reached the lancers, the door opened, and Anya stood there. "So . . . you finally made it." Anya offered her blinding and false smile. "Jeslek will be pleased to see you. Do come in. You must have had a cold ride."

"I've had warmer." Cerryl used the boot scraper and brush by the door before stepping into the house, finding himself in a hallway twice the size of the cot where he had spent the last two seasons and with a ceiling nearly four times higher.

Anya closed the carved door of stained dark oak.

"You had more trouble taking the city than anyone thought, then?" Cerryl asked, his tone mild.

"We could have done this last spring." Anya shrugged, and the smile faded.

"I imagine Jeslek had his reasons."

"He had the thought that it might be better not to have to rebuild the city." Anya's brilliant smile returned. "As I told you a long time ago, Cerryl, appealing to people's better nature almost always fails. They respect but force. So . . . it's better to use what force you must quickly and get on with it."

"I see that the High Wizard came to that decision as well."

"He had no choice. Hydlen provided few lancers and no levies to speak of. Nor did Lydiar. The perfect of Gallos grudged every body that came down the river. Even the second-promised levies from Certis were late and few."

"And the Black who commanded the blue forces . . . Brede . . . his name has even reached my armsmen . . . he was far better than expected?"

"Armsmen talk too much at times, Cerryl. Best you not put too much stock in rumors."

"I will remember that." Cerryl nodded. "I take it that the High Wizard—and you—will be occupied this winter."

"I see you understand, even without being here."

"We were tasked to protect the supply road and your flank. We did so."

"You did well, Cerryl." The smile broadened. "You eliminated almost a quarter of the Spidlarian lancers and never boasted a line about it. Jeslek was impressed."

"Yes, I was." Appearing in the doorway behind Anya, the High Wizard smiled at Cerryl. "Would you join me?" Jeslek's hair was as white as ever, still shimmering as it caught the light from the candles in their sconces on the wall. His sun-gold eyes glittered as before, but an air of age and tiredness surrounded him, and dark circles had grown under his eyes. An unseen haze, as if of chaos dust, surrounded him. "Anya, if you would finish that scroll about the division of duties . . . as we discussed? Bring it in when you are finished, if you would."

"I will."

Cerryl thought he saw a slight softening of Anya's hard smile but for an instant before she turned.

Jeslek turned, and Cerryl followed him into what had once been a private library. Half the shelves were bare, and books were stacked randomly among the rest of the polished wooden shelves that took up two full walls. A low fire glimmered in the hearth, and the warmth of the room was welcome.

Jeslek filled another goblet with a dark red wine from the decanter on the silver tray that rested on the corner of the massive table-desk— supported by four wooden pillars, each carved into the shape of a mountain cat. "You look like you could use this."

"It's been a long year . . . longer for you, though, I imagine." Cerryl took the goblet.

Jeslek seated himself, not behind the desk, but at one side of the circular table ringed by four wooden armchairs. "Sit down."

Cerryl sat and, following Jeslek's example, took a small sip of the wine. He avoided frowning, sensing that the vintage had already begun to turn . . . and that it should not have done so yet.

"Yes . . . a long year . . . and a longer winter for us both."

Cerryl raised his eyebrows.

"You and Fydel have a task or two here. Anya and I—and Eliasar—have more than a few elsewhere in Candar."

"Ensuring we get more support next spring?"

"Of course. Much of this year was a facade. I had to let them wind enough rope around their own necks." Jeslek took another swallow of wine and laughed once more. "Unless Fairhaven sees more tariffs and levies, there will be new rulers in a few lands. Enough of that." The High Wizard smiled, then extended a wrinkled and stained scroll. "These were the terms I offered Elparta. Read them."

The younger mage accepted the battered scroll and unrolled it, his eyes flicking across the words, some smudged, others blurred as if water had fallen on the scroll.

> . . . from the honorable Jeslek, and the commanders Grestalk and Xeinon . . .

"Who are Grestalk and Xeinon?" asked Cerryl. "I've never heard of them."

"The commanders of the Certans and Gallosians. Go on; they're not important." Jeslek took another swallow of wine, a healthy one.

Cerryl tried to hurry through the scroll.

> . . . beseeching that the citizens of Elparta, in the interests of justice and mercy, lay down their arms and pay homage to the greater hegemony of Candar . . .
>
> . . . that the river gates be destroyed and the water piers be open to all . . . that the battlements be cast down . . . that unmarried women be made available as consorts for . . . that all followers of the Black heresy, including the officers of the Spidlarian Guard who have committed atrocities and used evil magical tools against the hegemony, be turned over to the honorable Jeslek . . . that reparations from the granaries of the city be made to the forces of the hegemony . . . that all able horses are to be turned over to the representatives of the hegemony for proper redistribution . . . that all members of the so-called Council of Traders be returned to the Candarian Traders' Guild for proper disciplinary action . . .

Cerryl tried to keep from swallowing as he laid the scroll on the polished surface of the table.

"What do you think of the terms?"

"I was not here," Cerryl temporized.

"No, you weren't. You think they're harsh. They are. Even Fydel, good loyal Fydel, swallowed when he read them. I made the terms as difficult . . . as difficult as I could." Jeslek smiled, even more broadly.

Cerryl's forehead wrinkled. "Why?"

"Because I needed to destroy Elparta. Because I needed to frighten off those who were honest." Jeslek laughed.

"Destroy Elparta? As a lesson to Lydiar and Hydlen?"

"Exactly." Jeslek shook his head, then refilled his glass. "You do see, Cerryl. Better to destroy two cities that will seldom benefit the Guild than one that will. Though that may be necessary. I trust not, but folk can be stubborn unto death."

"I see that," Cerryl grudged. "But frightening the people?"

"After all the dead and wounded, and all the nasty devices the blues used . . . whatever happened in Elparta would not have been good. You cannot control soldiers who have been ambushed and attacked for seasons. Not without killing a number, and then they won't fight well for you in the next effort. So you make sure that most of those who would fear you leave." Jeslek shrugged. "I even told them that I offered honorable terms, especially given the depredations committed upon all Candar, the unfairness in trading, and the slaughter of defenseless traders." The High Wizard laughed, then coughed, once, twice, before clearing his throat. "That's also why I didn't want you around."

"Oh." Cerryl could feel his guts tightening.

"You get to put the city back together. You are the mage in charge of Elparta, the one to restore it and to ensure keeping the peace. You wanted to bend the Patrol's rules to benefit people. Here you can make or break the rules any way you want . . . so long as you get the city back together by late spring."

*After this . . . ?* Cerryl did swallow.

Jeslek ignored Cerryl's almost inaudible gulp. "Fydel will deal with the Spidlarians, should it be necessary. You are to work together, if required."

"I see."

*Thrap.* After the brief knock on the door, Anya stepped inside. "I have what you asked for." She walked over to the table and extended a single sheet of parchment to the High Wizard.

Jeslek motioned to the vacant chair to his left and began to read silently. Anya sat and waited, her face expressionless.

"Yes, this will do." His sun-gold eyes glittered as he handed the parchment to Cerryl.

The youngest mage took the document and began to read.

> ... and know ye all that the commander of the city and all that
> be within it shall be the honorable mage Cerryl ...

*A long, long winter ...*
From where she sat between Jeslek and Cerryl, not looking at either
man, Anya's eyes glittered.

# CV

If he had to take over as city commander or council chief or whatever,
like it or not, Cerryl needed some building that could serve as his quarters and as a place where lancers and others could meet with him—one
separate from Jeslek's building and where he wouldn't freeze once the
ice and snow came. He needed such a place soon, since Jeslek was
already readying his departure—with a goodly portion of the White
Lancers who had taken Elparta.

Cerryl had found Hiser and given him the task of locating possible
dwellings, ones where adjoining or attached dwellings could be used
to house Hiser's and Ferek's companies—and ones close to Jeslek's pu-
tative headquarters, even if Jeslek would not be in Elparta.

Now, as the fall rain misted down around him, Cerryl leaned forward
in the saddle and looked down a wide avenue—for Elparta—just on the
north side of the slope that held the High Wizard's quarters toward a
large, but comparatively more modest, dwelling set behind a low wall.

"This one ... well, it be the best Ferek or me could find." Hiser
coughed. "Better than those leaking inns by the river. Smells, though.
Everything does."

Cerryl rode slowly the last hundred cubits, stopping short of the
wall. The house was sturdy enough, despite the red roof tiles that had
cracked in the upheavals that had tumbled the city walls. The front
stone wall rose nearly six cubits. On one side the carriage gate had
ripped off the iron brackets, although the smaller wrought-iron foot
access gate remained locked in place. Behind the carriage gate was a
stable separated from the main house by a courtyard.

After easing the gelding through the carriage gate, Cerryl tied his
mount to a hitching post under the overhanging front eaves of the stable
and dismounted. Hiser and two lancers quickly did the same and then
led the way through the light rain to the front door.

One of the lancers turned the bronze door lever and pushed the door open. The odor welling out immediately turned Cerryl's guts, and he stepped back for a moment to see if the light breeze would help clear the stench. While the worst did dissipate, Cerryl found himself breathing through his mouth as he stepped into the green-tiled and walnut-paneled front foyer of the dwelling. The four drawers of the oak chest set against the right wall hung out, except for the third, which rested on the floor, various colored linens strewn around it.

The single floor chest in the sitting room had also been ransacked, with shards of pottery sprayed across the green tiles and the braided gold rug in the center of the floor.

Cerryl repressed a retching gag as he stepped past the settee and through the squared archway into the small study adjoining the sitting room. Three bodies, already putrefying, lay on the pale green ceramic tiles between the corner table-desk and the circular table.

One had been—he thought—a young woman. The others might have been her parents. He tried not to swallow as he gathered chaos.

"Darkness," whispered Hiser.

One of the young lancers ran for the front door, and Cerryl could hear retching outside.

*Whhtsttt!* The firebolt removed the putrefying corpses and the worst of the odor.

"Open the shutters, and the windows." Cerryl walked to the nearest window, opening the shutters and then the glass. Unlike most dwellings in Elparta, the house did have blown-glass windows, with shutters both inside and outside the sliding glass.

For a time he stood before the open shutters, letting the cold and damp air flow around him and into the rear study. The study would serve as a conference room—it had a circular table and even a corner desk.

He turned and crossed the sitting room, going past the carved balustrade of the narrow staircase to the second floor. The dining area was to the right of the kitchen and partly to the rear.

"Who do we have that can cook?" Cerryl shook his head, his thoughts going back to the three bodies. Had the young woman/girl been raped and killed? Or had the three killed themselves? The doors did not appear to have been forced, and the limited looting could have come later, but Cerryl wasn't sure that meant anything.

*Maybe they thought their wealth would protect them?*

Cerryl frowned as he stepped through the kitchen with its neat worktables and peered into the pantry—also undisturbed. Whoever had lived in the house had been well-off, wealthy even. *And innocent of everything but ignorance.* Despite Jeslek's cruel "terms," they had chosen to stay. How many others had, preferring near-certain death to exile?

The more he saw, Cerryl was convinced, the less certain he was about the wisdom of anything.

The dining area was untouched, as were the three bedchambers upstairs, with the exception of a single small chest, less than a cubit square, that lay smashed on the landing upstairs. A single silver that had rolled against the top of the balustrade indicated what the chest had once held.

Yet clothes had not been taken, nor any of the silver dishes in the sideboard in the dining area. Was that because there were so many empty houses and so comparatively few lancers and levies? Or because coins were easier to carry and hide?

Cerryl turned and studied the largest bedchamber from the small upper hall landing—four-poster bed, with solid dark wood posts at each corner, a silk-covered chair in one corner, two matching wardrobes with a full-length wall mirror between them, two windows, each shuttered and framed with maroon silks, and a door to a bathing chamber. *And three bodies . . .*

Cerryl walked down into the front foyer. Hiser followed him. Both lancers waited by the still-open front door. A faint green tinge suffused the face of the younger blond lancer.

"This looks good. We need to keep airing it out for a while. What about the houses on each side?" Cerryl looked at the blond subofficer.

"The dwellings on each side be not quite so good," confessed Hiser. "Better than those below, mayhap."

Cerryl smiled grimly. The work required might keep the lancers' thoughts off other matters. *Maybe.*

His eyes drifted in the direction of the study, and he hoped that the odor would fade before too long. He tried not to think about how many more bodies there had been—or might be.

# CVI

The High Wizard is expecting you." The lancer subofficer opened the door as Cerryl walked toward the guards stationed at the end of the short hallway. The candles in the smudged wall sconces were unlit, leaving the corridor dim and smelling faintly of burned wax.

Cerryl stepped through the door into the private library of the mansion that Jeslek had appropriated and eased into the chair across the circular table from the High Wizard, glad for the warmth from the hearth. The books remaining on the shelves behind Jeslek had been rearranged and no longer appeared randomly piled on their sides.

Anya and Fydel were already seated, Anya to Cerryl's left, Fydel to his right. A decanter of wine sat on a silver tray, with a single empty goblet beside it. Anya, Fydel, and Jeslek all had partly filled goblets before them.

Fydel's fingers tapped the polished wood of the conference table, once, before Anya raised her eyebrows.

"We can begin." Jeslek smiled.

"I am at your command." Cerryl returned the smile, then reached for the decanter and half-filled the remaining goblet. While he did not need the wine, the gesture was important, and he took a sip of the wine, an amber vintage, unlike that he had been offered when he had first arrived, but one also verging on turning to vinegar. *Too much chaos around Jeslek.*

The slightest hint of a smile touched the corners of Anya's mouth, while Fydel tapped the table once more.

"You will do your own commanding soon." Jeslek glanced from Fydel to Cerryl, then back at Fydel.

Anya kept her eyes averted from both Cerryl and the square-bearded mage.

"I've written it down and sent it to Kinowin and Redark," Jeslek said with a smile. "Fydel, you are to defend Elparta and to take the fight to the Spidlarians, as necessary. Cerryl, you are to work at rebuilding Elparta, and you are to keep the peace. You may conscript locals as necessary for building and rebuilding."

Cerryl nodded. That was an option he didn't like, but he also doubted that he would find all that many carpenters and masons in the lancers—and fewer still who would admit to such skills.

"*If* it appears that the renegade Black commander—this Brede—is preparing for a massive attack, Fydel, you *will* summon me immediately." Jeslek's eyes flashed. "Is that clear?"

"Yes, High Wizard." The timbre of Fydel's voice verged on that of boredom.

"In like terms, Cerryl, you are to rebuild Elparta so that it can serve as our staging base for next year's attack. The river piers must be rebuilt, and enough housing for 50-score lancers and 250-score levies."

Cerryl nodded. *Two hundred fifty score?* "What about supplies? And coins?"

"You will have 1,000 golds, as will Fydel. You will have to raise provisions and supplies locally. The Guild will continue to pay the lancers, but their pay will be held, as normal, until they return to Fairhaven."

Cerryl held in a wince. The held pay was not going to go over well with the lancers, and that would mean trouble with peacekeeping and the locals.

"The men need some coins," Fydel finally said in a low voice.

"Use your golds as you wish." Jeslek shrugged. "I am releasing all the levies except the levied lancers from Hydlen. I will be taking ten score with me. That leaves you with twenty-five score." His eyes fixed on Fydel and hardened.

*They lost fifteen score lancers in taking Elparta?* Cerryl pursed his lips. *Fifteen score? This Brede is better than anyone will admit.*

"As you command, High Wizard," Fydel responded politely.

"I am going to raise the coins and the armsmen necessary to take the rest of Spidlar in the spring. Personally." Jeslek's sun-gold eyes did not glitter but seemed cold and flat, like a serpent's. "Anya will be assisting me in this winter's preparations."

Anya still refrained from looking directly at either Fydel or Cerryl.

"You may all go." With a lazy smile, Jeslek stood. "You each have much to accomplish in the days before Anya and I depart."

Cerryl took a last small swallow of the wine he had barely tasted, then stood quickly, before the other two.

Jeslek remained standing by the table. The lancer subofficer closed the door after the three left the library.

Outside, Anya stepped up beside Cerryl as he walked along the hall and into the foyer. The scent of trilia and sandalwood accompanied her, as always. "You're no longer 'young Cerryl.'"

*Were you ever?* "Why do you say that?" Cerryl took his stained white jacket from the peg on the coat holder and slipped it on.

"The bit with the wine goblet. You didn't even hesitate. Or the blunt question about supplies." Anya smiled. "You intrigue me more than ever, Cerryl."

Cerryl returned Anya's smile with one equally bright and false. "You flatter me. You are the intriguing one."

"Oh, stop flattering each other." Fydel snorted. "You're both false as tin trinkets. And as useful."

"Cerryl will be very useful to you, Fydel," Anya answered with a softer smile. "You'll be free to pursue any blues you can find while he's worried about masons, and bricks, and planks—and piers and peace-keeping."

Cerryl wished it were going to be that simple, but he had his doubts, strong ones.

Fydel snorted a second time. "The winter will be long, even with what must be done."

"You two will manage." Anya offered a last smile.

Cerryl inclined his head to the redhead, then to Fydel, before leading the way out into the clear and cold afternoon. Despite the brisk wind, the miasma of death still hung over the city.

Cerryl swung into the gelding's saddle, wondering how he could accomplish all that Jeslek had laid upon him. *Does he want you to fail? Again?* The brown-haired mage nodded, his eyes somewhere beyond the street as he rode back toward his quarters.

# CVII

Cerryl looked at the blank scroll on the corner desk, then at the darkness that lay beyond the shuttered windows. The house he had taken was quiet, and even in the adjoining dwellings he suspected most lancers were sleeping, except for those on guard duty.

SSsss... The oil lamp hissed momentarily, then sputtered and hissed again. He glanced at it, wondering if the reservoir were empty, but the hissing died, and the yellow glow from the mantel continued to fall across the empty dun expanse of the parchment.

The White mage suppressed a yawn. It seemed like he ran from dawn until after dusk... dealing with so many things he'd never thought of, not only supplies and fodder, but tools, smithies for weapons, and even nails or bolts. How did you replace planks without some fasteners, especially when the only substitute was treenails, and they didn't work that well for barely skilled lancers and peasants?

He rubbed his forehead and looked down again.

For only the second time in almost three seasons, he could send Leyladin a message that would reach her, if he finished it before morning, when a messenger and lancer guards left for Fairhaven. Yet he hadn't the faintest idea where to begin. Or rather, he had so much to say.

Finally, he began to write, smiling as he scripted the first line.

My dearest Leyladin...

After that, the words got easier, enough so that before long he was reaching for a second sheet. Then the words got slower, and he had to turn and trim the lamp wick twice before he signed the bottom of the second sheet and laid it aside to dry.

After rubbing his forehead, sitting in the quiet of the study, ignoring the changing of the two lancer guards outside the front door, he picked up the first sheet, and his eyes skipped over the lines as he reread what he had written:

... have good quarters here, although I am troubled by how I came by them. It was not my doing, not exactly... so long since we have had a true roof overhead... yet I always thought of you... as you must know from my earlier message and from my glimpses through the glass . . . tried not to intrude . . . but I have missed you . . . more than I ever would have known . . .

He shook his head. That wasn't quite true. Even before he had really met her, she had been important to him. *What drew you to her . . . and her to you? Order and chaos? The need for some sort of balance?*

After a moment, he continued to reread his words:

. . . Elparta lies in our hands, and I am supposed to return it to a semblance of prosperity, but there are few masons and few woodworkers among the lancers and almost no crafters at all among the wretched souls who survived the place's fall . . . I found one mason's apprentice with a crushed hand and an old fellow who'd been a carpenter once . . . little enough that I know, but it is more than many of the men I must direct . . .

. . . already we have had some light snow, and the winter promises to be cold indeed. I shudder to think what it must be like along the shores of the Northern Ocean . . .

. . . I have no idea when we will be returning to Fairhaven. It could be well into next year, if not longer . . .

*Longer?* Momentarily he wanted to pound the desk—or something. Yet nothing had happened exactly as he wished. Even getting to know Leyladin had taken far longer than he had ever thought possible.

. . . however long that may be, you know what I feel and how strongly, and no words will convey what you have felt, and I would not try to reduce such to letters upon parchment . . .

*Besides, unlike Leyladin, you don't know who will be reading what you write.* She—or Layel—had effectively owned the guard who had delivered her scroll to him, a scroll he still kept with his possessions, a scroll whose green-inked sentences he still read and reread.

After another yawn, he rolled the scroll and, after heating the sealing wax over the top of the oil lamp, sealed it and laid it on the desk to be sent with the next dispatches to Jeslek in Fairhaven. Then he blew out the lamp and turned toward the stairs. Tomorrow would come—cold and all too soon.

# CVIII

Cerryl walked from the covered porch of his dwelling out into the light and cold rain and along the brick walkway to the masonry house beyond the courtyard wall of his dwelling. There a handful of lancers milled around a wagon drawn by a single bony horse.

The rain—small drops that felt partly frozen—carried a slightly sour odor, or perhaps the moisture drew the scent of recent pillaging and death out of the ground. Cerryl frowned as he heard the mutters.

"Tools . . . supposed to use these?"

"Worse 'n road duty . . ."

"It's the mage!" called a voice.

The lancers stepped back, and Hiser rode forward and reined up beside the wagon horse. "We got some tools in the wagon there, ser. And some shutters, at the back. Shutters—need to replace the ones on this side of the dwellings here, all of them. Some fool ripped 'em off the brackets so hard that the wood splintered."

"It was rotten," Ferek added as he rode up and joined Hiser. "Half the town is rotten. Too much rain. Rains every day here."

"I sent men to get shutters from buildings that were too damaged for anyone to use," Hiser explained.

Cerryl glanced at the two men standing nearest the side of the wagon.

"The ones we got, they need to be cut down," said a burly lancer. "Got a saw here that might do."

Cerryl studied the saw, then shook his head. "That won't do, not if we can find a better one. It's a ripping saw. We need one with finer teeth, about half that big."

"Ripping saw?" Ferek's mouth opened.

Hiser grinned, then wiped the expression away.

"A ripping saw rough-cuts planks, going with the grain rather than across it. Use those teeth on those shutters," Cerryl winced, "and you'll rip the wood up almost as bad as the ones you can't use." He stepped toward the wagon, rummaging through the indiscriminate piles of hammers, adzes, pry bars, mallets, and, in the corner, several other saws. He pulled out one, a smaller saw. "See? The teeth are smaller, finer, and closer together. Use this to shorten those shutter frames."

It would have been faster to do it himself, but he was one person. If they would just use the crosscut finish saw or knew what tools to use, without his looking over someone's shoulder all the time, more would get done. He couldn't do the work they were supposed to do. It wouldn't leave him time for what he had to do.

"You heard the commander," snapped Ferek.

"Lancers be not crafters," mumbled a lancer near the rear of the wagon. "Didn't ride to Spidlar to do no sawing."

"You didn't?" asked Cerryl, flicking the smallest flash of chaos fire past the complainer.

"Sorry, ser!" The lancer stiffened.

Cerryl wanted to shake his head. *How many are like that? Unwilling to do things if they think it would make others think less of them?*

"Make sure the roof gets patched, too," Cerryl reminded Ferek before turning to Hiser. "You bring a squad and come with me to the river piers. I'll be riding out in a bit. Those need work, if we want supplies from Gallos."

"Yes, ser."

Cerryl walked back to his quarters, then to the stable, where he saddled the gelding. He needed to inspect the river piers more closely, to see what needed to be done to get them ready to handle the barges once spring came. *Or now?* From what he could tell, they didn't have enough provisions for more than a few eight-days. He didn't want to have to raid the countryside if there were any other way.

He patted the gelding's neck, led him out into the courtyard and mounted, then rode out through the carriage gate. The sound of hammers, and a saw, echoed from the lancers' dwelling. Cerryl permitted himself a tight smile.

"Ready, ser," offered Hiser as he rode up with a squad of lancers.

Cerryl nodded and turned his mount.

"Men are not happy about fixing up Elpartan houses."

"Right now, who else can?" Cerryl snorted, letting his voice carry. "It rains most of every day, it seems, and we've driven off most of the able-bodied locals. Those who might be hiding nearby we won't find, and winter's coming. We're in this war because Spidlar and the traders don't pay their tariffs. So where are we going to get the coins to bring in laborers—or crafters?"

"Couldn't the High Wizard order some here?"

"How? The prefect of Gallos or the viscount will find some way to avoid doing it or send us people who are worse than our lancers and cost the Guild coins we don't have. If we bring crafters from Fairhaven, how could we not pay them? If we don't, they'll disappear, and they won't flee back to Fairhaven, and then we won't have crafters, and neither will the folk at home."

Hiser gave Cerryl a strange look but only nodded.

Cerryl understood the expression. The subofficer wondered why the High Wizard had even started the war.

"That's why the High Wizard didn't want to use chaos on Elparta,"

Cerryl offered. *And why you're stuck trying to put it back together. Maybe Anya was right. Maybe it was better to use a lot of force quickly.* He forced a long, slow breath. *And maybe there's never any good answer.*

More of the fallen stone, timbers, and bricks had been cleared from the main route westward toward the river, but the streets remained mostly deserted. Cerryl saw but one dog, a brown mutt that slunk down an alleyway as the riders passed, tail nearly between its legs.

The middle river gates were on their heavy iron supports—or had never left them—and were open to the piers. The stench from the piers was strong, despite the increasing rain—a mixture of rotting foliage, fish, and other decaying matter, mixed with the smell of mud. Mud was piled everywhere, over the splintered and broken planks that had once formed the deck of the piers and been cast against the rabbled river walls, up almost to the top of the tilted and shortened stone pillars that had comprised the base of the piers. Beneath the pillars, and under the mud, Cerryl could sense that most of the pier bases were solid.

Jeslek's flood or whatever it had been had piled so much mud against the solid stone bases of the piers that the river was now flowing more than ten cubits from the ruins of the piers.

Cerryl studied the jumbled mass of planks, stone, and mud. Could he use chaos—or loosen order enough—the way he had in the road battle, so that the river would carry away the mud?

"Be hard to put them back together," murmured Hiser.

Cerryl dismounted and handed the gelding's reins to the subofficer. The mage walked forward, then back to the pile of huge stones that had been the river wall. There he concentrated, working on loosening the bounds of order, shifting them beneath the pier bases and to the river walls, leaching order out of the mud heaped against the remaining stone pillars.

*Unnnnnhhhh . . .* The mud shifted, ever so slightly, and then seemed to slump. Bubbles frothed up through the gray-brown soupy mess.

For a time he just sat down on one of the larger stones from the wall, holding his head in his hands, while stars flashed across his vision.

The rain began to fall more heavily from clouds that had darkened, unnoticed by Cerryl, and mixed with the droplets were ice pellets that bounced off the oiled leather of his jacket.

At last, Cerryl stood and made his way along the edge of the fallen river wall to where Hiser and the squad waited. Hiser's eyes were on the mud and on the river water, which seemed darker than before.

Cerryl remounted and followed the subofficer's eyes with his own, noting that the fizzing and bubbling continued and that the river was eating away the slumping mess from around the pier pillars and bases. He nodded, then massaged his forehead. *Should have eaten before you came out here.*

"The mud's going . . ."

"Don't believe that . . ."

Cerryl blinked, then turned to Hiser. "We still need planks to refinish the top of the piers and some logs for the round posts . . ."

"Bollards," supplied a voice.

"Bollards," agreed Cerryl, turning.

A wiry man in tattered gray stood on the mud-smeared river wall, a good ten cubits to Cerryl's right. A sabre leaped into Hiser's hand.

"Greetin', ser mage. You want to put the piers right again?"

Cerryl nodded.

"Best you use your tricks to shift that bar upstream some, then, or 'fore long you be having the same mud back around the pier columns."

*Bar?* Cerryl's eyes flicked upstream, finally catching sight of a mud bar or sandbar slightly to the west of midstream.

"Water comes off the bend and splits . . . Slow stuff drifts to the east," added the spritely old figure, as if everyone should have understood his words.

"Did you used to run the piers?"

"Me? Not a lead copper's wager. Jidro, at your service. Few years back was lead boatman for Virot's barges."

Cerryl let his order-chaos senses range across the man, then nodded. "You want a job? Being in charge of rebuilding and running the piers?"

"Aye, and you'd turn me into ashes first time I displeased you."

"I don't do that unless people lie to me or attack me."

Jidro grinned. "Won't live forever, and I'd like to see 'em run right. But need one of your lancer subs to give orders. No one listens to an old fart like me."

Cerryl grinned, then glanced toward Hiser. Ferek was too stiff. "Hiser . . . let's see what Jidro can do for us."

"Ah . . . yes, ser." An expression between horror and relief flitted across the eyes of the blond subofficer.

Again Cerryl hoped he'd read things right. *More hope . . . never quite knowing.*

# CIX

Cerryl stood at one end of the table, then stepped back, his eyes raking over Teras, Ferek, and Hiser. Senglat was absent. *Probably sneaking off to find Fydel.* "I want that man tied to a post right in front of the gate outside and all the lancers mustered out, right on the street here, on foot."

"Now?" asked Teras.

"Now. I'll be out shortly, as soon as he's tied to the post. You can all leave and prepare." *Sounding like Jeslek, you are.* Cerryl concealed a wince, not moving until the small study was empty and he stood alone, alone with his thoughts and the faint odor of decay that would doubtless take years to dissipate totally.

The murmurs from the officer and subofficers were loud enough that he could hear they were talking, but not loud enough for him to pick up the words. It didn't matter. The lancer had been caught right after he had murdered a local woman because she wouldn't comply with his wishes. Then the fellow had bold-facedly lied to Cerryl, and denied the murder.

The slightly built mage shook his head. If he let the man off, his authority over the lancers would begin to erode until he'd have to do something drastic to regain it. *Anya was right . . . in this situation.*

When he saw the prisoner being marched from the makeshift cells in the cellar of the barracks house and the lancers forming up, Cerryl pulled on his jacket and stepped out into the cold and windy day, walking just outside the wrought-iron gate.

From where he was roped to a post wedged between two large cobble stones and braced with several other stones the lancer prisoner, a gag across his mouth, glared at Cerryl. The man probably could have loosened the post if he had struggled enough, but he still would have been fastened to what amounted to a heavy log.

"The men are here—all we could find quickly, ser," announced Teras, his voice carrying over the slight whistle of the wind.

"Thank you." Cerryl cleared his throat, then waited as he heard hoofs. A trace of a smile played across his lips as he sensed the chaos that accompanied the two riders.

Fydel galloped up, Senglat beside him. The square-bearded mage's face was red, almost livid, as he dismounted and marched up to Cerryl. His voice was low, pitched at Cerryl and not to carry. "I'm the one in charge of the lancers and what they do."

"I'm in charge of the city," Cerryl answered quietly. "Your lancer broke the peace, and lancers answer to the Patrol, even in Fairhaven. It's no different here."

"Why are you doing this?" asked Fydel. "I won't let you."

Cerryl raised shields and chaos before answering, his voice also low. "You won't stop me, Fydel." He smiled as the older man stepped back.

"Jeslek will hear of this."

"I'm sure he will. He doesn't care. All he wants are results. He wants Elparta rebuilt and the tariffs from its trade. If my way gets things done, your complaint doesn't matter. If it doesn't," Cerryl smiled ironically, "then it's minor compared to my failure."

"You're worse than Anya."

"Perhaps. Now . . . will you stand back and let me finish? It would be better if you did not make a scene."

"Jeslek *will* know of my displeasure."

"I am certain he will . . . if you choose to let him know. If you think, upon reflection, that is wise." Cerryl stepped forward, ignoring Fydel, his eyes beyond the lancer tied to the post. He raised his voice. "I ordered that no man, woman, or child in this town be hurt unless they attacked one of you. This man not only beat and killed a woman, but he lied to me about it. She did not threaten him; she did not wish to be used by him. He disobeyed, and he lied. He will pay the price." Cerryl nodded brusquely, then raised chaos.

For first time the lancer began to struggle, lunging against the ropes and the post—realizing that the slender mage meant his death.

*Whhsttt!* The firebolt engulfed the prisoner, flaring into a brief column of flame and greasy black smoke. Within instants, only white ashes drifted in the cold air.

Cerryl nodded to Teras. "You may dismiss them." His eyes went to the still-mounted Senglat. "You are dismissed as well, Captain."

Senglat's eyes flickered from Cerryl to Fydel and then dropped. "Yes, ser."

Cerryl remained almost rigid until the lancers had begun to move and until Senglat turned his mount down the street toward the makeshift stables.

". . . means what he said."

". . . other mage looked like the little one kicked him silly."

". . . Hiser said he was tough."

". . . one they kicked out of the Patrol 'cause he was too mean . . . that's what Yurit heard."

Cerryl looked at Fydel, whose color had gone from livid to near-white.

"I see why Isork wanted you off the Patrol."

"Do you?" Cerryl turned. His head ached again, and he felt exhausted, more emotionally than physically.

Fydel opened his mouth, then closed it. After a long pause, he spoke. "You cannot accept things as they are. You want them to be as they should be. Men are not as they should be but as they are."

"They won't be any better by doing their worst," Cerryl answered. "Neither will we." *But what is "better"?* He wished he knew.

Leaving Fydel and his mount in the street, Cerryl walked slowly back into the quarters building, back past the immobile guards and into the silent structure.

Force . . . maybe Anya was right, but Cerryl didn't have to like it. Not at all.

# CX

Windswept piles of snow had drifted against the stone fence-wall on the eastern side of the road, flakes swirling and shifting across the surface of the drifts in the light winter wind. Behind the stones were trees, mostly saplings, and the stumps where larger trees had once stood. The sound of a score of mounts' hoofs echoed off the frozen clay of the road as Cerryl and the lancers rode north.

Downhill from the western side of the narrow road, a stream burbled, ice-fringed, but its dark water clear in the center. Splotches of snow dotted the narrow field beyond the streambed, and trees with winter-grayed leaves rose behind the field.

"The place is around the next bend," Hiser announced.

As he passed the midpoint of the gentle curve in the road, Cerryl leaned forward in the saddle. A narrower road curved eastward rising beside the stream. Both road and stream cut through the middle of the field. The wide berm of stone-faced earth and the rough-planked building beside it were the first signs of the mill. A single large timber barn stood to the left of the mill and an unpainted house uphill of both, with a thin line of smoke rising from the chimney.

The arrangement of the mill and the outbuildings looked little like Dylert's, where Cerryl had spent his years after leaving the mines and Uncle Syodar and Aunt Nall, yet the feel was similar.

While there were recent tracks on the road to the mill and house, all the plank-sided buildings were shuttered, all the doors fastened tight. A dog's tracks crossed a patch of windblown snow before the low one-story house, but no dog was in sight. The plank walls of the house were water-stained, and the roof sagged.

Cerryl wanted to shake his head as he mentally compared Dylert's mill and the house before him. "Let's see if anyone's here."

At Hiser's nod, one of the lancers dismounted and, hand on sabre, used his free hand to pound on the door. Cerryl waited, but there was no answer.

"Try again. Say who ser Cerryl is," ordered Hiser.

The lancer pounded on the door. "Ser Cerryl, the city commander of Elparta."

Again the door remained closed.

Cerryl could sense no chaos, but he felt exposed. Then, he was always feeling exposed anymore. "I'm Cerryl, and I'm a White mage, and I don't mean any harm—unless you won't meet with me."

The door opened but a span. Cerryl could see the heavy chains.

"Yes, ser?"

"Come on out. If I wanted to, I could burn down the door, but it wouldn't do either of us much good."

Hiser smothered a grin.

Slowly, the bearded man eased out into the chill wind, and the door shut firmly behind him. "Mill's closed. No way to get logs down till spring."

Cerryl glanced at the bearded millmaster, then nodded at Hiser, before dismounting and stepping up to the taller man. Disliking it, but knowing the necessity, he raised equal order and chaos from the area around, letting it smolder around him. His gray eyes fixed the millmaster's pale green ones.

The miller's eyes widened, and he looked at the rut-frozen ground.

"Let's take a look at your mill."

The miller glanced at the score of lancers and at Hiser's hard blue eyes. "Ah . . . as you wish, ser mage."

Two lancers, sabres out, led the way as the stocky man walked ponderously along the frozen red clay to the planked door in the middle of the building. He opened the door and paused. "Dark inside. But one lantern and no striker."

"Hold up the lantern," Cerryl said dryly, waiting until the miller did before focusing a touch of chaos on the wick.

The lantern flared into light. The millmaster swallowed.

"Inside," Cerryl suggested.

One of the lancers took the lantern from the miller and stepped into the mill. The millmaster followed, and then came Cerryl.

Cerryl studied the mill floor, covered with sawdust that had to have been there since fall—or even summer. The few racks flanking the blade, wrapped in oiled cloth, were empty.

"Now the storage barn there." Cerryl gestured in the general direction of what he knew had to be the curing and storage barn.

With a deep breath the millmaster turned, and the four walked from the mill across the road and to the sliding door. The bearded man's hands fumbled as he unlatched the big door and pushed it sideways.

Perhaps a third of the racks contained planks, mostly smaller cuts, though Cerryl noted perhaps two dozen heavy oak planks that might work for refurbishing the piers. After walking to that rack and checking the planks, he turned and left the barn, then waited for the millmaster to slide shut the heavy door. The wind whistled more loudly as the four walked back toward the house and the still-mounted lancers and their subofficer.

Before the house, Cerryl turned once more to the bearded man. "We need timber. More than what you have here. You need your mill. You have no logs to cut, but there is enough water in the river to run the blade. The ice isn't that thick, and the mill is undershot anyway. It was designed to work in the winter."

"Ah . . . yes." The miller glanced at Cerryl.

"I once worked in a mill. Do you have a wagon and a team?"

"Yes, ser." The millmaster's eyes darted toward the outbuilding to the west of the long house.

"Then you will turn that wagon into a sledge. Remove the wheels. I will send a half-score of able men to help you fell and move the logs. If we get timbers and planks from those logs, you will get golds. Not many, but more than if I have to burn the mill. The choice is yours." Cerryl forced a smile like Anya's—hard and bright.

"You drive a hard bargain, ser mage."

"No. There are many who lost everything. You get to keep what you have and work hard for a few golds. Most would envy you."

The bearded man's eyes did not meet Cerryl's.

"Best you prepare," Cerryl said firmly. "You will have workers tomorrow or the next day."

"Yes, ser." The resigned tone was barely audible.

Cerryl ignored it and remounted the gelding.

As they rode back down the narrow road, Hiser glanced at Cerryl. "You promised men."

"The troublemakers . . . Bring them out here tomorrow. The first one that makes more trouble, bring him back to me."

"Ah . . ."

"I'll kill him with chaos," Cerryl said flatly. "In front of all the lancers. Don't think I won't. And any others who lay a hand on the locals, except to defend themselves."

"Ah . . . after the last one . . . you won't have trouble, ser." Hiser grinned raggedly. "What will you do when the troublemakers reform?"

"I'll think of something." Cerryl shrugged. "Or maybe we'll have enough planks, or maybe the locals will want planks, and the miller can pay some of them." He flicked the reins.

*Planks and timber will be the least of your problems.* Of that he was certain.

# CXI

Cerryl reined up by the south gate to Elparta, where the heavy wooden gates had been rebuilt and replaced on the gate pillars. The damp wind seeped through the oiled leather of his white jacket. He shifted his weight in the hard and cold saddle as he studied the river walls, the tumbled stones still sprawling away from the low wall cores that had been shifted and tilted in places by Jeslek's use of chaos on the River Gallos. The tumbled section ran northward to the middle river gates and then farther downriver to the north city gates.

After a moment, Cerryl turned to Hiser, mounted and waiting on his left. "We need to work on those . . . the river walls."

Most of the houses on the hill where he and his lancers were quartered had been repaired and reshuttered, if crudely. So had the dwellings in the area to the north and east of the south gate—not a hundred cubits from where he surveyed the river and where Fydel had quartered the majority of the White Lancers remaining in Elparta.

"What about the other houses?" asked Hiser.

"They'll have to wait." *Besides, if we get the walls and all the piers back, come spring, there will be people returning and paying crafters to rebuild—or doing it themselves.*

"Ought to wait," grumped Ferek. "Fools, all of 'em."

*Fools? Or just fearful?* "Perhaps. It doesn't matter. Finishing the piers and then the gates and the river walls comes next. Without trading facilities, the city will suffer more in the years to come."

"Should suffer," murmured Ferek under his breath.

Cerryl ignored the comment. "Tomorrow, have them start on the river side, all the way past the barracks houses, up to the trading gate— the middle one. After that, we'll see."

"That be several eight-days' work."

"I imagine so." Cerryl flicked the reins. "We'll go by the Market Square on the way back. Didn't you say people are showing up to trade?"

"Some," answered Hiser cautiously.

"When they think we're not looking," added Ferek.

The three, followed by four lancer guards, rode along the avenue from the south gate toward the center of Elparta. Away from the river, the smell of fish and mud dwindled, but the air seemed smokier.

As he neared the edge of the Market Square, Cerryl slowed the gelding. One of the stores—a chandlery—had been repaired, although the door was shut and the windows shuttered. A shutter on the adjoining cooper's shop clattered slowly against the mud-splattered plaster of the wall, moved back and forth by the wind.

A bellow, inchoate but loud, echoed across the seemingly empty square, followed by a scream and another, sharper yell.

Cerryl glanced around, then at Hiser.

Before either could speak, a man in a green vest and an oversized and open brown cloak ran out of an alleyway, darting around a pile of brick and mud. He dashed toward Cerryl. "Ser mage! Help! They'll kill me, they will."

Another man, swinging a sabre, his belt undone, scabbard banging against his leg, charged around the rubble and after the ginger-bearded and vested man.

"Halt!" bellowed Ferek.

Both the bearded man and the man chasing him slowed, then stopped as they saw the six lancers with unsheathed blades. The sabre-swinging man was a lancer, Cerryl could see, despite the afternoon shadows that lent an air of gloom to the dilapidated square.

The vested and bearded man turned to Cerryl. "Your lancer . . . he took out his blade and he threatened me. He said if I did not have my daughter . . . service him . . . he would kill us both."

Cerryl glanced at the unbelted lancer, who had sheathed his sabre.

"It's a lie!" yelled the lancer. "Ser," he added quickly as he saw the white cloak.

"He said he would kill us both, I swear," insisted the man with the curly beard and gold earrings.

Behind the two men were another pair of lancers, dragging a woman forward.

"What have you to say?" Cerryl's gray eyes focused on the single lancer.

"They're lying. She's a trollop and a cutpurse and—"

"See this cut? Do you see it, ser mage?" demanded the man in the vest, pointing to a short slash across his chin that dripped blood onto a stained shirt that might have once been white silk and onto a dirty brown cloak. "Your lancer did this to me."

Cerryl looked at the woman, struggling in the arms of two lancers who half-dragged, half carried her toward Cerryl, the subofficers, and the four lancer guards. One of the lancers lugging the woman kept looking down at her open cloak and ripped blouse, which showed half-exposed full breasts.

"He tried to kill me," insisted the bearded man.

"They . . . she offered . . . They tried to kill me . . ." stuttered the accused lancer, glancing from the bearded man to the woman.

Cerryl fixed his eyes on the woman. "Did you steal the lancer's purse?"

"I stole nothing."

"Did you offer yourself to him for coins?"

"He forced himself on me." The woman drew herself up as much as possible with the two lancers restraining her.

"She had a knife, ser," added one of the lancers holding the woman.

"What about the knife?" Cerryl asked.

"I had no knife. What would I do with a knife against such a brute?"

Cerryl smiled tiredly and turned to the lancers. "Bring her out into the street here. Let her go and stand away from her."

The two men looked at each other, then frog-marched the dark-haired woman forward, abruptly releasing her.

Cerryl seized chaos and flung it, almost contemptuously. *Whhhsst!* Where the woman had stood was a pillar of fire.

The man in the green vest ripped himself out of the hands of the lancer and started to run.

Despite his headache, Cerryl forced himself to concentrate.

*Whhssst!* A second firebolt created another heap of flaming charcoal that subsided to white ash.

Cerryl looked at the stunned single lancer. "They lied. You did also, but not so much. If I find you like this again, you'll join them." His eyes went to the two unknown lancers—from Fydel's forces probably, since he recognized neither. "Tell your comrades."

"Yes, ser."

Cerryl glanced at Ferek, then Hiser, before turning the gelding toward the low hill that held their quarters.

"Darkness-fired lucky, you were . . ."

"Coulda been you . . ."

"Fair . . . he is . . . cold as the Westhorns, too."

Cold? Cerryl almost laughed, half in frustration. *You'll be the most disliked mage in Candar the way things are going. Or the second most disliked, after Jeslek.*

He leaned forward and patted the gelding's neck. Horses didn't talk back or mutter behind his back. At least, his didn't.


# CXII

Chaos by itself guarantees neither prosperity nor the failure of prosperity; chaos guarantees but life, while order in excess must lead to death.

The nature of man is that of chaos, and not of order, for man is alive, as is chaos, and the goal of order is perfect stillness and all parts of a whole in an unchanging array.

Yet chaos unchecked is as ruinous to a prosperous land as order unchecked, and the excesses of man can be checked successfully only by the application of chaos bounded by order.

Order applied directly to that which is man will retard, if not destroy, that spirit of life nurtured by the flame of chaos; likewise, all life upon the world is nurtured by that flame of chaos that is the sun itself.

A land bound to chaos may fail to prosper, but it will not destroy itself, for chaos is as life; a land bound to order must, in the end, destroy itself, and all around it, for order is like the ice of the north in the times of the Great Chills, seeking always more order, until nothing lives within its scope.

A great mage must strive always to use chaos for prosperity, that is, growth and change bounded by the chill of order, yet never must he pay obeisance to order, for order will take his spirit and leave him a shell of what he might have been, as a mighty city empty of all souls, as a seed without kernel, as a hearth without flame . . .

> *Colors of White*
> (Manual of the Guild at Fairhaven)
> Part Two

# CXIII

In the private study, empty while he waited for Teras, Cerryl stood over the conference table and concentrated. The silver mists of the glass swirled, then parted.

Leyladin stood in the corner of the front foyer of the Halls of the Mages in Fairhaven. With her was the dark-haired Lyasa, and the two talked, apparently quietly, for there were few gestures. Abruptly Leyladin turned her head slightly and smiled but for an instant, and Cerryl knew she had sensed his presence through the glass. Lyasa raised her eyebrows, also momentarily, and Cerryl released the image.

He left the mirror glass on the table and walked through the archway from the small study into the front sitting room and up to the window, where he opened the shutter. Cold welled off the cloudy panes, intense cold, for all that little snow had fallen upon Elparta in the past eight-day.

The avenue beyond the front wall and the personal and carriage gates was empty for the moment. Cerryl shivered, though he was not cold, thinking of the lancers who had been disciplined and the villagers who worked for a few coppers—conscripted in effect—on restoring the walls and gates of Elparta.

One instant Elparta had been a functioning city on the river, the next a ruin. *Why? Because rulers disagreed . . . because the Guild insisted on existing and because people like Rystryr and Syrma and Estalin wanted golds more than prosperity for their people. And what of Anya and Jeslek? Are they any different, save that they seek power? Or the traders like Jiolt and Muneat?*

Cerryl snorted to himself. "The snare of power is that you think you do it for prosperity for all when it is for your own benefit."

"Ser?" asked the lancer standing inside the foyer.

"Nothing. A mage musing to himself." *As if it mattered, as if you will ever have that kind of power.* He shook his head. *You're deceiving yourself. You have power, if not so much as a Jeslek.* Still, he was having trouble with the limited power he had. He was trying to rebuild a city and keep order, and the lancers—at least some of them—hated him and the locals hated him because he represented Fairhaven.

And none of them really even understood Fairhaven. *You think that's surprising? Half the Guild doesn't.*

Teras stamped inside the front foyer, then closed the carved dark wooden door behind him. "Sorry being so slow, ser."

"That's all right." Cerryl waited until the big lancer hung his riding jacket on one of the pegs in the foyer, then turned and walked back to the study, sitting at one of the chairs beside the conference table. He gestured for Teras to sit down as the captain passed through the archway from the sitting room.

"Thank you, ser." Teras kept his eyes on Cerryl as he seated himself carefully, gingerly, as if he feared the chair might break under him.

"How are the quarters' houses faring in the cold?"

"About the same as barracks anywhere. Warmer than outside and colder than most would like, except for those raised in the hills, and they say it's too hot." Teras offered a rueful grin.

Cerryl nodded. "How are they finding the food?"

Teras shrugged. "They complain, but they know you eat what they eat. That suits them."

The captain had not mentioned Fydel, and Cerryl decided against bringing that question up. Fydel was using coins gained somewhere to improve the fare served at his private table, and all the officers knew that.

"It's plain," Cerryl said with a laugh. "I'm trying to get some dried fruit and nuts and more cheese, and coins to buy more eggs from the locals."

"You cannot take eggs from a peasant." Teras laughed.

Not when you couldn't even find the chickens, you couldn't, reflected Cerryl. "Teras? Why do you think we're here? In Elparta?"

"That'd not be wise of a captain to guess at the reasons of the High Wizards, ser. Begging your pardon." A grim smile crossed the hulking lancer's face, and Cerryl understood, again, why Teras remained a captain and would always remain a captain.

"I understand." In turn, Cerryl smiled. "From your viewpoint as a captain of lancers, after the work crews finish repairing the river walls, what should they do next?"

"Clear all the streets that yet have rubble in them. Let the locals repair dwellings as they wish or choose not to. Then if, as you say, the Guild and the lancers need to maintain a garrison here, we should have the workers build a proper barracks and stables. By the south gate, I would judge."

"That may have to wait until after spring. I was charged with having the piers and the river wall repaired first, and work on the wall is slow," Cerryl answered. "If I accompany the High Wizard in the spring, I will suggest the barracks to him."

Teras nodded, as if he expected no more.

Cerryl almost frowned. Was that the answer? Spread out the members of the Guild so that their presence was accepted and understood—and backed with lancers as necessary? He wanted to laugh. While it might work, who would listen to him? All the powerful mages wanted to be in Fairhaven, where the prestige and the power seemed to lie. *Is it that way in all lands?*

He forced his attention back to the lancer captain and on learning what else he needed to know.

# CXIV

The sound of the gelding's hoofs was muffled by the span or so of snow that coated the cobblestones of the avenue from the south gate. Cerryl glanced over his shoulder, barely able to see the four lancers acting as his guards through the snow that had begun to fall as he had left the sawmill—snow and cold that helped block off the lingering odors of decay and death and pillaging, snow that gave him a headache, if not one so sharp as from rain.

*Good thing you don't need too much more in the way of lumber . . . not until spring, and then there won't be enough.* He hoped he could put off worrying about lumber until spring. He had enough other problems to worry about—and far sooner.

Snow kept building up on the collar of his jacket, seemingly faster than he could brush it away, and then melting and oozing down his back. *Because you didn't think to wear a hat.*

One of the next problems was rope. "How could anyone dock a boat or barge without rope?" Jidro had asked. Even the chandlery had none, or so little—fifty cubits' worth of light line—as to be worthless. And then there was the lack of firewood. With no real woodlots within a kay of Elparta and the snow getting deeper, stocks of seasoned wood were nearly gone. Fydel, of course, had merely insisted that it was Cerryl's job to supply firewood—and everything else.

One supply barge had arrived from Gallos—surprisingly—but it had carried mainly barrels of flour and some excessively salted pork, and a half-dozen large rounds of cheese. The lancers might not starve, but they would complain, more than usual.

Cerryl swallowed the exasperation he felt, and his eyes flicked toward the last of the quarters' houses on his left. Before long—another four hundred cubits or so—they would reach the street that led uphill toward the dwelling serving as his office and headquarters.

The faintest hint of a taper glimmered through cracks in the shutters of the dwelling ahead on the left—the house used by one of Senglat's subofficers to house his company. Cerryl frowned, trying to recall the man's name. No, it was a woman, one of the few subofficers who was. Jrynn, that was it.

"Ser . . . ?" The voice was soft, gentle . . . feminine

Cerryl turned his head, hesitating momentarily. He sensed not only a figure in the alleyway to his right blurred by the white curtain of snow and the all-too-early gloom of a winter's eve but also a muted sense of chaos—and another form behind the first.

*Thwunnnggg.*

He threw himself sideways in the saddle even before the sound of the crossbow echoed off the walls and uneven stones of the narrow alleyway, then turned the gelding toward the figure—or figures. One reached for something—another crossbow?

Cerryl grasped for chaos, fighting the deadening effect of the snow, fighting the twisting in his guts, as the gelding quick-trotted toward the narrow passage between the ruined structures on the eastern side of the avenue.

*Whhssstt!* The muted, dampened firebolt seemed to crawl through the white curtain, and Cerryl struggled to gather more chaos, gasping as he did, almost as though he were underwater and fighting his way to the surface of a raging river.

He summoned more chaos, flinging it as well, silently, through the whiteness that seemed to retard and muffle his efforts.

Behind him, other mounts followed. "Ser? What is it! Ser?"

Cerryl reined up, abruptly, as the second figure toppled sideways, feet skidding sideways. Cerryl's breathing was ragged, and he felt drained. The kind of effort he had raised should have destroyed an entire dwelling. It had not, only burned away part of the shoulder and chest of the woman who had called and the side of the man's face and left a charred hole in his chest.

Cerryl tried to catch his breath. He looked at the two figures, almost sadly.

Once the woman had been beautiful, the man probably well built. The remnants of a uniform were visible under the ragged brown cloak.

"Do you recognize him, Buetyr?" Cerryl asked the lancer who had drawn his own mount up beside the gelding.

"No, ser. Not much left of his face." The swallow was audible, despite the muffling effect of the snow.

Cerryl waited, letting his strength rebuild. *A friend of one of the troublemakers? The troublemaker who had deserted? A local who had stolen a uniform? What about the woman? Who knows? The only thing certain is that whatever you do will disturb someone.*

"Now what, ser?" asked Buetyr.

"A moment," Cerryl said tiredly. "A moment." The snow sifted down past his collar again, and he shivered. Then he slowly, and gently, channeled more chaos toward the bodies lying on the thin blanket of whiteness.

*Whhhstttttt . . .* The last firebolt drifted across the bodies.

After the momentary flash of light and heat, white ashes mixed with the falling snow, both drifting in the gentle and cold wind that gusted along the street, sweeping ashes and snowflakes, lifting them, shifting them.

Cerryl flicked the reins and turned the gelding back toward his quarters, knowing that once more there would be speculations about his harshness and questions about what he had done to merit such an attack. *No one wants justice . . . or fairness . . . just their own comfort.*

The snow swallowed his deep breath, as it had swallowed much of the chaos he had flung, and buried the ashes of the two he had killed.


# CXV

Cerryl slipped into the high room that overlooked the river walls, the building that Fydel had declared as his headquarters as soon as Cerryl's crafters had reinforced and repaired the frame timbers and replaced the shutters and the glass in shattered windows. Cerryl had to admit that the room and the two wide windows did provide a useful view of both the river walls and the southern gate. The middle trading gate was too far north to see.

The younger mage studied the river walls where the work crew still toiled in the late-afternoon shadows. Small as the crews were, they might be struggling with the stones as the weather permitted until close to spring. Although the past eight-day had been warmer, enough to melt away some of the snow in the midpart of the day, Cerryl could scarcely count on the semithaw lasting much longer.

"You asked for me to join you." Cerryl turned toward Fydel, who had remained seated behind a table that had clearly come from some other dwelling, ornate and trimmed with brass as it was.

The square-bearded wizard studied the unfolded parchment on the table. Beside it lay fragments of blue wax from the seal that had closed it. Beyond him the smoke-smudged stones that might once have been white framed a large hearth in which burned a pile of ample logs. "The Spidlarian Traders' Council sent a message."

Cerryl nodded, waiting, feeling the draft around his trousers, a draft that showed how much his apprentice crafters did not know. Whistling outside the window, the wind still did not drown out the clink of masons' trowels and stones. The candles in the three-branched candelabra flickered with the gusts that found their way around the ill-fitting window.

Fydel stood and walked to the cloudy glass of the window. Below, the conscripted village troublemakers and the lancer disciplinary cases toiled with the stones of the walls, slowly dragging them back into position for the masons. Dark clouds overhead promised more snow or possibly freezing rain, but neither yet fell.

Finally, Cerryl, hunched in a heavy white wool cloak that Hiser had presented him from somewhere, spoke. "What are they offering?"

"Just about everything to save their necks," laughed Fydel. "They'll turn over any of the 'unfaithful'; effectively disband the guards by reducing them to a handful of squads; open the roads to our traders."

"Why aren't you taking their offer?" asked Cerryl.

"You assume too much."

Cerryl laughed softly. "I'm assuming nothing. You won't take the Spidlarian Council's offer. I'd just like to know why."

"Isn't it obvious? Why hand it to Jeslek? He's back in Fairhaven, enjoying fires, good food, and a few other pleasures." A wide grin revealed large white teeth. "Who knows? We might get a better offer before spring."

"We won't. What you're hoping is that Jeslek will have to face some mighty Black. Like this Brede? Or that the smith Dorrin will turn out to be greater than Jeslek thinks." *Or that I'll make more mistakes.* "That won't happen."

"It could. The smith has produced some nasty weapons."

"You don't believe that."

"No." Fydel smiled. "But there's no reason to make it easy for Jeslek, is there? No real reason to hand him an easy victory after he's muddled through a year of doing nothing, is there?"

"What about the levies? Why kill them off unnecessarily?"

"You're too soft, Cerryl. What are a few hundred peasants one way or the other? Especially peasants from Hydlen and Gallos."

Cerryl shook his head but said nothing.

"Here. Read it. Tell me if I'm wrong." Fydel reached down and picked up the scroll and handed it to the more slender White mage. After Cerryl took it and began to read, Fydel reseated himself at the table with his right side to the hearth.

The sunlight dimmed, and the room seemed to cool immediately as the first of the gray and white clouds from the north passed before the sun.

Fydel looked up only when Cerryl set the scroll back on the table before the older mage. "Is it not as I said?"

"It is." Cerryl frowned.

"You seem disturbed."

"Concerned. Concerned." Cerryl stepped closer to the hearth, but not to Fydel. "The traders do not sound like men who have fought off another land for a year. They do not write as men who have mages and war leaders from Recluce fighting for them."

"Perhaps the Black Isle has abandoned them. Recluce has done that before."

"The smith remains in Diev, and he forges strange things out of black iron. I've seen that in the glass." Cerryl turned. "Have you not told me that your patrols are still attacked, if by small numbers of blue lancers?"

"We've lost but a half-score since the turn of the year. Nothing."

The younger mage shrugged. "Nothing, but the tactics remain as they were, and that would suggest that their Black warleader remains here in Spidlar."

"What are you saying, Cerryl?"

"Nothing." Cerryl shook his head. "Perhaps you should take their terms. Or make a counteroffer."

"And let Jeslek . . . ? No."

"Then send him the terms. Ask for his advice."

"Why should I do that?"

"So that you don't give him another excuse to get angry at you."

Fydel pursed his lips, then fingered his beard. "Perhaps I should, although it may take some time for their message to reach the High Wizard. The Easthorns are closed, except for the Great White Highway through Gallos, and it will take eight-days for a messenger to reach there."

"As you see fit." Cerryl nodded. "Might I be of other service?"

"Only if you can get the walls completely repaired, so that we don't need so many patrols and sentries."

"We're working on that."

"Good."

"I will talk to you later." Cerryl stepped away from the hearth and nodded to Fydel before departing. As he walked down the stairs and out into the chill where the gelding was tied, the wind whistled and the sound of stonework echoed through the window. Behind him, in the high room above, the candles flickered in the late afternoon.

The bright first yellow-orange light reflected off the newly dropped snow, through the slits at the side of the shutters and into the sitting room, and then into the study—cascading across the glass and disrupting Cerryl's concentration.

He blinked twice, then rubbed his forehead, letting the mists in the screeing glass dissipate. He looked straight down but saw only his own reflection—thin brown hair, narrow chin, straight nose, gray eyes with faint circles beneath them—his own image and the image of the dark-beamed ceiling above.

For the fourth day . . . he could not find Leyladin in his glass. There might be many reasons. She could be in a place where the glass was blocked, like on a ship or traveling a large river or somewhere amid hills filled with order and iron, or she could be shielding herself, as Cerryl could do if he worked at it. There were reasons, but her continued absence bothered him.

He walked to the sitting room window and closed the front shutters—slightly ajar—all the way. Ignoring the lancer guards in the front foyer and the chill that held the room, he returned to the polished wooden table and the blank glass. Was he losing his ability to seek out Blacks? Had he used chaos too much, careful as he had tried to be?

He concentrated once more.

The silver mists swirled, then dissipated to reveal the redheaded smith of Diev, tongs in hand, sliding a chunk of highly ordered iron from the forge onto an anvil. A striker stood in the background, extending a hammer to the smith.

A puzzled look appeared on Dorrin's face, and Cerryl let the image lapse. Like Leyladin, the Black could sense a glass seeking his image.

But where was Cerryl's blonde healer? *Careful . . . she's not yours. She's not anyone's.*

He took a deep breath. *Maybe tomorrow.*

# CXVII

Why did you want me here?" Fydel stepped from the foyer into the sitting room. He stopped short of the archway into the study where Cerryl stood beside the circular table, empty except for the screeing glass.

"I wanted you to see something before Jeslek arrives."

"He won't be here for another eight-day."

"I would say less than five days." Cerryl gestured for Fydel to study the glass in which he held an image. "Look."

In the glass appeared the redheaded smith. Dorrin and an older man stood beside a cart. The contents of the cart could not be discerned, but the image rippled with the force of unseen and concentrated order.

"He's a Black. He's calling forth order. What else is new?" Fydel's voice contained equal parts of boredom and scorn.

"He's calling forth nothing," corrected Cerryl. "That's from the black iron in the cart."

"He's wasted all that order, sinking it into that much black iron. What can he do with it? You can't work black iron, not once it's ordered." Fydel straightened, as if to dismiss the image and the redheaded smith.

"Look at what's behind him," suggested Cerryl. He felt the sweat building on his forehead with the strain of holding the image against the twisting of the massive order displayed through the glass. *How can Fydel be so blind?*

"It's an old scow on blocks."

"It's being refitted and all that black iron is going into it."

"Some sort of order device?" Fydel laughed. "To use against us? What good would it do? That's a ship, and he's in Diev. We're attacking down a totally different river. He's wasting his time."

"How many lancers did you lose last summer? To those hidden black iron traps? And to that Black armsleader?" Cerryl's voice was pointed.

Fydel flushed above his wide beard. "He never fought. He just rode away except when he could kill defenseless lancers."

"The glass says that they're gathering more of their own lancers, and levies." Cerryl released the image in the screeing glass and blotted his steaming forehead on the lower sleeve of his heavy white shirt. "How many lancers and armsmen do we have here?"

"Now? Not quite 25-score lancers. Only 10-score footmen."

"And Jeslek insists that we will have 250 score after the turn of spring?"

"More like 300."

"If it's like last summer, we'll lose nearly half—and that's without whatever that smith can do."

"It won't be like last summer. We'll just burn everything, if that's what it takes. We'll march people in front of us again. Let them kill their own." Fydel offered a mocking smile. "Was that what you wanted me to see?"

"Yes." Cerryl returned the smile. "Before Jeslek returned. So that we both know you know what the smith is doing."

Fydel's smile faded. "You think you're clever, Cerryl. So did Myral, and Kinowin. One's dead, and the other's dying. Clever doesn't set well in the Guild. Sverlik thought he was clever, too, and the old prefect filled him with iron arrows. Jenred was another clever one. He was so clever that Recluce is around today and everyone calls him a traitor."

Cerryl forced a smile. "I'm not clever, Fydel. If I were clever, you wouldn't know what I did. Anya's the clever one."

"We aren't talking about Anya, little mage."

Cerryl raised his order shields, just slightly, ready to divert any chaos that the dark-bearded mage might raise. "We were talking about clever, Fydel."

Fydel turned his back to Cerryl, then looked over his shoulder and added, "Jeslek doesn't like clever. I don't either." He turned and lumbered out, his white boots heavy on the wood floor of the front room and foyer.

Cerryl stood in the silence for a short time. *Amazing how much less friendly Fydel has become as you've become more accomplished.* He smiled ruefully and sadly, then blinked several times, before bending his head forward, trying to stretch all-too-tight neck muscles.

He glanced down at the polished wood of the table, smeared at the edge where Fydel had rested his big hands, and at the mirror glass upon it. He still hadn't been able to find Leyladin in the glass, and his stomach turned at the thought that something might have happened to her.

With a deep breath he walked to the foyer and took his leather riding jacket off the polished walnut peg, pulling it on in quick movements. At least, he could ride down to the piers and the trading gates and check on the latest progress on the wall. *You can do that. You can't find the woman you love, but you can get walls and piers built. And kill people to keep others in line.*

His lips tightened as he marched out to the small stable to groom and saddle the gelding.

# CXVIII

Cold and gray, leaden, the River Gallos swirled past and under the refurbished piers of Elparta, around the forward stone pillars sunk into the riverbed, half-rushing, half-almost-thudding against the stone groins that contained the water and supported the rear of the piers.

Cerryl stood on the southernmost of the refurbished piers, where the wind blew out of the west, nearly straight into his face, disarranging his thin brown hair and surrounding him with the metallic odor of river, mud, and the hint of rotten vegetation.

Already the fast-moving clouds from the west covered more than a quarter of the green-blue sky, and the air seemed more chilled than it had at dawn. *Another storm.*

Behind Cerryl, the trading gates stood open. There was no reason to close them, given the state of the river wall, where the work crews still toiled, some two hundred cubits farther north, to rough-repair the city walls. Two squads of lancers waited, mounted, by the open trading gates. With them were a half-dozen spare mounts, since Cerryl had no idea how many might be accompanying Jeslek and who, if any, might need a mount.

According to Cerryl's screeing at midmorning, the five barges should have already been nearing Elparta. He wished he could have gotten a better image in the glass, but all the water around the barges made screeing difficult, sometimes impossible, with the shifting blackness of order that running water seemed to create. He shifted his weight from one foot to the other, then glanced sideways at Fydel.

Fydel continued to look southward—upstream, ignoring Cerryl's momentary scrutiny.

Cerryl turned and walked a few steps back toward the wall, then out to the end of the pier once more, passing Fydel.

"The High Wizard will arrive." The square-bearded mage offered a smile closer to a smirk. "Jeslek wears best in his absence. Especially for those who would be clever. Do not be so eager for his return."

It wasn't Jeslek—but there had been something about the barges in the glass, something . . . and Cerryl had not been happy to discover that he still could not find Leyladin in the glass. An eight-day before she had been riding somewhere with her father's traders, and now—now she had vanished. Did that mean she had taken a sea voyage? Cerryl turned and walked back toward the gates, then back to the end of the pier. Jeslek might know about Leyladin. The High Wizard had to know.

Cerryl paced the pier a dozen times or more before a call rang out from the lookout on the south tower: "Boat ho!"

The gray-eyed mage strained, watching the leaden water, squinting for some sign. Then the barge appeared. A thin green and gold banner flew below the ensign of Fairhaven—a trader's banner. Cerryl smiled. Had Leyladin managed to send something else? *What?* He shrugged—it didn't matter. That she had was what counted, because that meant she was all right.

*You hope.* He pushed away the thought as Fydel walked across the rough-sawn planks to stand beside him.

"Best we seem pleased," said Fydel, almost dryly. The older mage gestured upriver at where yet another barge had appeared. "Perhaps we should be. The High Wizard has doubtless brought us more than flour and salted pork."

Cerryl nodded. Although he enjoyed good food, he also remembered the lean years at the mines, and the past winter's fare, while plain, had been far better than that of the winters of his early youth.

On the upper level of the wide-beamed barge, above the mounts in tight stalls, above the bales and crates, stood the High Wizard. Cerryl swallowed. On Jeslek's right stood Anya, but on his left, a pace removed, stood a figure in green. Leyladin's short golden hair fluttered above her shoulders in the chill wind, and Cerryl felt his own pulse thundering in his ears, in his entire being. He edged forward on the pier, closer to the bollards.

As the rivermen jumped off the lead barge and snaked heavy hemp lines around the crude log bollards, Cerryl glanced at the second and third barges, packed with armed footmen, looking better than the levies of the summer before, if not as professional as the White Lancers. But his eyes went back to the blonde healer and the smile that made the cold day of late winter an early spring.

"A surprise for you, I see." Fydel laughed. "Were there such for me."

Cerryl couldn't help feeling a touch of sadness for the square-bearded mage, foolish as Fydel was to be attracted to Anya. "It comes when you do not expect it."

"For some."

Cerryl stepped almost to the edge of the pier planks as the boatmen tied the barge in place.

Jeslek was the first onto the pier. Although ruddier than when he had left Elparta in early winter, he appeared thinner, if not quite gaunt, and some of the circles beneath his eyes remained. "Fydel, Cerryl—you have made much progress." The sun-gold eyes merely sparkled, and he nodded as he surveyed the rebuilt piers and the river wall.

Leyladin vaulted over the gunwale of the gray-timbered barge, and Cerryl leaped forward to steady her. He caught her arm, and they stood there, on the heavy crude planks of the river pier, less than a cubit apart, as if neither could believe the other's presence.

"I can't believe . . ." Cerryl's mouth felt dry.

"Neither can I."

"How . . . ?" he stammered.

"Let us say that Kinowin's tongue and Father's golds were persuasive." Leyladin's hands reached out and took his.

He squeezed hers, wanting to draw her closer.

"Leyladin has already proved most useful." Anya's smile was tighter yet slightly less false than usual.

Cerryl turned, jarred by the redhead's words. He hadn't even sensed her approach, but close as she stood, the trilia and sandalwood were overpowering.

"I did what any good mage would do for others." Leyladin's gentle smile turned as hard and false as Anya's, and her green eyes glittered like frozen emeralds.

"We are all appreciative, Leyladin dear, especially young Cerryl, I'm sure." Anya turned to Jeslek even before finishing her words.

Leyladin's lips tightened for a moment.

"Another reason for shields?" His fingers squeezed hers again.

The chill left the healer's face and eyes. "I don't need them now." She slipped forward, disengaging his hands and wrapping her arms around him in a firm hug. "I missed you."

"Missed you."

For a time, they just held each other.

The pier shuddered as the second barge rebounded from it and then against the ropes. Even as he released Leyladin and turned toward where Jeslek and Anya stood talking to Fydel, Cerryl couldn't help but feel some satisfaction as the barge was tied into place against the new solidity of the pier.

". . . few more attacks, but we only lost a handful of lancers . . . Cerryl has been busy supporting us with all the rebuilding . . . good at support."

Cerryl wanted to wince at the belittling comment but didn't, forcing a smile as he and Leyladin, still holding hands, stepped toward the other three.

The pier shivered again as the third barge was moored downstream of the first two. Cerryl glanced out at the river, seeing that yet another barge made for the lower piers.

Jeslek followed his eyes. "Just the first. A mere fifteen score. Prefect Syrma has committed to sending a hundred score within the next three eight-days. We yet have another fifteen-score lancers two days south of here."

*How did he do it?*

"How? I suggested that he would not want the fate of Elparta to befall Fenard. I also told him that there were a dozen mages that could do so and that the Guild would put up with no more nonsense."

"He also turned the subprefect into ashes at dinner—and the arms commander and about ten enraged captains," said Anya dryly.

"Anya offered some assistance." Jeslek smiled. "Prefect Syrma decided that cooperation was preferable to annihilation."

Both Cerryl and Leyladin continued to smile faintly, but Cerryl could tell she felt the same emptiness as he did.

For all that Fairhaven offered, was the only way to force its prosperity on the other lands of Candar? Lands that unceasingly wanted the benefits of prosperity and good roads without contributing to them.

Seeing a lancer captain Cerryl did not recognize, Jeslek gestured abruptly. "Get the mounts off first."

"Aye, ser." The captain turned and called back to a figure in purple standing on the bow, "The mounts be first!"

"The mounts, aye. Up with the ramp."

Two rivermen slid a wooden ramp into place between the barge and the pier.

"The walls are new," Leyladin said.

"Look to the north, at the end there. That's the way it all was," Cerryl said.

A shadow fell across the piers, accompanied by a gust of wind, cold and foretelling yet more snow before the turn of spring.

"Your mount, High Wizard," said a lancer, leading forward a bay with crimson and white livery, although some of the white trim was almost yellow. "Been watered, but I'd not ride far."

"Only to my quarters." Jeslek eased himself into the saddle, and Anya had to hurry to mount and ride alongside him. Behind the two rode a good score of lancers who had been on the barge.

Fydel stood back, a sardonic smile on his face.

As he turned to watch the High Wizard depart, by the left gate Cerryl glimpsed the spritely white-haired Jidro, a smile on his face as he looked at the piers and barges.

Another lancer appeared with a black mare. "Lady Leyladin, our thanks."

"I am glad I could make things easier." The healer smiled, then mounted.

Cerryl walked alongside Leyladin as she rode the several dozen cubits to where his gelding was tethered next to the squad of lancers headed by Hiser.

As Cerryl swung up into the saddle, Hiser eased his own chestnut forward. "Ser? You be heading back to quarters?"

"Yes. The healer will be coming with me." Was he being too abrupt? But where else would she stay? He turned. "If that's all right?"

"I'd say that would be best." Her lips almost curled into a smile, and her eyes did smile.

"... don't think she'd be with anyone else," murmured Fydel in the background.

Cerryl guided the gelding through the open trade gates toward the main avenue, and Hiser and his squad fell in behind them. Leyladin rode so closely that their legs almost brushed.

Cerryl found his eyes wandering to her. "What did you do for the lancers?"

"Brought some dried fruit, nuts, some good travel bread, and cheese." Her voice faded out as they rode past the refurbished quarters' dwellings and turned onto the avenue, where most of the damage from Jeslek's attack remained untouched. One house stood gaping like a skull, shutters gone, door vanished. "Is it all like that?"

"More than half of Elparta. It's been hard enough to get the piers rebuilt and the gates and walls—and enough houses to quarter everyone." Cerryl coughed. "With another thirty score coming in ... I don't know. The winter's long here, and it's not over yet."

"Most will not linger here that long," prophesied Leyladin.

"If the Spidlarians do not hold them back."

"There is yet another duke in Hydlen, and this one will send levies."

"Jeslek and Anya paid a visit to Hydolar?"

"No. Eliasar seized Renklaar. The port belongs to Fairhaven now."

Cerryl nodded. That made sense. If the Hydlenese valued coins more than loyalty, then take that which controlled their coins. *Should Fairhaven take Lydiar? And Ruzor—after Spidlaria?*

"That was Sterol's idea. I don't think he thought Jeslek would heed it, but he did." Leyladin laughed, softly, bitterly.

A flurry of white flakes shivered from the clouds, and the wind picked up until it whistled intermittently.

"I'm glad you got here before the storm."

"You didn't know I was coming, remember?" she teased.

"I can still be glad." Cerryl gestured. "This way—up the long, narrow street there."

"Is it far?"

"Less than a kay."

*Whuff!* Leyladin's mare sidestepped as the wind blew a scrap of gray cloth across the way before them. "It's so ... empty."

"Jeslek's terms were hard. Most of the people fled. A few have returned."

"Your terms aren't so hard?"

"I try to apply the Patrol rules here, even to lancers. Sometimes I haven't been that popular."

"Why? The rules are fair."

"I've executed three or four lancers and several locals. One lancer raped and killed a local woman—a harlot, and she shouldn't have stayed, but that didn't mean she could be killed."

"Still trying . . ." She turned in the saddle and smiled sadly. "Even if you became High Wizard, you'd be disappointed."

"Probably more so. Things wouldn't work out, and I couldn't blame Jeslek."

They turned onto the short hilltop lane that held the quarters' dwelling.

"There, at the end."

"I like it better up here," Leyladin affirmed.

"Jeslek's is the big mansion—over there to the north. There's a back lane, and it's about two hundred cubits."

"Don't tell him. Make him ride the long way."

"I'm the one who goes to him." Cerryl's mouth quirked. "Remember?"

Leyladin giggled as they reined up by the carriage gate. They groomed both the mare and the gelding and put them in the two adjoining stalls in the small stable of Cerryl's quarters, then made their way through the light snow into the front foyer, stepping past the two lancer guards.

Cerryl turned. "Zoyst, Natrey, this is the Lady Leyladin—one of the few healers. She'll staying here."

"Yes, ser."

"I'm pleased to meet you both." Leyladin smiled warmly.

Though neither guard returned the smile, Cerryl could feel their reserve lower. *She can do that, and I can't. They respect me, I think, but everyone loves her. Almost everyone, except Anya.*

Cerryl gestured toward the front sitting room.

"These are your quarters? I expected . . ." She crossed the room and peered through the archway at the desk and table in the rear study.

"Something more like a lancer's?" Cerryl asked. "I do have a few rooms to myself, but I eat what the lancers eat."

"And you make sure they know that, I'm sure." Leyladin's eyes twinkled. "You don't sleep here, do you?" She gestured toward the conference table.

"I spend more time here." He paused, then added, "Oh . . . I'll show you." He took her hand, and they walked to the foyer and the narrow steps up. "Up there." He pointed to the top of the staircase.

"Do you mind if I look?"

"There are two other bedchambers up there. One is empty. I mean . . . there's a bed and everything."

Leyladin smiled again. "I understood." She started up the steps, and, after a moment, Cerryl followed.

The healer looked into the bedchamber on the left, then crossed the landing and stepped into the larger chamber. "This is lovely." She studied the four-poster bed, the small settee, and the curved rails of the wash table. "You've even kept it neat."

"There's nothing like the showers of the Halls," Cerryl said, "and I have to heat the water with chaos."

"You'll be . . . good . . . to have around." The healer took a half-step toward the still-shuttered window, then turned, still smiling.

"Are you hungry? There are some biscuits and cheese in the kitchen. Nothing like Furenk's around here. I'm not sure there ever was." Cerryl started for the doorway and the steps down to the kitchen.

"Cerryl?"

He stopped.

"You may have seen me through your glass, but I haven't seen you in more than a year. You don't have to rush off after biscuits."

"I do," Cerryl confessed. "I'm starving. I haven't been able to see you in the glass for more than an eight-day. I haven't eaten much."

An even softer smile appeared. "I actually worried you? I just wanted to surprise you, and I didn't want to worry you. It was work, holding those shields on the road."

"You surprised me."

"I could stand something to eat." She shook her head. "But there's something more important."

Cerryl froze. What had he overlooked?

"Nothing like that." She stepped forward. Not only did her arms encircle him, her lips on his, but her body was against his as well, far warmer, far more yielding, and far more demanding . . .

*Forget about biscuits* . . . His arms went around her.

# CXIX

Cerryl glanced over at the blonde head on the pillow beside him, then leaned back in grayness before dawn. *After all these years . . . why now?*

". . . waited all these years . . ." Leyladin's voice was thick with sleep, but she turned toward him. ". . . you waited, too."

"I saw you in the glass . . . more than a half-score of years ago." He propped himself up on his left elbow to study her, and his fingers traced the line of her chin.

"I didn't know who you were, then."

"I didn't know who you were, either."

"I haven't changed much."

"You still like green."

Leyladin wrapped her shift around her as she sat up against the headboard, a pillow behind her.

"You don't need that," teased Cerryl. "The shift, I mean."

"Oh?" She arched her eyebrows.

"You didn't last night."

"That was last night." The archness of her voice broke into a laugh. Cerryl laughed with her.

After a moment, she cleared her throat. "Oh . . . I'd better tell you. Kinowin made me promise."

"Promise what?" Cerryl didn't want to talk about Kinowin or Jeslek or anyone else.

"He had a message, one he didn't want to write down." Leyladin shook her head. "He's getting old, like Myral did. He was always so tall and strong, and now he's a little stooped, and he has to concentrate when he walks so that he doesn't shuffle."

"So quickly?"

"It happens quickly." Her eyes misted as she looked at Cerryl.

He shivered, knowing yet another reason why she had come to Spidlar.

"It's not that—yet." Her voice thickened. "Life is short enough . . . It's too short."

Cerryl was already discovering that. "Ah . . . what?"

Leyladin swallowed. "He said . . . you did not need to fight Jeslek. Just follow Myral's teaching about keeping chaos from you when you channel it, and you'll do what Myral expected."

"I wasn't thinking about fighting Jeslek."

"Kinowin didn't think so, but he wanted you to understand that Anya is the real danger to Fairhaven."

"Because she doesn't believe in it and because she's using her ties to Jiolt to influence the traders?"

Leyladin shook her head ruefully. "Why am I telling you this?"

"Because I might not have known and because it helps for someone else to think the same thing and because I trust you and Kinowin." He paused, thinking about the silksheen he had never been able to follow up on—that he had *known* went to Jiolt. "Besides, a lot of what I know about Anya is from what I sense but couldn't ever prove. So it helps to know others have discovered things or feel the same way." Cerryl's stomach growled—loudly.

"I suppose I should let you eat." Leyladin leaned forward and her lips brushed his cheek.

"If you want to abuse me like you did last night . . ."

"Abuse? Who abused whom?"

Cerryl found himself flushing.

"You're handsome when you do that."

"Do what?"

"Blush." Leyladin grinned. "It goes all the way down."

Cerryl knew he was red at least from the waist up. "You."

"Go on. You get dressed first."

"Me?" Cerryl swallowed, realizing that any more byplay and he'd only embarrass himself more.

"You can figure out what we'll eat while I'm dressing."

"Oh."

"Let a poor woman try to regain a little mystery."

"Mystery—that you'll always have." Cerryl put his feet on the rug around the four-poster bed, then walked to the wash table. The water was cold, and he took a moment to infuse it with chaos.

After shaving and dressing, he emptied the water out the north side window, where it did little damage, adding to the icy pyramid against the brick below, and refilled it.

"Close the window . . . please."

"I'm sorry." He closed the window and heated the water until it was almost steaming, even though his head was throbbing.

"Dearest . . . you didn't have to do that." Leyladin leaned forward, and Cerryl didn't care about the headache.

"You—you are impossible."

Suddenly he swallowed. "You know what I feel . . . some of the time."

"I didn't need much to know that." The playful smile vanished, and she nodded. "At times, you know what I feel. It happens, sometimes, with mages."

Cerryl sat down on the edge of the chair. "I just thought I was imagining."

"No . . . dearest. Why do you think I'm here?"

"Because I'm impossible?" He forced a smile.

"You know better than that."

This time his smile wasn't forced. He leaned over the bed and kissed his blonde healer, this time on the lips. "I'll leave you to your mystery."

"Go get something for us to eat—if you know how."

"I manage."

"Good."

Somehow, the gray day felt sunny as he clumped down the stairs in his heavy white boots.

# CXX

The wind outside had stopped wailing earlier in the day, as had the last of the snow flurries. The heavy snow of the past two days remained drifted across most of the streets of Elparta, except where the patrols had packed it into a second pavement—or ice.

Inside the mansion, the fire in the library hearth—where two fresh logs rested upon a heap of coals—still had not removed all the chill of disuse from the room. The High Wizard remained wearing a crimson-trimmed white wool cloak. Jeslek surveyed the table in the center of the library, the room that had again become his command post. His eyes went from Anya to Cerryl to Leyladin before finally settling on Fydel. "I received your message, just before we departed Fairhaven. Why did you feel disinclined to accept the terms offered by the Spidlarians?"

Fydel fingered his curly black beard and looked at the High Wizard. "I did not trust them. After I talked with Cerryl, I trusted the terms even less."

"Oh?" The High Wizard's gaze fell on the youngest mage. "Cerryl, what did you say that so swayed your comrade, the elder mage?" Irony crept into Jeslek's voice.

Cerryl offered a smile he wasn't sure he felt. "I do not recall the exact words, but there were several matters that bothered me. First, the Spidlarians fought for every span of ground, yet suddenly they offer terms that open the land to us? They offered terms that no land has ever accepted when conquered, not willingly.

"The viscount and the prefect are our allies and supporters, yet they avoid keeping their promises. Spidlar is an enemy that offers more than our declared friends? Why should we expect more from an enemy? Also, the smith mage Dorrin continues to forge implements and parts of something with so much black iron that the order nearly twists the glass when I view him. The attacks on our patrols continue, even now."

"With such logic, and such a high opinion of our declared friends, Cerryl, you would have Fairhaven take on all of Candar, and I doubt we can do such." Jeslek chuckled, albeit bitterly.

*Why not? It might be easier than all this posturing and dissembling.* "I never suggested such, High Wizard."

"Why is it that I mistrust words when my title is employed?"

Fydel covered his mouth with a hand, suggestive of a hidden smile. Anya's eyes brightened.

"I would not know, ser. You asked my reasons."

"Then what did your words suggest? Properly suggest?"

"I think that the large traders of Spidlar would offer anything to keep trading, but their armsmen might not be bound by such."

"Nor Recluce, either," suggested Jeslek. "Have we heard more from them?"

"No," answered Fydel.

"Just as well. Cerryl may have been right this time." Jeslek looked toward Cerryl. "Would you put another log on the fire?"

Cerryl nodded and slipped out of his chair. He took one log from the wood box built into the hearth and eased it into the fire, then followed with a second before returning to his chair.

"For the conquest of Spidlar we will need more mages with firebolts," Jeslek stated. "I have requested that another dozen mages join us before we begin the attack."

"Who?" asked Fydel.

"They are largely junior mages—your former assistant Buar, Myredin, Bealtur, Faltar, Kalesin, Ryadd, those are the ones I recall. Eliasar added some others."

"Why so many?" Faltar frowned.

"I intend to make an example of Spidlar so that we do not have to do the same to Hydlen, Certis, or Gallos."

Anya's smile broadened. "Hydlen deserves such."

"I would rather have Hydlen's golds than its corpses, dear Anya." Jeslek coughed once.

"So would I," murmured Fydel. "Gold is more pleasant to smell and more useful."

"Corpses do not hold onto their golds," countered Anya, "unlike traders. And traitors."

"Enough," snapped Jeslek. "Corpses don't earn more golds. Live traders do. Besides, the decision has been made." He inclined his head, fractionally, in the direction of Anya and then Leyladin.

The redhead rose smoothly from the chair, almost sinuously. "Fydel and Leyladin and I will depart then, since you have nothing else for us to hear or to undertake."

A puzzled look flitted across Fydel's countenance, but Anya took his arm with a smile. Leyladin offered a faint smile to Cerryl as she rose. After the door closed, Jeslek leaned back, but his eyes remained hard and glittering, fixed more on the roaring fire than upon the younger mage.

"The healer was most helpful, and I am certain she will remain so . . . so long as she holds to her course as a Black. And her sire supports the Guild and its efforts."

"I do not see that changing," Cerryl said carefully. "Layel is well aware of the advantages the Guild offers one such as him."

"What of the healer? Will you bed her until she is gray?"

*I don't see Anya's talents being changed by whom she beds.* "There is no reason why either of us should change. Not according to *Colors of White* or aught else I have studied." Cerryl kept his voice level.

"Too much closeness to a Black will weaken you," Jeslek's voice was flat. "You are not so strong as you consider yourself."

"I do not consider myself strong in comparison to you," Cerryl replied bluntly.

Jeslek laughed. "Ah, Cerryl, always honest about power. You deceive yourself about the healer, but not about power."

*But I do deceive about power.* "I try not to deceive myself where power is to be considered." *I try not to.*

Jeslek shook his head. "Go. Go and bed her . . . or whatever you choose. You are young, and you will see. Naught I can tell you will change that. Just remember. I have told you. Power is more true than any wench, and power is fickle indeed."

"By your leave?" Cerryl stood.

"By my leave . . . but throw another log on the fire before you go."

Cerryl was beginning to sweat, but Jeslek had still left the cloak wrapped around him. "Of course."

Jeslek did not even look up from the table and the glass before him when Cerryl left the library.

Did all White mages worry about their power being corrupted by close association with order? Or did Jeslek fear that Leyladin would make Cerryl somehow stronger? Cerryl concealed a frown as he stepped out into the corridor to find Leyladin.

# CXXI

Followed by the four lancers who trailed him everywhere, Cerryl reined up short of the section of the river wall where the work crew toiled in the sunlight, an afternoon warmer than any since fall. The crew numbered eleven, all locals of some sort.

The spritely white-haired Jidro set down an iron pry bar and walked toward the mage. "Best day in seasons, ser mage."

"I would agree. How are things going?"

"The boys and I'll have the wall 'side the river be finished afore long," Jidro said. "Took a mite longer than I'd thought. My recollections are better than my skills, these days."

"You've done good work, Jidro." Cerryl felt at his pouch, then extracted a silver, leaning down from the saddle and extending the coin. "This is extra."

"Ser." Jidro bowed. "I be thanking you, and saying that never did I think to get a bonus from a White mage."

"There's more work, if you want it."

A puzzled look crossed Jidro's face. "Word be that you folk be moving on."

"We are, but the other walls need repairs. Nor are the new sewers along the main avenues complete."

"I be willing, ser."

"Good. Kiolt is the one to see. He's a lancer subofficer. I'll tell him to expect you. If you have any trouble, I'll be here for a time yet." Cerryl turned his mount.

"Thanks to ye, ser mage."

"Thanks to you, Jidro."

Cerryl rode back along the avenue, noting that two men worked on another house across from the river wall. Both avoided looking at him and the lancers who trailed him.

"What was that all about?" Fydel had reined up just beyond the pier gate and waited for Cerryl. Four other lancers waited behind the square-bearded mage.

"Finishing the repairs."

"I don't see why you worry about the walls and the streets so much," said Fydel. "In another few eight-days most of us will be gone, headed downriver. You, too, this time."

"I know. But we have to leave a detachment, and I persuaded Jeslek to leave a few dozen golds to finish the important repairs. Kiolt has agreed to supervise them. His father was a mason."

"Why?"

Cerryl smiled. "Because it's cheaper than having to conquer the place again."

"We'll have to anyway, if it comes to that. People don't remember what happened last eight-day. You expect them to be grateful for fixing the damage we caused?"

"No. I think the locals here might remember that we can destroy or create, and the choice is theirs."

"Tell that to Jeslek or the Guild members in Fairhaven." Fydel flicked the reins and turned his mount to walk back toward the south gate.

Was Fydel right? Were most people so unperceptive? Or was it that too many White mages were contemptuous of the everyday people? Cerryl pondered as he rode up the hill. Pattera, the little weaver girl, had tried to warn him, years ago. Had he ever done one thing to repay her?

Cerryl winced at the recollection. And what of Tellis—who had taught him the art of scriving and made it possible for him to be a mage? *That's not so bad . . . He nearly threw you out when the Guild started looking for you.* Still . . . Tellis had helped him. *Are you any better than Fydel?*

Cerryl wasn't sure he was—or that he could answer himself honestly.

Back at his quarters, Cerryl stabled the gelding, glad to see that Leyladin's mare was in the adjoining stall. That meant she'd returned from her investigations to see what healing herbs and roots she had been able to find—or dig up from the partly frozen ground. He walked to the front entrance, where he nodded at the guards, stationed on the covered brick stoop outside the foyer now that the weather had improved.

"Zoyst, Natrey, everything all right?"

"Yes, ser. Glad to see the sun, ser," answered the darker Natrey.

"So am I." The mage stepped into the foyer, blinking for a moment as his eyes adjusted to the comparative gloom.

"Cerryl? Is that you?" Leyladin came down the steps slowly, rubbing her eyes. "I must . . . have fallen asleep."

"You've been healing more than you should. Your body is telling you need the rest."

"So many of them are so young."

"So many? Is Jeslek sending out scores already?" Cerryl frowned.

"No. There were just two, but I looked at all the others, and . . . many will die. One—he had a slash in his arm. The other—he took an iron shaft in the chest."

"Iron?"

"It was meant for Fydel, I think. From a crossbow."

*Iron shafts for mages?* Cerryl shivered. The advance into Spidlar could prove costly.

"You have to be careful," she said, stopping on the next to last step, so that she was taller than Cerryl, and putting her arms around him.

Cerryl saw the darkness in and around her eyes. "What about you? You can't spend so much of yourself on every lancer."

"I know," the healer acknowledged again. "I know. But I knew I could . . . this time. Was I supposed to let him die?"

"You'll have to let some die." *If you want to live.*

"It's hard. I didn't think it would be this way. I did, but I didn't." She squeezed Cerryl. "I wanted to be with you, and I wanted to help. Kinowin said it would be hard."

Cerryl returned the hug, then relaxed his hold so that he held her but loosely. "That's why some healers can't handle battles and wounds."

"I can see why." A faint smile appeared and faded.

"How is the lancer?" Cerryl wanted her to think about her success, not the pain.

"He'll be all right."

"But not for this season."

"No. He'll have to stay in Elparta."

"He may be one of the lucky ones." He squeezed her to him, again gently, then released her. "You need to rest. Have you eaten?"

"I had some cheese and some of the bread when I got back—and some of the joint."

"Good." He pointed upstairs. "You need rest, Lady Leyladin."

"Don't 'lady' me." She offered a mock pout.

"Then get some rest." He grinned.

She started to retort, then yawned. "Light! . . . You might be right."

"I am—once in a great while."

Leyladin stifled the yawn, then leaned forward and brushed his cheek. "This time . . ." Then she touched his cheek. "I know you care."

He watched until she disappeared at the top of the stairs, then turned and went to his study. He stared at the glass on the polished wood of the round table.

After a moment, he stepped forward, seeking the red-haired mage amid the silver mists of the glass. Dorrin was not in his forge, but upon the seat of a wagon, with another seated beside him—apparently a young-faced man wearing a broad-brimmed hat. In the wagon were objects wrapped in canvas, objects that radiated order even through the glass, so much that the image shimmered and wavered. After an instant, Cerryl let the picture fade.

The smith was bringing more infernal devices somewhere—doubtless to the Black warleader. *More devices to kill . . . and we will respond with chaos fire and lancers and more levies than the blues can raise.*

Cerryl sat down in the chair that faced the archway and the front window. His eyes ignored the glass before him on the table but did not see either the brick wall before the dwelling or green-blue sky beyond it.

After a time, the foyer door opened, and Natrey called, "A Mage Faltar to see you, ser Cerryl!"

"Send him in." Cerryl rose from the table and hurried into the sitting room toward the foyer.

At Faltar's name, Leyladin scurried down the steps from the second bedchamber she had claimed as her work space, even though the small desk was barely wider than a three-span plank. Then, as she had that morning, she spent a good half of each day checking the worst illnesses among the lancers, when she wasn't seeking out things like willow bark, astra, or brinn.

"Faltar . . ."

"Cerryl! Leyladin!" A broad smile beamed from the thin blond mage. "I'd hoped to find you together."

Leyladin offered a surprisingly shy smile.

"Can I get you something to drink?" asked Cerryl.

"Water is about all we have," apologized Leyladin. "Cerryl doesn't eat much better than his lancers."

Cerryl offered a shrug. "What can I say?"

"Don't," suggested Faltar.

"I'll get the water." Cerryl pointed across the sitting room. "Why don't you two sit at the round table?"

Both were seated in the small study when he returned with a pitcher and three goblets. "It's chaos-cleaned and chilled."

"Almost as good as ale," said Faltar.

"No," said Leyladin. "But the company is good. How was your trip?"

"Cold, especially west of Fairhaven. So cold that even Bealtur kept his mouth shut. I really didn't expect to be here." Faltar grinned sheepishly. "I've not been that industrious since you two left. Kinowin pulled me off gate duty and sent me off with the lancers. He told me to practice raising chaos and firebolts—if I wanted to get through the war. It is a war, isn't it? I didn't see that much going on, but we came through Gallos. The rest of the Easthorns won't be clear for eight-days. There were places where we still had to dig through snowdrifts."

"It is a war," Cerryl answered. "We still lose a few men every eight-day. The blues use archers and traps, and there aren't that many of them. They're hard to find."

"Do you have a place to stay?" asked Leyladin.

"Me? They put all of us mages—the three actually—in the guest house beside the High Wizard's headquarters. Jeslek met with us for a moment. He told us not to get comfortable in Elparta." Faltar glanced around the study and back through the archway. "It's hard to believe you're the city commander or Patrol chief or whatever here."

"Until we start the advance north," Cerryl answered.

"You're going?"

"Jeslek has been most insistent on that."

Leyladin nodded in agreement.

"You, too?" Faltar turned to the healer, eyebrows raised.

"What good is a healer where she can't heal people?"

"You can't heal everyone," protested Faltar.

"No . . . but I can hold back chaos for quite a few, and that way, more will recover."

*How many?* wondered Cerryl. *And for how long?* "Is anything happening in Fairhaven?"

Faltar gave a crooked smile. "Redark always says that he'll send a message to the High Wizard. Kinowin doesn't say much of anything, but usually he does something, quietly. The Guild raised the tariffs on traders, and one or two of the smaller ones sold off their stuff—what they could—and packed up. Piotal said he was going to Sarronnyn. I don't know what happened to Ziant. The poorer ale is up to four coppers at The Ram, and I wouldn't guess what it is at Furenk's." The blond mage spread his hands. "What else do you want to know?"

"Who are the others who came with you?" asked Leyladin.

"Buar and Kalesin. Bealtur, Myredin, and Ryadd are coming with the next group. Kinowin said others were coming later with Eliasar, but he's still in Renklaar. I guess he has to set up a Patrol there and a council or something for Gorsuch to use to run the place."

"Gorsuch? I thought he was in Jellico."

"He was, but Jeslek sent Disarj to replace him there—and Lyasa as his assistant. She wasn't too happy about that, said she'd end up doing everything."

Cerryl laughed. "She will, and that's why she's there."

"Having two mages around will make Rystryr more careful, too," suggested Leyladin, brushing a strand of blonde hair off her forehead.

Cerryl pursed his lips, worrying about the circles and the darkness under her eyes. *Trying to heal too many . . .*

"Myredin's not too pleased about being ordered to Spidlar, and you should see the new apprentice from Lydiar."

"Oh . . . ?" asked Cerryl. "I take it this apprentice is a woman."

"She's a redhead, and sweet, too."

Cerryl had to wonder about that. Faltar had fallen for Anya, once, as well. "Anya, without the . . . self-centeredness?"

"Anya was never as bad as you thought, Cerryl, but Viedra . . ." Faltar smiled even more broadly.

"I hope for your sake she makes it," offered Leyladin. "What about Heralt?"

"He's gone to Ruzor to help Myral's sister. You knew that Shenan was the Guild trade representative there, didn't you?"

"I'd heard something like that . . ."

"Jeslek doubled the representatives in the ports where there happened to be just one mage."

"Has anyone heard what Sterol is doing?"

"He stays to himself on the lower level of the White Tower. It's like he waits for something to happen."

*For Jeslek to fail? So he can claim the amulet again?* Cerryl refilled the goblets. He had much to learn about what had happened in Fairhaven, and Faltar would report what happened as it had. *Except for redheaded women.*

# CXXII

Around the circular table in the private library sat three White mages, a Black healer, and the High Wizard of Fairhaven. A low fire nearly guttered out in the hearth, sending thin intermittent trails of grayish smoke into the room.

Jeslek rose from his chair at one side of the table. Despite nearly two eight-days spent recovering from his trip from Fairhaven, dark circles rimmed the sun-gold eyes, but those eyes retained their flaring intensity as he surveyed the room.

"The plan is simple enough." Jeslek pointed to the map pinned to the easel, a map redrawn to combine Cerryl's screeing maps and older ones. "The combined lancers will sweep the two river roads. Once they have cleared the roads, or when they contact any massed enemy forces, we will use the river barges to transport the levies downstream to attack."

"What about all those traps the blues use?" asked Fydel.

"Those are road traps." The High Wizard smiled. "That is Cerryl's charge on the west river road, and Buar's and Faltar's on the east. We will not subject the bulk of our forces to such devices and stratagems. Cerryl has some considerable skill in detecting Black devices. He and his light lancers will scout in advance of the main body of lancers. Cerryl is not there to fight. He is there to discover traps and stratagems. If large blue lancer forces are present, he is to call up the full lancer forces under Captain Teras and under Gallosian overcaptain Grestalk. For now. Shortly Eliasar will be joining us to act as field commander."

Jeslek turned to Fydel. "You will command the lancer forces on the eastern bank and support Buar and Faltar as Teras will support Cerryl."

Fydel nodded slowly. "They are not so skilled as Cerryl."

"That is why I have put all three of you on the east bank. Lady Leyladin will remain with me and the bulk of the forces. Anya will begin with us, but she will handle the fast cavalry reserves, for anything unforeseen." Jeslek cleared his throat. "Have you any further questions?"

"How soon will we begin?" asked Cerryl.

"Three days from tomorrow morning. All should be ready tomorrow, but it will not be." Jeslek gave a knowing smile.

"Do the blues expect us to move now?" asked Fydel.

"They do not seem prepared," answered Anya. "Most of their forces remain near Kleth, except for the few patrols that harass us here."

"Their commander may have something else in mind," Cerryl volunteered. "So far, he has not been caught unprepared."

"Do you have any idea what that might be, Cerryl?" The momentary look of irritation on Jeslek's face faded into an ironic smile. "While this Brede is a good commander, he is young, and he must defer to his superiors, the traders. They do not wish to hazard their few remaining forces far from Spidlaria."

"He is not that good," mumbled Fydel under his breath.

"We have moved more ships into the Northern Ocean," added Jeslek, "to keep them from getting blades or supplies once their stocks run low. Their crops were not good last year, and they're short on mounts for their lancers and light cavalry."

"Have you discovered more about the smith?" Anya asked Cerryl.

"He has made some devices of black iron and carted them to Kleth, as I told the High Wizard an eight-day ago." Cerryl paused to swallow. "I cannot tell what the devices are, except that they hold great order. They feel like the one you recovered last year, so far as I can tell."

"That is why we will scout all the roads first," emphasized Jeslek. "Even our scouting forces should outnumber any Spidlarian horse you might encounter. This year, this year . . . we already have enough arms-men and horse to put them to flight, and we have more marching to support us."

*You said something like that last year.*

Leyladin's eyes widened, and Cerryl could tell she had understood the feeling behind his thought. He hoped no one else had.

"If you have no other inquiries, you may go and prepare for our departure." Jeslek nodded.

Once outside the headquarters mansion, Cerryl and Leyladin mounted and rode slowly through the warm misting rain, back to the quarters they would soon be leaving.

"Jeslek's not as well as he could be," murmured the healer.

"Too much chaos?"

"I don't know, but I would judge so. He could still muster enough power to bring down Kleth and Spidlaria." Leyladin eased her mount closer to Cerryl's gelding. "He does not seem quite so close to Anya. Did you notice that?"

"No," Cerryl admitted. "He still turns to her."

"It is not the same."

Cerryl wanted to roll his eyes but refrained.

"I felt that." Leyladin laughed. "You think I'm silly, but I'm not. You need to watch her even more."

That—that Cerryl could definitely accept.

# CXXIII

The shadows of the trees to the west fell across the river road, covering the low brush and open ground between the road and the woods. In places, green sprouted through the few patches of dirty snow remaining from the long winter.

For nearly two kays the road curved back toward the river and the higher wooded hills that separated the packed clay from the water. Cerryl studied the hills alongside the river, frowning. His head throbbed from a day in which he had struggled to extend eyes and senses out around the patrol, not always successfully. Something about the hills bothered him and had from the moment his patrol had followed the road away from the river. Yet some of the Gallosian levies had been following the river road, since not all the levies could be transported on the barges and flatboats Jeslek had commandeered.

Cerryl glanced back over his shoulder. He hoped the forward pickets—half his force—didn't have too much trouble during the night, but what use was clearing a road if you let the enemy return to it? Even so, the blues might circle the road. Cerryl shook his head. The ground was too soggy and the undergrowth too thick for much of that.

His eyes dropped to the young lancer riding beside Hiser, who struggled to remain in the saddle, blood oozing through the shoulder dressing, his head lolling, then jerking into awareness—and pain. Hiser tried to wave away the circling flies.

"... wish Leyladin or camp or something were closer ..." Cerryl's eyes studied the empty road. Still no sign of the camp.

"He's still with us, ser," Hiser said. "Not too much farther ..."

Cerryl didn't look back at the other saddle, the one onto which a body was strapped.

The river ran to Cerryl's left—eastward as his patrols retraced their steps back south toward where he hoped to find the day's encampment. The advance had slowed. After making nearly fifty kays in the first eight-day, they had covered less than fifteen kays over the past three days. *And lost four men already.*

Several thin lines of smoke appeared above the trees to the left, around another curve and apparently beside the river.

"Can see the camp ... not too much farther," Hiser repeated.

Cerryl turned to the lancer beside him. "Dyent, ride ahead and see if you can find the healer. Tell her that we have a lancer with a deep shoulder and chest wound."

"Yes, ser." Dyent urged his mount away from the main body.

*Hope she's not too exhausted . . . Is it fair to ask?*

Cerryl stood in the stirrups momentarily, trying to stretch his legs, to shift the soreness. He hadn't ridden so much in seasons. *One season, but it had been a long winter.*

Leyladin was waiting as Cerryl's lancers rode in toward the fires. "Here! Bring him here."

The raggedness in her voice tore at him. "Can you help him?" he whispered as he swung out of the saddle, stumbling when his boots hit the not-quite-even ground. *Please don't do too much . . .*

"I won't." Her eyes and senses went to the dark-haired and pale young lancer that Hiser lifted out of the saddle and onto the pallet Leyladin had waiting—on the edge of an area holding more than a score of other pallets.

*What happened?*

"Too much." She touched his hand and then stepped over and knelt beside the lancer.

Hiser hovered over the pallet.

Cerryl straightened. He couldn't help either Leyladin or the lancer. Neither could Hiser. "Hiser, the healer will do her best for him. We need to get the men set up and the mounts watered and fed—and rubbed down."

"Ah . . . yes, ser."

"We need to make sure they get fed." Cerryl took a deep breath and a last look at Leyladin. The healer in green looked frail, somehow. Cerryl swallowed, then forced himself away.

Once the men were settled, the mounts on a tie-line, and Cerryl had set his lancers up to be fed at the end cook fire, he walked toward the more central fire where he saw Faltar and Buar standing.

"What happened today?" Cerryl glanced up the gentle slope to where the wounded had been gathered. He could see a flash of green, but little more. "All those wounded . . ."

"We lost almost a whole boat of levies and some archers today," Faltar said tiredly, turning and pointing down at the river.

"Said it was bad," murmured the dark-haired Buar.

Cerryl looked at the boats. The forward craft bore scars, as though it had been slashed with a blade, and most of the stain and varnish had been ripped off the upper deck. The right side of the upper deck railing and the pilothouse were both gone.

"How?"

"You know those slicer things they use on the trails . . ." Faltar glanced at Cerryl. "Stupid of me. I'm tired. Of course, you do . . ."

Cerryl nodded.

"The black iron ones that smith made . . ."

"Dorrin," Cerryl said, lowering his voice. "I told Fydel and Jeslek that he was making more black iron devices."

"Well . . . he did. They put something like those horse slicers along the river. Fydel and Jeslek are down there now—looking at it."

"So where were you?" snapped Anya, marching from the silk tent on the flat ground above the river. "They were set up on your side of the river, great Cerryl, and you were nowhere around."

"We were on the road," Cerryl answered. "Taking arrows."

"They slipped up along the river, and you didn't even see them?" Scorn dripped from the redhead's voice.

Cerryl sighed. "I have only so many lancers. The road splits from the river. I told you that this morning. Jeslek told me to follow the road because Eliasar has to send most of the Gallosians that way. I did."

"You were wrong. Eliasar was wrong. Follow the river."

"How?" asked Cerryl. "If I take a force through that underbrush without a road, the blues will take out most of my lancers before I can even see or sense them."

"You have an answer for everything."

*You wish you did . . . at least for her.* After a moment of silence, Cerryl said, "I don't pretend to have answers I don't know. There weren't any blues on that part of the river when we passed where the road turns west."

"Of course not. They waited until you passed."

"If you know so much, Anya," said Faltar tiredly, "why weren't you there? Jeslek said you were in charge of reserves and supposed to take care of things like that."

Cerryl's eyes almost popped out with Faltar's words, words he'd never thought he'd hear. Maybe young Viedra was good for Faltar.

Anya's pale eyes turned icy gray. "You'd best concentrate on the east river road, Faltar."

"I will, Anya." Faltar smiled tiredly. "It's my task, and I do my best at my tasks. I don't have time to do others."

Buar's eyes had traveled back and forth between Anya and Faltar, getting wider as the conversation went on.

Anya turned full toward Faltar, and Cerryl couldn't help but smile as he watched Jeslek approach from behind the redheaded mage.

"Both of you will learn—"

"I'm certain we have all learned a great deal, Anya," said Jeslek smoothly. "Tomorrow, you will patrol the riverbank ahead of the boats in those areas where the road swings away from the water." The High Wizard paused. "Unless you would rather take over Cerryl's duties and have him patrol the banks?"

Anya's face was blank for a moment before the broad and false smile reappeared. "I would be most happy to patrol the banks. Now . . . if you would excuse me." She turned and walked uphill, more to the north and away from the horses and the wounded men.

"We should have watched the river area more closely," Jeslek said mildly. "Try to think of anything else unusual, and let me know, if you would." The High Wizard turned toward the white silk tent.

*That's as much of an admission that he should have heeded your warnings as you'll ever get.* Cerryl's mouth slipped into a crooked and cynical smile that immediately faded as Leyladin slipped out of the growing dusk to stand beside Cerryl.

She touched his arm gently, and her eyes were rimmed with blackness. "I did . . . what I could. He . . . I think . . . if he's still here in the morning."

The gray-eyed mage put an arm around her. "Are you all right?"

"I'm all right." She took a slow and deep breath before the deep green eyes fixed on him. "I can't . . . heal all of them . . . just try to keep the chaos out of their wounds." She sighed.

"All of those I saw?"

A slight sob escaped her. "So many . . ."

"You need to eat. You need the strength."

"We've got rations over there," suggested Faltar. "We had some earlier. Mostly bread and cheese, some mutton, could be cold by now."

"Cold or not . . ." Cerryl guided Leyladin toward the cook fire and the lancer standing there.

"Lady healer . . . here." The lancer extended a slab of mutton on a half-loaf of dark bread. "There's cheese here, too. Whatever you need." After a moment, he seemed to see Cerryl. "Ah . . . you, too, ser."

"Thank you," Cerryl said.

The two accepted the fare and stepped away to sit on a fallen log that had been dragged to one side of the cook fire.

"I can see who the lancers value," Cerryl added with a laugh, brushing away a large mosquito, once, and then again.

"They value you," Leyladin mumbled, "in a different way."

*Maybe.* Cerryl ate slowly, and Leyladin finished her meat and bread before he was half through his fare. He looked up. "Go get some of the cheese. There were some dried apples, I think."

"I didn't know I was that hungry."

"Healing is hard work," he pointed out. "Any use of order or chaos is."

Leyladin slowly stood and walked toward the makeshift serving table, a plank between two forked posts, where she sliced off a chunk of white cheese and took a handful of dried apples.

"Anything else you'd like?" asked the lancer cook. "More mutton?"

"No . . . thank you. I'm feeling better." She offered a smile. "Thank you."

Cerryl stood and joined her, cutting himself some cheese. "A little more than an eight-day and still more than thirty kays before we see Kleth."

"Then another hundred-fifty kays or more to Spidlaria?"

"More or less." Cerryl brushed away another hungry mosquito, circling through the growing darkness toward him. "You worry about the killing? Going on and on?" *How could anyone not worry about it?*

"I do." Leyladin waved at another mosquito. "The old books talk about Black being ordered and healing." She shook her head. "How is order any different from chaos when it's used to kill? They killed more of us today than . . . I don't know. Does it matter?"

Cerryl finished his chunk of cheese and put his arm around her. "The goals matter. They have to." *Because power can be abused, by either Black or White? How do you ever know that you're not deceiving yourself and abusing power? Are we doing the right thing?*

"We think so. I suppose they do as well." Leyladin took another deep breath. "I need to lie down. I don't know if I'll sleep, but I can't stand up much longer."

"I left my bedroll by the mages' fire."

"I can offer to share my quilted ground cloth with you, ser."

Even through the darkness, Cerryl could sense the smile. "Those are the best words I've heard today. I would be most grateful to accept."

They walked slowly uphill.

# CXXIV

With the growing warmth of the day and the white-orange sun pouring down through the clear green-blue sky, Cerryl unfastened his jacket, shifting his weight in the saddle as he did. He rode slowly, letting the gelding walk another hundred cubits or so before he reined up. The lancers before him reined up as well, their eyes searching the spring green of the bushes beside the road and the damp clay of the road itself for fresh tracks.

Cerryl tried to extend his senses, searching for any trace of black iron or chaos of some sort, wishing in some ways that Leyladin were alongside him. Her senses of order would have been useful. Then, she was safer with the reserves, especially with the scattered arrows that arched over trees—or from across gullies—anywhere there was no possibility of quick pursuit.

The light breeze out of the north still bore a trace of chill along with the smell of damp soil and new growth. The higher parts of the ruts in the road had turned a lighter brown where they had begun to dry, but much of the road was the darker brown of damp soil and clay.

Cerryl glanced toward the shoots in the fields to the west of the road, wiped the sweat off his forehead, and nodded to Hiser. "Another two hundred cubits—or three if it seems clear." He glanced toward the woods that began somewhere short of a kay ahead on the left side of the road, then toward the thin line of trees perhaps 150 cubits downhill on the eastern side of the road. The trees stood a dozen cubits above the River Gallos.

"Yes, ser." Hiser flicked his mount's reins.

Cerryl did the same, and the two rode slowly northward.

Patrolling the roads, again, and after almost two eight-days of plodding down the road to the west of the River Gallos, Cerryl had discovered nothing, not a single black iron trap.

*Of course, the moment you don't, there will be something.*

All the traps had been on the river itself, as if the smith Dorrin had belatedly recognized where the true danger lay.

Cerryl tried to use his eyes and his senses as they rode closer to the woods that began ahead on the west side of the road, the sort of place that would be ideal for another attack by the Spidlarians, for all that, they had not even seen a hoofprint in kays.

*Thwing! Thwing!* A series of arrows flew past—except one that slammed into the lancer riding beside Hiser.

Cerryl jerked his head around. Concentrating as he had been on seeking order foci, he really hadn't sense the approach of the blue archers.

"There they are!" Hiser stood in the stirrups, gesturing toward the side trail that wound toward a gap in the woods ahead on the west side of the road.

*The narrow side trail . . .* Cerryl's eyes flashed toward the trail, his senses following.

A half-score of riders started forward at a fast trot that threatened to become a gallop.

"LANCERS, HALT!" Cerryl yelled.

The riders continued, though Hiser reined up in confusion, glancing at Cerryl as if he could not believe his ears.

*Whsstt!* Cerryl lofted a firebolt over the heads of the riders, far enough that it sprayed harmlessly across the damp clay. "HALT! You worthless dark shadows!"

The lancers milled to a halt, and Cerryl took a deep breath and rode forward. "Back!"

". . . why's he want to go first?"

". . . let him . . . be target . . ."

One step at a time, Cerryl took the gelding onto the narrow trail, trying to keep eyes and ears and senses all searching.

*Thwinng!* This time Cerryl ducked even before he heard the arrow, and he could feel where the archer might be.

*Whhhstt!* The firebolt arced over the vegetation in the direction from which the shaft had come.

"Aeiii . . ."

Was there a line of greasy black smoke? Cerryl wasn't certain, but there was no doubt about the sound of departing hoofs that followed the firebolt and the short scream.

He kept the gelding to a walk, but there were no more arrows. As he had suspected, around the curve was something—something metallic and very ordered. He reined up and beckoned for Hiser to join him.

The subofficer wiped the dampness from his forehead as he halted his mount beside the gelding.

"There's a trap about two hundred cubits ahead," Cerryl said quietly. "I don't feel anyone around, but we'll have to go slowly."

Finding the trap was anticlimactic. Two thin wires so black as to be invisible, especially with dust raised by mounts in the air, ran across the trail. On one side, wedged behind a fallen tree trunk, was a black iron bar to which the wires were secured. At the other end of the wires was a second bar, nearly two cubits long, set in the fork of a tree.

Once they had loosened the bars, two lancers slowly wound the wire around them while Cerryl studied the area with both his senses and his sight.

*Nothing.* Nothing except a black-smeared section of ground on the trail fifty cubits beyond the trap, an area three cubits across where nothing remained but ashes.

"Frigging blues . . ."

The blue raiders had left nothing, except the first casualty they had taken in two eight-days. Cerryl eased the gelding back toward the main road until he found Hiser. The subofficer was strapping a body over a saddle—the lancer who'd been riding beside him.

"What do we do, ser? If we could ride after them . . ."

"We would have lost more lancers."

"But we're not getting to them."

Cerryl had no real answers. If they proceeded slowly, they'd lose some lancers to arrows. If they hurried, so as to keep the blues from having time to set things up, they wouldn't lose as many to shafts, but every so often they'd lose a lot to traps. "We're taking their land. Before long, they won't have any place to run."

"Hope it's not that long. Begging your pardon, ser." Hiser gave the rope a last knot and swung into his saddle and gestured to the lancer with one arm bound from an arrow taken earlier in the day. "Muntor, you hang back and take care of the mount here."

"Yes, ser." The sandy-haired lancer look the rope lead from Hiser.

"Back to the main road, ser?" asked the subofficer.

"Back to the main road," Cerryl confirmed. *Back to patrolling and being targets, and all because . . . because why?*

He shrugged. The answers that had seemed simple in Fairhaven seemed almost irrelevant along a booby-trapped river road in a war no one really wanted and yet one that no one seemed able to avoid, a war that seemingly sucked in more and more from Fairhaven—Leyladin, Faltar, and a half-dozen young mages without, Cerryl suspected, the real talents to see order traps or avoid the iron crossbow bolts that could prove fatal.

*Then . . . can you keep avoiding them?*

# CXXV

After rubbing down the gelding, Cerryl walked slowly to the canvas awning—not really a full tent—under which the wounded lay. Leyladin was bending over another lancer he did not recognize. Even from where Cerryl stood a dozen cubits away, the light of the low afternoon sun on his back, he could sense the order she mustered.

He wanted to tell her that she couldn't heal them all. No healer could. Instead, he waited until she straightened.

She walked toward him as if she had sensed him, a gentle smile in place. "I felt you riding in."

"You felt me?"

"If you can find me in a glass, can't I sense you when you're near?"

He reached out and squeezed her hand. "I'm supposed to meet with Jeslek and the others . . ."

"The other Whites?" Her eyebrows lifted in a query.

"That's not my choice."

"I know. Sometimes, it's hard." Her eyes swept the area under the awning.

"Because we create death and you attempt to heal?"

"No." The blonde cocked her head slightly to the side. "The Blacks are killing more than we are right now. The Guild needs order as much as chaos, and the old parts of *Colors of White*—they don't say it in quite that way, but it's there. These days, with Recluce the enemy . . ."

"No one seems to understand that order also belongs in Fairhaven . . ." Cerryl's eyes flicked toward the white silk tent set on a level grassy bench farther down the slope toward the gray water of the River Gallos.

"You have to go. I know."

"I'm sorry. I wanted to see you."

A trace of a smile reappeared. "I'll see you later."

He squeezed her fingers a last time before he turned and headed downhill, taking a deep breath.

The smell of burning wood was everywhere—faint but omnipresent. He rubbed his eyes gently as he neared the tent—guarded by a pair of lancers.

One nodded slightly. "Mage Cerryl?"

Cerryl returned the nod and eased under the flap held up by poles as an awning. Anya looked up as Cerryl stepped into the tent. Fydel, Anya, and Jeslek sat around the camp table on stools. Cerryl took the last stool, across from Jeslek and between Anya and Fydel.

"Good that you could join us," said Jeslek.

"It was a long day, ser. I just got back."

"How many more did you lose?" asked Anya.

"None today." After a moment, he added, "That worries me. I wonder what else they plan."

"They will indeed plan something else. The traders have told their field commander, Brede, the young giant from Recluce, to hold Kleth," Jeslek announced quietly. The tent billowed overhead.

Fydel nodded. Anya smiled brightly, and Cerryl smiled politely, with a deferential inclination of his head to the High Wizard.

"Where is Sterol?" Anya's smile suggested to Cerryl that she well knew the answer but raised the former High Wizard's name for some scheming point.

"In Fairhaven, I presume, which is fine with me. We really don't need another set of schemers." The High Wizard paused. "Your refusal of terms from the Council was brilliant, Fydel, even if you didn't mean it that way."

"I'm so glad you found it so." Fydel smiled.

"It forced them to decide on an early defense, in order to plan their escape if it failed. Traders would always rather run than fight. This Brede of theirs is better than they deserve, young as he is, and they'll squander his talent—and him. It's a pity."

"A pity? You intend to spare him?" asked Anya, her tone almost idle.

"Demon-light, no. After what he's done to the levies . . . and the lancers from Hydlen and Gallos? Politically . . . that's not wise."

"What about your elusive smith? Hasn't he cost you even more than their commander?" Anya added, "Drawing wire . . . much good it will do . . ."

"It cost us less than fourscore levies to get through his river traps, and we control the river all the way to Kleth. Brede is more dangerous."

"He's only a soldier, no matter how good," reflected Cerryl. "Your smith may have more tricks planned. He has carted some more black iron devices to Kleth."

"Perhaps . . . but they will not save Spidlar." Jeslek smiled again.

"We could lose nine of ten levies and still outnumber the blues. We should not have to spend anywhere near that number—but we could."

"The smith might cost us that," suggested Cerryl.

"How? You are losing but a handful of lancers for every ten kays of road you clear," Jeslek observed. "I expect Eliasar on the morrow, and we are less than twenty kays from Kleth."

*The last twenty could be the costliest, for both lancers and mages.* "And almost two hundred from Spidlaria:"

"Spidlaria does not matter, not now," said Jeslek. "Once Kleth falls, we will have Spidlaria within a pair of eight-days—or sooner."

Anya's smile was bright, hard, and particularly false. As Cerryl saw it, Anya reminded him of a viper or the drawings he had seen of the stun lizards of ancient Cyador.

# CXXVI

A light mist drifted from the low and gray clouds, cool but not cold, as Cerryl rode slowly down the west river road. A hundred cubits to his right was the line of trees marking the river. Ahead on the left side of the road was the hamlet where Jeslek had told Cerryl to round up whatever peasants he could find. *Do you really want to do this?*

He wanted to shake his head, knowing that Jeslek would march the people ahead of the levies toward Kleth. The idea of using innocent people as shields turned his stomach. *But so do Black traps using unseen wires to gut and kill young lancers.*

Cerryl glanced at the cots as the two companies of lancers rode up. The door to the first cot—a one-room thatched dwelling with a mud-brick chimney that rose a good two cubits above the topmost part of the thatch—was closed, and the single set of shutters was fastened shut.

"Voyst! Check the doors," ordered Ferek.

Cerryl could feel the ironic smile creep across his face as the lancers checked cot after cot, only to find no one present.

Ferek eased his mount up beside Cerryl. "We can't be rounding up village folk or herders or anyone, ser," complained Ferek, "not if there be none to round up."

Cerryl glanced around the hamlet. "Every building is empty?"

"Yes, ser. Not a soul around. Not even a cat or a pig."

"Then we won't find anyone in the next hamlet, either." Cerryl's ironic smile faded. "We'd better check one more, though. So we can tell the High Wizard that they've all fled."

"You think so, ser?"

"I'm sure of it."

The second hamlet, five kays farther north along the west river road, was as vacant as the first had been.

"Let's head back," Cerryl told Ferek and Hiser. "There won't be people in any hamlet or village from here to Kleth."

"That 'cause they knew what the High Wizard did to Elparta?"

"I'd guess so." Cerryl turned the gelding, and they rode back through a day that had turned warmer and damper, under clouds that were beginning to lift. He could feel the sweat building under his shirt, even though it was early in the spring yet.

The road remained empty, with a deserted feeling, all the way back to the latest camp by the river, slightly less than fifteen kays south of Kleth. One of the barges was missing, being pulled upstream to Elparta to return wounded and bring back more supplies.

As Cerryl dismounted by the tie-lines for the light cavalry, he saw Faltar walking toward the area where the cook fires were being set up. "Faltar?"

The thin blond mage turned. He had a bruise across his cheek and a short, scratchlike slash on his forehead. "Oh . . . Cerryl."

"What happened to you?" Cerryl tightened his lips as he saw the ugly purpling blotch. *Is that because you worry that Faltar doesn't have enough chaos strength for what he's been tasked with?*

"Caltrops—hidden in shallow water where a little creek crossed the road." Faltar started to shake his head, then winced, as if the movement hurt. "Can't sense order under running water, and who would have thought . . . ?"

"Your mount?"

"Went down, broke a leg. I went with her, most of the way."

"Caltrops—dirty nasty things," murmured the dark-skinned Buar, riding up and dismounting. "Lost three mounts and a lancer. No arrows, though."

"Everything in war is dirty and nasty." *Especially if it happens to you.* "Do you need Leyladin to look at that?"

"No. I brushed the cut with a touch of chaos, and there's nothing she could do about the bruises." Faltar offered a crooked smile. "I do need to find another mount, though. I'm supposed to ride in the middle group of mages. You know, with Myredin, Ryadd, and the others? And Bealtur, of course. We get to fry the countryside."

Cerryl winced.

"Someone told me that everything in war is nasty." Faltar grinned at Cerryl.

"You're right," Cerryl conceded. "Let's just hope it doesn't last another year." The midday sun had finally burned away most of the mist and was beating down as if it were almost summer when he turned toward the river to find the High Wizard.

Before seeking out Jeslek to report his inability to gather locals to serve as targets, Cerryl stopped by the awning tent, which held but two lancers. One held his arm while Leyladin checked the leg of the other—white-faced and stretched out on a pallet. All those previously wounded had already been sent back to Elparta the day before.

Cerryl eased toward the healer.

"Oooohh!"

"There," said Leyladin. "Just don't move until I can bind it." She turned to the second lancer.

"The bone . . . I can see it."

Leyladin turned, her eyes lighting on Cerryl. "Cerryl . . . could you give me a hand here? I need you to help me straighten his arm and hold it in place while I set the bones in place and bind them."

"Just show me what you want."

Leyladin raised her eyebrows. "Here. Hold like this . . ."

Cerryl followed her instructions, trying to keep the arm in place as Leyladin used her senses, a fair amount of force, and her ordering to reset the bones where she wanted them. In the end, the lancer lay unconscious on a pallet, his breathing hoarse, while sweat streamed down the mage's face and neck.

"Thank you." Leyladin was pale. "I couldn't do that if I had many who were wounded."

"I can see why." He guided her to the one stool, under the shade of the awning. "You need to sit down."

"Why are you back so early?"

"The peasants fled." He shrugged. "So I couldn't round them up to act as our advance guard."

"That doesn't seem to bother you." Leyladin took a swallow from her water bottle and offered it to him.

"Thank you." He took a small swallow. "I'm bothered, and I'm not. I don't think peasants or croppers should take attacks meant for armsmen, but I don't like seeing our armsmen and lancers killed by nasty Black tricks because the Spidlarian traders won't pay tariffs to support the roads that help their trade."

"People are people," she said tiredly. "The traders want more coins. The Guild needs to survive. The viscount and the prefect and the dukes want to stay in power and live well, and there's not enough coin for everyone to do what they want. So they fight."

*Is it that simple? There's not enough, and they fight? Except that leaves even less when the fighting's done.*

"You're right," she answered his thought. "But the winner has more, and the losers can't do much about it. I'll be all right. You need to find Jeslek. We can talk after that. I'll find something for us to eat."

"Thank you."

She smiled, and he had to smile back, although his smile faded once he turned. As he walked toward where Jeslek's tent was being set up, Cerryl could still sense the pain that Leyladin had felt as she had straightened and bound the lancer's arm. *Is that what it feels like? No wonder she's exhausted all the time.*

Anya stepped from under the small tree where she and Jeslek had been sitting on stools. "You were supposed to round up the peasants and hold them at the hamlet."

"I can't round up what isn't there."

"You didn't turn up any peasants? Did you warn them off?" asked Anya.

Jeslek stood, blinking as he stepped forward into the sun. "I doubt Cerryl would do something that foolish, Anya. Would you, Cerryl?"

Cerryl ignored the High Wizard's sarcastic tone. "Someone else warned them. Spidlarian lancers, I'd guess, from the tracks."

"And you just turned around?" asked Anya.

"No, we checked the next hamlet and some of the cots beyond that. They were all empty." The younger mage gave an apologetic smile he didn't feel. "All of the hamlets and villages from here to Kleth are empty, I suspect."

"Cerryl has a feeling for such, Anya. I am quite sure that he is correct. We will have to adjust our attack accordingly, and I am most certain Cerryl will be of great assistance." Jeslek turned his eyes on Cerryl. "You may go. I will summon you later."

"Yes, ser." Cerryl turned, ignoring the coldness in Anya's eyes and the set to her jaw.

Jeslek had always been devious and self-centered, but he appeared to be developing a streak of almost wanton cruelty. Did being High Wizard do that? *Sterol had been far more direct . . . and trustworthy.* And Cerryl hadn't cared much for Sterol, but he cared far less for what Jeslek seemed to have become. That would get worse, too, long before they reached Spidlaria or even Kleth.

# CXXVII

The mist rose off the edges of the River Gallos, shrouding the far bank as Cerryl squeezed Leyladin a last time.

"Remember what Kinowin said," she whispered. "Do what you must do, but no more." Her lips brushed his cheek as she stepped back, still holding his hands in hers.

*That will be hard.* "I understand, but it's going to be hard." He released her hands and stepped away from the shadows of the healer's tent, walking downhill toward where the others were gathering, feeling her green eyes on his back.

Faltar nodded to Cerryl but did not speak. Cerryl nodded back, offering a smile of encouragement, one he wasn't sure he felt.

Standing by the High Wizard's tent, Anya surveyed the group, then turned and murmured something Cerryl could not hear. Clad in whites that shimmered in the gray of predawn, Jeslek stepped from the tent. His red-rimmed but still glittering sun-gold eyes raked across the mages assembled there. A half-pace back stood the squat Eliasar, his face impassive. Behind him was the goateed Bealtur, who glanced away as Cerryl looked toward him. On the gradual slope above and behind the mages were the captains and overcaptains, some in the green of Certis, some in purple, some in gold and red, and one in the cyan of Lydiar.

"Today, we begin the advance to take Kleth," began the High Wizard. "The blues are gathered there, and once they have been crushed there is no other bar to our redemption of Spidlar. Eliasar or Anya or I have talked to each of you about your duties, but I will parse them out again so all know what the others' tasks are."

As Jeslek paused for a moment to let the words settle on the group, the faintest tinge of orange light glimmered on the eastern horizon.

"The heavy cavalry of Gallos will be the van proper . . ." Jeslek's eyes flicked from the overcaptain with the broad purple sash downward to Cerryl. "Cerryl, since we have no peasants to march before the levies, you and your light lancers will patrol the road before the main part of the vanguard. Your task is to detect any Black sorcery. Buar will work with you."

Cerryl nodded.

"Behind the van will follow the first of the heavy levies, those of Gallos, then the first section of White mages. They will burn the fields back away from the road." Jeslek snorted. "There will be no cover and no crops. Let them suffer." His voice rose ever so slightly. The sun-gold eyes glittered with the same intensity, despite the red that rimmed them. Chaos smoldered around the High Wizard, more chaos than ever, so much chaos that Cerryl's own eyes wanted to twist away from Jeslek.

"Then the lancers of Certis and the Certan foot . . ."

Cerryl continued to listen, but his thoughts drifted from the High Wizard's words. At times, the whole purpose of the Guild seemed fruitless. How could anyone bring prosperity to lands where rulers and greedy traders wouldn't even pay for the roads that brought them prosperity? And how could Jeslek think that mere destruction would force them to change their minds?

". . . you know your orders. Carry them out." A line of fire sparkled upward toward the orange-tinged puffy clouds and dark green-blue sky.

Cerryl turned and began to walk toward his lancers, where dust already rose and mixed with the smell of horse droppings and cook-fire smoke.

"Lot of horse and foot out here—good thing they don't have mages to throw firebolts," said Ferek, looking down from the saddle.

*They've got a Black mage who might do worse—except I don't know what that might be.* "We'll have to make sure they don't have something else hidden." Cerryl turned as he saw Buar approaching.

"Do you know what we're seeking?" asked Buar.

"No—except that it will have order surrounding it, as if it were black iron or something like that." Cerryl finished checking the girths, which seemed tight enough, not that he was the most expert of horsemen, if far, far better than a year before. Then he mounted. "Are we ready?"

"Yes, ser." Both Hiser and Ferek nodded as they spoke.

The dampness from the winter ice and the melted snow and ice had vanished days earlier, and the horses' hoofs already raised dust as Cerryl's lancers turned northward on the west river road.

"Doesn't the road get better?" asked Buar, drawing up beside Cerryl.

"Four, five kays up, or so," Cerryl answered, trying to get his thoughts off more distracting subjects—like Leyladin and the growing chaos around Jeslek and the shortsightedness of various Candarian rulers. "That's where it widens."

Two scouts rode past the column on the shoulders of the road, leaving low dust trails in the still morning air. Two scouts, Jeslek's concession to some prudence.

The Gallosian heavy lancers had moved onto the road behind Cerryl's force, and from behind them came cadenced marching songs and the measured step of the Gallosian foot. The column plodded northward along the river road. The sun crept higher into the eastern sky, bringing more light and increasingly unwelcome warmth to the land, the road, and the riders. Nothing moved anywhere except the riders and the armsmen, northward toward Kleth.

As the sun climbed, Cerryl struggled to keep his eyes and senses on the road. The line of packed clay curved eastward in an arc that followed the river, then curved back westward. To the west of the road were fields, showing even shoots of green, green that Faltar and the others would sear as they had those already left behind the column.

As they rode around the curve to the west, Cerryl studied where the road ahead changed. As he had seen in the screeing glass, the last ten kays, those closest to Kleth, were almost like a White highway, with oblong paving stones, radiating a faint order, set edge to edge. The paved center of the road itself was nearly fifteen cubits wide, enough for two wagons abreast.

"Better here," said Buar.

"Looks to be so."

The paving stones looked normal enough, and the low stone walls were set back more than ten cubits from the edge of the paving stones. The walls were just a shade less than two cubits high, hardly tall enough to harbor the invisible knives that the blues had placed in more wooded areas. *Not unless they can make them invisible or they're aimed at the horses.*

Cerryl rode at the front of the van, on the western side of the road, with a lancer between him and Buar, who rode the eastern point. As they neared the beginning of the paving stones, Cerryl tried to get a feel for the road. He could sense nothing out of the ordinary except the faint nagging order of the oblong paving stones—and that this part of the road was not new, but old. Had the entire road been paved at one time? Or had the traders run out of coins for paving?

". . . like one of ours."

". . . don't even think it."

The gelding's hoofs struck the paved way, and Cerryl continued to study the wall and the paving stones, yet all he could sense or see were the stones and the strong residual order they held.

"Riders ahead!" called one of the scouts riding but a hundred cubits ahead of the column and along the shoulder of the road.

Cerryl strained.

A small company of blue lancers appeared from behind a low hill, riding at an angle to the road. They reined up abruptly, drew bows, and loosed a double handful of shafts.

Cerryl raised a chaos barrier, struggling as he did to trace any possible order concentrations.

*Whhstt!* A shaft tumbled past Cerryl, its momentum killed by his barrier.

*Thunnk!* A second shaft plowed into a lancer somewhere behind the mage, who winced at the sound.

As quickly as they had halted and loosed their shafts, the blue lancers wheeled and rode northward.

Cerryl forced his senses onto the road, even as Teras sent forth a line of Gallosian cavalry to pursue the blues, who swung around the curve in the road that brought it more eastward. Cerryl's eyes and senses picked up the Spidlarian lancers on the crest of the hill toward which the road curved and climbed—the lancers and something else. The Black mage—the smith.

Cerryl's guts tightened. Why would the smith be with the blue lancers? Cerryl's eyes surveyed the road, but it remained a road, oblong paving stones and all, a road flanked by a stone wall, nothing more. Even his senses could discern nothing besides the faint order of the stones.

*But why is the mage here?* Cerryl turned in the saddle. The columns marched along behind him and the vanguard, with Jeslek so far back that even the High Wizard's banner was unseen. The riders and foot soldiers stretched two kays back toward Elparta, led by two squads of cavalry just behind Cerryl's small group, cavalry under the purple banners of Gallos.

Behind the combined vanguard were the first Gallosian levies, and behind them was the first group of White mages—those headed by Ryadd. Around Ryadd, there Cerryl sensed the reddish white of chaos marshaled but for destruction and the tongues of chaos that leapt forth, blackening and shriveling the grass and the shoots in the fields beyond.

The Gallosian lancers slowed as they caught sight of the larger blue force on the top of the low rise.

Cerryl blinked. The Black mage remained with the lancers on the hill ahead. *Why?* Yet Cerryl could still find no sense of inordinate order, no sense of black iron—just the confusing order of paving stones and wall stones.

"Darkness!"

At the exclamation, Cerryl flicked his eyes to his right and back as a Gallosian lancer pulled a suddenly lamed mount out to the side of the column. The single laming did not slow the advance of the purple banners of Gallos, nor that of the white banners that followed, shimmering in the sun.

As the vanguard approached the long, gentle incline, the column slowed ever so slightly, and Cerryl felt mounts moving closer to the gelding. He had the insane urge to spur the gelding clear of the column, despite the mounted blue-clad lancers on the knoll ahead.

Teras bellowed another command, and another score of Gallosian and White Lancers pulled to the side of the road and began to ride forward to reinforce the first detachment sent after the blues.

*CRRRRRuuummmmmmpppp!!!!* Earth, stones, bodies, blood . . . undefined shreds sprayed skyward. Cerryl felt the ground shiver under the gelding, wondering, his eyes darting over his shoulder, at the explosion *behind* him.

"How . . . ?" demanded Buar, puzzlement and anger flashed across his face.

Cerryl opened his mouth, then shut it, ducking.

*CRRRRRuuummmmmmpppp!!!!* A second gout of colored soil, stones, and flesh erupted into the sky.

*CRRRRRuuummmmmmpppp!!!!* By the third gout of gore, Cerryl found his eyes seared from the pain that had blasted through him, and he tottered in the gelding's saddle, glancing rearward again.

The first line of white banners had vanished, along with the second group of levies and the third. From pits below the knoll perhaps a score of archers appeared and began to fire upon the vanguard and the remaining Gallosian levies.

Cerryl stood in the saddle, urging the gelding forward. "Back off! Back off!"

The vanguard circled, then charged the knoll, right into the storm of arrows.

Cerryl's mouth was dry, his orders to back off ignored.

Of the mounted Gallosians but two remained, and they rode back toward the decimated Gallosian levies, already retreating, back toward the green banners of Certis.

Cerryl glanced around, back at the bodies, at the suddenly organized and milling forces, at purple banners being reraised. Then he looked northward, at the now-empty knoll, empty as if the Black mage and the blue lancers had never been there.

*What happened? How could it happen?* Cerryl had never felt any strange type of order, or even an untoward concentration of order, but whatever the smith had done had been concealed beneath the paving stones. *How could you have failed so badly?*

He glanced toward the space where the young White mages had been riding, but . . . amid the carnage . . . nothing moved. Nothing. The sparks of power that had been mages—nothing.

*Faltar!*

*How . . . ?* That question would not go away, not for a long time . . . if ever.

He swallowed again, his throat still dry. His eyes flicked back at the gap in the column, and his lips tightened. *You were supposed to find such traps, and you and your lancers were supposed to be the ones who triggered them—not Faltar. Not even Myredin and Bealtur.* Sweat ran down his forehead, burning his eyes, but he didn't bother to wipe it away.

Faltar—Faltar shouldn't have been killed by the Black mage's trap.

"Now what, ser?" asked Hiser.

Cerryl didn't have an answer, and his eyes went to the messenger that galloped toward him, one doubtless ordering a re-forming of the attack force.

The messenger kept trotting along the road when, spying Cerryl, he eased his mount toward the mage. "The High Wizard . . . ser . . . camp at the bend in the river . . . to the east there. Already scouted, ser."

"Thank you," Cerryl rasped.

"About time," Hiser muttered. "No sense in milling around here. Blues are gone."

Cerryl's eyes went back, but nothing moved. The white banner that had flown so freely lay broken across the eastern low stone wall of the road. *Just a broken banner . . . explosions . . . and a broken banner . . . and Faltar was gone.*

The trumpet signals confirmed the orders, and Cerryl nodded to Hiser.

"Off the road, to the east!" the subofficer relayed.

Cerryl rode slowly beside the subofficer. He looked but scarcely saw the two kays of the side road to the campsite, where, doubtless, Jeslek and Eliasar would re-form the force.

Once there, Cerryl went through the motions of ensuring the two companies were organized and stood down but found himself standing stock-still, apart from his men and subofficers, in the middle of men and mounts and tents and wagons, almost without thoughts.

At the sharp sounds of a mallet striking a hard surface, Cerryl jerked his head toward where a pair of lancers erected the white tent of the High Wizard. Beyond the tent, Jeslek dismounted, handing his mount's reins to a lancer.

With a deep breath, Cerryl finally stepped toward Jeslek, barely remembering to hold his shields in readiness, although a part of him didn't care.

"Ah . . . Cerryl . . ." Jeslek just looked at the younger mage. "Your failure was costly. Six young mages . . . because you could not discern the trap of this Black mage—even after all your warnings of his cleverness."

*What can you say? That you tried . . . that he couldn't have done better? You still failed, and people—including Faltar—died.* Cerryl looked blankly at the High Wizard. "I know."

"Is that all you can offer?"

What else could Cerryl say?

From behind the partly erected tent Anya stepped toward the two mages, a cold smile on her face, a chill and half-satisfied expression.

"The peasants might have been more effective," suggested the white-haired mage, eyes glittering.

"Yes, ser." Cerryl felt numb. *Why couldn't you find that black iron or whatever it was? Why not?*

"Finding those devices was your responsibility," Anya added. "You failed on the river, and you have failed here."

"I failed here," Cerryl admitted. *Not on the river.*

"And what will you do about it?" asked Anya. "That will not cost us any more mages?"

Cerryl wanted to shrug but didn't.

"I am certain Cerryl will be most happy to lead the vanguard all the way to Kleth," Jeslek said. "Will you not?"

"I will do my best." Cerryl's voice was flat, and he lacked the energy to make it more convincing. *Faltar . . . how . . . ? How could you have failed Faltar so miserably?*

"You will do what is necessary," Jeslek said coldly, turning. "I will talk with you more later, when you have had time to reflect on the seriousness of your failings."

"They were grievous failings," Anya murmured to him. "You have much to atone for."

*Not to Anya . . . but for Faltar and those who relied on you.*

Cerryl stood alone in the late-afternoon sun, looking toward the river he did not see, still half-dazed, half-wondering.

"I heard," Leyladin offered quietly.

Cerryl wondered how long she had stood behind him.

"I was supposed to discover those devices." He turned, then swallowed. The healer could barely stand, so drained was she—from trying to heal those injured by the explosions he had failed to prevent. He took her arm. "You need some rest . . . something to eat."

Not only had he failed Faltar, but his failure had put greater demands on Leyladin. His lips tight, he guided her toward where the cook fires were being set up. *They'll have something for a healer . . . they will. They must.*

# CXXVIII

The stars, pinpoints of light in a black-purple sky tinged with green, began to fade as gray seeped from the horizon. A few insects rustled and chirped in the short spring grass. Cerryl stood in the shadows of a tree he did not recognize, looking out almost sightlessly from the low bluff overlooking the gray waters of the River Gallos.

"You got up early," said Leyladin, slipping through the darkness to stand behind him, encircling his waist with her arms.

"I couldn't sleep. I was supposed to find whatever traps the smith laid. I didn't. Faltar, Ryadd, Myredin, Bealtur . . . the others with them, some I didn't even know, they're all dead."

"You've found most of his traps."

"I didn't find the ones on the river, and I didn't find whatever he put under the road. Jeslek and Anya were not kind in their words. I cannot blame them." Cerryl took a deep breath.

"Do not be too kind to Jeslek. He put you out there to trigger such traps." Leyladin snorted softly. "In that, he failed as much as you, and for that I am most grateful. Anya only looks for ways to show you have failed, whether you have indeed or not."

*But you did fail . . . and Faltar, your first true friend . . . he died.* Cerryl shook his head. *You can't bring him back.* "The smith used the order of the paving stones . . . the order of the darkness-damned paving stones . . ."

"You told me that," Leyladin said softly. "Going over it won't help. What could you do differently?"

"If the levies and the mounts traveled the shoulder of the road, I could sense anything in the ground itself. It was the paving stones . . . something about them."

"Then tell Jeslek that."

"It won't help Faltar."

"No, it won't," she agreed. "You did the best you knew how then." The healer paused. "Sometimes, our best isn't enough. Even for mages and healers. It's hard to accept that."

*Sometimes our best isn't enough . . .* "Yes . . ." The word dragged out. *But it should be.*

"You're a better mage than most, Cerryl. Better than any, I think. You're still a man. Even the ancient White demons failed at times, and so did the dark angels." The healer tightened her arms around him, letting the warmth of her dark order enfold him.

Cerryl kept looking at the dark gray waters of the river, flowing northward to the cold Northern Ocean. "I'm not a demon or an angel. I'm a mage."

"They lost friends, too, I'm sure. They were people, too. They hoped; they dreamed; and they failed and conquered."

Cerryl swallowed. "I haven't been that much help on this . . . whatever it is."

"What good will it do if you turn your back on all this now? Would you leave Anya and Jeslek to their devices?"

"They'll do as they please." He pursed his lips.

"Someone's coming," she whispered.

They stood in the dimness by the tree as two other figures walked the path below them.

"I don't understand, Jeslek. You raised those mountains, you brought Axalt down into rubble, yet you won't use chaos against these worthless traders." Anya's sharp voice carried uphill. "You were too gentle on Cerryl . . . for his failures."

"I do not have to justify what I do. But, to please you, dear Anya, I will." Jeslek's voice oozed irony.

Cerryl winced. Didn't Anya understand?

"She still thinks she brought down Sterol," Leyladin whispered in his ear.

"Best it remain so." Cerryl smiled bitterly to himself. "I would not be the one to tell her otherwise."

"Axalt was a city of parasites, adding to the cost of trade and siphoning off coins that better should have gone to Fairhaven. Likewise, the middle highlands of Gallos were worth little to any but herders.

Spidlar, on the other hand, is rich in farmland, rich in timber and even in metals. Those make the land valuable, and you wish me to turn it to cinders?" Jeslek laughed once, harshly. "I will bring down another city as I did Elparta, but only if that will place all Spidlar within our hands."

"You are letting lancers die."

"Lancers will die. That is their job." After a moment, Jeslek added, "Besides, the prefect has sent fivescore Kyphran lancers and an additional tenscore heavy foot. He would rather send those of Kyphros. They are less loyal than those from the north of Gallos." The High Wizard turned and gestured. "Cerryl! Come on out. I can sense your chaos blazing."

Leyladin let go of his hand, and Cerryl stepped from the shadows of the tree and began to walk toward Jeslek.

"I see you, too, could not sleep long." Jeslek's words were mild, far milder than those he had used upon Anya.

Unseen chaos coiled around Anya, almost as strong as that which entwined the High Wizard, but the redhead did not speak.

"So . . . how do you propose that we avoid these latest traps?" asked Jeslek. "I presume you have thought upon this."

The younger mage repressed a sigh. "Ser . . . I have checked. He can only hide that much black iron under something ordered—like the paving stones. The ground is dry, now, and if we march beside the walls . . ."

Jeslek nodded, his eyes cold, as Cerryl explained. Beside the High Wizard, Anya's pale eyes made the High Wizard's seem warm.

# CXXIX

In the shadows cast by the late-morning sun, Cerryl stood behind the higher earthworks on the top of the rise to the south of the slightly higher hill where the Spidlarian forces were dug into an entrenched circle. The west river road from Elparta to Kleth angled up the slope from southwest to the northeast. East of the hill that held the forces of Fairhaven were the bluffs overlooking the river, and to the west the hills sloped downward into the Devow Marsh, which stretched westward a good four kays. Farther west of the marsh were the Kylen Hills, rugged and filled with potholes and crumbling sandstone ledges.

Overhead, high, thin clouds gave a gray tinge to the morning. A light southerly breeze barely lifted the banners of the White forces but carried the odor of burned fields.

Pushing his senses outward, Cerryl had tried to find the smith. The glass had shown that Dorrin rested in an earthworks somewhere, and Cerryl had determined that the Black mage was somewhere on the opposite hillside, but he could not sense where. That bothered Cerryl. The last time the Black smith had been present had not been pleasant, either. *Not pleasant?* An ironic and self-mocking smile crossed Cerryl's lips. *Faltar would have said more than that . . .* Except Faltar would have forgiven Cerryl. *Will you be able to forgive yourself?*

From midway down the hill sounded a wavering horn, the first signal of the assault to come.

Cerryl glanced sideways to where Jeslek stood, flanked by Anya and Fydel, all looking over the berm of the earthworks to the north. None of the three moved as the horn sounded a second time, even as gouts of chaos fire flared from the ramparts fifty cubits below the one where Cerryl stood.

*Whhhsttt! Whhhssst! Whhstt!* The globules of chaos splashed across the hillside and the Spidlarian earthworks.

Cerryl sensed little change and could hear no screams, but earthworks were a good shield against chaos fire, although several thin lines of greasy black smoke spiraled upward. A second line of fire followed the first.

The horn signaled once more, and silence followed—for a long moment before the purple banners of Gallos surged uphill toward the lower front line of timbered trenches where the outlines of Spidlarian pikes and halberds waited.

Cerryl frowned at the speed and the ease with which the Gallosian armsmen smashed over the first line and through the trenchworks.

"See!" snapped Jeslek. "They have the first line already."

Fydel lifted his eyebrows but did not speak.

On the far hill, the purple banners pushed uphill, reaching halfway to the higher Spidlarian emplacements. Scattered arrows fell across the attackers, downing an armsman here and there but scarcely slowing the assault.

*CRUUUMPPPPPP!!!!* The hillside erupted, sending huge gouts of earth and chunks of timber skyward. And bodies . . . and part of bodies.

Cerryl smiled grimly. Yes, the smith had been there.

Jeslek turned toward Cerryl. "You did not sense that."

"Again," added Fydel.

"I could not get close enough to sense that. I warned you that the smith was there." *This failure is not yours. Others, yes, but not this.* Cerryl tightened his lips.

"No matter. It will not change matters."

Anya's broad and false smile underscored Jeslek's words. The High Wizard glanced back at the hill opposite.

Fydel held Cerryl's glance for a moment longer, then gave a scornful smile. Cerryl forced a pleasant smile in return.

Abruptly Jeslek turned to Fydel. "Darkness with this measured approach!"

"It was your idea," observed Anya.

"So? I can be wrong." Jeslek looked across to the hillside that resembled an instantly churned and plowed field.

"You can? I never would have guessed it." Anya's voice was bitter.

"Fydel," ordered Jeslek, "tell Eliasar to have all the levies march over the mined ground there. Bring up some more."

"What?"

"The one thing we know is that they can't have planted more of those devices where they already exploded. And we don't want them to retreat and mine another section of hill or field."

From where he stood Cerryl silently agreed. Even Fydel nodded at the logic.

"Everything that smith has done requires advance preparation. We can't give him any more chances. Order the charge. Pour everything into that point. And keep the troops moving."

"Yes, Jeslek."

"I mean it. Keep them moving."

As Jeslek turned to survey the battlefield, Anya and Fydel exchanged glances. They nodded. Then Fydel hurried out from behind the earthworks and downhill toward the small tent that held Eliasar and his glass. Cerryl had scarcely seen the older arms mage in the whole campaign, except from a distance.

Shortly another trumpet sounded, and the green banners of Certis flowed downhill through the already-trampled grass of the swale and upward through the explosion-plowed ground that had held earthworks. Before the Certan levies reached the second level of Spidlarian emplacements, another hail of arrows flew downward, cutting down as many as a third of the Certan forces.

Then a wave of blue armsmen swarmed from hidden trenches flanking the attack, slashing inward. Just as suddenly, the blue attackers retreated to their trenches, leaving the scattered remnants of both Gallosian and Certan forces.

Whhsstt! Whssst! The belated firebolts caught but a few of the laggard blue armsmen.

Another trumpet sounded, echoing from the south to the north, wavering but insistent. Cerryl glanced upward, half-surprised that the sun had dropped past midday.

"Another charge!" snapped Jeslek. "They can't hold forever."

Fydel had hurried back toward the High Wizard, then frozen as he heard the order. His eyes flicked back to the lower berm. Yet even before the trumpet died away, as though Eliasar below had heard the High Wizard's words, a set of golden banners rose, and yet another wave of armsmen began the charge uphill toward the next set of Spidlarian earthworks.

Fydel shrugged and slipped back beside the High Wizard.

More shafts arched from the top of the Spidlarian emplacements, falling in among the remaining Gallosians and Certans and touching the advancing ranks of the Kyphran levies. The Kyphran armsmen surged upward, before the gold banners slowed at the second line of trenches, stalled by a redoubled volley of arrows.

Cerryl watched as the Gallosian heavy lancers appeared and charged the southwestern side of the hill, sweeping up the Spidlarian flank.

*WWhhsstt! Whhhstt!* More firebolts flared across the higher trenches, the trenches that sheltered the blue archers, and the volleys of arrows faltered and died away. With fewer arrows striking them down, both Kyphran levies and Gallosian horse moved uphill steadily, the levies taking the second line of trenches and the horse nearing the sides of the upper emplacements.

The Gallosian cavalry turned the end of the upper Spidlarian earthworks, sabres beginning to cut down the blue foot from behind.

"Good! Good!" Jeslek beamed as he saw the second line of blue defenders being swarmed under from above and below.

Yet, seemingly from nowhere, two companies of Spidlarian heavy horse charged downhill and struck the Gallosian horse from behind, bringing down perhaps a third of the purple lancers on the initial sweep. Even from across the field, Cerryl could see and sense the blond giant who led the force—Brede.

Because of the chaos of confused and mingling forces, the White chaos fire died away, and as it did, blue archers reappeared, and more of the deadly shafts poured into the Kyphran foot.

"There! There's that Black wastrel!" Jeslek pointed, gesturing to Anya, then to Cerryl. "The middle of the upper works there, by that little pine. Chaos fire!"

Cerryl mustered chaos and flung it across the small depression that was too small to be a true valley, his bolt splattering along the back side of the earthworks just before Anya's.

"More!" ordered Jeslek. "More!"

Cerryl threw another firebolt, as did Anya, and a smaller bolt followed from Fydel.

Had they caught the Black armsleader? Cerryl doubted it.

The Kyphran levies continued to slash upward and through the second line of Spidlarian emplacements, more slowly because the Gallosian horse had turned and fought back the blue cavalry.

Only scattered blue horse remained between the Gallosian lancers and the uppermost line of blue defenders when another company of blue riders appeared, charging down at an angle toward the purple lancers.

Cerryl moistened his lips, seeing the large blond-haired figure leading the blue charge, a figure who once again stood out somehow even from where the mage watched from hundreds of cubits south. The blues knifed through the remaining Gallosian horse, and sunlight glittered on their blades, blades that rose and fell with swiftness.

Another volley of arrows cut through the Kyphran levies still assaulting the middle earthworks.

"More chaos fire! On those darkness-damned archers!" demanded Jeslek.

Cerryl took a deep breath and loosed another firebolt. His was followed by ones from Anya and Fydel and an enormous firecloud from the High Wizard.

The fire seared the space between the second and third blue earthworks, turning most of the blue horse—and a few remaining Gallosians—into torches. Oily black smoke circled skyward, clouding the afternoon sun.

"Now! Attack!" Jeslek's commands were more screams than orders, but the trumpet picked up his intent, and the thin, piercing notes signaled another assault.

The Kyphrans, backed now by Hydlenese levies and horse, continued uphill, cutting into and slowly pressing back the last thin line of Spidlarian defenders.

"Chaos fire—on the right!"

Cerryl obliged, trying to ignore the growing headache, the knives that cut through his skull with each new attempt at flinging chaos fire.

The White horse, now a mixture of forces from Certis, Gallos, and Hydlen, charged up the left side of the hill toward the crest. A few scattered arrows flew toward the lancers, but only a handful of riders fell.

Jeslek summoned another firecloud, searing the area of earthworks to the northeast from where some of the remaining blue archers had loosed shafts. No more arrows rose from blue bows.

Just as the mixed White Lancers neared the crest of the hill on the southwest side, a squad—or less—or blue horse, led once more by the giant Brede, appeared from behind a berm and swept westward. For a time the White forces fell back.

"Chaos fire! The leader!" ordered Jeslek.

Cerryl, Fydel, and Anya obliged, but more than half the blue horse had retreated before chaos fire splashed across the ground short of the last line of Spidlarian defenders. Still, a handful of Spidlarian mounts and riders were torched, and more black smoke circled upward.

The levies from Hydlen almost merged with those from Kyphros, and one wing had turned the right flank of the upper line of defense. The combined White cavalry regrouped and moved uphill, close to encircling the last of the blue forces.

"Now! More chaos flame. In the center!"

*Whhsttt! Whhst!*

The order trumpet sounded; the horse of the combined Fairhaven forces began the charge, the charge Cerryl knew, somehow, would be the last.

The White forces barely reached the top of the low hill when, again, the opposing blond commander appeared at the head of the smaller force of blue lancers, a force that split the White horse like a shimmering blue arrow.

A small pocket of Spidlarian archers appeared below and behind the White horse and began to cut down White Lancers from the rear.

"There!" snapped Jeslek.

Three quick firebolts silenced the last blue archers.

With few blue lancers and no archers to blunt their advance, the Kyphran and Hydlenese foot cut through the last of the trenches, then continued upward toward the crest of the hill.

Only a handful of blue lancers remained, then but one, and yet none of the Gallosians seemed able to bring down the tall blond figure.

"Enough!" Jeslek hurled a last firebolt.

Cerryl held his breath as the huge firebolt seemed to arc ever so slowly over the hundreds of cubits that separated High Wizard and Black commander. Fire splayed everywhere, rolling out from the flame-splashed figure of Brede and enveloping the nearer Gallosian lancers as well. Even as the Black commander flared toward ash, his blade spun end over end . . . and buried itself in a Gallosian lancer.

Cerryl blinked . . . and swallowed, knowing he should be relieved. *But are you? Do you know that Jeslek is a better person?* He shook his head. No matter how gallant and skilled the Black commander had been, he had been defending the wrong side.

"It's over," said Jeslek.

Cerryl massaged his neck and forehead, not certain that such was the case. Stars flashed intermittently before his eyes, and his head throbbed and throbbed.

"We need to see what remains," Jeslek declared. "Find your mounts, and we will follow Eliasar."

"Little enough remains," said Anya. "Little enough."

Cerryl walked down the back side of the hill to look for the tie-line that held the gelding, ignoring Fydel walking beside him.

"He was too good to be an exile," Fydel stated, "the Black war-leader."

Cerryl did not reply, realizing that he could not sense the Black mage, Dorrin the smith. Yet he knew that he would have known had the other died in the battle. *So where is he, and what will he next do?*

"How could be have been an exile?" asked Fydel once more. "They wouldn't have exiled anyone that good in battle."

"Maybe that's why," Ceryl answered. "He had to be an exile. Why else would he have fought as though he had nowhere else to go?"

Fydel had no answer.

Cerryl had questions, though, all too many, questions that swirled inside him even after he mounted and rode behind the other three. *Why would the blues order a suicide defense so far from Spidlaria? Why were the blue traders so opposed to Fairhaven when the White City meddled so rarely in how other lands governed themselves? Why would Recluce force out people like the Black warleader—or the smith?*

The smith was order in himself, a force so black as to be untouched by the slightest hint of chaos. *And he was exiled from the isle of order?*

Wearily Cerryl rode around the hill and after the High Wizard and Eliasar. He felt even more exhausted when they reached what remained of the battlefield. No Spidlarians emerged from earthworks, nor moaned, nor offered surrender—only bodies, everywhere, some splattered with blood, some not obviously touched, and others merely heaps of charred meat.

Anya's head turned at one point, and Cerryl wondered why as her gaze lingered on a seared patch of ground just short of the crest. The Black leader? But why? She had never met him.

The sun was touching the western horizon as Jeslek reined up at the crest of the hill held that morning by the Spidlarians. Beyond lay a small city—Kleth.

Eliasar turned in the saddle and looked at Jeslek. "Honored High Wizard, we cannot afford another battle such as this." The squat arms mage wiped his forehead as sweat oozed from hair plastered against his skull with dampness. "We have lost more than half our force."

"Two-thirds," suggested a voice from somewhere in the officers behind Eliasar.

"You won't have any more battles at all," Jeslek said. "Only a few skirmishes on the way to Spidlaria. They have no troops to speak of left."

"I hope to the light you are correct."

"I am," snapped Jeslek. "We move to take the whole river valley first. Leave a small force here to guard the road to Diev. Once we secure Spidlaria, we'll take Diev. We saved most of the best White Lancers."

"As you wish."

Anya and Fydel exchanged glances.

Although Cerryl's face was politely impassive, he doubted that the battle for Spidlar was truly over. Not with the redheaded smith still somewhere beyond Jeslek's control—and Anya's.

# CXXX

Under a sky that held both dark clouds and bright stars, Cerryl looked down at the pallet where Leyladin lay, either sleeping or insensible. The dark order that had flamed so strongly within her was but a faint shadow. Her breathing was shallow and ragged at times.

Three thousand Spidlarians had died, at least, and twice that many from the combined forces of Fairhaven under Eliasar. Unable to help or heal any more than the too many she had already saved, Leyladin had collapsed long before Cerryl had made his way back from the carnage, leaving Eliasar and Jeslek their triumph in entering the near-deserted streets of Kleth.

Cerryl sat by the end of the pallet and, with his eyes closed, massaged his forehead. Exhausted as he was, he found he could not sleep, unlike his poor healer. He could sense that sleep was beginning to restore her, but it might be days or weeks before she dared heal again.

Cerryl opened his eyes and stared into the darkness, ignoring the moans from the healer's tent more than a hundred cubits away, hoping that he had moved Leyladin far enough that she would not be disturbed. He reached out and touched the covered pitcher of chaos-heated and purified water, just to make sure that he had it nearby should Leyladin wake.

*Faltar . . . what have we done?*

Sounds suffused the camp—the murmur of a sentry, the coughing of an armsman, the *whuffing* of a restless horse on the tie-lines to the west, the muted rush of the River Gallos as it flowed over the broken rocks above Kleth. Yet to Cerryl the sounds were as silence, compared to the clangor of the day—a clangor fueled by both chaos and order.

Chaos had held. The smith had fled back to Diev, and Jeslek's mighty army would pour down the River Gallos to Spidlaria—and the presumed treasures it held—and Spidlar would fall under the shadow of the White City.

"Ohhh . . ."

Cerryl jerked upright, then patted Leyladin's shoulder. "You're all right."

"Thirsty . . ."

He offered her some of the water.

She swallowed, several times, then murmured, "Thank you," before dropping back into sleep.

His eyes went toward the star of the south, bright, green-tinged, and unblinking, watching as the fast-moving clouds covered it, then passed, leaving its light unchanged.

*Is that life, being a star, no matter what clouds your light?* Cerryl chuckled, bitterly but softly so as not to wake Leyladin. A light like a star? Hardly. He was but a mage with ideas that were less than popular, a mage with power and reluctant to use it after seeing how all who employed power seemed more and more to misuse such.

*And yet . . . without power . . . nothing will change.*

He closed his eyes and massaged his neck with his left hand, ears alert should Leyladin wake again.

# CXXXI

Great and mighty Spidlaria," snorted Fydel from the mount to Cerryl's right as they neared the southern edge of the city. The city gates to Spidlaria were scarcely that—two featureless red-stone pillars less than five cubits high, without even brackets, set apart and not connected to any sort of walls. Unlike the river road from Elparta to Kleth, the road from Kleth to Spidlaria had been paved the entire way.

"They were great enough to cost us thousands." Yet for all that, reflected Cerryl, perhaps Jeslek had been right. Nowhere on the ride northward to Spidlaria and the Northern Ocean had they seen another Spidlarian armsman or lancer. Cerryl's efforts with his screeing glass had shown some scattered figures, but none gathered into a body, and the scouts had found none at all.

"Most were levies," murmured Fydel. "No great loss. A gain, even, if we must fight those who supplied them."

*Faltar and Myredin weren't just levies . . . and the levies were men as well. So was Bealtur, even if he hadn't exactly been a friend.* Cerryl looked up several ranks to the head of the column, where, behind the vanguard, rode Jeslek, his whites gleaming in the full summer sun, seemingly cool. Anya and Eliasar flanked the High Wizard, Anya as cool-looking as Jeslek, while Eliasar's whites were damp with sweat.

Cerryl blotted his brow with his sleeve. He wanted to look backward to see if he could find Leyladin, even though he knew she was probably a kay behind him at the end of the column with the wounded who could ride, and far out of sight.

Once through the gates, Cerryl glanced from one side of the avenue to the other. More than half the buildings were of plastered planks and thick timbers, structures with heavy shutters and narrow windows— windows narrow to keep out the cold winter winds that blew off the

Northern Ocean. Despite the growing warmth of the day, the shutters were closed, as were the doors.

"No one to welcome us," said Fydel with a laugh.

The shadow from a white and puffy cloud passed across the column, offering Cerryl but momentary relief from the early-summer sun. "They probably don't feel welcoming."

"No, but some of their women will be, one way or another."

Cerryl nodded sadly, recognizing the truth of Fydel's statement, another inevitable result of war. *All because the traders wanted to make more profit at the Guild's expense.* But was it? Even thinking about the complexities of trade and Recluce and the roads, he wanted to shake his head. *No wonder everyone wants simple answers.* But simple answers, he'd learned, were usually wrong, incomplete at best.

"They deserve it," Fydel said, more loudly. "Don't think they don't."

"Fydel! Cerryl!" Anya's voice cut over the clatter of hoofs on the stone pavement of Spidlaria. "The High Wizard bids you join us." Without overtly acknowledging the summons, Cerryl urged his mount past the two lines of lancers, the leather of his stirrups almost rubbing those of the lancers.

"The conies cower in their burrows, as if to ignore us." A tight smile appeared on Jeslek's pale face, and his eyes glittered. "Fairhaven will not be mocked." The sun-gold eyes focused on Fydel. "Send forth the lancers to bid all the traders to gather in the square before the wharves. Say that any who do not answer the High Wizard will forfeit their lives."

"Yes, ser." Fydel inclined his head.

"They might feel their lives are forfeit already," suggested Cerryl from where he rode behind Anya, wondering how Jeslek knew there was a square by the wharves. Then he realized that the High Wizard had doubtless viewed Spidlaria in his glass, perhaps many times.

"They might indeed. They thought they could flee if Kleth fell, but I knew that." Jeslek laughed. "I had all the ships of the north sent to stop them. And now we will collect the golds that will repay the Guild for its trouble."

*Except golds won't bring back Faltar and Myredin or the lancers or the thousands of levies who died.* Cerryl said nothing, just letting his mount follow the column past silent and shuttered shops and dwellings until they reached the lower square above the wharves.

Jeslek reined up at the edge of the square, then turned in the saddle toward Anya. "Find a chair and an awning, whatever, to make it more comfortable." His eyes went to the blocky Eliasar. "You make it safe for me to receive the merchants here."

Eliasar nodded once, brusquely, then turned his mount away, riding to the harbor side of the square. "Captains—to me!"

Jeslek turned his eyes on Cerryl. "You assist Anya."

"Yes, ser." Cerryl eased his mount toward Anya's.

Anya flashed the smile Cerryl detested. "You know shopkeepers, Cerryl. Perhaps you should find an appropriate chair and awning." She turned away, as if there were no question that Cerryl would find both.

A cabinet maker and a chandlery—where would he find those? After a long deep breath, he turned the gelding and rode back to his lancers. "Hiser, Ferek, we're searching for a cabinet maker's shop."

Hiser shook his head, and Ferek shrugged.

"We'll just look for a sign—or a local." *A sign will be easier to find with everyone cowering behind barred doors.* "Let's head back south. I thought it looked like an artisans' area back a half-kay or so."

The subofficers flanked him, and the lancers fell in behind him as he turned the gelding. They rode on the left side of the main avenue, almost single file past the rest of the White Lancers still riding toward the harbor square.

Cerryl raised his hand to Leyladin as he and his lancers passed the last of the Fairhaven column headed toward the square.

"What now?" The healer flashed a sardonic smile.

"Searching for some things for the High Wizard," he answered. "We're setting up in the area around the harbor square. I'll try to see you later."

She nodded, and Cerryl continued.

After more than a half-kay of riding down the side streets, he reined up outside a shuttered building that displayed a small sign depicting a chest above a plane and a chisel.

"Hope his work is better than the sign," said Ferek.

So did Cerryl. "Knock on the door."

No one answered.

"Tell them that either they open the door or I'll burn it open," Cerryl said loudly.

A rasping from behind the door drew a smile from Ferek and a headshake from Hiser. The door slipped open, and a man peered out.

"Are you the cabinet maker?" asked Cerryl.

"Please, ser wizard . . . spare my consort . . ." The cabinet maker had short gray and ginger hair that clung to his scalp in tight curls and a short, curly beard more gray than ginger. He stared up at Cerryl.

"Are you the cabinet maker?" the mage asked again.

"Spare us . . . my consort," stammered the man.

*What have they been told?* "I'm not interested in your consort," Cerryl said tiredly. "I'm trying to find the best armchair I can—one for the High Wizard."

"I cannot afford to keep what I make . . ."

"I know." Cerryl turned to Hiser. "Guard his place. I don't want his family or his consort touched."

"Yes, ser." Hiser nodded.

"Have one of your men lend a mount to the cabinet maker." Cerryl focused on the artisan. "Who has your best chair, the one most suitable for the High Wizard of Fairhaven?"

"Reylerk, the trader, ser wizard."

"Fine. Get on that mount and lead us there."

"Ser?" The artisan's eyes went from the closed door of the shop to the mount from which a lancer Cerryl did not know dismounted.

"Get onto that mount," ordered Hiser.

Cerryl wiped his damp forehead and waited for the man to mount. "Now . . . where does this Reylerk live? Show us."

"Ah . . . to the north, ser."

"Fine. Lead the way."

As they rode along the narrow lane and then back out along the wider avenue, Cerryl studied the shuttered dwellings and shops. Clearly, the folk of Spidlaria—those who remained—feared the worst.

Reylerk's dwelling was on the hilly section of Spidlaria north of the wharves, up a winding but paved lane. The gates were closed.

"Behind the gates . . ." stammered the cabinet maker.

Cerryl nodded at Ferek.

"Open the gates!" demanded the subofficer.

No words answered the order.

Cerryl shrugged and mustered chaos, focusing it into a tight beam at the point where the two gates joined.

*Eeeeee-wwhsssst!* When the flash cleared, the gates slowly shivered apart, a half-cubit missing from each edge, and sagged to the stones.

After a moment two lancers used their mounts' shoulders to edge the timbered gates open, and Cerryl and Ferek rode into the courtyard, a courtyard paved with large red oblong stones, smooth as a table. Opposite the gates rose a dwelling, the lower floor of the same red stone, the upper of plaster and timber. As in every other dwelling in Spidlaria, the shutters were closed—except for one on the upper level that appeared to be cracked.

*Thrung!*

An arrow buried itself in the shoulder of Ferek's mount, and the lancer subofficer struggled to control the horse.

The closing of the once-cracked shutter told Cerryl from where the arrow had come, and he responded with a second chaos bolt. *Eeeee! Whsssst!* A man-sized hole appeared in the second story of the dwelling, and a charred figure tumbled onto the courtyard stones.

"Another arrow and you're all dead!" roared Ferek. Somehow he'd managed to work the shaft from his mount's shoulder.

Silence greeted his statement.

"Open the front door!"

The carved lower door swung open, but no figure showed.

"Out! All of you!" boomed Ferek.

A heavy, red-faced, and bearded figure in green silks waddled out from behind the door and stood on the portico outside the doorway. An equally rotund and white-haired woman followed, and shortly two older serving women cowered behind them. None looked at the ashes or at the charred figure that had once held a bow.

"Ser wizard . . . spare us. Please spare us," begged the man, presumably Reylerk.

"Why?" Cerryl asked with a snort.

The trader gulped. "We have done nothing except defend our land."

Cerryl urged the gelding forward, then reined up a few cubits short of the short shadow cast by the house. "You took advantage of the roads Fairhaven built, but you refused to help pay for those roads. You traded with our enemy and used the roads we built to sell the goods you bought to others. You sent men out to kill us and to die, and now you wish to be spared."

The fat and bearded man looked down.

"And you remain here because you would not be safe among those who fled because you brought the war to Spidlar out of your own greed."

Reylerk did not look up, confirming Cerryl's suspicions.

"I'm not here to pass judgment." Cerryl motioned to the wood-worker. *Except that you just did.* "Go find the chair of which you spoke." He turned to the trader. "If this man is even scratched, I will reduce your dwelling and all in it to ashes." The mage smiled coldly. "Including the daughters and sons you have hidden within."

"Let Besimn take whatever he wants . . . Let him do it!" screamed the trader. "Do not harm anyone!"

Cerryl gestured for the cabinet maker to enter the dwelling. Besimn trembled as he dismounted and walked toward the open door.

"It's not for Besimn," Cerryl said. "It's for the High Wizard. Might you have some red silk or velvet hangings?"

"Ah . . ."

"I see you do. Please have your consort and the serving women fetch them for us."

The three women scurried into the house, as if they feared the lancers would follow, the oldest looking back over her shoulder so fearfully that her shoulder rammed into the door frame.

"They've got much hidden in there." Ferek laughed. "Young girls, too. Pretty girls."

"That might be," Cerryl grudged, "but Jeslek wants the chair and the hangings, and the girls weren't the ones who shot the arrow."

"Ser?" Ferek's question implied more.

"If we have to rule these people, it won't help if you ruin their daughters. The fathers, they created the problem—not the children. We'll not harm the children." Cerryl stared at the trader.

The trader swallowed silently.

"You, trader, are to proceed to the square by the wharves. If you are not there shortly, we will find you, and your life will be forfeit. There is no escape from Spidlaria."

"And my family?"

"The High Wizard is not interested in punishing the innocent." Even as he spoke the words, Cerryl wondered exactly what he meant. In a war, was any adult in a trader's family totally innocent? Had the luxuries they enjoyed led them to persuade Reylerk to support the Traders' Council's defiance of Fairhaven? Had the trader's consort kept silent? Or had she protested? How could anyone really know?

Reylerk licked his lips nervously.

Besimn staggered out with a high-backed chair nearly as big as he was. Cerryl smiled as he saw the red velvet upholstery. "We'll need a cart."

"Ah . . . in the stable, there is a wagon," volunteered Reylerk, his voice unsteady.

Ferek gestured, and two lancers urged their mounts toward the small building to the left of the dwelling.

Shortly the three women scraped through the doorway with a long roll of red velvet, hurriedly folded and rolled.

Once the chair and hangings were loaded into the wagon, Cerryl looked at the trader. "You can drive your wagon. You're coming to the square anyway."

The woman in silks went to her knees. "Spare him, I beg you."

"That is the High Wizard's decision." Cerryl turned the gelding and started out of the courtyard, a courtyard that felt strangely confining.

Ferek rode another lancer's mount, and the lancer sat on the wagon seat beside the trader while the wounded mount walked behind as the wagon creaked after the lancers. Besimn rode along ahead of the borrowed wagon, swaying uneasily in the hard saddle.

"They're leaving . . ."

Cerryl could hear the disbelief in the whispered words. He turned in the saddle. "Fairhaven has some small honor—unlike the traders of Spidlar."

*Faltar . . . you were worth a dozen of this man . . . and those like him.* Cerryl's lips tightened as he rode back toward the square.

The sun hung low above the hills on the western side of the harbor before Jeslek finally appeared and took the ornately carved chair under the red velvet hangings that Cerryl had commandeered. Anya and Eliasar stood on each side of the chair.

Still mounted, with his lancers as guards, Cerryl watched from a good fifty cubits back, his eyes flicking across the traders.

"Shall we begin?" Jeslek raised his eyebrows.

The two heavyset traders knelt on the paving stones. Sweat dripped from their brows, leaving dark splotches upon the stone. Beside one was a small wooden chest.

"What have you to say?" Jeslek pointed to the trader with the chest.

"The Council is no more, honored High Wizard. Spidlar is yours. We submit to your will. Here—" The gray-bearded trader gestured to the chest beside him. "This contains my golds. I would offer what you think fair as tribute to Fairhaven."

A shuffling of feet from the traders massed behind him indicated their unease with the statement.

"You offer tribute only because you could not flee," suggested Jeslek, his voice almost indolent in tone.

Cerryl glanced toward the harbor to where four ships remained tied at the wharves, sails furled.

"I will spare you," said Jeslek. "I will not spare your fortunes. All but a fifth part of what you have belongs to the Guild. All but a fifth part of anything that any man has in excess of fifty golds belongs to the Guild. And any man who lies will lose all that he has—and his life as well."

The High Wizard turned to Anya. "Ask the one on the left."

"You say that this chest contains all your golds. What else have you hidden?" asked Anya.

"There is little else, sers, a few coins perhaps, some silver plates ..."

Anya's eyebrows lifted.

Cerryl winced, knowing the trader lied, knowing that Anya knew he lied as well.

The redhead glanced to Jeslek, who nodded fractionally.

"You lie," said Anya.

The trader started to jerk his head up, as if to protest, when Anya's chaos fire exploded across his body.

The other trader flung himself sideways, cowering on the paving stones. "I brought no golds, High Wizard, but they are yours ... yours ..."

"Do you have the temerity to insist that whatever chest you may offer holds all your wealth?" Jeslek's words were almost lazy.

"No ... no, ser. I have a ship, but it is somewhere on the Western Ocean, and there are other hidden chests. I have some horses and other possessions. Others in my family may have secreted small things, but what I do not know." The man's voice trembled.

"You see?" Jeslek smiled and looked at the half-score of traders guarded by the White Lancers. "He found it much easier to tell the truth. It is really not that difficult." The red-rimmed but glittering sun-gold eyes flashed toward the heavyset trader standing behind the prostrate trader and at the front of the remaining traders. "Is it?"

The trader bowed and stammered, "No, sire. No . . . sire."

Anya stood behind Jeslek's shoulder, and a cold smile crossed her lips.

Cerryl repressed a shiver at the smile, keeping a pleasant expression upon his own face as Jeslek motioned for another trader to approach.

# CXXXII

Jeslek sat in the chair Cerryl had taken from Reylerk. From the head of the long table that dominated the narrow dining hall of the largest stone house in Spidlaria the High Wizard surveyed the mages seated on each side. "People from everywhere in this miserable trading land—saving the traders—they all wish to submit and get on with their lives, except for that miserable place to the west." Jeslek fixed his eyes upon Cerryl.

"Diev?" Cerryl ignored the sweat dribbling down his neck and concentrated on Jeslek.

"That's where your precious smith is holed up. He won't escape this time."

*My precious smith? How did he become mine? Because I couldn't detect what no one else could, either?* Cerryl glanced from Jeslek to Anya to Eliasar, then down the table past Fydel, Syandar, and Buar toward Leyladin.

"What do you plan?" asked the scarred arms mage.

"We will march on Diev—all of us except you and a few of the remaining mages. I've sent for some more junior ones to help you—Lyasa and Kalesin. You will keep a third of the White Lancers and half the levies and hold Spidlaria . . . make it into a proper place. The blockade ships will make sure this Dorrin doesn't flee by sea." Jeslek turned to Leyladin, seated at the last place at the table. "You, healer, should plan your trip to Lydiar on the vessel leaving on the morrow. Duke Estalin's son ails once more."

"It will be days . . ." began Cerryl.

"It may well be," snapped Jeslek, "but Estalin is among the few rulers who truly acknowledge Fairhaven, and, unlike some, he asks but little."

A frown crossed Anya's face. "What if you need—"

"I am the High Wizard, dear Anya, and I know what I need." After the briefest of pauses, he added, "And when I will not."

"Spidlaria may yet harbor those who wish you harm," Anya pointed out.

Cerryl held a frown at the words, words that seemed false and calculated to irritate the High Wizard. Beside Fydel, Syandar looked from one mage to the other, his eyes darting back and forth with the conversation, his mouth firmly closed.

"There are many who wish me harm. Wishing does not make it so, Anya, as you above all should know." The sun-gold eyes were flat as Jeslek spoke. "The four of us—you, my dear Anya, Fydel, and our most dutiful Cerryl—will depart tomorrow to reduce Diev to the rubble it should already have been. You, Eliasar, will begin the work of turning Spidlaria into a city of which the Guild will be proud. Syandar and Buar will assist you."

The arms mage nodded. Beside him, the black-haired Syandar nodded quickly.

Jeslek rose. "There is little else to be said, and the day waxes hot, far too hot for a place that is so chill in the winter. Anya, attend me."

Cerryl and Leyladin exchanged glances, and Cerryl knew that the healer felt as he did as they rose from the table.

The side door in the wainscoted and paneled wall closed behind Anya and Jeslek, leaving the other mages standing around the table.

"That's clear enough." Fydel rolled his eyes, then fingered his beard momentarily. "We're all here to do the bidding of Anya and the High Wizard."

"Just the High Wizard, I think," corrected Eliasar. The arms mage turned to Cerryl. "Too bad you won't be staying. Your experience in Elparta and with the Patrol would be most helpful."

Cerryl shrugged. "Jeslek needs someone to . . ." He never finished the sentence because he really wasn't sure exactly what Jeslek wanted of him.

"To do the dangerous mage work," Leyladin filled in.

"All magery is dangerous, Lady Leyladin," said Eliasar dryly. "Even healing, as you have discovered."

"Around Jeslek, of course it is." Fydel shook his head. "I need to talk to the captains."

"We need to talk first, Fydel." Eliasar's voice was cold. "Now." He glanced at Syandar. "You stay."

Fydel's lips tightened, but he merely answered, "We do need to agree on which forces should go and which should stay."

Cerryl and Leyladin nodded to the other three and slipped from the dining hall. Once into the main foyer, they headed for the door to the courtyard and then walked through the small rear gate from the grand mansion overlooking the harbor and down the paved lane. Cerryl glanced back, and the dark slate roof tiles glittered above the wall almost like shining water in the rays of the summer sun. "It's more than twice as big as your father's house."

"Most traders' houses elsewhere are. Those of the powerful factors, anyway."

A faint and cooler breeze, bearing the scent of sea and harbor refuse, greeted them as they reached the back side of the harbor seawall.

Cerryl blotted his forehead on his sleeve. "Cooler here."

"Let's walk out that way." Leyladin pointed toward the breakwater that angled out into the harbor perhaps a kay northward.

Cerryl took her hand as they turned. "Why is it that nothing turns out quite the way you thought it would, even when it does?" He scanned the area, but the seawall was empty, except for the lancers on guard near the piers.

She laughed, gently, humorously. "Because you know more than when you first hoped for something."

"I suppose so. I always thought that being a White mage would solve all my problems."

"Now you have more problems?"

"It's not that," mused Cerryl, fingering his chin with his free hand. "Viental and Rinfur and I—back when I was a mill boy—we worried about whether we'd have warm clothes for the winter and enough to eat and, sometimes, whether we might get hurt, but we didn't want to think much about that. Now, I have more than enough to eat, clothes I couldn't have dreamed of, and a beautiful woman I wouldn't have dared to look at—and I still worry. I probably worry more."

"That's because you can do more about your life."

"Can I? Or do we just think we can?" Cerryl cleared his throat, then squeezed Leyladin's hand. "I used to think so, but what can even the High Wizard do? If he didn't fight this war, or something like it, no one would pay tariffs in a year or so, and the Guild would have a bigger war or problem."

"You really think so?"

"Jeslek created mountains upon mountains—and I still had to kill the old prefect of Gallos. He—we—took down two towers of Hydolar and killed one, maybe two dukes, and the Hydlenese are still grudging their obligations."

"You're just saying that everyone is bound by the world and the bounds are less obvious but just as real when you have wealth or power?"

"Something like that." Cerryl stopped under the shadow of some kind of oak, almost more a tall bush than a tree, that had grown out of the jumble of rocks at the inshore end of the breakwater.

"There's one good thing about when we talk," offered Leyladin, looking toward him.

"There are several good things." Cerryl grinned.

Her green eyes danced for a moment. "No one thinks we're talking seriously."

"Who says we are? Or that we have to keep talking that way?"

"I do," she answered firmly.

Cerryl gave a long and dramatic sigh. "About what?"

"You have that tone, ser mage. The one that asks if we can get through with your philosophizing and my trivial questions and get on with lust." Leyladin's red-blonde eyebrows arched.

Cerryl choked, then coughed his throat clear.

"Jeslek's not the same," she offered, pursing her lips for a moment.

"I know, but I don't know how, except there's more chaos around him all the time."

"So long as Anya's there," suggested the healer.

"Besides Anya. And he was definitely but politely ordering Anya around, more than he used to do."

"He doesn't trust her. I wouldn't. She used to sleep with Sterol, and maybe she still does when she can."

"Is he still in the White Tower? Sterol, I mean?"

"He's biding his time," Leyladin said. "He hasn't given up hope of reclaiming the amulet, no matter what he says."

"About Jeslek. . . . I won't be able to ask you once you go. So what should I do?"

"Do what he asks, so long as it's not dangerous to you, and wait. And never be alone with Anya. Not without lancers or someone around."

"I already learned that."

"See that it stays learned."

"I will." He paused, then took both her hands in his. "Now . . . can we enjoy a little tiny bit of lust?" he asked plaintively.

Leyladin laughed. "A tiny bit."

"That's all I ask."

"That's all you ask to begin with," she corrected, but her face turned to him, and their lips met under the shifting shadows of the young oak.

# CXXXIII

On the flat beside the river, lancers were striking the silk tent shared by Jeslek and Anya and rolling the silk walls into bundles. On the shady side of the pine tree, on the softer needles where he had laid out his bedroll, Cerryl concentrated on the glass.

When the silver mists parted, more reluctantly than normal, Cerryl beheld a ship, a strange vessel moored in a channel or quay area beside a shipwright's works. The sense of black iron infused the ship—the same feeling that Cerryl had gotten from the wagon the smith had driven to Kleth before the last battle. Between the road traps and the battle, Fairhaven had suffered greatly from the smith's devices, and now the ship was another creation of worry.

Cerryl let the image fade, then fingered his chin. He was glad, in a way he could not explain, that Leyladin was on her way back to Lydiar—on one of the White ships that had patrolled the Northern Ocean and sealed off any flight by the Spidlarian traders, or those who had waited until the last moment, anyway.

Finally, he made his way downhill to where Jeslek stood in the morning sunlight.

"You look troubled, Cerryl," Jeslek observed. "More troubled than you have, and you have looked troubled of late." A raw smile appeared and vanished.

"I have been using my glass, as you requested, ser. The smith is doing something with a ship—and it involves order and black iron." Cerryl shrugged. "What he does I cannot determine, but the black iron he brought to Kleth cost us dearly."

"I recall." The High Wizard nodded. "I appreciate your diligence, and as we near Diev, Anya and I will consider what we might best do."

"There is even more order and black iron in that vessel," Cerryl persisted. "I cannot tell what it may be, as it is in a ship on the water, but I like it little."

"One ship cannot make that much difference," said Jeslek with an indulgent smile. "We will deal with it. Besides, if he does flee, the blockade ships will capture his vessel—or sink it."

"If they do not," added Anya, "then he is gone and will trouble us and Spidlar no more." Her pale eyes fixed on Cerryl. "Best you make ready to ride. We have many kays to cover."

Cerryl ignored her order and turned to Jeslek. "I will see what I can discover in the days ahead." He nodded, then turned away.

# CXXXIV

Cerryl reined the gelding in at the top of the rise, glancing toward the woods on either side, then to the northwest, along the line of the undulating road, unable to see more than a kay ahead through the light afternoon mist that turned the horizon into a shifting gray curtain. The damp brought out the scent of fir and pine in the woods that had flanked the road for most of the day's travel.

Not only was the hilly and winding road that led from Kleth to Diev empty of all traffic, but also the rain and weather had erased all sign of horses or wagons, as if no one had traveled that way in eight-days.

Cerryl and his lancers comprised the vanguard. *As usual, when Black Order threatens.*

The main body of the Fairhaven forces followed nearly a kay behind. He took a deep breath, trying to sense any trace of concentrated order or black iron, but throughout the two days from Kleth he had seen nothing and sensed nothing, and the road had remained deserted. The few cots near the road were also deserted. *As if we were a destroying horde, or something.*

"Are you sure this is the way, ser?" Hiser glanced at the worried mage.

"It's the right way, all right. We're about halfway to Diev."

"It be unnatural quiet. Even when I was in Gallos and the High Wizard raised the mountains . . . saw some folk. Not many, but some." Hiser leaned forward in the saddle, peering at the road ahead through the warm misting rain that had barely dampened the dust. "Still no one out there."

"There won't be until we get nearer to Diev."

"What about the blue armsmen?" asked the subofficer. "What happened to them?"

"Not very many survived the battle and Kleth, and most of those came this way. That was over three eight-days ago. Some fled along the coast out of Diev." Cerryl shrugged, still studying the downhill stretch of the road ahead with both sight and senses, neither of which revealed anything but trees and underbrush. "Those who didn't . . . I guess they're pretending to be peasants or something else." He urged the gelding forward. "This section seems clear." *You hope.*

Hiser eased his mount along beside Cerryl's. "Ser, beggin' your pardon, but we been fighting here for two years, and I don't see as why everyone's so feared of you mages. I mean, the way you rule. You don't do much different as from other rulers."

Cerryl laughed, softly. "But we do. We cast chaos fire, and most of us can tell if someone lies to us. Chaos fire is something most folk can't raise, and that creates fear and envy."

"But . . . arrows'll kill a man just as dead. Blades and lances, too. Or the flux."

"People fear what they don't understand, Hiser. That's why many White mages and common folk fear Recluce, too." Cerryl's eyes flicked toward the upslope that lay beyond the narrow brook that wound under the stone bridge at the bottom of the incline in the road. "No one wants someone around who can tell when he lies. We all lie, and truth is something every man or woman fears." He shifted his weight in the saddle and shrugged. "Then, people don't want to pay for what the Guild does. They want the roads and the prosperity, but they want someone else to come up with the golds. The Guild and Fairhaven cannot survive for long without the roads and their tariffs, and places like Spidlar want to use the roads to sell cheaper goods from Hamor and Recluce without tariffs. The Guild hasn't been challenged in a long time, and people have forgotten what a chaos war can be like."

"Like as they won't forget this one."

"They will, as soon as they can." *Unless the Guild changes things.* He paused. Was that what Jeslek had once had in mind?

Cerryl glanced through the mist, which had begun to turn into true rain, wondering if Leyladin had reached Lydiar, wondering what really lay ahead in Diev. Did the smith have more devastating devices? Another surprise? Or would Diev fall as Spidlaria had?

A gust of warm rain carried the scent of pine to him as the gelding's hoofs clattered on the narrow stone bridge.

# CXXXV

In the orangish light that came with dawn Cerryl walked toward the silk tent that stood several-score paces from the herder's dwelling, not quite a house but more than a hut or a cot, where he and Fydel had spent the night.

Beyond the tent, trails of smoke from the cook fires spiraled into the sky, and the odor of cooking mutton hung in the still air. Cerryl swallowed, half-hungry from the smell, but not sure how well even more of the heavy and strong meat would settle. *Better heavy food than none.* He scratched at a vermin bite on the back of his forearm, from some insect that had escaped the chaos dusting he had given the squalid dwelling. He stepped carefully, knowing his boots threatened to slip on the rain-slicked and trampled grass, or on horse droppings, if he were not careful.

"Chaos or not, you didn't get them all," muttered Fydel, several paces behind the younger mage, scratching his own bites.

"Better than what it might have been."

Fydel grunted in response.

Cerryl circled around the High Wizard's tent, making for the cook fires. "Our High Wizard and his aide are not stirring yet."

"They've been stirring all night, no doubt." Fydel snorted. "Let us see if there's something to eat."

They joined Hiser and Teras by the cook fire, where Cerryl took a joint that was hot and dripping. He stood by the cook fire, alternating mouthfuls of hard bread and tough mutton, leaning forward enough that the juice didn't drip on his whites. Fydel chewed more noisily, but neither spoke while they ate. Ears alert, Cerryl listened to the scattered comments of the officers and subofficers around the nearby fire.

"... move so slow ... nothing here."

"There wasn't much there, either, when the blues used that order fire to wipe out a couple-dozen-score levies and some mages ... what's your hurry?"

"Just want to get it over."

"... so you can get killed sooner in another war, say with the Hydlenese?"

Cerryl found himself smiling crookedly at the last words.

"You think we'll have to take Hydlen, too?" asked Fydel.

"We'll have to do something. I'd wager soon rather than later, but that rests with the Council and the High Wizard."

"The Council will follow Jeslek."

"As it should be," interjected Anya.

"Good morning." Cerryl turned and inclined his head.

"Morning," Fydel grunted.

"Cerryl ... Fydel, Jeslek would like to meet with you now." Anya's voice was cool, preemptory, and she turned with the last of her words and walked back toward the white silk tent.

"Full of herself," mumbled Fydel through a last morsel of bread.

*She always has been, even when she first beguiled you.* "Perhaps, but Jeslek is not patient these days."

The two followed Anya back to the tent.

Inside, Jeslek sat on a stool before the small table, sipping wine from the single goblet. "Come in. We have much to do today."

Standing at his shoulder, Anya nodded.

Cerryl and Fydel stepped forward and stood across the table from the High Wizard.

"Cerryl, you have found no traces of the Black one's works along the road, is that not so?"

"So far," Cerryl replied cautiously.

Jeslek frowned. "A moment, and I will return." He stood. "Anya, you may proceed. You know my wishes."

Cerryl repressed the frown he felt. Jeslek had left hurriedly. A touch of the flux? Shouldn't the High Wizard have been able to control that?

"The harbor and center of Diev lie less than ten kays ahead," Anya said. "Cerryl, have you screed the town this morning?"

"I did. Before I ate. The smith had left his forge and was at the shipwright's on the harbor. I could see no bodies of armsmen, but those around him did bear arms."

"Not enough to trouble us," Fydel said. "A mere handful, and against our force . . ."

Cerryl frowned. Had he heard the sound of boots on the hard-packed mud and gravel?

Anya smiled, broadly and falsely. "Cerryl, I know you have so many important things to consider, but the High Wizard will need your sage advice when he returns."

Cerryl wanted to wince at the sickly-sweet tone and cover the red-head with chaos. She seemed to be acting more and more as if she were the High Wizard.

"Now . . . when we get ready to head out, Fydel, remember it's not too far until we reach that homestead. Don't fire it. The High Wizard wants to study it first—the one with the brush barricade around it and the charred cottage in front."

Cerryl nodded at the reference to the smith's place, although his screeing had shown it appeared to be empty and the smith was at the shipwright's—or he had been earlier.

"That is your precious smith's place, is it not?" asked Jeslek, returning to the tent, chaos swirling around him.

"This Dorrin is not my smith," Cerryl replied evenly. "He's left there for the shipwright's."

"It matters not. He can't escape our ships." Jeslek dismissed the smith with an offhand gesture.

Cerryl frowned, shifting his weight from one foot to the other. He could sense a change around him—a concentration of something—order? He turned to the side of the tent where the silk billowed ever so slightly. The air wavered. "Look! Over there!" As he spoke, he lifted his shields, wondering what good they would do against an order master even as he did.

"Concealment!" blurted Anya.

Fydel's mouth merely dropped at the appearance of the red-haired smith almost right before them, carrying something that looked like a short and heavy crossbow without the bow. The device was pointed at Jeslek.

The High Wizard gestured at the smith, and chaos swirled, beginning to build. *WHHHsssttt!* The firebolt flared past the smith and burned through the tent silk.

*Crack . . . thump . . . whummmmmmmPPPPTTTTTTTT . . .* Another kind of order-cased flame flashed from the smith's device toward the High Wizard.

Simultaneously Jeslek hurled a wall of chaos toward the slight figure who had invaded the tent. *EEEEEEEEIIIIIIIIIiiii . . .*

As the order-forged flame of the smith and the High Wizard's chaos met, incandescence seared through the tent, rending the silk walls. Despite his shields, Cerryl felt himself being hurled backward through a vortex of order and chaos that shivered the air and ground.

Darkness blanketed him.

He found himself lying on charred silk looking upward at a sky that seemed far darker and more cloud-filled than when he had entered the tent. Slowly, wondering how long he had lain there unconscious, he staggered upright in the cold rain that pelted down around him. He fingered his whites—definitely wet, and that meant he'd been down for a time, at least.

*Thurrrrrummmmmmmmmmm . . . thuruummmmm . . .* Winds buffeted the few sections of the tent still in place, and thunderclaps shook air and ground alike, but both seemed to be lessening.

"Jeslek! Jeslek!" Anya's voice was shrill, perhaps the first time Cerryl had heard it so.

Heavy droplets of rain continued to lash from the near-instant clouds, so heavily that Cerryl had to blink as he lurched toward the center of what remained of the High Wizard's tent. Then ice pellets rattled down in a quick flurry before vanishing.

Cerryl took a deep breath and sent forth his senses, trying to see if any traces of the smith and his dark order remained. *Nothing . . . What did he do, that he could strike so quickly and be gone?* The light cloak was similar to what Cerryl had used himself, but had he failed to recognize it because it felt different when used by an order wielder? *Does it matter now?*

He stopped, looking over where Jeslek had been. Jeslek was gone. *Jeslek gone? The greatest . . . or most powerful White mage . . . perhaps ever? Gone?*

Cerryl took a step, then another, still searching for the High Wizard.

Anya stood by the shattered remnants of the small table, binding her arm. Fydel rose from one knee behind her.

Cerryl tried his order-chaos senses again, but there was no trace that Jeslek had ever been there, except for the gold amulet that lay amid the disintegrating pieces of a white tunic. Nor was there any sense of the order that bespoke the Black smith. The only body was that of a White guard. Cerryl shook his head. *Jeslek dead . . . like that?* He glanced at Fydel.

"He's dead . . . gone," Fydel affirmed.

Cerryl rubbed his forehead, and his fingers came away slightly streaked with blood.

"It happens." Anya stooped and lifted the gold amulet from the pile of dust and clothes on the trampled and burned grass. Stepping around the dead guard's body without even looking down, she dangled it toward the bearded White wizard with the gash across his forehead. "Would you like it, Fydel?"

"Darkness, no! Give it to Sterol."

She turned to Cerryl. "Would you—"

Cerryl stepped back, almost involuntarily. "It's past time for games, Anya. Sterol should have the amulet returned to him. Especially now." *How can she just ignore Jeslek's death? Did he mean that little? Is she that cold?*

"Don't tell me that you two brave and strong White brethren are afraid of a poor Black smith and healer who must stoop to stealth and murder?"

Fydel looked away.

Cerryl did not, instead meeting Anya's eyes. "He was rather effective, wouldn't you say?" His arm gestured at the pile of dust that had been Jeslek, the two bodies, and the missing side of the tent ringed with charred patches. "There were three of them—just three, according to Jeslek. Between them, they've destroyed more than half our forces, a half-dozen of the White brethren, and the High Wizard. Just what would happen if they had decided to have sent a few more—perhaps older and more experienced order masters and Black warriors?" Cerryl's smile was crooked. "For such reasons, I would prefer to defer to one of great experience, such as Sterol."

"Do we wait for him . . . to finish this rabble?" snapped Anya. "No! Cerryl, you need to lead the pursuit of the smith. Now!"

"No. I think not. I think we can proceed—but slowly." *Jeslek . . . gone? Like that?* Cerryl felt his thoughts were running in circles.

"You are always so cautious, Cerryl," Anya said brightly, her voice tight. "Do you think that the Council—or even Sterol—would let the blues get away with this? The High Wizard has been killed, and you wish to proceed slowly. Oh, so slowly."

"When one cannot rely on sheer force of chaos, dear lady," Cerryl forced out the deliberate words, "one must needs be cautious."

"Bah . . . let's get the troops moving." Fydel blotted the blood from his forehead and stepped through the space where the tent wall had been. Then he paused and pointed toward the remaining two bodies on the ground—those of the guards who had stood outside the tent. Fire flared, and only ashes remained. With another snort, Fydel marched toward the hut where the march captains waited, not even looking back at the other two mages.

Anya and Cerryl raised their eyebrows simultaneously, even as Cerryl turned toward Anya.

"Well, Cerryl?" asked the redhead. "Are you with us, or will you remain here and be cautious?"

"I'll be ready to lead the vanguard shortly. As the High Wizard's most trusted and valued assistant, you should draft the scroll to the Council—and Sterol—and then direct Fydel, as you have already been doing. Perhaps you should also inform the armsmen that Jeslek is dead. It might be a good idea, you know?" Cerryl turned and walked heavily across the damp and matted grass toward the tie-lines where Hiser and Ferek and his lancers waited.

Beyond the first tie-line, Fydel had mounted and was talking to the march captains.

*Is this wise?* Cerryl glanced back toward the ruined tent, then up at the dark clouds that had already begun to disperse. He kept walking.

"Ser? What happened?" asked Hiser as Cerryl neared his detachment.

"The Black wizard killed the High Wizard. He got away in the storm and the chaos."

"Killed the High Wizard?"

"He killed the High Wizard . . ."

". . . High Wizard's dead."

". . . can't believe that . . ."

". . . light help us now."

"Enough!" snapped Cerryl. "It wasn't his order powers. He used an order-based crossbow or something. Then he ran away and hid in the storm." Cerryl stepped up to the gelding and fumbled for the glass packed in his saddlebags. *You're not about to go charging off after that smith until you know what he's doing, Anya or not.*

He found his hands shaking ever so slightly as the impact of Jeslek's death began to settle on him. *Jeslek dead?* What *had* the smith done— and how? How could they just march into Diev? Then, how could they not—if the Guild were to be respected? The Guild had to be bigger than the High Wizard.

Cerryl pulled out the glass and set it on the clay, concentrating and ignoring the headache he hadn't even realized that he had.

When the silver mists cleared, Cerryl took in the scene—an unmounted horse circling in the water behind the strange craft that was the smith's, the fighting on the deck of the smith's ship, and the smith dropping a blue armsman with a staff, then dropping another before taking a slash and staggering. As the White mage watched, the last figure in blue pitched forward, and the smith sagged onto the deck. Sails furled, impossibly propelled by something churning the water beneath the stern, the ship edged out the channel toward the breakwater.

"What the darkness is it?" demanded Ferek.

"A dark creation."

"Cerryl?" called a voice from a mounted figure riding toward him.

Recognizing Anya's voice, Cerryl released the image. "I was checking where the smith was. He's on his ship, leaving the harbor at Diev."

"No matter," snapped the redhead. "The blockade ships will take care of him and his ship."

*I wonder.* A faint smile creased Cerryl's mouth, an expression that faded as he recalled the dead Spidlarian armsmen on the ship. *The smith is far more ruthless than even Jeslek—or Anya.* "We can't. Not now that he's at sea."

"Then get on with it."

Cerryl nodded, packed the glass, and then swung clumsily into the saddle. His head throbbed. "Hiser, Ferek . . ."

"Yes, ser."

Cerryl ignored their doubtful tones, his headache, and Anya's eyes upon his back as he rode to the head of the column. *Jeslek . . . dead?* He forced his concentration on the task ahead.

# CXXXVI

The three mages stood on the edge of the quay, looking out into the empty harbor of Diev. The cool breeze off the water cooled them but carried the odor of dead fish and other decay—possibly bodies washed under the piers.

"We need supplies," said Anya. "Cerryl, send out a force to gather what we need."

"We can't pillage everything," the younger mage noted.

"Why not?" Fydel asked. "They killed half our men. They don't deserve any better."

Cerryl refrained from noting that earlier Fydel hadn't much worried about how many levies had died in taking Spidlar. "If we keep taking things, we'll never govern this place. We wouldn't keep seizing things from the farmers around Fairhaven."

"This isn't Fairhaven," said Fydel. "Never will be."

"Maybe we'd better think about making it so," answered Cerryl quietly. "The other way hasn't been working all that well lately."

"That will be the noble Sterol's decision, as you keep reminding me, dear Cerryl," answered Anya in an overly sweet voice. "I do not care how you obtain provisions, but provisions we must have. You seem best fitted for it, and Fydel must organize patrols to keep order."

"I'll take care of it." *All Fydel knows about peacekeeping is how to kill peacebreakers.*

"I am so sure you will, Cerryl. You always do." Anya flashed her bright smile. "You always do."

"Just do it," added Fydel.

"We'll need some of the golds we took from the traders in Spidlar."

"You wouldn't if you just took them," pointed out Fydel.

"Where would we get provisions next eight-day?" asked Cerryl. "Or the one after that?"

"You can have some golds," conceded the redhead.

"Thank you, Anya." Cerryl nodded, then walked back along the quay toward the spot where Ferek and Hiser and their lancers waited. His eyes drifted to the harbor, where but a day before a ship had moved to the sea without sail, under the power of some device, some engine, developed by the smith.

Cerryl offered himself an ironic smile. If the smith but knew what change he had already wrought. *That may be but the beginning.* The smile faded into a frown as he neared the two subofficers.

"You don't look too happy, ser," observed Hiser.

"We get to find provisions—without pillaging and disrupting things," Cerryl answered as he mounted. "So I suppose we'd better see if there are any traders left around."

"Traders?"

"I'd rather have a local do the hard work. Besides, they probably know better where to find things—especially since we'll be able to pay a little."

"Where do we start?" asked Ferek.

"At that warehouse there." Cerryl pointed toward a timbered building several hundred cubits to the west of the end of the quay.

When they rode up, Cerryl could tell the warehouse had been stripped. The door hung open, and the shutters had not even been closed. "We'll try another."

They tried almost a dozen. Of all the buildings that had held factors or traders, only the chandlery remained occupied, and a thin trail of smoke wound upward from the chimney.

Ferek gestured, and a lancer dismounted and pounded on the door. After a moment, the door, recently reinforced on the outside with heavy planks, opened a crack.

"Open for the mages of Fairhaven," snapped Ferek.

A thin figure scuttled out under the overhang of the extended second story. "Sers . . . we have but little."

"That's what you all say," said Ferek.

"Sers . . . true it is . . . true indeed."

"You are the trader Willum?" asked Cerryl, reading the carved sign-board.

"No, ser . . ."

"Where is he?"

"He . . . ser mage," stammered the thin-faced figure, "he was killed by bandits more than a year ago. I was his clerk. I help his widow and young sons."

Cerryl concealed a wince. He had no doubt who the bandits had been. He glanced toward Hiser. "Hiser, you and your men work with this fellow to round up whatever supplies are left. Have him keep track of them, and we'll use his warehouse to store them." Cerryl looked at the trembling clerk. "You work with us, and you and the widow and her children will be fine."

"Yes, ser mage . . . yes, ser."

"Thank you." Cerryl nodded at Hiser, then turned to Ferek. "We need to check out the last two at the end of the short wharf there."

Ferek remounted, and half the lancers followed as Cerryl rode through the summer heat toward the still water of the back harbor, not all that far from where the smith had launched his vessel.

The vessel was still at sea, for Cerryl could not find it in his glass and would not be able to do so, he suspected, until the smith ported, wherever that might be.

The sound of the lancers' mounts echoed hollowly on the pavement, reminding Cerryl of just how deserted the city—or port town—had become. Was that what always happened in war?

He shrugged. He'd promised Leyladin to do what he had to do and say little, but he'd already said too much beyond that, he feared. His eyes landed on the warehouse ahead, apparently abandoned like the others. *A long day . . . many long days to come.*

# Colors
## of
## Change

# CXXXVII

Cerryl . . . what do you want?" Anya asked idly from where she stood by the railing of the *White Flame* beside Cerryl.

"What do you mean?" Cerryl's eyes flicked from Anya toward the bow.

Just aft from the short forward raised deck, Fydel stood, the wind blowing his dark hair back, a big hand on a rigging cable, confident-appearing in the cool sea air under the bright green-blue sky.

"Jeslek wanted to be the greatest and most powerful White mage ever. What do you want?" Anya asked again.

The thin-faced mage glanced back at the headland beyond which lay Diev, now in the hands of Syandar. Eliasar had agreed that the three should return to Fairhaven with the amulet, but by ship, so that all the lancers could remain to help keep the peace in Spidlar. Cerryl had the feeling that the older arms mage had almost been happy to see them leave and allow him to get on with putting Spidlar firmly under the thumb of the Guild, as he had in Renklaar.

"I'm not sure I know," Cerryl said. "I wanted to be a White mage ever since I was a child, and I am." He shrugged and offered a wary smile.

"Cerryl, you have bigger goals than that."

"Well . . ." Cerryl paused. "I think Fairhaven needs to be stronger for Candar to prosper, because none of the other rulers think beyond their own borders. If they don't, sooner or later, Recluce will, in fact, rule Candar without ever sending a single armsman."

"Do you see Prefect Syrma or Viscount Rystryr allowing that?" Anya laughed, a hard and brittle sound. "They will fight their endless little wars and slaver over a few chests of golds while their merchants sell all that is dear to the traders of Recluce."

"If matters change not," Cerryl conceded, "that will happen. I'd like to change matters. I cannot say I know how, or that I could even if I did possess that knowledge. Look at Jeslek."

"You seem to be saying that Candar cannot prosper if the wars are endless," Anya answered. "Do you really think anyone can change what people are? Most are greedy fools. The best are smart and greedy."

"I can't gainsay that, either," Cerryl admitted. "That is why I cannot see any land, any force, but that of Fairhaven being able to impose rules that will allow prosperity for all. Nor will Candar prosper without the rules and harmony such as those of the White City."

"Do you really think that is possible?" A touch of scorn colored her voice.

"Look at Fairhaven—or even Elparta. Neither has folk begging in the streets. They are cleaner, and the average soul is happier."

"The traders are not."

"In Fairhaven, the traders prosper." Cerryl grinned in spite of himself, wondering just how Anya would twist the conversation to her ends.

"They're as bad as those elsewhere and, given the chance, would build palaces on the backs of the poor and the Guild."

"The Guild does not give them the chance."

"The Guild cannot be everywhere." Anya tossed her head as if to dismiss Cerryl's observation. "Nor can it dictate everything to its traders, not if it wishes to hold to its powers."

That observation bothered Cerryl, another feeling that, again, Anya had more to do with the traders than anyone in the Guild knew—or, at least, wanted to pursue. He refrained from shaking his head as he recalled how he had been dissuaded from following the missing trader and the stolen silksheen—although it was clear that trail had led to Jiolt, whose son was consorted to Anya's sister.

As the *White Flame* pitched through a trough, Cerryl reached out and steadied himself on the rail.

"Let us say that you," continued Anya, "or some High Wizard does unite Candar or the east of Candar. After him, then what? More squabbles and wars? What is the purpose of such a great achievement? To end up withering away like Kinowin or Myral or being killed like Jeslek? Or to turn what you have done over to another like Sterol to dither it away?"

"You think so little of Sterol?" Cerryl smiled.

"Sterol is what Sterol is," Anya responded. "Just as Jeslek was."

After a moment, Cerryl spoke. "You asked me, but what do you want, Anya?"

Anya flashed the smile that Cerryl distrusted. "I think we want the same thing. We want something that gives meaning to what we have done—something that will have meaning after we are gone." She shrugged. "Is that not what anyone wants?"

Cerryl mistrusted the shrug but remained silent.

"Some folk find such in their children, but that is hard for mages, and especially hard for a White mage interested in a Black."

"We've managed."

"Children would likely kill Leyladin, so strong are both of you."

Anya offered another shrug. "So you must find a meaning to your life in other fashion."

"What about you?" Cerryl countered.

"I could have children. A White can have children by a White. I could have had Jeslek's child, or yours."

Cerryl wanted nothing to do with that line of talk. "I suppose we'll have to find other means of making a mark."

"Like all the other mages who have tried, Cerryl, your mark will survive for a time, then vanish—just like this sea swallows all traces of those that travel on it."

"I will have tried."

"Just like Jeslek. Or Myral. Or Kinowin. Or Jenred the Traitor. And for what? Best you think long about that, young Cerryl." Anya turned to watch the whitecaps—as if to say that she wished to talk no more.

After a moment, Cerryl nodded to himself and walked forward and across the gently rolling deck to the other side of the bow from Fydel. Once more, he needed to think.

# CXXXVIII

The most honorable Sterol—he is now in the High Wizard's chambers." The guard—Gostar—glanced from Cerryl to Fydel, never looking at Anya, though she carried the amulet in the leather pouch.

The three walked up the steps.

Another guard, a young one Cerryl did not know, stood on the topmost landing. He turned and rapped on the door. "Three mages to see you, ser." Upon hearing something, without turning, the guard opened the door for them to enter.

The High Wizard's room remained what it had always been—a large personal chamber that contained a desk and matching chair, several white wooden bookcases filled with leather-bound volumes, a table in the center of which was a circular screeing glass, and four chairs around the table. At the far end of the chamber was an alcove, which contained a double-width bed and a washstand. Against the stone wall at Sterol's left hand was another small table holding but a large bronze handbell and a pair of white gloves.

Cerryl wanted to shake his head at the differences between the quarters and receiving spaces of the High Wizard and those of the other rulers of lands in Candar. Instead, he studied Sterol—still broadshouldered, if the shoulders were slightly more stooped, a head taller than Cerryl. Sterol's hair remained iron gray, if thinner, and his neatly trimmed beard matched his thick and short-cut iron hair. His face was ruddy, almost as if sunburned.

Brown eyes that appeared red-flecked studied Cerryl for a time, then Anya, and finally Fydel. "You bring me the amulet, I presume?"

"Who else should have it in these times," asked Anya, "save the one who held it well?" She stepped forward and extended the leather pouch.

"Thank you." Sterol took the pouch, removed the sign of his office, and slipped it over his head. The golden amulet hung around his neck, as though it had never left. He gestured to the table but did not sit but stood over the glass with his back to the open window.

The High Wizard's eyes fixed on Cerryl. "If you would be so kind as to call up the image of your smith's vessel?" Sterol's voice was smooth, so smooth that Cerryl wanted to wince.

"He is not my smith, honored Sterol, but rather Jeslek's." Cerryl offered a polite smile. "I will certainly try to locate the vessel."

The large glass on the conference table silvered over, then cleared to reveal a vessel, sails furled, moored to a black stone pier. Clouds gave the image a dark cast.

"Land's End—on Recluce," the High Wizard said flatly. His voice lowered as he asked, "How did you incompetents ever let this happen?"

The three White mages looked at the table with the mirror, then back to the High Wizard. Cerryl wasn't about to speak, not this time, and he waited, forcing his lips to remain shut.

Finally, Fydel spoke. "He built a ship that can run into the teeth of the wind. The *White Storm* went aground trying to catch him."

Cerryl nodded in agreement, stepping back from the others ever so slightly.

"Why didn't they at least fire his ship?"

The other two looked at Cerryl, and he had to answer. "They weren't carrying canvas. He'd stripped the topside, and this engine thing somehow pushed or pulled them away. They skirted the sandbars all along the coast until they got to the gulf, where the winds changed. Then they lifted sail, and with the engine and sails no one could catch up."

"Wait an instant. You said they didn't have sails."

"The sails were furled," explained Anya. Her voice was cold, cutting. "This engine device of his is as hot as chaos and bound in black iron."

"How does it work?"

"We don't know, exactly," Cerryl said, "save that it requires black iron and burns coal."

"Wonderful. Just marvelous. We now have a renegade Black wizard who can build an engine that nullifies our whole blockade of Recluce, and his ship is sitting at Land's End." Sterol sighed. "Well . . . you three and Jeslek did it. You'll have to live with it."

Anya raised her eyebrows.

"Really, Anya. Are you that dense? Have we ever had any success against Recluce proper?" The High Wizard smiled coldly. "You three incompetents can leave. You had better hope that the Blacks on Recluce hold the price of asylum on their fair isle as no more Black engines."

"Or . . . ?" asked Anya.

"I told you. Now, all of you, please go away." Sterol fingered the gold amulet. "So I can determine how to address this problem that you allowed the late Jeslek to create."

"We?" sputtered Fydel.

"I certainly had nothing to do with it, and I have ensured that the Guild well knows that. Good day."

Cerryl turned with the others, stepping out onto the landing. Whom could he talk to? Leyladin was still in Lydiar.

"Now what?" asked Fydel as Sterol's door closed behind them.

"I'm getting cleaned up," Anya said. "I'm certainly not waiting for Sterol to find some disagreeable chore for me."

"Just like him," mumbled Fydel.

Slowly, Cerryl walked down the stairs behind them, letting them get farther and farther ahead. Once he was on the White Tower's lowest level, he turned to the right and made his way back to Kinowin's door.

He knocked.

"Come in, Cerryl." The overmage's voice was strong.

Cerryl opened the door and stepped into the room—so different from that of Sterol or from what Myral's had been. Myral's quarters had been filled with books and Sterol's bare of all but essentials. Kinowin's walls were filled with the purple-oriented colored hangings, and his books remained limited to a single four-shelf case on the wall beside the sole window. Even the table that held his screeing glass was covered with the green-trimmed purple cloth.

A gaunt, almost emaciated white-haired figure sat in the chair behind the table. Cerryl forced himself to smile. "That's a new hanging, isn't it?"

"Yes, Shenan sent it to me from Ruzor. She misses her brother, but she was wise not to return." A painful smile crossed the once-powerful figure's face. "You don't have to force the smile. I know seeing me like this must be a shock."

"It is," Cerryl said quietly. "Leyladin said you were nearly as old as Myral, but I didn't really see it."

"I'm not quite *that* old, but my years are limited." The overmage paused. "I used more chaos than Myral when younger."

"Are you sure you're all right?"

"I get tired more easily, but I don't have a cough like Myral did, and my bones are still solid, and they say my tongue has gotten sharper." Kinowin smiled crookedly. "Did you see Leyladin?"

"She's in Lydiar. I took a ship with Anya and Fydel, and . . ." Cerryl shrugged. ". . . I really didn't want to go charging into the duke's hold."

"Good." Kinowin nodded. "She's fine, but it's better that Estalin and Sedelos not know about you yet."

"Sedelos?"

"Sedelos has been the Guild adviser to Estalin since the turn of last year. If you showed up, he'd have had a scroll back to Sterol within days, and you don't want anything like that going to Sterol right now."

The younger mage frowned.

"Cerryl—best you be careful. With Jeslek gone, there is no one to brook Sterol, and he needs you not as a foil to Jeslek. While you could best Sterol in wielding chaos, you would have little support from the older members of the Guild—save me and Esaak. We count for much less these days."

"You're the overmage."

"It's an honor, not a power."

After the momentary silence that followed, Cerryl asked, "What do you think I should do now?"

"You don't really need this old mage's thoughts. Just keep doing what you are. Do what Sterol asks in a way that won't hurt you or Leyladin or the Guild—and wait. Never trust Anya or Fydel or put yourself in their power. Don't make any more enemies in the Guild. Oh . . . and pay all the debts you owe. Even those you've forgotten."

"That's all?"

"You'll find that doing those things will take all the skill you possess for the next few years, especially remembering the forgotten debts. After that, it will get easier." Kinowin's face sobered. "One more thing . . ."

"Yes?"

"Find me a unique purple hanging somewhere."

They both laughed.

"Now . . . you need to eat and let everyone know you're back—the way you want to tell them."

Cerryl rose.

"Don't forget to draw the golds you are due. You also get double pay for the time you were in Spidlar."

"I didn't know that."

Kinowin's eyes twinkled. "There are still a few things I can tell you. Not many, but some."

"More than you think."

"Less than I think," corrected the overmage. "Now . . . go."

As Cerryl walked down the steps to the main foyer of the entrance Hall, his thoughts returned to the golds—near on three years' pay in golds. That was hard to believe. Kinowin had also mentioned debts—forgotten debts—and Cerryl had a few of those. *Ones you'd rather forget...*

He kept walking, back toward his dusty room.

# CXXXIX

The shadows of the fast-moving clouds cooled the air and brought a hint of fall to Fairhaven as Cerryl walked down the Avenue toward the main Patrol building. Debts to pay—even forgotten ones, and those that involved no coins—he had more than he'd thought, but Kinowin had never steered him onto a false course.

A single horse clopped along past The Golden Ram, pulling an empty farm wagon. It could have been his imagination or poor recollections, but the streets of Fairhaven seemed less busy than when he had left for Spidlar, and he still wasn't quite sure whether he recalled more bustle than had been the case or whether the war and the trading from Recluce had, in fact, reduced the traffic.

He turned south and walked swiftly, enjoying the cooler breeze.

The Patrol building was unchanged, and Cerryl paused momentarily in the rectangular and spare entry hall, taking in the two halls angling from the corners farthest from the entry, the backless oak benches, and the closed double oak doors on the back wall. The featureless and time-polished granite floor was still dull gray, and the only light came from the windows that flanked the entry door.

One of the two guards glanced at Cerryl.

"Cerryl to see Patrol Chief Isork, if he's in."

"I'll see, ser."

The patroller walked down the short hall, spoke through the open door, and then returned. "He'll see you, ser."

"Thank you." Cerryl made his way to the familiar small room, no larger than six cubits by ten.

Isork, pudgy-faced and muscular, glanced up from the flat table desk on which rested a stack of parchmentlike papers, an inkwell, and a quill holder, and a single volume. "What brings you here, Cerryl?"

"I just got back from Spidlar a few days ago." Cerryl forced what he hoped was an easy-looking smile. "I had some time to think. So I came back to thank you."

Isork frowned. "For what? Throwing you off the Patrol?"

"No. For giving me the chance in the first place and for *only* throwing me off the Patrol." Cerryl grinned. "You were most generous under the circumstances."

"Well . . . word is you did a good job of running Elparta. You must have learned something here." Isork's voice remained neutral.

"I learned a great deal. I just didn't learn to apply it fast enough. I did want to let you know that." He added quickly, "I'm not asking to be brought back. I think I could do the job now, but that would set a very bad example for the future."

Isork smiled wryly. "You have learned. It shows all over you, and it's a shame, but I hope the Patrol will be with you whatever you do for the Guild. Do you think you'll stay an arms mage?"

Cerryl almost shook his head. Surprisingly, he'd really never thought of himself as an arms mage, though that was clearly what he'd become. "I don't know. For now, I'll do what the High Wizard and the Guild wish of me." *Especially since I have little real choice.*

"None of us have that much choice in the colors of White we wear." Isork stood. "I wish you well, and I hope you'll come back from time to time."

"I will." As he left, Cerryl understood something else. Isork had not asked more because the Patrol chief was waiting to see if Cerryl would come back again. *One done, and more than a few to do.*

# CXL

Cerryl sat at the freshly polished flat desk in his room, a room that seemed far smaller than when he had left it.

"After having a mansion as your headquarters in Elparta," he murmured with a self-deprecating smile, "your perceptions might just change." *Quite a change from an orphan happy to have a closet to himself.*

He looked at the glass, then concentrated until the image of a coach filled the glass, and from what he could tell, the coach was well past the turnoff for Howlett and not all that far from Fairhaven.

Cerryl set aside the glass with a half-smile. Leyladin was indeed on her way back to Fairhaven, and with the clear roads she should be at her father's mansion before evening. Cerryl glanced out at the late mid-afternoon sun, then stood and stretched.

He paced across the narrow confines of his quarters. Sterol had sent a messenger ordering Cerryl to stand ready to attend the High Wizard. He couldn't very well leave the Halls, and he had to wonder what the High Wizard wanted, especially after Kinowin's warning nearly an eight-day earlier. Yet, until now, nothing had happened, and he'd been left to himself.

The sharp knock echoed through the room.

"Yes." He took two steps and opened the door.

The messenger in red peered up at him, almost fearfully.

"Mage . . . Cerryl, the High Wizard would see you now."

"I'll be right behind you."

"Yes, ser." The messenger looked decidedly unhappy with that phrase.

"Go on. I'll be there."

Without a word, the youth raced back toward the stairs and the White Tower. Cerryl walked quickly, but not enough to raise too much of a sweat in the muggy heat.

Still, Sterol glared as Cerryl entered the High Wizard's chambers. "You took long enough." Although the High Wizard was seated behind the conference table, he did not gesture for Cerryl to sit.

"I came immediately. I did not run because I wished to be ready to do your bidding." Cerryl could smell the scent of trilia and sandalwood, but Anya was not in the chamber.

"You do little bidding but your own, Cerryl, from what I can tell." Under the iron-gray hair, Sterol's red-rimmed eyes were unblinking as they studied the younger mage. "So . . . what is the Guild to do with you? You are an arms mage who is hopeless with weapons. You are a Patrol mage who cannot return to the Patrol. You are yet too young to train apprentices in the sewers and too experienced to continue as a simple gate guard."

Cerryl frowned, as if in thought. "I could assist one of the over-mages. Or I could continue to follow what the smith does in Recluce and what he plans. Or I could help supervise the younger gate guards."

Sterol smiled. "Perhaps you should do all three. Report to Kinowin and tell him that he is responsible for your accomplishing all three duties successfully. He is in charge of the gate details, in any case. Should the smith do something that merits my attention, you will first tell the overmage. You are not to disturb me without his approval. Do you understand?"

"Yes, honored Sterol."

"Go find Kinowin and inform him."

"Yes, ser."

"I do not wish to see you, or hear of you, except as Kinowin sees fit. You are far too full of yourself for one so relatively inexperienced."

"Yes, ser."

"Don't think you're deceiving me with your politeness, either."

"What do you wish?" Cerryl asked. "The High Wizard merits courtesy."

"Just go."

Cerryl nodded and turned, ready to lift his order/chaos shields at the slightest hint of chaos from Sterol, but he left the topmost level of the White Tower without either chaos or more words from the High Wizard.

Kinowin was in his quarters, much as Myral had been, as if he had been waiting for Cerryl and his orders from Sterol.

Cerryl immediately repeated his conversation with the High Wizard, concluding, ". . . so I am your charge."

"The High Wizard wants you kept well away from him . . . well away. That is as much Anya's doing as his."

"She had been in his chamber before me."

"She is there most often, far more than merely to pleasure Sterol or herself. Leave that aside. There is little either of us can do about that at the moment. In order to please Sterol, we will follow this pattern. Report to me either before noon or before the evening bell each day on what the smith has done. On the even days you are to visit and inspect, unseen, the gate guards in whatever order you see fit. At the evening bell, report anything that needs addressing. On the odd days, see me after breakfast for anything I may need help with. The evenings are yours, and I hope you spend little of them in the Halls." Kinowin smiled. "Use what days you have; the life of a mage is short enough."

"Ah . . . thank you."

"Go. You can start tomorrow." The older mage cocked his head and smiled. "She should almost be at her father's, and you might wish to greet her. The flower sellers are still on the square."

Cerryl stood. "By your leave?"

"By my command, if necessary."

Cerryl fled, hiding the smile.

# CXLI

Cerryl paused at the end of the walk, wondering if he looked like some fop or schoolboy, with the fragrant white roses wrapped in green ribbon.

The carved front door opened, and Layel stepped onto the stoop and gestured to the mage. "Cerryl . . . I take it from your presence that Leyladin is coming home."

"That's what the glass shows. Her coach was just beyond the north gates when I left the Halls."

"Please join me. There's little enough point in your standing out here in the heat, and I don't want to have my daughter attacking my lack of courtesy." The balding blond trader laughed.

Cerryl stepped out of the heat, past the silent houseman Soaris, who nodded, and into the comparative cool, following the older man to the front sitting room—the one graced by the portrait of Leyladin's mother. After laying the flowers on the side table, Cerryl took the settee.

"How long have you been back?" asked Layel, settling into an upholstered armchair.

"A little less than an eight-day."

"I imagine you're finding that Fairhaven is not quite the city you left, though it has changed but little." A slight smile creased the factor's lips.

"More that some folk I left are not quite as I recalled," Cerryl admitted guardedly. "I don't find that Fairhaven itself has changed, and it compares most favorably with what I have seen elsewhere."

"People often make the city—or a person."

"You mean Leyladin? I was looking for her before I even knew who she was."

"She told me. Can't say as I understand, but she has always been the one who followed the shaded path. Wertel—he would have been a factor had he been born a cobbler—and Aliaria and Nierlia . . . well, they've enjoyed having their own households."

Cerryl tried to place the names. Wertel had to be Leyladin's older brother. She had mentioned her two sisters, but he hadn't recalled either's name until Layel had mentioned them.

"You two are in a difficult position," Layel said.

"A Black and a White in love, you mean?" Cerryl frowned. "I suppose it's also created problems for you."

The factor leaned forward in the big chair, eyes more firmly on Cerryl. "More here than elsewhere. Wertel trades on the impression of connections, and you are not unknown—or unrespected—but he runs things in Lydiar and not in Fairhaven. Duke Estalin depends on mages, and Sedelos favors trade." Layel glanced toward the door. "Did you hear a coach?"

"No. I don't think so." Cerryl paused, considering the other's words. "You seem to be saying that the Guild is not so favorable to traders as it should be."

"We pay higher tariffs than those who trade from other lands, yet they use the same roads and are free to enter the city on payment of a mere pittance. We can enter any city, but our costs are higher, as our tariffs are." Layel blotted his forehead with a blue cotton cloth. "Then, there are those factors who appear more favored than others, if you take my meaning."

"I'd heard such," Cerryl said carefully, "but never seen it." He paused, thinking of how Sterol had used Kesrik's purported attack on Cerryl as an excuse to exile Kesrik's trader father. "Or perhaps I saw such and did not recognize it."

"It is there, if observed carefully."

Cerryl could suddenly sense a gathering presence, a bright darkness, and he stood, gathering the roses to him. "She's almost here."

The slightest of frowns appeared on the trader's face. "I'd not heard the coach."

Cerryl picked up the flowers, eased toward the door, and was at the foyer when the sound of hoofs on stone came through the window.

"Not even a glass." Layel stood more slowly.

Cerryl hurried down the walk and then to the side courtyard where the coach had pulled to a stop. The door flew open, even before he had quite reached the mounting block.

Standing on the whitened granite block, Leyladin looked down at Cerryl, then at the roses. "Flowers . . . you never brought flowers before."

"I missed you." He felt himself flushing, looking into the dark green eyes, seeing the reddish blonde hair, the fair skin, and, most of all, the order and the understanding behind the fine features.

"You're sweet." The healer looked at her father, who stood a pace or so behind the mage. "He is, you know."

"He's also got some wit. We were talking while we waited for you." Layel looked at Cerryl. "Go ahead. Embrace her. Kiss her. You're as much consorted as you can be."

This time, Leyladin flushed. "Father, I can't believe you."

"Too old to deceive myself, or let you do it." The trader grinned.

Cerryl stepped toward the mounting block, and she stepped down into his arms, and they did embrace, ignoring the late-afternoon heat.

How long Cerryl wasn't sure, except he heard Layel clearing his throat.

"Now that you two have greeted each other, I'm for eating. Meridis has doubtless scraped something together."

"Give me a moment to wash off the worst of the road dust," Leyladin offered as she and Cerryl separated. "I'm hungry, too. I won't be long."

"Not with your mage waiting, I'd wager."

"Father . . ." Still blushing, she took the roses as Cerryl handed them to her again. She and Cerryl held hands and walked toward the front door.

Both Meridis and Soaris stood in the entry hall beyond the foyer.

"Meridis . . . he brought roses." Leyladin smiled. "Could you . . . while I wash up?" She extended the roses to the older woman.

"I'll put them in the good crystal vase, where you always like them," said Meridis. "Now, don't be dallying. The supper's ready."

"I won't." The healer reached out and squeezed Cerryl's hand. "Cerryl, Father, I'll meet you in the dining hall. I won't be long."

"I believe I have heard words like that before." Layel's words were gentle, teasing.

"You have, but I won't be." With the last word, she slipped down the hall and out of sight.

Cerryl followed Layel through the sitting room.

"You felt her, didn't you?" asked the trader. "She said you two could do that. So close, and yet you dare not have children."

Cerryl winced. "It might kill her."

"She told me such, and she will have none but you."

"I'll have none but her."

They had barely reached the table when Leyladin appeared, still wearing her green trousers and silk shirt, with the black vest that seemed even darker than black itself in the fading light of day and the glow cast by the oil lamps in their wall sconces.

"I said I would not be long."

"And so you did." Layel seated himself at the head, and Cerryl and Leyladin sat on each side, across from each other.

As Layel poured the cool white wine into the three goblets, Cerryl looked across the table into Leyladin's dark green eyes. "How was your trip back?"

"The highway was almost empty."

"More and more like that these days." Layel nodded morosely.

"Trade is bad?"

"So little I'd not be calling it trade. Enough of that." He raised his goblet. "To both of you being home."

"To being home," echoed Leyladin.

Cerryl raised his goblet with a smile, without words, and they drank.

Meridis set three platters on the table. "The cold spiced fowl and the chilled pearapples and the riced beans. Nothing to be making you hot on a warm evening."

"What will you be doing now, Cerryl?" Layel eased the fowl platter toward his daughter.

"The High Wizard gave me some duties to carry out for Overmage Kinowin, probably until he can find somewhere distant to send me." Cerryl went on to explain in very general terms his assignments. ". . . and that means reporting every day on what the Blacks are doing with that ship."

"It truly moves against the wind?" Layel frowned.

"It does, and sometimes faster than a normal ship."

"A ship such as that, well, many be the traders who'd find a use for such."

"I cannot see how Recluce would allow a chaos engine, even one bound in black iron," ventured Leyladin before taking a bite of the fowl.

"In time, in time, a better ship will turn any trader's mind," mumbled Layel, "and your White brethren forget that the Black ones are traders first and order mages second."

*Traders first and mages second.* "And you think the Guild puts magery first and trade second?"

"Power first, magery second, and trade a poor third," suggested Layel. "Yet trade builds power. That the Black ones have discovered. All power is built on coins, and coins come from goods, and goods can but be sold through trade."

Cerryl ate a mouthful of the sweetened and chilled pearapples, thinking about Layel's words, about all the golds he had seen in Gallos and even in Spidlaria.

"Father would have been a great lord elsewhere." Leyladin laughed. "Wertel will make him one yet, from all he does in Lydiar, over Father's protestations."

"Fairhaven is my home," grumbled the trader. "Yet only the old overmage understands how what I do benefits her."

"Kinowin?"

"Aye, but he'll be gone in a handful of years, and then that spawn of Muneat's dead brother will turn the city over to Muneat and Jiolt."

"Anya?"

"That's the one. She plays Jiolt like . . ." Layel shook his head in disgust. "Muneat sees through her, but he's near on a score of years older than I am, and his boy Devo—well, he couldn't count golds with his fingers."

"Anya tried to play Jeslek." Cerryl glanced across the table.

"And he's dead," Leyladin pointed out.

"Sterol uses her. I don't think he's taken in."

"She'll find a way to turn the Guild against him," predicted Leyladin. "That's why Jeslek was trying to make that smith in Diev your problem."

"So is Sterol." Cerryl nodded slowly. "I have to follow the smith with the glass and report every day."

"She's clever," mused Leyladin. "If you don't keep track, then you'll be in trouble. If you do, and everyone knows it, then Sterol will have to do something."

"I worry about that," Cerryl admitted.

"We can't do anything tonight. Not about Anya. How are Aliaria and Nierlia? I need to see them." The green eyes danced. "They should meet Cerryl."

"You're going to be an aunt again. Nierlia says this one will be a girl and she'll name her after you."

The hint of darkness crossed the healer's face, followed by a smile. "I'll spoil her."

"Not any more than Nierlia will," suggested Layel. "Oh . . . and Aliaria's oldest—I can never remember her name—Aliaria has her taking guitar lessons from some music master who claims he's from Delapra . . ."

". . . she doesn't have any rhythm . . ."

". . . Aliaria thinks it will improve her chances for a good consort . . ."

". . . barely over a half-score years . . ."

Before Cerryl knew it, the small talk had drifted into silence. Layel stretched and yawned almost ostentatiously. "I think I'll be leaving. I need to write a scroll to Wertel before the evening's over so that it can go on the morning post coach." He stood. "You might find the front room more comfortable, but you two are young, and you'll find whatever suits you."

Meridis appeared, as though she had been waiting. "Be best if I could clean all this before I have to burn every lamp in the place."

Leyladin laughed. "We're being directed."

"No one directs you, Daughter!" called Layel from the door to his study.

The two mages—White and Black—stood and walked into the sitting room, where they paused. Meridis had arranged the roses in a crystal vase on the low table beneath the portrait of Leyladin's mother.

"You don't mind that they're there?" the healer asked.

"No . . . why?"

"Mother loved roses. I haven't been so good as I should."

"Wherever you would like them."

Leyladin touched his hand, and they crossed the entry hall into the darker front room, where not a single lamp was lit against the growing late-summer dusk. They sat on the long settee that faced the open windows, and the cooler evening breeze wafted around them.

"How is Estalin's son?"

"He's fine, for now. He'll need healers all his life, at times. He's not that strong."

"I'm glad you could leave."

"I don't know as I could. I told Sedelos that there was nothing to be gained by my staying and that he could summon me were I needed. I knew you were coming home, and I wanted to see you."

"Sterol is High Wizard now."

"Anya is the one to watch."

"I know." Cerryl refrained from repeating Anya's words about children.

"We can talk about the Guild tomorrow." Leyladin paused. "Can you stay . . . here?"

"For now," he said.

"I meant at night."

"Yes." He grinned in the dimness. "I'm glad you want me to."

"You really can?"

"Kinowin almost ordered me to. He said my nights were free and he expected me not to waste them in the Halls."

"He said more than that."

Cerryl nodded. "He said a mage's days were too short."

Leyladin's arms were around him. "They can't be. They can't be. You can't be like Myral and Kinowin. You have to use more order and less chaos. You can't leave me. I won't let you."

His eyes misted, and for a time he held her in the growing darkness of the front room.

"I meant it," she finally whispered.

"I know. You'll have to help."

"Any help you need."

He tightened his embrace, then brushed her lips with his.

"Bringing the flowers . . . that was sweet. Thank you."

Silently Cerryl thanked Kinowin.

"And thank Kinowin for me, too." Her dark green eyes danced, brighter than any lamp, as she reached for his hand to lead him to a silk-hung bedchamber—one he had but seen in a glass.

# CXLII

Cerryl stepped into his quarters at the back of the rear Hall. He sniffed. The scent of trilia and sandalwood was faint but unmistakable. What had Anya been seeking?

He cast his senses across the small room, the space he used only for work in the days since Leyladin had returned from Lydiar, but could detect no concentration of chaos or even of order. He shook his head. Perhaps for the first time in his life, he truly had no secrets, and the redhead clearly thought he did.

He closed the door and sat at the desk, studying the screeing glass for a moment before concentrating on finding the smith and his vessel. When the silver mists cleared, the glass showed Dorrin's ship anchored in a rough bay off a low and marshy point of land. Where?

Cerryl scratched the back of his head, then tried again.

It took Cerryl most of the remainder of the morning to discover that the Black ship lay off the southwestern tip of the isle of Recluce, no-

where near even a town. There were several tents and what looked to
be several dwellings or structures under construction.

He tightened his lips. What exactly the ship's movement meant he
didn't know, but Kinowin needed to know as well. Perhaps the overmage might have some ideas. If the smith and his followers were building a town or another port . . .

Cerryl pursed his head, finding it hard to believe that the smith had
done so much so quickly. Then, this Dorrin had helped destroy half the
forces sent into Spidlar, killed Jeslek, built an engine that moved a ship
against the wind, and escaped the blockade. What was building a town
in a few days compared to that?

Letting the image fade, Cerryl massaged his neck and forehead before heading to see Kinowin. It was almost noon by the time he stepped
into Kinowin's room amid the gathering of purple hangings.

"You have a disturbed look." Kinowin touched the purple blotch
on his cheek, almost absently.

"The smith has moved his ship to the southern end of the accursed
isle."

"Away from Land's End. Some might say that is well."

"It lies at anchor in a small bay. There are tents on the land and the
beginnings of buildings."

"A town for him and his followers, you think?" Kinowin smiled
faintly.

"I would guess so, but it is too early to tell."

"Then it is too early for me to tell the High Wizard aught except
that the ship has been moved. One should not disturb His Mightiness
with mere speculation."

Cerryl raised his eyebrows at the heavy irony in the overmage's
voice. "Speculation."

"Ah, yes, speculation." Kinowin made a sound halfway between a
laugh and a snort, and for a moment he looked cadaverous. "I suggested to the High Wizard that this vessel might prove useful for trade,
and he suggested that he had little time to worry about what might be
when he was gathering a force to break the latest Duke of Hydlen to
rein."

"The latest?" *How many have there been in the last few years?*

"Another cousin. Afabar, I believe. He is from Asula, one of the
ancient towns that claims the purest line of descent. He also has the
support of the traders of Worrak, Pyrdya, and Renklaar. There are few
traders of coins outside of those cities."

"He refuses—the new duke—to pay tariffs?"

"He has not said anything—by messenger, by scroll, or in any other
fashion. Fairhaven does not exist for him. You recall Derka?" Kinowin
leaned back in the chair.

"He went back to Hydolar."

"The Council made him mage adviser, but he declined and vanished—quickly—and they sent Elsinot."

"The new duke killed him somehow?"

"How did you guess?"

"Mountain cats don't lose their claws," Cerryl said dryly.

"So Sterol does not wish to deal with mere speculation at the moment." Kinowin's mouth quirked. "I will tell him that the ship moved and that you will watch closely. I will also tell him you are out inspecting the gates this afternoon. I suggest you do so, and that after you do, you make your presence known to one of the gate mages."

Cerryl nodded. "I should give Sterol no excuses and no offense."

"Not until you must."

"Also . . . Anya's been in my quarters when I've been gone."

"That surprises me even less than the movement of the smith's vessel."

"I should ignore her but leave nothing that I would not wish Sterol to see?"

"You understand, Cerryl. Unfortunately, that is the way matters will be for a time. After you eat, be on your way. I will be meeting with the High Wizard in the early afternoon." Kinowin grinned. "Did she like the flowers?"

Cerryl flushed. "She did." Then he grinned. "And she said to thank you also."

"Hang to her, Cerryl. She is worth all those in the White Tower, this old overmage included. Consider yourself fortunate, and waste no days . . . or nights."

Cerryl flushed even more brightly.

"Go." Kinowin laughed gently. "I'll not tariff you more."

# CXLIII

Cerryl studied the empty Avenue, his eyes flicking around the square. Despite the infrequent street lamps, the whitened granite of the Avenue held and reflected enough light, even at midnight, that Cerryl's borrowed mount had no difficulty in making her way from the Artisans' Square up the narrower Way of the Lesser Artisans. The shops of the first crafters were as he had recalled, including the old potter's, but the one that had held the weaver's shop—where he had first seen Pattera—

that now held yet another potter, if the emblem over the door were true.

He guided the mare down the alleyway—*past all the sewer catches*—toward the rear gate to Tellis's house. Outside the courtyard, Cerryl sat in the saddle, then fingered the leather pouch—a small handful of golds, but a few golds were all he had. *Not all by any means, but you have other debts to pay, and now is not when you should be poor again, either.* Self-deception? *Probably.*

He smiled in the darkness, not quite sardonically, as he swung down from his mount, which he tied to the gate. He looked in all directions, but all the nearby windows were dark. Then, letting the light-blurring shield rise around him, he opened the gate from the alley and eased across the rear courtyard. Rather than open the common room door, Cerryl tied the pouch to the door latch and cloaked it in a faint illusion, one that would break the moment a hand touched the latch and one that would not hold past midmorning.

He wondered if Tellis and Beryal or Benthann would guess who had left the pouch. One way or another, it didn't matter. *Another debt paid . . . as best you can for now.*

He retreated to the gate, which he closed, and then untied the mare and remounted. The faint clop of hoofs echoed down the alley and then along the Way of the Lesser Artisans as he retraced his path back to the small stable behind Layel's small mansion. The air remained warm and still, the Avenue empty, except for one White mage and his mount.

Once back at the stable, he dismounted and led the mare to her stall. He brushed her quickly in the darkness, then closed her stall and the stable door, making his way through the gloom back to the door on the south side of the house. He unlocked it with Leyladin's key, then relocked it behind himself. His steps were not quite noiseless on the marble floor, but no one roused—or called out—as he opened Leyladin's bedchamber door, then closed it behind him.

"You weren't that long. How did it go?" asked Leyladin sleepily as he undressed and then slipped under the single sheet, more than enough for the warm night.

"It was too little and too late, but . . ."

"Better than not at all." She touched his lips with her finger. "Tellis? The weaver girl?"

"Tellis. The weaver has moved."

"I'll ask Soaris to see if he can find her. No one should know you're the one who's looking. Especially Anya."

*Especially Anya.* "Thank you."

"I'm glad you are who you are." Two warm arms slipped around him, and their lips met.

*So am I . . . after all these years.*

# CXLIV

$S$itting at the other side of the round table, the gaunt Kinowin sipped some early cider from a mug.

*Just like Myral. Does age do that?* Cerryl's eyes lingered on the mug.

"The apple juice helps." Kinowin smiled. "I used to wonder that myself. Now, I know. What more about the smith?"

"He is building a town. I wasn't sure to begin with," Cerryl admitted, "but in two eight-days he has the beginning of another port town. The Blacks are letting him do it; some are even sending timber and supplies"

"Maybe it's just a way to get a second good port," suggested the overmage, fingering the collar starburst with the fingers of his free hand. "The waters are smoother in the winter there."

"They've even got a timber wharf, and the glass shows walls and footings for a stone quay or something. He's working on the bay, making it bigger, but with some kind of order force."

"You can't use order that way," Kinowin pointed out.

"He used some kind of order force to kill Jeslek," Cerryl countered.

"Are you sure he just didn't use order to contain that force?"

Cerryl shrugged. "That might be, but he's as Black as they come, with no trace of chaos. How did he come up with that kind of force? Chaos is the only force I know of that's so strong."

Kinowin fingered his clean-shaven chin, his eyes going to the purple and blue hanging on the wall above him. "Cammabark or explosive powder, I'd guess, and he put it inside black iron so none of you could spark it off with chaos fire."

"What if he builds something bigger than what he carried?"

The overmage offered a wan smile. "If he doesn't, someone else will. That's usually what happens."

"He could use it against our lancers or—"

"That won't work," Kinowin replied. "He can only forge so much black iron. He couldn't possibly forge enough to take on even a few companies of lancers. It has to be a limited weapon." He laughed. "Good against mages and little else. This Dorrin didn't remain in Diev. You'll also note that Sterol avoided talking to you three about his weapon."

"I wondered, but that's not something you ask the High Wizard." Cerryl laughed once, softly.

"Just watch to see if the smith is building something else. In the meantime, I will tell Sterol about the town and the new harbor," Kinowin said. "Now that we're sure. I only told him that the ship had been moved away from the part of Recluce, where there were towns. He laughed at that."

"He won't laugh now."

"No. He'll try to blame you. That's why I won't tell him until I've written a short scroll about it and given a copy to Redark and a few others." Kinowin offered a wry grin. "It will be later this afternoon. We can't afford to allow him to claim we delayed unduly."

"Then what?"

"You give me a short written report each day—dated, you know, fiftieth day after the turn of spring . . . first day after the turn of summer."

"What will that do? He'll still want to blame me."

"I'm sure he will. But he can't, not with the reports. So he'll send you somewhere, and it won't be bad for you to be someplace else for a while."

Cerryl wasn't certain he wanted to be somewhere else. He hadn't had that long with Leyladin, and here the overmage was suggesting they be separated again.

"Remember," Kinowin said gently, "you wanted to be a White mage."

The overmage's words hung in Cerryl's mind long after he had left the tower and was riding out to the south gate for another inspection.

*You wanted to be a White mage . . . but did you have any real choices?*

*Yes . . . you just didn't like any of the others.*

# CXLV

Cloaked in the light-blurring shield, the one that would not scream his presence to an alert gate mage, Cerryl stood in the early-afternoon shadow of the guardhouse beside the north gate.

Another of the younger mages he did not know paced along the upper balcony, looking down and out at the empty White highway that stretched north and then eastward to Lydiar. The gate mage rubbed her forehead, then her neck, before pacing back across the worn stone tiles, the same tiles Cerryl had paced in years past. It scarcely seemed that long ago, before Spidlar had become more than a name on a map and a wiry smith had killed the most powerful chaos mage in generations.

Cerryl focused his eyes on the gate mage, who had seated herself on a stool. Below her, the three duty guards stood in the shade of the gates, not a dozen paces from him.

"... slow ..."

"... always slow anymore, except for the post coaches ... some of the factors' wagons ..."

"Don't see many wagons out of Certis or Gallos these days."

"Hydolar, neither ..."

Cerryl nodded to himself. As Layel and Leyladin had also noted, the roads were almost empty, except for farmers bringing produce to Fairhaven, and such slow commerce was unusual at any time, particularly in summer.

Then, there was the problem of the Black smith. Each day Cerryl screed the southern tip of Recluce. Each day he wrote a report, and each day more dwellings and structures were appearing in the smith's town on Recluce. Kinowin had reported such to Sterol, but the High Wizard had done nothing—at least nothing that Kinowin had relayed or that Cerryl had perceived.

Nor had Cerryl found any more traces of Anya's presence in his room in the Halls.

The quietness that filled the Halls of the Mages bothered Cerryl. Something had happened—or would happen. He just hadn't been able to see what it was or might be.

His eyes went back to the gate mage. She had stood and begun to pace again—as he had so often.

# CXLVI

Cerryl stepped into the overmage's quarters. Kinowin was standing by the table, beside the purple wall hanging with the blue arrows. His face was impassive.

"What's the matter?" Cerryl concealed a frown. "Did I do something wrong?"

Kinowin shook his head. "You did nothing wrong. I have been requested to bring you to the High Wizard."

Cerryl did frown and began to raise, slightly, his order shields.

"You won't need those. Eliasar was killed. Sterol is sending you to take his place." The overmage offered a grim smile.

"Me? To get me out of Fairhaven? How did it happen?"

"That and because you are the best one to send. You know the land better than any others here. You're strong with chaos. Although you've taken great pains to conceal that, Sterol is no fool, and more perceptive about that than either Jeslek or Anya."

"And I'm away from you."

"That, too, but you don't need my advice, not that much, anymore."

"I don't know about that," Cerryl protested. "What happened to Eliasar?"

"Iron crossbow bolts . . . that's what Lyasa's scroll said."

"Lyasa? She's there. She could handle things. Or Syandar. What happened to Buar?"

"Neither the older members of the Guild nor the folk of Spidlar would take kindly to rule by Fairhaven under a woman. That also wouldn't give Sterol an excuse to send you there. As for Syandar, he's all right as an administrator, but he can scarcely muster enough chaos to light a fire. And Sterol already sent Buar back to the blockade fleet."

"I think I'm going to Spidlaria."

"Sterol has insisted on confirming that—as soon as you arrived." Kinowin gestured toward the door. "Shall we go?"

The two walked up the stone steps, Cerryl being careful to walk slowly, all too conscious of Kinowin's heavy breathing, marveling sadly at how quickly the big and powerful mage had become a gaunt old man. *Will that happen to you?*

The guard on the landing outside the High Wizard's quarters opened the door and announced, "Overmage Kinowin and Mage Cerryl."

Sterol did not rise from where he sat at the table, with his back to the open window. The light summer breeze had not carried away all the scent of sandalwood.

"If you would sit." Sterol inclined his head to the chairs across from him.

Cerryl waited for Kinowin to sit, then seated himself.

"I presume the overmage has told you that I would like you to go to Spidlaria and complete the tasks Eliasar had begun." Sterol's words were deliberate, evenly spaced.

"Yes, ser."

"I would like you to find those responsible for his death and ensure they are executed publicly."

"I will do my best on that," Cerryl said cautiously.

"You do not promise that so readily."

"If those responsible come from Recluce or beyond the West-horns . . ." Cerryl shrugged.

"Young, but cautious." Sterol steepled his fingers for a moment, then cleared his throat. After another silence, he continued. "You are younger than would be best for what I have set before you, but caution may assist you. The malefactors of the Black Isle have cost us grievously." Another pause followed.

Cerryl forced himself to wait.

"There will be a blockade ship waiting for you in Lydiar, Cerryl." Sterol looked mildly across the circular table. "You will leave on the post coach in the morning. I will draft a scroll with your commission. You may obtain it from Kinowin in the morning."

"What do you expect from me?" Cerryl brushed back hair he feared was thinning like Myral's had. "In Spidlaria."

"Anya reported that you had managed to set matters right in Elparta. I expect the same in Spidlaria. After Syandar and Eliasar reduced Diev, Eliasar sent Syandar to Kleth. Syandar will remain there, but he will answer to you. Kalesin remains in Spidlaria and so does Lyasa. With their assistance I'm sure you can manage. We look forward to the resumption of tariff coins."

"There are not likely to be many ships in the near future."

"The Guild and the Council are confident you will find a way to resolve the problem." Sterol's words were flat, their tone indicating he had said what he would say. "I expect written reports on your progress each eight-day." The High Wizard stood.

So did Kinowin and Cerryl.

They walked back down to Kinowin's quarters. There the overmage settled into the chair behind the table. Cerryl remained standing.

"Sterol wants either the tariff golds or a way to blame me," suggested the younger mage.

"He needs the golds more," Kinowin said. "He has been going through those set aside for lean times, and there are but a few thousand left."

*A few thousand—once you would have marveled at that number of golds.* "How long before those set aside are gone?"

"I do not know, but no more than a half-year, less if Rystryr and Syrma delay their tariff payments." Kinowin laughed, half-humorously, half-bitterly. "Sterol can no longer stir their fears with the threats that Jeslek could."

"He can suggest that they could vanish as have other rulers."

"He already has," Kinowin said. "How long can he use such a threat before he must carry it out? A year? Two? One cannot remove rulers too frequently, or they ignore the threat because they fear they will be removed whatever course they follow."

"Hmmmm . . . So what would you do were you the High Wizard?"

"Try to gather more coins and spend less. Let matters settle so that traders again fill the roads."

"And try to make sure than outland traders pay the surtax on goods from Recluce?"

"That is more difficult because the ships for the blockade are costly."

"What should I avoid in Spidlaria?"

"Being too lenient and too understanding. Remember, all men and all traders—and all women—serve themselves above others." Kinowin gave a crooked smile. "No matter what they profess or how earnestly they affirm their allegiance. Study the coins and follow their course, not the words of the men who gather them."

"Should I seek for Leyladin to join me?"

"Not unless it appears that you will be in Spidlaria as the mage adviser for many years."

Cerryl nodded. "I am being sent as the head arms mage, then."

"If that. Your power is what you make it."

"I'd better make ready."

"Spend most of that time with the healer." Kinowin's smile was faint, almost self-mocking. "Trust the words of an aging mage there, Cerryl."

What sort of love had the overmage known and relinquished—or lost? Cerryl nodded. "I will."

"Then be on your way."

Cerryl gave a last nod and departed. On his way back to his quarters, to pack what he would need, Cerryl paused at the archway to the Meal Hall, looking in at the double handful of apprentices scattered across the tables. He knew not a single one—that was how out of touch he was with the Halls. Even Kiella had become a full mage and stood gate duty. Idly Cerryl wondered if the redheaded apprentice sitting by herself was Viedra, the one poor Faltar had fallen for before he'd left to fight in Spidlar.

Myredin and Faltar, and even Bealtur, were dead. Of those who had become mages when Cerryl had, only Heralt and Lyasa were left. Heralt was still in Ruzor with Shenan. Of course, Cerryl would be in Spidlar if Heralt ever did get to Fairhaven. *You'll probably spend the next ten years in Spidlar, so long as Sterol is High Wizard—or whoever Anya maneuvers to succeed him.*

Cerryl swallowed. How could he have been so stupid? Anya had wanted him to take the amulet in Diev. If he had, then he and Sterol would have been at each other. Even if Cerryl had prevailed, he would have had to rely on Anya for her contacts, especially with the large trading families, and politicking to keep the older members of the Guild, or enough of them, behind him. But he probably wouldn't have prevailed—Anya would have seen to that.

He frowned. He had to do something. Did he dare to take the chance? Then he shrugged and turned, hoping he could find the redheaded mage.

Anya surprised him. She was in the Library, poring through a thick and ancient tome. "Cerryl."

"Anya. Have you a moment?"

Anya flashed the broad smile, and the scent of trilia and sandal-wood flowed around him. "For you, Cerryl, I can spare a moment."

"I am most grateful."

They walked to the fountain courtyard. There Cerryl walked into the shade in the corner where the falling water would mask their voices.

"What do you want?" For once, Anya was not smiling as she turned to him. Her eyes darted to the far corner, toward the door from the main Hall.

"I'll be but a moment. I was thinking, and I wanted to thank you."

"I don't know as I merit thanks." Puzzlement and interest appeared in her pale eyes, eyes neither quite green nor blue.

"After Jeslek's death, you offered me the amulet, in a way. I think I understand why now, and I appreciate the gesture. I'm leaving for Spidlaria in the morning to take Eliasar's place, but I wanted you to know that I did appreciate your suggestion."

"Thank you, Cerryl." A faint smile appeared and vanished. "Is that all?"

"Well," he added, "you seem to work well with Sterol. But you know where you can reach me, and Leyladin can get me a message if you need something I can provide."

That brought a faint smile, one not quite real, but one with a hint of self-satisfaction and wistfulness, an expression that faded as she spoke. "I forget at times how young you were when you became a full mage. You continue to grow. I thank you for your offer." The bright smile appeared. "You had best be readying yourself."

"I will."

Together they turned back toward the rear Hall. Once inside, Anya slipped toward the Library and Cerryl toward his quarters. He packed what he thought he might need—including two sets of whites, small-clothes, spare boots, and his ragged-edged copy of *Colors of White*—and set it on the narrow single bed.

Then he left, walking quickly through the Halls and up the Avenue toward the Market Square, before turning left at the side street leading to Layel's dwelling.

Soaris opened the door, his eyes widening slightly as he beheld the White mage.

"Is Lady Leyladin here, Soaris?"

"I believe so, ser. Would you come in?"

"Thank you." Cerryl followed the blue-vested and huge man into the sitting room.

"I will tell her you are here. It may be a moment."

"Thank you," Cerryl repeated. He did not sit but studied the portrait of Leyladin's mother, studying the blue eyes that seemed to follow the beholder.

Leyladin appeared nearly immediately—wearing green trousers and a light silk shirt without a vest. Her red-gold hair was ruffled, half-disarrayed. "It's barely afternoon." The usually dancing green eyes were somber and fixed on Cerryl's gray orbs. "What happened?"

"Eliasar was killed. The High Wizard is sending me back to Spidlaria to take his place. Tomorrow."

"Tomorrow?"

He nodded.

She was silent, then stepped forward and slipped her arms around him. For a time, they just embraced.

Then the healer eased back, her arms still loosely around him. "This is all a ploy to get you out of Fairhaven . . . and to discredit you." Her voice was low, pitched as if to keep it from others.

"I know. Making me responsible for obtaining and collecting tariffs when there's no trade. Why me?"

"Neither Sterol nor Anya wish you around." She snorted. "You might actually come up with the tariff coins. No one else could, and the way we're losing mages, you're already one of the few really skilled ones left."

"Recluce is winning this war, if it is a war." He paused. "I told Anya you could get me a message if she needed one."

"You what?" The healer stiffened.

"I worry about Kinowin's health, and I'm not so sure about Sterol. It's just a feeling. He's not quite the same, and I don't know why. Anya can be counted on to preserve herself."

Abruptly Leyladin smiled. "You're more devious than you let on, dear mage. You implied that she could count on you if something happens."

"I suppose I did. Was that wrong?" Cerryl frowned.

"No. Not since you told me." Her eyes narrowed. "But when did you tell her this?"

"Just before I came here."

"Ah . . . coming from another woman to me?"

"That's not . . ." He grinned as he realized she had been teasing. "You!"

"You'd best remember that."

"I promise."

"Now . . . I know you have to leave early in the morning, but you are staying here the rest of today and tonight."

"Are you sure?" asked Cerryl, grinning in spite of himself.

"Of that I'm quite sure."

They both smiled . . . bittersweet smiles.

# CXLVII

The *White Serpent* pitched forward, riding the downside of the swell before spray cascaded over the bow. Cerryl swallowed hard, hanging onto the heavy wooden railing and glancing toward the west, wondering if his stomach would hold for the remaining two days of the voyage from Lydiar to Spidlaria.

The ship was a faster way to get to Spidlaria, but not terribly comfortable, especially in the heavy swells.

"How ye be, mage?" The ship's second stood at Cerryl's elbow, standing there without holding onto anything.

"Fine." Cerryl forced a grin. "Except I don't seem to be able to walk anywhere without holding on."

"Must be a storm to the northwest . . . a mite unseasonable this far north in summer. Hope the Black ones haven't been calling their storm mages." The second gestured off the starboard bow quarter, almost into the sun that beat down out of a green-blue sky that held but the faintest hint of high, hazy clouds. "Don't ye worry. We'll have ye ashore afore the worst reaches this far south."

"Good." Cerryl paused. "Did you see the Black ship—the one that needed no sails?"

The second's face clouded. "Aye. Demon-driven it was, and the Black one skirted the reefs and left us near becalmed. The mages' fire—it washed over the ship, scarce touching it. Evil as anything I ever saw upon the deep, that it was."

"It's anchored off Recluce," Cerryl volunteered.

"I'd wish it were anchored twenty-score cubits deep." The second laughed. "Not that chaos listens to a poor sailor." With a nod, the man turned back aft.

If the Black ship worked, Cerryl knew, there would be more on the Eastern Ocean, just as there had been more chaos mages once the ancients had unleashed the White power, just as Recluce had become inevitable after the fall of Westwind.

He glanced to his left, in the general direction of Fairhaven. He hoped Leyladin would be all right. Once at sea, with the swirls of order and chaos, he couldn't use his glass, even in the times when the ocean was calmer.

Kinowin would watch out for her, and Anya wouldn't seek her harm, scheming as the redhead was, because Anya wouldn't want to upset Cerryl, not while she still had uses for him.

The reluctant arms mage's lips quirked. *You'd almost rather deal with the Black smith than with Anya—except that you have no choice.*

The *White Serpent* pitched again, and his fingers tightened on the railing.

# CXLVIII

In the early-afternoon sun, Cerryl set the two packs down beside the railing where three crewman wrestled the gangway into place. He inclined his head to the dark-bearded master of the *White Serpent*. "Thank you, Captain."

"My duty, mage."

"I appreciate it." Cerryl offered a smile.

"You be one of the few who do." A wintry smile crossed the man's face. "These days."

"We'll try to change that."

"You do, and we'll all be pleased."

Cerryl gave a nod and reclaimed his packs.

A stocky mage with sandy blond hair—a man about Cerryl's age or even slightly older—stood on the wharf. On the stone pavement at the foot of the wharf waited a detachment of White Lancers—mounted in formation. Cerryl thought he recognized Hiser as the subofficer leading them.

The mage stepped forward as Cerryl carried his two packs down the plank to the heavy-planked wharf.

"Mage Cerryl? I'm Kalesin. Are you here . . . ?"

"The High Wizard sent me to replace Eliasar."

A momentary expression of dismay crossed the other mage's face. Cerryl extended the scroll. "As sealed by Sterol."

"The High Wizard commands." Kalesin took the scroll.

"Inspect the seal and open it," Cerryl said.

"Here?" Kalesin glanced to the *White Serpent*, then to Cerryl.

Cerryl began to muster both chaos and shields.

Kalesin swallowed and looked at the red seal. He fumbled open the scroll, and fragments of red wax sprayed across the planks of the wharf. His eyes went to the signature first, then to the words. He read the words twice. "You are the arms mage of Spidlar. But there is no mention of a mage adviser."

"Right now, there is no one to advise," Cerryl pointed out.

"The Traders' Council . . ."

"Yes . . . I'll need to see them. One at a time. Then the traders who have remained—and any who have come from Diev or Elparta or Kleth." Cerryl gestured toward the lancers. "Shall we go?"

"Ah . . . yes, ser."

Cerryl could tell the words were bitter in the other mage's mouth and stopped. Kalesin took two steps, then turned and halted.

"Kalesin."

"Yes?"

"Perhaps you should remember a few things. I am here with the blessing of the High Wizard and of the Council. I also have the support of Anya, the assistant to the High Wizard. I'm better with chaos and order than you are, and I've had more experience as an arms mage." Cerryl softened his voice. "And I strongly doubt that I will remain here after I've returned Spidlar to prosperity. I suspect that is why the High Wizard wished you to remain."

"Ah . . . yes, ser."

Cerryl forced a smile. "I did not wish to come here, and you did not wish me here in this position. But I doubt it will be long, and it would be best that we work together so that I complete what needs to be done."

"As you wish, ser."

Cerryl wanted to blast the other but only smiled again. "We have much to do." He resumed walking toward the waiting lancers.

After a moment, Kalesin scurried to catch up with Cerryl. When the two mages reached the stone seawall from which the wharf projected, Kalesin looked up at the lancer officer. "Captain Hiser, Mage Cerryl has returned as arms mage to continue the work of Eliasar."

"Welcome back, ser." Hiser's smile was warm, almost one of relief.

That worried Cerryl. "It's good to see you. I'm glad you're a captain now."

"A mount for the arms mage." Hiser gestured, and a young lancer guided a chestnut mare forward.

Cerryl fastened both packs in place before mounting, then swung into the saddle. "I presume Eliasar took over the mansion that Jeslek used."

"That he did, ser," answered Hiser quickly.

"Then I'll follow his example."

"Forward!" snapped Hiser.

Cerryl studied the harbor square as they passed along the east side—the shops bordering the square open, but only a few passersby visible. A sense of hush, of expectation, hung over the area. Cerryl liked that feeling not at all. "Has it been like this since Eliasar was killed?"

"Yes, ser. Too quiet, if you be asking me," answered Hiser.

"I don't want any of the men traveling anywhere in groups of less than four."

"Yes, ser." Hiser nodded grimly. "I'll be letting the other captains know."

"Teras? Senglat?"

"Teras be here. Senglat serves the mage Syandar in Kleth."

"What about Ferek?"

"He be a subofficer under Senglat now."

Cerryl kept the nod to himself. Eliasar had been smart. Then, the scarred arms mage had been smart about most things, and his death worried Cerryl. Worried him more than a little with the feel he was getting for Spidlaria.

A half-score of lancers guarded the walled mansion on the low hill that overlooked the harbor. A pair stood by the double doors as Cerryl dismounted and neared.

"Good day, ser," said the one on the left.

"Good day to you—" Cerryl struggled and recalled the man's name. "Natrey. Is Zoyst here, too?"

"Yes, ser. He be my replacement."

"I know I'm in good hands. The High Wizard sent me back to carry on what Eliasar started." Cerryl offered a smile and a nod, then stepped into the two-story entry hall, still half-amazed at the wealth of the traders outside Fairhaven.

"His study," Cerryl suggested.

Kalesin turned down the hallway to the left of the marble staircase, stopping at a small door some fifteen cubits to the left of the double doors to the dining hall. "Eliasar used the dining hall for meetings but the study here for his own working space."

Cerryl opened the door and stepped inside, noting the scrolls still stacked under a stone paperweight shaped like a mountain cat. The side walls were wooden shelves filled with leather-bound volumes, and a wide window behind the desk offered a view of the harbor. The study was so warm that Cerryl had begun to sweat, and he stepped past the desk and opened the paired windows. Then, turning, he studied the ancient desk, polished wood, adorned with various bronze protrusions—an elaborate and ugly piece of good workmanship. "Sit down."

Kalesin took the single armless chair on the other side of the desk.

"Tell me exactly how Eliasar was killed. Exactly."

"It wasn't anything special." Kalesin shrugged. "I mean the way it was set up. Eliasar inspected the barracks, the ones we took over from the blues, every six-day. He was riding over there, and someone put three iron bolts in him."

Cerryl nodded, even as he again wanted to shake Kalesin. "Three bolts? Did they strike him all at once?"

"Pretty much, it seemed. He was ashes before long, before I got there."

Cerryl turned his eyes full on the sandy-haired mage. "Did you have any thought that something like this might happen?" He concentrated on applying his truth-reading skills to the other.

"No, ser. I mean . . . we knew the traders were not pleased with the edict that all sea trading had to be carried out here and inspected by me."

"Three crossbow bolts—and they all hit at once. What does that tell you?"

"There were three crossbowmen."

"How good were they?"

"They had to be good."

"Doesn't that seem strange in a land where most armsmen were killed or had fled?"

"Ah . . . when you put it that way, ser. Ah, yes."

"Was there any reaction from the traders?"

"No one said anything."

"Did you talk to them?"

"Not about Eliasar's death, except to tell them that nothing had changed."

*But it had . . .* From what Cerryl could tell, Kalesin was telling the truth, and that meant that whoever had planned Eliasar's death had understood both the Guild and Kalesin's obvious limitations. That meant Cerryl had to act immediately.

"Kalesin . . . I wish to see every factor in Spidlaria, and every trader. I also want a listing of the assistants to each of those traders. Not all the assistants, but the ones who are important, who might take over each factor's house if the factor died. Oh, and I want to see them starting tomorrow. Make sure Reylerk is here, but not the first one I see."

Kalesin swallowed. "They will not be pleased."

"The High Wizard is not pleased. The Council is not pleased. The Guild is not pleased. You might suggest to those who wish to demur that Diev is no more because a mage died." Cerryl smiled coldly. "And suggest to them that they would not like to suffer because one of their brother traders was unavailable to meet with the arms mage of Spidlar."

"Yes, ser." Kalesin's words were resigned.

"You had best be going to arrange those meetings. Make sure that a full company of lancers is on duty outside here before they arrive." Cerryl let the smile fade. *You sound worse than Anya . . .* He stood. "When you have all the arrangements made, come back and inform me. Bring a list that holds the names of all those I will see—and those you could not find. Best there not be many of the latter."

"Yes, ser." Kalesin backed out of the study.

Once the door closed, Cerryl sank into the armchair behind the too-ornate desk. *You're where you don't want to really be, with an assistant who thinks he should be Eliasar's successor and a bunch of local traders who hate Fairhaven and probably would pay to kill every mage in Spidlar if they could get away with it. And you're supposed to come up with a way to improve trade and tariffs.*

# CXLIX

Morning found Cerryl in the study munching through cheese and hard biscuits and studying the stack of scrolls and papers Eliasar had left behind, many of them lists. Lists of shops, lists of existing provisions, lists of provisions needed, lists of names, some without even the sketchiest of explanations.

Abruptly he looked up. Lyasa! She was somewhere around, and he had yet to see her. He rang the handbell.

Kalesin peered in.

"Kalesin, where is Lyasa?"

"Ah . . . she's been in charge of the patrols maintaining order in Spidlaria and on the roads."

That made sense, from what Cerryl had seen of Kalesin so far. "Get a message to her. I'd like to see her at her convenience early this afternoon. How are we coming with the merchants?"

"The merchants and factors are waiting, ser." Kalesin inclined his head, then handed Cerryl a sheet of rough brown paper. "Those are the ones who cannot be found."

Cerryl glanced down the list. None of the names meant anything to him, and that would be another problem. He rolled the list and slipped it into his right hand. He stood and walked around the overornate desk. "You had the table moved? So that I can see them in the hall?"

"Yes, ser."

Cerryl walked toward the former dining hall. Hiser and four lancers stood waiting outside the carved and polished double doors.

"Natrey and Jlen will stand by you inside, ser," Hiser said. "Foyst and Lyant will guard the door."

Kalesin glanced from Hiser to Cerryl, then back to the lancer captain. The mage assistant moistened his lips. "Four . . . ?"

"I suggested six, ser, but the master arms mage convinced me four would be enough." Hiser smiled. "With a full company outside."

"These people . . . they . . ." Kalesin's words trailed off.

"We've lost enough mages in Spidlar," Cerryl said. "And I'm going to put a stop to it." *Just like Jeslek was going to conquer the place and like*

*Eliasar was going to put it in order?* He pushed open one of the double doors and stepped into the former dining hall, glancing at the big chair, standing alone in the long room. "I'll need a small table here, to the side where I can write." He could feel and sense the repressed sigh and anger from his reluctant assistant mage. "I think I mentioned that earlier, Kalesin. I would appreciate it if you would take care of it now." *You sound like Sterol—or Jeslek. Does power do that? Or is it the frustration that comes with trying to do more than you have time for or knowledge about?*

Kalesin bowed and left.

After the door closed, Hiser glanced from the closed door to Cerryl.

Cerryl nodded. "I know." He smiled wryly. "I'm guessing that you have concerns about our assistant mage."

"Begging your pardon, ser . . . and it not be a captain's place . . ."

"Go ahead. You're more interested in my health than he is."

"He is most wroth that you were picked to succeed Eliasar. The lancers are not."

"Let us hope they continue to feel that way." *Especially since you have no real idea how to fix the mess that Spidlar has become.*

Kalesin returned, followed by two lancers, one bearing a side table and the other paper and an inkwell, quill, and stand.

"Did you get that message off to Mage Lyasa?"

"Yes, ser."

"I hope so. We're old friends." Cerryl offered a cold smile that he hoped showed Kalesin that Cerryl was well aware the message had not been dispatched. "I'm ready to see the first of the traders."

Flanked by two lancers with bared blades, Cerryl sat in the chair he had once claimed for Jeslek, looking down at the thin black-haired and bearded trader who had walked in and stood a good five paces back from Cerryl. The man bowed his head deferentially, although Cerryl could sense the defiance.

"Your name?"

"Joseffal."

"You factor what?"

"Today, ser, I factor nothing. There are no ships, and the people have no coins."

Ceryl could sense the lies. "You mean that you report no factoring and you try to keep it hidden?"

Joseffal did not raise his eyes. "The great White wizard took the most part of what all of us had."

"What did you factor?"

"Cloth, ser. Wools, linens, silks, velvets."

"You didn't factor . . . say . . . crossbows?"

The bewilderment from within the trader was clear. "No, ser."

"Do you know any armsmen who have been in Spidlaria recently?" Cerryl persisted.

"No, ser. Except those in white." The sweat dribbled down the side of the man's face, but his words remained true.

Cerryl unrolled the paper Kalesin had given him. "What do you know about Yerakal?" He'd picked the name at random.

"Yerakal?" Another puzzled expression crossed Joseffal's face. "He left long before even Kleth fell."

"What did he factor?"

"He was a wool factor, ser. Just wools, from everywhere in the world."

"What about Hieraltal?"

Joseffal swallowed. "Ah . . . he left also."

Cerryl could sense the man's apprehension, but his words came across as true. "And he was one of the ones who factored arms for Spidlar? Like crossbows and blades?"

"Ah . . . I'd be only guessing, ser, but some said he made golds on blades and bolts."

"And he's never returned?"

"No, ser."

Cerryl asked about another three factors on Kalesin's list before nodding. "We will have another talk about what you're really factoring later, Joseffal. You may go."

As the trader bowed and turned, Cerryl glanced at Kalesin. "A moment before the next."

"Yes, ser."

Cerryl dipped the quill in the inkstand and began to jot down notes about Joseffal and the "missing" factors. Then he nodded.

The second trader was burly, but he, too, kept his eyes averted as he stepped into the converted dining hall.

"Your name?" Cerryl asked.

"Aliaskar, ser wizard." Aliaskar had a high, thin voice, surprising for such a big man.

"What do you factor?"

"Clay, ser."

Cerryl wanted to laugh. Of course, with the need for pottery, china, and storage urns, someone had to factor clay.

"What do you know of crossbows?"

Aliaskar frowned under his lowered brow but answered, "They kill people. Beyond that, I little . . ."

Cerryl nodded and continued as he had with the first factor.

After each factor, he made notes on the sheets of paper.

Midday had neared when Reylerk stepped into the converted hall, bowing as he stepped forward, clearly not recognizing Cerryl. "You summoned me, master of Spidlaria?"

"I summoned all the traders and factors. You are Reylerk?"

"Yes, ser. That I am."

"And what do you factor?"

"I once factored many things—timber, rare and precious woods, even the spidersilk from Naclos. Now there is little to factor and few who would buy such." Like the others, Reylerk avoided Cerryl's eyes.

Cerryl looked at Reylerk. "What do you know of how the mage Eliasar was murdered?"

"I know nothing . . ." The portly merchant's words trembled, as if to reinforce his fear—and his lies. He coughed several times, dryly, as if forcing the cough, and his hand went to his mouth.

"Tell me what you know of crossbows."

"They are weapons, ser." The factor coughed again. "Save they are little use to a trader. They take too long to reload."

"That is true. Have you traded in crossbows?"

"No, ser."

Cerryl could sense that the crossbow subject was making Reylerk nervous, though the man hadn't lied outright, from what Cerryl could tell.

"Have you met any crossbowmen in the past few eight-days?"

"No, ser." Reylerk coughed and put his hand to his mouth again.

That had been an outright lie. "Reylerk . . . I spared you once. You are lying to me. Now . . . did you help plan the murder?"

The merchant gulped convulsively once more, swaying. Abruptly he collapsed on the stone tiles of the floor.

"Kalesin!" snapped Cerryl, sensing the ebb of both chaos and order that signified death.

The door opened, and the sandy-haired mage walked in. "Darkness!" His eyes went to the contorted figure. "Poison?"

"It would appear so." Cerryl shook his head. "Have the body removed and dragged out past the others. Then turn it to ashes in the square."

"Me . . . in the square."

"Why not? Announce that he was one of those who plotted Eliasar's murder. He was, but he wasn't the only one." Cerryl gestured for Hiser, who had peered inside the chamber. "Hiser. Kalesin will need an escort. This merchant admitted that he had helped plan Eliasar's murder. He swallowed some poison before I could discover more. Kalesin is going to announce that in the square and then turn chaos on the corpse."

"His . . . family . . . they will not . . . like that," offered Kalesin.

"I'm sure they won't. But the High Wizard would be most offended if he received an honorable burial after killing one of the most respected mages in Fairhaven." Cerryl fixed his eyes on Kalesin. "Don't you think so?"

"Ah, yes, ser."

"Hiser, have one of your subofficers provide the escort for Mage

Kalesin. I would like you to usher the remaining traders in to see me, as Kalesin was doing, while he is occupied."

"Yes, ser."

Cerryl waited until Kalesin left with two lancers and Reylerk's body. Then he nodded at Hiser, and the questions resumed.

As Cerryl suspected, he learned little more about Eliasar's death but a great deal more about which factors had traded in what—and received continued false protestations that no trading was occurring in Spidlaria.

He finished interviewing the factors Kalesin had rounded up early in the afternoon and retired with a pounding headache to the study. He carried a tray of bread and cheese and wine that one of Hiser's lancers had gotten for him.

Lyasa was waiting, sitting in the straight-backed chair. She stood and offered a sheepish smile. "I sneaked in. I hope you don't mind."

Cerryl closed the study door and looked at Lyasa. The circles under her olive brown eyes were as dark as her black hair. "Sit back down before you fall over."

"I look that bad?"

"Worse." Cerryl offered a wry smile. "Tell me about it." He set the tray on the edge of the desk closest to her. "Have some."

"Thank you."

He poured out wine, some into the goblet for Lyasa and some into the mug he used for water for himself. "You were going to tell me how bad things were and why."

"Eliasar thought you could just ride lancers around and kill peacebreakers and then people would get the idea. It hasn't been working that way." Lyasa took a deep breath, then reached for the wine.

"I got that idea. What's been going wrong?" Cerryl took a swallow from his mug, then broke off a chunk of bread.

"Nothing. Nothing's going right, either. People are sneaking away along the coast into Sligo, or into the Westhorns through what's left of Diev, or up the river woods into Gallos. Almost no one comes to the chandleries or the shops here—not during the day. I can see figures at night, but I can't stay up all the time, and Kalesin doesn't have the night sight."

*There is much Kalesin doesn't have.* "I am not surprised. He was not pleased when I showed up to take over Eliasar's job."

"He wouldn't have been. He's a lot like Kesrik."

Cerryl nodded, recalling the blond apprentice mage who had held far too high an opinion of his modest abilities—until, played by Anya, he'd run afoul of Cerryl and the High Wizard.

"What were you doing this morning?" Lyasa asked.

"Interviewing traders, asking questions, truth-reading—and getting a terrible headache."

Lyasa laughed.

"And the feeling that I'd have an even bigger one if I knew what I should."

"Maybe you know more than you think you do."

Cerryl refilled her goblet and added some wine to his mug. Then he ate another chunk of cheese. "Do you recall Reylerk?"

"The big old trader?"

"He was involved with Eliasar's death. I started to get close to asking questions, and he took poison. He died right in the hall."

"That's bad."

Cerryl stood and looked out the open window, blotting the sweat from his forehead. The study felt close. "I hadn't even threatened him. He knew I was truth-reading him."

"And he poisoned himself? Why?"

"Why do you think?"

The dark-haired mage moistened her lips. "You want me to guess. Well, I would wager that he knew something and he knew you could find it out and he didn't want to let you know it."

"A trader self-willed enough to kill himself? An attack against us?" He eased back to the massive desk.

"I would say someone he feared more than you, perhaps someone who threatened his family," suggested Lyasa. "As mages, we don't always understand how strong family can be."

"Some of us don't have family, but I can look at Leyladin and see where that might be the case." He took a sip of wine and used his belt knife to cut several small slabs off the block of yellow cheese. "Have some."

The black-haired mage took a chunk of cheese and began to eat.

"I have to wonder," Cerryl mused, "why someone would care enough to threaten Reylerk. Or what he would care enough about to kill himself to keep me from finding out."

"That shows we have a big problem."

"We already knew that." Cerryl turned and looked out at the harbor once more. After a few moments, he turned back. "I'm not very good at intrigue." *But you're getting better, unfortunately.* "Some of this is obvious. The traders know we can tell when they lie. One of the most powerful traders takes his own life rather than let me question him. No one is doing any trading or even buying things in the city."

"Recluce?" Lyasa finished her water.

Cerryl reached forward and refilled the goblet from the pitcher, then shook his head. "They've been used, just as we have. Jeslek and I played right into Rystryr's hands. I can't prove the viscount is the one, but it feels right."

Lyasa shrugged helplessly. "You may be right, but I don't see it."

"First, take the crossbow bolts. Someone tried to kill me with a crossbow when I was in Jellico. Eliasar was killed with three at once. Now . . . Sverlik was supposedly killed by Lyam. Remember, he was prefect of Gallos before Syrma? It took over a dozen archers—archers, not crossbowmen."

"What are you pointing toward?"

"Bear with me." Cerryl turned and took a swallow of the clean but warm water in the goblet. "Axalt—Axalt controlled the direct land trade between Spidlar and Certis. Axalt is no more. Then, there is Gallos, now split in twain by those Little Easthorns raised by Jeslek, with much of the High Grasslands burned to ashes. And Hydlen, rent by struggles over who would be duke ever since the untimely death of Berofar and then his son. Of course, Ferobar might have been a strong duke, too, except I was sent to kill him and I succeeded. Spidlar—Spidlaria is the best port on the northern coast, and it had strong free traders. Diev is gone . . ."

Lyasa's mouth opened. "Everything that has happened . . . it all helps Certis and its traders."

"The glass would show it that way . . ." Cerryl paused. "Shyren . . . when I found the golds in his bedchamber, he said that I was just 'his' tool. I thought he was referring to Jeslek. I don't think so now."

"Rystryr?"

Cerryl nodded. "Then there's Jiolt. Layel said something about his cousin being the largest factor in Jellico."

"Anya's sister is consorted to Jiolt's son."

"It's all like a spiderweb. You can barely see it except if you look at it in a certain way." Cerryl shrugged. "That may not be the proper way, either." *And sometimes you can't even see things. You can only sense them, like the way in which Anya used her ties with Jiolt to set Kesrik after you when you were an apprentice . . . and there was no way to prove it and never will be.*

"Best you send Kalesin to Kleth, then."

"Kalesin?"

"Once . . . he and Anya . . ."

"Has she bedded every mage in the Guild?"

Lyasa laughed. "She's tried every one, except the women, and she'd try that if she thought it might benefit her."

"What about Syandar?"

"He's not bad—like Myredin, I'd guess."

"Then we don't want Kalesin with him. We'll have to be Kalesin's keepers."

Lyasa brushed short black hair off her left ear. "Put that way, I would agree he should stay, like it though I do not."

"What do you think? About the whole situation here?"

"We're losing as badly as at the beginning. We aren't getting any golds from Spidlar. The lancers are on edge, and they feel it's but eight-days before we lose another mage."

"It will take years for Spidlar to recover, and Certis will benefit?"

"Gallos, too, if not so much."

"And the Guild is already weaker."

Lyasa nodded.

"We aren't going to do it this way any longer."

"What have you in mind?"

"I don't know. Yet." Cerryl could feel the chill in his eyes, the anger colder than chaos was hot. "But I *will* stop it. Without letting Anya and Sterol learn what I know."

Lyasa shivered.

# CL

With the dim light of late twilight fading, Cerryl looked at the image of a blonde healer in the glass for a long moment, savoring the smile offered by Leyladin, wishing, once again, that they were together before letting her visage fade.

The stacks of lists and papers remained on the study desk—a set of papers larger than those left by Eliasar. Cerryl had read them, all, and, for the most part, they were just that—lists. He picked up the shorter list, the one for the evening, the one that held Lyasa's suspected night-time traders.

He'd already ridden by the shops earlier in the day, beside Hiser at the head of a routine patrol, marking them in his mind, trying to assess which might be the most likely. He'd not told Hiser the purpose of the ride, nor Lyasa the reason for the list. The less anyone knew about what he planned, the safer he would be. Spidlaria was far more dangerous than Kalesin could know. *Or than he cares.*

With a deep breath, Cerryl stood, then stepped past the massive desk and out of the study into the hallway. "Good evening, Natrey."

"Evening, ser," answered the lancer guard, remaining alert, his eyes on the entry hall and the front door.

"How have you found Spidlaria?"

"It be an unfriendly place, ser. Folk'd spit at you, dared they to."

"They've never been that friendly, I fear." Cerryl nodded. *They'll be less friendly before they become more so.*

"Yes, ser."

"I'm going upstairs." Cerryl turned and walked toward the staircase until he was out of the guard's direct line of sight and only a dozen cubits from the barred side door.

Where to? The chandlery? The reluctant arms mage turned toward the side door out of the dwelling. He eased the light-blurring shield around him—the illusion protection that caused people's eyes to slide past him, as if he were a wall or something so commonplace that he were not even to be noticed. Then he slid the bar enough so that he could open the door and step outside.

Using the blur shield would keep Kalesin, were the other mage even around, from sensing Cerryl's presence.

Cerryl paused in the rear courtyard, drinking in the coolness of early evening for a moment. With sunset, the breeze had quieted, but it still blew off the cooler waters of the empty harbor.

He walked quietly to the rear gateway and stepped through the archway and down along the walled passage to the street below the house. He halted in the deeper shadows of the arch that opened onto the street, one of the four that led to the harbor square.

A lancer patrol rode by, the hoofs of the four mounts clicking on the stone pavement. Once the patrol passed, with the blur shield still around him, Cerryl slipped along the side street toward the chandlery Lyasa had placed on the list.

On one side was a cooper's and on the other was a structure without markings. All three buildings were dark. The chandlery's door was shut and presumably barred, the shutters fastened, but Cerryl could sense order and chaos within, the order and chaos of people.

As he watched from the nearby alleyway, a woman walked quickly toward the side of the building, where she rapped on a narrow door—a cellar door—before she darted inside the door quickly opened and quickly shut.

Cerryl edged toward the low steps that led down to the cellar, remaining shadowed and shielded. He waited, and shortly the door opened and closed quickly once more. The woman scurried past Cerryl, not even sensing him behind his shield, and down the street, staying in whatever deep shadows she could find.

How long he watched and waited Cerryl was not sure, except that the next prospective purchaser did not come soon. The big man almost waddled up to the cellar door and rapped heavily. Cerryl slid up behind him, then stayed behind the other's bulk as he lumbered into the cellar.

Once inside, Cerryl stepped to the side in the momentary darkness.

"Who you . . ." The man who uncovered the lamp on the table blinked and frowned. "Thought you had someone with you."

Cerryl could smell hot and damp wool, probably from the moist cloth used to mask the lamp. He eased into the corner of the room, trying to blend with the gloom away from the single lamp set on the narrow table.

"Just me, Tyldar. Got any cheese?"

"That I do, but don't be showing or telling it around. Be a silver for a quarter wedge."

"Steep, that be."

"Know anyone else has cheese?"

"Where did you get it?"

"Would I be telling you that now?" Tyldar laughed softly. He removed an oblong rock from the wall and reached into the opening, apparently releasing a catch or lever, because a section of stones swung open.

"Clever there."

"Old trick—put rocks from the tailings from the worked-out coal mines there and no mage, Black or White, can tell what's there. Said they hid Black healers there in the Days of Fire."

Cerryl frowned. Days of Fire? He'd never run across that before. It wasn't in any of the histories.

"Here you be." The chandler pushed the wall back into place with his hip, then set the quarter wedge on the narrow table.

"You think those Whites'll ever leave?" The buyer extended a silver.

"Thank you. When they run out of mages, they might. Some folk are saying they haven't got that many. The latest one—he's pretty young."

"He figured out Reylerk quick enough."

"Luck . . . had to be." The chandler glanced toward the door.

"Well, best be out of here."

"Check the street."

The lamp was covered, and the man who had bought the cheese cracked the shutters. "Clear-like."

"Be off, then."

Cerryl nearly tripped on the boots of the man he followed but stepped back into the shadows.

The buyer glanced around. "Darkness . . . swore . . ." He shook his head, then began to walk quickly away from the harbor.

Standing in the shadows, Cerryl frowned. He could have the lancers seize the merchandise, but what good would that do? He couldn't track down everyone who sold goods secretly. Besides, what he needed was for them to be sold in public, so that there would be a clear trail of goods on which the tariffs could be levied and collected.

Finally, he nodded, then began to walk down the street toward his second observation—the basket maker's two blocks north.

# CLI

Lyasa and Hiser stood on the other side of the desk.

Cerryl stood behind it because there was but a single chair opposite him. "As I told Lyasa earlier, Hiser, the traders are trying to keep us from collecting tariffs by pretending no trading is taking place. Most everything is done at night."

Hiser scratched his head. "Can't say as it makes sense to me. Some folk won't go out at night. Sooner or later mages like you will find out."

Cerryl shrugged. "I'm going to try something. In some of the places, I know where they've hidden their goods. We're going to make them buy and sell in the light of day."

Hiser raised his eyebrows.

"The usual way—the one I'm so adept at. Trade and pay tariffs or lose your goods and your life." Cerryl snorted.

"Will this do any good, ser?"

"It can't do any less than doing nothing," suggested Cerryl. "It won't be enough, but we're working on the next step. We'll need two companies this morning. We'll surround each shop so that no one can escape, and then Lyasa and I—and a half-score lancers—will present the alternatives." He nodded at the lancer captain. "If you would get the companies ready?"

"Yes, ser." Hiser smiled. "They'd like to see something happen."

"Good." *Let's hope it happens the way you think it will.*

After the study door closed behind the departing captain, Lyasa looked at Cerryl.

He gestured to the chair. "We have a few other things to talk about."

"You don't think this morning's work will solve everything?" Lyasa sat down.

"No. Would you help me?"

The black-haired mage smiled warmly. "Just for asking, rather than ordering, I'd be happy to. What do you want?"

"After we finish today, I want you to use your screeing glass—you can use it, right?" His eyes flicked to the window at the sound of hoofs in the courtyard outside. "I want you to track several merchants and let me know if a group of them is meeting somewhere. Whenever you find that out, find me, and let me know right then."

"That doesn't sound impossible."

"Not quite. If you're like me, you'll have to spend some time riding or even calling on them to get to know them."

"You have to do that?"

"Unless it's someone like the smith who radiates so much order that it doesn't matter." *Or Leyladin, who you found with a glass before you knew who she was.* "Or Jeslek, I suppose, though I never tried. That didn't seem wise."

"Or Anya?"

Cerryl shuddered. "I never wanted to know."

"You're still too honorable about some things."

"What I'm planning here isn't totally honorable."

"They didn't give you much choice. Neither will Sterol, but that wasn't what I meant."

"I know." Cerryl turned from the window and lifted the top sheet of crude brown paper. "We'd better get ready. Can you track these people?" He extended the list.

Lyasa took it. "I can try."

"Thank you."

They left the study and took the side door to the courtyard where Hiser and the lancer companies were forming up.

"You do one thing that Jeslek and Sterol didn't understand." Lyasa stopped by the mount being held for her.

"Oh?"

"You don't rush into things, but once you decide, you act."

*Then why do you feel like you're rushing?* "Sometimes, there's little choice and waiting can only make things worse." Cerryl swung up into the saddle. "It's still hard to know those times."

"You're doing fine."

*Maybe . . .*

By the time the column entered the harbor square, Ceryl could sense the eyes on him, Lyasa, and the lancers. He felt as though silent messages had crossed all of Spidlaria, which they probably had. As they reined up before the chandlery, Cerryl turned in the saddle. "Hiser?"

"Ser?"

"Remember, I want the chandlery surrounded. I want no one to escape, but unless someone flees or attacks, I want no one hurt."

"Yes, ser." Hiser turned. "Blades and lances ready!"

The chandler opened the barred door even before Cerryl and the lancers set foot on the narrow front porch.

"Ser . . . we have nothing." The chandler stepped back and gestured to the empty shelves of the store. "The war took most of what we had, and the lack of trade has taken the rest."

"Chandler, I don't like lying. I know you care little for Fairhaven, but you will respect her. Follow me." Cerryl gestured to the lancers, then to the chandler.

"Ser . . . where . . . ?"

"To find some goods you can sell." Cerryl let a grim smile cross his face as the chandler and his consort exchanged glances. "To the back room there."

"Ah . . . yes, ser."

The back room had more shelves and was as bare as the front had been.

"Open that." Cerryl pointed to the inside cellar door in the small back room of the chandlery.

"That is but for the cellar, and bare it is, as you will see."

"I'd like to see that." Cerryl turned to the lancers. "Half with me. The others make sure no one leaves." He followed the chandler and his consort down the creaky wooden stairs.

"You see, ser?" The man gestured to the bare clay-floored room, where only the small table remained from Cerryl's night visit.

Cerryl walked straight to the wall, removed the oblong stone, and fumbled for a moment before pulling the lever. The narrow door swung open.

The chandler paled.

"So . . . you had no goods to sell, chandler?"

"None so as I'd tell you . . . White thieves . . ."

Cerryl let chaos appear on his fingertip, then grow into a sword of flame. He let the slightest touch of chaos flash toward the outside door, leaving a blackened slash in the wood. "I could do that to you. I won't. Believe it or not, I'm not going to take your goods. I'm not even going to take a single coin out of that strongbox you have here." Cerryl smiled. "I'm not going to kill anyone. I will say one thing. If you do not put those goods back on the shelves upstairs within two days—all of them—then . . . then you will answer to me. And I will have to find someone else who will sell goods during the daytime and not under the cover of darkness."

". . . kill me . . ." The murmur was nearly inaudible.

"You are not the first who has been discovered, and you will not be the last. Spidlar was a land of traders, and it will be again. You can be one of those, or you can choose not to be."

Cerryl walked up the steps and out the front door to where Lyasa and Hiser and the bulk of the lancers waited, mounted and stationed in groups around the building. With a smile, he mounted. "Leave a half-score here. I don't want anyone coming with a wagon and carting off all the goods. If people come and buy, that's fine."

While Hiser talked to the subofficer of the detachment that was to remain, Cerryl glanced at Lyasa. "They won't do anything for a time—to see what happens."

"Would you?" Her eyebrows arched.

"I wouldn't. But I know White mages hate being crossed."

She laughed softly, and Cerryl had to grin—until he thought of how many more shops lay ahead of them.

When Hiser eased his mount back toward the mages, Cerryl said quietly, "Now . . . the wool factor's place—Joseffal's." Behind him, he could hear a few murmured comments from the lancers.

"Tough little bastard . . ."

"Blues'll find out . . . knows everything."

*Not nearly a tenth part of what you need to know . . . if that.* He forced himself to keep the smile in place as he urged the gelding forward.

# CLII

In the late-afternoon light, Cerryl stood just inside the study door and studied the pile of scrolls and lists. He knew it hadn't grown, but he hadn't decreased it much, either. Finally, he settled behind the desk. After four days, he'd barely finished his initial round of publicly "discovering" goods, and his legs ached. So did his head, and from what he could tell, no goods had appeared on any shelves.

*So . . . do you start executing people?* He took a deep breath.

Before long, he needed to meet with Lyasa and talk over what he could do next without destroying whole cities the way Jeslek had. *You're beginning to understand why he did, though. Destroying things is a lot easier than getting cooperation. But destruction didn't raise tariff coins, at least not after what you grubbed from the ruins.* He took another deep breath and let it out as someone knocked on the door. "Yes?"

The door opened, and the sandy-haired Kalesin peered in. "This arrived from the High Wizard, ser." Kalesin bowed slightly as he extended the scroll.

"Thank you." Cerryl paused. "How are you coming on that compendium of shops and traders?"

"Ah . . . another day or so, ser, I would say. It's hard to find out about some of the shops that are closed."

"Keep working."

The door closed, and Cerryl studied the scroll, opened and resealed, from what he could tell, probably by his good and faithful assistant Kalesin. With a twist of his lips, he broke the chaos-mended seal and began to read:

While you have been in Spidlar but a few eight-days, we must reemphasize the need for coins with which to repay the costs of the campaign so unwisely undertaken by our predecessor. We direct you to consider some form of local tariff or surtax, as you see necessary . . .

*In short, send coins—lots of coins—and Sterol isn't that particular how you obtain them.*

Cerryl wanted to snort. Bleeding the beaten land to death wouldn't solve the problems Fairhaven faced, as if Sterol or any of those in the Halls really cared. *Except Leyladin . . . or Kinowin.* He looked at the words and set the scroll on the desk, closing his eyes for a moment.

Lyasa burst into the study, breathing hard. "Five of them—Menertal, Zyleral, Tillum, Sirle, and Halak—are meeting in the back room of that public house off the main square."

"Now?" Cerryl stood, almost losing his balance before turning and glancing toward the courtyard. "I'd better get there."

"You—you're the arms mage."

"Who else can do it? Besides, I have no intention of letting them see me."

"At least, let Hiser bring a troop somewhere close."

Cerryl had to admit that made sense. "Can you find him? Or some lancer subofficer you trust? Have him waiting in the corner of the square closest to the public house."

"I can get Suzdyal's company there first."

"Fine." Cerryl opened the study door and brushed past his guards and out into the courtyard.

As Lyasa headed toward her mount, Cerryl walked along the narrow passage from the courtyard to the lower street, lifting the shield that caused people's eyes to shift away from him. Once on the lower street, he forced himself to move quickly, but deliberately, so that he'd not be winded when he reached the square and the public house. *What do you hope from this?*

"An improvement," he answered in a murmur, suspecting that was unlikely. *But you have to try.*

The weathered signboard outside the public house bore the image of a brown boar with oversized yellow tusks and smaller letters beneath in Temple tongue—"The Brown Boar."

The White mage took another deep breath and stepped through the open door. A few eyes glanced toward the door but slid away from the eye-blurring shield. Cerryl tried not to swallow as he caught a glimpse of mail beneath a stained shirt and several daggers almost lengthy enough to be shortswords. The near half-score of men in leathers who sat around the tables in the main room were anything but indulgers.

*This isn't sensible . . .* Then life wasn't sensible. The blur shield around him, Cerryl edged across the floor toward the two doors in the rear. A few men glanced in his direction, and one burly man frowned, then blinked.

A serving girl walked around Cerryl without realizing she had.

"... don't like this. Whites got lancers everywhere ..."

"They don't want to fight." The speaker laughed. "Figure they fought enough already ..."

The front room was filled with the odor of smoke, cooked fat, spilled ale, and unwashed bodies. Cerryl began to muster chaos as he moved slowly but deliberately toward the back—keeping away from the tables that held the disguised armsmen.

The door to the back room was closed. Cerryl raised a full light shield and settled into the darkness, letting his senses tell him about the room beyond the door. Five men sat at the table in the rear room of the inn, and a single guard stood on the other side of the door.

With a wry smile, the mage opened the door and stepped inside—unseen even as all eyes turned to the door—and then around the guard.

"What ... ?"

"Probably blew open. There's no one there."

"Make sure it's latched, Dignyr."

*Clunk!* The guard shut the door, and Cerryl slipped into the corner, deciding to remain in darkness and to listen for a bit.

"This latest thing of his—telling them to sell or lose everything—some folk won't hold with us, Menertal. You can't ask them to."

"We can ask what's necessary. If the Whites can't get coins, they'll lose."

"Not before destroying Spidlar."

"Why don't your ... 'friends' kill this one like the last? There aren't that many mages outside of Fairhaven?"

"This one is harder to get to than the old one. His lancers respect him. And he never tells anyone when he'll be going somewhere."

"Anyone can be killed ..."

Cerryl continued to listen.

"We have to do some of this ourselves."

"The hard part."

Cerryl took a deep breath and began to muster as much chaos as he could draw around his shields.

"Look in the corner!"

*Whst! Whst! Whst!* ... Chaos flared across the room, in six quick flashes that centered on the guard first, then the traders around the table. The chaos flashed so quickly that there was not a single scream or exclamation.

Cerryl felt the world twist around him, and for a time he just leaned against the wall gasping. When he looked up, his shields down, the center of the room remained a drifting pile of white ash.

He walked heavily to the door and gently unlatched it, raising his blur screen as he stepped aside and let the door swing open. The pounding in his head bit through his skull like a disintegrating sawmill blade. He gritted his teeth and waited.

"What happened?" One of the armsmen in the main room bolted to the open door. "Everything's gone!"

After the first rush to the door, Cerryl waited and eventually slipped through an opening, ignoring the exclamations from the disguised armsmen. Trying to hold his guts and the blur shield together, he walked slowly back along the main street and around the corner to where Lyasa and the lancers waited. He dropped the shield with relief, ignoring the few gasps.

The lancer subofficer reined up beside Lyasa was a dark-haired and hard-faced woman—one of the few women subofficers in the lancers, Cerryl suspected. Beside Lyasa was Cerryl's mount.

"You're all right?" asked the black-haired mage.

"I'm fine." *Sort of . . .* He swung up heavily into the saddle, trying to ignore the weakness in his legs, the pounding in his head, and the faint queasiness in his guts.

"This is Subofficer Suzdyal. Mage Cerryl." Lyasa raised her eyebrows. "Now what?"

"They ought to have arms ready," Cerryl said.

"What did do you?"

"Arms ready!" snapped Suzdyal. Blades and white-bronze lances glittered in the late-afternoon sun of the fading summer.

"Let's just say that the plotters all vanished."

"All five?"

Cerryl offered a twisted smile. "That's my one skill—removing people who are difficulties. I have to use it too much."

"I wish more leaders did," said Suzdyal dryly. "You expecting a riot or something?"

"No. Let's ride down the side street to the public house."

As the formed-up lancers approached the public house, several of the disguised armsmen stopped on the street.

"Armsmen, all right," said Suzdyal. "Locals'd run and get cut down from behind. What'd you want us to do with them?"

Cerryl looked at Lyasa, then looked at the five men standing before the sign of The Brown Boar. He raised his voice. "Let them go, unless they cause trouble. If they do, kill them."

One of the leather-clad armsmen started to open his mouth. The man next to him elbowed him in the gut and spoke. "He meant nothing, ser mage. We'll be going peaceably."

"Good. Spidlar is going to stay peaceful, and people are going to start trading again—out in the open. Those who think otherwise won't be around long." Cerryl offered an icy smile but kept his eyes fixed on the men until they slowly began to walk down the street away from the lancers.

Every so often one or another would glance back over a shoulder.

Cerryl kept scanning the area, for anything that might cause problems, with both senses and sight, but could find nothing.

When the shadowed street stood empty, silent, Suzdyal gave Cerryl a quick look. "They'll tell the others."

"And?" Cerryl finally wiped the dampness off his forehead.

"There won't be so many eager the next time some fop flashes silvers before them."

Cerryl hoped not. "I think we can head back."

Suzdyal and Lyasa nodded.

# CLIII

With Suzdyal's lancers behind him and Lyasa beside him, Cerryl rode slowly around the square, glancing at the handful of people who moved from shop to shop. Three or four buildings remained shuttered, but most were open, despite the air of sullenness, almost of shock.

The day was cooler than the hot late-summer days that had preceded it, with high hazy clouds and a warmish wind out of the south that brought a dryness to the city. Spidlaria wasn't as bustling as it doubtless had been once, but people were going through the motions of buying and selling. Sooner or later, because sneaking around was exhausting, most would return to normal—except that there wasn't enough trade.

"They're doing what you wanted," Lyasa said, her voice dry. "They don't like it much."

"They'll get used to it," answered Suzdyal. "They had to realize that Fairhaven was something different from Gallos or Certis."

"Because they always used trade as a weapon before?"

The subofficer nodded, her eyes on three men at the corner of the square. "Those three. You might want to ask them a question or two, honored mages."

Cerryl's eyes flicked to the hard-muscled trio as he guided his mount toward them, flanked by lancers with drawn blades. Cerryl looked into the tall and bearded man's flat brown eyes. "You wouldn't be from Certis, would you?"

"No . . . ser."

Cerryl knew even Lyasa could feel that lie.

"And you wouldn't still be on the viscount's payroll, would you?"

The man's eyes flickered to the two lances centered on him. "No . . . ser. Don't know no viscount."

Cerryl smiled and looked to the second man, shorter and burly in stained gray battle leathers. "How about you? Did you come from Certis, too?"

"No, ser."

Cerryl laughed. "You're both lying. The viscount paid you to come here and help the old traders cause trouble. Most of them are dead. You keep this up, and you'll be dead, too. Of course, if you want honest work, you could come to the headquarters and talk to Mage Lyasa. We'll need some honest and experienced men as patrollers."

Abruptly he could sense something wrong, and he turned to see the crossbowman on the roof. *Whhst!* As the first charred figure fell, Cerryl wheeled the gelding and surveyed the square.

*Whhst!* The second crossbowman tumbled from the side porch of the basket maker's shop.

Cerryl continued to scan the area, as did Lyasa.

When Cerryl looked back at the two men, he had to concentrate to keep his legs from shaking. Both were pinned against the chandlery wall with lances against their chests. Several townspeople peered around the corner, watching, waiting for him to kill the disguised armsmen.

"*If* . . . if there is one more attempt on anyone from Fairhaven," Cerryl said loudly, and coldly, "your lives, if you are seen again, are forfeit. We are trying to heal Spidlaria, to put the city back to work. You, and your friends from Certis, seem more interested in destroying it. Is that because Certis fears the folk of Spidlar? I wonder."

Cerryl turned and nodded to Suzdyal. "Let them go. This time."

He could feel the eyes on him as he, Lyasa, and the lancer column rode away from the chandlery and then toward the square on the way back to his headquarters.

". . . White bastard . . ."

". . . don't cross him."

"Fair in his own way . . ."

"Call destroying five factors fair . . . had to be him . . ."

"Certis—he was certain on that."

"Lies . . . all lies . . ."

". . . don't know about that . . . don't know at all."

Cerryl cleared his throat and looked at Lyasa. "You think I was too easy?"

"Maybe."

"No, begging your pardons, mages," offered Suzdyal. "Killing the bowmen was fair. Killing a man on the square would have angered 'em so they'd not think."

Cerryl hoped so, but he was hoping far too much. Among other things, he needed a trader, a good trader—like Layel. He pursed his lips. Well, Layel wouldn't have much competition in Spidlaria.

"You have an odd look on your face," Lyasa observed.

"I'm thinking about bringing in a trader—and giving him Reylerk's establishment."

"Layel?"

"Why not?"

"You are a dangerous mage," Lyasa said, almost straight-faced.

"Can you think of anyone else?"

"Not that the Guild—and you—could trust." Lyasa paused, then added, "If he will do it, your redheaded friend will not be pleased."

"Because she's Muneat's niece, you mean?"

"She's *very* close to some of the traders, one in particular."

"And every other man with something to offer," Cerryl added dryly.

The black-haired mage laughed.

Cerryl paused, realizing Lyasa knew more than he did. "Which one is she so close to?"

Lyasa raised her eyebrows. "It's only been said . . ."

"I understand."

"The one who is father to her sister's consort."

Cerryl nodded. *Jiolt . . . again.*

After dismounting in the headquarters courtyard, Cerryl hurried back to the study and began to write. He needed a good trader—and one he could trust. *Will Layel see it that way? Will he consider it worth his while?*

Who knew? All Cerryl could do was offer the opportunity.

When he was finished, he had one of the guards summon Hiser.

The blond captain inclined his head as he entered the study. "Yes, ser? I understand you had some trouble earlier. I'm sorry I wasn't here."

Cerryl shook his head. "Subofficer Suzdyal handled it well, and you can't do everything."

Hiser looked relieved.

"I do have a small task I'd like to entrust you with." Cerryl extended the small sealed scroll. "I need this to go to the factor Layel in Fairhaven. I do not wish Kalesin to be troubled with it."

"I imagine we could send it with our courier, ser." Hiser grinned. "I can make sure it's the last scroll he gets, as he's leaving."

"That would be good. I'm hoping that the trader Layel might be able to help us settle Spidlaria. It would be better if none knew this." Cerryl shrugged. "He might not wish to do so, and that could cause problems. Or he might, and that would cause other problems."

"I understand, ser." Hiser paused. "I'm glad it was Suzdyal. Prytyr

would have done well, also. The others . . . some I don't know as well
as I should."

"Others you do," replied Cerryl. "I'm glad I got a good one." He
paused. "And thank you."

Hiser inclined his head, then turned.

Cerryl looked at the stacks of paper and scrolls, then stood and
stretched. He was hungry, and the papers would be there later.

# CLIV

Cerryl closed the door of his study on his way to one of his frequent
but irregular and unscheduled rides through Spidlaria. He hadn't done
a noon ride in a while, nor one in the rain. He hoped the headache that
the light rain gave him wouldn't get worse, but he couldn't afford not
to keep inspecting the city, and he couldn't do it only in good weather.

"Cerryl!" Lyasa's voice carried an urgency as she marched toward
him, her whites as spotless as ever, despite the early-fall rain that had
come and gone all morning.

"Yes?"

"Suzdyal's lancers caught a man running from the chandlery—the
one where you made them sell their goods."

The way Lyasa spoke, Cerryl had the feeling he wasn't going to like
what came next. "And?"

"The chandler—Tyldar—he said nothing was the matter, but he had
blood on his apron and a freshly bound wound on his arm. He kept
insisting that he'd cut his arm himself."

"He's afraid to talk." Cerryl sighed. "All right. Where's the man
who ran?"

Lyasa smiled. "He and the chandler are in the reception hall—with
lancer guards."

"You know me too well," Cerryl complained.

"Not as well as Leyladin, but well enough for this."

"Wait a moment. I need a list." He turned back to the study.

"A list?"

"Of the larger traders still alive and in Spidlar. Kalesin's effort, the
one you cross-checked."

"You think one of them is behind this?"

"If it happened to be planned . . . yes." Cerryl opened the door and
retrieved the list, then closed the door and nodded to the lancer guard.

"I don't know how long I'll be, Foyst. Don't let anyone in—unless I send Mage Lyasa back."

"Yes, ser."

As they walked toward the reception/meeting hall that had once been a dining hall, Lyasa added, "I wouldn't have thought of that so quickly. We don't have a Patrol here. You're really the only one with Patrol experience."

"We do need a Patrol, but it won't work if Fairhaven supplies the patrollers."

"It won't work if we don't control it."

"We'll talk after I see these two."

Outside the reception hall were a score of lancers. Cerryl raised his eyebrows.

"I thought it better to be safe," she answered.

"I do hope it's not that bad." He opened the door and stepped inside to find another half-score of lancers, two with barred blades flanking the chair set behind a flat table.

Cerryl took the chair and looked out across the empty table at the man the lancers had caught—burly, short-haired, and with a flatness to his eyes. While the arms mage was certain he hadn't seen the man before, the accused peacebreaker was of the same type as the disguised armsmen hired by the five traders Cerryl had turned to ash.

Lyasa eased up behind Cerryl's left shoulder.

"Would you care to give your name?" Cerryl didn't care if the man did or not.

"Hystryr."

*Not too bright . . . a clear Certan name . . .* "What were you doing at the chandlery?"

"I wasn't there."

"That's your first lie," Cerryl said quietly. "Did someone point out Tyldar—the chandler? Did someone point him out to you?"

"I wasn't there," the man repeated.

"That is your second lie. Was it a trader who paid you to harm the chandler?"

Hystryr's eyes flicked to the lancers with barred blades flanking Cerryl and to Lyasa. "I don't know what you're talking about."

Cerryl pulled out the list he had thrust into his belt. "Was it Nussal?"

"I don't know what you're talking about."

"Querialt . . . Yurtal . . . Kestrisal . . ."

Cerryl stopped and turned to Lyasa. "Go with Hiser or Suzdyal and a full company of lancers to bring in trader Kestrisal." He beckoned her nearer and added in a low voice, "As soon as you have the trader, bind his hands *immediately*, and don't let him put anything near his mouth."

"Yes, ser." A grim smile appeared on Lyasa's face as she straightened, then turned and left the reception hall.

The color drained out of Tyldar's face. Hystryr looked dumbly at Cerryl, his eyes avoiding the chandler.

Cerryl smiled. "You don't understand, do you? You've seen but a fragment of the power of the Guild." His eyes went to Hystryr again. "While we're waiting for trader Kestrisal, you can answer a few more questions."

The bravo straightened slightly. "I don't know nothing."

"Were you promised gold by the viscount's officers . . . ?

"Did you do other . . . work . . . for Kestrisal . . . ?

"For other traders . . . ?"

Cerryl plodded through a long series of questions, the reactions of the bravo providing greater certainty that Rystryr had indeed been attempting to subvert the Guild's hold on Spidlar, but the bravo showed no reaction to other names.

As Cerryl questioned the bravo, the chandler's expression varied between fear and horrified interest.

Cerryl broke off the questions when the reception hall door opened. The bound trader who had to be Kestrisal struggled as the lancers set him on the stone tiles a good dozen cubits back from the table.

Cerryl mustered the slightest chaos flame, letting it elongate toward the angular trader. "I suggest you stand there quietly."

Kestrisal stiffened, and his goatee quivered.

"This bravo from Certis has indicated—unwillingly, I must admit—that you directed him to harm the chandler Tyldar. Did you do this?"

"Of course not," sneered Kestrisal. "I'm scarcely that stupid."

"Like your tool . . . Hystryr"—Cerryl had to struggle for the bravo's name—"you lie."

Kestrisal looked at Cerryl impassively.

Cerryl looked at the list. "Did Querialt have anything to do with this?"

There was neither answer nor reaction.

"Yurtal?

"Sieral?"

Cerryl smiled. "Note the name of Sieral." Behind him, Lyasa nodded, and Cerryl continued down the list.

Although the trader refused even to speak, Cerryl could see the slow deflation of the man.

Finally, Cerryl stopped the questioning of Kestrisal and turned to Lyasa. "See if you can find the other four and bring them here."

"Yes, ser."

As the black-haired mage left, Cerryl turned back to Kestrisal. "We might as well discover what else we can."

The factor's eyes dropped.

"Were you approached by agents of Viscount Rystryr of Certis?

"... of the prefect of Gallos?

"Were you promised the support of Certis for a new Council of Traders on which you would serve?

"Were you given golds to continue to oppose the Guild ..."

Cerryl finally paused and had one of the lancers bring him water, so dry was his throat. He had barely resumed when the next trader appeared, also bound. Cerryl motioned for Kestrisal to be moved aside and began to question Sieral, repeating his questions, ignoring the growing headache the effort engendered, but nodding to himself as Sieral silently confirmed the pattern.

With each of the two succeeding traders, neither of whom would speak, the arms mage continued his efforts. Finally, he stopped and cleared his throat. He was getting hoarse from all the unaccustomed talking.

Cerryl studied the four bound traders, then the bravo, and finally the chandler, before his eyes went back to the bravo. "Hystryr, you are to be kept in chains until you can be sent back to Certis."

The bravo flinched but remained stolid after the one reaction.

Cerryl fixed his eyes on the wounded chandler. "Tyldar, you are to receive ten golds in damages from each of the strongboxes of these four traders. You are to use half of those golds to buy goods for sale to others. Is that clear?"

Tyldar gulped. "Yes, ser."

Cerryl paused, then continued almost conversationally. "As for you four, I'm tired of dealing with people who use golds to buy life and death, without even understanding what happens to the people. I'm tired of people who will destroy their entire land to keep a few extra golds in their coffers and then claim they do it for the land they've ruined. And I'm especially tired of people who lie to me and to themselves. You will die by chaos at sunset."

He turned to Lyasa and murmured, "In the harbor square."

She paled. "Someone will try to kill you."

"It has to be public."

Kestrisal lunged forward, only to be felled by the flat of one of the lancer's blades across his temple.

Ignoring the fallen trader, Cerryl turned to Tyldar. "You may go. The golds will be sent to you."

Tyldar raised his eyebrows.

"Did I lie to you before, chandler? Have I not done exactly what I said?"

Tyldar looked down.

"Go!"

After the lancers had dragged off the five captives, Cerryl rose from the chair and made his way out of the reception hall, blotting his sweating forehead in the main hallway outside.

Kalesin stepped forward. "What do you think you're doing, dragging all these traders in here?"

Cerryl just looked at him.

Kalesin waited.

"I'm getting rid of all the ones who've plotted to thwart the Guild and to kill Eliasar and me. Do you have a problem with that?"

"How do you know they're the ones?"

"I know, Kalesin." Cerryl forced a smile, hard as it was because of the pounding headache that had come with the extensive effort to truth-read the factors and merchants. "Don't ever question what I *know.*"

"I see, ser." Kalesin inclined his head. "By your leave."

"By my leave."

"That one hates you," Lyasa murmured, joining Cerryl. "This making a public execution in the harbor square could get you killed."

"Not if we do it right now. Someone has to order it and pay someone. That takes time. These traders won't do it themselves. Not any of the ones still here in Spidlaria."

"I hope you're right."

So did Cerryl.

"It will take most of the lancers . . ." Lyasa pointed out.

"That's fine. It should be worth it. I wish we'd been able to get that last one, but Sieral, was he the one who said that Byal had already fled?"

Lyasa nodded. "I'd better make ready for the spectacle. It's well past late afternoon. We'll need to hurry."

"I'd better get a bit of rest so that it will be a spectacle."

They exchanged nods, and Cerryl headed back to his study to rest his voice—and for something to eat and drink.

# CLV

As the sun touched the waters of the harbor, Cerryl looked from the makeshift platform to the four traders who stood bound in the center of the harbor square. The square and the adjoining streets were filled with every lancer Hiser and Lyasa had been able to muster. Lancers— and the few archers—watched every street and every building.

Cerryl cleared his throat and began to speak, trying to get his voice to carry. "All the people of Spidlar were warned about deceiving the Guild and refusing to pay tariffs. You deceived the Guild and refused to pay what you owed. Two of your cities were destroyed. Your armsmen have been killed or fled. Yet after that, your predecessors still refused to pay what was owed. They died, and yet you refused to learn. The Guild wants a better life for all people in Candar—not just for a handful of greedy and selfish traders in Spidlar. But you thought you knew better. You would destroy your own people for a few more golds. My words mean nothing to you. Perhaps others will learn from them." Cerryl paused but for a moment, then focused raw chaos on the four.

*WHHHHSTTT!!!*

The pillar of flame lit the square, flaring nearly fifty cubits into the air.

Without even waiting for the flames to die, Cerryl hastened off the platform and through the flickering shadows cast by the fire that had succeeded the chaos. He mounted the chestnut awkwardly, but quickly, and Lyasa and Suzdyal's guards escorted him back to his headquarters, through streets that seemed empty, save that he was all too aware of the eyes that had rested on him through shutters and darkened windows as he had passed.

Not until Cerryl was back in the headquarters dwelling and into his study did Lyasa take a deep breath. "You can't keep appearing like that."

"I can't hide. That will make them think they can drive us out." Cerryl sank into his chair, massaging his neck.

"If anything happens to you, they *will* drive us out. Oh, the High Wizard won't call it that, and the new Council of Traders will pay some token golds, and things will return to the way they were."

"It can't happen like that." Cerryl's voice was tight.

"Why not? You're not the first mage who's tried to change things. It's never worked. Look what happened to Jeslek."

"I have to try." *You don't have any choice . . . because if you return to Fairhaven as a failure, you're dead . . . sooner or later.*

"You're stubborn."

"Probably."

Lyasa slumped into the straight-backed chair with a sigh sounding of both relief and exasperation. "Cerryl . . . I've never seen anyone use a truth-read like that before."

He rubbed his forehead. "It's demon work. My head's splitting."

"You don't take compliments easily, either."

"I'm sorry. I've mistrusted them for a long time, especially after working with Jeslek," he added. "All I have is water. Would you like some?"

"Please."

"You could do what I did. All you do is set up the questions so that they have to deny what you think is the truth. Untrue denials are easier to read. It's not evidence, really, and I'd get in trouble if I were in the Patrol in Fairhaven for acting just on truth-reading. Here ... I have to do something."

"Will it work?"

He shrugged. "They either change or get killed, or I get killed. But if I remove enough of them—always from the top—some of the more common merchants and the people in the street may get the idea that the Guild's not after them."

"You grant them vision they do not have."

"We'll have to give it to them." *Somehow ... someway ...* He kept massaging his forehead, hoping the force of the needles that stabbed at his eyes would at least lessen.

Lyasa poured a mug of water and sipped it, and the two sat in the darkness, neither looking toward the embers in the center of the harbor square.

# CLVI

The stocky blond mage stood on the other side of the study desk from Cerryl, a separation for which Cerryl was more than glad. "I don't understand. You killed a bunch of traders, and now the people are back in the streets." Puzzlement crossed Kalesin's face.

"I didn't kill many average people. I didn't kill the bravos, except for those who tried to kill me. I didn't kill the chandler." Cerryl shrugged. "After a while, even stupid people get the message." *Except for you, Kalesin.*

"There aren't any ships in the harbor," Kalesin pointed out almost smugly.

"It takes some time for word to get out." Cerryl smiled gently. "There was a coaster yesterday, and we did collect a few golds. That's more than anyone else has collected." He stood and glanced out the unshuttered and open window into the cool and clear early-fall day. "I need to take another inspection ride."

"You do a lot of that, but you don't drill the troops the way Eliasar did."

"I can't. I don't know how. I'd waste my time and theirs." Cerryl gestured for Kalesin to leave the study before him. "So I let Hiser and Teras do it. They know their tasks."

"You're supposed to be an arms mage," said Kalesin as he stepped outside into the hall.

"That's true." Cerryl frowned for a moment. "If I get the task done, no one is going to question whether I drilled lancers. If I don't succeed, they won't praise me for drilling them, either." He nodded to Kalesin. "I'll expect your report on the sawmills tomorrow. Then, you can start on what we discussed about the wool growers."

"Yes, ser."

Cerryl walked briskly toward the courtyard, leaving Kalesin in the hallway.

# CLVII

Cerryl reined up outside the long one-story timbered building and dismounted. Two of the score of lancers did also. While the arms mage disliked the continual guard, he couldn't argue with Lyasa, Hiser, Teras, and Suzdyal about the necessity of the precaution. *Not yet, anyway.*

The cold rain continued to fall around him as he stepped under the overhanging eaves that sheltered the crude plank door. Cerryl knocked and waited until the door opened.

The burly bearded factor stepped back away from the door, back into the long room with the huge vats. "Ser mage . . . I have done nothing . . . nothing wrong." His voice was thinner and higher than Cerryl recalled.

Beside the second vat stood a younger man, also bearded, watching Cerryl with wide eyes.

"I know," Cerryl said gently, not pressing into the building. "Unlike many factors and traders I have encountered in Spidlar. And *Certis*," he added with a slight emphasis. "You are an honest man."

"Factoring clay and fuller's earth, one must be honest," admitted Aliaskar.

"Might I come in?"

"Of course." Aliaskar backed away another few cubits.

The two lancers followed Cerryl in but stepped to the side.

The mage blotted the dampness off his forehead, taking in the odor of earth and clay, then looked at the clay factor. "You have noticed that the lancers have not bothered you or the other merchants who have continued to work their businesses?"

"That is what folk say," Aliaskar replied cautiously.

"Have they bothered you?"

"No, ser mage."

"So long as I am here, and so long as you pay any tariffs you may owe, they will not bother you, or any who follow your example."

"Those are fair words . . ."

"But you doubt them. I would also were I standing where you stand," Cerryl admitted. "You can choose to believe me or not. Trade is what holds Candar together, and trade travels the seas, the rivers, and the roads. Without good roads, trade is less and more costly. It takes more time to reach those places without river ports or seaports."

"That be true, mostly."

"Fairhaven built the roads, and many have used them, but many of the wealthier traders of Certis, Spidlar, and Gallos did not wish to pay for their use of the White highways."

"I've heard that some were not allowed to use those highways."

Cerryl frowned, thinking of the lady trader who was apparently the consort of the smith Dorrin. "That also might have been true. I do not think it is so now." *Not if I can do anything about it.* "That meant that the traders of Fairhaven paid more and could often not match the prices of traders who did not pay."

Aliaskar nodded that he had heard what Cerryl said, not necessarily that he agreed.

"Yet when the Guild asked these traders of Spidlar and Certis and Gallos to pay tariffs, we were ignored or mocked. We asked again and were ignored. We tried to warn folk without killing many."

"Like as the mountains the old wizard raised in Gallos?"

Cerryl nodded. "That encouraged the prefect of Gallos to ensure we received the tariffs. But not the Traders' Council of Spidlar. They bought goods cheaply from the Black isle and then used the roads we built to sell those goods without even paying the tariff." He shrugged. "In the end, we had to fight. We would rather not, and so long as the tariffs are paid there will be no fighting."

"Your words make sense, yet many would claim that the tariffs go for luxuries of the White City."

Cerryl laughed, harshly. "You can believe me or not, but the High Wizard of Fairhaven lives in one large room at the top of a tower. In Fairhaven, the richest merchant's dwelling is a quarter part the size of Reylerk's mansion. Yet we have no beggars, nor do people starve in the streets. You or anyone can travel there and see." He paused, then added, "I was an orphan apprenticed to a scrivener, and the mages took me in. The mage Lyasa comes from no wealth or position. Nor does the overmage Kinowin."

Aliaskar frowned, then studied Cerryl and the lancers. "I do not know. You have done what you said you would do. You have not lied— not that I know. Yet . . ."

Cerryl nodded. "I am not asking anything except that you think about what I have said. There is one thing more you should know. I have encouraged some of the larger factors from eastern Candar to come here and to set up their warehouses." *One—so far—but he doesn't have to know that.*

"You expect them to be more loyal?"

"No. I expect them to understand that all of eastern Candar must abide by the same tariffs and rules for trade. If this does not occur, in the end Candar will suffer." Cerryl smiled crookedly. "Of course, that means that the factors can't line their purses with golds that should have gone to build roads to help traders large and small."

"I must think, ser mage," Aliaskar said.

"That is all I ask." Cerryl nodded a last time. "I will trouble you no more." He inclined his head. "Good day."

"Good day, ser mage."

As the door closed, Cerryl caught a few words.

". . . most strange, Ziersar."

The arms mage hoped so.

After he walked through the cold drizzle and remounted, Cerryl pulled out his list, studied it, and then replaced it inside the oiled white leather jacket.

"Viskarl—charcoal factor." *Darkness . . . how many days will this take?* Too many, but he had to convince a good portion of the remaining factors and merchants that he and Fairhaven were halfway human and not White demons, at least not all the time.

# CLVIII

Cerryl had finally given up and had another chair brought into the study, and both Lyasa and Kalesin sat across the ancient desk from him in the gloom of another gray and cloudy fall morning.

"We have another twenty golds from tariff collections," Lyasa announced. "We're nearing a hundred for this season."

"Twenty golds. Sterol will not find that adequate," prophesied Kalesin. "Nor even five score or ten score. Not after a mere three and a half score for the summer."

"He won't," Cerryl agreed amiably. "But another coaster from Suthya entered the harbor yesterday, and Tyldar told me that yet another was sailing here out of Quend."

"Still . . ." murmured Kalesin.

Gloomy as Kalesin was, Cerryl knew the stocky mage was right. Both Sterol and Anya would find his performance inadequate. They probably already had and doubtless would have sent his replacement, save for the fact that there wasn't anyone any better to send. *Not yet.*

"Another coaster will help," Lyasa said.

*Now . . . if Layel would only arrive—or send someone—or Wertel.* "A full trader from Hamor or Sarronnyn would help more," Cerryl admitted. "But we have more than half the fall remaining."

*Thrap!*

"Come in."

Subofficer Suzdyal peered in, holding a pair of scrolls. "For you, ser."

"Thank you." Cerryl rose.

Lyasa took them and handed them to him. Kalesin eyed the scroll with the crimson ribbons speculatively.

Cerryl ignored the look. "I haven't seen your wool factor report."

"I have two other factors to visit."

"Perhaps you should."

"One remains in Kleth."

"Then visit the first and complete the report. The other might remain in Kleth for seasons."

"Let us go, Kalesin." Lyasa rose from her chair. "The arms mage has much to do, and so do we. I do, I know."

After the two mages had left, Cerryl eased open the first scroll, glad that Teras or Hiser had made sure it came directly to him. The High Wizard's seal crumbled away, as though it had been invested with far too much chaos.

Cerryl, greetings—

The three-and-a-half-score golds which you sent were, the Council finds, most disappointing for one of your skills. As arms mage of Spidlar you are expected to regain all those golds unpaid by the traitors . . .

Cerryl wanted to grit his teeth. Four parts out of five of the old traders' fortunes had been taken by Jeslek and sent to Fairhaven even before Eliasar had taken over from Jeslek. By the time Cerryl had arrived, every stray gold had fled or been hidden who knew where. He forced himself to continue reading.

. . . greater efforts will be required in Hydlen, and Spidlar must be brought into line and speedily, so that at least half of the lancers there can be returned to Fairhaven and mustered for the spring campaigns . . .

*Campaigns? In Haydlen and where else?*

We look forward to at least a thousand golds before the turn of the year . . . Our wishes and those of the Council for your success in carrying out your duties . . .

The scroll was not even signed by Sterol but by Anya, "at the direction of the High Wizard, His Mightiness Sterol."

"His Mightiness?" Cerryl took a deep breath. What did Sterol expect? Or Anya? It had taken over two years to destroy Spidlar, and now the High Wizard expected great flows of golds in less than two full seasons? After Jeslek had plundered the great fortunes? Except for that onetime rape of Spidlar, Cerryl doubted Fairhaven had ever collected 4,000 golds in a year from Spidlar—or a thousand in a full year. *That was the problem, though.*

He took several deep breaths to calm himself before opening the second scroll—the one with the green ribbons, the one he hoped would be more cheering. The greeting alone lifted his spirits.

> Dearest—
>     I have sent this with Hiser's courier and trust it will arrive in a timely fashion.
>     Father is preparing to undertake the task which you had suggested, and I hope that you will see the results—if you have not—before long. You have asked much, although we both think that you suggestions will be helpful for all of us. The climate there may be better for his health in his declining years, also. Wertel agreed with that, as do I . . .

Declining health? Cerryl swallowed, wondering if Anya and Muneat and Jiolt were already making matters more difficult for Layel in Fairhaven—and for Leyladin. *Not if . . . how . . .* He hadn't seen such in his glass, but Anya's maneuverings wouldn't be obvious that way.

> We all wish you both the best and look forward to seeing you before too long.

He smiled at the "love" with which Leyladin had signed the missive, but the smile faded as he considered all the implications of both scrolls, separately and together.

After rereading both once more, Cerryl stood and glanced out through the window into the almost cold fall day. The clouds were darker, promising more of the cold rain that seemed so common.

# CLIX

As the first ship eased toward the wharves, Cerryl dismounted and walked to the seawall, watching. His guards eased their mounts behind him but did not dismount. The fall wind blowing off the Northern Ocean carried the odor of salt and a chill that foreshadowed a cold winter.

Cerryl kept his jaw in place as the two ocean traders were tied to the wharves, both bearing the green and gold banners of Layel's trading house. The two heavy-laden cargo ships were the first trading vessels so large that he had seen in Spidlaria since his return.

A balding blond figure in blue, flanked by a pair of guards in green, stood near the bow of the inshore vessel and gave a single wave to Cerryl. The arms mage and administrator of Spidlar walked down the wharf to where the gangway was being wrestled into place, conscious that his guards had dismounted and followed him, weapons at the ready.

Layel stood on the deck by the top of the gangway. "I see you have guards now—just like the High Wizard. You've come up in the world, Cerryl." The factor laughed.

"If having enemies is a sign of position, it's one I could do without."

"If you would join me in my cabin—or the one I took from the master?"

"The ships are both yours?"

"Aye. There are two others that sail out of Lydiar, but Wertel manages them, and well, too."

Cerryl hopped onto the plank and then onto the deck. The guards followed as the mage and factor walked to the rear deckhouse.

Layel opened the narrow door and gestured to Natrey. "You can look in."

The guard nodded and made a brief inspection, but both guards remained in the passageway outside the cabin when Layel shut the door. Cerryl sat in one of the chairs around the gold oak table that was bolted to the polished plank floor.

"Trust my ship more than anywhere else," said Layel.

"More than most places," Cerryl agreed.

"Both my daughter and the overmage pushed me here—against my initial judgment," said Layel.

"I agree with them," Cerryl said.

"I do as well, from what I've since learned. Fairhaven is no place for an honest trader, not while Sterol is High Wizard and Anya sits by his side."

"What happened?"

"Scerzet . . . did Leyladin tell you of him?"

Cerryl shook his head.

"He died—sudden-like—and Muneat and Jiolt ended up with his warehouses and stock, settled with his heirs. Folk said that the Council suggested that there were too many traders in Fairhaven." Layel gave a wry smile. "About that time, your offer looked more tempting."

"That I had not heard of."

"I doubt many folk have, but it happened all the same." Layel cleared his throat. "Be hard starting here, even with the ships and the golds."

"Perhaps not so hard as you think." Cerryl offered a smile. "In return for your help in restoring trade in Spidlar I am giving you the dwelling, the warehouses, and the lands of the leading factor in Spidlar."

"What befell him that he has no need of such?"

"He plotted to kill Eliasar, and then me. And lied about it. When I questioned him, he took poison. I executed ten others who were part of the plot. Things have run better since then, but we need some larger traders, with ships like yours."

"And you would hand over his lands and facilities for me to do what I would do anyway?"

"I have a condition," Cerryl admitted.

"Just one?" Layel raised his eyebrows.

"Two, I suppose. I want you to be loyal to Fairhaven—not to the High Wizard, whoever that may be—and I want you to set up trading here as if Spidlaria were Fairhaven, except with lower tariffs, say a twentieth part, except for the surtax on goods from Recluce. The mage Lyasa is serving as the mage in charge of the lancers who will make sure the tariffs are collected."

"Do you intend to send all the tariffs to Fairhaven?"

"We are setting aside some to pay our lancers here." Cerryl offered a lopsided smile. "And for a few other matters—such as repairs to the wharves and the harbor."

"Sterol won't like that you are charging lower tariffs. Or not sending every last gold back to the White Tower."

"The only ones who know that are you and the traders, and me and Lyasa. Lyasa won't tell, and I can't see traders complaining that their tariff levels have been lowered."

"Ha! That you have the right of, even here. No trader worth his coins would mention a word of such, even in this cold place." Layel glanced toward the closed porthole. "It can get terrible cold here."

"Better cold than dead, and you would be if you had remained in

Fairhaven too much longer. You are Leyladin's father and Muneat's and Jiolt's rival."

"And," Layel raised his eyebrows, "the father of your consort. You and I know that's so, for all the words saying Whites have no consorts." He waved aside Cerryl's protest. "None of those are good to be at this moment, that is true." Layel fingered his chin. "Yet I wonder about her."

"They need her skills, and, since she can muster no chaos, she is seen as no threat."

"My head says you are right, but my heart is troubled."

"I do worry."

"She frets over you, she does, and fears that you need return afore long."

"I doubt Anya or the High Wizard wish my return."

"What the High Wizard may wish may not be best for you or the lands." Layel shrugged.

"True." Cerryl stood. "Do you wish to see what you will work with before you decide on what to do with your cargoes and coins?"

"Always in a hurry, you young folk are." Layel rose with a grin.

"I'd like to see a certain healer, and I can't until I get this land back on its boots." Cerryl opened the cabin door.

"Like I said." Layel's grin broadened.

# CLX

At the sound of footsteps on the chill and polished stone of the hallway floor, Cerryl turned.

Kalesin walked quickly toward Cerryl and the pair of lancers outside his study door. "I'd like to talk with you, ser." The smile that followed the words was false and forced.

"I was headed out to accompany Lyasa on an inspection." Cerryl reopened the study door and stepped inside, moving behind the desk to put some space between him and the other, but not seating himself.

Kalesin closed the door with a dull *thud*. "I know that, ser." His eyes were hard as he glanced at Cerryl. The stocky blond mage's eyes were cold, above a body that had thickened in the seasons since Cerryl had returned to Spidlaria. "I don't understand. What have I done to displease you? You're letting her handle the tariff coins and supervise the lancers, and she's not even an arms mage."

"She is good at what she does," Cerryl said evenly. "I give you those things to do that you do well." He paused. "Many of the tasks you do are the same sorts that I did for Jeslek, or Kinowin, or that Anya does for the High Wizard."

"I proved I was capable of more for the honored Eliasar," Kalesin replied firmly.

"You may well have," Cerryl said gently, "but what we are capable of doing is not always what needs to be done. I need the lists and the locations of merchants if we are to ensure that we can collect taxes and tariffs. Such a task is tedious, but it is necessary, and it takes a mage who can use a glass."

"I can do more than that," Kalesin insisted.

"I'm sure you can. But if you did more, you would not be doing what needs to be done." Cerryl tried to make the smile friendly.

Kalesin's lips tightened, and he was silent.

"Is there anything else?"

"No, ser." After another pause, the blond mage asked, "By your leave?"

"You may go."

"Thank you, ser." Kalesin turned and opened the door.

Cerryl followed him into the hallway.

As Kalesin stepped away from the study door and walked toward the main entry of the building, the blond mage's fingers tightened around the hilt of the long dagger in his belt, a long iron dagger, with a heavily wrapped tang and a thick scabbard.

Cerryl concealed a frown before he turned to the guard. "I will be riding to the large barracks with the mage Lyasa and the lancers from one of Captain Teras's companies."

"Yes, ser."

The arms mage walked quickly out to the courtyard, trying to make up for the delay caused by Kalesin's interruption.

Lyasa stood by her mount, holding the mare's reins and those of Cerryl's gelding. "You don't have to come with me, you know?"

"If I don't show up occasionally when you inspect the barracks and the lancers, they won't remember who I am." Cerryl took the leathers and mounted the gelding.

Lyasa gestured toward the gate. "Kalesin just rode out of here. He was angry."

"He's angry most of the time, these days. He wants to do great and challenging things when what we need is painstaking and tedious chores. I try to keep a close watch on him."

Lyasa urged her mare toward the open courtyard gate, and the cold wind ruffled her jet-black hair, blowing it back off her ears. "I hate to say this . . . You'd be better off if he were in Fairhaven."

Cerryl flicked the gelding's reins to catch up with her. "I can't send him back. They'd probably send someone else and then call me up before the Council. They'd claim I sent him away because I was taking the coins. Like I thought Shyren had. Those are the coins we have yet to collect. So I give him things to do that need to be done, things that he can't foul up without my knowing immediately."

"He knows that, and it just makes him angrier."

"Do you have any suggestions about Kalesin?"

"Oh, Cerryl . . . all you can do is watch him."

*For now.* "I know."

The hoofs of the horses clicked on the hard and cold stones of the street that led to the main barracks.

# CLXI

Cerryl watched from the study window as Kalesin once again rode angrily through the courtyard and out through the front gate, a half-score of lancers at his back. The cold wind flicked intermittent flakes of snow past Cerryl's face, reminding him of how much earlier winter came in Spidlar—and of how much colder it would be. His eyes drifted to the harbor, where one of Layel's ships remained moored. The other had left for Sarronnyn, in hopes of picking up dried fruits and surplus grain and returning before the winter storms struck the Northern Ocean and it began to ice over. Then both would leave on a long voyage somewhere over the winter, for Layel noted there was little point in maintaining an idle ship.

*How long . . . how long before you can get Spidlaria somewhere close to being a normal city again?*

He laughed softly. That wasn't the problem. His problem was that he wanted Spidlaria to be more like his image of Fairhaven and what it could be. *That will be hard, since all the Council wants is repayment of the golds spent to conquer it.*

Once he was sure Kalesin was safely on his way, Cerryl stepped out of the study past the guards and toward the stairs that led up to his bedchamber—and the ones on the third floor used by Kalesin and Lyasa.

Before touching the door lever, Cerryl studied the door with his senses and his sight, but there were no traps or chaos concentrations in the locks or elsewhere. After a moment, he pulled the new leather gloves from his belt and slipped them on. They would keep any sense of order or chaos from him from remaining on whatever he might touch, a trick Kalesin had yet to learn from all the chaos residue Kalesin had left on all the scrolls he had intercepted and scanned.

Cerryl pressed the door lever and stepped inside the corner room.

Without moving anything, he looked over the small desk and the three stacks of papers, each held down by a fired clay weight in the shape of a shield. The inkstand needed refilling, which surprised Cerryl not at all, and the quill could have been sharper. The lamp mantle, was coated with soot.

Cerryl finally lifted a paperweight. The first two stacks of papers held nothing but rough copies of the lists and reports he had requested of Kalesin. The third stack was shorter and dated back to before Cerryl's return. Several sheets held columns of numbers. Cerryl studied the numbers and the names opposite them. From what he could tell, the sheet held a listing of merchants and tariffs they had paid. Most of the names were unfamiliar, except for a handful like Tyldar, whom he knew as smaller merchants.

He leafed through the rest of the stack, but none of the sheets held the names of the more important—and largely dead—factors. Cerryl pursed his lips. "Interesting."

He surveyed the room, then found, in a box in the bottom of the wardrobe, another stack of parchment and paper, and those seemed to be personal scrolls to Kalesin, largely in a feminine hand. Cerryl studied them and sniffed them, but neither the hand nor the scent was Anya's. *Skeptical you are.* The signature on those read: "Zylariae."

He frowned. He was wrong. There was a faint scent of trilia and sandalwood in the wardrobe. He tried to follow his nose, but all he could determine was that the scent lingered around the lighter wool cloak hanging on one of the side pegs. But there was no sign of a scroll, and none of those in the box carried that scent.

Cerryl shook his head and scanned the letter scrolls, as quickly as he could, looking for some hints—of anything. Phrases from some letters struck him as he hurried through them:

> ...must be patient, dearest... No mage reaches high position quickly...
> ...he is from a coinless hearth and will not understand the true power of coins... For that deficiency you cannot blame him, but you must be wary...
> ...trust not the redhead, for all she promises...

Cerryl nodded. That opinion was widely held.

> ...many think highly of him, and he is most powerful but tries not to show that power...
> ...a mage loved by a healer cannot be totally stupid nor without intelligence. You MUST be careful...

That was the last scroll, and he replaced the sheets in the box carefully, hoping Kalesin was as careless with his memory as he had been with everything else.

Cerryl could discover nothing else save several sets of whites, and personal toiletries, including scented soap, and a white-bronze razor.

After he slipped out of the room and closed the door, Cerryl frowned as he walked down the steps to his own bedchamber. Eliasar had not collected much more than a few hundred golds, if that, and most of those had come from the smaller merchants and traders.

*That follows. Did Eliasar start after the old large traders then? Was that why they sought help from Rystryr or whoever?*

Either that or Kalesin had disposed of the papers that had held the tariff collections from the larger traders, just as he had received something from Anya recently—and had destroyed it or hidden it somewhere.

Cerryl took a deep breath.

Once more, he did not know as much as he should, except that his instinct not to trust the blond mage had been sound and that he had to exercise even more care. And again, he was reminded that where power and traders were concerned, evidence of *anything* was hard to come by. *You have to trust your senses.*

That was hard, too, at times.

# CLXII

*T*hrap!

Cerryl concentrated on the glass before him, letting Leyladin's image fade and focusing on the outside of the door. The silver mists swirled and revealed a stolid-faced, stocky blond mage. "Come in, Kalesin."

"Ser, here are the scrolls from the courier for you." Kalesin extended three scrolls.

"Thank you." Cerryl rose and took them.

"We only mean to please, honored Cerryl."

Even without looking closely, Cerryl could tell that someone had sliced the seal on at least one of the scrolls and then reheated it. Cerryl studied the other mage impassively. "I appreciate it, Kalesin."

Kalesin inclined his head, then turned and left.

Once the door shut, Cerryl studied the scrolls more closely. One was sealed with a purple wax, the second with red, and the third with green. All had been opened and resealed.

"Let's read the worst first." He broke the seal on the one from Sterol or Anya and skimmed through it, centering on the key phrases:

... wish to remind you that the turn of winter approaches and that the Council expects at least several hundred golds in tariff revenues, with the balance to follow by the turn of the year at midwinter ...

That missive had been signed and sealed by Anya at the direction of "His Supreme Mightiness, the High Wizard Sterol." There was more, but all in the vein of reminding Cerryl of the urgency of tariff collections. He set the first scroll on the desk and opened the second. As he had suspected from the purple wax, it was from Kinowin.

Cerryl—
I would like to remind you that you promised to bring me, if possible, a purple hanging from Spidlaria. I am doing my best to look after the one in green silk that I feel you entrusted to me, though I know that was not precisely your intent. As with Myral, age has begun to creep upon me, and I may not be a fit custodian for all that much longer ...
I would like to see the handiwork Myral promised you would bring me before too much longer ... The handiwork is important, and though some will quibble over the coins, good workmanship outlasts coins.

Kinowin

Cerryl swallowed, set the second scroll down, and hurriedly broke the seal on the third, a seal he suspected had been cut and resealed twice.

Dearest—
I know that you have had great duties laid upon you, but I thought you would like to know that Mother is close to the end. Knowing how you have respected her, it might be best that you return to Fairhaven as quickly as you can, if possible. Kinowin can no longer leave his quarters, now, as you suspected might happen. I have no one to assist me now that Father is helping you in rebuilding factoring in Spidlar, and Aliaria and Nierlia are occupied with their children and legacies ...
If this is not possible, I understand. It may be hard to explain to certain relatives, particularly one niece who left a message suggesting that if you respected her judgment, you should has-

ten homeward—as if you had ever jumped to her scented wishes.

As always, we all miss you.

Leyladin

Cerryl looked at the words of the scroll again. He frowned. The words were in Leyladin's hand. The order behind them was Leyladin's, but she never would have said something like that, especially such nonsense. His regular screeing of her showed her in no danger, and her mother had died long before . . .

"You're stupid, Cerryl." He nodded grimly. The message was the same as what she had written—get back to Fairhaven—but the other words, the reasons, were there for whoever might have opened and read the scroll, and the niece had to be Anya—she was Muneat's niece and wore too much scent.

Cerryl studied the scroll, looking with his senses for the slightest touch of chaos on the inner parchment—and finding it. Lyasa had not been around, and the chaos was too fresh for it to have been anyone other than Kalesin who had opened the scroll.

He stood and walked into the hall. "I'm going out for a bit of air."

"Yes, ser."

Instead, once around the corner, Cerryl raised the blur shield and started up the stairs to the third floor.

As he had suspected, Kalesin was seated at the small desk in his bedchamber on the third floor.

When Cerryl stepped into the room, closing the door behind him, he let the blur shield drop. "So what are you sending to Anya? Or is it Rystryr?"

Kalesin rose and turned slowly, bringing the long iron dagger around. "I'll use this on you, if I have to. You can't order me around, Cerryl. I've been a mage longer. They sent you here to get rid of you. You aren't going to sneak home and leave me with the mess you've made. And you're not proof against cold iron, no matter what—"

"Why not? You'd like being in charge—"

As Kalesin lunged forward, Cerryl didn't even hesitate but slammed the focused light lance into the blond mage's chest.

The sandy-haired mage flew backward, his dead face frozen in surprise.

Cerryl played chaos over the body carefully, trying to ensure that no trace of the man remained, except for the white ashes that would dissipate and the dagger that had fallen to the floor.

Then he rearranged the desk back in the order in which Kalesin kept it. He picked up the dagger and set it alongside the third stack of paper, leaving everything neat, except for the half-written scroll, which he read quickly.

> Anya—
>
> Cerryl has become insufferable . . . He has received a scroll bidding him return to Fairhaven . . . from that blonde harlot . . . and another one from doddering old Kinowin, begging for a hanging before he dies . . .

Cerryl wanted to shake his head. Kalesin had been more stupid than Cerryl could have imagined, and that meant that Kalesin hadn't been any real danger at all, except as Anya's tool. *How many tools has she?* He tucked the half-written scroll under the blotter and replaced the quill and inkstand.

With a deep breath, and ignoring the incipient headache his order and chaos manipulations were bringing on, he cloaked himself in the blur shield and slipped down the steps until he was in the shadows of the main corridor outside the study.

"Natrey?"

"Ser? How did you get there?"

"I walked." Cerryl smiled. "Have you seen Kalesin?"

"No, ser. He left your study a bit ago . . ."

Cerryl frowned. "He was supposed to bring me something, but I haven't seen him."

"You want me to send some of the boys to find him?" Natrey grinned.

Cerryl forced an amused smile. "Perhaps you should. Perhaps you should." He let himself back into the study and forced himself to wait, rereading the three scrolls until he had them committed to memory.

Kinowin was clearly telling him that the overmage had been able to shield Leyladin, but that wouldn't last forever, and Leyladin was practically ordering him to return as quickly as he could get there.

Cerryl continued to wait.

Finally, there was a knock on the door.

"Yes?"

Foyst peered in: "Ser? We can't find the mage nowhere. His mount be in the stable, his dagger be on his table, but he be nowhere."

"Are you sure?" Cerryl put a shade of annoyance into his voice. "He was supposed to bring me a report on the golds taken by the older traders before they fled or were executed. He had those records."

"Ser, beggin' your pardon . . ."

"It's not your doing, Foyst. I'm not angry at you." Cerryl pursed his lips. "Have you seen the mage Lyasa?"

"Yes, ser. She was riding in."

"Good. If you would tell her I'd like to see her . . ."

"Yes, ser."

Cerryl offered a quick smile and a nod. The door closed.

He waited, but not nearly so long, before Lyasa, still in her white cold-weather jacket, stepped into the study.

"You were asking for me?"

Cerryl looked at her, then shook his head. "Kalesin has vanished. None of the lancers saw him go. I'd like you to come up to his room with me."

"You're worried?"

"Yes."

"You should be. I warned you, you know."

As he stood, Cerryl shrugged. "I know. I did what I could." *That is true enough.*

The two walked hurriedly up the two flights of steps, with Foyst following. Both mages kept scanning the staircase and landings.

Once on the third floor, Cerryl looked around the room, as if he had not seen it earlier. "He left in a hurry, and he left everything behind." He stepped toward the desk. "There's something here." Cerryl pulled out the half-written scroll from beneath the blotter and began to read it. He shook his head and handed it to Lyasa.

"Read this." Cerryl wandered to the wardrobe, looking through it cursorily. "Everything seems to be here."

"This looks like his writing." Lyasa's eyes widened as she read. After a moment, she looked at Cerryl. "I told you . . . What are you going to do?" She paused. "You suspected he would leave, didn't you?"

"He was nervous when he gave me the scrolls." Ceryl laughed ruefully. "I forgot to tell you. I got a message from Anya demanding more golds and one from Kinowin suggesting I get back to Fairhaven, however I could. Both scrolls had been opened—most recently—and resealed with chaos. I sent the lancers after Kalesin . . ."

"He must have known you'd find out."

"You'll have to be *most* careful," Cerryl told her.

"*I'll* have to be . . . You're leaving?"

"If I can, I'm returning to Fairhaven, before it's too late. If it's not already."

"Sterol will try to kill you."

Cerryl nodded. "But if I stay here, I'll be even deader, because he'll take Leyladin and Kinowin, too."

"I could go."

He shook his head. "If matters don't go well, I may need a friend outside Fairhaven." Cerryl didn't like deceiving Lyasa, but she'd be safer not knowing how Kalesin had disappeared. The scroll Kalesin had written was enough to warn her, and she could say, truthfully, if anything happened to Cerryl, that she had known nothing about Kalesin's disappearance.

"How?"

"I'm going to ask Layel for a trip on one of his ships. He might just agree."

"When it's his daughter you're trying to save?" Lyasa laughed. "You shouldn't have any worries on that course."

"Not until I get to Fairhaven." *Then my real troubles begin.*

# CLXIII

Cerryl glanced past Layel, past the polished wooden railing of the *Western Sun,* toward the dark gray waters of the harbor and beyond, toward the Northern Ocean.

Layel clapped Cerryl on the back. "Best I stay here, but Wandrel will get you there." The balding trader grinned. "Better quarters here, and the crew is safer, too. The *Western Sun's* a good ship."

"I'm sure she is:"

"Besides, this way Wertel can send back more of that dried fruit and those tools and blades I agreed to get for the sawmill fellow. Still think he can make the kind of planks that the Sligan yards need, and that will mean more golds in tariffs."

Cerryl gave a half-smile. "I'm glad you came here."

"Except for the cold . . . I am, too. Don't have to worry about what Muneat's doing or whether I can get haulers or wagons . . ." Layel laughed. "Could talk your ear off, and you best be going." The balding trader frowned and looked directly at Cerryl. "You sure you don't want some guards once you get to Lydiar?"

"No. Just a pair of mounts. No one will remember I was there."

"Mage stuff?"

"Magery," Cerryl confirmed.

"You coming back soon?"

"Probably not." *If you're successful you'll stay, and if you're not . . . you'll be dead—or mind-blind and working on the road crew.*

"Feared of that. Well . . . you know how I feel. Try to keep that daughter of mine in line."

"More likely, she'll keep me in line."

Layel nodded a last time, then climbed slowly over the railing and scrambled down the gangway to the wharf. "She's yours, Master Wandrel."

"Single up the lines!"

Cerryl stepped back and watched as the crew began the effort to take the *Western Sun* out of the harbor and back to Lydiar.

*Toward what?* Cerryl had kept checking the glass, watching Kinowin and Leyladin, but both seemed to continue their daily routines, from what Cerryl could tell, and he dared not use the glass on those he distrusted the most, fearing that alone would tell them too much.

His eyes went to the north and the colder waters of the Northern Ocean beyond the breakwater.

# CLXIV

Cerryl sat in the chair in Leyladin's bedchamber, half–nodding off. He really needed to sleep, but he didn't dare, not until he knew she was back in the house. Both horses were groomed and stabled, more quickly than he'd anticipated, because he'd been too tired to refuse Soaris's help. Cerryl had washed and changed, since he hadn't liked the way he'd smelled and he could do that while he waited.

Outside the bedchamber window, the fall wind whispered through the late afternoon, not nearly so cold as in Spidlaria, though the trees had shed the leaves they would shed and the winter leaves had all grayed, giving the forests along the White highway between Lydiar and Fairhaven a depressing gray look, since no snow had yet fallen.

He jerked awake and glanced toward the door. The mansion remained silent, except for the muted clanking from the kitchen where Meridis labored over something. He dozed off slightly, until he heard a door through his stupor and immediately awakened, glancing around.

The bedchamber door opened, and Leyladin, still wearing a dark green woolen cloak over her healer greens, burst into the room. "You're here! How did you do it? No one knows where you are." The dark green eyes contained both love and wonder.

Cerryl smiled, feeling not nearly so tired. "A little magery. You remember I showed you?" He didn't feel like explaining in detail how the blur shield didn't alert chaos wielders and made those who used screeing slide over his image.

"That was a long time ago . . . and you still amaze me."

"I'm here, and glad no one knows. Very glad." *For more than a few reasons.*

Her arms went around him. "It's good to hold you."

"It's good to be held—and to hold you."

After some moments, she stepped back. "Father?"

"He's fine. He's already set up and bringing in golds, mumbling the whole time about how he's too old to do it and how Spidlaria is too cold. Then he figures out some other business to set up and someone else to run it for him. He thinks he can sell timber to Spidlar."

Leyladin laughed. "Father."

"He's safer there, I think. He's a trader, and they'd rather have a trader, even one from Fairhaven, than armsmen and lancers and mages."

"Fairhaven . . . you don't think it will be safe here?"

"For your sisters . . . it's safe. For your father or you or me?" Cerryl shook his head slowly, then drew her close again, holding on tightly.

After a time, she disengaged herself. "How are you going to take on Sterol? Even Kinowin says you have to."

"Meet with Anya tomorrow and go straight to his quarters."

"That's dangerous, trusting her."

"I won't tell her I'm here. You send a messenger asking her to meet you in the fountain courtyard, but I'll be there." Cerryl shrugged. "I can defeat Sterol. That's not the problem. I don't want anyone to know I can do it. If anyone realizes I have that kind of power, they'll turn on me because I'm so young—and so inexperienced."

"You're scarcely inexperienced."

"That's what they think, and I don't want to take on all the older members of the Guild. Anya needs *someone* to run the Guild for her. It might as well be me."

"You're playing a dangerous role, dear one. Trusting Anya for anything is like playing with a serpent."

"Tell me." He rubbed his eyes. "Except Sterol is getting worse."

"Both Kinowin and Anya warned me about Sterol. Kinowin even suggested I stay away from the White Tower these days. I'm glad you're back."

"Did he . . . Sterol . . . ?"

"No . . . nothing like that."

*Yet.* Cerryl swallowed.

"Sterol is controlled by Anya." Leyladin smiled sadly. "He doesn't even know it. She says things so that he'll do the opposite of what she says and not realize that's what she wants."

"That's the problem with her. Do you oppose her or support her? How do you ever know quite what she intends?" Cerryl glanced toward the growing darkness outside the bedchamber windows, stifling a yawn.

"Have you eaten?"

"Not enough."

"Not nearly enough." Her eyes danced. "Not for tonight."

Cerryl couldn't help grinning.

# CLXV

Cerryl waited in the shadows of the pillars beside the entrance to the Council Chamber, on the way to the fountain courtyard, where he could see the courtyard, but not where Leyladin had told Anya she would be. Because heavy dark clouds swirled over the city and no lamps had been lit in the Halls that morning, the entry foyer was dark, gloomy.

*Most fitting in some ways.* Cerryl glanced down the rear corridor of the foyer but could see no one nearing or in the front part of the fountain courtyard. He maintained a slight version of his blurring shield, not wanting to be seen nor to draw attention.

Two messengers in red scurried past.

"Redark . . . couldn't decide if he wants . . . water or wine . . . then changes his mind."

"Better than the High Wizard . . . claims wine spoils before he can drink it . . . blames us for bringing it." The second crèche-raised messenger glanced over her shoulder, his eyes skipping past Cerryl as if she had not even seen the mage.

"Quiet . . ."

Coming the other way was a student mage, one of those Cerryl didn't know, a dark-haired young man with a wispy goatee, of the type that poor dead Bealtur had tried to cultivate. The apprentice also passed without noticing Cerryl.

A red-haired figure descended the steps from the tower, then moved silently down the center of the foyer toward the rear archway into the fountain courtyard.

Cerryl let Anya pass before stepping out of the shadows and dropping the shield. "Leyladin's not coming. I prevailed upon her to request your presence."

Anya turned and flashed her bright smile. "Why . . . Cerryl . . . you have grown even more cautious."

"Coming to Fairhaven was not cautious, Anya. Best I be cautious when I can."

"You also have skills some know little about. I sensed no one nearby."

"That was because you sought Leyladin and not me."

"There's always more to you than meets the eye."

"Thank you. I would hope so, since not that much meets the eye. When one is not physically imposing and does not swirl vast amounts of chaos around . . ." Cerryl shrugged, then drew her back next to the pillars, not into the shadows, for that would have alerted the suspicious, but along the side of the thoroughfare, as though their meeting were merely a conversation begun in passing.

"You wish something of me?"

"I received a message." Cerryl raised his eyebrows.

"Ah . . . yes. Perhaps I was precipitous. Or just wished to see if you would keep your word." Anya's smile faded.

"I would suggest you gather those you can trust to stand ready when we go to see Sterol."

"He will not wish to see you."

"You will not request that. You will bring me."

"And if I do not?" Anya's smile was almost coy.

Cerryl forced a shrug. "Then you will suffer through many more years of Sterol as High Wizard . . . until he grows tired of your taking pleasure elsewhere—if he has not already."

"Do not be so coarse, Cerryl. It does not become you." Anya arched her eyebrows. "How would you be any different? I assume that is what you want?"

"I have Leyladin, and that leaves you free to pursue . . . what you wish, besides power, of course."

"There is a certain attraction to that—but that assumes you can defeat Sterol."

"If I cannot, well, then you and Sterol are well rid of me, and you can claim I forced you to bring me to the White Tower. Sterol will believe that of a female mage."

"You are getting more devious as you age, Cerryl."

"I have watched you, Anya, to learn what I can. Why did you really summon me?"

"Because this time the amulet has poisoned him." Anya lowered her voice to a murmur, and her bright and false smile dimmed into something sadder—and truer.

"His scrolls seem the same to me," Cerryl said mildly. "Impatient and self-centered."

"Do you believe that? Truly?" asked the redhead. "Once he talked, as you have, of making Fairhaven great again. Now he demands golds and berates the rulers of other lands, and we must send lancers to protect the mage advisers—or recall them. He does nothing about the Black demon smith who fled to Recluce."

"Where is Gorsuch? Still in Renklaar?"

"Where else? He can control the port there, and there's less danger than in Hydolar. Duke Afabar is even more unpredictable than his predecessors, but he's Asulan, and they're known for that."

"Disarj is in Jellico?" *Lining his purse as Shyren did, no doubt.*

"You know that already, Cerryl."

"So . . . what else has Sterol done that shows this . . . poisoning?"

"He's turned a messenger to ashes because the lad brought him sour wine. He's done the same to two apprentices." She paused. "One might have merited it, but even Broka was aghast at the second. Esaak remonstrated with Sterol, and the High Wizard threatened to send Esaak, at his age, to Naclos. Then he asked him to report on the sewer tunnels from the Halls." Anya paused.

"And what of the problem of the smith and Recluce?"

"The Guild asks for action, and he will not act. I have asked, and he will not act."

*So Anya does want to act against the smith. She really does.* "He does not listen to anyone?"

"Has he ever? Need I say more?"

Cerryl nodded slowly. From what he could tell, every word Anya spoke, she had believed. Some he even believed. "No. Who can you call upon . . . today?"

"Today we could summon but Fydel, dear faithful Fydel, and two of the younger mages—Isepell and Rospor. You did not chose the best of days."

Cerryl inclined his head. "Shall we go? Fydel must be somewhere near."

"We might as well."

They passed no one Cerryl knew on the way to the rear Hall that held Fydel's quarters, but that was because there were few indeed left in the Halls that Cerryl knew—Kinowin, Esaak, Broka, Redark, and Kiella, now that the apprentice had been made a full mage. All the others Cerryl had known were either in the peacekeeping Patrol—and not in the Halls—scattered across Candar or dead. *Which is why you need Anya.*

Fydel's mouth opened, then closed as Anya and Cerryl stepped into his quarters.

"Cerryl has returned to put things to rights with Sterol," Anya said briskly, without her usual smile. "We need to move quickly."

"Now," added Cerryl.

"I like this not." Fydel paced back and forth across his narrow room. "If Cerryl cannot defeat Sterol, we are dead."

"If Sterol remains High Wizard, you are dead," Cerryl said bluntly. "He already knows Anya would rather spend her time with you than with him. He only waits for a way to assign you some impossible task, such as becoming the new mage adviser to Duke Afabar."

Fydel fingered his beard. "I will stand ready, but I don't wish to be in the meeting."

"You would not be there for this," Anya said quietly. "I must ask him to act on the Guild's wishes, and he must refuse. There must be a reason."

"He will not act against Recluce," Fydel said.

"Then that would be best. We can claim that we will." Cerryl smiled. "Now . . . you could do one favor before that?"

"I like that less yet."

"Gather Isepell and Rospor to stand with you."

"Why me? They're Anya's supporters."

"Exactly," offered Cerryl. "Should anyone see Anya gathering them . . . whereas if you do . . ." *Of course, that's not your reason. You don't want Anya out of sight until the deed is done, but they don't have to know that.*

"Ah." After a moment, the square-bearded mage asked, "Then what?"

"Bring guards with iron chains. Tell them that the High Wizard needs them for a problem."

"Sterol won't submit," Anya said.

"No," Cerryl admitted, "but the guards and chains will keep others from asking why three mages wait outside Sterol's quarters."

Fydel nodded. "And we can be totally innocent if this fails. Not that I expect either of you to fail, but . . ."

"You would rather not fail with us." Anya did offer the bright smile.

"Let us make our way to see the High Wizard," Cerryl said, offering his own bright and false smile. "Fydel will gather the others and follow. Will you not, Fydel?"

"Your wishes—both of yours—are my command."

Anya and Cerryl left Fydel's small quarters and began to walk back toward the front Hall and the White Tower.

"You know, Cerryl, Fydel is most pleased that you have an arrangement with the healer. It does make matters . . . easier."

"It does," Cerryl agreed, "and that will not change."

"Fydel will be pleased."

As they left the second Hall and stepped into the fountain courtyard, Esaak appeared, saw Cerryl, and stepped away hurriedly, but not toward the front Hall.

"Best we not delay," Cerryl said.

"You've said that before." Anya's voice was testy.

Two apprentices backed away as Anya and Cerryl crossed the foyer toward the steps up to the tower, though Cerryl knew neither.

At the topmost landing, outside the High Wizard's apartments, the guard Gostar's eyes widened as they went from Anya to Cerryl and back to Anya. "Sers? He . . . said he did not wish . . ."

"Is he alone?" asked Anya.

"Yes, Mage Anya."

"Then he will see us. And there will be several other mages following with guards to take care of Sterol's needs." Anya stepped forward and opened the door. "Sterol! I have a surprise for you, a rather unforeseen and pleasant one."

Cerryl followed Anya, closing the door.

Sterol rose from behind the table, chaos building and billowing around him. "A surprise? Cerryl? So . . . you have brought our recalcitrant mage home to the High Wizard for judgment?"

"I thought you might like to see him. You may deal with him after you answer the question that Redark and Kinowin prevailed upon me to ask." Anya's tone was languid, almost insolent.

"After? Who tells me what I should deal with and when? Are they so weak they would not trouble themselves to ask?" Chaos crackled around the iron-haired High Wizard, so much that Cerryl wondered how the man had not already aged into dust.

"The Council wants to know what you intend to do." Anya's eyes dropped to the blank mirror upon the table. "They are getting restless."

"They wish? Do they know what they wish?" Sterol gestured, and the white mists appeared and vanished. A view appeared in the glass, so solid that it might have been painted there, a view of a black ship moored at a pier in the narrow inlet, with five black stone buildings on the hillside above. "Look. Have you ever seen anything so clear?"

"No."

Cerryl, standing well back, almost to the window, shook his head ever so slightly, but his eyes did not leave the High Wizard as he quietly and slowly raised his shields, without raising chaos. *Yet.*

"I haven't either. What aspect of the Balance created that monster I don't know . . ." His eyes flicked to Cerryl. "Save that you let him escape."

Cerryl did not answer.

"The Council is worried," Anya persisted. "They want you to do something."

"Fine! What am I supposed to do? Send a fleet out against Recluce? What good will it do?" Sterol snorted and looked at the image in the mirror on the table. "The old Black ones won't respond. Should we attack the island? Do you know what black iron swords do to our White Guards? Do you want one of those things he built blowing you into shreds? Like the great Jeslek?"

"The Blacks are divided," said Anya quietly. "They want this Dorrin to disappear as much as we do."

"That may be, but how does that explain all the people helping build this new town? He didn't carry them all on that little ship. And they're all still Blacks. That means he isn't creating any chaos on Recluce, the demons know why . . ." Sterol rubbed his forehead.

"Why can't you send a fleet? Recluce doesn't even have a half-score of warships, if that. They don't like fighting. And most of those ships are spread across the oceans."

Sterol massaged his forehead again, then touched the amulet that rested against his chest. "Haven't you heard a word I've said?"

"The Council wants some action, Sterol." Anya's voice was sharp.
The hint of a frown crossed Cerryl's forehead.

"With what do they wish for me to pay for such action?" Sterol's
eyes went to Cerryl. "We receive no golds from Spidlar. Disarj sends
scrolls but fewer golds than did Shyren."

"The Guild members mutter. They say nothing when you are
around, but they mutter."

"Cowards—all of them." The air crackled with chaos. "And they
send you, a woman. You are supposed to be my assistant, not their
lackey." The High Wizard lifted the amulet. "Here. You take it. Be my
guest, O lackey of Redark and Kinowin."

The redhead looked at the amulet, then at Sterol. "I won't be tricked
like Jeslek."

"Either shut up or take the amulet," Sterol snapped.

Anya's hand lifted, then dropped. Finally, she sighed. "Someone has
to do something."

"Why?"

"Do you intend to do nothing while this . . . oddity . . . builds so
much order into black iron that Recluce will dominate the Eastern
Ocean forever?"

"I don't see that much of a threat." Sterol laughed. "He can't live
forever. Why spend golds we don't have on a threat that won't hurt
us?"

Anya laughed, harshly, metallically. "You know . . . those were Jenred the Traitor's exact words? Creslin didn't live forever, but he lived
long enough so that you—the High Wizard of Fairhaven—are afraid to
take any direct action against Recluce. Will you be the one who's remembered for letting Recluce dominate all of Candar?"

"No." Sterol chuckled, bitterly, and laid the amulet on the table
beside the mirror. The image of Southpoint vanished. "You want action.
Take the amulet—or give it to someone else."

"I'm asking you, Sterol."

"And I'm refusing. Have those lackeys come to me."

"Fydel!" Anya nodded toward the door, and three guards appeared,
all bearing chains. Behind them stood three White wizards.

"How predictable, dear Anya. You would all chain me rather than
act yourselves." White chaos fires swirled around Sterol.

By the window, Cerryl lifted his shields, then focused the tight
white light lance.

The redhead's eyes burned; her fingers tightened on the white-
bronze dagger.

Fire, white flames, and swirling mists filled the room. The mirror
upon the table exploded, and two of the guards shriveled into dust on
the white-powdered stones. A single blaze of light flared through the
dust, boring through the shields raised by Sterol.

Abrupt and sudden silence fell across the tower.

As the remaining white smoke subsided, Anya picked up the amulet, glancing down at the pile of white dust that lay within the white robes and white boots. She turned and extended the amulet. "Here. You earned it, Cerryl."

Cerryl looked at her sadly. "No. You earned it, but I'll wear it for you." His eyes flickered to the white powder on the stone that vanished as he watched.

"Good. We need to plan the attack on Recluce."

"As you wish. Bring me a plan, and we will implement it. I need a moment." He gestured.

After a moment, the sole remaining guard eased his way back out of the chamber. Then Fydel, Rospor, and Anya stepped outside the tower room. Anya closed the door behind her, leaving Cerryl amid the white dust and the residual chaos.

*Has any High Wizard died in his sleep? Can anyone really rule the White City? And you think you can unite Candar?*

His laugh was short—and bitter. In time, he slipped the amulet over his head.


# CLXVI

Cerryl stood looking out the White Tower window at the clouds that threatened rain and massaged his forehead, hoping the rain would hold off, hoping Anya wouldn't return too quickly. He fingered the amulet. *Hard to believe you wear it, but keeping it will be even harder.*

He turned and studied the room. It needed cleaning and the removal of Sterol's effects—among other things.

"High Wizard, the Lady Leyladin," Gostar announced through the door.

Cerryl opened the door immediately and swept her inside. "You shouldn't be here. How did you get here?"

"I came here to the Halls right after you left this morning. I stayed down with Kinowin. I couldn't help you, but I wasn't going to leave you, either." The green eyes that sparkled so often were somber. "The word is out that you and Anya and Fydel have destroyed Sterol and that you were the compromise choice to be High Wizard."

"Scarcely a ringing mandate, but it's better that way." *And the only way you could possibly succeed as High Wizard . . . if you can.* Cerryl laughed ruefully. "I understand why you're here, and I love you." He paused. "I do worry, and I didn't want you in danger."

"I'm safer here than at the house. You have guards." Her eyes danced mischievously. "Besides, right now, who would attack the High Wizard?" The green eyes turned somber again. "You're safer from Anya if I'm near."

Cerryl couldn't argue that. "I am, but are you?"

"For now. It will reinforce her belief that you need a woman to support you, you weak-willed White noodle." The healer grinned.

"Noodle? I'll show you—"

"You need to meet with Kinowin."

"You change the subject too much." He waited.

"Send a messenger for both Kinowin and Redark," she insisted.

Cerryl looked around, then finally located the handbell on the side table. He rang it.

"Ser?" A young messenger peered inside the door, his eyes wide, almost fearful.

"If you would, please inform the overmages Kinowin and Redark that I would greatly appreciate their presence here at their earliest convenience."

"Yes, ser." The door closed swiftly.

"You're so fearsome," Leyladin said ironically. "If they but knew ..."

"They do. Everything was going as it had. I returned, and suddenly there is a new High Wizard—or a very young mage claiming to be High Wizard. All those who once knew him—except the Council and Anya and a suspect Black healer and a few ancient Whites—are gone."

"You are more cynical."

"More realistic, I fear." Cerryl glanced toward the door.

"That could be. What will you do first ... after this meeting?"

"Get the Guild to acknowledge me. Then start working on changing trade in Candar."

"You sound like Father."

"He's right about trade."

"He is ..." Leyladin smiled.

*Thrap!* "The overmage Kinowin, ser."

"Have him enter."

Kinowin stepped through the door. Despite his gauntness, his shoulders were straight, and his gray eyes were intent, with the hint of a smile buried there. "Cerryl—or should I say 'honored High Wizard'?—greetings, my best wishes, and my condolences." He bowed slightly to the healer. "Especially condolences to Lady Leyladin."

" 'Cerryl' is more than sufficient, old friend." The new High Wizard gestured to the round table. "Please sit. We're awaiting Overmage Redark."

Kinowin settled into one of the seats, and Leyladin sat beside him.

"You intend to have Leyladin here?"

"Absolutely. I'm a weak-willed compromise for High Wizard who needs a healer nearby."

Kinowin laughed. "Anyone who knows the healer knows the lie of that." After a moment he added, "Some will claim that you will be too soft on Recluce, if you listen to a Black."

"That is possible, but I would have them judge by my actions."

Kinowin frowned. "You are not going to allow Anya her head in invading Recluce?"

"Let us see what the season brings." Hating the immediate temporizing, Cerryl offered a smile as he seated himself with his back to the window, facing the door.

"You have something in mind?"

*Much in mind . . . but whether it will play out as you wish, that is something else.* "Some thoughts."

"He has grown more cautious in what he utters." Kinowin nodded toward Leyladin.

With another knock, Gostar announced, "The Overmage Redark."

"Have him come in." Cerryl stood and gestured to the single empty chair. "Please join us, honored overmage."

"Honored Cerryl." Redark inclined his head, and the ginger beard bobbed. "This has been a surprise, truly a surprise, but not necessarily an unwelcome one, though change is always unwelcome to some." He cleared his throat as he sat down at the table. The pale green eyes flicked to Leyladin but centered back on Cerryl.

"We need a full Guild meeting," Kinowin said, "within the eight-day."

"Many could not be contacted and return," protested Redark.

"They should not leave their posts, not at the moment," Cerryl said as he reseated himself. "In Spidlar but Lyasa and Syandar remain, and their presence is necessary. With the trade problems, both Gorsuch and Sedelos must remain watchful."

"Besides," Kinowin added dryly, "how will their presence change matters? Half of those elsewhere would favor Cerryl, and the others know him not."

"Mages belong in Fairhaven," Redark replied, "except when they are needed elsewhere."

"That is often these days," Kinowin observed.

Leyladin smiled faintly but did not speak.

"It may become more necessary in the days to come," added Cerryl.

Redark raised his ginger eyebrows.

"Recluce must be respected in Candar before it will be respected in Recluce." Cerryl made a vague gesture. "How to accomplish that we will discuss in greater detail later." He smiled. "For now, we need to discuss whether you and Kinowin feel that immediate changes are necessary within the Halls."

"The younger mages . . . the apprentices . . . they protest the sewer training," offered Redark.

"Who handles that now? Or is it still—" Cerryl glanced at Kinowin.

"Alas . . . I am still working with Kochar and Kydasl on the sewers."

Cerryl knew Kochar from when he had been an apprentice but had never heard of Kydasl.

"Kydasl was an assistant in Renklaar, but Gorsuch thought he might better serve the Guild in Fairhaven, and Sterol suggested he could one day take over the sewer cleaning and training."

Redark nodded. "He is inclined to be most fastidious."

Cerryl concealed a wince. "I think we all disliked sewer training, but it is necessary." He smiled at Redark. "If you have some thoughts on exactly how we might improve that training, I would find them most welcome."

"I will think on it," promised Redark. "There is also the question of whether the tariff structure for gate medallions might best be improved so as to raise the revenues . . ."

The last thing Fairhaven needed to do was discourage farmers and traders from entering the city. Cerryl nodded. "Perhaps you could prevail upon Esaak to show what revenues might be raised with changes at both higher and lower levels and how that might affect the number of wagons entering the city."

"Esaak . . . he is inclined to lower the tariffs." Redark frowned.

"I see." Cerryl paused, then added, "Ask him to show all the possible numbers and golds received so that we might review them. And the numbers for past years as well."

Redark nodded. "I will."

Kinowin covered his mouth for a moment.

"We also need to consider refurbishing the Guild Hall . . ."

*That's the last thing golds should be spent on . . .* "Perhaps dealing with that would seem too presumptuous for a new High Wizard." Cerryl knew the meeting was going to last far, far longer than he wished—or needed.

He could sense the smile hidden behind the bland expression of interest shown by Leyladin, but he nodded at the ginger-bearded overmage to continue.

# CLXVII

Cerryl felt exposed as he sat in the front row of the Council Chamber. He could feel Anya's and Fydel's eyes on his neck . . . and countless others' as well. *Never imagined you'd feel this alone amid so many mages . . .*

Kinowin, erect and broad-shouldered still, despite the gauntness of age, marched up the side steps and then to the center of the polished gold-shot marble dais of the Council Chamber. Behind him by several steps followed Redark, his eyes shifting nervously from the marble floor to Kinowin and down again.

The two waited for the whispers to die away.

"The first order of this meeting is to affirm Cerryl as High Wizard." Kinowin nodded toward Redark.

The second overmage smiled quickly and faintly, as though he would rather have been anywhere else.

"Is there any member of the Guild who wishes to propose another member as High Wizard?" questioned Kinowin.

A few murmurs followed the inquiry, and Cerryl wondered who speculated about what but did not turn his head.

"Does any member of the Guild propose another for High Wizard?"

In the silence that followed, Kinowin surveyed the chamber, looking methodically from the gold oak desks and red-cushioned gold oak seats at the front to the white granite columns at the sides for any who might be standing under the swagged crimson hangings. Finally, he announced, "Seeing as no other candidate has been proposed, as overmages and representatives of the Council we declare that the new High Wizard is the most honorable Cerryl." The aging blond mage motioned for Cerryl to take the dais.

Cerryl forced himself to rise deliberately, calmly, and mount the dais. Once before the assembled mages, he bowed, noting in passing that with each meeting the numbers were fewer, the ages younger. *Which is why you stand here and why you need to do something.*

He straightened, forcing himself to pause, to let the silence draw out before he spoke, to survey the mages as though he could look into each heart. Finally, he spoke. "It is right and customary for a High Wizard to thank the Guild for its support, and I do so with gratitude."

He waited for another moment, his eyes studying the chamber once more. "We, all of us, face a time of change in Candar. We did not seek that change, but we must address it. The overmages and I will be seeking your assistance, and your wisdom, in continuing to undertake the steps necessary to strengthen the Guild and to ensure that all of Candar respects you. This was the goal of both Jeslek and Sterol, and it will be my goal."

Cerryl bowed slightly again. "I will not deceive you. The Guild faces dangers greater than any known in recent years, and we must work together in overcoming them. I am most confident that we possess the will and the power to do so. And we will." He waited, knowing there would be questions, hoping he could defuse them.

"Honored High Wizard," began a figure in the back, one Cerryl did not know, "can you tell us exactly how effective all the golds poured into the trade blockade have been?"

"For the most recent details we would have to ask Sedelos and Gorsuch, since they observe the largest ports in eastern Candar," answered Cerryl, trying to ignore the veiled sarcasm of the speaker. "From what I have seen, the blockade has been most effective in keeping goods from Recluce out of Lydiar and Spidlar and, more recently, from Hydlen. The Council and I will be looking into ways to reduce the cost of such efforts."

"High Wizard," asked Fydel, his voice blunt, "nearly a score of mages have been assassinated by agents of various rulers. What do you plan to do to redress such wrongs?"

"We have totally destroyed dissident traders and their Council in Spidlar. We have replaced the larger local traders there with traders from Fairhaven loyal to the Guild. We have begun to obtain tariff golds for the first time in years. In turn, we will address the wrongs of other lands." Cerryl smiled.

"Honored Cerryl," asked Huroan, the second in command of the Patrol, "folk have said that you started a Patrol in Spidlar. Is that so?"

"That is so. The Patrol has worked well for Fairhaven, and it seemed that it would work well for Spidlaria. Fairhaven has much to offer Candar, and for those offerings it should be repaid."

A smile flitted across the Patrol mage's face before he sat down.

The thin and angular Broka rose, almost languidly. "Your words bespeak both the need for action and a certain . . . caution, High Wizard. Which can we expect?"

Cerryl managed to keep from choking or even showing his surprise at the double-edged bluntness of the question. "How about caution when it is merited and action when it is necessary?" He offered a self-deprecating grin. "I'm sure that you and the overmages will make your feelings known about which course you feel is appropriate when." Before another question could come up, he bowed again. "I thank you all for your interest, and your support, and I would ask that any of you who have recommendations or advice let the overmages know, and we will address them as we can." He stepped back and nodded to Kinowin.

"The High Wizard having been selected, and there being no other business before the Guild, the assembly is ended."

Cerryl shook Redark's hand, then Kinowin's. "Thank you both."

Kinowin's eyes twinkled. "The year ahead will be most interesting."

Cerryl feared he was right, all too right.

# CLXVIII

Cerryl sat with his back to the window, Leyladin in the seat to his right and Anya across the table. The shutters were closed against the rain and the damp, chill air.

Cerryl massaged his forehead once, then forced himself to keep his hand from his throbbing forehead.

"What do you plan to do about Recluce, Cerryl?" The heavy scent of sandalwood and trilia drifted across the table from the redhead. "Now that you are High Wizard?"

"Make preparations as I can." Cerryl shrugged. "First, we need to raise more golds."

"Raise the tariffs, then." Anya waved off the need for golds.

"Perhaps I should put it more clearly, Anya. I do not like Fairhaven suffering. We are suffering because we must maintain the roads and some of the ports. That costs golds. We are short of golds not because the tariffs were too low, but because Certis, Spidlar, and Gallos were not paying all they owed. Spidlar is paying now, and the revenues are increasing every season. To obtain the golds necessary to support an attack on Recluce—even a sea battle to destroy their ships—we need more golds. I cannot obtain more golds by raising tariffs rulers do not pay. I cannot fight another war that will cost more golds than we have to obtain golds."

"Then what will you do," Anya snorted, "cautious Cerryl?"

"What Jeslek wished to do and Sterol did not understand. Gain control of the major trade ports and thus raise more golds."

Anya raised her eyebrows. "Oh?"

"Between Sedelos and the trader Wertel in Lydiar we have almost doubled the tariff golds there in the last season. And I am working on a plan to increase the tariffs that Certis pays."

"We will have golds in a year, but no power."

"If we have no golds, Anya, we shall be powerless even sooner."

"At least, you have the right idea." Anya turned to the healer. "You should encourage him to act, Leyladin."

"I am sure he will act," the healer said gently. "And he will weigh your words most heavily. He always has."

"From you, those words have great meaning, and some small comfort." Anya frowned as she stood. "Very well, I will bide, and tell Fydel and the others that you are raising the funds necessary to confront the Blacks. I can also tell them that you have been hampered by Sterol's extravagances which left the Guild's coffers near empty."

"They were indeed near empty," Cerryl affirmed. *If not precisely for those reasons.*

"And it is good you do not plan to tax further our own traders." Anya bowed. "They will appreciate that." She turned. "By your leave?"

"I would hope so." *Especially Jiolt.*

Once the door closed, Leyladin shook her head. "She wants you to attack Recluce."

"I can't do it now, even if I wanted to. She knows that."

"She will keep pressuring you."

"Of course. That is how she will destroy me. She will make the Blacks the enemy, as Jeslek did, and if I fail to destroy them, then she will blame me for the traders' woes and those of the Guild and find another High Wizard." *Unless you can turn her schemes.*

Leyladin reached for the goblet of water. "She may, even with your understanding."

"I know. I can only do what I can, and I can do nothing without more golds and tariff coins."

"Father and Lyasa sent more than you expected."

"Nearly a thousand golds, but that will be all until next summer, I fear. The ice grows now on the Northern Ocean. Tyrhavven will stay clear of the ice for another few eight-days, perhaps longer if the weather remains not too cold."

Leyladin reached out and squeezed his hand. "You didn't think it would be this way, did you?"

"I knew it would be, but I had hoped otherwise." He took a sip of water, then stood. "I need to walk through the Halls. I cannot remain cloistered in the tower, not when so few know or recall me."

"I will return to the house. It would not be well for a Black to accompany you." She paused as she rose. "I do expect you for dinner, and you are not sleeping here."

"Yes, dearest lady." He had to smile.

Leyladin returned the smile.

# CLXIX

Cerryl turned in the chair and glanced out the Tower window. The winter clouds threatened cold rain or wet snow, but nothing was yet falling from them, nor was his head throbbing.

"The mage Heralt," declared the guard outside the door.

"Please have him come in." Cerryl stood, moving from behind the table, still amazed after more than a pair of eight-days that he was the High Wizard and that people were deferring to him. *Except they defer to the title and the position, not to you.*

Heralt looked much the same as when Cerryl had last seen him—short brown curly hair, olive eyes, and a trace of diffident shyness. There were the beginnings of lines in his forehead and dark circles under his eyes. "High Wizard."

"Please sit down. Would you like some wine?"

"Please."

Cerryl poured a half-goblet of the white—for some reason it kept in the tower better than the red or the rosé—then sat down. "I appreciate your making the trip here at this time of year."

"As the High Wizard commands."

Cerryl wanted to sigh. Instead, he said, "Please save the ceremony for the public. You're still Heralt, and I'm still Cerryl, and I need your help."

"Mine?" The surprise in Heralt's voice shocked Cerryl. "What can I do? I'm not that powerful. You know that. That's why they sent me to Ruzor to count ships and cargoes and be Shenan's assistant."

"I need every mage's help, but you have skills that will be most useful in the seasons ahead. These are skills few mages have."

"I cannot say what those might be," confessed the olive-eyed young mage.

"Heralt, is your father still trading?" Cerryl found himself standing, then pacing back and forth across the stone floor of the High Wizard's apartment, still half-bemused that the quarters—and the position—were his.

"No, ser. He died last spring."

"I'm sorry. I didn't know. And please . . . I'm just Cerryl here. I know the proprieties have to be observed in public . . . but this isn't public."

"It's hard . . . the High Wizard."

"You didn't expect a friend to be High Wizard so soon?"

"No." Heralt grinned. "I thought you might be one day, but not so soon."

"I'm High Wizard because the Guild is threatened and weakened. Whether the Guild survives or not depends on whether we can enforce the tariffs throughout Eastern Candar. I've sent Lelyadin's father to Spidlaria, and Lyasa and Syandar are working with him to rebuild the trading and factoring system there. Between Duke Estalin's debt to Leyladin and my support of Wertel—"

Heralt looked blank at the name.

"Another trader from Fairhaven, and Leyladin's brother," Cerryl explained. "Lydiar is obeying the tariff rules, and the Guild has taken the port of Renklaar. East of the Westhorns, that leaves three places—Ruzor, the two smaller ports of Hydlen, and Tyrhavven. Now, if we can ensure the tariffs are collected in Tyrhavven, that will give the Guild control of all tariff coins across the whole north and east coasts, except for Worrak, and the blockade ships can be used for other things—controlling smugglers . . ."

"And an attack on Recluce?"

Cerryl shrugged.

"I'd rather go on one of the ships."

"Heralt . . . you understand trade. When we were both apprentices, you explained it to me. The Guild needs you in Tyrhavven. I need you there. I need someone who can understand things and keep the traders in line."

"They won't listen to me."

"They will if you're my representative and if you have tenscore lancers behind you and a pair of apprentices to assist."

"Who . . . the apprentices?"

"You can pick them. Then tell me, and I will summon them to meet you here, so that it is clear that they go with you by my command."

"Tyrhavven is that important?"

"More important than you know. Also, if you hear *anything* about the viscount moving troops into Sligo or mustering them, let me know. Do not wait for confirmations or reports."

"I see you trust him highly."

"I found him taking the bulk of the road tariffs for his own use, but that was during the war with Spidlar and Jeslek would not let me act on what I discovered, save to remove Shyren and one of the viscount's ministers. I doubt that replacing a minister changed anything. The tariffs from Certis have continued to decline."

"But Tyrhavven?"

"We now control the ports of Spidlar and Lydiar. From where else can Rystryr and his traders obtain trade goods from Recluce and Hamor?"

"The Sligan Council will not be pleased."

"They will not, but I will send another twenty-score lancers if need be and blockade Tyrhavven, and I have already let messages be intercepted and sent to their traders indicating such." Cerryl shrugged. "Since I am known as the mage who butchered the leading Spidlarian traders . . ."

"Do you think Rystryr will send lancers?"

"That is possible, but he knows that the Guild removed his brother and that three Dukes of Hydlen and the prefect of Gallos have been removed."

Heralt's mouth opened. "That . . . I did not know . . ."

"Rystryr may send crossbowmen against you—he did against me and against Eliasar—but he will do little that can be tracked to his lair. So . . . you must be careful." Cerryl smiled crookedly. "Do you still wish to go to Tyrhavven?"

"How could I not go? Would that not make me mage adviser there?"

Cerryl nodded.

"And what else do you want me to do once I am there?"

"If your lancers get restless for action, have them patrol the roads—against brigands and smugglers." Cerryl added dryly, "Those tend to appear once we start seeking to change the way matters have been."

"And they once wore green?"

"Some have. Fydel and Shyren gave Rystryr that idea."

"Tyrhavven still sounds better than Fairhaven or Ruzor."

"I hope you find it so." Cerryl slowly stood. "I'll leave my quarters here with you."

Heralt raised his eyebrows.

"I walk the Halls, talk to folk . . . that sort of thing."

"Oh?"

"I have to. No one knows me. Both Sterol and Jeslek took pains to keep me away from Fairhaven and out of sight when I *was* here."

Heralt nodded slowly. "That is why you allow Anya such latitude?"

"Unhappily . . . for now."

"Best you be careful. She has many allies that she has cultivated for many years. You must know that."

"Leyladin reminds me most often." Cerryl's tone was wry.

"Listen to her."

"I do."

Bental, one of the newer tower guards, watched as Cerryl and Heralt stepped out.

"I'll be somewhere in the Halls," Cerryl said.

"Yes, ser." Bental nodded.

They had no more than descended into the front foyer before Cerryl sensed that Redark had appeared, hurrying down the steps behind them to catch Cerryl.

"High Wizard ... ser ..."

"I will see you later, Heralt." Cerryl gave a twisted grin before smoothing his face and turning to Redark.

"Yes, ser." Heralt bowed and turned toward the rear of the front Hall.

"Yes, Overmage Redark?" Cerryl waited.

"Ser ... I just received a scroll from Gorsuch, in Renklaar." Redark raised his eyebrows. "A very important scroll it is, but you had already left your quarters."

"I do need to be visible at times, Overmage. What did mage adviser Gorsuch send you that was so vital?"

"He is requesting at least one of the blockade ships off Spidlar be reassigned to patrol the waters off Renklaar and especially around Pyrdya. There are more smugglers there now."

"I can't say that I am surprised." Cerryl nodded. "Since Spidlaria is iced in or will be shortly, the *White Serpent* and one other ship could be sent to patrol the area off the Ohyde River delta and off Pyrdya. Draft the dispatches, and have them ready for me this afternoon." Cerryl waited, then asked, "Does Gorsuch have other difficulties?"

"Ah ... he suggests that Renklaar is a strenuous post and that perhaps another mage would be helpful."

Cerryl fingered his chin. "Hmmm ... I do not know who we could spare to aid him at this very moment, but he is indeed skilled. Perhaps we could review those junior mages on gate duty? If you would, brief me on them—their strengths and skills—then we could meet with them in the next eight-day. Tell Gorsuch we value his long-standing efforts and we are working to send him assistance."

"Ah ... he would like to return to Fairhaven ..."

"That could pose a problem. Would he rather be in Jellico? We could send Disarj to Renklaar? Or Ruzor? Shenan might be persuaded to go to Hydlen." Cerryl smiled brightly. "What do you think, Redark?"

"I would have to consider that."

"I'd like your thoughts on that. Perhaps we could discuss it this afternoon when you tell me about the junior mages."

"Ah ... yes."

"Good." Cerryl gave a broader smile. "Until then."

He left the front Hall and crossed the fountain court before he was accosted again—this time by Broka, the thin mage who had once taught Cerryl anatomie.

"High Wizard."

"Broka. You have a thought upon your mind?" *Upon a very devious mind?*

"Yes, honored Cerryl. You may recall that I asked whether you would choose caution over actions or the reverse. You responded fairly, if cautiously." Broka bowed his head very slightly.

"I would prefer to act when the actions will have the effect we all desire," Cerryl answered. "Acting for appearance wastes coins we do not have."

"Like Kinowin, you are concerned over golds?"

"I am concerned for the Guild. Golds are necessary to assure the Guild's future." Cerryl offered a faint smile. "I would that it were otherwise, but controlling chaos does not pay lancers nor purchase grain."

"So long as the Guild comes first . . ." Broka nodded.

"It does," Cerryl affirmed. "The good of Fairhaven is uppermost in my thoughts."

"I look forward to when your actions will bring the desired results."

"As do I."

Broka gave a sidelong nod and slipped away in the stealthy and angular fashion that had always made Cerryl think of him as lizardlike. Cerryl made his way toward the Meal Hall, even though the noon bells had not quite rung.

The young High Wizard surveyed the Hall. Almost as though he could sense Cerryl's eyes, Esaak glanced up from the corner table in the Hall. Cerryl made his way through the empty tables and settled down across the round table from the older mage. "How are matters working out with Redark?"

"You may be the most mathematically inept High Wizard the Guild has ever had." Esaak looked at Cerryl, almost blankly, before a trace of a smile appeared. "But you are not *that* inept."

"Redark does not understand why we cannot raise tariffs. He will not listen to me." Cerryl shrugged. "He will not believe matters unless they are put before him in a fashion he cannot deny. I know of no one other than you who can do so."

"I appreciate your trust, High Wizard." A broader smile crossed Esaak's lined face. "I also imagine you have no objection to my sharing my calculations with anyone who is interested." The heavyset and white-haired old mage scratched his ear.

"Not at all. I would appreciate seeing them before they are widely shared so that I know what you have calculated."

"You know what I have calculated, I imagine. Lower tariffs in Fairhaven and broader and lower tariffs in the ports will gain the Guild more golds." Esaak sighed, then lifted the mug of ale before him, slurping down a healthy swallow. "The difficulty is not the calculations, but the explanation of why this is so."

"A twentieth part of fifty-score pies gives one more pies than a tenth of fivescore pies," suggested Cerryl.

"You wish to write the explanations, High Wizard? With your gift of words . . . ?"

Cerryl laughed, easily. "If I wrote them, no one would believe them. You are esteemed and respected."

"You are a dangerous flatterer, ser." Esaak smiled broadly. "I will complete the calculations and essay to educate the overmage on pies and golds." He nodded as Cerryl stood.

"Thank you." With a nod, Cerryl stepped toward the serving table, where the youths in red were setting out what looked to be mutton stew—a lamb stew that had not changed since he had first come to the Halls and heard Faltar complain about it.

*And you wish he were still here to complain.* Cerryl's eyes burned as he turned from the serving table and began to walk back to the White Tower. *More than ever you wish that . . .*

# CLXX

Cerryl peered into the study commons, noting the three apprentices studying there, then slipped into the corridor, using his blur screen to avoid attention.

He passed back to the front Hall, where he waited a time, watching messengers in red passing, some other apprentices, and, finally, a mage he knew, if but slightly. He waited until the red-haired Kochar was almost abreast before dropping the screen. "Kochar?"

"Ah . . . oh, I'm so sorry, ser. I didn't see you." Kochar half-bowed and stepped back away from the High Wizard.

Cerryl offered a pleasant smile and beckoned to the redhead. "You're on gate duty now, are you not?"

"Yes, ser. The eastern gate." Kochar's eyes did not quite meet Cerryl's. "Except for today."

"That was my first gate duty," mused Cerryl. "You still get farmers coming through?"

"Ah . . ."

"Not that many?" prodded Cerryl.

"No, ser."

"You sell many medallions?"

"Not one, ser." Kochar paused. "I've only been on gate duty for a half-season, and it is winter."

"Still," mused Cerryl, "they must have some provisions laid by to sell somewhere. Do not some ask about medallions?"

"There was one, an older man, but when he heard it would cost five coppers, he said he'd take his chances at the square in Howlett or even Weevett."

"What did you say?"

"Wasn't much I could say, ser, was there?"

"Not now. We'll be trying to change that." Cerryl paused. "Anyone tried to bring in perfumed oils packed inside timbers? They're hard to sense if they're not in leaded pottery."

"Ah . . . not that I know."

"You never know what might be in a wagon." Cerryl nodded. "I won't keep you."

"Yes, ser. Thank you, ser." With a bow, Kochar backed away.

As soon as the young mage's head turned, Cerryl concealed himself with the blur screen.

Kochar glanced back once and almost stumbled when he could not see the High Wizard. Cerryl smiled to himself. *One way or another . . . you'll get them thinking you can be anywhere.*

Cerryl crossed the fountain courtyard, ignoring the chill wind and raw air, and then along the corridor and into the library, watching a young woman in the red-trimmed whites of an apprentice who pored over a familiar map. It took him a moment to put name to face.

"What are you trying to find?"

Her eyes widened as she saw the amulet. "Oh, ser, honored High Wizard . . . ah . . ."

"I know. You've been told not to seek help from any full mages and now you have the High Wizard questioning you." He gestured toward the map stretched on the table before her. "That map is familiar . . . It was the first big map I did—for Jeslek, even before he became High Wizard. I had to find out where Tellura, Meltosia, Quessa, and a few other places in Gallos were. What is your task? That you can tell me." Cerryl smiled.

"I'm to find a place called Asula and one called Telsen."

"Who set the task?"

"Overmage Redark, ser."

"Add two more," Cerryl said gently. "Diev and Axalt. You may ask anyone why they are important, but not their location."

"Yes, ser." The tone was not quite resigned.

"What do you think about the Black Isle?"

"The Blacks are our enemies."

"So it has been said for many years," Cerryl answered. "It will be for years to come. Yet most arms mages have died in Candar with few Blacks nearby, and never have the Blacks sent lancers or armsmen into Candar."

"Ser?"

"All enemies are not those who are the most convenient to name." Cerryl smiled enigmatically. "I wish you well on the map. Diev was somewhere in Spidlar, by the way, and Axalt in the Easthorns."

"Was?"

"Good day, Meylal." Cerryl stepped back past the bookcase, drawing the blur shield around him, so that he would appear to have vanished.

# CLXXI

Cerryl glanced around the lamp-lit and silk-hung bedchamber, so similar to the first view of Leyladin's chamber through his glass and yet so different in ways he could not describe but only feel.

"You look tired," Leyladin said, standing behind him and rubbing his shoulders. "Your shoulders are tight. Lie down on the bed."

Cerryl was glad to comply, easing off his boots and stretching out on the green coverlet. The breeze coming through the shutters that were cracked but a fraction of a span was chill yet held the hint of approaching spring.

The healer's long fingers were firm but gentle as she massaged the tight muscles between his shoulder blades and spine. "Your muscles are like iron."

"That's from wondering who will appear behind me every time I leave the tower." *And if they'll see through your blurring screen.*

"You don't have to walk the Halls of the Mages that much."

"I don't? How else do I establish that I could know anything and be anywhere? I'm not a mighty mage like Jeslek was, or a planner and plotter like Anya is."

"You're getting pretty effective. Kiella drew me aside yesterday. She wanted to know if I knew how you managed to slip through walls."

"I wish I could sometimes." Cerryl sighed, enjoying the kneading that relaxed and loosened his shoulders.

"She also said that someone had told her that you had removed all the traders in Spidlar. No one had seen you do it, nor knew how you had, not even to this day." The healer's fingers moved down his back.

"That feels good." After a moment, he added, "I'm not getting respected but feared? Is that it?"

Leyladin laughed. "Both, I would say. That's not too bad for a mage almost no one knew a season ago."

"From nothingness to High Wizard in a single season."

"Better that than the other way around."

Facedown on the soft bed, Cerryl closed his eyes. He wanted to shake his head.

"You can't have as much power as the High Wizard has and expect to be loved," she said quietly. "Except by me and a few others who really know you." After a moment, she added, "That's true for everyone, really."

"I suppose so. Sad, isn't it?"

"Yes, but we won't change that."

*Not if you want to change Candar, we won't.* He let his breath out slowly and tried to concentrate on the firm and gentle touch that had begun to relax a body all too tight.


# CLXXII

Cerryl glanced at the scroll sent from Heralt.

> ... now that the ice is out across the entire Northern Ocean, the wagons have begun to roll in from Certis. I have stationed a full company of lancers at the harbor with one of the apprentices there all the time. Otherwise, cargoes would be loaded and unloaded without tariffs being paid ...
>
> ... with this should come a small chest of golds, nearly 400, to follow the 200 sent three eight-days ago ...
>
> There is a certain sullenness ... yet acceptance when we mention your name to the Certans ... as though they know of you by more than name ... as though they now know that the full surtax will be collected ... Records here show that such was not so last fall ... still concerned that the viscount may attempt something ...
>
> ... have seen no Black traders ...

Cerryl let the scroll roll shut. He stood and walked to the open window, looking out at the white and green of Fairhaven, thinking about Heralt and the continued tariff and trade problems. His use of the glass showed no movement of Certan troops, and the tariff collections sent from Jellico by Disarj had increased somewhat over the previous year, but not to the amount Cerryl suspected was truly due. Sooner or later, he'd have to deal with both Rystryr and Disarj, but that problem would have to wait.

His eyes went to the pile of scrolls. So far matters had continued to improve in Spidlaria and Lydiar, and despite complaining, Gorsuch remained dutiful in Renklaar. The Duke Afabar continued to send obedient scrolls—and golds—from Hydolar. Shenan confirmed that more trade was appearing in Ruzor, but without more mages or lancers she could not ensure that all the tariffs were being recorded and paid.

"How long that will last . . ." Cerryl twisted his lips in a private and wry smile.

*Thrap!* "Overmage Redark."

"Have him come in." Cerryl turned from the window and the warm breeze.

"Greetings, High Wizard." Redark bowed after he entered the High Wizard's apartment. The pale green eyes peered at Cerryl above the ginger beard as the overmage seated himself across the table. "You are often seen around the Halls, or so I am told. Yet you are like a shadow."

"The High Wizard must cast a long shadow . . . don't you think?"

"I had not thought of it in quite that way."

"The overmage Kinowin," announced Gostar from beyond the white oak door to the chamber.

"Have him join us," Cerryl answered, raising his voice.

Kinowin walked in, with no sign of the stiffness Cerryl knew the older overmage felt, and sat to Redark's right. "Greetings, High Wizard, Redark."

"Greetings," Redark answered, not quite dourly.

Cerryl glanced from the white-and-blond-haired Kinowin to Redark. "You requested this meeting, Overmage. Perhaps you should begin." He took a sip of water from the goblet, then poured water for both overmages.

"Ah . . . yes, ser." Redark took a sip from the goblet before him. "There is no doubt, ser, no doubt at all, that you are the most powerful mage—in a quiet sort of way, you understand. But not all understand your power, and you are young . . ."

Cerryl smiled. "I understand."

"At first . . . well . . . every High Wizard must take some time." Redark shrugged. "It has been more than a season since you assumed the amulet, and spring has turned, and summer is upon us."

"And?" asked Cerryl politely.

"Recluce . . . the Black Isle remains aloof. Their traders ply the Eastern Ocean, and they carry cargoes that should be from Candar. You have spoken well and often—"

"Their traders, or those receiving goods in Candar, now pay the full surtax," Cerryl answered mildly.

"Those ships are few," protested Redark, his voice rising slightly. "Many feel that the time to act has long passed. Were it not for having had three High Wizards in near as many years . . ."

"I do understand. The time to act will come. That is why you and Kinowin will explain to the Guild at the next meeting why we are not recalling any of the White Lancers or mages from Spidlar."

Redark frowned. "We are not? They have been there for near on four years. They should be gathered for the attack on Recluce."

Cerryl forced a broader and more winning smile, then nodded toward Kinowin. "I am but following the path laid out by my esteemed predecessors and by you and Kinowin. All of you foresaw the need for Fairhaven to gain control of the northern traders. That was to assure that the shipping tariffs and the surtax were paid. I continue to defer to your expertise. We have, of course, finally managed to do something about Tyrhavven, so that the viscount has not been able to use that port and the Sligan traders to evade his tariff responsibilities, as he once did. But Rystryr will not continue to pay those duties unless we keep the lancers to support Heralt and his assistants."

"Ah . . . I had talked with young Anya," Redark went on in a modulated voice. "She is of the opinion that Recluce remains the greatest danger facing the Guild."

"She is indeed quite knowledgeable," Cerryl said smoothly.

"She continues to be most concerned about Recluce and the threat which the Black Isle poses."

"As are we all," Cerryl agreed.

"There are a number of mages who feel this must be addressed above all," Redark continued, leaning forward. "I fear you do not appreciate the intensity of feeling."

An amused smile flitted across Kinowin's face, vanishing before Redark straightened to await Cerryl's response.

"I understand that, and we are working on plans to do so. This effort to gain greater control of trade is part of that plan. It will enable us to raise the resources to deal with Recluce."

"Would you be so kind as to explain, ser?" Redark's brow furrowed.

"I had thought Sterol and Jeslek would have been more forthcoming," Cerryl said, "but they had much with which to occupy their talents. We now have nearly a score of ships upon the Northern and Eastern Oceans, enforcing the tariff rules. Is that not so?"

"Ah . . . somewhat slightly less than that."

"And if we remove these ships and place them in a fleet to attack Recluce? What happens to the golds we have been collecting?"

"Ah . . . are you suggesting that they might not be collected? That they would defy the High Wizard?"

"I have noticed that in the past the Guild has had trouble collecting golds anywhere that we did not have several mages and detachments of lancers. That was true even when Jeslek was High Wizard, and he was the most powerful chaos wielder in many generations." Cerryl smiled apologetically. "I cannot see why that would change unless we changed something else."

"What do you propose changing?" Kinowin asked, as if to forestall any objection Redark might have.

"By using friendly traders, detachments of lancers, and junior mages with knowledge to ensure all ships that port in Eastern Candar pay their just tariffs, we have begun to do two things. You see that, of course." Cerryl favored the ginger-bearded overmage with a smile. "We can free the older and more experienced mages for service against Recluce, and we can free the ships we have been using to enforce the tariffs for an action to blockade Recluce itself, to strike at the heart of the problem."

Redark frowned.

"But . . . you know all this." Cerryl smiled. "It has taken me some time and study to comprehend the brilliance of what you all had devised, and for that I beg your indulgence. I am now working to complete the plan so that we may have enough warships free of tariff-collecting duties to assemble a true fleet."

"How long might this take?"

"I doubt that any would wish to serve on the ships of a fleet too small for the task at hand. Still, I would suspect that we should be ready to assemble a fleet by summer's end."

"Might I tell Anya of this?"

Cerryl forced a cold and bright smile. "It might be best if Anya were to speak to me directly. I would hate to have something I said taken falsely, and so would you, Overmage." He paused. "Would you not?"

"Ah . . . yes. I can see that." Redark did not quite stammer. "What might I convey, then?"

"That I share your concerns, and hers, and that I look forward to meeting with her about just those concerns." Cerryl rose, to signify the end of the meeting.

"Might I trouble you for a personal matter, ser?" asked Kinowin quietly. His eyes went to Redark.

"By your leave?" said the younger overmage.

"By my leave. If you have other thoughts on how we might speed the assembly against Recluce, I would be most glad to hear them over the next eight-day or so." Cerryl fingered his chin as if thinking. "Oh . . . you might tell Anya that I am working on something, but that I said she should hear it from me, given her interest and expertise."

"Ah . . . that I will."

Cerryl maintained the smile until the white oak door shut.

"You are getting dangerous, Cerryl." Kinowin shook his head. "But words won't stop Anya and the older mages who wish to sit in Fairhaven and collect their stipends."

"I know." Cerryl's voice was bleak. "I know."

"You also play a dangerous game in admitting to an attack on Recluce. Even Sterol knew such would be foredoomed."

"The attack will fail," Cerryl admitted, "no matter how many ships are used." The crooked smile that he found coming more often appeared. "That is why the fleet must carry some of the more experienced and older mages."

"That, too, might be fraught with risk."

"Life is fraught with risk." Cerryl shrugged. "I am but a young High Wizard who will do his poor best to restore the luster of the Guild."

"You'd better practice the humility more," Kinowin suggested.

They both laughed.

# CLXXIII

Cerryl looked at the weaver. The man's lined face was haggard, and two children looked up from the corner beyond the floor loom. Despite the open shutters, little breeze flowed into the hot room.

"I've come to pay a debt," the mage said.

"I do not recall, ser." The man kept his eyes downcast, away from the mage's whites and away from the golden amulet that hung around Cerryl's neck.

"Are you the consort of Pattera?" asked Cerryl gently.

"She is dead, honored ser."

"I had heard." Cerryl extended the leather purse. "Once, when we were children," he lied, "she gave me what coin she had, and those coins made all the difference. I've been away, and I would that I could have repaid her. These are for her children."

The man looked up, warily, not taking the purse.

"I have not seen her in years," said Cerryl, setting the purse on the edge of the worktable, "but a White mage must pay his debts, for better or worse. I would that I could have repaid this debt earlier. Much earlier." *And in person . . .*

"Who might you be, honored ser?" asked the weaver, his voice barely audible.

"My name is Cerryl. I was once an apprentice to Tellis the scrivener, when Pattera and her sister lived off the Square of the Artisans."

"You are among the mighty . . ."

"And I bother to repay a debt?" Cerryl shook his head. "This acknowledges the debt. I owed Pattera that debt, and that can never be repaid." He paused, studying the single hanging on the wall, a small rug of red and green. "Did you do that?"

"Yes, ser."

"Could you do one in white, purple, and some shades of blue and maroon? With the same type of design?"

"I could, ser."

"How much?"

"I could not charge a high mage . . ."

"You cannot afford not to charge one." Cerryl gave a short laugh. "What would you get for that one?"

"Two silvers, ser."

Cerryl could sense the truth of the answer. "Fine." He fumbled in his belt wallet before extracting a gold and extending it. "I would like a hanging like the one on the wall, with the finest wool you can obtain here in Fairhaven, in purple, maroon, white, and blue. The most striking color should be the purple."

The weaver swallowed.

"It is to repay in small part another debt." The High Wizard nodded. "In three eight-days?"

"Yes, ser . . . Your Mightiness. It will be ready. Yes, ser."

"Thank you." *You still have to find a way to repay the debt to Brental and Dylert . . . somehow.* After a nod, Cerryl walked out to the waiting lancers, his eyes and senses scanning the area. *Will you ever be able to walk or ride the streets of Fairhaven openly without a guard?*

He swallowed, wishing he had been able to find Pattera earlier, wishing . . . "What use is wishing?"

"Ser?" asked the lancer subofficer who held the reins to Cerryl's mount.

"Nothing. Just the musings of a mage." *One who continues to find that not all dreams are quite what he dreamed they would be.*


# CLXXIV

Redark suggested that I should see you, Cerryl, dear, and here I am." Anya brushed back a strand of near-perfect red hair as she settled down across the round table. "Would you pour me some of the wine?"

"I would be most happy to." Cerryl filled her goblet half-full but set that pitcher down and refilled his own with water.

"You know, your wine does not turn so quickly as did Jeslek's." With her words drifted the heavy scent of sandalwood.

"I have less chaos to swirl about me." Cerryl shrugged. "I suspect it makes a difference."

"Almost a season has passed, and you have made no moves against the Blacks or against that smith who cost us so dearly." Anya's voice was level, not quite throaty, as she looked across the table at Cerryl. "And you sent a message through Redark, rather than to me."

"I am sure you understand, Anya. Redark is one of the overmages. Would you like to be one?"

"Overmage . . . that does sound intriguing. I will have to keep that in mind, dear Cerryl. After you keep your promise to deal with the Black Isle."

"What would you suggest?" Cerryl's tone was mild, inquisitive. He looked toward the tower window that was but ajar, observing the painted wooden rose that did not move with the cool breeze that passed it.

"You cannot let such acts go unpunished, you know."

"We razed Diev, and neither the city nor the harbor remains. The old cities of Kleth and Elparta are no more but rebuilt as we wished. Spidlaria does whatever we wish—willingly. In the last year, we have added another half-dozen ships to the trade blockade of Recluce." The High Wizard smiled politely.

"Sterol did much for the blockade."

"I have released ships from station off Spidlaria to assist those in the Eastern Ocean."

"So you have, dear Cerryl." Anya took a languid sip of wine. "So you have."

"I take it you believe that more should be done?"

"You are so unfailingly polite and attentive, Cerryl. It's one of your charms."

"I am so glad you find it so. Are you suggesting that an expedition against the Black Isle or at least Southpoint is in order? A fleet, perhaps a firing of the new city being built by the smith?"

"It is so refreshing not to have to outline the details. Sterol was so dense about it."

"I know." Cerryl's voice was dry. "Would you like me to propose this officially in the next Guild meeting and appoint you to develop the plan—under my direction, of course?"

"Of course." Anya leaned forward and touched his cheek. "You are so understanding, Cerryl. So understanding."

"We do try, Anya. We do try."

"You will need a good commander." Anya smiled again. "I would do it, but you know how sailors feel about women on board their ships. So I will have to do what I can from Fairhaven."

"You have done a great deal already." Cerryl temporized.

"The only thing . . . Cerryl . . ."

"Yes?"

"It would have been nice to tell me first."

The High Wizard returned her smile with one equally false. "I did, Anya. Neither Redark nor Kinowin knows the details we have just discussed. After all, I had thought it would be something you would be most interested in, and I would not have wished to discuss details with another first."

"You do so understand, Cerryl. My friends will be pleased." She took another sip of the wine. "All my many friends in the Guild."

"I would hope so. I would also hope that they—and your friends among the traders—understand such expeditions do require golds for their support."

The flicker of a frown crossed Anya's face at the mention of traders but vanished nearly instantly. "Golds—golds are gone tomorrow. No one will recall how you gathered the golds, Cerryl. They will remember but what you did with them." Anya rose. "I will not trouble you longer."

*Not at the moment.* Cerryl stood.

After the redhead had departed, he turned back to the window, studying the White City. Was it always that way? No one considered the cost laid on the laborer, the crafter, or the factor—or the men and women who died—just the great and glorious deeds, where all who took part were either great heroes or equally great villains. "Of course . . . people change but little."

The heavy tower door opened, then closed after Leyladin slipped inside.

"I can smell your friend. I would have come earlier, but I wanted to retain what I'd eaten."

"I've had only water," Cerryl said.

"I can stand her less and less." Leyladin's lips were tight.

"I know." Cerryl sighed. "I know. I'm doing the best I can."

"Are you putting her on the flagship?"

"She's made it clear that she won't go and that her *many friends* support her in that. I'll put Fydel there and a few supporters on the other ships. If I could put Disarj there as well, or . . ."

"It would have been better if she went," Leyladin said, "but, as you always say, you can do what you can do and no more."

"That doesn't mean I do not hope for more."

"Myral did, and much good it did him." Her tight expression softened. "Though you have already done more than he had wished."

"Less, I think."

"You will . . . once you can deal with Anya." The healer took Cerryl's hands, squeezing them gently with cool fingers.

*If I can deal with Anya and her many supporters . . .*

# CLXXV

In the late-summer twilight, Cerryl walked quietly along the Avenue, his form half-shielded by the blur screen, a slight headache remaining from the afternoon thundershower. At the steps to The Golden Ram, he turned and entered the inn, slipping along the wall and up the steps to the second level of The Golden Ram and through the half-ajar door into a private room.

Five mages sat around the table, two on each side of Anya, the space across from her empty.

Anya frowned. "I thought I heard someone."

The four men glanced around, their eyes sliding across Cerryl as though he were not there.

"Close the door."

A thin-faced and brown-goateed mage rose quickly to comply.

Cerryl smiled to himself. *Always someone else is there to do her bidding.* Cloaked and blurred in the shadows, he listened.

"We have to act soon. The High Wizard—the younger mages claim he is everywhere and that he must be older and wiser than he is, that he hides his true appearance."

"Zurchak . . . Zurchak . . ." Anya shook her head disapprovingly. "Do not believe every word you hear on the wind. The High Wizard has but two strengths, and both are formidable. He can raise shields strong enough to stop any order or chaos forces known to any but perhaps the great Jeslek. He also can sense where the golds and silvers flow. Other than those traits; he is a normal mage. He does not drift through walls. He does not hear his name murmured on the wind. For darkness' sake, he sleeps with a Black healer, and he could scarce do that if he bore mighty chaos within him."

In his cloaked and shadowed corner, Cerryl nodded to himself.

"Cerryl the cautious. He does nothing unless he has calculated and planned."

"Caution is not always without merit, Muerchal," observed Anya, the tip of her tongue touching her lips after she spoke. "He is High Wizard, and the Guild has more golds than when he took the amulet."

"Golds . . . golds are not glory. They don't bring the Guild or us power or respect." Muerchal snorted.

"They do pay our stipends," added the goateed mage. "There is much to be said for that."

"If Cerryl the cautious were bolder, the Guild would be more greatly respected, and the golds would flow in," retorted Muerchal.

"Perhaps . . . perhaps when you are High Wizard, you can make that happen," suggested Anya, smiling broadly.

"I will. Even as overmage, I could do more than doddering old Kinowin or Redark the repeater."

"Muerchal—you talk so much now, but when you get in the chamber we won't hear so much as a whisper."

"You will. You will, Aalkiron."

"We'll see." The goateed Aalkiron snickered.

"What about you, Aalkiron?"

"I'll leave the words to you, Muerchal."

"Enough . . . enough," Anya said. "The High Wizard has promised that there will be an attack upon Recluce. Should he fail to address that, we must question his resolve."

"He will address it, at great length, and with many words," suggested Zurchak. "If the words mean anything new, that is another question."

Cerryl's unseen smile was crooked. *Your time is getting short, shorter than you would like.*

"Others—older mages—will listen with care as well," Anya replied. "They have been more patient, but they will take it amiss if nothing definite is promised."

"They will take it amiss?" Muerchal laughed. "And then what? Will they ask for more and more words?"

Cerryl decided that Muerchal needed to serve somewhere outside of Fairhaven, preferably aboard a ship—a small ship that was barely seaworthy.

After a time, when a serving woman appeared with more wine, Cerryl slipped from the upper room. He walked silent and unseen up the Avenue and past the Halls of the Mages, nearly to the Market Square. Then he turned westward toward Layel's dwelling.

Leyladin was waiting in the front room, the one with the portrait of her mother. "What did you discover?" She stood and offered an embrace.

Cerryl returned it, adding a kiss, before responding. "Anya and her group of younger acolytes will indeed push me to commit to the attack on Recluce. She says she has also talked to some of the older mages, Broka and Fydel, I'd guess, and perhaps Gyskas and a few others. They want action as well."

"So long as others' blood is shed." The healer led the way to the silk-hung bedchamber and closed the door behind them.

"That has been the case since I was a student mage, and doubtless before that." Cerryl sat on the small chair and began to pull off the heavy white boots.

"Do you want anything to eat?"

"No. I'm not hungry."

"Not hungry?" The dark-green eyes danced in the light of the single lamp lit in the bedchamber. "I don't know that such is good. What can I do with a mage without hunger?"

"Woman . . ."

"Do not forget that, my highest wizard. I have waited long, and the season you have been back is too short . . ." Her eyes went to the second boot as it thumped on the green rug that covered the polished floor stones. Then she smiled. "No one notices that the High Wizard still wears the heavy working boots of a patrol mage."

"There is much they do not notice," Cerryl said with a grin, "and probably that is for the best—for us."

"Best they do not notice your evenings." Leyladin stepped forward, her arms encircling him as he rose.

# CLXXVI

Cerryl surveyed the Council Chamber for a long moment, letting the murmurs die away, faint words muffled by the heavy crimson hangings swagged between the gold-shot pillars that framed the chamber. "A number of you have exhibited great patience in refraining from demanding that I act at once against Recluce." The High Wizard offered a broad smile. "That patience is to be rewarded."

"Hear! Hear!" The words came in a low whisper from somewhere in the back benches. "Cheers for Cerryl the cautious."

"I appreciate the confidence, Muerchal, though your words were not much more than a whisper." Cerryl's normally mild voice filled the Hall. He was glad for the time he had spent slinking through the Halls and elsewhere, listening, unheard, noting and keeping track. His eyes fixed on the far left corner. "Do you agree, Zurchak?"

Cerryl couldn't help but note the smile—quickly smothered—from Kochar at the end of the second row. "I am announcing that the steps we have taken to secure tariff payments from the north coast of Candar have indeed worked, and that the Guild has received the largest such tariff payments this summer that it has ever gotten." Cerryl let golden light sparkle—momentarily—from the amulet at his neck. That had been one of Leyladin's suggestions. "We have also reduced the number of ships in the Northern Ocean and shifted them to patrol the waters of Worrak and Ruzor. Tariff collections in both ports have increased as

well. They have increased greatly." He paused to let the words penetrate.

Beside Anya, in the center of the fifth row, Fydel shifted his weight,
almost as if the square-bearded mage did not wish to be noticed.

"At my direction," Cerryl continued, "the noble Anya has been and
will be developing the plan for the attack on the new port city on Recluce. As many of you know, Anya has been one of those most concerned about the Black Isle. She has been most insistent that the Guild
deal firmly with Recluce, and I felt that, with that insistence, she would
work to develop the strongest possible attack on the Southpoint port.
She has had much experience in Guild campaigns, from Gallos to Spidlar to Hydlen." Cerryl gestured toward the redhead. "If you have suggestions, or information that would be helpful, please convey them to
her. She has worked long and hard to make all aware of the menace of
the Black Isle. She served Sterol and the mighty Jeslek well in their
efforts on behalf of Fairhaven and against Recluce. To her, nothing is
more important than the Guild vanquishing Recluce." Cerryl offered a
slight bow, pausing before asking, "Is there other business before the
Guild? If not . . . overmages, would you join me?"

Kinowin stepped forward and onto the dais, followed by Redark.

"Now that the business of Recluce has been handled for now," Cerryl said, more warmly, "let us bring in the new mages."

Cerryl waited on the dais, Kinowin to his right, Redark to his left,
as Esaak escorted the three figures in the tunics of student mages forward and down the center aisle of the chamber.

"High Wizard, I present the candidates for induction as full mages
and members of the Guild." Esaak's voice rumbled, and he barely managed to avoid coughing before stepping to the side.

Cerryl stepped forward, looking down at the three student mages
he'd scarcely known. They'd come from the crèche and gone through
training while he'd been in working for Jeslek and then in Spidlar for
the better part of three years. After a short silence, he nodded, calling
forth the names, "Eidlen, Dumal, Ultyr . . . you are here because you
have studied, because you have learned the basic skills of magery, and
because you have proved you understand the importance of the Guild
to the future of all Candar . . ."

Cerryl wondered if they really did, if any of the Guild members in
Fairhaven itself—except Kinowin—truly understood what Fairhaven
and the Guild offered for the future of Candar. ". . . we hold a special
trust for all mages, to bring a better life to those who follow the White
way, to further peace and prosperity, and to ensure that all our talents
are used for the greater good, both of those in Fairhaven and of those
throughout Candar." Cerryl paused.

"Do you, of your own free will, promise to use your talents for the
good of the Guild and for the good of Fairhaven, and of all Candar?"

"Yes," answered the squat and bushy-haired Eidlen.

"Yes." Dumal squared his painfully thin shoulders.

"Yes." Ultyr was a small blond girl/woman with the same dark green eyes as Leyladin had.

"And do you faithfully promise to hold to the rules of the Guild, even when those rules may conflict with your personal and private desires?"

"Yes," answered the three, nearly simultaneously.

"Do you promise that you will do your personal best to ensure that chaos is never raised against the helpless and always to benefit the greater good?"

"Yes."

"And finally, do you promise that you will always stand by those in the Guild to ensure that mastery of the forces of chaos—and order— is limited to those who will use such abilities for good and not for personal gain and benefit?"

"Yes."

"Therefore, in the powers of chaos and in the sight of the Guild, you are each a full mage of the White Order of Fairhaven . . ."

Cerryl raised that shimmering touch of chaos to brush the sleeves of the three—and the red stripes were gone, as if they had never been, as had been the case when he had become a full mage.

"Welcome, Eidlen, Dumal, and Ultyr . . ." Cerryl smiled at the three and then studied the mages behind them. "Now that we have welcomed our newest mages, our business is over. All may greet them."

Murmurs, and then conversation, broke out across the chamber. Cerryl's eyes took in Anya, leaning to one side and whispering to Fydel. He forced his smile to remain in place and stepped off the dais toward the three young mages, each of whom carried a half-bewildered expression.

Dealing with Anya could wait. *For the moment . . . only for the moment.*

# CLXXVII

As soon as she seated herself at the table in the High Wizard's quarters, Anya raised her eyebrows. "Come. Show us what your precious smith has done now, Cerryl."

"I would be most happy to show you what Jeslek's precious smith has done," answered the High Wizard, pausing to blot sweat off his forehead with the back of his hand. He concentrated, and the silver mists formed, then parted.

A small schooner with sails was tied at a sturdy stone pier. The ship's sails were furled, and a black pipe protruded from the main deck. Beside the schooner was a small two-masted fishing boat and, on the other side, another ship, jet-black, without masts, but with a slant-sided deckhouse, an open cylinder behind it, and smooth, curved hull lines. Workers attached black metal plates to the rear of the Black ship's deckhouse. The three White wizards studied the scene in the mirror.

"What in darkness is it?" asked Fydel.

"Do we really want to find out?" Cerryl's voice was sardonic. "You can sense the order he has poured into the iron."

"Cerryl dear, you are so cautious. Look at the hillside. Those are tents beyond the first houses. Clearly, this . . . settlement is scarcely begun."

Fydel raised his eyebrows. "The stone buildings appear rather solid, Anya."

"As do the piers," added Cerryl.

"You . . . men! If you can call yourselves that. We need to stop this before the Black Council decides this smith should build more such vessels. Right now, all he has is two small ships and a fishing boat and a few buildings. We wait much longer, and it gets that much harder."

Cerryl cleared his throat. "Anya, we are not in the Council Chamber. The Guild has agreed to your plan. The southern fleet is already gathering in the Great North Bay. Within the next two eight-days, depending on the winds, it will be ready to set forth—exactly according to your plans." He offered the redhead a broad smile. "What else would you have us do?"

"You are too accommodating, Cerryl." Anya's voice was smooth. "But I appreciate your thoughtfulness. I do trust that the fleet's departure will be as you have projected and that there will be sufficient troop support to level this Black settlement."

"You wish to prove to the Blacks that we can strike even upon their beloved isle?"

"It would aid our effort, would it not?" asked the redheaded wizard.

"If you so believe, then I bow to your wisdom, and I will make certain that all understand your words and observations." Cerryl inclined his head. "I will ensure that the fleet leaves as you have planned. With some lancer detachments aboard."

"Thank you." Anya stepped back and inclined her head. "By your leave, Highest of High Wizards?"

"Of course." Cerryl inclined his head in return, standing and watching as she left, waiting until she was outside his apartments.

Fydel waited impassively until the door shut. "You push her too much, Cerryl. With all her supporters, she could have your head tomorrow."

"Perhaps. But would you want this position? Now, particularly?" The High Wizard looked down at the amulet, then turned and glanced out the window into the hot late-summer day, where the white-orange sun burned through the green-blue sky. *Too bad you cannot remove her as you did Lyam and the others . . . but too many in the Guild know of your skills that way, and all would turn on you . . . now, anyway.*

Fydel shook his head.

"Only the young bulls like Muerchal would want to be High Wizard." Cerryl laughed and turned back to Fydel. "Mages like Disarj, Gorsuch—even Heralt and Lyasa—would have him turning in circles within days. Old and cautious as Kinowin and Redark are, either would be a far better High Wizard."

"They don't wish to be," suggested Fydel. "It takes strength and skill, and cunning. You and Anya are the only ones left with such, save Gorsuch and Disarj, and both of them are rock lizards." Fydel stood.

"You have your strengths," Cerryl pointed out. "I would like you to consider being the fleet commander."

"Me? If all is not well with the ships . . ."

"Anya will blame me, and then you." Cerryl frowned, then added, "You have seen me. You know I do not lay my failures on others."

The square-bearded mage shook his head. "You do not, but Anya would."

"If you do not command, then she will seek someone like Muerchal or Zurchak—and then, should anything be amiss, she will blame you for not putting your expertise to work for the Guild." Cerryl grinned lopsidedly. "After she blames me before the entire Guild for not insisting that you take the post."

Fydel laughed. "Best I make preparations to go to Lydiar." His face clouded, then cleared, and he nodded somberly. "By your leave?"

Cerryl nodded in return. As the door closed, Cerryl's eyes went to the papers on the side of the desk, with the commission for Brental from Wertel, who, at Cerryl's request, had found some buyers interested in quality-cut timbers and planks. *You hope that it will help more than a little.* Brental had been as good as his father to Cerryl when the High Wizard had been a sawmill boy there.

*Can you repay them all? Probably not, but you have to try . . . just as you have to try to be the best High Wizard—knowing you can't be.*

# CLXXVIII

I understand Cerryl has suggested that you command the fleet." Anya glanced across the table to Fydel, then at Cerryl. Her pale eyes avoided Leyladin. "I thought I was directing the plan."

"I have followed your plan, Anya." Cerryl poured more water into his goblet and then into Leyladin's.

Even as Leyladin took a sip of the chaos-cleaned water, the healer's dark green eyes never left Anya.

"Then, you will direct the fleet, Fydel." Anya smiled winningly. "I had wanted you, but I had hoped the High Wizard would let me tell you that."

Cerryl kept his face impassive.

The wizard with the square-cut brown beard frowned, looking from the High Wizard to Anya. "You want me to go against that demon ship? It's seaworthy now, and it moves faster than the other one."

"It's only one ship, and you'll have a dozen well-armed war schooners," Anya replied. "Besides, you don't even have to land. Just use your skills to fire the town."

"What if the . . . whatever he is . . . comes after us?"

"You sink his ship," Cerryl said quietly. "I recall your once saying that would be possible were you in command. You're the wizard in charge."

"Fine. I'll need some more assistants."

"Pick whom you need. Except for Lyasa and Heralt—I need them to make sure the tariff coins keep flowing from the northlands. Let me know, though, and I'll inform those you pick."

Fydel pursed his lips, then inclined his head. "By your leave?"

After Fydel had departed and the tower door had closed again, Cerryl massaged his forehead and looked out the window into the cold rain pelting Fairhaven. "Demon-damned rain, always gives me a headache."

The redheaded woman sat, legs crossed, before the table. The circular mirror that lay upon the white oak was blank. She smiled, first at Leyladin, then at Cerryl.

"You really don't care if we win, do you?" asked Cerryl.

"What ever gave you that idea?"

"Everyone who supported you has been given a position on those fleets. At your request. That's a page from Hartor's book."

"You've read a great deal of history. It makes you much more appealing." Anya paused. "I did not select them all. Some you added."

"That is true, but was that not what you wanted?" The High Wizard fingered the amulet once worn by a High Wizard named Hartor and more recently by Sterol. "If they win, they owe you—"

"They owe you, High Wizard."

"That is so thoughtful of you." Cerryl inclined his head to Anya. "Humor me, if you please, and listen. You owe me that, at least."

Anya smiled faintly, but only with her mouth.

"If we somehow destroy or humiliate this Black builder of magic ships, then all your supporters will be indebted. If this unknown Black proves as great as, say, Creslin, then no one is left to challenge you. And," Cerryl added wryly, "like Hartor, no one will want this position for at least a decade, or until their memories grow somewhat fainter. You are rather astute, Anya dear." He paused. "Of course, if they fail, but return, then I will follow Sterol."

"Then why did you accept my proposition?" Anya asked.

"Why not? All life is a gamble. Besides, like Sterol, I suspect attacking Recluce is doomed to failure."

"You admit that and yet are sending out those fleets?"

"I could be wrong." Cerryl smiled.

"So you could." Anya returned the smile, stood, and stepped around the table toward him, lips parted. She bent down and brushed his cheek.

Cerryl took the kiss, and the swirl of sandalwood scent and chaos, without wincing.

Anya glanced at Leyladin. "I trust you do not mind, healer. He has been most helpful."

The White mage's smile was broad and false.

"I am glad for you, Anya." Leyladin's eyes were cold, her voice level.

"You are such a coward, Cerryl." The redhead stepped away.

"That is one way of putting it, and I admit it." He laughed gently. "If there were anyone else . . . anyone who could be High Wizard . . ."

"There isn't." Cerryl smiled as falsely as she had. "Not who needs you."

"You must remember that, especially before the next *full* meeting of the Guild," Anya said, overly sweetly, inclining her head briefly to Leyladin. "And you also, healer."

Cerryl did not wipe his cheek until the door shut.

"I hate her. Did you have to let her do that?"

"Let her kiss me? No. I could turn her into ash and have half the Guild at my neck."

"You're stronger than all those left here."

Cerryl nodded. "But I can't fight them all, day after day. You know I'm working on it. If I let Anya humiliate me in private . . . well . . . there's less chance she'll expect what's coming."

"She's planning more than a confrontation before the Guild," predicted Leyladin. "There aren't that many who will follow her. Not if you show your power."

"Probably, but what is she planning? I've checked with the lancers and the lancer officers. The companies that were loyal to her were the ones I sent to the southern fleet. Every one of her four young mages— Muerchal, Zurchak, Aalkiron . . . and the other one . . . I can't remember his name . . ."

"Giustyl," Leyladin supplied.

"They're with Fydel and the fleet. Broka is also her tool, but I can't do much about him. Still, he's about the only older one left here, except maybe Gyskas, and I can't see what he sees in her . . ."

"Lust . . . sex." The healer smiled. "Even High Wizards have been known to experience it."

"Woman . . ."

"Well? Can you deny it?" Her smile grew broader.

"No." Cerryl frowned. "We'll have to watch those two closely, but neither is that strong in chaos."

"Treachery of some sort, then." Leyladin frowned. "I think I'll have some of Father's trade guards watch the house at night."

"That couldn't hurt. Should we sleep here?"

"At the house, they can't tell where you sleep. It's order-spelled against most glasses now. Besides, if Broka and Gyskas are involved, are you any safer here?"

"Probably not."

"You *could* remove her . . ." Leyladin suggested, tentatively.

"That wouldn't work well for the future. By now, everyone knows that I can remove people without anyone seeing anything. If Anya disappears, it all points to me. And I can't hold on as High Wizard just by sheer force. Removing people without the support of the Guild . . . look what happened to Sterol at the end. No one even said a word. They were all relieved. I have to position Anya as totally unreasonable . . . and leave her without supporters."

Leyladin raised her eyebrows. "If you look too much to the future, we may not have one."

"I know. I know." *The longer you're High Wizard, the worse it seems to get. No wonder Sterol was so arbitrary.* Cerryl took a deep breath.

# CLXXIX

Leyladin sat up in bed, then slipped in the darkness from under the quilt and coverlet to the window, where she peered through a crack in the shutter—out at the heavy fat snowflakes that followed the afternoon's cold rain, leaving a thin coat of slushy snow on the bushes and the ground.

"There's something out there," she whispered.

Cerryl climbed out of the silken sheets, wearing but a loose nightshirt, still groggy. He'd barely gotten to sleep, and deep as his sleep had been, it had not been restful. He shook his head, throbbing from the storm. Despite the pounding in his skull, he could sense something beyond, not exactly chaos, not exactly order.

"A lot of iron . . . I can feel that," she added in an even lower voice.

"Iron . . . weapons." Cerryl blinked and rubbed his forehead.

*Thurummmm . . . thurrummm . . .* The thunder of the snow shower rumbled across Fairhaven and through Cerryl's skull as he pulled back the inside shutters and fumbled open the window.

Had there been a muffled yell . . . a *clank* of some sort?

Through the heavy flakes of snow, the intermittent glow of the single outside house lamp glinted off dark iron. Figures in dark leathers slipped along the shadows by the wall, and a heavy pounding came from the front of the house.

"Cerryl . . . there must be twoscore armsmen out there, and . . ."

*And someone mustering chaos.* Concentrating was hard, with his sleep-befogged mind and headache. *You have to concentrate . . . you have to . . .*

"I know . . . there's a pair of mages—I don't know whom, though."

"He's at the window there!" hissed a high male voice.

Cerryl frowned. Despite the headache he began to muster chaos, as much as he could.

*Whhhstt!* A firebolt flared toward the window, curving away and splatting against the bricks of the wall.

Cerryl swallowed. He hadn't even sensed the chaos. Leyladin's shields had diverted it while he'd been fumbling, trying to create a larger chaos focus through the ground and storm.

Leyladin touched his hand lightly, letting her dark order support him, adding to his shields, actually shielding him as he worked. "Go on . . . You can do it."

*Can you? You have to.* Ignoring the two sets of pounding—a heavy hammer against a door and storm-chaos and conflict within his skull—Cerryl struggled to raise the chaos he needed.

*Whhhstt!* Another chaos bolt flamed toward the window, and again Leyladin diverted it.

Cerryl could feel the strain she was under, trying to deal with chaos and his impossibly slow reactions. His eyes burned, and each of the armsmen in dark leathers seemed to have split into two armsmen.

The ground rumbled, once, twice, and he smiled grimly as the chaos he had called forth infused the area around the house.

*Ssssssss!* Orange-white flame seared upward through the ground, and steam hissed into being, wreathing the factor's dwelling. Curtains of black-shot white chaos fire played around the walls and wavered across the ground. Gouts of steam flashed into the dark night air.

"Aeeeii!! . . ." The screams of men being chaos-roasted filled the night, and the ugly unseen reddish white chaos of death rolled across the ground, swirling against the bricks of the dwelling.

*Whhhssst! Whssst!* Two more firebolts flashed toward them, and this time Cerryl diverted them, his senses on the two figures that stood, seemingly impossibly, amid the chaos storm that filled the night.

*Whhhsst!*

The High Wizard straightened, taking a slow breath, and focused a narrower beam of chaos.

The first figure flared like a white candle struck by molten iron. The second turned but did not take three steps before another white candle flared in the darkness.

Cerryl bent forward, his hands on the wooden sill.

Leyladin's fingers trembled on Cerryl's forearm, then tightened. "Finish it . . ."

Cerryl closed his eyes to shut out the painful double images and concentrated on widening the swath of chaos to include those armsmen already retreating, even those trying to scramble over the stone walls.

*SSsssssss!*

The muscles in his arms and thighs tightened, almost cramping into knots. Outside, the ground steamed, so much that the air felt like a hot and damp summer night, shot through with an occasional brief gust of chill wind.

Leyladin tugged gently at Cerryl's arm. "There's no one out there, but the front entry . . ."

The healer at his side, Cerryl walked heavily but quickly toward the front door, holding some fragments of chaos ready.

A leathered figure leaped across the tiles of the front Hall—almost reaching Cerryl before a golden light lance burned through his chest. Cerryl and Leyladin jumped back as the dull thud and clunk of covered plate mail echoed through the dwelling.

Both glanced around.

"I don't see anyone else," she whispered.

Squinting through double images and eyes that stabbed pain, Cerryl swept the hall and foyer with sight and senses but could see no one. They eased toward the open front door and the lamp that spilled faint light across the still-steaming ground.

"There were two running toward the square," Leyladin said.

"We'll have to let them go," he answered hoarsely.

Leyladin bent and studied the body in green livery lying in the front foyer. "Gleddis . . . he once carried me on his shoulder."

Cerryl noted the sledge and heavy chisel on the stone stoop, and chunks of wood gouged out of the door frame. "I'm sorry."

"Lady? Ser?" Soaris padded up behind them, trousers thrown on over a nightshirt but barefoot. "Are you all right?"

"Yes," Leyladin answered simply. "They killed Gleddis."

Soaris studied the fallen guard, then peered out into the now-still night, squinting to see beyond the faint semicircle of light thrown by the door lamp. "He saved you, and allowed ser Cerryl to destroy the others."

*None of the armsmen would have been here, except for me.* "Sometimes that's cold comfort." Cerryl's words were heavy.

"He would not have died, had he not wished to do his duty." Soaris studied the ground. As the wind from the storm rose and the ground dried and cooled, white ashes swirled up and mixed with white and fat snowflakes. Farther from the house, the flakes had begun to stick.

Cerryl looked out beyond the doorway, through the double images and the reinforced headache. "Soaris . . . ?"

"Ser?"

"I can see our intruders left some weapons and metal implements. If you would not mind . . ."

"I would be happy to gather them, ser. If nothing else, ser Layel could resell them at a profit."

"You should not have any trouble." Cerryl massaged his forehead above his eyes.

"I would think not, ser."

"Thank you, Soaris," Leyladin said softly.

Cerryl walked slowly through the front Hall. His legs barely supported him, and he took several steps into the front sitting room, where he sank into the nearest chair. His eyes were pain-seared, so much so that the images—when he opened his eyes—were doubled and tripled.

"You'll be all right." Leyladin said.

"Not . . . without . . . you . . ."

Slowly, as she kneaded his shoulders and neck, the shaking subsided. The double images remained, if not so pain-seared as immediately following his use of focused chaos. His head ached, more than he could recall, perhaps more than ever, or perhaps just more than he wanted to recall.

Soaris passed through the front Hall again, this time wearing boots and a jacket.

"Anya. It was Anya." Leyladin added, more softly. "I told you she planned something. She's one of the few that know you don't handle chaos as well in storms."

Cerryl refrained from nodding but tightened his lips, thinking about his comments to Anya about a storm only days earlier. "Stupid . . ."

"You did fine."

"You can't let anyone know anything, can you?" This time he did shake his head, if minutely. "For a bit, she'll have to think we don't know her connection. Until I can discover whose armsmen those were."

"She gets away with too much."

"Not this time," Cerryl promised, his voice cold and distant. *Not this time . . . but we do it my way.*

# CLXXX

As the tower door opened, Cerryl turned his eyes from the white blanket that covered the city to the man who entered the High Wizard's apartment.

The overmage bowed to Cerryl. "You asked for me, High Wizard?"

"Kinowin, I'm still Cerryl except when formality requires it, and this isn't one of those times. Please sit down and join us." Cerryl gestured to the seat at the table beside him and across from Leyladin.

"There are rumors . . ."

"Doubtless all over the Halls. I've summoned Senglat since his lancers were the last in Certis. I've also summoned several traders. With large detachments of lancers to ensure the traders honor their . . . invitation."

A puzzled look crossed the overmage's face as he sat beside Cerryl.

"What sort of rumors have you heard?" asked Leyladin.

"Oh, that the High Wizard summoned chaos to entertain you . . . that Broka could stand the new High Wizard no more and has left Fairhaven . . . that were Fydel here, he would be wearing the amulet . . . those sorts of things."

"Anya," said Leyladin.

"I fear she has discovered what I am doing," Cerryl commented, "and would raise discontent against me as quickly as she can."

"Broka is not anywhere to be found," Kinowin pointed out.

"That is not surprising, since he attacked Leyladin's dwelling last night, along with another mage—I don't know who." Cerryl shrugged. "We will have to play this out, and that is why it is best you are here."

"It would be wiser to have Redark here."

"Perhaps." Cerryl's voice was cool.

"No," added Leyladin.

Kinowin nodded to her. "I bow to you in this, lady."

Cerryl pointed to the pair of fire-darkened iron blades, blades with even the wrapped leather of the hilt grip burned away. "What do you make of those?"

"Armsmen's blades. Not ours. Probably from Certis, possibly Gallos."

"We—or Soaris—collected several score of those last night." *Along with a few other items, like two white-bronze daggers*

Kinowin's eyebrows lifted. "You must be doing something correctly, Cerryl. It takes most High Wizards several years to generate such enmity."

*Thrap* ... After the knock, the door opened a crack. "Overcaptain Senglat."

Cerryl beckoned for the lancer commander to enter.

The nearly bald overcaptain stepped up to the other side of the table, bowed, then straightened. "Ser?" His eyes took in the overmage and the healer.

"Are you missing any armsmen, Senglat?" Cerryl kept his voice level, almost idle, not looking to his left where Leyladin sat, nor to Kinowin at his right.

"No, ser."

Leyladin nodded her reaction that the overcaptain told the truth.

After pulling on heavy leather gloves, Cerryl lifted one of the blades from the table. "Would you look at that?"

Senglat stepped forward and took the blade, his eyes ranging over it, weighing it, before he replaced it on the wooden surface. "That be a Certan blade, ser. The tang is curved so, and the blood gutter, here, is shorter and wider." Senglat frowned. "How did you come by this?"

"Several-score armsmen attempted to attack the healer's dwelling last night. Only their blades and coins survived, but the coins were all struck in Fairhaven." *New silvers, no less.*

"Several score?"

"It is hard to tell, but we did recover forty-two blades." Cerryl smiled.

"There were forty-two outside armsmen in Fairhaven? That is hard to believe."

"No," Kinowin said quietly, "there were forty-two armsmen who carried Certan blades."

"I am not sure either is good." Senglat tightened his lips, then licked them.

Cerryl nodded. "I'd like you to stay." He nodded in the direction of the empty seat. "Pull it around some."

The overcaptain concealed a frown but eased the chair to his left, then seated himself, carefully, beside Leyladin.

"We will be hearing from some traders next," Cerryl said.

The first trader to enter the apartment quarters was a wiry man dressed entirely in gray except for a wide green leather belt. Chorast bowed. "I am honored to be here."

"I hope so," Cerryl said. "Have you hired any additional armsmen lately?"

The small and wiry man blinked, then cocked his head sideways. "Why, honored High Wizard, would I be doing such in winter when I factor less and collect less? No . . . I have not."

"Have you had any armsmen disappear lately?"

Chorast blinked again. "No, ser."

"Have you heard of other factors looking for armsmen?"

"Not in more than a season. I heard that Loboll sought some guards for his shipments to Suthya last fall."

Cerryl wanted to nod to himself. The trader was confused inside, but his answers had been truthful. "How are you finding trading in Fairhaven?"

"They say that you seek truth more than most High Wizards, Your Mightiness, and maybe that be so . . ." Chorast paused and smiled.

Cerryl laughed. "Well put, Chorast. That means it's hard, and you think it's going to get worse, and the last thing you want to do is tell that to the High Wizard."

"There been times worse."

"But not many. Why are you staying?" Cerryl leaned forward.

"Fairhaven's my place, Your Mightiness. And . . . well, you took care of Layel, and folk say that you're making the surtax stick in the out ports. First time in my life, anyway." The hint of a smile appeared and vanished as the wiry trader's eyes met Cerryl's.

"I am working to make it better for trade—and fairer across Candar."

"Be true that you raised tariffs in Spidlar, ser?"

"Some. They're half of here," Cerryl admitted. "I'd like to have all traders and factors pay the same."

"You do that, and the honest factors—I'm a scoundrel but an honest one, ser—they'd never want another High Wizard."

Cerryl nodded. "You've told me what I needed to know from you. If you think of something that might help all traders . . . come and see me." He smiled. "Or send me a scroll if you think proximity to the High Wizard might be testing your judgment."

Chorast smiled as he bowed. "By your leave, Your Mightiness?"

"You may go, honest scoundrel." Cerryl was grinning as the door closed.

"He told the truth," Kinowin said.

"I know." Cerryl glanced toward Leyladin, then Senglat. The overcaptain shook his head. Leyladin offered the faintest of smiles.

The next to enter was the trader Muneat. Somehow, despite his deep blue tunic and trousers and the silver-trimmed blue boots, he looked far smaller than Cerryl recalled. *Remember, you were a scared apprentice scrivener then.*

"Your Mightiness . . . I am here at your command." The trader touched his silver mustache as he straightened. "I cannot recall when a High Wizard . . . requested a factor's presence . . ."

"Nor on such short notice?" Cerryl offered a crooked smile. "I must apologize. These are not the best of times, for either factors or the Guild."

"I must admit that I am also pleased to see the honorable overmage, the overcaptain of the lancers, and the healer." Muneat permitted himself a brief smile that stretched a third part across his broad and jowled face.

"All are known for their honesty and fairness, I admit," Cerryl responded. "There have been strange circumstances in Fairhaven lately, and their fairness is necessary." He paused, fixing his eyes on Muneat, wondering just how much the man knew. "Have you purchased the services of any new guards or armsmen lately?"

"No, Your Mightiness. In winter, after a year such as this?" Muneat's eyes flickered, even as he kept them on Cerryl.

"Might you know of some traders who have?"

"I do not *know* of any."

Cerryl caught the faintest emphasis on the word "know" and continued. "Perhaps you have heard rumors or surmised that another trader has hired armsmen in recent eight-days?"

"If you listen long enough, Your Mightiness, you can heard any rumor that you wish. Coins and facts and goods, those be the staples of a factor, not whispers in the streets or rumors." Muneat fidgeted, and his hand moved, as though he wanted to blot his forehead or brush back the long silver hair above his ears and below the shining bald center of his skull.

"Oh, you have heard rumors of armsmen?"

"Yes, Your Mightiness, but you hear those when times are bad."

"Might they have been about Chorast?" Cerryl paused. "Or Layel? Or Loboll? Or Felemsol?" Then, after a lengthy silence, he added, "Or Jiolt?"

"I can't say as I've heard that any of those have added armsmen lately." Muneat offered a tight smile.

"Jiolt is related to you through consortship, is he not?"

"He is, and he is a fine factor, and a good consort and father." Muneat smiled more broadly, offering the smile more to Kinowin and Leyladin than to Cerryl.

*What do those have to do with treason and plotting?* Cerryl wanted to shake his head. Being good at what one did and loving one's family didn't mean either innocence or guilt. "I am sure he is all of those." *And more.* "I do appreciate your time, your forbearance, and your assistance."

For the first time, Muneat looked disquieted.

"You may go, Factor Muneat." Cerryl paused, then added, "And I do hope you still enjoy *The Wondrous Tales of the Green Angel.*"

Muneat bowed deeply, his face nearly frozen, then bowed again and turned.

When the door had closed, Kinowin cleared his throat. "He was fine—except for lying about Jiolt—until your last words. What did they mean?"

Cerryl laughed. "I wanted to let him know something. Many years ago, he purchased that volume from Tellis the scrivener. I thought he should understand that I knew that."

Leyladin laughed softly.

Senglat swallowed.

After a moment of silence, Gostar announced, "Factor Jiolt."

The door closed behind the handsome factor with a dull thud.

Jiolt's ruddy face sat atop a muscular and trim body clothed in a dark green that emphasized both his well-trimmed beard and his hair, both sandy-colored and shot with silvered gray. He bowed and then offered a smile that was warm, friendly, charming, and totally false. "Your Mightiness . . . overmage, overcaptain, and . . . healer."

Cerryl knew that Jiolt had used the last pause to insinuate that Leyladin was somehow less worthy than the three men. He smiled broadly. "Factor Jiolt, I cannot tell you how pleased we are to have you before us."

"And I am most pleased to be able to assure such pleasure."

"There have been strange circumstances in Fairhaven lately, as I am most certain you above all others understand," Cerryl said mildly. "Have you purchased the services of any new guards or armsmen lately?"

"In the depth of winter, after a year such as this?" Jiolt's sandy eyebrows arched. "I am a factor, and hiring armsmen to guard shipments one cannot make until spring or later is a certain way to ruin."

"Perhaps I was not so clear as I might have been," Cerryl said, sensing the growing tension around the factor and beginning to raise the chaos he might need. "Have you been involved in obtaining the services of armsmen? Say, Certan armsmen?"

"Certan armsmen?" Jiolt laughed.

"I will ask once more," Cerryl said, his voice chill. "Did you act in one way or another to hire armsmen to aid your niece's plot against the Guild?"

"Absurd . . . that is . . . totally absurd! What do you mean by asking me that?" The sandy-haired trader drew himself up.

"I'm asking because some armsmen from Certis caused some trouble last night. That trouble involved your niece and Certis, and you deal with both. Did you pay them?"

"Ser High Wizard, I must confess that I know nothing of this. I am a respected trader . . ."

The light lance burned through Jiolt's chest even before he had raised the thin iron throwing dagger. The dagger clanked on the stones of the floor, just before Jiolt collapsed onto it.

Kinowin, swift and graceful still in his gauntness and age, was beside the dead factor almost before the body lay still.

Senglat was on his knees by the dead factor nearly as quickly. The overcaptain rolled the factor over. "Don't touch the blade. It's smeared with something."

"Poison, no doubt." Kinowin's voice was dry. "The blade is black iron. Nasty dagger to use on a White mage."

Senglat glanced up at Cerryl. "Begging your pardon . . . High Wizard . . . but he had barely raised the knife . . ."

"He knew Cerryl would kill him," Kinowin said, straightening. "He had to have known, once he was summoned."

Senglat's face clouded.

"It's not that," Kinowin added. "Jiolt was plotting against the Guild and the High Wizard. If he fled, then all would know he was guilty, and his golds and trading vessels and warehouses would be forfeit and his family sent into exile. He would die in any case." A sad smile crossed the overmage's face. "No one has ever escaped the High Wizard, and Jiolt knew that."

"Oh . . ." said Leyladin. "So he forced Cerryl to kill him."

The overcaptain's mouth dropped open. "But . . . will his family . . . ?"

"How?" asked Cerryl. "There won't be any proof. If I act against his family now . . . for what he did . . . how will that be received? The Guild would lose all support among the factors."

"Jiolt knew Cerryl could tell he was lying," Leyladin interjected. "He didn't want the High Wizard to learn more."

Senglat shook his head, then slowly rose. "Perhaps I should leave . . ." He looked down at the body once more.

"No," responded Kinowin, "not yet. You are honest, and all know it. If you are asked, you are to tell exactly what you saw." He added after a brief pause, "It would also not hurt to mention that other traders left unharmed or with praise."

Cerryl leaned forward, his hands on the table. "Senglat... if you would, have someone contact Jiolt's son—Uleas, I believe. While I would prefer other... arrangements, it is best to be politic in these things. And if you would have a summons sent to the overmage Redark and the mage Esaak, I would greatly appreciate that—while the over-mage, the healer, and I take a moment or two to recover."

Kinowin nodded.

Senglat half-turned, shaking his head. "How did you know?"

"That's the task of the High Wizard," Kinowin answered for Cerryl. "Would you sleep better knowing what His Mightiness knows?"

The overcaptain paused and thought for a moment. "I do not think so."

"Nor would I." Kinowin walked to the tower door. "Gostar! Send for the guards at the base of the Tower. And a messenger!"

Senglat lifted the dagger, using a square of cloth, careful to touch but the weapon's hilt.

Cerryl stood back and watched, as did Leyladin.

Once Senglat had left with the guards and Jiolt's body and the heavy door closed, Leyladin stood and put her arms around Cerryl for a moment. Then she stepped back.

"You don't like doing this, do you?" asked Kinowin.

"No. It has to be done. I can't have either Anya or the old factors running Fairhaven, though." He held onto Leyladin's hands for a moment before adding, "Anya will be here shortly."

"Why? She wouldn't come before... when any of her little plots failed then." Leyladin's puzzlement showed in every feature.

"How many other plots were there?" asked Kinowin.

"Enough," Cerryl answered. "She will be here. That's why I wanted Esaak and Redark. All she has left are threats."

"For the moment. Then she'll start with some more gullible young and old mages." Leyladin's laugh was short and bitter. "Unless you do something."

"I promised," Cerryl said heavily. "I did, and I keep my promises."

Kinowin nodded. "Let us hope that kept promises do not bury you, Cerryl."

"I know." Leyladin touched his cheek with her fingers. "I won't say more."

Even before she lowered her hand, there was another knock on the tower door. "The overmage Redark."

"Send him in."

Redark stepped into the Tower room, fingering his ginger beard, then glanced toward Kinowin. "I saw Jiolt's body..."

"He tried to attack the High Wizard with a poisoned dagger," Kinowin said. "We thought you should be informed."

"Jiolt . . . he is most temperate . . . a good man with his family . . ." Redark shook his head.

"That may be, but the dagger was most real," Cerryl replied. *Why do people think that loving family precludes murder and treachery?*

"That . . . it is hard to believe . . ." stammered the ginger-bearded overmage.

"The dagger was poisoned," Kinowin added. "Overcaptain Senglat saw that as well."

"Poisoned?" Redark paled.

Esaak entered through the door that had not closed, puffing. "I hastened, High Wizard . . . overmages . . . healer."

"Good." Cerryl gestured. "If you all would sit . . ."

"The High Wizard . . ." mumbled Esaak.

"The High Wizard needs to stand." Cerryl walked to the window, looking out and trying to compose himself.

*Thrap!* "The mage Anya," announced Gostar.

Cerryl nodded and turned. "Have her come in."

Anya's boots clicked on the stones as she marched toward the conference table, ignoring the four seated at the table and staring at Cerryl, who remained before the window. "Why did you bring Jiolt here? What happened to him?"

Cerryl shrugged. "He lied to me. Then he tried to kill me with a poisoned throwing dagger. A black iron dagger. He's dead. What do you expect?"

"He's dead? You murdered him!" Anya's eyes widened. "You . . . murdered . . . him . . . You! You miserable excuse . . . No, No, NO!!!!" She lurched toward Cerryl, chaos fire flaring at her fingertips.

Cerryl raised full order-chaos shields, as did the other mages.

Abruptly Anya snuffed the flames. "Not . . . you . . . not that way. Not for you, Cerryl. High Wizard," she corrected herself as her eyes flicked to Kinowin and then to Redark. The redhead swallowed, looking at neither Esaak nor Leyladin. "You just killed him? The most powerful factor in Fairhaven? When trade is already so bad?" Her voice moderated by the end of the last question, turning cool and hard.

"If a Patrol mage can pass judgment, then so can the High Wizard," suggested Cerryl. "I will report on what I discovered to the Guild."

"You will report . . . you will report . . . you will discuss . . . you will talk . . ." Anya clamped her jaw shut and glared at the High Wizard, then glanced toward Redark. "And you let him do this . . . this abomination?"

"Ah . . . I came but later."

"How terribly convenient for you all." Her eyes went back to Cerryl.

"Just how do you expect to remain as High Wizard doing this . . . sort of thing?"

"I may not, Anya, but I couldn't exactly ignore it when Rystryr sent a half-company of armsmen after me in Fairhaven now, could I? Or when a factor from Fairhaven helped him?"

"I'll have the whole Guild throw you out! You are High Wizard because—"

"Anya," Cerryl said quietly. "Have you noticed that Broka is absent today? Or that the armsmen Rystryr sent to support Jiolt have vanished? Or that all your supporters are with Fydel on the ships? Or that both an overmage and the overcaptain of the White Lancers were there when Jiolt lifted a poisoned dagger against the High Wizard?" He paused. "Not even their worst enemies would accuse Kinowin or Senglat of lying." After a moment, he smiled. "Oh . . . I expect that the fleet has reached Southpoint already—or it will shortly."

"I hope for your sake, dear Cerryl, that it is successful." Anya flashed a tight false smile. "Even that may not be enough to save you."

"You may be right, Anya, but even the weakest of High Wizards has to do what is best for Fairhaven."

"Best for Fairhaven . . . ?" The redhead closed her mouth and stood before the table silently for a long moment. Then, she looked straight at Cerryl. "By your leave." As she turned and left the Tower room, Anya avoided looking anywhere even near Leyladin.

The door thudded shut and vibrated on its heavy hinges.

"Perhaps you were a bit hasty . . . High Wizard," suggested Redark.

Cerryl glanced toward Esaak. "You have much experience, Esaak? What do you think?"

"I think, High Wizard, that Anya is most angry and will seek any and all to have you removed."

"Perhaps so . . ." Cerryl shrugged. "Yet it remains that Anya had ties to Jiolt, and Jiolt lifted a poisoned dagger—a poisoned iron dagger—against an overmage and the High Wizard."

"Ties, but not proof," suggested Redark.

"Exactly," suggested Cerryl. "Did I do other than listen? Did I threaten?"

A faint smile crossed Esaak's face. "You were most patient. Even Sterol would have turned her to ash."

"I do wonder how Rystryr's lancers found their way to the healer's dwelling in a storm. Especially now." Cerryl shrugged. "That is all we know, and you all have been helpful. I will summon you when it appears as though our fleet will engage the Black forces. For now . . . I would like some quiet."

"I would suggest that as well," said Kinowin, standing and moving toward the doorway. "By your leave?"

Esaak and Redark rose as well.

Once the overmages and Esaak had left and the heavy door had thudded shut, Leyladin turned to Cerryl. "Why did you have them present when she accused you? What did you gain?"

"Now . . . none of them can tell each other that Anya has done nothing." *And since three cannot keep a secret, word will spread, and not in the way Anya would like.*

"You should have locked her away." Leyladin said. "She and Jiolt were lovers. They had to be. She was truly upset. I've never seen her react that way. She'll try to kill you, as soon as she can."

"She can't best me directly," Cerryl pointed out, "and there's no one left she can lure into trying. Besides, if she does it now, all will know, and she'll lose any support she may have left." He shrugged slowly. "I can't tell you why, but I know I cannot remove her at this moment, not without being distrusted by all." *You need the story to spread, first . . . and it will.* "There is no proof that Jiolt and Anya were conspiring, nothing beyond what you and I or Kinowin could sense by truth-reading, and who would believe that?"

Leyladin sighed. "She'll find someone else to poison against you."

"Not before the attack on Recluce." Cerryl shrugged wearily and added, "If she can, then they're the sort I'd like to know about before sending them out into Candar."

"You're still serious about that, aren't you? About spreading the Guild all over Candar?"

"Most serious. There's too much plotting and too little use of the Guild's power with most of the Brotherhood here."

"More will die."

"Probably," Cerryl admitted. "They'll die for the good of Candar and Fairhaven, though, instead of dying in Hall plots and schemes."

"You have to stay, High Wizard. You cannot if plots such as these continue. And what if the fleet fails?"

"I will be most surprised—pleasantly so, but most surprised—if any fleet should succeed in inflicting any real damage upon Southpoint or the smith's vessel." Cerryl slowly turned toward the window, stretching tense muscles.

"And you let it go?"

"How else could I prove to the Guild the futility of attacking Recluce?" *How else indeed . . . and how many will die to prove that?* Cerryl swallowed and took a deep breath. He turned and looked out across the snow-covered city—indeed a White City. Truly a cold white city, with a cold White High Wizard.

# CLXXXI

Cerryl slowly surveyed those around the table—Kinowin, Redark, and Leyladin—with the new young mage Ultyr standing slightly back, beside a stool Cerryl had asked to be brought in.

"Are you ready?" Cerryl asked.

"Yes, ser." Ultyr stepped forward and squinted.

Slowly, far more slowly than if Cerryl had sought the image, the mists in the glass parted and showed ships upon a dark blue sea. The small Black craft without masts or even a bowsprit, a craft that radiated order, drove through the low and rolling swells toward the larger ship—the *White Serpent*, Cerryl thought. One of the smaller war schooners downwind of the *White Serpent* veered to port, as if the mage on board had sensed the deadliness of the Black ship.

"Darkness, it *looks* evil," murmured Redark.

The Black warcraft eased alongside the *White Serpent*, and the *Serpent* tacked, but the Black ship followed the *Serpent* and pulled alongside easily. A flash of light and something more streaked toward the *Serpent*, and the bowsprit shattered into fragments. The *Serpent*'s bow swung port, and the big schooner wallowed as the forward jib and the remnants of the bowsprit sagged into the gulf waters.

A series of fireballs streamed from the near-becalmed *Serpent* against the black iron plate of the single Black vessel, but all sprayed harmlessly from the dark metal. Three more of the black weapons struck the rear of the *Serpent*, and before long it had begun to list. Occasional fireballs flashed from both the *Serpent* and the surrounding ships, without effect, as the small ironclad continued to circle the larger schooner.

"More than a dozen vessels, and nearly as many mages, and they do nothing," muttered Redark.

"It does not appear as though they can," observed Kinowin. "They cannot approach closely enough for their mages to be effective, not without risking our armsmen as much as the Blacks' men—and our ships even more."

Abruptly grappling hooks flashed from the Black vessel, followed by a flurry of dark arrows that cleared a section of the *Serpent*'s deck, with black-clad armsmen swarming onto the ship. Cerryl and the others watched silently. A dark figure, smaller than the armsmen, appeared with a staff, apparently walking across the deck toward a White mage who cast firebolts that missed.

"That's Fydel," murmured Leyladin.

"He can't even stop one Black," protested Redark.

"That's the Black mage who built the ship," Cerryl said. "Jeslek couldn't stop him, either."

Several firebolts arched from the two nearest White ships, one falling short, a second splattering on the black iron ship, and a third burning through the sagging bowsprit rigging of the *White Serpent*.

"They can't get close enough," mumbled Redark.

*Not with that much black iron there,* reflected Cerryl silently.

What exactly happened none could see in the glass, save that in the end the Black mage struck Fydel with a staff and turned the White mage into ashes. Then the Blacks abandoned the sinking *White Serpent,* and the Black vessel swung toward a second White ship.

Another volley of whatever weapons the Black mage had developed turned the second war schooner into a flaming pyre upon the waters of the Gulf of Candar.

As the flames rose, more than half the White fleet turned from the Black vessel.

Cerryl continued to watch as the black iron ship approached the third vessel. Parley flags rose on a short staff on the Black craft and on the White ship. Something was passed to the White ship, and the Black craft turned and headed back toward the harbor at Southpoint.

"Ser?" Ultyr stood pale and trembling, shaking like a gray winter leaf in a storm.

"You can let the image go," Cerryl said, feeling guilty. "Sit down." He poured a glass of wine and extended it. "Here. You need this."

The glass blanked.

"Thank you, ser." The young mage took the goblet, sank onto the stool, and drank slowly.

"We can fight them again," Redark said. "Then . . . perhaps we should not." He shook his head.

Cerryl glanced at Kinowin.

"The firebolts were useless against that ship," noted the older overmage. "They could have destroyed every one of our ships—with one vessel."

"They didn't," said Leyladin.

"I don't think the smith wanted to," Cerryl said slowly.

"Didn't want to destroy us? He cannot be that charitable, not after what they tried to do with their traders," objected Redark.

"I've been thinking," Cerryl mused. "It wasn't charity. How many White mages have died in the past few years? Almost a score and a half, maybe more, and we've only found a bit over a third that many apprentices who have become full mages. That ship of his, and everything he makes, concentrates order. There has to be a balance. We know that. What if he did destroy another half-score of our mages?"

Kinowin nodded slowly. "He might create a truly great White mage—or several more."

Redark frowned but did not speak.

"No, it wasn't charity. The Blacks are not charitable." *Nor are you.* After a moment, Cerryl stood. "There's not much more we can do at the moment, is there?"

"Not at the moment," agreed Kinowin. "The Guild will need a report."

"And reasons, High Wizard," suggested Redark.

*Reasons? How about Anya's scheming?* "You might ask Anya how she might better have planned the attack," suggested Cerryl blandly.

Redark frowned as both he and Kinowin rose.

Kinowin nodded and said, "The attack was indeed her idea—and Jeslek's, I suspect, though we will not ever know that."

"It was the will of many," suggested Cerryl, standing and ushering them toward the door, "but not necessarily for the best of many—or Fairhaven. I will be reconsidering many things." He smiled.

Once the heavy door had closed after the departing overmages and Ultyr, Cerryl turned to Leyladin. "Now I have to deal with Rystryr. He's begun to mass lancers and foot. This will make matters worse because he will take the sea battle against the Blacks as an indication of weakness."

"You haven't let his acts be known," Leyladin pointed out.

"No. Kinowin knows. For the others, I had to wait until the Recluce matter was settled."

"Is it settled?"

Cerryl shrugged. "For all but Anya and a handful. Dealing with her and her followers comes next. Then I will have to alert Redark and the Guild about the dangers of Certis. We will use some of Esaak's calculations . . ."

"Do you really think Rystryr will try to take Sligo?"

"If he can get away with it—or thinks he can." Cerryl rubbed his forehead. "And eventually, that will mean more meetings and efforts to persuade others of the danger."

Leyladin stood and stretched. "I'm sorry. I don't know how many meetings I'll be able to observe. My lips will be bloodied."

"It's hard for you not to speak."

"Only when people are being stupid."

"All meetings bring out stupidity. So do . . . It doesn't matter." Cerryl shook his head.

"What were you going to say about Certis?" prompted Leyladin.

"Rystryr will try to take Sligo, if he can. The glass has already shown that Disarj has convinced Rystryr that this is the time to act, when the Guild is the weakest. Or maybe Disarj let Rystryr convince him. Rystryr is beginning to mass forces at Rytel. So I've already sent a scroll asking Disarj to go to Tyrhavven to confer with Heralt."

"Will he do that? With Rystryr thinking about invading Sligo? Disarj, I mean?" Leyladin squinted as she glanced out the tower window into the bright light of the clear winter day.

"Disarj would not come to Fairhaven—not now—he would find an endless well of excuses. Besides, Rystryr has doubtless prevailed upon Disarj to go to Tyrhavven. If Disarj thinks he can overpower Heralt, then . . . perhaps armsmen would not be needed, except . . ."

"To help the Sligan Council keep 'order'?" Leyladin's tone turned ironic.

"Of course. That way Certis would regain a port to avoid the tariffs and more golds to stand against the Guild."

"What will stop him?" Leyladin raised her eyebrows.

"I will." Cerryl laughed, harshly. "Then we will destroy his forces—if we must."

"You sound like Jeslek."

"No. I tell you, and only you. Jeslek told the world. I will tell everyone that I'm going to Tyrhavven to review the trade and tariff problems and to confer with Heralt. Everyone will think I'm displeased with him. I will claim that I hope to work out something. As my critics have said, I will speak many, many words."

"Convincing everyone that you do not intend to act," predicted the healer.

"I've dispatched Kochar and Kiella to Tyrhavven to support Heralt, and also told them to be very polite to Disarj should he arrive earlier than expected."

"The Guild—some of the older mages will say you're just using this . . . Black Order thing . . . as an excuse not to fight Recluce," said Leyladin.

"Some will," Cerryl admitted. "Most of those remaining will say so most quietly. I will listen and talk to them—privately. After I deal with Anya."

"What will you tell them?"

"What will make them happy. I will *not* tell them that all prosperous lands are based on a combination of acceptance and force. Fairhaven and Recluce are no different."

"We're no different from Recluce? Darkness forbid that the High Wizard of the White City admit such." A lazy smile crossed her full lips. "Surely you must be jesting."

Cerryl returned the smile. "Each person wants in his heart for everyone to believe the way he does, but everyone has different beliefs. Some form of force is necessary to ensure lands do not fall apart. Recluce uses the force of order; we use the force of chaos. Both are force." He shrugged. "They exile those who will not accept their way—unless, as in the case of this Black engineer, the exiles have enough force to change things. We allow people to think as they will, unlike the Blacks. We only force those who do not keep the peace to flee—or we kill them. The Blacks exile those who even think the wrong way and let others do the killing. It's still death, one way or the other. But we're more forgiving and more honest about it, I think."

"What of those who can accept neither your rules nor those of the Blacks?" Leyladin frowned.

"Each man and woman wants rules that are suited for them. Can we have a thousand sets of rules in a town of a thousand? Even fifty sets of rules in a village? It's better to have a few absolute rules than many that attempt to deal with all that may befall people."

"A few simple rules?" Her eyebrows arched.

"The Patrol rules are a good start. We need to bring the idea of patrollers elsewhere. More patrollers and fewer lancers, especially in Fairhaven."

"You don't intend to keep that many lancers in Fairhaven?" asked Leyladin, eyes twinkling as though she already knew the answer.

"Why?" Cerryl inclined his head. "If we need more than fifty score to defend the city, we will already have lost any war. If we cannot hold together Candar east of the Westhorns, then we cannot hold Fairhaven. Life must get better for the people beyond Fairhaven. They must be our responsibility—"

"Why are they the Guild's? Some will surely ask that."

"Because their own rulers will not do what is best. We will."

"The Guild would not. You will," said Leyladin. "Just as you will deal with Anya—now that you have undermined much of her support."

"Not much . . . but enough." *You hope . . .* Cerryl turned to the window, where, from outside the White Tower, came the faint wail of the late-winter wind.

"Let us hope." Leyladin took his hand.

Both looked into the clear and cold afternoon.

# CLXXXII

There you have the fleet," said Cerryl, nodding toward the glass in the center of the table. A dozen ships bearing the red thunderbolt banner straggled back into the Great North Bay. Cerryl raised a finger, and the image vanished from the mirror. "Now what do you suggest?"

"You send out another fleet, this time one that will follow orders. That is, if you wish to continue as High Wizard," Anya said lazily from where she half-reclined in the chair across the table from Leyladin and Cerryl. Anya's eyes focused not on Cerryl, but past him and on the high gray clouds visible through the tower window beyond the table. On one side of the table rested a deep basin of cold water.

"Sterol was right," Cerryl added, his voice conversational as he looked at the box on the small side table, a box containing a gold-painted iron amulet.

"Don't tell me you're going to let that nobody on Recluce humiliate us?" Anya's voice took a harder tone. "After what he did to Fydel . . . and to Jeslek? You'll let it pass? And stand up and tell the Guild that?"

"There is a Balance, and we can accept it or fight it. Everyone who has fought it has lost. The trick is to make it work for you."

"You sound like you're weaseling out, Cerryl. We can't have that." Anya sat up straight in the chair but did not rise to her feet.

"Why don't you listen, for a moment? It won't hurt." *You really don't think she will, do you? She's convinced that you won't ever act against her.* Cerryl stood and walked to the window, glancing toward the cold gray clouds, then back at the redhead.

"I'm listening." The words were cold, yet white flames lurked behind her eyes.

"This smith-wizard builds machines. Those machines must contain chaos-fired steam or water. That means they embody great, great order. If he builds many of his machines, he increases the amount of chaos in the world. That would increase our power more greatly than his, because his order would be locked in those machines."

"So you would encourage him to build those machines? To attack and destroy our ships? That would certainly increase chaos. How much good it would do us is another question." Anya rose like a pillar of white flame.

"He won't do that." Cerryl gestured at the now-blank mirror. "He could have destroyed the entire fleet with his little Black ship. He didn't. He's certainly no weak-willed Black idiot either. Weak-willed idiots don't fight head-on. He destroyed Jeslek and Fydel one-on-one—Fydel with a staff, not even that iron clad chaos of his."

Cerryl turned slowly, almost indolently, and stepped over to the small side table. His back to the redhead, he slipped off the amulet he wore in a quick motion and set it on the table. He opened the wooden box and removed the painted amulet, concealing a wince as the metal burned his hands, not badly, but enough to sting. He had to get back to using less chaos . . . somehow. "Besides, you saw his ship. Even if we could board it, what could anyone do? Our White Lancers couldn't even touch half of it with all that black iron."

Anya eased out of her chair and stepped toward Cerryl's back. "It's too bad you'll follow Sterol, Cerryl dear. You'll see once the fleet mages return."

Leyladin stiffened but did not move.

"I don't think so." Cerryl lifted the amulet and turned. "But here, you wear it. You always wanted to." With a quick gesture he dropped the gold-painted iron links around her neck.

Anya lifted her hands, then screamed as a circle of flame burned away the gold paint and the white cloth beneath it. Her hands reached for the hot iron, but Cerryl grasped her wrists and nodded toward the door.

"I'm not quite as dense as I look, dear Anya. And while I'm not as powerful as you believe you are, or Sterol did, I do occasionally think." His voice rose. "Gostar! Hertyl!"

The three guards who hurried through the tower door and across the white stone floor bore chains of heavy and cold iron in their gloved hands.

"You need me!" the redhead screamed as the additional heavy iron chains slipped around her.

"Indeed we do. You will make a perfect example for future would-be schemers. You will look ravishing once your image is captured for display. Most fetching." Cerryl smiled and inclined his head to the guards. "Good day, Anya."

The redhead straightened, ignoring the pain of the cold iron. "You don't understand, Cerryl. I can *see*. See like Myral. No matter what you do, it doesn't matter. I know. I saw you in this room with the amulet. Why do you think your aunt and uncle died? Why did those brigands attack you in the sewer? Despite everything I did, all my actions brought you here." Her face twisted in pain and rage. "Don't you see? Everything you do is for nothing. Fairhaven will fall. It will melt under a sun you cannot even think about. Everything you want to do will end as ashes. It's all worthless! You're worthless."

"Good day, Anya," Cerryl repeated, watching as the leather-gloved guards wrapped the cold iron chains around the redhead.

As the door closed, he plunged his hands into the basin of cold water, taking a deep breath as the water soothed his hands.

Leyladin stepped up beside him. "With all that iron on her, she'll die before the Guild meets."

"I know," Cerryl said soberly. "That is proof she could not maintain the balance necessary for a mage. It will also relieve everyone of having to make a decision . . . and leave the blood on my hands."

"Sometimes . . . you can be cruel."

"Sometimes a High Wizard has to be cruel. No one listens otherwise. Anya didn't listen at the end, either." He shivered. *Will you listen? Or will you become like all the others?*

"Was she right?"

Cerryl offered a harsh laugh. "Of course she was . . . in a way. Everything ends. Fairhaven will fall. So will Recluce. Cyador and West-wind fell. But she was wrong about what it all means. The end is always the same. That's why what we do *does* matter. Good or bad, we die. If we bring some light and prosperity into the world, isn't that better than there being less light?" He dried his hands on his trousers, ignoring the red blotches on his fingers.

"Some would say, then, that power for one's self is all that there is." Leyladin's eyebrows lifted momentarily.

"Some would. I wouldn't. Power for one's self is hard to amass and harder to hold. Where are Jeslek? Sterol? Anya?" He shrugged. "Myral died as peacefully as he could have. Kinowin is still here. So are we." *So far . . .*

"So far," she repeated. "And I am with you."

"I'm glad."

The healer touched his hands, and the soothing darkness spread across his skin, lifting the discomfort. "She was screaming about an image."

"I'm having her statue put up on the ledge. I did promise her that, and I keep my promises."

"You didn't set one up for Myral."

"No, I didn't. He was more than an image . . . much more."


# CLXXXIII

The High Wizard dismounted at the alley gate, and the pair of lancers checked the courtyard before he crossed the rain-puddled stones and entered the small common room that had once seemed so spacious.

Beside the table stood a wide-eyed boy of less than a handful of years and a woman.

"Is that you, Cerryl?" Benthann's voice was hoarse, and the once-blonde hair was mostly gray, the blonde like streaks of sunlight against gray autumn clouds.

He nodded.

"Why did you wait so long to come back?"

"Because had I shown any affection toward you or Tellis or Beryal, my enemies would have used you. The only way I could show my gratitude was not to come." He smiled, not concealing the twist to his lips. "I did what else I could."

"The golds in the leather bags?"

"Yes."

"I thought they might have come from you."

"Your son?" He inclined his head toward the towheaded boy. "He is handsome."

"Like I was once, I suppose."

"Yes. I always looked at you."

"I know." Her eyes dropped. "You're not here just for me."

"I need to thank Tellis. I owe where I am to him. Because he took in a mill boy and made him a scrivener."

"He won't know what to do." Her voice was low. "He's in the workroom."

"Where else would he be?" Cerryl looked at the boy. "If you need help . . ."

"Only if I really need it."

"If you do . . ." He nodded and stepped through the archway.

Tellis was bent over the copying desk as Cerryl stepped into the workroom, but the scrivener's head jerked up. "Ser? I did not see you enter. My apologies, ser, my apologies. Have you seen the latest copies of the *Histories*?" Abruptly the scrivener stopped, his eyes on the golden amulet. "Oh, Your Mightiness . . . what can this humble scrivener—"

"Tellis." Cerryl laid a manuscript on the table. "It's been a long time, but I'd like you to make three copies for me. If you would . . ."

"Of course, honored ser. Of course."

Cerryl wanted to wince at the politeness, the servility, the near-groveling. "As I told Benthann . . . I owe you my life and more, and until now there was little I could do to repay it, except through purses left by stealth. I am sorry . . . but I do try to repay my debts."

After a moment, Tellis looked at the manuscript. "Your letters are wide . . . honored ser."

"They were not, once upon a time." Cerryl grinned crookedly. "If you could find some of the green leather, I would appreciate that. Oh . . . and if you can finish them by the turn of summer, your fee will be ten golds—for each of the three I need."

"Some, honored ser, pay their debts, and that be what a good scrivener would hope for. You'll have your three, and all in green."

Cerryl finally nodded, knowing that to say more would not help. "Thank you. For everything." *For life, for Leyladin, for the chance to become what I have . . . for not making it too hard to try to repay debts . . . old debts.*

"Thank you," he repeated before, with another nod, he turned to head back to the White Tower.

# CLXXXIV

Cerryl stood before the table as Kinowin and Redark entered the High Wizard's official apartment, which had come to serve mainly as a meeting and conference room, since Cerryl and Leyladin continued to spend evenings at her dwelling.

"Thank you both. I've requested your presence for the Council to meet with the last of Anya's . . ." Cerryl paused, searching for a word, then added, "acolytes."

Redark glanced to where Leyladin stood by the window.

"The healer is most helpful in discerning shades of truth," Cerryl said politely.

"Ah . . . yes." Redark cleared his throat.

"Before they arrive, you should read this." Cerryl handed the scroll that tingled from the order that filled it to the older overmage.

"What is it?" asked Kinowin as he seated himself to Cerryl's right.

"A request for terms from the Black mage."

"Terms? He asks us for terms?" demanded the ginger-bearded Redark.

"Not exactly. I'd rather you read it. Then we can talk," said Cerryl.

After a moment, his face blank, Kinowin handed the heavy parchment to Redark.

The younger overmage read the document and returned it to Cerryl. "Can we trust him?"

"Considering that he can destroy any ship upon the seas, do we have any choice?"

"As I understand this," Kinowin said, "he is proposing that we reduce the surtax on goods from Recluce to three parts in ten but will open the new port at Southpoint to any ships from Candar that do not carry White mages onboard."

"I took the liberty of having Esaak do some calculations," Cerryl explained. "Our factors will do better at three parts in ten. That is high enough to protect the wool growers."

"Why would the Blacks do that," asked Redark, "if their ship is so mighty?"

"Like all of us, they must eat, and they cannot compel our ships to port there," said Cerryl.

"Because they need the grains and oilseeds and they can still charge more for those cargoes in Recluce. But they have to be able to sell something in Candar. They can't travel one way in ballast," suggested Kinowin.

"We can tell the Guild that we have gained trading rights in Recluce and that more trade will be coming to Candar." Cerryl smiled. *Besides, it doesn't matter now that you're getting control of the tariff collections.*

"We lost . . . and you're going to claim a victory?" Redark frowned.

"We didn't lose. The Black can't build enough ships to stop us from blocking their traders. If this keeps up, we both lose. So they give up something, and we give up something."

"But . . . most of the trading on Recluce is at Land's End." Redark glanced at Kinowin.

"That will change," predicted Cerryl. "Besides, do you have a better proposal? We only lost two ships this time. How many will we lose if we don't agree? And how much will it cost us to keep up a blockade of the Black Isle?"

Redark shrugged. "I defer to the High Wizard."

Cerryl wanted to sigh. Instead, he smiled. "The Guild needs to pick the battles it can win. By reinforcing our mage advisers with lancers in all the major ports we can collect more in tariff coins. That is a battle we can win, and we are winning."

"The viscount and the prefect will protest."

"Probably," Cerryl admitted. "We now control Lydiar, most of Hydlen, Sligo, and Spidlar. If we do not have to blockade Recluce or our own coasts against Black traders, we can use those ships to quarantine Ruzor and Worrak. Neither Gallos nor Certis can muster the arms to stand against us now."

Redark wiped his forehead. "You . . . you planned this from the beginning."

Cerryl nodded. "I had help from many, but . . . yes, I did. By controlling the roads and the ports the Guild can unite Candar, at least that part east of the Westhorns. With the use of the screeing glasses, the White highways, and mages in the major ports and trading cities we can bring down any ruler who will not pay his tariffs and trade fairly."

"The viscount . . ."

"I know," admitted the High Wizard. "We will deal with him next, but this agreement will free the ships and armsmen to do so."

Redark glanced from Cerryl to Kinowin, then back at the parchment before him. "You have dealt with . . . other rulers before . . . to the Guild's advantage. I must defer to that expertise."

"Dealing with Certis will be easier than with Recluce," confirmed Kinowin.

"Thank you, Overmages." Cerryl nodded. "Now . . . let us see Anya's acolytes."

Redark cleared his throat and glanced at Kinowin once more but did not speak.

"How many of Anya's young followers are actually left?" asked Kinowin.

"Aalkiron was on the second ship that was fired by the Black mage's weapons. That leaves three—Muerchal, Zurchak, and Giustyl."

"You'll see them all at once?" Redark adjusted his chair.

"Why not? I'd rather we not spend too much time on them." *And you might not have to ash them all that way.*

"You'll pardon me, High Wizard," said Kinowin, "if I raise some shields?"

"They will be reasonable, I am certain," offered Redark. "How could they not be ... ah ... given their position?"

"What is their position?" Kinowin's voice was smooth.

"That ... they were supportive ... of Anya," admitted Redark.

"So far, they have not done anything against the Guild," Cerryl said. "Because of their closeness to Anya, I asked them to appear before the Council."

Leyladin had moved her chair back and closer to the wall, next to the side table, as though she wanted to be disassociated from the three Council members.

Cerryl raised his voice and called, "Send in the mages!"

The three young mages entered the chamber and stood abreast facing the table, with the bull-necked Muerchal at Cerryl's left, Zurchak in the middle, and the rail-thin Giustyl edging even farther to the right, as if he wanted to distance himself from the two others.

"The three of you are here because there is some question of your loyalty to Fairhaven and the Guild." Cerryl's voice was mild, almost conversational.

"After facing that black iron fire in the gulf?" Muerchal squared his broad shoulders, but his green eyes fixed on Redark, not on Cerryl.

"I did notice that a number of ships turned from the Black vessel long before it could have been a threat," Cerryl pointed out.

"Mine did not," said Giustyl quietly. "We brought back the Black's message."

"What did it say?" asked Muerchal, almost belligerently.

Cerryl tilted his head. "It was for the Council—a request for terms beneficial to both the Guild and the Black Isle."

"Beneficial to you, perhaps, Your Mightiness." Muerchal's contempt was not even veiled.

Once again, Cerryl wanted to sigh. Muerchal was not only stubborn but stupid. "You seem to forget that you stand before the Council, Muerchal." He kept his voice mild.

"The Council? Two dodderers and a schemer?"

Cerryl could sense the chaos rising around Muerchal and raised his own shields, extending them to protect Leyladin as well.

*Whhhsttt!* Fire flared around the three Council members and past them toward Leyladin, then subsided.

Redark shuddered, and sweat had beaded on gaunt Kinowin's forehead.

Cerryl glanced at Muerchal as the burly mage began to focus more chaos. Without so much as raising his hand, the High Wizard concentrated, and a line of golden light seared through Muerchal's shields. The young mage crumpled onto the floor, but before his body even struck the stone it had begun to shiver into fine white ash, so much chaos had Cerryl directed there.

In the silence, Cerryl studied the sullen Zurchak and the silent Giustyl. "If I were Anya, or Sterol, you would be dead beside Muerchal. I am not either, nor like them."

"So you will chain me in cold iron to soothe your conscience?" asked Zurchak ironically. "Your Mightiness?"

"Darkness, no." Cerryl laughed. "Did you see what happened? Could you have stood against me?"

"No . . . no, ser."

"Light, no . . ." murmured Giustyl in a voice so low as to be almost inaudible.

"I propose sending you—Zurchak—and a score of lancers to Summerdock. You will watch the traders there; and you will send a report every eight-day. You will tell me what ships have entered the port, what have left, what cargos were loaded, what were unloaded. You will report on anything you think will harm or benefit Fairhaven and the Guild. Several years from now, if you do well, you may be moved somewhere closer to Fairhaven—Ruzor, Worrak, perhaps Tyrhavven."

Zurchak's face remained impassive, but the darkness had vanished from his eyes.

"I give second chances," Cerryl said quietly. "I do not give third chances."

"Muerchal would be alive now," added Leyladin from behind the Council, "had he not raised chaos against the High Wizard."

Cerryl looked at the thin-faced Giustyl. "You will go to Biehl and do much the same."

Giustyl nodded.

"I do not expect gratitude. I do expect obedience." Cerryl offered a crooked smile that felt false. "If you attempt to betray the Guild, you will die, and you will never see that death approaching."

Kinowin cleared his throat, loudly. "I would not interrupt the High Wizard in most matters, but you two should know something before you leave. Despite walls and guards, three rulers and a score of well-protected traders‧ who schemed against the Guild have vanished into chaos over the past five years. The High Wizard does not make idle statements." The older overmage smiled. "You should also know that I have never troubled myself to deceive. Nor do I now."

Giustyl swallowed. Zurchak's lips tightened.

"Are you willing to serve the Guild faithfully and well?" Cerryl asked. "And to build its strength throughout Candar?"

"Yes, ser."

"Yes, Your Mightiness."

"You may go." The High Wizard waited for the two younger mages to leave. The door closed.

"Will they obey you?" Redark twisted to face Cerryl.

"Who knows?" Cerryl laughed softly. "They'll be far enough away that almost anything they do will help the Guild. If it doesn't, then we replace them with those who will obey."

Redark frowned.

"What will protect them is the reputation of the Guild. If they betray the Guild and it becomes known . . ." Cerryl shrugged. ". . . one way or another they'll die. Few people trust White mages who stand alone."

"Another ruler?"

"If they leave Candar, fine. If they remain, they die."

"You are more cruel than Sterol, Your Mightiness," observed Redark.

"Cruel? I think not. I ask members of the Guild to serve faithfully and well. I accept honest mistakes. I punish treachery. Is that cruelty? Or will you and others think it cruel because I will not allow a mage to attempt to betray the Guild a second time? Because I do not play games with intrigue?" *Except you have . . . You just wish you didn't have to.*

"I think . . . Cerryl," Kinowin said gently, "the noble Redark has been so accustomed to . . . indirection . . . that he finds your methods somewhat too refreshingly direct. Perhaps he and I should talk." The older overmage stood. "By your leave?"

Cerryl rose as well. "I will see you both later."

The High Wizard and the healer waited until they were alone.

"Kinowin is going to explain a few things," Leyladin said, her eyes twinkling. "Like how you won't tolerate scheming and bribery and a few other time-accepted practices."

"There are only a few mages left who know much of that." *Thank the light!*

"There will be fewer who know such, and more honest mages."

"The Guild will see to that," Cerryl said.

"No, the Guild will not," Leyladin replied, repeating her earlier words. "You will. We will."

Cerryl knew her words were a promise, a long-delayed affirmation of Myral's visions and Kinowin's hopes, and the challenge that would occupy him for as long as he lived. He glanced toward the healer and the deep green eyes that enfolded him.

*As long as we both live.* With that thought, Leyladin smiled.

Cerryl felt her thought and smile, though his eyes traversed the winter lands beyond the White Tower, and the spring to come. *So long as we both live.*

CANDAR

GREAT
WESTERN
OCEAN

REG